MW01602760

# Grace of Day

S.L. Naeole

Grace of Day

© 2010 by S.L. Naeole

All rights reserved.

Published by Crystal Quill Publishing

All of the situations and characters in this novel are fictional. Any similarities to actual people or situations are completely coincidental and wholly unintentional.

S.L. Naeole

Visit my website at www.slnaeole.com

ISBN-13: 978-1461074243
ISBN-10: 146107424X

"*But our love it was stronger by far than the love*
*Of those who were older than we-*
*Of many far wiser than we-*
*And neither the angels in heaven above,*
*Nor the demons down under the sea,*
*Can ever dissever my soul from the soul*
*Of the beautiful Annabel Lee.*"
~ Edgar Alan Poe

.

For All The Fans

Thank you for being there with Grace, from beginning to end.

## PREFACE

The smell of fear and domination were overpowering. I could not close myself off to it as I struggled to breathe amid the chaos that reigned around me. The violence that was the beating of my heart only further drove my mind into a downward spiral of confusion and grief as I forced myself toward the dark visage that stood before me.

I could not take my eyes off of the sinister smile that seemed to stretch from ear to ear, pleased at the pandemonium that danced around us, oblivious to the standoff that was taking place at its core. My fingers twitched at my side, the temperature dropping so suddenly: I didn't have time to feel cold. It was time. I had chosen this, after all. This was my destiny, my fate.

My chin raised defiantly, my eyes narrowed, and I took the final steps toward the last decision I knew I'd ever make.

## ONE WEEK

"You've got to be kidding me!"

I stared at the sheet of paper in my hand. The creases where it had been neatly folded to fit cleanly into its envelope sliced in half the short and simple note.

"I'm not graduating?"

The warm hand at my waist lifted away and took the letter as I looked away, a blank expression on my face even as my jaw hung in disbelief.

"Dear Miss Shelley," his gentle voice read. "We are sorry to have to inform you that you did not meet your science requirements for graduation. The final grade submitted by your biology teacher, Mr. Branke, does not qualify you to attend the ceremonies to be held in one week. You may, however, attend the summer biology class to make up this credit and obtain your diploma at a later date. If you have any questions about this, please call the office during regular school hours. Sincerely, Mr. Patrick Kenner."

"Robert, what the hell am I going to do? I can't *not* graduate!" I wailed as I snatched the letter back and reread the printed text. "Ooh, I bet Mr. Kenner just laughed like a psycho when he signed this. I can't believe this—why would Mr. Branke fail me?"

*I think you know why.* The words filled my head, the sound of them much louder than if they had been spoken aloud, and I felt my mouth crinkle up in an annoyed purse.

"I wish you'd answer me like a normal person would," I complained, shoving the letter into its envelope and then shoving the envelope into my backpack.

"Whether my answer was given to you in the 'normal' way or the way that is normal for me, it doesn't change. You know why he failed you. It wasn't right, but there's nothing we can do about that. You're just going to have to attend summer school."

I raised my eyes to Robert's sterling stare and felt my heart skip several beats before it finally settled back into its normal rhythm. He gifted me with a lazy smile and tipped my chin up with an intent finger. His dark lashes framing those gilt irises were hypnotizing me, and I felt myself swallow my retort while he chuckled before bending down to press his lips onto mine.

"You might not have said it, but I know what you wanted to say. You should know better by now..." he whispered when he pulled away.

"Well, I can't help it sometimes. Whenever I see that smile, I think about...that."

His eyes widened as he saw the image I formed in my mind, and I felt the blush creep across my cheeks when his lids grew heavy with the same heated desire that I knew was boiling through me.

"Grace, we promised to be good."

"Yes, we did, but that was before I learned that I'd have to spend four weeks in summer school," I pointed out. "That pushes everything back an entire month. I don't know if I can wait five weeks, Robert."

"Patience, Grace."

I huffed. "Patience? There's no such thing right now—we're working on borrowed time, Robert."

He sighed and turned away before standing up to begin pacing. There was lots of room for that now that the bookshelves that lined the wall of his room had been removed, its contents packed up and shipped to his family home in England. The white walls had not remained bare for long though; he quickly filled them with dozens of black and white photographs—some of the two of us, others of scenes from Heath, the town that we would call home for only two more months.

One photograph featured a shot of his sister Lark as she posed happily with her husband, my best friend Graham. Their expressions were joyful, their eyes fighting against looking at the camera and at each other.

I couldn't help but smile at that carefree image, the radiating love so obvious and blatant it was hard not to reach out and try to grab a hold of it. Beside it was another photograph, this time of Graham and me. I was straddled on his back, and his head was turned back, looking up at me as I looked down at him, our smiles mirroring each other the way best friends' smiles often did.

He had no idea that, come the end of summer, I would be spending the last days of my life in Europe with Robert while he was just beginning his brand new life with Lark. It was a difficult decision to come to, but one that had to be made. Graham had to remain ignorant of everything—his life had already been put in danger once—and I couldn't take the risk of it being put into danger twice because of me.

"Grace, you know that it's not because of you," Robert interrupted my thoughts.

"You're wrong. Sam didn't take him because of you. He didn't take him because of what he meant to you—he took Graham because of what he meant to me," I told him with little hesitation.

The look on Robert's face was a pained one before he turned away from me, and I immediately felt contrite for my thoughtless words. Sam had been Robert's mentor and the closest thing to a big brother as any of Robert's kind could have, and the knowledge that Robert had taken his life in order to save mine still weighed heavily on him.

I stood up and walked over to him, wrapping my arms around his shoulders as I stood behind him, my chin resting against the blade of his shoulder. "I'm sorry," I whispered.

"Don't apologize, Grace," he murmured in a downtrodden tone.

"I would do it again and again each time were I given a chance to do it over because I knew it was the right decision."

"I know," I mumbled into his shirt. "But that doesn't make it any easier for you to deal with."

His body twisted around so that he was facing me. I lifted my gaze to his and saw the residual sadness there, and my heart ached for being the cause. He brushed the side of my face with the back of his knuckles before sighing, long and deeply.

"Grace, when I see you, when I hear your voice, every single second of sound, every minute I get to take in the sight of your smile or the brown of your eyes makes it easier to deal with. I never thought I'd get this much time with you—every moment is a blessing, and I don't plan on wasting it with thoughts of something that I wouldn't change, so please, stop feeling guilty and enjoy the fact that we're together. Okay?"

"Okay," I replied glumly, knowing that this wasn't the end of this conversation. Not by a long shot.

"Grace..."

"Sorry."

He smiled and placed a gentle kiss on the top of my head. "I think I should get you back to your house now—my mother will be returning shortly."

At the mention of his mother, my body stiffened. I pulled away and immediately began to gather my things, shoving the letter into my backpack, along with my books, and headed toward the large window that faced the backyard. "I'm ready."

The sadness that had filled his eyes then spouted from a different source, a source that pained him far more deeply than anything else. It brought the burning sting of tears to my eyes when I saw his grimace turn dark and broody. He hadn't forgiven Ameila for her betrayal.

"It's not just that, Grace," he countered, my thoughts obviously being sifted through.

"I know," I sighed as he scooped me up into his arms before

kicking the window open and stepping out. "I know it's not just that, but I don't blame her for what she did. I would have done the same thing."

"Don't say that," he demanded; his grip suddenly stronger, his body rigid.

"It's the truth, Robert. I wouldn't want to lose you either, and I'd do whatever it took to keep you safe—no matter what. I think I've proven that already."

He bent his knees a fraction of a degree before pushing off, the burst of speed forcing air to push down on me, and I nearly lost my grip on his neck before his hands compensated with a slight shifting, bringing me even closer to him than usual.

"You've proven to me that you love me more than your life, Grace, and I have never felt more undeserving than I do right now—you just got some bad news and I'm wallowing in my own self-pity—how can I make this up to you? Would you like me to fail a class as well so that we can be in summer school together?"

I looked into his face with shock, seeing the sincerity in his eyes and started to laugh. "Are you serious? No one is going to believe that you failed a class—any class—so I don't think that would work. Besides, it's too late anyway. You'll graduate like you're supposed to, and I'll just have to deal with this. I just can't believe that Mr. Branke failed me!"

"*He* didn't fail you, Grace. Mr. Branke wasn't himself anymore. Who he was died that night in the hospital parking lot," Robert reminded me.

"Well, I highly doubt whoever was in control of Mr. Branke really thought it would matter whether or not I failed since he or she obviously figured I'd be dead by now. This grade is from the original Mr. Branke, the one who hated me because I accused him of running me over."

Robert sighed and shook his head. *You're going to be stubborn about this, aren't you?*

"Don't use that mind stuff on me—I'm serious about this!"

*So am I. This is the only way you'll listen to me when you're like this. Whatever grade Mr. Branke intended on giving you doesn't matter; we'll never know because he was never allowed to give it. You forgave Erica upon her death—why not Mr. Branke?*

I scowled and looked away as I sent my own thoughts back to him. *Because he wouldn't forgive me.*

This response was an obvious surprise to Robert, and it showed by the way we slowed down, our bodies stilling in the sky as he adjusted me so that he could see my face better. "Are you serious?"

"Yes."

"That's the pettiest thing I've ever heard come out of your mouth."

"I didn't say it out loud," I pointed out before we suddenly dropped from the sky, plummeting toward the ground at a speed that took my scream from me before it had a chance to leave my lips.

We landed on the ground with such force, the pavement beneath his feet cracked, sending chips of gray rock flying up around us. I felt the jarring stop all the way through my body, the shock of it causing my teeth to gnash harshly in my mouth, and the pain created an instant headache.

My feet were placed on the ground, and I stumbled before toppling over and landing amid a small pile of rubble as Robert stood over me, one hand in his hair, disheveling it even more than it already was, the other hand at his waist, his posture one of disbelief and pure disappointment.

"What. The. Hell." My voice was filled with anger, and I glared at him from where I had landed, my hands stinging from the rocks that lay beneath my palms.

"A man died before he had a chance to make right any of the wrongs he had done—wrongs that I knew he would have liked to have corrected—and you can only think about what he didn't give to you? You have the luxury of knowing when you're going to die, Grace—he didn't. I've never seen you act so selfishly before."

I dusted my hands against my thighs and then struggled to stand. "Look, I know it's selfish, but aren't I allowed to be selfish about my feelings for once? Aren't I human enough for that?" I asked before looking around to see where Robert had landed and seeing that he had placed us at the end of an empty street, vacant lots waiting for new homes that had yet to be built.

"You're human, Grace. Too human, in fact," Robert lamented.

"*Too* human?"

"Yes, dammit" he muttered before grabbing me and bringing his mouth down onto mine fiercely. I lost all train of thought and simply reveled in that moment as his mouth possessed mine.

Finally, after what felt like both forever and not long enough, his mouth lifted slowly, his lips curled up in a satisfied smile. I was dizzy with emotion, my breathing affected by him as always, my heart stuttering inside of my chest so quickly, I knew that sooner or later, it would sprout wings and fly completely out of my chest.

"I understand your need to feel the way you do, Grace. I understand you want to be selfish, you want to possess thoughts that you've always believed were wrong. But I also know that you know what it's like to not be able to tell someone something because they're no longer here. You know what that feels like, to have missed an opportunity, or to have one taken from you. Please try to see that for Mr. Branke, this was the same for him; he never had the chance to make right the wrongs he'd done."

I was still reeling inside from his kiss—at least, that's what I told myself—when I nodded and told him "alright" before leaning against his chest, my ear pressed against the solid wall of muscle and sighing at the familiar and comforting sound of silence that existed behind it.

"Are we ever going to talk about it?" he asked quietly, his hand stroking my hair as we stood on that broken sidewalk together.

"Talk about what?" I murmured, oblivious to what he was referring to.

"About your mother."

I shook my head, pulling my lip between my teeth and clamping down on it as I fought against the urge to begin railing against her aloud as I had done silently when I was alone.

"Grace, sooner or later we're going to have to talk about it."

"I don't want to talk about her."

"Grace-"

"Robert—how about, I talk about my mother when you're ready to talk about yours?" I interrupted.

He quieted almost instantly, and I smiled smugly at his silence. He chuckled and soon, that laughter floated into me, lifting my spirits considerably before they came back down and settled with the weight of reality.

He was right. Sooner or later, we would have to talk about it. It just wasn't going to be right now. Right now, what mattered was that I had five more weeks of school left, which meant that all of our plans would be pushed back. Or would they?

"What if we got married anyway?" I said suddenly.

"What?"

"What if, instead of waiting until I get my diploma, we just go ahead and get married anyway? I'm eighteen and you're...definitely legal. What if we just got married?"

"You mean, elope?"

"Yes!"

"Are you serious?" The pitch in his voice showed a twinge of nervousness that I'd never heard before, and I felt my excitement at this new idea drop down several notches.

"No. No, I'm not," I said, before looking away and instantly filling my mind with several false thoughts all at once, effectively splitting them down the middle and forming a wall around what suddenly made my heart begin to pound a frightening beat beneath my T-shirt. I looked at him and smiled when he nodded.

"Good, I'm glad. The wedding was supposed to be small anyway, so we can push it back a few weeks—I'm pretty sure your father will be ecstatic with that, even if the reason won't make him all too pleased. This will work out, Grace."

"Yeah, yeah it will," I replied softly.

"Come on, let's get you home. I'm sorry for the detour, love."

Once again, I was scooped up into strong arms, and soon we were sailing across the sky toward my home. I hid my disappointment when we landed in the backyard, this time the impact absorbed wholly by Robert. I walked into the kitchen nonchalantly; Janice stood in front of the stove with a spoon in her hand, stirring something in a large pot.

She turned to look at us, her face flat, emotionless. "How'd you two get here?"

"Um…we just dropped in," I said quickly before pulling Robert toward the living room where I was certain Dad was sitting.

*Why didn't you say we flew in?*

I looked at Robert and realized that I had lost my concentration, and his thoughts were free once more to penetrate my mind. *She and Dad have come to a compromise—she won't leave him if he doesn't bring up the subject of angels, demons, zombies, or eggplant ever again.*

"Eggplant?" he said aloud.

My eyes widened as I turned a quick glance behind us to see if Janice had overheard, but thankfully, she was too engrossed in whatever was in her pot to notice. *Yeah, eggplant. That health food kick she went on during her pregnancy has made her swear off certain foods for life. Just saying them makes her nauseous—eggplant especially.*

"Robert, Grace," Dad said when he saw us. He pressed a button on the remote control in his hand while shifting a sleeping Matthew over onto his other shoulder with the other. "I didn't hear your motorcycle or the car, so I'm guessing you came in some…other way, Robert."

"Yes, sir." The look on Robert's face told me without words that the thoughts running through my dad's mind weren't pleasant. They weren't pleasant at all.

"Well, that's going to have to stop. Janice wants a sense of normalcy to return around here, which means no more flying in, no more misting, no more late night visits to Grace. Is that understood?"

I felt my eyes bulge at Dad's list of demands. "Wait—you *knew*?"

He looked at me with a rather bored expression on his face. "I was born Electus, remember? I knew what Robert was the moment I saw him; I knew exactly what was going on."

I choked down my response when Robert spoke up then. "And yet, you did nothing to stop us. Why?"

Dad looked at Robert with anger in his eyes before turning to look at me, his anger dying away as sadness took over. "Because I knew that you wouldn't do anything to hurt Grace."

"That's because I love her."

"I know you do, son. I know you do, which is the only reason I can stomach seeing the two of you together—especially knowing...what I know."

Robert's hand tightened around mind before loosening. "Thank you, sir."

"Well, I suppose you two want to talk to me about next week, and what happens afterwards, right?"

Dad's voice had suddenly grown surly, and I felt my knees begin to shake as the letter in my backpack grew heavier and heavier. Robert said nothing, instead waiting for me to tell him the truth.

"Well, what is it? I've already given my consent to this wedding, and I've pretty much reached the conclusion that nothing I say or do is going to make you change your minds about what happens afterwards-" His voice cut off and he looked away, too emotional to continue.

Afterwards. How strange that the rest of my life could be compacted into a simple adverb. What happened afterwards was something that Dad knew he could not prevent from happening no matter how he felt. Robert and I looked at each other, and sad smiles crossed our lips as we both shared a silent understanding of what it was we were doing. Neither of us could live without the other, but one of us would have to.

I was born specifically to die; that's how it was explained to me.

My mother had been an angel, like Robert, but living with my father meant more to her than living forever. She gave up her divinity and immortality to be with him, and then gave her life to have me. Because of this, I was human in every way except one: I had a call; the divine reason for every angel's existence. I had to let the person I loved most in the world take my life so that his own call could be fulfilled.

Robert had fought against it, we both did, but it was stronger than we were. In the end we gave in; only I didn't die when I should have, and he couldn't kill me when he had the chance. And so here we stood, suspended in our fates as time pressed on with neither of us knowing when the signs that our time was running out would reappear. But we accepted that when it did, this time we would not fight it. It hurt too much.

"Dad, I…I've got some bad news."

I paused to gather my strength, but this seemed to confirm whatever suspicions Dad had already formed in his head, and his expression turned angry once more as he pointed an accusatory finger at Robert. "You bastard! I trusted you! How could you do that to Grace?"

"Dad!" I shouted, angry at the fact that his booming voice had woken up Matthew who now wailed against Dad's shoulder, upset that his nap had been disturbed. I reached for Matthew and took him from Dad's arms, patting and cooing to him softly as I glared at Dad's beet red face.

"My God, Dad, really? Do you really think that we'd do something like that after everything we've been through?" I groaned.

"Well, what else could it be? Bad news when it involves two normal teenagers is one thing; a parking ticket, a broken condom— those things are fixable. Bad news when it involves my daughter and an angel could only be one thing," he responded as his breathing normalized a bit.

Janice, who had rushed out of the kitchen at Dad's outburst, returned to her pot, once again ignoring what was going on to maintain her self-imposed "normalcy". I frowned at this but knew that there was no real point to mention how I felt about it. Instead, I gently rocked Matthew in my arms and tried to explain as calmly as I could what had been detailed in my letter from Mr. Kenner.

Dad's reaction was mild. Actually, he was rather giddy about the entire thing because he came to the same immediate conclusion that Robert had: we'd simply have to postpone the wedding until after summer school. When Robert openly admitted that he shared this opinion, he and Dad suddenly became occupants of the same shared ground.

"I think waiting an additional month is fine, Robert; better than fine. This is probably the best news I've received all day."

"Thank you, sir."

The sudden pleasantries and politeness were too much for me to take. I headed upstairs to put Matthew down. As I passed my bedroom door, I saw my cap and gown hanging on the closet door where I had left it after bringing it home.

I placed Matthew into his crib and waited a few moments while he settled, imagining what it would have been like to graduate with the rest of my class, before tiptoeing out of the room. I returned to my room and flipped on the light.

"Jeez, Stacy!" I gasped when the light revealed the waxen figure of my friend Stacy Kim standing in front of the closet door. She'd chosen to be my friend when everyone else refused, and through everything she had remained a loyal friend.

Even through death.

The pale color of her skin might have looked normal during December, but it was the beginning of summer, and she looked like she'd spent the past year living in a cave.

"Sorry, Grace. I just needed a place to rest for a while," she groaned as her head leaned back and a visible sigh left her body.

"I don't understand; you look so...tired," I said to her, concerned, as she slowly began to sink down to the ground, her knees giving way to the exhaustion that her body was fraught with.

"I am," she replied, her voice fainter now.

16

"What's the matter?"

She looked at me and the woebegone expression on her face was a clear indication that whatever it was, it wasn't good.

"I can't do it," she uttered, her tone utterly woebegone.

"Do what?"

"Do this. Be…this. Be what I am, what this…is. I can't do it, Grace."

I moved over to her and sat beside her, taking her cold hand into mine and squeezing the clammy flesh. "Is it that bad?" I asked, knowing that personally, the idea of becoming one of the undead wasn't exactly a *good* thing, but it was better than being completely dead. At least, that's what it felt like at the time. That's what we all believed.

"I thought I could deal with this, you know? I thought that being an erlking wasn't going to be that bad—I'd drink a little blood from a bag, like Ambrose said, eat a rare steak or something and then I'd be alright, I'd be great, but…it's not."

I'd never asked Stacy what it had been like, what she had gone through. Dr. Ambrose, the erlking who had given Stacy a second chance at life when the cancer that she had been fighting since childhood returned, had insisted that the transition would be much easier to deal with than the actual transformation. But it appeared that the opposite was true.

"Talk to me, tell me what's wrong," I told her as I pushed aside the hair that had fallen into her face so that I could see the exhaustion that plagued her eyes and darkened them even more than they already were.

"I…I thought that when everything was done, when the whole change thing was over that I wouldn't have to feed for a while—Dr. Bro said that I could go up to a month without needing to feed; he said that I wouldn't even realize that anything had really changed inside of me. But it's not true. I'm always hungry, but I can't drink that bagged blood."

"Why?"

"I don't know. Dr. Bro thinks it might be because I was virtually dead before the change happened, so my body probably won't recognize and accept altered blood. He believes that the only way I can feed properly is if I take fresh blood."

I squeaked. "That means you…"

She nodded and looked away, ashamed. "When Dr. Bro bit me," she scratched the crook of her arm, "the kid that was working with him used this syringe to pump blood into my mouth. I remember that I couldn't move, I couldn't tell them to stop; I just laid there and tried not to choke to death, which seems ridiculous because I was dying one way or the other, right?

"And, this might seem gross, but the taste of the blood…it didn't seem right to me. It didn't taste like how it does when you prick your finger and stick it into your mouth, or when you bite your tongue and it bleeds. It tasted…spoiled. Can you believe that? Can you believe that I would know what spoiled blood tastes like?"

She paused then, as though the next part was physically painful to recall, much less mention. When she began to speak again, I knew why.

"Lark…she told Dr. Bro that something was wrong, that she could hear my thoughts going in and out and that I was screaming inside of my head. I don't remember that at all—I don't remember any part of that—I only remember that she kept looking at me and telling me that everything was going to be okay. Dr. Bro started to check me out, doing the usual doctor stuff; that was when I began to vomit up all that blood.

"It kept coming out and I smelled it, Grace, and it smelled…dead; like something rotten…or worse. That was when I knew that I wasn't alive anymore. But I couldn't believe it. I didn't *feel* dead. I didn't feel any different at all; I still don't. It was like I just woke up from a bad dream and couldn't tell what was real and what wasn't.

"Dr. Bro and Lark, they were too busy arguing about what might've gone wrong to notice. And that kid—that poor kid who was there helping Dr. Bro, the kid who had tried to feed me that nasty blood—came to check on me. I could see his face, see how terrified and curious and jealous he was all at the same time, and when I looked at him, the only thing I could think about was how good he smelled, and how good he must taste.

"It happened so quickly, I couldn't stop myself-"

She stopped talking and began to sob, her hands covering her face in shame as her body shook with the tortured and violent sounds that came out of her. I wrapped my arm around her and tried to bring her close to me, to comfort her the same way that I knew she would have comforted me, but her reaction was the rude awakening that I had not been expecting, though should have been prepared for.

She pushed me away roughly; so roughly in fact that I crashed into the wall behind my bed, having slid several feet from her. My head slammed into the painted surface, the crack filling my ears with a pinging that brought with it the speckled and blurred vision that I had almost—and morbidly—grown accustomed to.

"I-I'm sorry," she moaned when she took in the surprised expression on my face. "I'm still not used to this strength yet... Oh God, I killed that kid, Grace. I killed that poor kid; I took his life and it made me realize that I can't do it again—I can't kill people! It's wrong; it's not who I am. I can't live like this; I can't be *dead* like this."

"So what does that mean? That you're just giving up?"

She looked at me and nodded.

"So, when you said you'd come to the wedding-"

"You and I both know that was never going to happen, Grace," she said softly. "I wish it was different but-"

Her head turned to the door, and I followed her gaze, seeing Robert standing there with a frightfully enraged look on his face as he took in Stacy's weakened state and my position in the corner.

"What happened?" he demanded to know as he glared at Stacy while gracefully leaping over the bed to reach me.

"Nothing," I told him reassuringly as his eyes scanned me for visible injuries—and not so visible ones—while his hands gently roamed the back of my head, feeling for the lump I knew was starting to form. "She's tired."

"She's hungry," he said darkly as he turned his head to focus his heavy stare onto Stacy. "You're starving yourself, aren't you?"

She nodded, but something in her expression changed as she stared at Robert, as though she was looking at him for the first time.

"I can't believe it," she whispered. "Dr. Bro said I'd see it when I got used to my eyes, but I didn't believe him…"

"What? See what?" I asked as I looked around Robert's stiff frame.

"She sees me," he answered before she could.

"Sees what?"

"Dr. Bro said that I'd be able to see all things dead and dying when my mind fully accepted the changes that had happened to my body. The new strength, the new speed, the new…sight; my brain had to adjust to these things, he said, because it was used to the human way of doing things. But I didn't realize what exactly he meant by that last part until now. You're dead," she said to Robert.

"No more than you," Robert replied.

"No…no it's different with you. You're not just dead. It's like it's…pouring out of you. God, if death was light then I'd be a light bulb and you'd be the…sun," she finished, too exhausted to continue.

"Grace, we need to get her out of here," Robert informed me as he slowly approached Stacy's still body. "She's starving; if she doesn't feed soon, she won't be able to control herself, and she'll attack the first living thing she sees—that's you."

"She…she doesn't want to feed," I said softly.

"I know that-" he looked at Stacy and quieted.

*I know she doesn't want to feed. She thinks that she can simply starve herself to death, but that's not how it works. When she's fed, she'll act like she normally does, but if she intentionally starves herself, she'll go mad, Grace. You saw what happened in the woods with that erlking. We need to get her to Ambrose now.*

My gaze latched onto Stacy's limp body and I sighed. I didn't want to reveal her secret, but there was nothing else I knew to do. *She can't eat that donated blood. She gets sick. She…she killed a boy…*

The air turned cold around us as anger flowed in and around Robert, affecting the air as he fought between the fire and ice of his emotions. *I told you this would happen. I told Ambrose. I can't allow her to kill people, Grace.*

I grabbed my blanket and wrapped it around me before I responded. *I know that. But what if she just drank the blood from people after they cut themselves or something? I read in a book once where there were people who did that sort of thing…*

Robert sighed and shook his head, the futility of my suggestion plain. *This isn't make-believe, Grace. An erlking's saliva is not just toxic, it's instantaneously deadly. Once it touches blood, it grows, spreads like a flood. If the blood is still on the human, it will leech into the bloodstream where it will attack the body in seconds.*

*There's no way to remove it, no way to avoid contaminating any wound with it if an erlking feeds from it. You can't suck it out, you can't wipe it off, and you can't disinfect it. And besides, the blood is only to mask the taste of the raw meat she needs to survive. Looking at her, I give her about a week before she starts rampaging, and if that happens, I have no choice, Grace…*

My head bobbed down once in understanding, but inside, my heart was caving in. I had done this to her. I had turned one of my best friends into a killer, thinking to save her life, and instead I had condemned it.

One week was all she had left. One week was all we had left.

## BY DESIGN

Stacy left while I was downstairs, but she left a note saying that she'd try to return later that evening to finish our conversation. I hid it from Robert and sighed when I realized what I had done. So much for starting clean.

Janice said nothing during dinner—which turned out to be a carefully prepared, and meticulously stirred pot of canned vegetable soup— and Dad simply watched as she spooned the tinny meal into her mouth, never looking at him, or us, instead staring blankly at some invisible spot on the table. Robert made several attempts to strike up a conversation with her about anything—the weather, sports, Matthew— but she responded only with flat smiles and semi-courteous nods before continuing to eat in silence.

When she stood up and announced in a monotone voice that she was going to bed, I offered to go up with her to check on Matthew. She looked at me and smiled sadly. "No, it's okay Grace. He'll be fine. He's not like you."

Those four little words caught me off guard, and I felt frozen in place as she sidled past me. Her steps were careful and slow, her shoulders hunched down with a depression that we had all seen coming on and yet had been unable to prevent from taking its hold of her. How could we? Dad had grown up with this life and had accepted its consequences, while I had willingly invited it into my life when I began my relationship with Robert.

22

But Janice had done neither. Instead, she had been pulled in unknowingly simply by marrying Dad and inheriting me as a step-daughter. No one explained to her the costs; no one told her that she could lose people she loved. Katie had been just the beginning—her sister's death at the hands of Sam was the initiation into the life that she had not volunteered for—and now she had to contend with the very genuine fear that at any moment, someone, some unseen figure from her nightmares could come swooping in to take from her someone else she loved, even before she had time to fully grieve Katie.

Initially, she seemed to have taken it all in very well, but as the days passed, one turning into several, several turning into weeks, she had grown even more sullen and reserved. The night when the seraphim came to our house to speak to Dad and me about what was expected of me now that Sam was gone had marked the noticeable beginning of Janice's descent. She stayed in her room for two days after that visit, emerging on the third day looking thinner despite having just given birth to Matthew only weeks before.

Less than twenty-four hours later, she began to remove certain things from the house, odd and seemingly inconsequential things that made little sense to me until I found the silver winged pendant that she'd bought for Matthew, its twin still hanging around my neck, in the trash atop a pile of torn photos.

She was purging the house of anything that reminded her of angels. Books, pictures, even the plastic Jell-O mold that Ameila had brought over last Christmas were dumped, buried in the garbage can that was then rolled onto the street for the trash guys the next day.

I tried to speak to Dad about this, but he brushed it off as her way of dealing with everything. "Does that mean ignoring her own kid?" I asked in retort and began to point out that she hadn't done so much as change a diaper in a week. The responsibility of caring for Matthew had fallen wholly on me and Dad. He changed his schedule around, working nights so that he could stay home during the day, while I took care of him while Dad was gone.

Janice acted like Matthew didn't exist, and now, after hearing her comment and seeing the vacant look in her eye as she said it, my chest and heart ached because she was acknowledging that our connection had been severed as well; she looked at me differently now. It was the first time I recognized the fact that Janice had never looked at me like that before, never spoke to me like that before; I had always been James' daughter to her, and that meant an extension of him to love. Now I was something else. I wasn't James and Abigail Shelley's daughter anymore. I was the daughter of James, electus patronus, and Avi, former angel. I was...different.

"Grace..."

Robert stood behind me and placed a consoling hand on my shoulder, but I brushed it off. "No. Don't say it's not true. I used to say that I was different because everyone else thought so. Everyone else made me feel like it was the truth and they were right; I *am* different."

I turned to look at him, and Dad, who now stood beside him with a distressed distortion to his face. "I'm not supposed to be like everyone else; Mom knew that. She never planned on me growing up and being normal. She never intended on me being like the other girls here because she knew that I wasn't. I'm not supposed to want the same things they do; I'm not supposed to have the same dreams. She stole the only thing I ever wanted from me; she stole having a normal life from me.

"But she couldn't leave it at that, could she? She had to steal herself from me too, and then made sure that no one else could have me either—not even you." I huffed with frustration. "She took everything from me because she *had* to have me, she *had* this big plan and it didn't matter how I felt about it. She ruined my life and I hate her for it! I. Hate. Her!"

I ran upstairs to my room, dashing away the fat, sticky tears that slipped past my lids, and threw open my closet door. I fell in front of it, landing roughly on my knees, and began digging through a large box that sat on the floor. I pulled out an old photo album that I hadn't looked in since before Matthew was born and took it to my bed. I opened it angrily and stared at the photos inside.

Each one that I had foolishly believed held an image of a supposed family member now revealed the truth to me as my mother's face appeared, clear to me as it had never been before. The smile on her face in every image seemed phony, forced, and yet even through the aged photographs I could see the pale aura of light that clung to her, extending outwards like a shadow would.

It was the sign that I should have noticed right away but didn't because I hadn't been looking for it. Why would I?

Furious at the betrayal that I finally could admit to feeling, I began to tear the photos out, methodically ripping each one into tiny pieces. When I came to the final few pages holding the most recent of the photos, images of the two of us together, I hesitated only momentarily before those, too, became confetti on the comforter.

It was when I reached the last page, the last photo slot empty with a caption written on the bottom hinting at the future she knew I would never have; the mocking words and the emptiness of the page taunted me until I screamed and threw the album at the window. I swallowed my cry of surprise when it sailed through the glass, shattering it and sending shards and slivers of my pain raining down outside and onto my floor.

As the tinkling sound filled the room, I became aware that I wasn't alone. Robert was with me, appearing the instant the glass cracked before it disintegrated; his arms were around me, holding me against him as tightly as he dared as I continued to scream, every ounce of anger and hate and disgust turning into piercing shrieks that escaped me and flooded the street.

I cried; wallowing in my self-pity until Matthew's equally pitiful wails just behind the wall beside me brought me back to the reality that no matter how I felt, no matter what I might still need to get out, I had a responsibility to someone else besides me.

Robert, his arms tense around me, waited until he was certain that I was done throwing things before he let me go to examine the scraps of paper that littered my bed. "You destroyed them all?" he remarked as he picked up the torn fragment of what looked like my left eye.

I sniffed, hiccupped, and then nodded. "She was trying to sell me a lie with that album. I thought this was her way of helping me to connect with my past, to help me understand the family she left behind, the family I couldn't know because they were too far away. Instead, every single photograph is a lie, even the one that wasn't there. I have no family from Korea—my God, I'm not even Korean! I don't know who or even what I am anymore. I tried to pretend that nothing had changed, but everything has. Everything has changed, and it took Janice to make me see that."

Robert once again took me into his arms and brought me against his chest, the embrace he held me in strong and supportive, yet there was also a sense of separation there that I didn't know I needed. I turned my head into the hollow curve beneath his chin and felt my body twitch with each hiccup, feeling it absorbed through him as he took within him my suffering.

"Janice is in a state of shock, Grace. She's been forced to accept a change in her life that no one should have to deal with. She loves your father, she loves you; she just needs time now to grieve for her sister, and for the life she once knew. She didn't mean what she said."

"I don't care if she meant it or not," I informed him. "I'm not like her. I'm not like you. I'm not like anyone; she was right."

"I wish I could make this easier for you," he said into my hair.

"There is one way…"

"Grace-"

"Robert, hear me out. If we got married right after graduation like we planned, I could stay with you, and then Janice wouldn't have to see me around anymore. That would make things easier for Dad, and it would make summer school a whole hell of a lot easier to deal with because I'd be coming home to you every day. We'd be free—no more sneaking around, no more floating into windows or misting under doors."

I looked at him hopefully, and he seemed to weaken ever so slightly before his iron reserve returned, and I was shut down. "No, Grace. We agreed that we'd get married after graduation."

"Yeah, but only one of us will be graduating, remember?" I grumbled before squirming out of his arms and assessing the mess I had created. "I guess I should go and get the dust pan or something to clean this all up."

"You're changing the subject, Grace. You always do that when you don't want to face something. What's wrong, aside from the obvious?"

I laughed before the tears started to fall down my face once more, my hands dashing them away frantically as my head tossed back and forth at the ridiculousness of my reason. "It's just that, I never really cared about graduation before, and now that I know I won't be going to mine...I've never wanted to go more. It's like a cruel, reverse psychology joke or something. I *know* I deserved to pass Mr. Branke's class, and to know that I won't graduate because of him—I feel so angry and so dumb all at the same time. Why didn't I keep my mouth shut about the shoes? Why couldn't I have just waited a couple of more days?"

"Because, despite everything, you're human, and as a human you make human mistakes. You saw what you saw and that doesn't make you wrong, just mistaken. You made it as right as you could, you apologized."

He touched the tip of my nose with a warm finger and then caught a tear in the palm of his hand, smiling as the crystal liquid turned solid, shimmering in the lamplight.

"This part of you, this special part of you that makes you different is what makes you feel things far more deeply than anyone else could. You feel hurt, love, joy and sorrow much more intuitively, much more sincerely than anyone else could.

"It's why you cannot help but feel so profoundly guilty about what's happened, even though you still cannot let go of the anger you feel toward Mr. Branke for not changing your grade when he had the chance. But I also know that you can forgive much more completely as well because this part of you doesn't just make you different; it makes you special."

He plucked the tiny tear drop from his palm and crushed it between his two fingers, turning the crystal into sparkling dust. He looked at me and playfully tipped my chin with his free hand. "Make a wish," he told me before a puff of air left his lips, blowing the dust toward the window. I watched the faint glitter float outside and quickly made a wish that I knew he could not hear.

"That's not fair," he exclaimed, while I laughed and shook my head.

"Uh-uh. It's my wish and if I want to keep it a secret, I can. Besides, it's bad luck to tell."

"Fine. If you won't tell me your wish, I won't tell you mine," he teased.

"That's fine with me since you'll probably end up telling me anyway," I teased back.

A mischievous smile crossed his lips before he tackled me and pinned me to the bed, my giddy laughter soon replaced with the rapid thumping of my heart. The silver ring of his eyes turned liquid, his pupils dilating as his gaze roamed over my face, fixating on my lips that parted when I realized his intent.

"We shouldn't do this," he groaned.

"No…we shouldn't," I agreed, my own voice nothing more than air.

And then his mouth was crushing mine, this kiss desperate, needy. Our promise to be good was quickly forgotten once the taste of his lips on mine, my lips on his, filled our senses. I could feel the weight of him and knew that nothing could ever feel so wonderful. That is, until he began to grow lighter. My hands that had flattened against his back, desperately trying to bring him closer, began to sink lower, into him,

28

through him. When they finally lowered down onto my chest, I inhaled deeply, taking in the sweet smelling mist that now hovered over me like my own personal fog. It trembled—actually trembled—as it drifted over my body and down the sides of the bed.

"Robert, don't do this again," I moaned when slowly the dark smoke disappeared.

"I have to," a muffled voice replied from beneath me after a period of silence passed.

Grunting, I rolled over and leaned my head toward the underside of the bed, pulling up the bed skirt and glaring at the glowing figure that lay behind it in the shadows.

"Hiding under my bed is pretty crappy," I told him as the blood began to pool in my face.

"You don't understand how difficult this is for me."

"I can imagine," I replied sarcastically.

His head turned to face me, his eyes glaring at the insensitive tone in my voice. "No. You can't. It physically hurts to deny myself being with you, Grace; almost as much as lying to you does. But *you* promised my mother that you wouldn't become intimate with me, and we promised each other that we'd wait until we were married before we did anything else…again."

"It was a moment of weakness when I made that promise with you," I huffed before pulling myself back up onto the bed. I stared at the ceiling and frowned. "You told me that if we waited just one more week, we'd never have to wait again. One more week, you said, remember? And now look at us—five weeks. One week has turned into five, and you're still hiding under my bed, talking about '*it hurts*'. Did you ever stop to think that maybe I hurt, too?"

I waited for his response, but when he said nothing I sighed and rolled over onto my stomach, letting my arm dangle to the floor. "I'm sorry. I just don't like rejection."

I wiggled my fingers and waited for his to reach out to take mine but he didn't. "Robert? Robert, I said I was sorry—all of this has just been a bit aggravating for me and knowing that I have to wait even longer isn't exactly making things easier. I'm not helping things, am I? Robert?" I slid off the bed and peeked beneath it, gasping when I found it empty. "Where'd you go?"

Standing up, I spun around in a circle, looking at every corner, every wall to see if he was merely hiding before heading to the window to look outside. "Ow, crap!" I yelped as my right foot dropped down and mingled with the forgotten glass on the floor. I fell onto the bed, clasping my ankle in my hands and watching the blood ooze from a large gash in my sole. A larger piece of glass was protruding from it, surrounded by smaller, tinier shards of sparkling pain that grew darker as the blood seeped through the tiny cuts they'd created.

A thumping sound came from Matthew's room, and I suddenly realized that the crying I had heard earlier had stopped. With nervous fingers, I pulled the largest piece of glass out of my foot and tossed it onto the bed. I hobbled toward the door and opened it, finding the hallway dark. There was no light coming from downstairs, and the light that should have been glowing from beneath Dad and Janice's door was absent. I turned to the left and limped to Matthew's door, grabbing the handle and attempting to turn it. It was locked.

"Janice?" I called out, but no response came. I jiggled the doorknob once more, and found it just as inflexible. "Janice, open the door!"

I pushed against the door with my shoulder but it wouldn't budge. Leaning down, I braced myself against it, planting my bleeding foot on the wooden floor and pushing, biting through the pain that shot through me as the glass embedded deeper, but the blood that had pooled beneath me caused me to slip, and I fell, holding onto the doorknob to keep from landing on my face. "Janice!" I shouted, and began pounding on the door.

From behind the wooden surface, I could hear muffled crying. This spurred me on, and I scrambled to my feet, limping away from the door a bit and then charging toward it, leaning my head and shoulder down and slamming into the dubiously solid door. The force of the impact reverberated through me and I fell once more. The wailing grew louder, and I shook off the pain to stand up once more, this time putting more space between the me and the door.

With a heavy, forceful grunt, I ran, shoving my entire right side into the door. It gave and I crashed into the room, tumbling into the closet door and bouncing off, landing on my back. A loud bang followed as the door slammed into the wall, the doorknob embedding into the plaster getting trapped there.

Groaning, I rolled over and reached for the crib, using it as leverage to pull myself up. Matthew lay inside, his legs and arms flailing as his red face and puckered lips warned me of the coming scream. My hip and shoulder were throbbing, while my foot felt like it was on fire. Ignoring the pain, I reached into the crib to pick the baby up, cradling him against my chest securely before turning around to take in the state of the room.

Janice wasn't there; the rocking chair that sat in the corner was empty. The window was shut, and the air in the room was stale and stifling. Matthew's diaper was full, his pajamas wet. He screamed in my ear, and I knew I had to remedy the cause of his discomfort before anything else. I worked quickly, removing his clothes and changing his diaper. Almost immediately, the baby calmed down, his cries turning into small whimpers as he adjusted to being dry and warm once more.

"Sorry, little guy," I told him as I put his wet clothes into his hamper and threw his diaper away. "I thought your mom was in here."

I limped toward the door, eased it out of the wall, and stared, astounded, at the evidence that the door was, indeed, locked. "You couldn't have locked it from the inside, so who did?"

Leaving bloody footprints behind me, I headed to Dad's door. I knocked, but no one answered. "Dad? Janice?" My hand grabbed the doorknob and turned it with ease, the door swinging open quietly into the darkened room.

"Dad? Are you awake?" The clock on the bedside table glowed a bright red, revealing that it was only ten minutes past nine. I reached for the light switch and flicked it, filling the room with soft light that illuminated the empty bed.

The bathroom door was closed, but a light was on beneath it. Gingerly, I padded toward it. I raised my hand to knock on the door but saw that it was open, a sliver of bright, white light peeking through. Gently, I pushed the door open. The bathroom, too, was empty.

"What the hell is going on?"

I left the room and made my way down the stairs. I reached for the switch at the base of the steps, flipping it on and watching as the living room was lit up.

Every room was empty. I thought that Dad hadn't come running to my room when he heard me screaming because he figured Robert would take care of it. Now I realized it was because he wasn't here. But neither was Janice and I *knew* that she had gone upstairs.

I heard the rattle of keys, and my body whipped around to face the front door, sighing with relief when Dad walked in, a grocery bag in his hands. "Thank God," I breathed. "Where'd you go?"

"To the store. I told you this morning that I'd be going down after dinner to check on the inventory," he replied as he walked past me into the kitchen.

"Oh, I must have forgot," I mumbled, following him and watching as he unpacked fruit and vegetables into the refrigerator.

"Well, given the news that you got today, I don't blame you. What's up with Matthew? Is he hungry?"

"No, he was wet. Is Janice bringing the rest of the stuff inside?"

His head popped out from behind the refrigerator door and I saw the alarm in his eyes. "You mean she's not here?"

"No."

The refrigerator door slammed shut, and he rushed toward the door that led to the garage, flinging it open and sighing when he saw that Janice's little, white SUV was still inside. "Did you check the bathroom? The doctor gave her the ok to start taking baths now that her sutures have healed."

I nodded. "I checked your bathroom, the hallway bathroom; Matthew's door was locked, Dad. She must have locked it, but why?"

"I don't know. Did you check the backyard?"

Together we headed to the kitchen door, Dad flinging it open and rushing outside while I flipped the backdoor light on, the yellow glow barely revealing anything outside.

"She's not here," he called out before returning. "Maybe she just went out for a walk to think about things. She does that sometimes. Grace—you're bleeding!"

He pointed to the floor, and I nodded. "I know. I broke the window in my room and then stepped in the glass," I explained. "I heard Matthew crying and thought that was more important."

"Good God, Grace, you got blood all over the house! Come on; sit down at the table before you make things worse."

He reached up onto the refrigerator to remove the first-aid kit and began to rifle through the various bandages and pads, pulling several out, as well as a tube of ointment and placing them all on the table.

"Give me Matthew," he told me, holding his hands out for the baby.

"I'm fine, Dad. He's asleep. I just need the glass out, that's all."

"You know, my eyes aren't that good—you might have a better chance with Robert; where is he?"

I shrugged my shoulders and looked away as a knowing look crossed over his face. "You made him angry again, didn't you?"

"Yes," I answered glumly.

"Sometimes, I'm glad that he's the one you've chosen, Grace. Only an angel could have the patience to be with you," he mumbled before he sat down and began his ministrations.

I sat quietly while he clumsily removed shard after shard of glass from my foot. I flinched when he had to dig around to reach a deeply embedded piece, but stayed silent, choosing instead to focus on the picture of Janice and Matthew that was held onto the refrigerator by a magnetic frame.

The touch of something cool and wet rubbed against the bottom of my foot, and then the stinging began. Once more, I flinched, but again I remained silent, not wanting to disturb the baby. Dad began to smear what I assumed was the ointment on the sole of my foot before he wrapped it up in gauze and pads, finishing it off with some surgical tape.

"Your right foot's gone through some hell this year, hasn't it?" Dad remarked as he lowered my foot to the ground and began gathering up the wrappers from the gauze and pads.

"Nothing it can't handle," I joked.

"Yeah, well, it's handled it very well...it's handled everything very well. Your mom would have been so proud...of your foot."

I looked at his face and saw the sullen look that had taken over his features, his eyes turning glossy as his gaze rose to meet mine. "Dad..."

"I'm sorry, Grace. If I'd been honest with you from the beginning maybe none of this would've happened-"

My head swung from side to side in denial. "Dad, stop. If you had told me about Mom and about you, I probably wouldn't have believed a single word of it. And even if I did, it wouldn't have stopped me from meeting Robert."

"I should've left this damn town after your mother died. I should've just taken you back to California when I had the chance..."

"Dad, Ameila would have found us no matter where we were; you know that. How...how could Mom say that she loved me when she knew she was only having me so that I could die?"

Two hands gripped my arms as Dad brought his chair closer to mine. "Grace, your mother loved you. She loved you so much, from the moment she knew she was gonna have you.

"She never stopped talking about you. She would talk to you while you were inside her. She knew you were a girl from the very beginningand named you before I even found out: Grace Anne. When she was four months pregnant, she told me that your eyes would be brown and that you'd have a dimple. She said you loved listening to music. It didn't matter what it was, your heartbeat would just slow down and you'd simply relax in her belly. She called you her peace.

"When you were born, that was the only time I'd ever seen her frightened; she didn't want anything to happen to you. Her doctor did a c-section, just like with Matthew only I didn't pass out. And when they handed you to me so that I could show you to your mom, she just cried and cried. She was so happy to see you, so happy to finally have you in her life. I'd never seen her that happy before; you were everything she ever wanted.

"I asked her about Sam, but she told me not to worry about him. She said that everything was going to be fine because you were here. I believed her then, and I still believe her now. Every single time I felt like everything was falling apart, that things were just too chaotic to deal with, you were there to make things okay, even if sometimes you're the reason for the chaos to begin with."

I laughed, startling Matthew whose hands rose up in angry little fists, mad at the disturbance. I patted his back and bounced him to help ease him back to sleep as Dad continued.

"When I got the call about the car accident, I knew that Samael had gotten to Abby. But I prayed to God that you were safe. I never prayed before in my life; I prayed that you were alright, that nothing had happened to you because I was prepared for the day when your mother wouldn't be around anymore—we both were—but I never thought for even one second that you'd be taken from me, too. Abby wouldn't have brought you into this world and shared you with me if she knew you wouldn't be in it for long.

"Your mother loved you, Grace. She loved you so much. You were her entire world, for every single second you were alive you were what she lived for, and I will never believe for a single moment that she intended any harm to come to you."

It was easy to believe him, the way he looked so sincere. He still loved my mother, even after learning the truth, and I envied his ability to do so. I could only compare it to the way I felt about Robert, how I had still loved him despite the deep betrayal I had felt upon learning that he had known that Sam had killed my mother, but nothing could equate the secret my mom kept.

"Dad...why didn't you tell me that Mom was pregnant when she died?"

He choked on the question, or perhaps the answer that he nearly blurted out, his hand dashing out to rub Matthew's back again.

"Grace...your mother and I both knew that no matter how miraculous her pregnancy was, it would never come to term. Her time was limited, and she knew that she was only ever going to have you. We didn't want to tell you that she was pregnant because we didn't want you to get excited."

"So you don't want to know why Mom needed Ameila's help to get pregnant with me but didn't need her help to get pregnant after that." I asked, curious now to know how he felt about what Ameila had done.

"No, Grace, I don't. I knew—deep down I knew that there was no way that you were mine biologically, but I didn't care; a father knows his little girl, and you *are* my little girl, Grace. However your mother was able to get pregnant that second time, it doesn't matter anymore. The only thing that matters is that you're here, that you're safe—that means more to me than anything else in this world."

"But it's only temporary," I reminded him sadly.

"Don't talk like that, Grace-"

"Dad," I interrupted, "I know that you want to believe that everything will work itself out, but it won't. You grew up around these people; you know what they're like. They don't deviate from their paths, from their calls. And I have my own call, Dad. I have my own call and it's not to stay alive."

Dad's face registered shock, and I felt foolish for not realizing that he didn't know. "Oh God, Dad, I'm sorry..."

"Why...why didn't you tell me?"

"I-I-I didn't think. I didn't think that it mattered."

"Grace Anne Shelley, you didn't think that it mattered to tell your dad that you have a call all of your own? This changes everything, Grace; you realize that, don't you?"

"How does it change everything?"

He reached for Matthew and took him from my shoulder. He stood up and walked into the living room. He placed the baby into his bassinet and then returned to the kitchen, sitting down and pulling his chair even closer to me.

"Grace, if you have your own call, that means that you're more of an angel than the seraphim have let on, and if that's the case, then they can't let you give yourself up to Robert—angels can't kill other angels."

"But I'm not an angel! I'm…I'm something else. Maybe I am one of those Nephilim things, or maybe I'm something else, but it doesn't really matter—I'm dead either way," I told him, my voice dripping with despair.

"Grace," he chastised. "You're not Nephilim; your mom wasn't an angel when you were conceived. If you're like anything, it would be like Robert, and his existence is welcomed by the Seraphim which means that yours is, too. That means that Robert cannot take your life."

My eyes watered as I tried to explain why this wasn't exactly a positive thing. "Dad, you don't understand. We both can't live. One of has to die and I don't want to live in this world if he's not in it with me. I watched him die twice and both times he came back because he wasn't meant to die, and I can't watch him die a third time; I'm not strong enough for that, and I don't ever want to be."

"Grace, you've survived so much, you've cheated death over and over again—that's supposed to mean something, don't you see that? Don't you see that you were meant to live?" he cried, his hands on my shoulders, shaking me gently but firmly, trying to press home his concern and his fear.

My tears fell down my face, hot and heavy as I shook my head at his words. "I'm not, Dad. I'm not. Robert wasn't born for me; I was born for him. I was born to die for him. I never cheated death, Dad. I never cheated him. I was waiting for him."

The minute the words left my lips, I realized what I had done, and my hands flew to my mouth, as though the simple act could somehow pull the words back in, erase them from Dad's memory, but it was too late. Dad's eyes bulged at this revelation, his face paling as the truth became scars in his mind and heart.

"Dad…" I began, but he shook his head.

"You knew…you knew all this time what he was, and you still…you still brought him into our house. You still brought him into our lives, into your life. Why? Why would you do that? Why would you put us in danger like that? Do you know the kind of evil that he's capable of?"

"He's not evil, Dad! He's not Sam! You said it yourself, he's Ameila's son—he'll do what's right!"

"Yes! What's right for him! Death is the only angel who has the power to kill indiscriminately without repercussion, Grace. His reach goes far beyond human life! If Sam had killed you, the seraphim would have found him guilty of overstepping his bounds by taking what was rightfully Robert's because when Death claims a soul, it's his and no one else's.

"He's the gatekeeper to heaven and hell; that's more power than all of the seraphim combined! He's not waiting around for them—they're waiting around for him! I cannot believe this, Grace. He's deceived you, led you to believe that he's good. This can't happen—you can't marry him!"

The acidic tone to his voice, the sheer broken spirit that spat those words out to me felt as though he had just slammed his fist into my chest. I couldn't speak, I couldn't breathe. I just stared at him.

"You can't marry Robert, Grace. I won't allow it," he ordered.

"Dad!"

"No! Don't 'Dad' me, not when your life is at stake. You're

going to tell Robert that the wedding isn't just postponed, it's called off. You're going to end your relationship with him, Grace, do you hear me?"

Angry. That's what I was; I was angry. "You can't tell me who I can and can't see anymore, Dad. I'm eighteen. I'm an adult."

"It wouldn't matter if you were eighty, Grace—no one should be getting involved with Death; especially a human!"

"Well, it's a good thing that I'm becoming less and less human the more I learn about myself then, isn't it?" I snapped, standing up so abruptly the chair fell from beneath me. "I don't have much time left, Dad. The call could come at any time, and when it does it'll be stronger and more demanding than before."

"How do you know that?" he asked angrily.

"Lem told me," I answered honestly.

"Lem?"

"Yes, Lem. That night he and Sera were here-"

"When did he say this? I didn't hear him say that."

I sighed and felt my shoulders slump as I realized that I had dug myself into a very deep hole of deceit when it came to my father. "He shared his thoughts with me. He knew that you didn't know about my call—I didn't even find out until that night in the park—and he didn't want any more secrets to get out, especially in front of Janice."

"You talked to Lem about this—Sam's father—but not to me, your own dad?"

His face told me quite clearly that he was hurt. The heartbroken expression that lined his eyes and his mouth with deep grooves hurt to see. "Dad…"

He turned away, unable to look at me, unable to acknowledge me, as my confession turned into a betrayal against him. He stood up angrily, somehow managing to avoid any eye contact with me, and headed toward Matthew's bassinet. He reached in and lifted his son out, gently cradling him, before turning and heading up the stairs.

I opened my mouth to say something, but what could I say?

Sorry? Sorry Dad that I couldn't talk to you about the little voice in my head that keeps telling me that I need to die? Sorry that the person I love more than my own life happens to be the one who's going to take it because he's Death?

Feeling utterly useless, I turned off the kitchen light and began to head upstairs. At the third step, I reached over for the light switch. My eyes did a quick scan of the living room and then I flipped the lights off, the darkness pooling behind me and swallowing the room.

Almost immediately, my hand flipped the switch back up, flooding the room with light once more. I rushed toward the closet door, the last thing I had seen before the lights went out. "Dad!" I shouted as I threw the door open before my cry turned into a horrified bellow that then dissolved into a whimper of dismay.

One side of the closet held shelves filled with linens that had been moved down here while Graham had been sleeping on the couch, but the other side held a bar where winter coats usually hung during the cold season. Except it wasn't the cold season. It was the end of spring, and there were no coats hanging up.

Instead, Janice was dangling from a noose made from the tie of a her robe, the blue terry cloth wrap hanging open, exposing her bruised and battered body. Her eyes were closed, her mouth slightly open, a dribble of spit glistening at the corner of her lips.

"What's wrong?" I heard asked behind me before I was roughly shoved aside. "Janice? Oh my God, Janice! Baby, no! No, God, no! Why? Why would you do this?"

Above us, the wails of baby Matthew could be heard but slowly faded as a buzzing began to fill my ears. I watched Dad struggle with Janice's body, his mouth soundlessly moving, his eyes blinking away at rapid tears that fell down, landing on his shirt and darkening the fabric.

My gaze traveled down to Janice's hand, and I saw the glint that bounced off of the small diamond in her ring. It flashed, once, twice as Dad finally got Janice down, her hand flopping onto his shoulder, the motion making the reflection look like a twinkling star. I blinked and shook my head.

"Dad."

I could hear my voice, but I heard no response from him as I once again said his name. "Dad. DAD!"

"What, Grace? My God, what the hell could you possibly want right now?"

"She didn't do this." My voice was calm, eerily so, and I knew that anyone normal should have felt frightened by that, but I wasn't.

"What? What do you mean she didn't do this? She hung herself in the closet, Grace! I don't have time for this," he shouted at me as he dragged Janice's lifeless body into the living room. "Call 911. Call 911 right now. She's still breathing-call 911!"

"O-okay," I stuttered before rushing to the phone in the kitchen, dialing the number and waiting for the operator to pick up.

As I began to relay the information to the woman who answered the call, I saw Dad begin compressions on Janice's chest before puffing air into her mouth. Seeing his desperation, hearing it in his voice brought back memories of my very own moment of desperation when it had been me on the ground, despondent, lost as Robert lay on the ground, his heart unmoving, dead in his chest.

"Dad, the ambulance is coming," I whispered as I hung up the phone. "They're coming."

He didn't hear me, though. He was bent over Janice's body, his own body shaking and quivering with the harsh sobs that tore through him as he continued his effort, his voice hoarse as he repeated her name over and over again between breaths.

"Grace…"

My head jerked up and I spun around. Robert stood at the kitchen door with a grieved look on his face, his arms held out to me in invitation.

"Robert," I whimpered before rushing to him, my hands needing to feel him, my arms needing to hold him. "She didn't hang herself. Someone did this to her; I know it."

I felt his head bob down once, confirming my belief. His embrace tightened around me, pulling me up against his chest to the point my feet were off the ground. *She's between life and death right now.*

"How do you know?" I asked into his shirt, too upset to look at him, too guilty...

*It's who I am, Grace.*

"And you didn't say anything? You didn't warn me or come help her?" I was stunned.

*I'm sorry, but there was nothing I could do. She isn't dead; not yet, but she's very close. And you are right; she didn't do this.*

"Dad believes she did," I whispered.

*And that's exactly what we will let him think. Whoever did this cannot know that you suspect differently. Keep your mind closed; say nothing to anyone about this. I will talk to Lark and see what she can find out.*

He pulled away from me so swiftly, I barely had time to register that he was leaving before he was gone, the faint remainder of a kiss lingering on my lips.

Robert wanted me to lie, which required that I lie to Dad...again. I hated doing it, I hated the idea of it, but the walls were closing in on us. The number of dead was growing bigger; first Katie; then Mr. Branke and Erica; and unless help got here soon, Janice as well. Only this time there was no Sam to blame. There was no definitive target anymore.

Katie's death had been an accident, a case of mistaken identity. Erica and Mr. Branke had been already been dead in all ways that counted long before their hearts finally stopped beating. What happened with Janice, on the other hand, had been intentional. This meant that whoever else was out there did not care about rules anymore. Whatever this person was planning, whatever their intent, the laws got in the way.

"The laws..." I breathed, my eyes suddenly widening with recognition. "That's it!"

# THE TREE

"Come on, Matthew, please, *please* stop crying!"

I walked toward one wall and bounced three times before turning around and pacing toward the opposite wall, repeating the same triple bounce, turning around once more and repeating the process all over again. It was three in the morning, I had class in four hours, and I was completely alone, trying to comfort a colicky newborn that sensed that he, too, was all alone.

Three days had passed since Janice was found in the closet. Dad was gone, spending all of his time at the hospital. Janice was in a coma and the prognosis wasn't good; she'd been without oxygen for a dangerously long time and the reality that there wasn't much that could be done was starting to weigh heavily on Dad.

Robert had not returned since that night, and I did not know if it was because of what Dad had said or because of what I had done. He wasn't in school, and though Lark continued to attend, she didn't acknowledge me. Only Graham continued to speak to me, our conversations the only part of the day that I looked forward to. With school ending, there was no real instruction during class, and so, many kids simply didn't attend. This made for empty classrooms, which was fine with me as I used that time to catch up on sleep.

Sixth period was the only class that required my full attention. Mr. Danielson, the drama teacher, refused to allow us to become complacent and instead had us participate in trust building lessons, memory building exercises, and so on. Normally, this would have made me grit my teeth, but with Chad, Dwayne, and Shawn—also known as Chips, Dips, and Salsa—it was difficult to find anything but enjoyment during this last hour of school.

And when that bell rang, I glumly headed home, riding the bike that had replaced my old one that had been destroyed almost nine months ago. The babysitter that I had hired to watch Matthew while I was in school was sitting on the couch folding laundry when I arrived. She was an old friend of Janice's who had babysat a few times before and didn't charge much.

"Hey Paula," I said to her, walking over to the bassinet and picking up a rather alert Matthew. "Hello, little man," I cooed. "What are you doing awake?"

"I just fed him and changed him, so he's quite content to just lay there and stare at the ceiling," Paula commented as she gathered her things, shoving them into her overly large handbag.

"Oh, here Paula-" I grabbed the crumpled wad of twenties in my pocket and handed them to her "-this is for today and for tomorrow. I won't be going to school on Thursday or Friday so you don't have to come and watch Matthew," I told her.

"What about graduation? It's on Sunday—did you want me to come on Sunday?" she asked, her eyes hopeful.

"No. I'm not graduating," I answered flatly.

"Oh. Well, okay then," she said with mild annoyance in her voice. "I'll see you tomorrow morning then. Oh, your dad came home about an hour ago and asked me to stay. He's upstairs; I think he got some bad news."

My eyes drifted toward the stairs and I felt a pain in my chest. "Okay, thanks for telling me. I'll see you tomorrow."

"Goodbye, Grace."

I watched her leave and then closed the door, Matthew squirming in my arm like a curious kitten. "Hey, what's the matter, little guy? Don't like my bony shoulder?" I quipped, shuffling him around a bit until he was more comfortable. "There, is that better? Do you want to go and say hi to Dad?"

I started toward the stairs when the doorbell rang. Annoyed, I turned around and returned to the door, peeking through the peephole and seeing an unfamiliar looking woman standing on the porch. Though the vision through the tiny hole was distorted, the size of her head exaggerated by the glass, it felt as though I knew her somehow. I opened the door and in the soft light of the afternoon sun, I felt my jaw fall in absolute amazement.

Standing before me was a woman who looked like the female version of my father. Her hair was brown, like his, but her eyes were a light, almost aquamarine shade of blue. She was a foot shorter than Dad, which made her far shorter than me, but she was him in every way—right down to the small cleft in her chin.

"Are you Grace Shelley?" she asked me in a surprisingly feminine voice.

"Yes," I responded. "Who are you?"

"My name is Jessica. Jessica Shelley. I'm James' sister."

"You must be mistaken," I corrected her. "My father doesn't have a sister."

"No," she said in a monotone. "He disavowed his family, but we never disavowed him, and now we're ready to welcome him back—he is needed home."

She pushed past me, her posture rigid with discomfort as she walked up the stairs, her movements and direction so sure it was as though she had been here before. I followed her, uttering protests and complaints with each step while Matthew grew fussy in my arms at my sudden change in mood.

She stopped in front of Dad's door and stared at it. "How is he?"

"Probably tired. He's been at the hospital all this time. My stepmother…something happened and-"

"I know what happened."

"Oh. Well, then you probably know that you coming to visit like this isn't exactly a good idea."

Her eyes narrowed, her brows pulling together as a frown formed on her face. "He's electus—we might lose our way for a while but we never lose that, and it never leaves us. He's made mistakes and has been punished for them. Now, he needs to realize that his family needs him, and that he needs us."

"Why are you doing this for us?" I asked her as she opened the bedroom door.

She looked at me and snorted in disgust. "I'm not doing this for you."

"But you just said-"

"I said that his family needs him—I did not say that it included you."

And then she was gone, disappearing behind the door that clicked as she locked it. I stood there, staring at the door mutely while I tried to figure out what she meant by that. How was I not family? Dad was my...Dad. And if she was his sister, that made her my aunt.

Before my thoughts could fully form, the sound of shouting could be heard from inside the room. Dad was angry, and so was Jessica. The yelling grew louder, and only then did I notice that it wasn't in English. Dad was speaking in a different language, one that sounded familiar.

"Dad speaks Latin?" I whispered, amazed.

Something large and heavy crashed against the door, the sound startling me and sending me flying back in surprise. I clasped Matthew to my chest as the crashing continued, mixed with the yelling that switched from Latin to English with frightening speed and ease. The door and the walls shook with the jarring sound of glass breaking, and my foot began to throb while painful memories flashed in my mind as the tinkling sound of glass shards spreading across cold tile could be heard from where I stood.

And just as suddenly as it started, it stopped. Everything was eerily quiet and a strange calm took over. When the door opened and a flustered Jessica emerged, she didn't look at me. She just walked downstairs, her footsteps heavy with anger. The front door was opened roughly and slammed with equal vigor, the whole house rattling with the force.

I took several steps toward Dad's room, being careful to avoid any glass and debris that might be on the floor. "Dad?"

"I'm here, Grace," his voice called from the bathroom, offering me an odd sense of relief after not hearing it for the past few days.

"Dad…are you alright?"

"I'm fine, kiddo."

I walked into his bathroom and gasped at the mess that lay on the ground, the large mirror that had taken up one entire wall now lying in reflective slivers around Dad's feet as he stood in the middle of what looked like a warzone. "Dad, what happened?"

He said nothing. His eyes were focused, staring at the wall where the mirror had been attached. I tip-toed through the mess—thankful that I was still wearing my boots—and whistled when I saw what he was gazing at.

"What is it?" I breathed as my eyes took in the large, intricate image that seemed to have been burned onto the wall, the design resembling a large, ornate oak tree, with dozens of expansive branches, free of leaves, that fanned out into smaller, tinier groups until there were hundreds, perhaps thousands of segments that were all labeled with strange lettering.

"It's our family tree," he answered with disdain.

"Our family tree?"

"Yes."

I brought myself closer. "Why is it on the bathroom wall, Dad?"

"Because it follows you no matter where you are, no matter who you try to be. It's a reminder for us—a curse really—to let us never forget that when we are born, we become bound by our family's vow to protect the angels. Our families were chosen thousands of years ago and given the blessings of never having to need or want for anything in exchange for perpetual servitude, regardless of how many generations the families extend.

"Even if we leave the family, even if we never take the test, this tree will appear like a brand wherever you call your home. When your mother and I moved here, it appeared after that first night. I couldn't have your mother see it so I covered it up with mirrored tiles. I stayed up all night doing it, and once it was behind a wall of glass, I tried to forget it existed, just like I tried to forget that my past existed. I almost succeeded, too."

He pointed at a small fork in a multi-tipped branch that hung so low, its tip nearly touched the floor. One thin line stretched out and split into another smaller, thinner one. "This extension…this is me, and this line is Matthew."

"She said that I wasn't family," I repeated as I crouched down to examine the foreign lettering.

"She would say that—it goes against the laws of the family to get involved with an angel, so to marry one is just unconscionable, even if the angel has lost his or her divinity. My relationship with your mother wasn't unique, Grace, but you are, and it doesn't matter what your mother was when you were born—children of an angel and human are strictly forbidden.

"EPs are just as rigid when it comes to their laws as the angels are; so to recognize your existence would be recognizing the breaking of one of our oldest laws. It doesn't matter what they think, though. I know that you're not what they fear. Your mother wouldn't have done that to you, to us."

I shifted Matthew to my other arm as I traced the branch that Dad said represented him up toward a dozen other shorter branches. "You have a lot of brothers and sisters," I remarked.

Dad nodded. "Twelve. Jessica is the youngest. The oldest was Joseph; he left the family when I was ten. He died a year later in a fire at a church. My parents never spoke about his death—they didn't speak

48

about him at all after he had gone. It was like he simply stopped existing. I assumed that it would be the same with me once I left."

"So what changed?" I asked softly. "Why did she come now, after all this time?"

He exhaled and pointed to his branch. "Do you see the difference between this one and the others?"

My eyes flicked back and forth between the larger group and the lone segment that represented Dad, taking in the only subtle difference that could be seen. "Yours is the only one that continues on...with Matthew."

"Yes. I'm the only one who's had a living child. Jessica came here today because she wants Matthew to take my place. My family is one of the few that protects the dark ones, but that protection comes with a price. For a few, it's too high a price to pay. It's why I left; it's why Joseph left," Dad explained. "As a child, you're told only the good things about angels, and you know that it's this incredible secret that only you and your family are aware of. It makes you feel special; it makes you feel like you're a part of something incredible and amazing.

"And then you take the test, you get asked the question that will change your life forever, and when all of your dreams come true, when you get everything you thought you wanted, you realize that the glory isn't without its own grievous stain. We're brought up believing that we'll be protecting the angels, beautiful creatures who are full of this awesome power that you would do anything to experience. Instead, we find out that we're protecting monsters who exist solely to cause pain and terror.

"'The end result is the same' I was told when I questioned why we were covering up some of the most heinous crimes imaginable. If it takes being scared or losing someone to get people to return to their faith, or to simply find it, then it's all right. 'The ends justify the means' they said, but I couldn't accept that—how could I?

"I had been taught that we were doing a good thing; all my life I believed that we were helping people to escape the nightmares of their godless lives, and then I find out that *we* were the monsters. This revelation was soul crushing, and everything I thought I knew suddenly lost its meaning. I had nothing. After a lifetime of believing and wanting something so badly... I was empty; I had lost my reason for being. It's why I left.

"The rest of my siblings found nothing wrong with what they were doing, and they paid the price for that. Every branch in this tree has stopped growing, the children have stopped coming. Every one of my siblings died except for Jessica, and now she's turning to me. They need me. More importantly, they need Matthew."

He looked at Matthew and then me, his eyes lingering on mine with a gentle sort of sadness in them before he touched the baby's nose with the tip of his finger. "I told Jessica that she and the family could go to hell. I'm not giving up my family—the family that I chose for myself—to help maintain a legacy I put behind me a long, long time ago. She said that the family was dying out, and I told her that I didn't care.

"What have those demons ever done for us? What have they done but destroyed the good in us? My brother Joseph was the first one to leave in over thirty generations. No one has ever chosen to leave the family, and he paid for it with his life."

My head perked up at this, and I asked, astounded at what he was saying, "You said he died in a fire. That fire wasn't an accident, was it?"

Dad's head jerked to the side, and I saw his hands ball up into fists against his side. "No. We possess their secrets. We possess their past in our history, and they cannot let us leave with it. Joseph was killed to set an example for the rest of us, and we were supposed to learn from it. I did. I learned not to get caught."

Matthew let out a deep sigh, and I looked down to see that he had fallen asleep. I couldn't help but smile at his blissful face and envy him the ability to just close his eyes and shut everything out without fear of consequence or the ugly visions of death and fear floating behind his lids.

"But you got caught, Dad."

"Not really. Sam didn't want me; he wanted your mother. I didn't realize that until it was too late, and now I'm paying the price for it twice over. I lost your mother, and now I'm going to lose Janice. If I do, you and Matthew will be all I'll have left. If I give him to Jessica and he ever decides that this isn't the life he wants for himself, what will happen to him?"

I grabbed a hold of his robe with my free hand, balling it into a fist and pulling it as I forced him to look at me. "Robert can keep him safe, Dad, he'll keep Matthew safe. He'll protect him from them."

"No," Dad growled. "I don't want him near you or Matthew."

"Dad, you don't know Robert if you think he's like all of the others," I tried to explain, but he cut me off.

"Grace, you don't know anything about them. You saw Sam, you saw him at his worst—as an Innominate—but you've never seen the others, the ones whose dark callings are so full of evil that they've changed themselves physically to resemble the darkness inside them.

"Samael, as evil as he was, was still your mother's son and still had some good in him. The others…they're demons, monsters that only care about causing harm and suffering. Robert leads them. He controls them. Millions of people die every single day in this world, Grace. How do you think he oversees them all when he's with you?"

It bothered me how little faith he had in Robert, how little he understood despite the lifetime of knowledge that he had about angels. "Dad, I know that what he is isn't exactly what you expected. I know that what he is bothers a lot of people, but no one more than him. You don't know what it's like for him, to be responsible for the deaths of so many people. Did you know that before he got his call he could heal people? Did you know that?"

Dad shook his head, doubt plain in the lines around his mouth as it drew into a grim line. "It's not possible—healers don't end up as dark ones."

"It's true. He could heal others. My God, did you never stop to wonder why I healed so quickly after being hit by Mr. Frey? Did you never stop to wonder why my burns disappeared after one day? It's because of Robert.

"Healing people was his gift, Dad. It was his ability, and when he got his call it...it's like the call took it away from him. Do you know how devastating that was for him? He went from being able to save lives to taking them. You know better than anyone that he couldn't choose his call anymore than you could choose whose family you were born into. How can you hold what he is against him when he's never done anything to give you reason to?"

The storm of emotions that displayed on Dad's face before he turned away from me pulled at every string in my heart. "Dad, Robert loves me. I know you cannot understand that, and maybe you never will, but please, please try to see that whatever he is, I don't care. I love him, and no matter how short my time is here, I cannot see spending it without him."

"How do you know he loves you, Grace? He's an angel—they can charm anyone to feel anything they want."

I shook my head in denial, the very idea so laughable, I chuckled. "Dad, you don't get it. He's never been able to charm me into doing or feeling anything. Maybe it's because I'm not completely human—I don't know—but I've never felt anything for him that wasn't real."

The air in the room was beginning to grow thick with Dad's doubt, and I knew that there was only one thing left to tell him. "He tried to get me to leave him, you know."

"What?"

He looked at me, and I could see the uncertainty in his eyes begin to waver, even if only slightly. This bolstered me, and I continued. "Last Halloween. He told me he didn't love me. He knew that I had been unsure about his feelings, and he used that against me by telling me that he didn't love me."

Dad's voice was raspy when he asked, "What happened?"

My gaze was steady, but my voice shook with emotion as I answered. "He died."

"That's not possible."

"It's true, Dad. I was there. I saw everything. I ran away from him when he rejected me; it was like Graham all over again, only a million times worse. I couldn't be near him; I couldn't even look at him—it hurt too much—so I ran. And that's when the screaming started. It was the most awful sound I've heard in my life. If dying had a sound, that would've been it.

"I followed those screams until I found Robert. He was in so much pain, and I didn't know how to help him; I didn't know what to do for him. He was dying and there was nothing I could do to stop it...that's when he told me that he'd lied; he did love me."

Dad's snort caught me off guard. "He was just saying that to make you feel better. *That* was the lie, Grace."

"No, Dad," I contradicted. "That wasn't the lie. It was the most significant thing to have ever happened to me in my life. He wasn't telling me he loved me to save himself—he knew it was already too late. There was no reason for him to say it to me, no reason to say it at all, but he did. I felt his heart stop and I thought that was it, my life was over.

"Robert had put me back together, he had given me a reason to see myself as something other than Grace the Freak, to believe that I actually deserved to be loved by someone, and now he was gone? Just like that? I couldn't believe it. I didn't want to believe it—it wasn't true.

"I hated him then, Dad. I hated him for making me love him; I hated him for telling me he loved me only to leave me without giving me a chance to love him back. He was dead, and hating him wouldn't do anything, but I had nowhere else to go emotionally. It felt like my own heart was dying—I would have died right there with him, Dad. I wanted to die right there—I prayed for it—because without him I knew that my life would be meaningless-"

"You barely knew each other!"

"I knew enough to know what he was and to know that he lied to protect me, despite what it would cost him. He died, Dad. He died, and I thought that was it—the world was going to end, and I'd never get to hear him say that he loved me again. Every single moment, every person that had existed then didn't matter to me anymore. My life was Robert; if he didn't exist anymore then neither did I. And then the most amazing thing happened."

"What?"

My face beamed, and I answered proudly, "His wings came."

"His wings? After he died? That's impossible-"

"It's not impossible. Nothing is impossible when you're talking about angels."

Dad's voice was a shadow of itself when he exclaimed in wonder, "That means…you're his wing-bringer."

I nodded triumphantly, a hot tear slipping past my lids and rolling down my cheek. "Lark and Ameila were there, they were there and they did nothing to help him. They just cried, and I got angry. I got so angry, at them, at him, at myself. I lost it, Dad. I lost it, and I began to hit him. I slapped him, punched him, I hit him and then hit him again until my hand started to hurt. And I kept hitting him and hitting him until the pain went away. I didn't care what it meant, I didn't care what it looked like—my entire life was gone because he was.

"And then something stopped me—*someone* stopped me. I thought it was a dream, a really bad nightmare when I looked down and saw that Robert was holding my arm. But it wasn't anything like that. Robert was alive—he was alive and all I knew was that he had come back to me. You don't come back to someone because you want to see them dead, Dad. You don't come back to someone because of something you said to make them feel better. You come back because you love them—you love them so much that it defies death and dying."

My chest was rising and falling heavily, the impact of my own words doing something to me that I knew Dad could not ignore—the notion that love could resurrect the dead was not one that was lost on him. I could see that it brought the question why, if he loved my mother so much, and she loved him as deeply, could she not return as well? Remorse came to me quickly at this revelation, but Dad saw this and his response was quicker.

"Grace, don't think that I now doubt the love your mother and I shared; I don't. Your relationship with Robert merely drives home the truth that your mother's time here was done. She had fulfilled everything she'd been created to do—the most important of which was to bring you into this world. But loving me—that was something she did all on her own. She chose to love me, to marry me, and give up eternal life to be with me. I cannot know that and not believe that she loved me every bit as deeply as you claim Robert loves you. However, knowing now what you have endured, the tests your relationship with Robert has been put through...I..."

"Yes?" I urged when his voice faded away.

"I suppose I must reconsider how I feel about him, if only because you love him that much."

My free arm wrapped around his neck while a whoop of joy left me, flew right out of my lips, startling Matthew, who had remained contentedly asleep through all of the other outbursts, and he expressed his disapproval with a plaintive wail. "Dad, that's all I ask. That's all I want, is for you to see him the way that I do," I whispered into his ear.

I felt Dad's head bob up and down, but I could also sense the rigidity in his body that had not yet let go. "I won't tell you that I approve, Grace—I don't think I'll ever be able to now that I know who and what he is—but...he's done more for you than his kind normally would-"

"Because he loves me, Dad," I finished for him. "Because he loves me."

"The pain an angel endures when they lie has been compared to being set on fire and having every nerve that dies out be reborn, only to be destroyed again in an endless cycle that increases with intensity—no angel would willingly endure that, even for love. What he feels for you must be something much, much more."

It was a strange thing, hearing Dad speak to me about what it must have felt like for Robert. I knew what it felt like—I had felt it inside of me. The screams had made it seem like my blood was exploding in my veins, and that my head was caving in even as it expanded to allow for the horrible visions that I had tried to block out. Sitting there, with my thoughts pulling from the air the memories that I thought didn't exist, I saw the images that hadn't been important enough, significant enough to recall later.

But now, now that I had opened myself up to them, they flew in, one after the other like raindrops making up a storm that shook me. "It's not true," I whispered before pulling away from my father and his confused expression.

"What's not true?" he asked.

"N-nothing," I lied quickly. "I'm just overwhelmed by all of this-" I pointed to the charred image in front of us "-it's so much to take in."

He glanced over at me skeptically, but turned his attention back to the blackened lines that told in vague detail the cost that dedication to the darkest of angels could wreak on a family legacy. "It doesn't matter what this says—or doesn't say—this is not my family. I gave up that life a long time ago. I cannot do anything about you—you've already made up your mind about this world—but I can do everything in my power to keep Matthew from being a part of it. He deserves a normal life, the life his mother and I want for him."

Dad's voice cracked at this last part, and his hand flew to his eyes, pinching them, fighting the burning and stinging I knew he felt behind closed lids. "Dad…"

"I don't know what I'll do if she dies. She'd been so distant since that night, and I don't blame her. I told her to leave me, to take Matthew and raise him far away from me and the mess that I had thrown her into, but she said no. She had gotten angry at me for even suggesting it, can you believe that? She was more upset at my suggesting she leave than at what she had just learned about who I was, about who we were involved with.

"She told me that she and Matthew were staying. She said that we were a family, and that she didn't care if the devil himself appeared and called me his uncle; she wasn't going to break up our home. I believed that if she wasn't screaming and trying to harm herself or Matthew that she was fine and just adjusting to things in her own way.

"I should have insisted that she leave. I should have insisted that she take Matthew and go somewhere. Because of my own stubbornness and willingness to believe that things could go back to normal, Matthew might grow up without a mother. What's going to happen to him if she dies?"

I grabbed my father's hand and pulled it away from his eyes so that he could see the earnest expression in my face when I told him, "Dad, she won't die. I won't let it happen. But...but if she does, I grew up without a mother, remember? You raised me all by yourself, and you did a very good job of it, too."

"What good came of it, Grace? You're in love with Death. How could I have done anything good if I'm going to be gaining the angel of death as my son-in-law? How can I introduce him to my poker buddies? To the people at work? 'Hey guys, this is my son-in-law, Death. Death, the guys.'"

I smiled at his half-hearted attempt at humor. "By knowing that I was able to find someone who loves me as much as you loved Mom." Almost at once, my tone turned somber. "And besides, if Robert and I are putting off getting married until after summer school, there probably won't be a wedding anyway."

Dad's eyes lit up with immediate recognition of what I had just hinted, and the theories rolled around in his head before he finally came to the right conclusion. "You think you'll be dead before the end of the summer?"

"I have no reason not to," I answered simply. "When I read the letter from Mr. Kenner, I suggested to Robert that we elope-"

"Grace Anne Shelley, you did not!"

I rolled my eyes at the outburst. "I did. But don't worry—Robert insisted that we wait because we had agreed to getting married after graduation."

"It's about time he did something sensible," I heard Dad mutter under his breath before coughing and then looking at me with seriousness in every line on his face. "You know that I still refuse to believe that you are going to die, right?" He waited for me to nod before continuing on, never giving me a chance to utter another sound.

"The call inside of you was postponed once—there's never been such a thing before, not that I'm aware of anyway, but then again there's never been one of you before—which makes me believe that it can be put off again, and again if need be, until-"

I cut him off, exasperated at his refusal to accept the unavoidable. "Until what? There is no 'until' here, Dad. It's not something that you can just put off! We did that and look at what's happened—Katie, Erica, and Mr. Branke, all dead. And Janice-"

"This has nothing to do with Janice!"

"It has *everything* to do with Janice, Dad! Janice didn't hang herself in the closet! Why would Janice refuse to leave you, only to hang herself a week later? She didn't do this to herself, Dad—Janice loves you too much to do that to you."

"If she didn't try to kill herself then who did, and why?" he demanded to know.

"I don't know, Dad," I answered softly, almost futilely. "I don't know."

# STONES

One week after Janice was found hanging in the downstairs closet, she was moved to a different hospital. It was one that specialized in severe brain injuries, where they could monitor her brainwaves and see whether or not she would recover. A part of me wanted to say that I knew someone who could figure that out just by closing her eyes, but I kept silent.

Dad set up the room exactly as she would have liked it and brought pictures of Matthew to put beside the bed. He opened the curtains to let in the light and adjusted a pillow beneath her head, being careful to not disturb the wires that floated around her head and down the side of her neck. He then sat beside her, forgetting everyone else in the room.

A hand slipped into mine, and I looked up into green eyes that smiled down at me. Graham had arrived at the house last night and had not left my side, insisting that as my best friend he belonged with me. It had brought tears to my eyes, and I could say nothing for a good hour, too overwhelmed by the need to tell him everything that had been running through my mind and the need to keep it all to myself until I had figured it all out. Instead, he began to tell me what I didn't have the courage to ask.

"You know, when you told me about this Sam person, I was expecting some kind of monster or something, some four-eyed, horned devil-looking dude who spit fire and stuff. Instead, he was like a blonde version of Robert, including the whole creepy sneaking-into-the-house-through-the-window part.

"He seemed friendly at first; I thought he was a friend of Lark's or something the way he talked about her, about her childhood. I felt comfortable around him, which I realize was probably stupid since I didn't know him, and Lark's never talked about any friends of hers except for you and Stacy.

"And then I felt this crushing sort of pain in my head, like I'd just been sacked by a three-hundred pound lineman. I know I passed out, and I remember thinking when I woke up that I was such a wimp for letting it happen. I wanted to do one of our epic face-palms, you know? That was when I realized I couldn't move. I didn't understand it. It wasn't like I wasn't trying; it was like my brain and my body were in two separate rooms.

"I couldn't even move my eyes. All I could see was the ground; it looked like I had been dumped in some hole, like I was trash or something. I stared at ants crawling in the dirt for what could have been hours—it actually made me miss French class, can you believe that? I started to get hungry and those ants were looking really good by then, which is really gross, and I can't believe I'm even telling you that, but then, I always tell you everything. I thought things couldn't get any worse after that, but I was wrong because right then a toe—a big, hot-pink painted toe—appeared in front of my nose.

"I knew that pink; Erica loved that color, talked about it all the time when we first started going out. I thought I was saved, and I tried to get her to help me, I called her name but it was like she couldn't hear me. She just stood there until someone else showed up."

"Mr. Branke," I filled in.

"Yeah—I recognized his shoes. I thought that at least he'd help me, but I was wrong. He stood there like a zombie. I didn't need to see his face to know that. I just...I felt it, which meant that if he was some kind of zombie or something, then that meant Erica was, too. And then like nothing, they started to move.

"They walked around me and picked me up, and I remember thinking 'wow, Erica's pretty strong'. They dragged me to this huge boulder—it looked like one of those rocks we saw in geography class in ninth, remember?—and then they leaned my back against it and pulled me onto it. I couldn't feel anything before then, and all of a sudden, it was like I was being pulled apart.

"Erica held my feet, while Mr. Branke held my hands, but it's not like it was necessary—I still couldn't move. That's when Sam came. When he looked at me, I knew why I was being held down. He didn't say anything, just smiled at me, like we were buds or something—I didn't even know he had moved until I felt myself hanging from Erica and Mr. Branke's hands. Sam had hit me; he hit me so hard, the force broke the rock underneath me, and I thought that was it, I was going to die because my insides felt like soup and that's never a good sign, you know?"

He stopped then to look at the innocuous grayish band that wrapped around his left ring finger. His finger twisted it, turning it around and around as his mind seemed to struggle to find the right thing to say.

"It's strange what you think of when you think you're dying. I saw Lark's face in my head, and I thought how lucky I was to have had her, even if it was for only a little while. She was everything worth fighting for, everything worth living for…which is why it felt weird that I had completely given up ever seeing her again.

"I felt like such a jerk, like I didn't deserve her, and that's when I saw your face take over hers, and seeing you in my head…it made my heart start racing, like it wanted to jump out and just take off, and I felt so guilty. I mean, I understand why it happened—you're my best friend, you're the reason why Lark and I are together in the first place—but it still made me feel like everything that I had thought I knew about myself was wrong somehow.

"Lark had her mother turn me, she had changed me physically so that I could be with her forever, but all I could think about right then was what did all of that mean if the last face I saw before I died was yours?"

The woeful look on his face gave me pause, and I tried to console the obvious feeling of betrayal he must have felt then, but he patted my knee and shook his head.

"Don't, Grace. Worrying about it now is pointless because I didn't die. Sam continued to beat me. It was like a game to him, to see how far he could stretch this immortality of mine until I broke. But no matter what he did, nothing changed. I didn't die, and after a while, it was like he got bored, and so the beatings stopped.

"But then the other one appeared."

"Other one?" I asked, alarmed.

"Yeah," Graham replied with a single bounce of his head. "Whenever Sam was around, even if he was wailing on me, he'd actually talk to me, you know? Like, use his mouth and say things. This one...this one didn't; it only used thoughts. I couldn't tell if it was a guy or a girl because I never saw who it was, and the voice in my head sounded like it was coming through an empty soda can or something, but just hearing it made my head hurt. It was like poison or something the way it would make me feel sick and dizzy afterward. And I couldn't see anything when it talked; the only thing I could hear was what was in my head—everything else got blocked out.

"You want to know the most messed up part? That voice told me that what was happening to me was nothing personal. Nothing personal, can you believe that? The two of them together took turns, kicking and punching me like I was nothing, like it didn't matter that I begged for them to stop, but it was 'nothing personal'.

"They broke my back; I felt my neck snap twice. I was scared that I'd never feel my legs again, but like Robert had said, I healed. It was crazy, but I could feel my bones pulling back together, like a slinky or something. At first, everything fixed itself in a minute or two, but as soon as I was better, they'd start hitting me again, and with each beating the healing took longer and longer.

"I guessed it was because the beatings weren't just lasting longer, they were getting more violent. I mean, I swear they almost tore my arm off, Grace. I felt my skin ripping, and you know what? It doesn't sound like it does in the movies, like a T-shirt tearing, or celery breaking. It sounds like gum being popped—that's what it sounds like; at least, it does to me. After figuring that out, it was pretty simple to work out why they were doing it."

I felt my head cock to the side, my jaw falling loose as I asked him why. A sarcastic sort of snort slipped past him before he responded.

"Because they wanted you to think that I was dying. They were timing it, Grace. They were seeing how much I could handle, and how long it would take before I healed so that they could create the biggest impact on you. They wanted to hurt you.

"When the other angel was around, if he wasn't…thinking to me, Sam would be arguing with him. Sometimes, he'd ask why they couldn't just kill me and pretend that I was still alive, but most of the time he just complained about you, about how much he hated you, how much he wished you had never been born. All I could think was why did he hate you so much?

"Lark won't answer my questions about what happened; she's still so upset by everything, and I don't know why, Grace. She and Ameila act like Robert's still dead or something, and every time I ask why, I get the run around because they don't want to tell me the truth. What's going on?"

The tone in Graham's voice had grown irritated, and the frustration that he felt was visible in the fists that he had balled in his lap. His jaw was clenched so tightly I could hear his teeth grinding against each other. I felt horribly pressed to tell him what he wanted to know, what *I* knew, but at the same time, I could barely understand any of it myself.

"Graham, you said that you were in a hole…when you were leaving to come to the field, did you see what kind of hole it was?" I asked, needing more information.

"I said it looked like a hole. After that first night, I saw that it was more like some kind of cave or something. It was dark, but not so much that I couldn't see anything. Oh, and everything echoed."

I smiled in appreciation and continued. "It sounds like you were in a sanctuary."

"A what-uary?"

"Sanctuary. The angels have this place…it's like their own panic room, where they can go to be away from everyone and everything. It makes sense that Sam would take you there. He knows that Lark would hear your thoughts no matter where you were…except in there because no one outside can hear what's going on inside. That means that he probably had you close by."

"It was kinda close, I guess. When I was in the car with Mr. Branke and Erica, I stared at the clock in the dash; the entire ride only took ten minutes."

"Did you tell Lark this?"

He shook his head and sighed, his hand fidgeting with the dark metal band on his left-ring finger once more. "I told you; she won't talk to me at all about this. She keeps saying that she doesn't want us to get any more involved, but how can we not get any more involved? You're my best friend, and hell, Robert's her brother! You've gotta talk to me, Grace. Tell me what the hell is going on because I'm getting nowhere with her."

I grabbed Graham's hand and forced him to stop twirling the ring. He looked at what he had been doing and grinned sheepishly. "Graham, Lark's upset, but I can't tell you what's going on with her because I don't know. I know she blames me for what happened, and I know she resents the fact that her call demands that she keep me safe. She's obviously chosen to ignore it, which I suppose she views as only a temporary thing. It's what I prefer anyway—I never wanted to come between her and her brother, ever.

"But I can't tell you anything else, Graham. I've already screwed up in that department once and it's come back to bite me in the ass— hard. I can't afford to do it again."

"Is that why Robert's not here?"

His question forced me to stop and think about that. *Was* that why Robert wasn't with me? Had my slip-up with Dad angered him? He'd said nothing the night Janice was found, which did little to ease my fears that perhaps that last kiss had been a goodbye that he couldn't say.

"I don't know. I don't know why he's not here. He said that he was going to find out what he could about what happened to Janice…he said he was going to talk to Lark-"

"Well, he hasn't been around the other house, that's for sure," he cut me off.

"He doesn't need to be around the house to speak to Lark," I reminded him.

"Yeah, well, it's not like Lark would tell me if she had spoken to him anyway. She and I haven't really spoken much since that night. It's been weeks, Grace, and the only thing she wants to do is…you know, *it*. Not that I have a problem with that, because it's always great, it's just that I miss talking to her. Like I said, she won't tell me anything."

"I don't know what to say, Graham. Maybe you should be with her right now, instead of me…"

"No. I belong with you right now. Besides, in a few weeks I'll be gone from this God-awful place so I've got to spend as much time with you as I can, right? Even if it means spending it in a hospital."

And I was never more grateful for him being around than I was right now. It was draining, seeing the sorrow in Dad's face and watching him teeter on the edge of hope and hopelessness every time he spoke to Janice's still body. Between trying to make sure that Dad didn't pass out from exhaustion, Matthew was fed, cleaned, changed, and loved, and not freaking out about not graduating, I felt like I was a thousand-years-old.

"Come on, let's leave him alone," I said, turning around suddenly and walking out into the hallway.

Graham's grip was sturdy and reassuring as I teetered from the dizziness of moving too quickly.

"Are you okay?" he asked, concern wrinkling his brow.

"Yeah, I'm fine. I haven't eaten anything yet, and I've been up since five. Hey, shouldn't you be getting home? You graduate tomorrow, remember?" I reminded him.

"Well, that's a whole twenty-six hours away. We still have one more thing to do today."

I was stumped as to what he meant when he took my hand and dragged me out of the hospital and toward his car. "You've got the sitter watching Matthew, right?"

"Yeah. I told her we wouldn't get back until after ten."

"Good."

We drove listening to the radio play some of the songs that took us through high school. It felt good to laugh and cry and be silly for a little while, completely forgetting what was going on in the world until I saw where we had finally stopped.

I climbed out of the car, and Graham grabbed my hand, dragging me through the grave stones toward a dip and a rise that led to one in particular, its vase filled with daffodils...her favorite flower.

"I don't want to be here," I argued vehemently.

"Grace, she's your mom. It doesn't matter what she did—or why—she's always going to be your mom. You can't stop loving her now just because you found out something bad about her."

"That's easy for you to say—the worst thing your mother's ever done is shack up with some guy ten years younger than she is," I threw at him.

"This isn't about me, Grace. This is about you—you've never been one to hold grudges against anyone. You've always found the ability to forgive people—hell, you forgave me and I know that I had a much lousier reason for hurting you than your mom did—so why can't you forgive her? Make peace with her while you have the chance. Life is short, Grace; don't waste a single moment of it hating someone for something you can't do anything about."

"I…I can't, Graham. You don't just forgive someone for ruining your life before it's even begun," I said simply.

"She's not just someone, Grace," he implored. "She's your mother, and she did what she did because she knew something that we could never understand. I might not have been able to hear everything that was said that night, but I do remember that if she didn't do what she did, you wouldn't be here, and I can't hate her for that. I love her for that—I love her for having you because my life would've sucked big time if you weren't in it, Grace."

"It would have only sucked because you wouldn't have met Lark," I scoffed.

"That's not true—if I'd never met Lark, I wouldn't have known what I was missing—but I would've missed you even if I didn't know you. You're my best friend, Grace. You helped me through a lot of tough crap with my parents; you were there for me when no one else was.

"You cheered me on at the games even when I sucked, and you never expected me to be anything but your friend—you never expected me to be the hero, or the star, or the popular one. Yeah, if you hadn't started dating Robert, I would've never met Lark, but even if I had, who I would've been without you would've been someone completely different, and she would've wanted nothing do with me. Your mom gave me the best gift in the world, Grace. She gave all of us the best gift in the world."

I wanted to believe him, I wanted to hear his words and let them be true, but it was impossible when I knew so much that he didn't. "I hope you still feel the same a thousand years from now," I said halfheartedly.

"God—a thou-a thousand—whew…I'm having trouble with that number. A thousand years?" he stuttered, looking at me with wide eyes and a slack jaw that looked about ready to fall off.

"What did you think 'living forever' meant, Graham?" I asked irritatingly.

"I'm eighteen—forever isn't exactly an official number...but a thousand? Is that possible?"

"Your *wife* is half-way there, Graham. Jeez, did you even think about any of this when you agreed to get married?"

"To be honest with you, I thought that turning was a great way to be all superhero-like and do the things that I've always wanted to do but was afraid that I'd get hurt trying. The fact that I get to have sex with Lark was also a bonus."

"Graham..."

"Hey, I love Lark, okay? If I close my eyes and try hard enough, I'm pretty sure that I can see myself with her for a thousand years...maybe. But this whole marriage thing isn't what I thought it would be. Everything's changed—I told you, she doesn't talk to me much anymore.

"Right now, that's okay, because I've got you, and the boys, and hell, even Chips, Dip, and Salsa hang around. But what happens when we're in Florida? What happens when I start college, and she's doing...whatever it is that she does when she's not pretending she's in high school? Is the only thing we'll have going for us gonna be sex?"

He shoved a distracted hand through his hair, the golden spikes crisscrossing into a disheveled mess as he sighed and stared at my mother's headstone. "I didn't know that this was going to happen, Grace. It feels like there's this big rock tied around my neck and it's pulling me down—and I hate to say it, but that rock is starting to look a lot like my wife."

"You don't mean that," I started, but he gave me a look that said quite unequivocally that he did.

"It's pathetic, isn't it? I haven't even been married a month, and already I'm complaining about it. I'm married to the hottest girl in the world, and every time I'm with her, I keep thinking about ways I can get away from her so that I can have a conversation with someone—anyone—and it doesn't matter what it's about. I even had a conversation with Ameila about Jell-O once. Can you believe that? Jell-O!

"What am I going to do once I'm in Florida? Who's going to sit down and watch Rocky Horror with me? Who's gonna stay up with me until the sun rises to talk about farts? What am I going to do without you, Grace? What am I going to do when you're not in my life anymore?"

A strangled sob got caught in my throat as I choked out two words that I had been rehearsing in my mind for weeks now, the only words that I knew I'd be able to say to him when this time came.

"You'll live."

## GRADUATION

Sunday came way too quickly. I wanted to hide in my room and not emerge until summer was over, but I couldn't do that to Graham— he was graduating in just a couple of hours and did not yet know if his mother and father would be attending, though I was pretty certain that Iris Hasselbeck would show up, if only to rub it in that her new boy toy was younger than Richard, which pained me because Graham didn't deserve to witness that.

Instead, I waited on the couch in the living room, wearing a simple white blouse with the skirt that Janice had bought me for Christmas, while Dad got ready. Matthew was in his carrier, his lids heavy after downing an entire bottle of formula.

"Okay, kids, let's go," Dad announced as he hurried down the stairs dressed in a suit that looked so old, it looked stained with dust.

"Is that what you're going to wear?"

His eyes lowered to his chest and then rose to meet mine. "Is there something wrong with it?"

"No. No, Dad, you look just fine," I said with an encouraging smile. "Let's go."

He bent down to grab the infant carrier and together we walked outside. Janice's little SUV sat outside in the driveway, and Dad took a moment to pause and stare at it before walking around and opening the door to his car. I followed, helping to keep the door open while he snapped Matthew in.

We drove to the school in silence, the obvious disappointment that my Dad still felt at my not graduating coupled with his worry over Janice, not making for very good conversation. I was tempted to turn the radio on but stopped myself a dozen times. The lot was nearly full when we arrived, but Dad found a stall, and we exited the car in silence. I could see the crowd of gowned students off to the side of the gymnasium, preparing for their last stroll as seniors, and I felt a longing that had never existed within me before.

I *wanted* to be a part of them. I wanted to be a part of this class that had ostracized me and excluded me from everything since grade school, and I couldn't understand why. They had gone out of their way to avoid me at all costs, only involving themselves in my life when the events held some sort of entertainment value. And yet, I still wanted to stand beside them and walk down the aisle with them, cheer them on as they stood up to collect their diplomas, and toss my cap into the air with them as we cut away the last ties to our childhood.

Instead, I walked into the gym with my father and baby brother and took a seat with the rest of the audience. I couldn't help but smirk at how fitting it was—I had always been on the outside looking in here at Heath, and that's exactly how I would leave it. I sighed in resignation as the music began to play, the pomp and circumstance of twelve years of schooling coming to a grand and bittersweet end.

\*\*\*

"Did you see my mom?"

"No, I didn't see her; is she here?"

Graham nodded, his head scanning over the crowd. "I saw her with the latest boyfriend—Kyle—he's only eight years older than we are, can you believe it?"

Dad clapped Graham on the shoulder and laughed subtly. "Graham, it doesn't matter how old he is. If he's making your mother happy, that's all that matters. Besides, we're not here to talk about her.

Congratulations, son."

"Thanks, Mr. S. You were always like a second father to me, so this means a lot," Graham gushed.

"I only wish that we could be celebrating the both of you graduating, but circumstances being what they are, I'm very proud of you."

"Have you seen Robert?" I asked quietly, while Dad busied himself with a fussy Matthew.

"Yeah. He's right behind you."

"Oh."

I turned around slowly and saw the warm mercury eyes smiling down at me, the impact of it hitting me squarely in my chest and causing me to tumble forward. Sturdy and sure hands grabbed me and pulled me into a soft and warm embrace that eased away the stiffness of worry and rejection that I had had bearing on me for a week now.

"I'm sorry," I murmured into the itchy polyester folds of his gown.

"Sorry for what?"

"For telling my dad about you."

He chuckled and squeezed his hand between us, pushing my chin up to face him. "Why are you apologizing for that? You didn't intend on revealing anything to him. It was an accident—a completely *human* thing to do—and I cannot blame you for being what you are."

"But...you stayed away. You didn't come to see me; you didn't come to check on me or anything. I-I thought you were angry at me."

His head dipped down and a quick pass of his lips over mine was followed by another soft laugh. "You silly girl." He straightened then and turned me around to face the stern and disapproving expression that was plastered on Dad's face as he stared at the two of us, a bawling Matthew in his arms.

"Hello, Mr. Shelley," Robert greeted warmly.

"Robert," Dad said coolly.

"Hey, it's my mom!" Graham interrupted with a whoop.

Iris Hasselbeck had worked her way through the crowd and

rushed to Graham with a mixture of tears and laughter distorting her beautiful features into something more comical. Her arms slipped around his back as she squeezed him, his own arms wrapping around her and hugging her with meaning.

"Wow—my boy is all grown up and not afraid to show some affection to his mom. I like this change in you—what's brought it about?" she tittered as she wiped away the dark streaky tears that had marred her makeup.

"Well, my, um…girlfriend, for one. And Grace," he answered proudly.

"Girlfriend? Where is she?"

"She'll be here in a moment," Graham insisted. "Mom, you remember Grace and her dad, right?"

Iris turned around and, as though she just realized that she and Graham weren't the only people in the gym, immediately plastered a smile onto her face that she reserved solely for the people she'd rather not speak to—and the narrowing of her eyes told me she knew that I was aware of this.

"Hello, James! It's been too long since I've seen you—you look like you've lost some weight, in all the right places, I might add. And who's this? Is this your son? He's a feisty one, isn't he? Just like his father—handsome, too! Hello, Grace."

The tone of her voice went from pleased, to content, to downright contemptuous in under a minute, and I couldn't hide my own contempt when her eyes took in Robert standing behind me, and her expression changed once more, her voice lowering into a sultry, almost hungry growl. She stepped forward, her hand reaching out in invitation.

"And who are you?"

"I'm Robert, Mrs. Hasselbeck," he answered politely, while refusing the proffered hand.

"Oh no, no; you call me Iris, Robert—I love that accent. You must be one of the new friends Graham's been telling me so much about. You must come out to dinner with us tonight to…celebrate." She looked downright covetous as she inched ever closer to him, ignoring Graham's embarrassed groan and my gasp of shock when she took my place in front of Robert, her once rejected hand now resting possessively on Robert's arm.

"I'm grateful for the invitation, Mrs. Hasselbeck, but I must decline—I've already made plans, as has Graham…isn't that right, Graham?"

Graham took his cue and nodded vigorously. "Yes. Yes, we've got plans, Mom."

Iris' eyes darted between the two young men before her and frowned. "Well, couldn't I join you? I mean, this *is* your graduation, and I did fly all this way to see you. What are you two planning to do?"

Graham stepped up beside me as Robert took my hand, the two of them grinning like loons as Robert replied, "We're going out to dinner with Grace."

"Grace? Hmm…did I imagine it or were you *not* a part of the procession?" she asked, her gaze scrutinizing me from head to toe.

"You didn't imagine it," I replied, my voice saccharinely sweet. "I wasn't allowed to graduate because of a missing science credit."

The icy laughter that crawled out of Iris' throat sent chills through me as her smugly lit eyes narrowed into dark slits. "How ironic, isn't it, that Graham's always claimed you were the smartest girl he knew and yet you're the one who's failed to graduate while my son here has not only done that, but will be attending college in Florida. And what will you be doing, Grace? Attending community college while working at your father's grocery store, I suppose? How predictable."

"Iris, I don't think what Grace does is any of your business," Dad interjected.

"Of course it is, James," she said in retort. "Graham's a good kid, who cares about his friends, but your daughter has a way of making people feel sorry for her when they shouldn't. I wouldn't be surprised if he told me right now that this mystery girlfriend of his that has yet to appear is none other than Grace."

74

The air grew chilled around us, a sudden and drastic dip in temperature that silenced almost everyone in the large gymnasium. Almost everyone.

"Grace is not Graham's girlfriend," Robert hissed, his voice a stabbing sound that sliced through my head and caused me to wobble on my feet. "She's my fiancée, the person I plan on spending the rest of my life with, and the only person who has stuck by your son when both you *and* your husband abandoned him. You criticize her, verbally insult her under the guise of concern for your son's welfare when in truth you do so because you envy how close she is to your son, how much she's been able to do for him despite everything about her you seem to find lacking.

"Your son loves Grace, and that should be enough for you to accept her because her place in your son's life won't ever change, no matter how you feel."

Iris fumed, her face growing red, her expression piqued. "I don't know who you think you are, but Graham is my son—I know him better than anyone, and Grace has never been anything more than a distraction. Once he's in Florida, he'll never think of her again—she's forgettable and always has been."

The next few seconds passed like a blur as I was roughly pushed aside, my feet—still unaccustomed to the added height that the heels I had chosen provided me—tripping over themselves. I squeaked as a pair of hands kept me from falling while a cape of dark polyester flew past me, blocking my line of sight until the disruption settled and I was staring at the back of Graham's head, Robert's arms wrapped around me protectively.

"She was forgettable to *you*, Mom," Graham shouted. "She was forgettable to you, but so was I. You forgot me when I didn't meet your expectations. You forgot me when I became a burden to you, and the only time you ever thought of me was when I could bring you some form of bragging rights. Grace is my best friend. She's always been there for me, even when I turned my back on her.

"I thought I'd tell you tomorrow before you left, but since it seems like I'm probably not going to be seeing you after tonight, I've decided that I'm not going to Florida."

At Graham's bombshell, Iris looked as though she had just swallowed a ping-pong ball: her eyes bulged and her mouth took on a lazy "O" shape that forced her tongue nearly halfway out of her mouth as a guttural sound choked its way out of her. I knew this look well, for it had also found its way to me.

"N-n-not coming to Florida?"

"Well damn, I thought you'd at least wait until I got here," an amused voice said from behind us.

"Lark!" Graham cheered, turning around and sweeping the beaming beauty off her feet, swinging her in his arms as he kissed her soundly. "You're late!"

"I'm sorry. I was delayed but I'm here now and so glad that I didn't miss the fireworks." She turned to face the glare of Iris' hooded eyes and smiled at her with the same false-sweetness that I had shown.

"Hello, Mrs. Hasselbeck. We've met once before, remember? At the homecoming game? A lot has changed since then, hasn't it?"

Iris nodded, her eyes instantly brightening at the sight of the beautiful girl standing in front of her. "It's always a delight to see such a lovely person such as yourself...uh..." The look on the woman's face showed without question that she was at a loss.

"Lark. My name is Lark. Robert is my brother, Grace one of my closest friends, and Graham here is *mon mari*."

"Mount Mary? Have you been hanging around that Donovan boy again, Graham?"

"I'm her boyfriend, Mom," Graham answered quickly, while I choked on the words that had obviously gone unrecognized by the irate and flustered older woman.

"Well, I suspected as much when she kissed you, but why does she know that you're not leaving and not me? I'm your mother—your decision affects me just as much—if not more—than it does anyone else.

Why are you staying in this hell-hole of a town?"

Graham looked at his mother and sighed, his face showing the disappointment that he felt with having to explain to his mother in such a manner, at such a time.

"Because I don't want to be around you, Mom. Not while you're like this."

An insulting sound came out of Iris' throat, and she glared at her son with such scorn I could almost smell his skin singing with the heat of it. "While I'm like *what*?"

"Like this, mom; thinking that you're some teenager, coming to my graduation and hitting on my friends? Where's Kyle or whatever your latest boy-toy's name is? Why didn't he come with you like you said he would?"

"He went back to the motel because I told him that I wanted to spend some time with you—alone—with your pretty little girlfriend before you came home with me. And I wasn't hitting on your friend—it's quite obvious that his standards are too low and-"

"See! Do you see what you just did there, Mom?" Graham snapped, his booming voice cutting her off and shooting across the gym, causing every head to turn toward the heated argument taking place mere inches away from me. "You just can't stop taking pot shots at Grace, can you? She's done nothing to you—absolutely nothing—and yet you continue to pick on her and insult her. Why? Why can't you just leave her alone?"

"Graham, it's okay," I said softly, not wanting the confrontation to grow any more rancorous, but it was too late.

"No, Grace. She's done nothing that the rest of this damn school hasn't done, but damn it all to hell, she was the adult. She has no excuse to treat you this way. No one here does, but if I'm going to get an honest answer out of anyone, it's going to be her. Tell me, Mom, why do you hate Grace so much?"

Iris was fuming, but the steam that had built up within her was slowly letting itself out, her once proud shoulders and chin sinking ever so slightly, bit by bit, until finally her eyes were lowered, and her grimace turned into a shameful frown that aged her quite dramatically.

"Because you always went to her. Even as a little boy, whenever something was wrong with you, she was the one you would turn to. Whether you were sick, or hurt, or just confused, you never came to me, your own mother. You would sneak out of the house and run to hers. I thought that it would fade, that this fascination with her would die, but it didn't.

"And when I saw the way that you would look at her sometimes, I...I couldn't stand the thought of her being a part of your life forever, Graham. She's not good enough for you—for any part of you."

"Now listen here, Iris, any man alive would consider himself damned lucky to have Grace love him—she's too good for all of them, especially your Graham—but your inadequacies as a mother should have no bearing on how your son feels about her. Especially since she's been there for him when you were too busy nailing your sister's pool boy!" Dad's angry and yet strangely calm reply filled me up with such warmth that I couldn't help the wide grin that tugged at my lips.

"Let's get going, Grace—we have reservations that we cannot miss," Robert interrupted, his hands sliding down my arms and filling my hands. "Mr. Shelley, I hope it's alright with you if Grace accompanies Graham and me for a bit of celebrating."

I looked at Dad expectantly, slightly fearful that he'd refuse the request on sheer principle alone. To my relief, he smiled and nodded in agreement. "She should be going out to celebrate—she's just slain the dragon."

I exhaled in relief and pulled away from Robert to throw my arms around my father, who patted me with one hand, the other one occupied with a snoozing Matthew. "Thank you, Dad," I whispered into his ear.

"You have fun, kiddo. This should have been your night, anyway," he said back, his voice cracking a bit.

"Are you going to be okay? With Matthew, I mean?" I asked,

suddenly aware that tonight would be the first time that Dad had been alone with Matthew, ever.

"I'll be fine, Grace—I had midnight feeding duty with you when you were a baby, so I think I might be able to handle one night alone with one who's a thousand times more relaxed than you ever were," he kidded.

"Thanks," I said again before kissing him lightly on the cheek. I pressed another soft kiss onto the top of Matthew's head before allowing Robert to pull me away from a still semi-seething Iris, her eyes still lowered, her posture still slack.

"It was nice to see you again, Mrs. Hasselbeck," I said before she disappeared behind a throng of people too consumed by the ceremony of graduation to care about any of us for more than a second or two.

We were nearly to the exit when a hand reached out to grab my arm. The grip was unusually strong, and I exclaimed in surprise at the person to whom it was attached to. "Shawn?"

"Grace! I thought I wasn't going to see you here—I'm so glad you came! Graham! Robert! Hey, Lark, too! I'm glad I got to see you guys! Listen, I wanted to invite you to my graduation party next week—do you think you'll come?"

"That sounds like something we'll make time for," Robert promised before pulling me away, leaving me to shout a quick and apologetic farewell before we were outside, the summer sun having long since set, leaving the muggy night sky to welcome us with its endless array of stars.

"So, when were you guys going to tell me that you all were speaking again?" I asked when we were standing in front of Graham's rusty Buick.

"We're not exactly speaking to each other," Lark corrected. "It's just that with what's happened recently, and what's going to happen, there really is no room for any form of animosity. Not now, anyway."

"What do you mean, what's going to happen?"

"You going to summer school, Grace," Robert replied before

Lark could. "Janice didn't try to commit suicide—that much we've figured out."

"We think that it might be a message," Lark added, though it was quite clear that she was not pleased with the idea of having to speak to either of us at all.

"A message to who? And about what?"

"A message to your father, to remind him that no one he loves is safe," Robert answered flatly.

My heart began its slow crawl beneath my skin as fear took over every other emotion save panic and anxiety, the slow, icy creeping of blood quickening as my breathing rapidly increased while the intake lessened with each inhale.

"We've got to go back," I told them in jumbled spurts. "We've got to go back and get my dad—we've got to keep him and Matthew safe!"

"Grace, he's safe. My mother is watching him," Lark informed me.

"What? Since when?"

"Since his sister arrived. We didn't want to believe that anything would happen so soon—it is why we were not as diligent with watching over your family as we should have been—but now that she's made herself known, it won't be long before the rest of the dark ones start arriving as well."

"D-did you just say dark ones?" My knees began to wobble, and I grabbed onto the roof of Graham's car to support myself as I grew lightheaded.

"I'm sorry, Grace. I thought we'd be able to postpone this for a few more months or so," Robert said in as consoling a manner as he could manage. "They're coming to see me."

"You? But why?"

"You know why."

I did. I knew why, but there was a part of me that still didn't want to believe it. I still refused to believe it.

80

"Grace…"

"Well, I don't," Graham spoke up then. "Why are these dark…whatever the hell you call them coming to see you?"

"They're the dark ones. They're Sam…only worse," Lark answered ominously.

"Worse? How the hell can anything be worse than that jerk-off?"

"You don't want to know."

"Dammit, Lark, why do you keep doing this? I'm supposed to be—no, scratch that—I *am* your husband. God, you know what I lived with, you know what kind of marriage my parents had, and now you're forcing us to have the same goddamned thing by not talking to me."

"You think I don't want to tell you the truth? You think I want to hurt you and drive you away?" Lark cried. "I'd tell you everything if I could, but there are rules, there are laws that I cannot break for anyone—not even you."

"Graham," Robert interjected; the tension far too thick for him to take any longer. "Lark cannot tell you because I've told her not to. While Grace's safety is paramount to me, so is yours, and anything that you learn from Lark could be used against both you and Grace, and I thought it best that you be kept in the dark about everything."

Graham's nostrils flared as Robert's words sunk in. "You're screwing around with my marriage, Robert. A husband and wife aren't supposed to keep secrets from each other. That's what ruined my parents' marriage—it's what got Grace's mom killed."

"I'm sorry, Graham. I thought—foolishly, obviously—that keeping you ignorant to what was going on would be the best thing for everyone. I see that I was wrong. I love my sister—seeing her hurt has hurt me far more than I could have imagined. Knowing that I am the cause of that pain only adds to the guilt I feel, and I take full responsibility for this, and any additional hurt and confusion that you will no doubt feel the further we go on with this.

"The dark ones are angels whose only purpose is to hurt and kill, Graham. They have no divine purpose—their ultimate goal is not to see the resurrection of faith in a person, but to see their fear and their terror, to hear their cries of pain and their pleas for mercy. And…they all answer to me."

Lark groaned, and I felt the words I had wanted to say lose themselves in my throat as Graham tried to digest what Robert had just revealed to him.

"Why would they do that? You're not like Sam—dude, you killed him. What the hell are you to them?" Graham asked.

"There's no easy way to tell you. I don't know how else to say it other than to just…say it. I'm-"

"Death. He's Death."

Four heads whipped around to look at the person who stood behind the rusted and dented green car, her face pinched with anger, her chest rising and falling with puffed up fury.

"S-Stacy?"

Graham blinked, his jaw hanging open in disbelief. "Is that…holy hell, is that really you?"

"Close your mouth, Princess—you're gonna catch flies."

"Damn! It is you!" Before any of us could stop him, Graham had Stacy in his arms, swinging her around once before quickly dropping her. "What the hell—you're like a slushie!"

"And you're still slower than two old folks doing the grody grope—thanks for shouting my name out loud in the middle of a parking lot, you idiot."

"B-b-but you're here…alive. What else am I supposed to do?"

"How about keep your mouth quiet?" she seethed before calming, a quirky smile pulling at the corners of her mouth before she threw a quick jab, her fist landing squarely on his arm. "It's nice to see you, too."

"Holy crap, ow!" Graham cried, grabbing his bicep and staring at her with a mixture of fear and amazement. "You're stronger!"

"And you're still a sissy."

"Okay!" Lark stood between the two and held her hands out to each of them, the gesture not meant to separate them but to quiet them as the gym began to empty behind us. "We can either continue this…joyful reunion here and expose Stacy to everyone, or we can leave and save everyone from being slaughtered because I'd rather they all die than have Stacy be found out. So, what's it going to be?"

"Whoa—harsh," Graham commented, returning to the car and opening the driver-side door.

"I'll just meet you there," Stacy said before disappearing.

"Meet us where?" I called out, already too late.

"It won't matter where if we don't get going," Robert said as he ushered me into the backseat of Graham's car.

"And we're all going in Graham's clunker?"

"It's only until we get to the house," Graham announced.

"Then what?"

"Then we fly."

## REALITY BITES

"Where are we?"

"Somewhere over Toledo most likely."

The night air was chilly, although that probably had less to do with the actual temperature and more to do with how high we were and how fast we were sailing through the sky. We'd been in constant motion for several hours, and I knew that I had fallen asleep at least once during the trek although for how long Robert wouldn't say. My hair whipped my face as I clung to his neck, afraid to look down, afraid to look anywhere.

"Where are we going? Are we almost there?"

"Yes, we are almost there, and as to where we are going, that is a surprise."

"Surprise?"

"Yes, a surprise. I had planned this all in advance a while ago to celebrate our graduation together, but I wasn't sure if you'd still feel like celebrating after learning about biology, and then after what happened with Janice, I thought it was best to postpone everything indefinitely. Lark heard my thoughts; she told me that to cancel everything would be a mistake. She said that if ever there was a time you would need cheering up, it would be on the night you should have walked down that aisle with the rest of your classmates. She was right."

"So...you're okay then, you and Lark?"

"We're working on it. I told her that I would make things right between her and Graham…and that I would try to make things right between her and Stacy."

He said Stacy's name in an almost venomous tone that forced my head away from the safe hollow of his neck so that I could look at him and see the displeasure he obviously felt at the idea. "You're never going to accept Stacy as an erlking, are you?"

He shook his head. "I can't. I can tolerate Ambrose and others like him—they have learned to cope with their problem and maintain the balance that my kind have set up—for all of us. But Stacy…she's acting like the first ones, that bloodthirsty generation that couldn't control themselves. She's killed again—did you know that?"

An icy tremor ran down my spine and he knew that I did not. "W-who?"

"A man who lived near the cemetery where her coffin's buried. She ate him, left only his head and his bones."

I swallowed in disgust before I asked the question that I hated to ask, but knew that I had no choice; the question needed an answer—I needed an answer. "Are you going to kill her now?"

A long gap of silence followed as his jaw stuck out, stiff and unerring. I waited for it to relax, even if only slightly, to give me any kind of reassurance that he wouldn't, but he kept the straight line of his disapproval set, the rigidity of it simply unmovable.

But…his voice was soft when he replied, "No."

The oxygen that had begun to turn toxic inside of me as I held by breath rushed out in an exaggerated sigh as that lone word did wonders to assuage my concern, my body suddenly remembering how to inhale and exhale again. "Can you tell me why?"

"Why I won't do it? Because the person that she killed had already been chosen to die. It was his time. Stacy…she preempted me by mere hours."

"How do you know it was her and not some other…thing?"

His head ticked to the side, a nonchalant motion that spoke volumes of how easily it had been done. "I recognized her scent."

"You knew it was her because of her smell?"

"Yes. She's dead, Grace. Because of that, she has a particular scent that distinguishes her from every other dead thing that still manages to live. The living dead recognize each other by this scent—it's their calling card."

"Is that how she knew what you were? Because you're...not alive either and smell different to her?"

His mouth curved up in a sadly bemused smile. "No. I may not be alive in the conventional sense, but I am not dead either."

"Well, neither is Stacy," I informed him.

"That's something we can discuss later...right now, I want you to look down."

Slowly, gradually, my gaze lowered until I was staring at the darkness below us. I could see the faint glow of lights that told me we were descending, and as the glow increased in intensity, the lights widening their arc, so too did the scent of something unfamiliar. As we came closer to the ground, I could make out a few buildings and a spattering of street lights that did little to reveal their surroundings.

We passed the outline of trees and homes that were far different from the ones in Heath, and as Robert slowed, I was able to take in the bright, yellow glow that sat in the middle of what looked like an emerald lake. Instead, as our feet touched the ground, I realized it wasn't a lake, but an expanse of jade green grass that, beneath the glow of a dozen antique gas lanterns swinging lazily above us, appeared to shimmer like any stone would under a lit flame.

A table set for five sat in the center of a canopy of wood so light, I would have sworn it had been whitewashed. The lamplight did nothing to mute the vivid colors that had been used to decorate the table, which displayed hues of blue and green in everything from the plates to the napkins.

A large column vase that sat in the center of the table held white, lily-shaped candles that floated in turquoise colored liquid. The table cloth was a shocking white, and the chairs that sat open and inviting around the circular table were covered in the same material, the skirt of each one flaring out, the white darkening into a gradient of blue that ended in a bright, cobalt trim at the bottom.

"Are we having dinner here?"

Robert looked at me and nodded in reply to my question. "Graham and Lark will be here shortly, as will Stacy."

"Where exactly is 'here'?"

"Don't worry about that now. Just enjoy the fact that we're here, with friends."

A low whistle to my left brought my attention to Graham, who stood in a loose shirt and pair of baggy pants, his hand holding onto Lark's tightly. I felt reassured by that, and a pleased and relaxed smile crept across my face.

"This set up looks sweet," Graham exclaimed. "All that traveling made me starved. Can we eat now?"

"We're still waiting for one more person," Lark informed him as she took a seat, her eyes scanning the darkness even as her brow pulled together in frustration.

Robert pulled out a chair for me, and I took my cue to sit, my hand waiting in open invitation for his when he took his place beside me.

"Stacy?" Graham asked as he clumsily tried to scoot his chair closer to the table.

"Yes. She's nearly here, although she will need a change of clothes after that swim," Lark answered him, her colorless eyes unmoving.

"Swim?" I questioned, receiving only a shrug in response.

"It's the only way to get here other than flying," Robert whispered into my ear.

"Oh."

"At last, she gets it," Lark murmured playfully before getting up, only to freeze and turn to face me. "On second thought, it might actually be better if you went and got her things."

I knew why she suggested this, but there was never anything to gain from running from your problems; Robert and I both learned that the hard way. Stacy couldn't be forced to forgive Lark for what she saw as a complete betrayal. The fact that Lark knew the truth about my mother, and what that meant to Robert and I had destroyed Stacy's faith and trust in her, and nothing as simple as speaking to her could fix what had been so irrevocably damaged.

"No problem," I said to her weakly, even as my conscience pricked at me to stay out of it, but her relieved smile gave me hope that perhaps, even if her relationship with Stacy could not be repaired to-night, our relationship could. At least, I hoped it could.

"There's no need to get me anything, I'm already dry."

I muted my surprise when Lark stood up, her steps taking her slowly toward the stark figure that stood in the semi-darkness. Stacy's dark hair disappeared in the slant of a shadow, but her pale skin could not be swallowed up, and the grim line that sliced her face in half told all of us that her time here would not be a pleasant one—especially if any of us tried to force a reconciliation.

"I'm so glad to see you," Lark said to her, her voice faltering at the end when she saw the cold, almost frozen look that Stacy threw her.

Graham approached, obviously eager to learn for himself what exactly had happened to Stacy. "Everyone thinks you're dead, you know. I was there, at your funeral—we all were—and man, it was heavy stuff. Like, global heavy. Your parents are going to flip when they see you. And Sean! He's going to give birth to his own holy cow when he learns that you're alright."

"So none of you guys told him, huh?" Stacy remarked icily. "I suppose I understand why, especially from *some* people-" she looked at Lark then with hooded eyes "-but it's time to stop lying. There's no room for it with all the crap we've gone through. Graham, you're not going to tell my parents or my brothers anything; they think I'm dead and that's exactly what I am."

"Dead people tell better jokes," Graham jested before letting out

88

a rather undignified snort and taking a jab at Stacy's arm. As quickly as he had done it, he was pulling his fist back with a piercing cry of pain. "What the hell?" His hand was mangled, his fingers bent at odd angles while his knuckles were split, the bony protrusions jutting out like teeth.

"Even turned, I still have an advantage over you," Stacy snickered.

"Yeah, but how? Jeez, it's like you're some kind of rock or something! Look at my hand!"

"Sorry, but you should know better than to just throw punches around this crowd, Graham."

"What do you mean by that, Stacy? You're the only normal one here—what's going on?"

Stacy's eyes flitted over to Lark's before a disappointed toss of her head told us all just how wronged she thought Graham had been. "You really didn't tell him anything, did you?"

"No. It wasn't the right time," Lark answered softly, almost ashamedly.

The answer was the truth—as far as truths went—but it didn't stop any of us from feeling the immense guilt at keeping Graham ignorant of what had truly happened to Stacy the day she died.

"Well, let me fill you in, Graham. See, I'm dead."

"What do you mean, dead? Dead-dead, or just pretending to be dead, like witness protection dead?" he interrupted.

"Dead, Graham; as in my heart's not beating, there's no blood pumping through my veins, and my skin is as cold as ice dead."

"But, that means you're a zombie. Or-or like a vampire or something! But that can't be right because you don't have fangs or red eyes or anything like that, so that means you're a zombie, right? Wait, does that mean you're going to, like, eat me or make me your zombie slave?"

I could see Robert's head shaking, and hear Lark's groan of embarrassment, but I understood where Graham's line of reasoning stemmed from—I'd had the same reaction. It wasn't his fault that he did not understand or know that what we pictured in our minds wasn't always what we'd see with our eyes.

"Graham," I spoke up then, knowing that out of everyone, I'd be the one most capable of delivering this news to him without acting like it freaked me the hell out. "Stacy's not a zombie. She's *like* a vampire, but she's not. She's what's called an erlking. She doesn't suck people's blood. She…she eats them."

Graham's head bobbed down a few times in acknowledgement of my words, and then his hand flew to his neck, his voice coming out somewhat squeaky and high-pitched. "You're not going to eat me, are you? Because I probably taste bad; really, really bad—I had a hot dog with extra mustard and sauerkraut for lunch—I'm totally pickled and full of preservatives."

Stacy's chuckle, followed by Robert's amused snort, seemed to ease the sudden tension that had appeared in Graham's face, though his hand did not lower any.

"I'm not going to eat you, Graham," Stacy reassured him. "As cute as you are, you aren't appetizing to me in the slightest, which is actually quite ironic, considering how badly I wanted my last meal and how physically unattractive he was-"

A deep rumbling sound brought about her immediate silence, and I gasped when a bristling Robert wedged himself between Stacy and me, his hands held out protectively, keeping me behind him. "You are mocking my generosity and patience, Stacy," he growled, his voice sounding unnaturally deep and foreboding.

"Oh get off of your moral high horse, Robert—you're no saint, not with what you do. You take lives every single day, whether you're there to do it or not. All of those people are inconsequential to you, their lives and what they mean to other people mean nothing; they're just part of your job. The only lives I've taken, I've done so out of necessity, and neither of them was worth a damn and you know it."

"Stacy, I thought—I thought that you couldn't do this anymore," I interjected. "You looked so pale, so weak the last time I saw you. You said-"

"I know what I said, and I meant it…at the time. When I left your house that night, I promised myself that I'd never do it again. I left with the intention of going back to see Dr. Bro and telling him to help stop all of this, to just end my life or fix me somehow. But before I could, I felt I needed to do something; I needed to see where that boy lived, I needed to try to make amends to his family. Every second that that boy's blood existed inside of me, it was like I could hear his voice in my head, screaming at me, making me feel even guiltier than I already was.

"I went to that boy's house—I don't know how I knew where he lived; I just did. I snuck into his room through his window and I looked around. You know what I found? That poor boy, that innocent boy that I murdered wasn't so innocent after all."

She lifted a hand to her face as a sneer marred her beautiful features, her fingers rubbing at her temple as she tried to massage away whatever image she had just conjured up.

"He was so young, I thought there was no way that anyone that young could be tainted—I was wrong. I was so wrong. I wanted to get a feel for who he was, so that I could mourn him the way he deserved, the way that *I* deserved. I needed to punish myself with his face and his life burned inside of me—I wanted him to be the last thing I thought about before I died.

"You know what I found? Pictures; hundreds of them; pictures of him doing things…horrible, gross things to little girls; so many little girls…and one of them was his sister, his own sister! I felt sick. I felt…dirty, betrayed by my own guilt, by my own conscience. I thought I was going there to make things right, and instead everything was wrong, everything was dirty and disgusting. I burned those pictures. I destroyed them, and I prayed that as they burned that the little girl who slept in the next room could finally find some peace now that the person she should have trusted was gone.

"When I left, I felt different—not so guilty anymore. I felt like, by taking that boy's life, I had done something good, something right.

He was young—can you imagine what he would have been like if he'd gotten older? What he would have done? The damage he could have caused? I thought to myself, if I had to kill anyone, if I *had* to do it that one time, why shouldn't it have been him? Why shouldn't it have been that monster?

"But then I started to worry—what if it happened again? What if I came across someone else and without thinking, acted? It was a fluke that that kid wasn't innocent—but what if he had been? What if he was the perfect kid, the Boy Scout?

"I left that house. My head was filled with so many questions, so many pictures that I couldn't see straight, I couldn't think. I started to walk around the streets of that boy's neighborhood. I passed by people who didn't know me, didn't recognize me. Some of them said hello, some waved, and I didn't feel anything—I didn't feel anything that I felt with that boy. I thought I was cured.

"I went back to see Dr. Bro and tried to drink that damned blood again, but it was disgusting. It was like drinking spoiled milk—I couldn't do it. Dr. Bro told me what I already knew—if I didn't feed soon; I wouldn't be able to control myself. He said if I killed another person, he'd have to kill me; I told him there was no need to wait; just stake me or whatever he needed to do so that I wouldn't hurt anyone else. He said it wasn't that simple, that it didn't work that way.

"I thought…I thought that if he wouldn't do it that I'd do it myself. I ran away again. I didn't even realize it had happened until my feet stopped moving and I was standing outside of this door. I'd never seen it before; I didn't even know where I was, or how long I had been running. I only knew that I needed—no, wanted—to go inside. I turned the handle and just walked in.

"It was like I was in a trance, and nothing I thought of doing could break me out of it—I didn't know where I was going, only that there was this smell that was so incredible, my mouth watered. It's kind of like that first time you walk into a bakery, and the smell of baking bread and cakes and cookies just slaps you in the face and you want to

92

taste everything.

"Only this wasn't a bakery—it was somebody's home. I followed the smell until I found it: a man in his bed, sleeping like a baby. He smelled so good. I didn't even think about what I was doing, or whether or not he'd wake up and see this strange person in his bedroom, smelling him like a starved animal. The next thing I knew, I was attacking him. He didn't fight much, really, which surprised me considering how big he was. He just struggled a bit; then he was too weak to do anything else.

"After…when I was done, I walked around his house. There were family pictures on the walls and books on the shelves. There was typical guy-stuff around the house like weights and skinmags, and his fridge had beer and steaks in it. I started to feel guilty again because I'd just killed this guy in his sleep and I didn't know why.

"I went into the basement. I went down those stairs and into that dark room like a kid goes into a toy store—you just go, you know? I turned on the light and whatever guilt I felt just vanished like the dark."

A cynical laugh came out of her while her head tossed from side-to-side at the images she recalled. "See, he had the same sickness as that boy, only he didn't just take pictures…he kept souvenirs. His basement was filled with freezers, Grace. I won't tell you what was in them—you can probably guess for yourself—but I knew. I knew what he had in them—I could smell it. He tried to hide it with a billion of those stupid pine tree things that Graham keeps in his bucket."

"Buick," Graham corrected.

"Whatever. They were hanging from the ceiling like a freaking floating forest, but they couldn't mask the smell of death—not to me. Right then I realized that I no longer felt guilty; I don't think I ever will again." She turned to focus her hard, cold gaze onto Robert's steely one. "And I don't think anyone would blame me either."

Graham's face was pale, but his eyes registered an understanding that he shared with Lark as they both nodded their heads in agreement. "I don't—*we* don't. I think it's cool, actually," he beamed. "You're like some kind of avenging erl…something. Ooh, you should get a costume!"

"Leave it you to find some way to make it into a comic book," Robert said with as little humor as he could manage before returning his focus to Stacy. "Whatever those two men's sins were, their lives were not yours to take. It's a crime, Stacy."

Stacy's mocking laugh rang out like a bitter bell. "In whose world? Yours? Grace's? Graham's? Mine? We don't live in the same world anymore, Robert—we never did—and even if that wasn't true, you're not angry at me for killing those people because their lives are gone; you're angry at me because you didn't do it yourself."

I expected denial, anticipated it. Instead, Robert responded with a laugh of his own. "I always thought Lark was the epitome of biting honesty. I see that she's been eclipsed." He sighed, as if a weight that had been settled onto him and refused to let go had lifted.

"You're right, Stacy. I am angry that it was you. Killing does not come naturally to me. It's not something that I relish doing, even when the death might be deserved, and so, when I see others do so without issue, I admit to feeling…envious, jealous even, which I cannot say I've yet mastered control over but I am far better at it now than I was the first time I experienced it."

"I'll say," I murmured when his sparkling eyes traveled to mine.

"So…are you going to kill me now, or after dinner?" Stacy asked, the amusement in her voice clearer now.

## STARRY EYED

"I think that, given the occasion, it might be better to wait," Robert answered, the good humor that had been so desperately needed finally making its appearance.

"Well, good, because I'm starving," Graham announced, his stomach agreeing with him loudly.

Robert turned to face me, his arm held out in invitation. "Shall we return to our table?"

I nodded and looped my arm around his, following him as he led our little group back to the empty table. Four chairs sat undisturbed, while one rested neatly, its back butted against the table's edge. Once more, I found myself seated, this time with Robert sitting on one side of me, Stacy on the other. Graham sat beside her, leaving Lark to sit between him and her brother.

As if from out of nowhere, a man dressed in black with a white cloth draped over his arm appeared. Behind him, a cart stood, its contents shielded from view by large, silver dome covers. There were only four plates, and as he placed them in front of us, I realized that Stacy would not be receiving one.

"What did you expect? That they were going to be serving me rare torso of creep?" she quipped when she saw my perplexed expression. "I won't be feeling left out, believe me. Just enjoy your meal."

As the covers were lifted off their plates, I could hear Lark's pleased sigh, and Graham's ecstatic holler.

"Alright! Ribs!" he hooted, shoving the napkin that had been rolled up beside him into the collar of his shirt, the clumsily draped cloth dangling between himself and the table.

I spied a white, rectangular looking object sitting on Lark's plate and stared at it perplexingly, wondering what it could be. Her head lifted as she answered, "Plain tofu steak, my favorite."

Beside me, Robert's cover was lifted to reveal an empty plate. "Where's your food?" I asked, confused, as the mountain of silver in front of me was raised away.

"I'm not hungry," he replied, looking at me anxiously.

I turned away from himand reached for the napkin beside me as my eyes turned to my plate. "What...?"

My plate wasn't empty. But, there wasn't any food on it either. Instead, a folded sheet of paper sat in front of me, its contents hidden away by its creases and overlapping edges. "What's this?" I asked as four sets of eyes focused their attention onto me.

"Open it," Graham said, smiling.

I reached for the white sheet and unfolded it. My eyes quickly scanned over the text, stopping midway when my I felt my breath catch in my throat, and my heart stumble in my chest at my name printed in block letters standing beside another name, the owner of which sat beside me, his hand reaching over to steady mine, which had begun to shake.

"How?" was all I could say, as my eyes drifted to the top of the document and read three times the title that scrawled across the top in old English lettering.

"Simple—I did an online search for where I could get one without you knowing. I personally don't care about the legalities, but I know that you would."

"Is this really real?" My voice was soft, meekly quiet as my fingers traced out the two words that I didn't expect could mean so much to me. "This is an actual marriage license?"

"It's real and it's ours. I'm sorry that it's not in some fantastical—or perhaps even more traditional—place of elopement like Vegas, but I thought that perhaps you'd prefer something a bit more low-key and personal."

I raised tear-filled eyes to his and nodded mutely. What could I say? He had been so vehemently against doing anything like this-

"I wasn't against doing anything like this at all," he interrupted my thoughts. "I merely wanted everything to be perfect. This isn't how it's normally done, you know."

"How what's normally done?" I asked as a hiccup of emotion took away the seriousness of my question.

"Getting married. It's supposed to be ceremonious, with flowers, and cake, and loved ones, and a-"

"Big white dress?" I added.

"Well, yes, to be honest. I know that this is something that most human girls dream of; you plan this almost from conception it seems."

"I've never even thought about it…not once," I admitted. "And if I were to start, the last thing I'd ever imagine would be me in a big white dress."

"That's why," Lark spoke up then, a broad smile taking possession of her face and lighting it up like a beacon. "I made you some white jeans instead." She held up a box that had been tied with a dark blue strip of fabric. "This is for you."

She passed it across the table, and I placed it in front of me. I looked at everyone, their expectant expressions encouraging me on silently, and hurriedly undid the bow that had been carefully tied together. The box wasn't that large, only a few inches deep and a foot square, but it didn't need to be as I discovered when I lifted the lid and gently pulled away the tissue that covered the objects that lay beneath it.

Carefully, I lifted a satiny blouse out of the box. Its color graduated from white at the base of the low neckline to the same blue as the ribbon. Beneath the blouse was a pair of white jeans, just as Lark said. They were soft and looked like just looking at them would make them dirty.

"Here, I want you to have this," Stacy said, taking my hand and pressing something cold into my palm.

My eyes traveled from her dark ones to the object that sat in my hand. It was a thin, silver-link bracelet with a single charm dangling from its very center: a musical note. "Stacy..."

"It's your something old—although I think Robert could probably qualify as that if you want to be more accurate."

"It's beautiful," I observed. "Where'd you get it?"

A wistful look crossed her face before disappearing almost as quickly as it had arrived. "My parents gave that to me when I was seven; they said it was to give me good luck. I suppose it worked, since I did get better shortly afterward. Funny thing is, it was always too big to wear, so I never did. Eleven years that thing's been sitting at the bottom of my jewelry box, and when I finally started to wear it, I didn't think anything of it. I had almost forgotten what it was, but then one day I realized that I wore it for the first time the day I met you.

"You were my first real best friend—that wasn't related to me, of course—and knowing you changed my life; knowing you saved my life. I think that on the day you make one of the biggest changes in your life that you should wear something that means something. I know it's not really fancy or anything, but-"

I wrapped my arms around her and held her close; held her tightly; held her like I was afraid that if I let go, she'd disappear forever. She couldn't finish her sentence, couldn't continue speaking at all. I didn't care that she felt like a Popsicle. I didn't care that, for the first time, it was she who felt awkward by the close contact. She was my friend.

"It's perfect," I whispered. "It's more than perfect, thank you."

It was she that pulled away, and her sheepish smile told me that she knew how I felt, even if she couldn't read the words in my head. She turned in her seat, her head looking away and her hand lifting up to rub her eye, a motion that I wasn't sure would brush away any actual tears.

Graham looked at her and then his eyes lifted to capture mine in its emerald gaze. "Well, I don't know if you had planned this or not, but I drew the short straw when it came to who would be your maid of honor. I'm supposed to help you get dressed and all of that girly stuff, so come on."

He stood up and came behind me, carefully pulling my seat away as I stood to meet him. "You're going to help me dress?" I asked warily.

"Well, not literally, but there are other things I'm good at doing," he said with a chuckle. I looked at Robert, and then at Lark, and finally at Stacy, and knew that this was how it was supposed to be. I followed Graham through a door that led into a rather plain looking room.

"What is this place?" I asked as I took a turn into another room that held a small bed and a table with a mirror hanging above it.

"Some cottage that belongs to an EP Robert knows."

"Do you know where we are?"

He nodded but gave me a knowing smirk as he said, "But I'm not telling you."

"Ingrate," I mumbled. Graham handed me the white box that held the jeans and blouse and turned around.

"Graham," I called out. There was a tremor of nervousness in my voice, and he detected it immediately.

"What's the matter, Grace? You're not getting cold feet, are you? Because that's what the guy's supposed to do, not the girl."

I shook my head and an uneasy giggle slipped past my lips. "I…I wanted to ask you what it…what it felt like."

"What what felt like?"

I clutched onto the small white box in my hands and stared at my fingers, watching their tips change color from pink to yellow and finally to white. "What it felt like to turn."

His face went from amused to horrified in a quarter of a second, and I would have laughed if it didn't cause me to feel equally as horrified. "Is it that bad?"

"No, no…no," he stuttered. "It's just—well, I don't know if I'm the person who's supposed to tell you."

My eyebrows rose as doubt settled into the line my mouth made on my face. "I think everyone else thought you were perfect for it."

Confusion crossed his features. "What do you mean? We drew straws. Stacy wouldn't know what it felt like, which left Lark and I, and I'm the one who drew the…"

It was amusing, seeing the dawning of recognition light up his eyes and bring his drawn brows even closer together before they fell slack and separated into arches that framed an amused expression. "I got played."

"Yes, yes you did," I laughed.

"Wow." He looked at me and sighed, his shoulders sinking and his posture bending forward, revealing to me how much he disliked this fact.

"Hey, if you don't want to tell me, I understand. It's probably something really personal."

"That's not it at all. It's just…well, I don't know if it's going to be the same for you as it was for me. What if I tell you something and it turns out to be worse for you? You're a girl-"

"What does that have to do with it?" "Sit down," he instructed, taking the box from my hands and placing its crumpled mass on the small bed. We sat down, the mattress having little give. Graham sighed once more and then began to speak.

"Ameila…she did that whole morphy-changy thing so that she would look like Lark. She said it would make it easier for me to handle the change. And…you know—I'm a guy. When I see a beautiful girl, especially one that's now my wife, and all I can think about is…well…*being* with her, things got…heavy. Ameila said that that was a good thing—and all I felt after that was warm, like I was sitting in a warm bath or something.

"I saw a lot of lights-"

"Lights?"

He nodded. "Yeah. Like, spotlights, you know? Everything got all light and bright and I couldn't see anything after a while. I heard this humming sound though, and my head started to fill up with pictures of people that I've come across in my life. Pictures of my mom, my dad, your parents; hell, even Stacy flashed by a couple of times—and none of them good times—but you were there the most, just like I told you when…you know."

"Yeah, I know."

"Anyway, the lights that I saw, they kinda faded, and then everything faded. That's what it seemed like, anyway. After that, it was like my mind was on rewind or something—no, no, it was fast forwarding, starting from the very beginning. It was like I was living my life all over again, every single second of it, no skipping, no editing, nothing. I even relived my dreams—can you imagine what that's like? Reliving the nightmares of an eight year-old?

"I saw things I didn't even realize I had seen, things I think I blocked out. Every second, it was like a day of my life went by, and the more I saw, the more I realized how awful I was. The things I did, the things I didn't do—especially when it came to you.

"I didn't understand when it started why it was happening, why I was seeing all of these things. But, by the time it was all over, I knew that I was seeing what the angels had seen—it was like I had to see who I was, and whether or not I actually deserved to be given the chance to live forever. I thought they were going to change their minds because I saw who I was—I was a jerk, Grace."

My hand rested on his forearm as my head tossed from side to side in a vigorous denial. "You weren't a jerk, Graham."

"It felt like it," he said softly. "It felt like I had done nothing to protect you. I had all this popularity, but I never used it to help you out, never used it to make your life at school easier. I should have, Grace. I should have done what I could for you."

"Why?"

"Because that's what you would have done. That's what you did! You stood up for me to Robert, and Lark, and Stacy. That's what a friend does." He was so adamant, I felt a rush of warmth fill me, and this transferred through my hand; he looked down at it, and then at me, his eyes soft.

"Remember when we were eight, and Mrs. Mackey got mad at you because those girls tore your dress? Remember she started freaking out all of a sudden?"

"Yeah. Yeah, I remember that."

"You were the one who stayed with her. You held her hand and you told me to go get help, even after what she did. You always were the generous one, Grace. You were the forgiving one, the understanding one, the patient one. I used to think how the hell could you stand me, how could you possibly deal with me? Of course, now I know what you are-"

"What am I, Graham?" I looked at him, my eyes wide with anticipation of his answer. "What am I?"

His mouth closed, his voice silenced as he realized his faux pas. And I felt guilty. He didn't understand. How could he? He didn't see the harm or the difficulty caused by what we'd all learned when my dad and Ameila finally told me the truth. But even the truth didn't give me the answers that I had been seeking.

"Graham, it's okay," I reassured him. "It doesn't matter what I am; not anymore."

"I screwed this talk up, didn't I?" he said with a half-hearted laugh.

"No, no you didn't. This is just how it is with us."

He shrugged and a little puff of exhalation whooshed out of him. "Anyway, when my memories finally arrived at the point where I met Lark, it was like everything was different. It felt different. Hell, it even *smelled* different. I didn't really understand why, or how—it just did. She changed my life that much.

"And then everything stopped. Everything just stopped and I thought that was it, but it got…really, really dark, like my head was empty or something. I couldn't think; I couldn't call up a single thought or memory. I couldn't even remember what light was supposed to look like, or what it was supposed to do. There was nothing in my head, nothing in my head at all, except for two things.

"You and Lark: my best friend and my wife. I started to panic then, you know. I had a wife—I had a wife! What was I thinking? I'm eighteen, still in high school, and I have a wife? And I was doing all of these things to be with her—getting married, doing this turning thing, and who knows what else—and what were the guarantees that our relationship wouldn't just turn into crap like it did with my parents?

"Oh God, Grace, that fear started to spread like mildew or something. What was I doing? What was I doing, getting married to someone I barely knew? What was I doing getting married to someone who wasn't even human?

"And what if I was making a mistake? What if I wasn't supposed to marry her? What if I was supposed to marry someone else? What if what I was doing was changing me, making me doubt myself, turning me into something or something I wasn't? What if turning would make me into some kind of monster who didn't recognize or care about anything?

"And then everything was gone. It was like my doubt had taken the only two things I had left away. I was alone and I suddenly felt really, really cold. And then hot, and it kept going like that, like I was being tossed from a freezer to a fire, back and forth until I thought if I didn't die from third degree burns, I would freeze to death and that my body would end up on one of those alien abduction papers they sell at your dad's grocery store.

"I was scared, I was in pain, and I was…well, I was hungry." He stopped then, and snorted. "That's how I knew that everything was okay. How could I be hungry if I was dying? How could I be different if I could still find time for food?

"Lark, her voice was in my head, and she told me to open my eyes, and for a second I forgot how to. I think I overloaded my brain or something with all of those memories and fears, but after a while I did eventually open my eyes, and Grace, it's like seeing everything lit up like a Christmas tree.

"Everything is so bright, so...shiny. I've never seen it before, you know, that glow that hangs around Lark and Robert—I mean, I kinda knew it was there, maybe they always seemed like they were unreal and...glowy—but when I looked at Ameila and Lark, I could see this awesome light around them. It was incredible! Have you seen it before?"

I nodded. "It's how I knew what Robert was."

"Wow. That's just...it's...."

"Yes, yes it is," I agreed.

He looked at me and grinned, this newfound connection between us obviously giving him something that he somehow felt we'd needed. "So yeah, that's about it. It wasn't that big of a deal in some ways, but in others it was a total mind game. I checked my fingers for, you know, frostbite and burns, but everything I'd felt was in my head. It was terrible for me, but you're like some kind of Olympics brain gold-medalist or something from what Lark's told me, so I think you'll be able to handle this without that big of a deal."

He seemed so pleased, so self-assured, that I was hesitant to ask him my next question, but I feared that if didn't, I'd never get a chance to, so I simply blurted it out.

"What's sex with an angel like?"

Watching his reaction to my question was like watching a geyser prepare to blast a million gallons of blistering hot water into the sky. His cheeks expanded and emptied rapidly with air, his eyes bulged, blinked, and bulged some more, and his face turned a rather embarrassing shade of red before darkening to an almost purple, strangled sort of shade.

A gurgling sound deep within his chest, followed by a muddled gargling that made no sense to me at all proceeded to fill up the silence left after my question, and I realized that I wouldn't get an answer from him that would satisfy me, or ease him of the obvious discomfort he felt, so I left him to compose himself and headed into the bathroom that stood at one end of the room to change.

I closed the door and smiled at my reflection in the mirror as I heard the unmistakable sound of a hand slapping against a sweaty forehead behind me—an act that was so Graham—and felt full with the knowledge that he had succeeded in being the best friend that he feared he had not. He had trusted me with his secrets, his experiences, and had done so without questioning his ability to trust me to keep them to myself. To know that I had someone like him in my corner was a completion of something I didn't know had been wanting.

Quickly, I undressed and removed the clothes that Lark had made from their crushed box. I pulled on the jeans, the fabric soft and clingy as it slipped over my hips. I tugged on the zipper and slipped the button through its hole and admired the fit. It was like I'd worn these a thousand times before.

"Only a blind angel could do something that impossible," I said to myself before slipping the blouse over my head. It fell over my skin like water, the hem hanging past my hips, almost like a mini dress. The sleeves ended at my elbows, dropping down in points, while just below my chest, a ribbon crisscrossed, ending behind me in a bow.

The neckline was as low as I thought, but it wasn't as revealing as I thought it would be because a lacy, almost gauzy silver panel sat between the fabric and my skin. White ribbon weaved in and out at my shoulders, and I saw that they actually held the sleeves to the blouse, leaving a small gap that exposed the bare skin between.

I slipped Stacy's bracelet onto my wrist and grabbed the tube of gloss that I had stuffed into the pocket of my skirt, passing a few swipes of color across my lips before I declared myself done.

And, despite the fact that I had done nothing more than add a bit of deepened shine to my mouth and straightened my hair, I could see that I looked different. Maybe it was the clothes. Maybe it was the fact that I knew that after this moment, everything about who I was would change. I was going to be married.

"Holy hell, I'm going to be a wife," I breathed. My eyes dropped down to my left hand, where the ring that Robert had given me sat, em-

bracing my ring finger like a lover would. Two small crystals were embedded into the braided, silvery white metal, each one a half that formed
a heart, symbolizing how Robert and I completed each other. It was a
notion that was more poignant given the fact that one crystal teardrop
came from him, while the other was my own. It was the one thing I appreciated, the only thing I appreciated, from being who I was.

The idea of being married should have frightened me, it should
have sent me screaming in terror, but I had faced death more times than
anyone should. I had faced death, and now I was about to marry him,
and I never felt more sure about anything else in my life.

I could hear Graham's words in my head, about how everything
he saw after turning had looked brighter. I knew I didn't need to turn to
see things that way. My future wasn't a long one, but it was going to be
spent with Robert, and that was enough to give me that same, starry
eyed outlook.

# THE VOW OF DAWN

"You look incredible," Graham managed to whisper as we stood at the doorway that would take us outside.

"Thanks," I murmured.

"Are you ready to do this?"

I nodded.

"Good. We're going to do a bit of walking first—don't worry about your shoes."

I looked at him and then my gaze traveled to the floor, smirking when I saw his pale feet planted on the floor beside mine. "Your feet are so white they're almost clear," I joked.

"Ha-ha, very funny. Your feet aren't exactly tan either you know."

"I know. They aren't as wild animal hairy either."

"You could always give yourself away," he threatened.

"Fine, fine. I'm sorry." I threw him an apologetic look that was far from sincere, and he snorted. I snorted back, and then we were walking outside again. The table was empty, the lights above swaying with the slight breeze that had begun to blow through. I could smell the scent of something almost briny, and as we headed past the threshold of the lights behind us, my feet touched something cold and gritty.

I didn't stop to question what it was, and instead trudged forward until I saw the soft glow of amber ahead. As we grew closer, the glow grew brighter, and only when we were mere feet away from it did I realize that it was coming from Robert, who stood beside his sister, the two of them giving off a vibrant light that stretched past them to reveal another person whose face was unrecognizable, though no less beautiful.

Stacy appeared from the shadows to the side of us, a small bundle of freshly picked wildflowers in her hand. "Here's your something blue," she said, her mouth curled up in a pleased smile.

The blossoms were closed to the night air, but it wasn't that difficult to see that a good amount of them were indeed blue. I reached out and hugged her, smiling myself when her arms didn't hesitate this time, and she held me just as closely.

"I'm happy for you," she whispered into my ear.

"Thank you for being my friend, and for being here," I whispered back.

She pulled away and headed toward the three bodies that stood just a few meters away, leaving me to stand alone with Graham, whose grin could not be avoided, even in the semi-darkness.

"Well, Frank," he said gleefully. "It looks like this is it."

"I suppose so, Rocky," I replied.

"Last chance to change your mind and run away with me."

"I'm not going to change my mind. I want to do this. Besides, I think your *wife* would be quite upset with the both of us if we decided that now would be a good time to finally decide we wanted to be with each other."

He chuckled. "You're right—it was a stupid escape plan. Okay then, let's get this show on the road." I looped my arm with Graham's and proceeded to take the steps toward a face that looked as expectant as I was sure mine did.

Robert was holding a flower in his hand, a white lily covered in deep pink spots, the ends of the petals merging into that same deep rose shade as it met the vibrant green of the stem. He was wearing a pair of black slacks and a white shirt, the first three buttons left open, and I could see quite clearly as he swallowed upon seeing my pleased smile.

Beside him, Lark stood, her hands holding onto a single yellow daffodil, its colors bright even in the dim glow. She stepped forward and handed the single flower to me. "For your mother," was all she said before stepping back, taking her place next to her brother.

"Thank you," I said, stunned and confused by the implied significance.

Shaking the thoughts that formed in my head, I approached Robert, nervous and joyful all at the same time. Graham unwound his arm from mine, and after a poignant pause, placed my hand into Robert's waiting one.

"Okay, man. I'm filling in for her dad here, so the only thing I can say is to just take care of her and love her or else I'll send your sister after you."

Robert laughed and patted Graham on his shoulder with his free hand, his eyes filled with mirth. "I promise, Brother."

When Graham stepped away, Robert's hand closed over mine, his other hand slipping the lily that it still held over my ear, the blossom now resting behind it. "So lovely," he said softly, his eyes glassy as he looked into mine.

Leading me forward a few steps, we turned until we stood in front of a man whose face was unfamiliar and yet not, his light, deep set eyes looking down on me with a kindness that I could almost feel. He had dark hair, probably not black, but definitely a rich brown that was just long enough to graze the collar of his shirt that, even in the dim light that was cast by the angels beside me, still told of its vibrant crimson shade, while a white sash draped over his shoulders like a snowcap.

His face lit up with pleasure as he looked at the two of us, and I couldn't help the blush that filled my cheeks when the kindness in his eyes shifted into something a bit…more. "What a beautiful couple—so devoted, so filled with promise. We'll begin in just a moment."

I looked at him quizzically and turned my gaze to Robert, who only smiled and winked. Knowing that there was no point in asking why we were waiting, I instead focused my eyes downward. My feet were sinking in a strange combination of cool, soft, and gritty that swam between my toes, even as it remained still. Tiny, tiny pieces of history clung to my skin and sparkled like diamonds, rich in their stories of what they had once been. I wiggled my toes and marveled at how they sank further into the ground, swallowed by it as surely as if it were water.

"Sand...we're standing in sand," I breathed.

A shot of warmth hit my arm, followed by a burst of light that stole my attention, turning my head toward it and catching the first glimmer of sunlight peeking over the horizon.

"It's time," the man announced, and I moved my head to look at him. In his hands he held a book that had not been there earlier. It was open to a page filled with characters that I could not make out. He smiled at me and stepped closer. His hand rose to pull the sash down, and he proceeded to bind Robert's and my hand together with it, his motions so quick I nearly convinced myself that I had closed my eyes and missed it completely.

"Now then," he said, "We are gathered here, friends and family, to witness this joining of two halves into the whole of one heart. Though they have not been long on this road together, their trials and the depth of their bond goes beyond any length that time might have afforded them.

"Robert, you have chosen to forgo the traditional vows and recite those that you have prepared yourself. You may do so now."

I was set into a panic then, when I realized that I would also have to say my own vows, but seeing my reflection in his eyes and how he seemed to absorb it into himself, his smile never leaving his face, I forgot my worry and fell into the lull of his voice.

"Grace, before I met you, I used to measure the worth of my days by the number of lives I could save. Years, too, too many years would pass by without a single one giving me any joy, any hope. The promise of something better never once showed itself to me. Every single moment that disappeared with time combined into a meaningless existence that held as much value for me as an endless night would to a blind man.

"And then you came into my life, and without even knowing it, you changed everything, altered everything in my world. You weren't the catalyst to the light returning to me. You *were* the light. You were the dawn that I had given up hope on ever breaking through the black that painted everything.

"All it took was one look at you and everything in my life took shape; the shadows of an endless and empty existence disappeared, the fear of never being anything more than what I was finally leaving me, only…when it was replaced, it wasn't with what I had thought I wanted. To be some great angel, to be some savior to the people of this world suddenly became worthless to me. Instead, I realized that what would mean the world to me was being what you wanted, what you needed.

"If I could make you happy, then I'd be a prince. If I could get you to love me, then I'd be a king. If I could spend the rest of my life loving you, then I'd be in heaven. And now that I have you here, knowing that you are happy and that I'm the reason, knowing that you love me, and knowing that I will spend the rest of my life loving you, I understand what it truly means to be blessed.

"I pledge to you my life, my heart, my soul—everything that is good in me is good because you've touched it, and I vow never to give you cause or reason to doubt your gift to me. You have blessed me with far more than I deserve, far more than any man, angel, or god deserves, and I vow to you never to take that for granted.

"The sun is rising, Grace Anne Shelley, and with it comes a new day. I wanted it to begin with our new life; the dawning of us, the start of our life together, not just as partners, but as husband and wife. You see the colors in the sky? All of the blacks, the blues, the purples, pinks, and reds—each shade is like an emotion—emotions that I'd never have felt if it weren't for you.

"They're memories and dreams that I would've never had if you had never entered my life. They're wishes that I've wanted for no one else but you. Everything that the dawn represents, I would have never known, never been able to appreciate, if there had been no you in my life, and so, as it approaches us, as it consumes us, I make to you my vow to love you, not only for as long as I live, but for as long as time exists.

"The dawn doesn't end here. It continues to push onward, over the horizon and around the world, endlessly giving the heart hope and the promise of something new. I will love you even long after that is gone and there is nothing left but my love for you. This I vow to you."

My face was a wet, soggy mess when he was done, and I tried unsuccessfully to wipe away the moisture, even as an emotional hiccup made its appearance within me. Robert's hand reached over and gently rubbed beneath my eyes, taking with it the damp and the solid tears that had been shed over the words that had acted like its lodestone, pulling them from me.

"Grace, would you like to say something now?" the man who stood there waiting anxiously asked.

I looked at him and then at Robert and knew that, as unprepared as I was, I did have something to say.

I took a deep breath and my mouth opened, allowing the words to flow out. "Robert, when I think about my life and what it was before I met you, I can honestly say that I would have been content to have continued on that way, feeling half-alive, loved and yet not. I thought that that was how life was and that's how it was supposed to be. I had lost so much by the time we met, and I had given up on knowing anything more because for me, the sun had set on my dreams and I couldn't even remember what a dawn looked like.

"And then there you were, and you filled my life with light like nothing I had ever seen before, but you weren't the sun. You were the moon, and you lit up my dark and dreary world like something out of a fairytale. I didn't think it was possible, but it was true, it was real. You gave me comfort through the darkness, and when the sun finally did appear, you didn't disappear behind it. Instead, you chose to shine brighter. You made it impossible for me to hide anymore. You forced me to see myself, truly see who I was. There were no shadows to hide in anymore.

"Everything that I thought I knew about who I was has been changed. I think that I was born loving you. What I feel for you, it's so strong, so unending that it's not just what I feel in my heart and in my head; it runs in my veins. Loving you came far too naturally to be something new. It's what I was born to do—I was born to love you, and I will do everything I can to live up to that expectation."

*You've already surpassed it.*

I blinked, because the words in my head had been unexpected. I giggled in surprise, and he in turn gifted me with a smile so filled with light that it turned my insides to jelly. We both turned our heads to the man who stood smiling over us, and he let out a broken cough and patted his eyes before focusing them onto the words in front of him, a sigh of contentment coming out in one long exhale.

"Do you, Robert N'Uriel Bellegarde, son of Ameila Bellegarde, take to your heart, Grace Anne Shelley, to be your bride in earthly measures as well as divine ones? Do you promise to bless upon her your faith, your trust, your devotion, and your love until the life within you ceases?"

Robert looked into my eyes and said firmly, "I do."

"Do you, Grace Anne Shelley, daughter of Avi and James Shelley, take to your heart, Robert N'Uriel Bellegarde, to be your groom in earthly measures as well as divine ones? Do you promise to bless upon him your faith, your trust, your devotion, and your love until the life within you ceases?"

My chin rose defiantly, my shoulders pulling back as I said with conviction, "I do."

"Then it is done. I pronounce you to be husband and wife, joined and bound together in matrimony that extends from this mortal earth to heaven itself. May it forever be blessed and may you always know the joy of each other. You may now kiss to seal your union."

Though I had imagined in the last few moments what this would be, what this would feel like, nothing that I could conjure could equal the deeply intense sense of completion and triumph I felt when

Robert smiled down at me before his lips gently grazed mine in a kiss so chaste, it could have been a dream. But it wasn't, because dreams never felt like this: real and vibrating through my skin like an endless breeze.

I watched as Lark handed the man in the red shirt the folded marriage license. He looked at, nodded, and then handed it back before bidding his farewells and disappearing as the sun crept across the sand, revealing the soft pink mist that he left behind.

"Was that...who was that?"

"An old friend," Robert answered as he took the license from Lark. He glanced at it, and I exhaled as I saw his signature appear beside his name. "Your turn."

He handed me the thick sheet of paper and I took it with shaky hands, accepting the pen that he slipped between my fingers. He turned around and offered his back to me, and I placed it against the solid plane of his shoulders as I searched for the line that awaited my signature.

"So...I sign my married name here, don't I?" I asked, and I saw Robert's head bob once before my eyes located the blank space that attracted my pen and my fingers, surprisingly eager and nimble as almost mindlessly, I signed for the first time my new name.

"Grace Anne Bellegarde."

As soon as the last swirl of ink was down, Robert had turned around and had me in his arms, the morning sun filling his eyes with a glittering halo of warm amber light emphasizing the silver irises that looked down at me lovingly. "The most beautiful name I have ever heard."

"Even more than Grace Anne Shelley?" I pouted playfully.

"Yes." It was an answer that was final, there would be no explaining it, and there would be no questioning it.

But I didn't want to, I realized, when he bent his head down and pressed an urgent kiss to the corner of my mouth. "Now then, Wife, how about a wedding breakfast before we leave?"

"Leave?" I asked, suddenly nervous.

"Yes. As lovely as all of this might be, there is still the matter of turning that has to be dealt with, plus we do still have to break the news to your father about all of this."

I groaned inwardly as I pictured the reaction that Dad would have upon hearing that Robert and I had eloped. "He's going to ground me for life."

"He might have been able to ground Grace Anne Shelley, but she doesn't exist anymore," Robert said encouragingly. "You're my wife now, Grace. As much as you love your father, and as much as he loves you, you're an adult now, and you are allowed to make your own decisions. He loves you and will respect that."

"How nice it must be to be so optimistic," I mumbled before turning to face the three eager and amused faces that watched us so carefully.

"Thank you guys, for being here, for helping put this all together, for being my friends," I said, my eyes prickling with tears.

"We're always here for you," Stacy said first, her arms taking me into a brief embrace.

"Are you leaving?" I asked, panicked.

"Yes—don't look at me like that, Grace. I wanted to be here to see you get married. I didn't agree to anything else." She looked at Lark with that last sentence and then quickly returned her eyes to me.

"You make a beautiful bride, Grace. I'm happy for you. Robert—take care of her." And then she was gone, rushing past all of us and disappearing into the water that was slowly lightening before us, the color changing as the sky grew brighter, bluer with each passing minute.

"Congratulations, Grace," Graham said, his voice awkwardly quiet as he looked at the stricken expression on his wife's face. "I think...I think your mom would have been proud of you."

"Thanks, Graham." I watched him as he turned to face Lark, who stared at me with her blank eyes, her mouth a thin line of disappointment and obvious dismay. "Lark..."

"Don't apologize for anything, Grace. I did this to myself. It's the cost of being what I am and avoiding it all at the same time. I can't have my cake and eat it, too. I can't keep secrets and expect everything and everyone to forgive me simply because it's what I'm supposed to do. Choices aren't just yours to have—Robert's proven that time and time again. I'll make things right. I promise you that, Grace. I will make things right."

It was a quick little thing, her arms dashing out to grab a hold of me and pull me to her, an embrace so brief, I could have blinked and I would have missed it. But I didn't. I wouldn't miss this for anything. Instead, my arms went around her for that fraction of time—selfish and grasping—and for a moment, a tiny, sliver of a moment, Lark was my sister. And then, all too soon, she was gone as well, Graham along with her.

I stood there, my feet in the warming sand, my eyes staring out over the water, wondering how it was that I could have just had the most incredible moment in my life and still feel so empty. "Will things ever be okay between them?" I asked aloud.

"I don't know," Robert sighed behind me, his arms wrapping around my waist, his chin resting beside my ear. "They share a common interest in your welfare, and despite how betrayed and hurt Stacy feels, she still cares greatly for Lark."

"You're not going to kill her, are you?" I asked warily, feeling my blood turn cold at the words that had just left me.

"Not if I can help it. She has to feed—and while I did not en-courage her change, I did nothing to stop it. For the moment, the deaths she has caused have not been unjust ones, and I cannot fault her for doing what I would have done myself—except for the whole eating part. However, if she ends up taking the life of someone innocent, I will have no choice, Grace. If the seraphim decide to hand down a rapid punish-ment, there will be nothing I can do to stop it."

I turned around in his arms and frowned. "That's not what my dad said. He said that the seraphim don't have as much power as you do—he said that you have more powers than they do combined."

He nodded. "I do have more power than they do, but power is

not the same as authority, Grace. If the seraphim decide that Stacy is to die, then she will die. They do not go back on their orders; they do not change their mind."

His hand rose to adjust the lily against my ear. "I'm sorry—this is not the time for that. We're alone now. What would you like to do?"

I flushed, my eyes suddenly needing to look anywhere else but at him. My head was filled with thoughts that I couldn't voice, suggestions that I felt embarrassed just thinking.

Warm hands surrounded my face and a soft sigh was my only warning before all I felt were lips and warmth against my forehead. "You're such a silly girl, Grace. I was hoping that you'd ask for me to turn you—but I can see that's the last thing on your mind. Well then, what shall we do first? Perhaps a bit of light misting?"

His voice seemed to fade away, and I turned to see his face begin to dissipate into a dark, smoky haze. "Robert, don't!" I blurted even as the fog began to curl around me, not leaving me this time, instead wrapping me up in its sweet smelling warmth.

*Is this what you wanted, Grace?*

I wanted to nod, to shout out yes, but the nagging feeling of it not being enough settled over me, even as the wisps that tickled my skin reminded me of the wonders that simple mist could do.

"We're not done," was all I could say, and sighed with a strange yet familiar mixture of relief and disappointment when the soft caress against my skin disappeared, and the firm grip of reality took hold of me.

"So. you're ready to turn?"

"It's why we did this, right?"

He didn't answer me. Instead, he scooped me up into his arms and slowly carried me back into the small, white cabin. In the light of morning, I could see that it was really sparse, with a front room and the one bedroom and bath in the back. A rudimentary sofa took up the majority of the floor space, while a mini refrigerator sat next to it, acting as a makeshift end table and range, holding both a lamp and a camp stove.

"How much do EPs get paid if they're living like this?" I wondered aloud.

"Thomas lives a rather extravagant lifestyle while he's with us, Grace, but when he's allowed his leave, he comes here. He appreciates the solitude and the lack of responsibility that this place affords him, and I admit it is quite relaxing and peaceful."

"So…is this where…is this where we…do it?"

He laughed, a full-bodied laugh that flowed out of him as easily as water from a glass, and I marveled at how he could be so nonchalant about this whereas I felt as tightly wound as an over turned screw. "If you want to know if this is where I turn you, the answer is no. I don't plan on waiting too long after turning you to finally make love to you, but it won't be on some itchy, lumpy mattress."

"Oh," I breathed, suddenly wordless. I looked down at my clothes and knew that I needed to change before we left. Dad saw me leave in one set of clothes; if he saw me in another, he'd automatically assume the worst.

"You don't have to change, Grace," Robert kidded as he placed my feet onto the wooden floorboards. "But if we don't hurry, your father is going to suspect something and that would be counterproductive for what we have planned."

It registered with me then that we weren't going to be telling my father anything. "You don't want my dad to know that we're married." It was a statement, a matter-of-fact statement that didn't need his acknowledgment to make it any more true. "Are we keeping this from your mother, too?"

A flash of something passed through his eyes, and then there was a peaceful calm that was so blatantly false, I could taste it. "We're keeping this from everyone who wasn't here."

"So, what happens when I turn? How do I keep that a secret? And why should I keep that a secret from my dad?"

"No one will know you've turned, Grace, or when you've turned. This is for your protection as well as your family's."

A slamming sensation gravitated from my chest to my head as his words echoed all around me. "Why? My dad's not just anyone, Robert! He knows what you are; he knows what we planned on doing. I'm tired of keeping secrets from him. All we've had are secrets—I don't want to start our marriage with them!"

The look of anguish on his face pained me, but I was too angry to let it affect me the way that it wanted to. "This isn't fair. If we'd gone through with a regular wedding like we'd planned, he would have known. He would have known everything, so why is now so different?"

"Because things have changed, Grace. This isn't a simple matter of me trying to prolong your life anymore."

I looked at him, and the pain that contaminated every feature in his face burned into my memory and told me more than his words could have. "You've seen my death, haven't you? You've already seen it, or at least know when it's supposed to happen."

He nodded, though the motion was so minute, it was almost imperceptible. "I've seen it. I've seen it a million times."

"Tell me."

He looked at me as though I had just asked him to destroy the world. "And so you did! Asking me to describe to you your own death forces me to accept it—I won't!"

My hand was cold, bloodless when I pressed it to the side of his face. "Please."

His fingers wrapped around my wrist, and as gently as he could, despite the anger I could see in his eyes, he pulled my hand down. "No."

"Robert-"

"It's not going to happen, Grace. You've chosen to die—I have to accept that because it's your choice—but I do not have to accept what I've seen. Not yet."

His voice was cracking, and the distorted sound created its own cracks in my heart as the memories of painful goodbyes that had turned out to merely be rehearsals for what still lay ahead replayed in my mind, each scene acting like a poison inside of me, tainting me and sending my

119

thoughts spiraling down into a depression that came on so suddenly, I didn't realize I was on the floor sobbing until I was lifted from it, Robert's arms wrapped around me so protectively, he could have been strangling my body.

"I'm sorry, Grace. I'm sorry."

"It's real, isn't it? It's real. This isn't just a bad dream—you and I aren't really going to live happily ever after, are we?" I hiccupped.

"We're going to be as happy as we can until the time comes, Grace," he vowed, his voice a harsh whisper against the curve of my ear.

"We have to at least tell my dad that we're married. I won't keep that from him, Robert; I won't."

"Okay."

Forgetting my clothes, forgetting the reason behind needing them, Robert carried me to the door and stepped out into the blazing summer sun that blinded me and forced my head into the shelter of his shoulder.

It was only the loss of the scent of water and sunned sand that hinted of our departure. I didn't open my eyes—they were swollen shut from crying anyway—and instead tried to remember that Robert was mine now. We were married, we had sworn to love each other and be with each other for the rest of our lives—and though the hiccups in my chest spoke otherwise, I knew that I didn't care about what loomed ahead for us. I had won this round, and that was one more than I had ever hoped for.

# A CIRCLE OF PROMISE

I spent the afternoon of my wedding sitting in front of the kitchen table, listening to Dad rail at Robert, tossing epithets and horrid accusations his way without a single care to how awful they were. He was angry—Robert had warned me about that—but it stemmed mostly from not being there to share in the moment with me. I didn't need Robert reading Dad's mind to know this. I could see it on his face.

"You've never done anything this stupid before. You've never acted without thinking before, Grace—this is so unlike you and I don't approve of it."

"Dad, whether you approve of it or not doesn't matter anymore; I'm married."

"For what, a few hours? That makes you an expert, does it?"

I bounced Matthew in my arms, the chubby infant content to suckle on one hand while the other clutched at my hair, tugging with every jostle. I kissed his rounded forehead and sighed. "We didn't have to tell you, but I insisted. I would've liked to have had you there but I knew how you felt, and so did Robert."

"Which is exactly why it shouldn't have happened!" he bellowed. "You're my only daughter. A father has a right to give away his daughter's hand in marriage—especially when that marriage is to someone who's more of a danger to her than anyone else could be."

"Dad!"

Robert, silent this entire time, spoke up then. "Mr. Shelley, if

Grace is in danger, it isn't from me. I love Grace. I love her in ways that you cannot imagine-"

"Because I'm not an angel," Dad spat.

"Yes, but it goes beyond that. I could have taken her away and you would've never found her again. Instead, I've taken on the responsibility of not only her safety, but also the safety of her family, who are now my family. Matthew is now my brother, you are now my father.

"You know that when an angel takes upon him a human mate, they sever the human ties with their family. My kind might be able to empathize with yours to an extent, but for the majority of us, familial ties are simply genealogical. There's little love lost between father and son, mother and daughter, as children aren't viewed by us as choices but as obligations.

"The relationship I have—had—with my mother was not the norm, so to want to embrace into my life, into my existence any family, it's because of the love that I feel deeply for your daughter and for those she loves."

Dad looked stricken, as though he'd just received the worst news imaginable, and I struggled for something to say to him but he lifted his eyes to me and shook his head, a warning to remain silent.

"Grace," he began, his voice choppy as his thoughts piled one on top of the other, fighting for dominance and release. "I'm sorry. It's been so long…it's been so long and yet I still believe some of the lies. Robert's telling the truth. You would be long gone from here—taken and turned without my knowledge. But he…he is his mother's son. I'm sorry, you two, for being so set against this. I know that it was wrong of me, but there's something to be said about being a parent who's already lost a child and a wife. I can't…"

He turned away from me, his hands dashing to his face quickly to wipe at tears that he was too ashamed to show. There was a stiffness in his shoulders that I took for pride, and though his head was bent down, I could see the stubbornness there that told me he was conceding a point to save himself from admitting any others.

"Dad, I know that this is hard for you. It's not exactly easy for me—I don't want to die. I don't want to give up all of this now that I have it, but if it means that you'll be safe, that you and Matthew will be safe, then it's something I've got to do."

His head whipped around so fast, the slight sag of his cheeks rippled from it. "It's not the responsibility of the daughter to keep her father safe. It should never have come to this."

And just as quickly as it came, the look of anger left him, replaced with a sullen, dejected acceptance. "I don't know what your mother was thinking when she allowed you to come into this world knowing that all of this would happen, but I have to try to understand that she had her reasons, even if it means hating it, and hating myself for doing it. I can only see this as my punishment for doing what I did."

"Dad, don't say that."

"Being human affords us a multitude of choices, many without consequences, but the ones that come with them are the ones we never avoid, and my choice cost you your mother and me my wife and unborn child. And now, all these years later it might cost me another wife and soon a daughter. That's the reality of being human, Grace. Angels admire and envy us our ability to choose what paths we take, but look at what we lose because of it."

He stood up and left the kitchen, his heavy, muffled steps dictating his destination as they moved up the stairs and above me. I turned to look at Robert, and I saw that the words had affected him just as profoundly as they had me, and there was no doubting that we would both lose so much because of the path our decisions have taken us on. My death, the death that neither of us could avoid, loomed over us like a storm cloud, always threatening to drench us, but never quite letting down because it wasn't yet the right time.

I hated it. I hated every single moment and yet, at the same time, I was thankful for this delay because it afforded me more time with the people I loved. It allowed me to…say goodbye.

Dad's return pulled me from my distracted thoughts, and I

stared at him, a befuddled expression forming on my face as he held out a small, velvet bag to me. "Take it," he said, pressing it into my hand, exchanging it for a slumbering Matthew.

"What is it?"

He didn't answer me, which left me to pull the bag's drawstring opening apart and dump out the tiny object that had lain hidden in the soft black folds. A circlet of pale silver lay in my palm, one that looked almost identical to the one that now rested on my finger. Etched on the outer ring was a strange looking symbol, one that looked like a circle with two pointed wings jutting out from either side, their origination point crisscrossing within the circle itself to form a diamond center surrounded by four large and two small triangles with rounded corners.

"That was your mother's. It was the only way I could identify her after the accident—her wedding band had completely melted and she never took that off. She got that ring when she finally grew her wings—you've grown yours and I think that she always intended that this come to you when the time was right." Dad's voice was wistful, his eyes glossy as he looked at the metal halo that sat in my palm, cool even against the warmth of my skin.

Robert picked it up between gentle fingers and turned my hand over, slowly removing the ring that cradled my ring finger before slipping my mother's on in its place. He slid the other on top of it, the two pale silver circles melding into one unified band, each one significant, each one different, but now seeming as though neither would be complete without the other.

"They're perfect," he sighed before bringing my hand to his lips, pressing a soft kiss against the knuckle above the two bands.

"Grace," Dad interrupted. "When the time comes for you to turn…don't tell me."

"Don't worry, Dad," I reassured him. "I won't."

His eyes clouded with confusion, and Robert sighed as he relayed to him what I already knew, the news coming as both a shock and a relief—neither of which I was currently feeling. "Grace doesn't seem to understand that this is for the best—this as much for her safety as it is yours and Matthew's.

"But who *is* trying to hurt her? And why?" Dad demanded to know.

"I wish I could tell you. I wish I knew," Robert replied, with anger tracing the concerned lines that formed between his brows. "It makes no sense that anyone would try to harm her when they know her death is so near."

"But how can they know that she's going to die and yet you didn't even know that her mother was Avi?"

Dad's question caught me off guard, words that had no meaning, no completion sputtering out of me as Robert sighed with a defeated sinking of his shoulders.

"It was kept from me just as Grace's parentage was kept from her. I never met her, and neither has Lark; we haven't met half of the angels that exist in this world. There's never been a need to."

"Yes, but she and Ameila were close," Dad reminded him.

"My mother's thoughts are very reserved and have been since my birth. She would've never shared what Grace's mother looked like with me or with anyone. If I was unaware of who she was, there was no need to even speak of her with me."

"Well, what about Sam?"

Robert's sigh was heavy with grief and disappointment. "In his thoughts, she was a grotesque shell that bore his face. She was a monster that was only recognizable because she was tied to him in some way. The only time I've ever seen her face is in Grace's thoughts, and in them Avi is Abigail: mother, wife, and most importantly, human because that's what she was to Grace. I believe that my mother wanted me to believe that as well."

"But why? Why would she do that if your mother knew what your role in all of this would be?"

Robert's gaze drifted from mine to Dad's, and his mouth moved slowly as he answered. "I think that my mother believed had I known the truth, I would have avoided Grace at all costs. And...she was right."

I heard the tick of my head whip up before I felt it, before I had even realized I had done so. "She was?"

As his eyes implored mine, Robert's grip on my hand tightened, as though he knew that all I wanted to do was pull away. "I knew the moment I saw you that I loved you, Grace. I might not have recognized the emotion for what it was, but I know now, and had I seen your face in my mother's thoughts and seen it accompany what it was that you had been born to do, I would have still felt the same way and I would not have risked your life for it. I love you too much—I *would* have loved you too much to have done that to you."

I could hear the waver in his voice, see it in the tremble of his lips, feel it in the tremor that traveled through him into my hand, which now felt like it was holding on to mine for support, rather than to keep me from leaving. "Every step we've been taking in our life has been to-ward each other—even if we had tried to avoid it, we would have failed."

He leaned in, and our foreheads rested against each other as our thoughts mingled, his filled with regret for the moment of hurt I felt, and mine filled with regret for causing his.

"My God, you two do love each other, don't you?"

I smiled, even as the tears that I had not known were there be-gan to fall, some absorbing into my jeans while others bounced off of my knees, plinking onto the tile below. I turned to face my father and saw that his eyes were just as red, just as glossy as I knew mine were. "Did you just figure that out now?"

"I think I've just been avoiding acknowledging it. I've always known—you wouldn't wear a dress for someone you didn't love."

He moved forward, and for a moment, I feared that he'd pry my hand out of Robert's, but instead his hand covered ours, and I felt the gentle squeezing as it transferred through Robert's. "I didn't like the idea of this relationship when it began but I knew that you wouldn't hurt my daughter, Robert. I knew that you would carry it along to its natural end. When I learned what that end was, and what you...are, I couldn't accept it. A daughter is supposed to fall in love with someone a father despises, but even though you are what you are, I can't despise you. I can't…hate you.

"I did my best to protect her and her mother. I failed with Abby, but I promised that I wouldn't fail with Grace. I realize now that she needs the kind of protection that I can't give her. I can protect angels, but I can't protect my own daughter. She needs you, Robert, and I'm thankful that you realized this before I did. I…I'm thankful to you, son."

Robert's face lit up at this sudden acceptance. It made my heart fill up with something unlike anything I had ever experienced before. I didn't know what it was, only that I was grateful for it being there. I didn't want to spend the rest of my life being pulled between Dad and Robert.

"And so you won't," Robert said aloud, my thoughts plucked from the air and answered before a question had been asked.

I beamed at the two of them, feeling elated and overwhelmingly relieved. "Dad, you don't know how much this means to me," I blubbered, my breathing soon turning into hiccups.

"Grace, the last thing I want is to spend the last few moments I have with you fighting. It would be pretty stupid of me to waste this time after all that I've lost already."

I threw my arms around him, startling poor Matthew into a pitiful wail. I rubbed the soft down on his head in an effort to comfort him but my main focus was on my dad, the ruddy complexion that had taken his face hostage was spreading as his emotions got the better of him as well.

"I love you, Dad," I said to him, kissing his cheek and squeezing him as tightly as I could. He'd had given me the only wedding gift I could have asked for, the only wedding gift I wanted which was acceptance of Robert for who he was.

"I love you too, Kiddo."

I was reluctant to let him go, unwilling to end this father-daughter moment that had surely not been plausible just a few hours earlier, but I did finally release him, even as my arms struggled to latch on to him once more. It seemed strange how, the further I grew away from him, the closer I wanted to be.

Dad began to bounce Matthew on his shoulder and looked at the clock on the wall. "It looks like it's Matt's feeding time, and you two have some packing to do I imagine."

"Packing?" I looked at him, unsure of what he meant by that. "For what?"

Dad looked around him and then let his eyes drift back toward mine. "You can't possibly mean that you're going to be staying here, under my roof as a married couple, can you? I mean, I know what the plan was, but everything's changed and I'm not going anywhere; especially not with Janice in the hospital."

"I-I…"

"What, you thought I meant packing for your honeymoon or something?" he asked, shifting Matthew to his other shoulder as he walked over to the refrigerator to pull out a bottle.

"I…I-I"

His eyes rolled—actually rolled!—and he shook his head. "Grace Ann Shell—excuse me, Bellegarde, you may be an adult, and you may be Robert's wife, but I am still your father and if there's one thing I know it's that you will not be going on any honeymoon before you graduate from high school."

I looked over at Robert and saw the bemused expression on his face, one that told me in no uncertain terms that he agreed. "You mean I actually have to go to summer school? As a married woman?"

I was dumbfounded. Shocked. Speechless.

Matthew starting bawling, and I reached for him to allow Dad the use of both his hands as he filled up a pot with water to warm up the cold bottle. "At least someone understands how I feel," I mumbled. Dad and Robert both chuckled, the new ground they had gained together holding much more firmly even as my grip on reality seemed to slip just

128

a bit.

## DEVIL IN THE DETAILS

Robert had my things packed in the same amount of time that it took me to throw my last load of laundry into the wash. Boxes were produced from out of nowhere, and everything I owned, everything that I had forgotten I owned was packaged neatly and tidily in seven boxes that sat on the floor by my bed, still dressed in the comforter that Janice had purchased for me.

I sat down near the nightstand and pulled open the little drawer. Inside was the old phone that I'd used to speak to Graham almost every night. It was obviously being left behind. The lamp that sat atop the small table was gone, and a dustless ring lay as a reminder that something had been there.

My closet was empty. I hadn't changed out of the white jeans I'd been married in, and already they showed signs of staining.

"Where are we going to take all of these things?" I asked, as I realized that we wouldn't be returning to the white room at the back of that large house that Robert had called home.

"That's exactly where we're taking all of these things," he replied to my thoughts.

"But doesn't that kind of go against the whole plan?"

His head bobbed down once, but he shrugged off the implication of it. "Things have changed. Janice's attack has forced your father to remain here with your brother. It's safer if we leave instead. If…when Janice recovers, she and your father will be moved somewhere safe as planned, but right now, it's best that they stay."

"I'm not sure I like that idea. I mean, your mom and Lem said that it was safer for them to go. Obviously they were right. If Janice and my dad had left earlier, she wouldn't be in some hospital bed right now.""

"They weren't right, Grace. Janice's attack proves that. If she can be attacked here, with angels—*seraphim*—constantly watching this house, then she can be attacked in any house."

I stared at him, silent and unwilling to address that rebuttal. He looked tired, something I had never seen on him before, and it worried me.

"Don't worry about me, Grace," Robert sighed, sitting down beside me, his hand covering mine. "This has been a very eventful twenty-four hours and I've yet to spend any of it with you quietly. I suppose I am weary from the need of it."

I looked at him and pulled him down with me as I lay my head on the pillow. His chest pressed against my back, his arms curling around me and bringing me in closer, the two of us forming a pose that was so familiar to us, so comforting and calming that in a short while, I fell asleep to the sound of my breathing.

***

Sleep is supposed to be restful. It's supposed to be something that restores you, replenishes you to take on the challenges that lay ahead of you in the waking world. If only it were so for me.

I knew I was asleep and dreaming when I could no longer feel Robert's arms around me and my room was no longer a cocoon where one last moment alone together was being shared. Instead, I was back in a strange hallway of what could have been easily mistaken for some sort of deranged funhouse.

A closed door stood behind me, its flowery shape with four distinct petals familiar and yet not. There was a leaf-shaped door to my left, and though I knew what was behind it because my memory wouldn't let me forget, curiosity pushed me toward it, my hand reaching for the brass doorknob.

I pulled away only when I realized that there was no doorknob—not anymore. As my eyes traveled further down the hallway, I could see that each door was now graced with a ribbon where their knobs should be, the red tongues hanging out and waving in a wind that I could neither feel nor hear.

With shaky fingers, I grabbed for the first ribbon, pulling it and feeling taken aback when the door opened, revealing an empty room. Gone were the carcasses of countless birds. Gone were the wings and the bloodied feathers. Even the table that had sat in the center was gone. The gray box that remained told nothing of the horrors that had taken place here.

I left the room and proceeded to open up every door, finding behind each one the same, empty space. The bird, the heart, the moon, and apple shaped doors were all opened to reveal bare rooms. It was the last door, the one that was shaped like a giant eye that caused my moment of pause. It looked no different than it had the first time I had seen it, but vastly different from the last time.

The outer golden ring that encircled a dark center was thick and vibrant. It almost glowed with an impossible light, even as the black middle tried to consume it. It had not changed, this hunger that existed for what it could not have. I stepped closer, my hand remembering the chill that had replaced all feeling when I had placed it in that dark hole, discovering that the way through the door was not by opening it but rather by going through it, into it.

But that was when I knew what lay on the other side. This hallway, these doors, they had all been the prison that had been built inside of Stacy's mind, a fortress to keep her from being discovered by those who would set her free; to keep her safe from me. This time, I knew nothing about what lay behind that door.

What I did know was that I didn't want to find out. I turned around, determined to leave this dream and never return. Instead, I gasped. The doors that I had opened were now shut and bowing outwards, stretching, creaking, their wooden surfaces splintering and cracking from the pressure that pushed against the other side. The ribbons that had opened them to me were now long and furling across the hallway, lapping at their painted facsimiles on the opposite wall.

It looked like five faces sticking out their tongues in defiance of something. Or…perhaps it was a mocking gesture. But to whom? I took a step forward and found myself unable to do so. I looked down and saw that the ribbon to the eye shaped door had wound its way around my ankle, tighter and tighter until there was a numbness in my foot that I was certain I would not have felt had I not seen it.

"Let go, you stupid ribbon!" I grumbled as I struggled to loosen the hold that the ribbon had on me. My fingers pulled at the red length but rather than ease up, it grew tighter. I jerked my leg, hoping the line would simply break and instead found myself on the ground, my eyes staring up at the ceiling of the hallway, a ceiling I had never seen before because I never had cause to.

"Holy crap," I breathed as I took in the sight before me.

An intricate mural that featured the figures of people crowded around one person—not a person; an angel—filled the lower part of the ceiling, while another showed a dark cloud hovering above them. It was heavy with consequences, that much I knew, and as my eyes traveled further I could see a wave rushing toward the people, but their backs were turned, their attention focused elsewhere. The angel that their faces were turned toward was faceless himself, but his hands were held out to them in supplication. He was their savior. He was going to save them from the consequences. But from what?

Ameila's voice filled my head, her words of what had happened millennia ago rushing back in their own tidal wave. The deaths of millions of people and angels alike, brought on by the greed and lust for power that the Grigori had. It was nearly the end of the world, nearly the end of humanity as it was known then, according to Ameila, and as I stared at the image above me, I could see the fear on the people's faces. I could almost taste their terror, smell it as they looked to the angel for guidance, for help, for rescue from the danger they felt, the danger they sensed but did not see.

The sharp tugging at my ankle broke my gaze away from the image above me, and once again, I tried to free myself from the ribbon constraints. I braced myself against the door with my feet and pulled the red length, wishing that I had a pair of scissors or a knife to cut it.

A plinking sound forced my head to turn, and as if it had always been there, a pair of shears now lay beside me. "Is this the part where I say 'curiouser and curiouser'?" I asked out loud before reaching for them and quickly snipping the ribbon, unraveling it from around my now purple foot.

As the blood began to circulate once more between my toes and the rest of my body, I stood, wobbling a bit and tilting my head back to gaze once more at the mural above me. I walked sideways toward the flower-shaped door, taking in as much detail as I could of the imminent destruction that would follow that wave and cloud as they both loomed over the people like promises.

Deadly promises.

A tightening around my waist drew my attention downward once more, and I found myself being enrobed in ribbons, wrapped in them like some kind of scarlet mummy. I struggled against them, but they were fast, faster than I was, faster than I could have been. My arms were held against my sides, immobile, and my legs were being squeezed together as the strip of red endlessly wound around them. My balance was thrown off, and as stiff as they were, my legs still buckled beneath me sending me crashing to the ground once more, only this time I could not prevent my head from slamming into the ground and sending stars to pop and fade in front of my eyes.

"Oh, God," I groaned as I tried to roll over. A wave of nausea hit me, and I turned my head, knowing that failing to do so could cause me to choke on the vomit that threatened to escape up my throat and out of my pursed lips. The doors seemed to rattle with glee at the pain that I felt, the sound of them creaking and cracking as they expanded and contracted filling up that hallway like a wooden thunderstorm that echoed in my head, playing the harmony to the melody of the ringing that filled my ears. And as the dots and stars began to cloud my vision, the scene above me began to change.

"What's going on?" I asked of no one. I saw the faces of the people in the mural change, their expressions remaining, but their features morphing into those that were familiar, those that put the sting of fear, the cold grasp of it into my chest.

Graham's face appeared, so did Dad's, and Janice's,. Shawn's, Stacy's, Mrs. Deovolente's; Ambrose's face was there as well. The only face that was missing was mine.

"No," I whimpered when I finally understood what the image was trying to tell me. "No."

It was that recognition that seemed to trigger what happened in those next few moments. As I lay there on the ground, unable to even writhe in agony at the pain I felt both on my body and in my heart, the doors finally had had enough of their abuse and gave in to the pressure that forced against them from the other side. They blew outward, shards of wooden daggers slamming into the wall opposite them and raining down on me as I lay powerless to their cutting ends.

I closed my eyes and prayed that that would be enough. My ears were ringing with the pealing sound of the explosion; even thoughts were drowned out. The smell of burnt and rotted wood floated in the air, attacking my nose with its itchy and pungent aroma, and I sneezed, forcing my head to fly up and back down again which sent sharp, shooting pains down my back and through my mind. It bounced around within me, endlessly cycling through as though that had been its intention all along.

And through it all, I remained silent. I waited until the air had cleared, I waited until the throbbing inside of me had ebbed just enough so that opening my eyes wouldn't hurt. I waited until my body could recognize the slack that had been given now that the ribbons had lost their anchors and slowly, gingerly shuffled my limbs around enough to escape their confines.

I rolled over, and promptly threw up. I managed to pull myself up to my knees and waited until the last, hacking heave, then wiped my lips on one of the ribbons before attempting to stand. It was difficult, the world seemed to tilt with every millimeter of motion, but I managed to place both feet surely on the ground, my hands held out for balance. I was able then to register the damage that had been caused around me and marveled at the destruction that lay at my feet.

The doors had been obliterated. All of them except for the two at the opposite ends of the hallway. Between them laid the remains of five doors, their vibrant colors now nothing but flecks of paint that had chipped off and littered the ground like confetti. The rooms that had been empty were now filled with thick, gray smoke that threatened to push forward into the hallway and suffocate me. But it didn't. It stayed, as though confined by some invisible wall, and instead swirled around in a tempest of heat and air that I could not see or feel.

With careful steps, I hobbled toward the opposite end of the hall, the flower-shaped doorway beckoning to me. My bare feet crunched through the debris of splinters and shards of wood that stabbed at my feet and brought cry after cry to the tip of my tongue, but I swallowed each one. I would not let my own pain defeat me.

When I reached the end of the hallway, the door that stood there was unscathed, its ribbon still pristine and shimmering in the light that came from nowhere and everywhere all at once. I reached for the ribbon and tugged, my head lifting to get one last glimpse of the mural above me.

Before the door opened, before the ribbon snapped me back to my waking consciousness, I saw something that caused my heart to stop. Behind the wave, behind the ominous cloud, stood a dark figure, its wings standing out, proud and full.

And black.

136

I opened my eyes to see the wall of my room, my bedroom door open, my nightstand still bare. Robert's arms still held me against him, and I felt him draw me toward him, turning me to face him. His eyes were stormy, a concern in them that I knew could only come from him having seen the dream for himself through my thoughts.

"You knew it was a dream and you still stayed. Why?"

"I have questions, Robert. I have so many questions about what is going on, what is happening to me—to us—that I won't pass up an opportunity to get answers, even if I don't like them."

His hand brushed against the curve of my ear as he tried to keep his disappointment in check, the words that came out of him slow and measured in their calmness. "I cannot protect you in your dreams, Grace. I cannot bring you back if you stumble into a dark place and can't find your way out."

"I'm fine, Robert," I insisted.

"No, you're not. You saw things—terrible things. You cannot expect me to ignore that."

I knew that he was referring to the vision of him, the dark figure that seemed to be causing that wave of destruction to head straight toward the people I cared about. "I don't understand what that image means, Robert. I don't pretend to know, but it's important."

"What if it means nothing, Grace? What if it's just the sum of your fears manifesting itself into something that will only terrify you more?"

"Then at least I'll know," I answered.

"So you admit that you're scared…of what I am"

And it was then that I finally recognized that what had clouded his eyes with fear was not what I'd seen in my dream. He was afraid of what I thought of him, and what those thoughts might result in.

"Oh, Robert," I breathed, before wrapping my arms around his neck and burying my face into the planes of his neck. *I am not afraid of you, or what you are. I might have been at one time, for a second, but that moment passed almost as quickly as it came.*

*If I'm afraid of anything at all about you, it's that you might find one day that all of this isn't worth it, that I'm not worth it, and that we've just been wasting time.*

Rough yet gentle hands pulled my head away from him, and I was met with the fierce gaze of disbelief and disappointment. *I will never believe that you're not worth this.*

Disbelief quickly turned into something more, something…fiery. I felt my lips part just an instant before his crashed down on them. It was like a whirlwind, the emotions that this kiss created, and all too easily, we became lost in it, pulled into its vortex that ensnared us and held us captive as hands explored and lips traversed skin and bone and flesh and heat.

When you can feel every line, every crevice, and almost smell the scorching of skin, you know that there's no power on earth that could match the heat that exists between you and the person you're with. This was why love was compared to the sun and the stars; you couldn't escape it; it was always there, even when your eyes were closed and you felt weightless.

Panting, Robert pulled away, his face flush with an impossible redness, while his skin shone with the slick glisten of sweat that could not have possibly been his. His eyes were dilated, the pupils wide and ebony black, endless, like the feeling that went on and on inside of me, even as my heart thrummed in my chest.

"It's not…fair," he finally managed to say in a breathless whisper.

"That's my line." It was meant to be mocking, but instead it sounded sad. It wasn't fair. This constant push and pull of our emotions, of our feelings, physical or otherwise, that we had to tiptoe around and fight off because of the consequences that had nothing to do with either of us.

"I wish I could turn you now."

"Then why don't you?" I looked at him with imploring eyes, wanting him to give in. Instead, he eased away from me.

"It's not going to happen tonight, Grace. We have things we have to deal with first," he allowed before sitting up and running his hands through his hair, the dark waves separating and gathering together, my heart skipping as the recent memory of that silk running through my fingers caused them to tingle.

Not wanting to start an argument, I sat up as well and pulled at the hem of my shirt, which had ridden up past my navel, exposing the pale flesh beneath it. "I guess we should get these boxes out of here," I suggested before standing up.

"Grace…"

I turned to face him, and the expression on his face was pained. "Yes, Robert?"

"It's not going to be forever, you know. It's not going to be like this forever. You'll be turned—soon—and then we'll be able to…we'll be together in that way."

I simply nodded and left the room, heading to the bathroom to splash cold water on my face and examine the damage that yet another round of denial had caused. There were circles beneath my eyes, and the red webbing that crisscrossed the whites of them made me look more haggard than tired. My skin was waxy, and I reached for the soap to scrub at it, hoping that I could erase the dullness with one turn.

Dissatisfied with my end result, I closed my eyes to my reflection and was greeted with the nagging image of the mural that had hung above me in my dream. It came to me in pieces, chunks that did not meet up anywhere because I had not been able to see their ends. Faces that had not been there before, emotions that had been blank filled up spaces that should have remained empty. The lines grew darker, deeper, as though they were on fire, burning through the plastered surface until they met the sky itself. I frowned and opened my eyes, sighing when the dark half-moons that framed them seemed to grow darker.

"So much for being a blushing bride," I muttered before turning off the light and heading back to my room. I found it empty of both boxes and Robert and felt for the first time the fear of leaving behind something that I had always known, something that had always been a part of me. My entire life was packed away in a few boxes, and my future, short as it was, awaited me outside of these four plain walls.

I took one look at my twin sized bed and turned to face the mirror on my dresser, seeing myself for the last time as the awkward and unaccepted girl who had lost and gained more than anyone deserved. With a sigh, I headed toward the door, closing it behind me and shutting out the past.

# FIRST NIGHT

"Are you sure you'll be alright?"

I nodded and allowed a small smile to form on my lips before I felt the gentle press of a kiss against them. Robert pulled away and then left, his call taking him away from me on our wedding night.

With a groan of disappointment, I began the task of unpacking my boxes, thankful that the shelves Robert had removed in anticipation of our leaving for Europe were now back. He had not replaced his CDs or other objects, instead leaving them bare for my things, and I gladly stacked what little I had on them, the books and movies that I had collected over the years barely taking up one shelf.

The clothes that I had brought with me were placed neatly into the drawers in his dresser that he had cleared out for me, and a closet located near the bathroom was now empty, awaiting the few garments I had that actually required hanging. I placed my toothbrush in the little urn that sat next to his sink and left my hairbrush at the edge of it, noting that I'd probably never need it again now that we were living together.

I looked into the large shower and smiled when I saw the bottle of shampoo that was the exact same brand as mine. By the time I had emptied out the last box, the sun had long since set, and the darkness in the house was emphasized by its emptiness. Feeling hungry, I rummaged through the refrigerator for something to eat and found a tray of prepared salmon.

After dressing it with a bit of lemon and ginger, I threw it into the oven and prepared a salad while it baked. I ate alone, sitting at the kitchen counter with a meal for two sitting before me, making me feel utterly pathetic. Knowing that Robert wouldn't return hungry—and probably not at all—I wrapped the fish in foil and cleared away the dishes, washing them and placing them in the rack to dry.

With a pitiful sigh, I gathered my things and prepared to take a shower. The water was hot, steaming, and it felt good to wash away the dirt and grime and residue of the past twenty-four hours. I washed my hair twice and stepped out of the shower, wrapping myself up in a thirsty towel while my hair dripped down my back. After brushing my teeth, I got dressed in a pair of boxers and a ratty T-shirt and reached for my brush, pulling it through the mess of tangles that rested on my head.

I drew out the brushing for as long as I could, hopeful that at any moment, Robert would appear and finish it for me. But, in what I assumed was just the first of many nights like this to come, he did not show. With disappointment flowing through me, I put the brush down and turned off the bathroom light.

The four-poster bed held clean, crisp white sheets that felt smooth against my skin. They were cool and helped to stave off the unnatural heat I felt charging through my skin. I looked over beside me, and the empty space brought me further into a depression; the smooth, unwrinkled sheets acted like a siren that blared to anyone who could hear just how alone I was.

"Some wedding night," my cynical voice mumbled to the air. "Why did I think it would be any different?" I turned to my side and grabbed the book that I had placed on the nightstand, flipping the pages until they came to a dog-eared section and fell deeply into the story, forgetting everything but what the words on the pages revealed.

This night repeated itself, over and over again, until almost a week had gone by. Shawn's graduation party was tonight, and I was determined to go, even though Robert had said with dismay that he could not. Graham arrived at the house with Lark to drive the three of us there, and for the first time in a week, I felt…happy.

Robert's return in the morning had brought little for us in the way of any private reunions. I had started summer school immediately, my days spent trying to recoup what I had lost in biology class. It came as a big surprise to me to see that Mrs. Deovolente was teaching the class, her inexperience in the subject obvious to the four of us in the classroom with her.

I was relieved when I saw that my fellow classmates were few and of the sort that did not look down on me for having met the same fate as they had. On the contrary, they felt bolstered by it. If I had failed, then it was surely because of Mr. Branke and not because of my grades, and they saw that as the cause of their failures as well. It didn't matter that they could not grasp the concept of the subject—not that Mrs. Deovolente's teaching methods helped any—because they felt vindicated, justified in their failure.

At the end of class, while they filed out to retrieve what time they had left of their summer vacation, I lingered behind to speak to the confused teacher, whose face showed embarrassment after having been corrected on her terminology twice—by me.

"Can I ask you why you're teaching a subject you obviously know so little about?" I asked her after that first day.

"I needed the money," she replied succinctly.

"But why couldn't you teach psychology instead? Why did you get stuck with biology?"

"Because no one else wanted to take this class; they offered a third more than they did for the other positions, and I needed the money. It's not that difficult to understand, Grace."

Her auburn hair burned a deep burgundy under the florescent lights above, and her eyes were a sharp green that glittered as she took in the amusement in my face. "I'm sorry. I know as much as you do that you don't belong here, just as I don't belong here. I'd much rather be at home with my cats, curled up with a good book and a cup of tea, just as I'm sure you'd rather be off with that handsome boyfriend of yours, hanging out at the pool or going shopping for college supplies."

I choked on my reply, instead nodding and allowing her to finish up while I left. Each day, I started a conversation with her at the end of class, each time learning a bit more about her until I learned that she was divorced and lived with two cats named Isis and Iago. She loved to read graphic novels, was a fan of Neil Gaiman, and had everything that he'd ever done. She was an avid fan of dark horror and had seen Rocky Horror Picture Show over a hundred times.

She was, to my surprise, exactly how I pictured I would have turned out before Robert.

"So, are you going to Shawn Bing's party tomorrow?" she had asked me yesterday as I helped to close the windows.

"Yes. I wouldn't miss it for the world."

"Well then, I guess I'll see you there," she announced before disappearing into her office.

It was that knowledge that kept me from feeling any more disappointed when Robert again informed me that he wouldn't be joining me that night at the party. I had come to expect it and told him to not worry about me, that I'd be with his sister and friends who wouldn't let anything happen.

"I know you'll be fine. That's Lark's call, remember? She's not going to let anything happen to you that you don't let happen."

So, dressed in a pair of jeans and a blouse that I had borrowed from Lark's closet, and wearing my trusty boots, I entered the Bing house and was led through a hallway and down into a basement that had been decked out in Christmas lights and balloons, a large banner reading "Congratulations Shawn" covering part of the facing wall. Beneath it, a DJ bobbed to the thumping beat of the music that blasted from the equipment he had in front of him, a fast techno rhythm with electric notes that caused the frantic gyrations of several people who had gathered in front.

Shawn was standing off to the side, speaking to a young, blonde girl with glasses. On his head was his graduation cap, the tassel blinking with multi-colored LEDs that had been affixed there, a modification that I did not recall seeing at graduation.

"Shawn!" I called out, waving as he turned toward my voice. He grinned and rushed toward me, his arms thrown haphazardly around me before quickly pulling away and sobering up as the blonde sidled up beside him, her hand clasping his arm possessively.

"Grace! I'm so glad you could make it! I see Lark and Graham over there, hey guys!" He waved to the two figures that stood off to the back behind me, and then returned his gaze to mine. "Grace, this is Heather, my-uh-"

Heather shoved her hand in front of me, her fingers stiff as she finished for him, "I'm his girlfriend."

I took her hand and shook it, noting that she was gritting her teeth through her smile, and I knew that I had not made a friend in her. "It's nice to meet you, Heather," I told her with a pleasant smile on my face, as though to demonstrate how it was done.

"So you're the one he took to prom"

"Yes. Are you the one who dumped him?"

My question surprised even me, and her sputtering and dagger-laced looks before she stormed off told me quite clearly that she had been. Shawn looked at me apologetically before rushing after her, his pleas falling on deaf ears as she moved through the crowd and disappeared.

I turned to find Lark and Graham and saw that they had disappeared as well. Sighing, I walked over to the refreshment table and poured out a glass of punch. It was there that Mrs. Deovolente found me. She was wearing a miniskirt and a flashy sequined top that tied around her neck, her back completely exposed and revealing a large tattoo of a cat's silhouette.

"Wow," I breathed. "That's a lot of ink!"

"Isn't it?" she replied before downing the red liquid in her clear, plastic cup. "It hurt like hell, too."

"How long have you had it?"

"Since I was eighteen."

I admired the sleek lines of the feline's body, the profile of the slinky back and long, curved tail making her seem taller somehow. "I don't think I could sit down and let someone attack me with needles like that."

"Oh, I didn't sit down for it either. They had to hold me down to get it done."

This admission caught me off guard, but she walked away before I could ask her what she meant. To my surprise—and to pretty much the surprise of everyone around her—she stepped into the throng of kids dancing and began to move along to the rapid beat, her hair flying about her head like a cloud of red smoke.

Feeling the need to speak to her, a need to know more, I forgot where I was and followed. I began to move awkwardly to the thumping and pulsating sound, leaning my head toward her ear so that she could hear me as I asked, "Who held you down?"

"My sister," she shouted. "We kinda made a pact to get the tattoos together, but I chickened out after she had hers done. She wasn't going to let me get away with it so she held me down while the tattoo artist scratched away at my skin until the pain in my back numbed and I simply gave up."

"That's awful!"

"Is it? It was my fault—I'd agreed and then reneged on the plan."

As the music grew louder, the tempo increasing, I saw that she kept up with it, her smile widening on her face, her eyes closed while her body moved to the music, as though she were in a trance. I couldn't keep up, my clumsy feet and useless hands unable to find any sort of rhythm to grasp onto.

"I'm going to get something else to drink," I said out loud and didn't wait for a response before turning away.

I walked around the basement, surprised at how large it was, and searched for Graham and Lark. As I rounded a dark corner, I saw them,

146

clasping onto one another in a tight embrace, oblivious of the world around them, their bodies and their minds attuned only to each other. I felt a pang of jealousy then. No, not jealousy. Envy. I envied them their freedom to be together, to be with each other without fear of consequences or intrusion from an outside source.

I wanted that. I'd been married for a week and hadn't so much as spent a night sleeping beside my husband. I'd barely seen him, and every moment that passed forced me deeper into the depression that had begun that first night. Knowing that I couldn't take it any longer, I turned away, needing to leave the close confines of the basement, the smell of sweaty bodies and spiked punch too much to take now that I had lost all reason for being here in the first place.

Upstairs, the pounding base could be felt through the floor, and I wormed my way outside into the fresh night air, thankful when my feet could finally find ground that didn't vibrate.

"Why aren't you inside?"

"Oh!" I uttered, startled by the voice and then by the face of the person who stood beside me.

"I'm sorry; I scared you. Lark's attention has been drawn elsewhere at the moment and it fell onto me to make sure that you are safe."

In the lamplight of the street, it appeared as if a deep purple halo surrounded the angel who stood before me, his hair pulled back with a leather tie. "Lem. I didn't know you were watching me."

"It's my turn. Sera, Ameila, I and a few others rotate between you and your father. He's at the hospital right now, just in case you were wondering."

He was dressed in black, causing him to almost disappear into the shadows, but it was impossible to miss the glint in his eyes as they twinkled when he smiled at me. "You keep your thoughts sheltered from me. I completely understand. After what happened between you and my son, I would keep my thoughts safe from everyone, including myself."

"I-I'm sorry about Sam," I said softly.

"Do not apologize for what could not be avoided. His path was chosen for him long before he took a single step."

My brows pulled together at this and I frowned. "You knew he was going to die?"

He shook his head and a half-smile formed at the corners of his cynical mouth. "I only know that whatever happens to us is what was meant to happen."

"Do you think that way about all deaths?"

An auburn brow rose above a silver eye and his mouth completed the curve as his teeth slipped past his lips, revealing themselves in a pleased grin. "You want to know if I think your death can be prevented. I think that when it comes to humans, your lives are as much tied to ours as ours is to yours. If you're meant to die, I do not see how it can be prevented. Postponed, maybe, but stopped altogether? No."

"What about those that have turned? Haven't their deaths been stopped?"

A small burst of laughter passed through him, and his hand reached over to his shoulder to dust off something that I couldn't see before he turned to answer me, his demeanor suddenly serious. "Those that have turned are no less susceptible to death than those that have not. Humans are still humans, no matter what they've been turned into. Their core is still the same."

"You don't like humans much, do you?"

His head cocked back, obviously stunned by my question. "I love humans. I feel that human beings are the most blessed creatures on this earth, and I will do everything in my power to keep them safe. I only feel disappointment in those that would give up the joy of appreciating life to live forever in a body that never ages, that never allows them the benefit of understanding just how wonderful it is to change, to grow old and become someone new, someone wiser. A lifetime of knowledge and experiences given up for a perceived eternity of pleasure is something that I cannot understand.

"Pleasure fades. Humans get bored very easily with things and are simply not capable of appreciating what it means to be immortal.

They want change, constant, constant change and for us, for my kind, change is non-existent. We don't change who we are, we don't change what we do. We can't. It's why, when one of you promises to love someone forever, to be with someone forever in order to turn, it usually ends up being a lie."

An intake of breath filled up the silence that followed that last statement. It was mine, and it was one in offense. "I didn't lie when I said that I would love Robert forever."

"That is debatable, Grace, since you haven't allowed anyone but those closest to you to delve into your thoughts and see for themselves whether or not your words are true, and how they feel about you would skew their opinion toward you, regardless of the truth."

"You don't think I'm trustworthy, do you? You think…you think I'm like my mother."

A flash of something passed through his eyes, but it faded too quickly for me to guess what it was. When his mouth turned down, and the angle of his shoulders dipped down, his posture drooping, I guessed it was pain.

"I loved your mother, but she couldn't love me. Her heart had already been promised to someone else, even if he did not exist yet, and I cannot hold that against her; it wasn't her choice."

The woeful look on his face caused an ache within me, and it surprised me to know that I had something in common with him, this unrequited love that he had felt.

"I loved someone who couldn't love me back," I confessed, my voice quiet as my heart remembered the sting of rejection, the burn of it slight, a mere memory now but still able to cause that ache inside of me.

"And what now? Has he realized the error of his ways? Does he regret turning you away, knowing what he has lost?"

I laughed in spite of myself and shook my head. "Yeah, right. He's in love with someone who's crazy beautiful. Even if I still wanted to be with him, I don't stand a chance."

"I don't see how anyone could be more beautiful than you are."

149

An awkward silence passed between us, and I struggled to find something to say, something that wouldn't acknowledge this odd compliment. Fortunately, he realized his faux pas and corrected himself. "I'm sorry. I see your mother in your face and for me, no one else could be more beautiful than Avi; please, forgive me."

His embarrassment was clear, and I did the only thing I knew how to in situations like this.

I punched his arm.

"Ow! Holy hell, ow!"

My fist—or what was left of it—lay clutched against my chest, my fingers bent at odd angles, twisted and bruising rapidly before my eyes. The expression on Lem's face showed nothing but shock as his eyes bounced from my face to my hand, up and down, until at last he settled on my face, too surprised to say anything while I whimpered at my quickly swelling hand.

"Grace? Oh God, what the hell did you do?" Lark was here, her face filled with dismay and concern as she pried my hand away from my chest, examining it and shaking her head.

Graham stood opposite her, his eyes throwing daggers at Lem, who still seemed unable to utter a single word. "What did you do? What did you do to make her hit you, man?"

"Graham-" I interrupted, but the pain cut me off.

"We need to get you to Robert," Lark announced, her eyes searching mine, her thoughts weeding through my head. "Lem, can you carry her?"

He looked at me with trepidation clear on his face. "If she doesn't mind."

"You don't mind, do you Grace?"

"I-I guess not," I replied, though there was noticeable doubt tingeing my voice.

Lark and Graham ran to his car, while Lem took my hand and pulled me into the shadows. I said nothing, didn't even let slip out of me a cry of surprise when my feet left the ground and I was in the air, my body cradled against the firm and broad chest that belonged to someone other than Robert.

This was different from flying with him. Robert sailed through the air like a bird, as though he and the sky were meant for each other. Lem's movements were jerky, turbulent even though the sky was still and no cloud could be seen. In the faint glow that radiated outward from his skin, I could see the tenseness in his jaw, see how rigid he held himself as he tried to hold me as carefully as he could; he was afraid that he would break me. I sensed it.

"You don't have to be so quiet," I said to him. "You can talk to me if you want to."

"You'll forgive me if I find it a bit…difficult to do so. I'm afraid that I can't quite fly and talk at the same time."

I chuckled. "That's okay. I can't quite do anything and talk at the same time. Everything else, I'm golden, but when it comes to talking, I'm a total klutz."

A small twitch pulled at one side of his mouth, and I reveled in that small victory. "Besides, you need to keep my mind occupied, otherwise I'm going to start thinking about how much my hand hurts—and it really, really, really hurts."

When he said nothing, when the tiny smile disappeared, I tried another tactic. *We can speak this way if it'd be easier for you.*

His head jerked down to look at me, surprise marking his face. *You would do that? To make me comfortable?*

I nodded. *Does it?*

He smiled, a glorious smile that made me feel that familiar twinge inside of me that…well, it frightened me, actually. "I think that if you're willing to open your mind to me, I should be willing to attempt to have a conversation in the way that makes you most comfortable. But I thank you for your attempt."

"Y-you're welcome?"

He laughed, and a rush of warmth filled me at the sound, the musical quality of it a symphony to the silence that I'd grown accustomed to this past week. I was so stunned by the effect it had on me that a tear formed and fell from my eye.

"I'm sorry—did I say something wrong?"

I shook my head at the perplexed tone that drenched Lem's voice. "It's not you. It's just me being a stupid human."

"You've spent far too much time with Lark I see."

It was my turn to laugh, and my head bobbed up and down in agreement. "It's that obvious, huh?"

"Very. You could probably do with more humor in your life— hanging around an undertaker or gravedigger might do the trick."

"What?"

"Hey, they're some of the funniest guys around; they have to be in order to do what they do."

"I guess that's true."

I felt our descent—more like drop—as we approached Robert's home, and our conversation ceased, silence once again filling the space between us. The house was dark, and I fumbled in my pocket for the key to open the front door as Lem set me down. He walked in front of me and grabbed for the knob, turning it with ease, the lock giving way beneath his silent manipulation.

"Well, I could have done that…if I had like…powers or something," I mumbled, following him into the darkened foyer.

"You're right handed, Grace. You couldn't get your key out of your pocket because it's on your right side—and if you couldn't get the key, you wouldn't have been able to open the door," Lem pointed out as he waved a hand, sending the lights all flickering on and filling the room with their hollow glow.

"Oh sure, point out my flaws; that's exactly what girls like," I quipped as I walked past him and headed toward the kitchen, flipping the light on with my elbow.

"Now see, that is something I could not do," he remarked behind me, watching intently as I pulled open the freezer door with my foot and removed the ice box from its holster. Kicking the door shut, I opened a drawer and removed a towel, filling it with several cubes of ice before pulling the corners up and twisting it on the counter, creating a makeshift icepack that I soon placed on my throbbing hand.

"Ahh," I sighed at the soothing chill.

"You're quite self-sufficient, aren't you?"

I glanced at his face and saw the look of awe that covered it and felt my mouth twist up with annoyance. "All I did was get some ice for my hand. That's not exactly being self-sufficient. Any idiot could do it."

"But you did it with one hand—and a foot. You did it as if it was all automatic. You didn't even need to think about it, as if there was no choice for you."

"Well, there really isn't. Robert's not here, and who knows when he'll be back. I've got to keep this swelling down otherwise I'm going to have to go to the emergency room, and if Ambrose isn't working then I'm going to have to figure out a way to explain why my hand is the size of the Goodyear blimp, and why it looks like black glass."

I held up my hand to emphasize my point and saw his face pull back in disgust. The honeycombed bruising had extended past my wrist and was nearing my elbow now. If it was allowed to continue, I'd be purple by sunrise.

"That is not…that is not normal," was all that Lem could say before he turned away, the sight obviously too much for him.

I couldn't help but compare his reaction to Robert's, the acceptance and concern unquestionable with him, whereas Lem's back was stiff, his aversion to the human injury obviously not something he could tolerate. I reached into the towel drawer and pulled out another towel, placing it atop of my hand and covering it.

"You can turn around; I covered it," I said to him, my annoyance growing by the second.

When he did, the relief on his face was so evident he couldn't hide it or deny it. Instead, he issued an apology, his hands held out in supplication as he stepped forward, his eyes avoiding the towel that was draped on my hand, water from the melting ice dripping beneath it and onto the floor.

"I'm sorry. I should have a stronger stomach for something like that, but it looks too much like..."

"Like the skin of an Innominate, right?"

When his eyes widened, I felt my face give off a visible shrug. "I know what it looks like, Lem. I've seen it on Sam, as well as on Robert. This is what happens to me when I get hurt. When Robert comes back, he'll make it go away. Until then, I'll just keep it here beneath this towel because I really don't like the way it looks either."

His shoulders lowered as he relaxed, my assertion running in line with his doing much to set him at ease. "Why are you so different?"

My eyes narrowed at his question. "What? What do you mean by that?"

"Well, you're unlike most humans. You're nervous, you're jittery and uncomfortable, and yet, you still try to make others feel less uncomfortable, pushing your own feelings aside as though they don't matter. You're unnaturally patient, even now, when Robert has not yet arrived despite knowing what has occurred. Anyone else in your position would be in no condition for pleasant conversation, much less attempting to ease anyone else's discomfort."

Feeling sheepish, I felt my mouth pinch up, my bottom lip swallowing my top in some vain attempt to mask my embarrassment. "I'm sorry. I get defensive every time someone says that to me. I don't know why I am the way I am. I guess I've always based how I felt on how others felt; if they weren't feeling alright then I wasn't feeling alright. I don't know any other way to be."

Lem turned my body around, forcing me to look squarely at him as he spoke. "You're not just human, Grace. Remember that. Your mother was an angel, no matter what she had become when you came into being. She passed on to you her divinity, the part of her that makes any of us as good as we are. What you are isn't different. I used the wrong term and I apologize for that.

"No, you aren't different. What you are is empathic. You feel what others feel more deeply, more completely. When they hurt, you hurt; when they're happy, you feel it, too. It's how we feel things. Love, anger...passion; as a human, it's amplified in you. Even now, you feel what I feel only you feel it ten-fold."

His hands on my shoulders burned, and I opened my mouth to ask what he meant by that when he disappeared, leaving me gaping at the empty space that still smelled of softness and warmth and smoke, like a cozy fire that had been put out by the morning rain.

"Well, I've got a knack for driving off male angels," I muttered to myself before the sound of a car pulling up and doors slamming could be heard from outside. Graham ran into the kitchen, his eyes darting back and forth as though looking for some danger that I was unaware of.

"Did Robert show up?"

His question answered itself when Robert arrived just moments afterward, his face filled with dark anger that, for a fraction of a second, sent a chill of fear through me before it was replaced with another emotion altogether.

"What have you done to yourself now?" he asked, the biting sting in his voice and the accusation acting like a slap in my face.

I pulled the towel off of my hand and raised it, unsure if I even wanted him to look at it, much less touch it.

"For Heaven's sake, Grace, couldn't you stay safe for one week?" he grumbled as he removed the icy rag and wrapped his hands around my broken fingers.

"So you've noticed that it's been a week? One week without my *husband*?" I threw back at him, unable to take the accusatory tone in his voice.

"Grace-" he began, but I cut him off.

"You think I hurt myself on purpose, don't you? You think I did this on purpose to bring you back here, don't you?"

He tried to deny it, but I saw that my words had more than truth in them, and it hurt. God, did it hurt. "Oh. My. God." I pulled my hand away from his and stormed down the rear hallway, opening up the bedroom door and slamming it shut behind me.

I collapsed onto the bed, angry, destroyed...broken. The soft knock at the door went unanswered. I stared away toward the window, ignoring the slow creak of the door swinging open, and the soft click of it shutting. I pretended that I didn't feel the dip in the bed as a weight pressed down on it, a body moving up against mine, arms enfolding me in an embrace I neither wanted nor wanted to be free of.

"I'm sorry," the voice whispered into my ear.

I closed my eyes to it, not wanting to believe it and yet needing to believe it. "You hurt me, Robert."

"I know."

"We've been married for a week and I've spoken to Lem more in one night than I have you these past seven days."

"I know. I'm sorry."

"This isn't what I thought marriage was going to be like—I didn't know what marriage was going to be like—but if I did, it wouldn't be this. I've spent every single night alone."

A hand, warm and strong, covered my bruised one, and I felt the heat flow through it and into mine as his other hand reached up to press against heart. I knew that he could feel every shuffle of my heart as his words replayed themselves over and over in my head, each turn hurting me just as much as the last.

"I'm sorry, Grace."

"Stop saying you're sorry."

"What would you like me to say?"

I turned my head so that I could see him. Kinda. "Don't say anything. Just stay with me tonight."

"Grace, I can't."

Defeated, I turned away. "Fine."

"Grace..."

"I said fine. Go. Leave."

The throbbing in my hand was already easing, and I knew that in a few hours it would be completely healed, with or without Robert there, so I moved away from him, standing up and heading to the dresser. I pulled open the top drawer that had been reserved for my things and pulled out a set of keys.

"What are you doing?"

He was beside me, my intent clear even if I hadn't said a word—or thought them.

"I'm not going to stay here alone another night, Robert. You might see nothing wrong with it, but I do. I can't be alone, night after night. I'm going to my dad's. If you want me, you can find me there."

He grabbed for my shoulder, but I knew him. I knew him too well, and I moved out of the way at that same instant. "Go and do what you need to do, Robert. I understand it, I accept it."

"Then why are you leaving?"

"Because I don't want to waste my last days on this damn planet going to summer school and then coming home to an empty house. I don't want to have to worry about getting hurt and having my *husband* come home and accuse me of doing it on purpose just to bring him back."

"I said I was sorry-"

I shook my head. "It doesn't matter. We can stop pretending that we're not married, Robert, because there's nothing to fake." I stepped toward the door, and I could see Graham standing at the end of the hallway, his eyes shadowed, Lark's relaying of my thoughts damaging him in the way only a best friend could.

He held his arms out to me, and I walked into them, allowing them to pull me away, my feet moving of their own accord through the kitchen and past the living room and finally outside. I felt myself being lifted into the front seat of Graham's Buick and buckled in.

I stared out of the window, telling myself that the blur that I saw was summer rain hitting the glass.

## FELINE INTUITION

"Are you sure you'll be alright?"

"Dad, I'll be fine. It's just to the school."

"I still say you should let me drive you."

I stood in the driveway, my feet planted on either side of my bike, and I shook my head at the suggestion. "I've got babysitters floating around here somewhere, Dad. If anything happens, they'll be there."

"I still don't like it. Robert should've never agreed to this. Busy or not, he's your husband and you should be with him."

A rough sigh passed through me, and I gritted my teeth at the lie Dad repeated back to me, the lie that I had told him to explain why he came home from the hospital to find me in the kitchen cooking breakfast two days ago. I couldn't tell him that I had left because after only a week, my marriage was an absolute failure. Not after he had accepted Robert into his life. I wouldn't do that—to either of them.

"Dad, he's got his priorities and I have mine. You said it yourself, I have to graduate. I can't focus on school if I'm stuck there worrying about him, and he can't focus on what he's got to do if he's worrying about whether or not I'm doing okay in school."

Another lie. It twisted up my insides to have to say it, but there was no hope for it now. I had dug myself a hole that would only get deeper—I wanted it to get deeper. At least there, I was safe. My lie was a small comfort because I felt if I repeated it enough, if others believed it as firmly as I hoped, that it would become true and banish the truth that

I refused to admit.

"How about I drive behind you? Make sure for myself?"

My eyes rolled, and I grimaced at the idea. "D-A-D!" I groaned, each letter turning into its own syllable. "Do you actually think having a car coming up behind me is going to make *me* feel safe?"

He paused for a moment, his response hanging on the tip of his tongue, and then sheepishly closed his mouth, suddenly aware of his mistake. "I'm sorry. You're right, it's a terrible idea."

"Thank you. Now, I've got to get going before I'm late."

Kicking up the bike stand, I took several steps backwards, the bike rolling beneath me, until I was in the street. I waved goodbye at Dad, the concern still marring his features, and then began pedaling down the road. My legs began to burn less than five minutes into the ride, and I knew it was because I had grown lazy, and I cursed myself for that.

My breathing soon grew haggard, and sweat stained my shirt as the morning sun grew angry above me, burning a red swatch down my arms. By the time I reached the school, I was a bag of sunburned jelly. I stumbled off of the bike, clumsy in ways I didn't know possible, and it took me several tries to get the lock on the bike before I collapsed in a heap on the sidewalk, unable to move or breathe without it hurting.

"Do you need help, Grace?"

A dark silhouette stood above me, the sun blocking out everything save the shade of hair that glowed a deep wine color in the soft orange haze.

"Hey, Mrs. Deovolente. Could you give me a hand?"

I reached up and took hold of the firm grip, pulling myself up to my feet, wobbling a bit before righting myself and thanking the woman who stood next to me now, her face filled with amusement. "It's been a while," I said, a rather bland explanation but the only one my lungs could manage.

"At least you didn't forget how," she joked before starting her stride toward the school doors.

"At least."

Together we walked into the cooled hallway of Heath High, the clicking sound of her pumps echoing in the strange emptiness. "I'm glad that I caught you before class started. Do you think we could talk…about the night at the party?"

"What about?"

She looked around, checking to see if anyone else was around, before she lowered her head, her voice lowering in kind, and whispered, "The tattoo."

"What about it?"

"It…I should have never worn such a revealing top. If word gets out that I was even at that party, much less dressed the way that I was, I might lose my job. You were the only one who attended that's still a student here—even if for only a few more weeks—and I'd like it if you kept what you saw to yourself."

This confused me, because nothing she had done or said or wore had seemed inappropriate to me in the slightest. "Okay."

"Thank you. It means a lot to me."

We walked in silence the rest of the way, and I took my place in the near empty classroom as she apologized for being late to the three other faces that stared, bored, at the whiteboard in front of us.

The next few hours proceeded as dully as possible, Mrs. Deovolente's usually cheerful voice dropping down to a sullen monotone that forced at least one student to fall asleep.

When the bell rang, I felt ten pounds heavier from just the weight of it, but I was also glad for it. Anything to keep my thoughts from being filled with Robert's accusation or his indifference, I told myself.

It had been three days now since I'd left, and he hadn't so much as visited me. I closed my eyes that first night back and waited for him to appear, waited for the dip in the bed, for the arms to embrace me, but nothing came. The next night repeated the same loneliness, and I realized by the second morning that it wasn't better, waking up alone in my father's house. In fact, it was worse.

"Grace, do you think you could stay a while? I have a question to ask."

My head lifted at this and I nodded enthusiastically. She noticed this and my head stilled, but it was too late.

"Don't want to go home so soon, do you?"

I looked at her and sighed. There was no hope in denying it now. "Not really."

"Trouble with your father?"

"No. No, things with my dad are great. He's…he's honestly the best dad a girl could want."

"Then it's trouble with your boyfriend, the handsome one. That's it, isn't it?"

No matter what my mouth wanted to say, my eyes screamed the truth out at her, and she nodded in understanding. "Guys are the bane to a woman's existence. What's been bothering you?"

"I don't—I don't know if I can talk to you about it."

"Has he been pressuring you? Is that it?"

I shook my head, as I laughed sarcastically. "If only…"

"You've grown apart then. He's planning on moving on—or you are. Is that it?"

"We're apart. We're always apart. Even when he's right there with me, we're not in the same room, and it wasn't like that before. Before, it didn't matter where he was, he was with me. He was right here." I pressed my hand against my chest, my heart slowly pounding inside.

"Perhaps it's for the best. You're young, Grace. You have your whole life ahead of you. College, marriage, kids. There's so much that you have to look forward to, with someone who will always be there for you. Maybe this is an opportunity for you."

"No offense, Mrs. Deovolente, but you don't know what you're talking about."

She eased back in her chair, obviously surprised by my response. "Well, excuse me, but I do take offense to that. I was young once too, you know. I thought I was in love when I was your age. I thought that the sun rose and set with the person I was in love with, but it turned out that I was wrong. I got hurt, and I let that hurt derail plans that I had made for myself. It took me a long time to get back on track, and I don't want to see the same thing happen to you."

"Trust me, it won't."

Mrs. Deovolente stood up and took careful, measured steps around her desk. She pulled the chair that was beside me out from under its desk and sat down in it. "I worry about you, Grace. I see so much potential in you, and when I see you looking as though your entire world is caving in around you, I feel it, too."

"Look, Mrs. Deo-"

"Call me Mel."

"Fine. Look, Mel, I'm not saying that you don't know what you're talking about for yourself. You're probably some kind of relationship guru in that department. You just don't know what you're talking about when it comes to me."

"Then help me to understand. Maybe I do know. Maybe, even if I don't, I can give you my opinion from another perspective."

As much as I wanted to, as much as I wanted to tell her and hear what she might think, I couldn't. Who was this person to me but a teacher? One whom I'd never see again and who couldn't possibly understand what it was like to love an angel?

"I'm sorry. I can't."

"Well, then tell me something you can. You said 'if only' when I asked about being pressured. Are you worried that your boyfriend isn't attracted to you?"

I gaped at her, my mouth hanging open like an empty pot. "I don't think that's any of your business!"

"I'm sorry. I didn't mean to offend you. But, if it's true, if that's something you're concerned about then I think I might be able to help."

"How can you help me?" I asked, doubt and aversion wreaking havoc with my tone.

"Well, for starters, have you ever thought of seducing your boy-friend?"

"I don't think this is something a teacher is supposed to instruct me on," I pointed out, but deep down, I was intrigued.

"Well, you *are* an adult, aren't you?"

"Being eighteen makes me legally an adult, but that doesn't mean that I'm any more comfortable with the idea of you giving me sex advice."

She held up her hands in defeat and gave me a wan smile. "If that's how you feel, then alright."

"What could you tell me anyway? You don't know Robert, or what he likes or dislikes."

I hadn't meant to say it. I didn't even realize that I had until the words had left my mouth and Mrs. Deovolente was responding.

"I might not know what Robert likes, but he is a guy, and all guys like knowing that you've made an effort at trying to look sexy for them. They appreciate that."

I snorted, an unladylike snort that was definitely not sexy. "I couldn't pull off sexy if you poured it on me. It's not possible."

"Well, have you ever tried?"

"No," I snapped indignantly.

"Maybe that's your problem. Maybe you need to entice him. Wear something provocative, something skimpy."

Instantly my mind was drawn to that night I had worn his shirt, and only his shirt. It had provoked an unexpected reaction, one that changed everything between Robert and I, and I could do nothing but acknowledge that in everything else, he had been able to resist what both of us struggled with. But was it that simple? Did he not come to me because of my choice in clothes?

"Have I struck a chord?"

My head snapped up, and I realized that I had been so lost in my thoughts my silence had told her everything she needed to know—there was no denying anything now.

Instead, I revealed a fear that I hadn't realized I possessed until it was past my lips. "Why am I not enough the way I am?"

The hurt in my voice, the visible hurt in the furrowing of my brow, and the painful twisting of my mouth brought her forward, her arms wrapping around me in a comforting embrace.

"If he doesn't find you attractive enough to be with the way you are then he's not worth your time. I'm sorry for even suggesting that you're the problem, Grace. That's a woman's worst mistake—I should have never even brought it up."

My body shook with rejection of her apology. "No. No, you were right. The only time we've ever...the only time we've done..." My words failed me, the subject so uncomfortable and private that my mouth could not complete the sentence.

"You don't have to say another word, Grace," she said mercifully. "Perhaps this is for the best. It's far better to remove yourself before you become too involved. There's a price to pay for getting too involved." Her voice trailed away, even as she pulled away, and I could see that there was pain in her eyes that seemed to mirror my own.

"Mel?"

"I'm sorry. This obviously is not the most appropriate conversation we should be having. I have to get going, Grace, but we'll talk more tomorrow. Alright?" With that, she stood up and hurriedly gathered her things before dashing out of the classroom, leaving me to ponder just what had happened to her that could have hurt her so badly that she'd be able to comprehend just how awful I felt.

I was also left wondering if perhaps her advice, regardless of whether or not she had retracted it, would work. Robert had always maintained a semblance of control, even when it appeared that I was the one who had drawn things to a halt. I never fooled myself once into thinking that perhaps if I had just kept my mouth shut that things would have been different—not when it came to that.

As I grabbed my backpack from the ground beside me, I frowned at the ideas that ran through my mind. Horrible ideas that left me feeling low in both spirit and body. The compliments that Robert had given me had always been seemingly never ending, but as I rifled through the memories of each one, each one that I so preciously coveted because they had been from him to me, I couldn't help but acknowledge that the majority of them were given when I was wearing something that wasn't…well, me.

I rode my bike home with slow, steady strokes, and with each marker that I passed, I counted yet another moment when the only compliments I received from him—or anyone—had been when I was dressed in something that I would not have chosen for myself. Each tick on the invisible chart that kept track of them seemed to scream at me just how foolish I had been.

Did I doubt that Robert loved me? Never. I couldn't deny that he loved me as fiercely as I did him. But by the time I reached my father's house, I realized that what I felt for him, this passionate need to be with him, wasn't something that he seemed to share for me.

It definitely wasn't the heated, unquenchable desire that Lark obviously felt for Graham and vice versa. They hadn't spent a single night apart that had not been forced upon them, and even when they were together, there was barely a foot of distance between them, their need to be close to each other far too strong to ignore.

I was a quivering, blubbering mess by the time I reached my room, my bed still a mess, my nightstand now bearing the duck lamp that I had borrowed from Matthew's room.

I lay down on the bed, too deeply embedded in my sorrow to hear the phone ringing in the drawer beside me. When Dad knocked on the door a few minutes later to tell me that the call was for me, I don't recall blindly fumbling with the drawer pull to reveal the phone, or even lifting the receiver up and pressing it to my ear.

My voice creaked as I spoke into the phone, "Hello?"

The person on the other end waited until the tell-tale click of the other phone being hung up could be heard, and then the sound of an odd voice filled my ear.

"Grace?"

"Yes?"

"This is Sean. Sean Kim. Stacy's brother."

"Oh." I sat up, my head instantly shoving aside the makings of my own self-pity party and quickly replacing it with the harsh words he had thrown at me, the cold stares, and the hidden threats. I treaded cautiously. "What can I do for you, Sean?"

"I need to talk to you. It's about Stacy."

"What about her?"

"This is going to sound crazy, and since I know *you're* crazy, I figured you wouldn't think this strange at all. I think Stacy's alive."

The phone fell out of my hands, slamming against the legs of the nightstand before coming to rest partially beneath the bed. I bent over it with clumsy hands, fumbling with it several times—pressing a button or two in the process—and pressed it against my head once more, my hands firmly holding it there, creating a vacuum between the clammy receiver and my sweaty ear.

"I'm sorry, I'm sorry," I apologized. "What makes you think that Stacy's alive? You saw her die. We all did."

"I saw her. The other day, while I was driving to Shawn Bing's house for that stupid party he was throwing. I saw her standing across the street. She was staring at the sky. I swear I saw her. I blinked—I freaking blinked—and when my eyes opened again she was gone. I need to know if you've seen her, too."

"Why would you ask me something like that?" There was nervousness in my voice that I hoped he could not hear. I hoped...

"Because you were one of her best friends, and I know that you've seen her, too."

"What?"

"At the funeral. I saw you looking at the window. Stacy was there—you saw her, too."

"Sean, I-I don't know what to tell you." My stammer was almost as bad as my grip on the phone, which continued to threaten to slip out

166

of my grasp at any moment, my fingers growing slicker by the moment.

"Look, just tell me the truth, okay? I won't tell my parents—they'd never understand anyway—but I don't feel like something's missing. I don't feel like she's gone, even though everything else says that she is. If she's not, then I know that you'd know for sure. I know that you'd know if what I'm feeling is me just being crazy or if there's something else going on."

He was vulnerable. I sensed it in his voice, his closeness to his sister unmistakable and firm, another connection that I now found I envied.

But how do I go about trying to explain something to him that was unexplainable? What did I say to him? Do I tell him the truth, or do I lie and tell him that he's crazy?

"Grace?"

"Yeah, I'm still here."

"She's not dead, is she?"

"She's dead, Sean. She's stone cold dead."

There was a silence on the other line that I did not like. And then a voice that was colder than I'd ever heard before. "You're lying." The click of the other end being slammed was nowhere near as deafening as that accusation, and I shivered from the implication that it brought.

I wasn't lying. It didn't matter that my words had a double meaning, and that he'd taken it for face value. Stacy *was* dead. She wasn't alive, not in the way that he'd accept, and there was no way I was going to reveal that to anyone. Not even her own brother, even if it cost me something that I had not yet realized I had to lose.

But sitting up now, with the phone still pressed against my ear, my thoughts an endless pit of doubt and hurt and confusion, I fought to regain some semblance of control over what I was going to do. Robert stained my thoughts like ink, turning everything dark. Sean was willing to fight for the possibility that his sister was alive. Why couldn't I fight for the possibility that Robert's need for me was as well?

Realizing that I was making a foolish gamble based on the crazed hopes of someone who despised me, even as he turned to me for advice, I went to the bathroom to wash away the evidence of my crying. I returned to my room only to grab my wallet from my backpack and shove it into my jeans pocket.

I ran downstairs and slipped out the door, grabbing my bike in the process and pedaling as fast as I could down the street.

"If I hurry, I can make it there before they close," I said to myself out loud, my destination clear, my intent clear, my nerves shot to pieces and scattering behind me like frayed ribbon.

# CRACKED

God, what a stupid thing to do. I paced the room, my bare feet padding on the soft carpet, my hands nervously clenching and unclenching the thin robe that hung around me like a scarlet curtain.

I hurried to the bathroom to check my reflection once more, unsure as to whether or not this would be passable, or whether I looked like some hooker circus clown prowling the streets for Johns.

After leaving Dad's house, I had pedaled like a mad woman to get to the mall. There were still a few hours before it closed and I needed every single precious minute to find what I was looking for. A woman with short, dark hair watched me enter the small store, near panic set on my face at the abundant amount of things that were lacking. Lacking in material, lacking in coverage, lacking in actual clothing; a store filled with nothing but things meant to entice and seduce was where I found myself after deciding to test out Mrs. Deovolente's theory.

I silently cursed her—and Sean—for being two separate reasons for why I had to try this approach because if it failed, then I'd know for certain where I stood with Robert ,and I dreaded the answer. I dreaded it as much as I dreaded the look on the saleswoman's face as she saw within me a virgin customer ripe for the picking.

"Hello, dear. Can I help you with anything?" she asked me in a voice that was all too sweet, all too kind.

"I'm looking for something…" was all I could say to her. I didn't know what I was looking for. What did one buy in a place like this that didn't leave them feeling cheap? Okay, after looking at the prices in here, cheap is the wrong word. Expensive. Very, *very* expensive is more appropriate. And poorer; definitely poorer.

"Is this a gift for someone else? Or is this a personal purchase?"

My head tilted to the side as I tried to decipher what she meant by gift when she smirked and added, "Or both?"

"Can it be both?"

"Oh, definitely," she said with a knowing smile. "You seem quite young to be looking for something of that nature, though. Do you mind if I ask you how old you are?"

"Eighteen," I answered stiffly.

"Well, that's the perfect age to start learning about what to wear when you want to feel provocative."

There was that word again! Provocative was what Mrs. Deovolente had used. Provocative was what I, in my boxers and tank tops, had not been. I wanted to be that word.

"Do you think you could help me?" I asked nervously, and the woman smiled at me like a sculptor would a piece of clay. She dragged me toward the back of the shop, and pushed me behind a pair of dark, striped curtains.

"You stay there and start to undress," she commanded. "I shall return with a few things for you to try on."

And when she said few, she meant a few dozen. I felt like an overused mannequin by the time she clapped her hands and cheered over a short, frilly gown of red that was so sheer, I could have sworn being naked felt more modest.

"You look divine," she said to me before handing me a robe that was just a tad bit more substantial than the gown. "You cannot just wear the dress, however. This must be seen first. Let the reveal be…slow. Let it be tantalizing and teasing."

I giggled at her voice, how she lowered it into something she intended to be sultry, and instead just sounded rough—phlegmy.

"Do I have to talk like you, too?"

She straightened her back, the offense noted, and she shook her head. "No. You can continue to giggle like a little girl and maybe that'll be enough. Or not."

She turned away to leave me to undress, and I immediately felt bad. My mouth had grown just as clumsy as my hands had, and I felt ashamed when I walked up to the counter to pay for the gown and robe and saw that the friendly smile that should have been there—even if only for the sale—had vanished, and was replaced by a stern line of thick disapproval.

"Thank you for your help," I said as the lady swiped the plastic card I gave her.

"You're welcome," she bit back before yanking the paper receipt from the register and handing it to me to sign.

The exchange was swift, clinical, and then I was out of the store and into the nearly empty hallway of the mall, the store gate slamming shut behind me. Realizing the time, I raced to find my bike, hidden behind a dumpster near the back exit, and I pumped my legs, pushing myself harder than I should have to get to the house.

As I expected, the house was dark. Using my key, I let myself in through the front door, closing it carefully before feeling my way through the foyer and into the kitchen of Robert's home. My feet knew the way from there and I followed them as they pulled me toward Robert's room. Only when I was safely inside did I turn the light on, revealing that everything was as it had been the day I left. My legs were throbbing, and I realized that I also stunk. I tossed the bag that had been clutched so tightly in my hand the entire ride here onto the bed and then dashed into the shower to wash off the exhaustion and funk that covered my body.

After wrapping myself up in a towel once I was done, I left the room to tiptoe upstairs into Lark's room. It was empty, and as quickly as I could, I walked to her vanity and swiped a tube of what I could only hope was a pleasant shade of lipstick. Knowing that I might not have that much time, I ran downstairs, slamming into the corner of the couch and letting out a not-so-muffled curse before I returned to Robert's room, closing the door and grabbing the bag off of the bed.

Carefully, I began to assemble myself in the red frock, the matching underwear causing me to shudder at its total lack of substance. The robe, I realized, was far more concealing than I originally thought, and I was thankful for it, even as I was angry that things had come to this point.

I felt uncomfortable, exposed, and nervous. I looked at myself in the mirror and saw that my cheeks were flush with something that I wanted to believe was excitement, but that I knew came more from shame than anything else. Shame that I thought this was necessary, shame that I wasn't enough.

The tube of lipstick in my hand turned out to be some god awful shade of red that was so bright, it made my lips look like they were on fire, but it was all I had.

And then the waiting game began. My brush, still sitting at the end of the counter in the bathroom, had been swiped through my hair over a dozen times, and I'd brushed my teeth enough times to hear them squeak.

I thought about what would happen, over and over in my head, playing out different scenarios to see which would be the most optimal, but each time I did, even my fantasies chickened out on me and stopped before anything could happen. Finally, I realized that standing in the middle of a brightly lit room would not be seductive at all, that the best light that I could possibly get would be from the high moon shining through the window, and so with a sigh that I hoped would not be the last, I flipped the switch off and waited.

By the time I had begun to pace, my bathroom dash to recheck my appearance now a distant ten minutes past me, an entire hour had gone by. What if he didn't show up at all? He had been busy, after all, and tonight should have been no different.

I sat down once more on the edge of the bed, needing to clear my thoughts before I ended up screaming with all of the "what ifs" that continued to bombard my brain. I lay down after a few more minutes, and soon found myself drifting off to sleep, the coolness of the night prickling my skin and triggering dreams that were unnatural in how they made me feel.

I woke up in a flushed heat, my breaths ragged and harsh. The sound of movement outside of the door forced my hand to my chest, to still the slamming of my heart and the audible rise and fall of my breathing.

A sliver of light cut beneath the door and when it opened to reveal a column of brightness, I stood up with an expectant smile on my face. Robert walked in, his devilish grin one that made my heart forget what I had been telling it to do, and instead began to gallop within me, a steady rhythm that sent heat to my skin in one tidal wave of excitement. How could a simple—yet expensive—piece of clothing cause such a reaction out of me?

I stepped forward, my hand falling from the edges of the robe, and I smiled at him, meeting his eyes and seeing a spark there that gave me hope.

And then the hope died.

The spark turned into shock, and then guilt, and then my eyes saw that his arm, the arm that should have been holding me, that should have been welcoming me home, was drawn behind him, his hand ending where another's begun.

My eyes traveled to another pair, these eyes shaded a brilliant violet, their sparkle, their shine telling me that she was filled with as much happiness and want as I was with heartache and betrayal. She was beautiful, her face heart-shaped and the color of creamed coffee.

She wore her hair down, the honey waves looking like a waterfall of gold past her long neck and her creamy shoulders that were bared by her slouched blouse. She was one of them—one of *his* kind; one he could be with. One he *wanted* to be with. Recognition hit her like a thunderbolt, and I saw her pale, her skin glistening as she turned to look at Robert and then back away from him.

I, too, backed away.

"Grace-"

I wouldn't let him speak. Hearing his voice was like hearing the echo of my heart shattering to pieces around my feet. "Don't. Say. Anything." It was a demand. It was an order. It was a plea.

I walked calmly to the dresser, a repeated action that I had not hoped to make yet again so soon after the first time, and I pulled out some clothes.

I walked to the bathroom, my head held proudly high, and I changed, not daring to look at myself in the mirror for fear of seeing the pain there and never being able to recover from it. I pulled on a pair of baggy jeans and a shirt that I remembered Graham buying for me a few years back.

I picked up the vile red garments and tossed them into the wastebasket, and then swiped at my mouth with a wad of toilet paper before tossing that, too, into the trashcan. I reached into the shower to grab my hair tie and pulled my hair into a quick and messy ponytail, and then, taking several deep breaths, stepped outside into the room where Robert still stood, the girl beside him hanging her head down low in shame.

I said nothing to either of them. I walked past them and through the house. I placed the key to the front door on the table inside the foyer and then quietly stepped outside. My bike still lay on the ground, a sign that Robert probably ignored because of the beautiful guest he had brought with him.

I picked it up and slowly walked it down the driveway. The gate was open, and I walked through it while the demon of betrayal mocked me with every step. I could hear in my head now all of the questions, the taunting thoughts that all repeated how it wasn't possible that someone like Robert would find me attractive, that he was just feeling sorry for me. And they all took on the voice of one person. The only person who had ever caused me to doubt Robert's love for me.

"You evil, bastard," I hissed. "Even dead you still manage to get to me."

174

I stopped then. Though I hadn't shed a single tear and had remained steadfast and stoic, my face felt heavy, swollen with emotions that had not been released. And that's exactly what I wanted to do. Only not alone, and not to myself. The bike slipped from my hands, and I turned around. Determined steps led me back to the house, the lights now all on, until I was back in Robert's room, watching an exchange between him and the beautiful angel.

Though it was silent, I could almost feel the words of accusation; hear them as though I could pluck them straight from the air. It was a fight between lovers, one that would not have existed if not for me. If I had remained at home and sulked like the good girl, the empathic girl who could not be happy unless everyone else was then they would be doing something else, and that pissed me off.

Their faces turned to look at me, and I saw surprise on the girl's face, surprise that made me feel somewhat triumphant. Her eyes narrowed as she tried to read my thoughts, but I gave her a smug smile that told her without words that she would not succeed. Pain had shut that door—I wasn't letting anyone else in there. Not anymore.

"She keeps her thoughts hidden, N'Uriel," she finally said aloud, her accent thick, her voice a smooth bass that surprised me.

"She's special that way," Robert agreed, his eyes focused on mine, his pupils thickening and thinning with each beat of my heart he heard.

"Why did she return? Ask her."

"Why don't you ask me yourself?" I said snidely.

"Because you're not worthy of being asked," she replied, her tone dark, the threat hidden in words that were never meant to insult because they were the truth.

"If you want to know, I returned because I'm not done here yet. I have some unfinished business with Robert. If you want to stay and wait until I'm done with him you can. Until then, I suggest you leave." My voice sounded different. Defiant, strong. It didn't matter that I was hanging on by a mere thread of stubbornness.

"N'Uriel, why do you bother with this trifling human child? Kill her and be done with it already—toying with her will do none of us any good." The angel with the violet eyes looked at me one last time and disappeared in a puff of vapor, the slow slide of it easing past me and out the door. I kicked it shut and then turned accusing eyes toward Robert.

"Grace-" he began, but I held my hand up to silence him.

"No. No, you're going to listen to me. You're going to listen to me, and you're not going to say anything to me. Not a single word because I'm not just some 'trifling human child'. I'm your wife. Even if it's only in name, it's what I am, and until that can be changed, right now you owe me that much."

When he said nothing, staring at me mutely, I continued. "I came here tonight because I thought that perhaps I've been going about this entire marriage thing all wrong. I thought that I hadn't been trying to look appealing to you, that I had failed at looking—provocative. I thought that if I came here wearing next to nothing, that you'd swear to never leave my side again, that you'd make love to me and that we'd finally be able to start our life together as a married couple.

"I realize now that I was wrong, and that I was stupid to think that you could look at me the same way I look at you. It's simply not possible, and I'm sorry for putting that expectation on you when there was no way that you could possibly meet it."

I stared at the ground while my mind continued to form the words that I wanted to say. When I looked up again, Robert was standing much closer to me. I didn't flinch.

"I don't want to continue to pretend that we're married—or not married—anymore. It should've never happened. I know you only did it to make me happy because I whined like a damn baby about it, but I'd rather have nothing at all and be content with that than sit at home alone every night and question everything that you've ever said to me."

"What are you saying, Grace?"

"I want...I want an annulment. We haven't consummated the marriage yet, which I guess was the plan from the very beginning, so there's nothing legally that can prevent us from having this marriage annulled."

"No."

"I'm not asking you, Robert, and you don't really have a choice. Tomorrow I'm going to start filing the papers-"

"It's not going to happen, Grace."

His eyes darkened, the storm had returned, and I struggled to keep my composure as his voice washed over me. "You aren't going to leave me. You're not going to end this marriage, not after everything that we've been through to be together."

"It was never going to last anyway, Robert," I reminded him. "I'm going to die. The call is going to come at any moment, and I don't want to spend what little time I have left waiting for someone who doesn't want me."

"But I *do* want you!"

"Not enough to actually be with me," I countered.

"You don't know what you're talking about."

"Of course I don't. You don't talk to me—you've been avoiding me and hiding from me and all that's left of you when you are with me is a shell, an empty shell."

"Grace, would you stop with this nonsense?" His hands gripped my arms, but I couldn't feel them. I was too cold inside.

"It's not nonsense! You left me, Robert. You brought me here to your home and then left me here. You came only to take me to school and then pick me up. You treated me as if I was your duty, rather than your wife. Every night I waited for you to come to me, and every night you were doing who knows what, and with who knows who?"

"Grace-"

"No, Robert. I'm done with the excuses and the half-assed explanations. I made an ass out myself tonight because I thought that wearing that stupid nightgown would make you want me. Now I see that I had it completely wrong. It wouldn't have mattered if I was standing butt-naked in the middle of this room when you walked in because you wouldn't have noticed anyway."

"I noticed! I noticed every single inch of you in that red negligee!"

My words caught in my throat. Was that what that thing was called? A negligee?

"Well good for you. It's on the bathroom floor if you want to keep it. I paid for it using your card," I snipped.

"That's unkind and unlike you, Grace."

"Yes, it is, and I really don't care. I've given up on trying to be what you want, Robert. Everything you've asked me for, I've done or given to you. You wanted me to turn, I agreed, and then you refused to do it. You wanted me to marry you, and I agreed, then you refused to do it because it didn't fall in lines with 'the plan'. You wanted me to wait for us to be together, and I did, and now I discover that while I've been doing all this waiting, you're bringing other women into your room.

"I'm done with this, Robert. I can't do this anymore. It hurts too much to pretend that it doesn't, and it hurts too much to pretend that what we have is anything but a great big joke." I pulled off the large sapphire ring from my right hand, and then the top silver band from my left.

I held them out in my open palm. "Here, take them."

"I'm not taking those from you."

"Take them or I'll drop them."

His hands left my arms and quickly snatched the two silver rings from my palm. But, rather than shove them into his pocket, or place them atop the shelf behind him, he grabbed my hands and slipped the rings back into place.

"You're not leaving me, Grace, and you're not going to continue to think that I don't want you."

"I can think what I whatever I want, especially if it's true."

He shrugged. "Well, then you're heinously and most embarrassingly wrong."

I looked at him and then at the door, suddenly realizing that perhaps confronting him like this was not such a good idea, His eyes caught what I had been looking at and with a swift wave of his hand, the door slammed shut. I rushed to it and pulled at the handle, twisting it every which way and finding that nothing I did would cause it to budge. It didn't even rattle.

"Open this door," I demanded.

"Not until you sit down and listen to what I have to say. I listened to you, after all, and if this marriage is going to work, then there has to be some balance involved."

I scoffed at his logic and reminded him of the reason why. "Balance? You think that bringing home another woman while you think your wife's away is balanced?"

"She wasn't just another woman, Grace. I had no plans on being with her, or anyone for that matter, except you."

"Oh please," I said with a roll of my eyes. "I saw the way she looked at you, the way you looked at her. You were holding her hand, leading her inside the same way you did me."

"Grace, sometimes you're so obtuse it's scary."

It was automatic. My hand lashed out, coming within millimeters of his face before his own hand grabbed my wrist and stopped its approach. "I was not bringing anyone in here to have sex with, or make love to. I was bringing Isis here to trap her."

"Is that her name? Isis?"

"Did you not hear me, Grace?"

"I heard you. Why would you need to trap her? She seemed willing enough to be with you."

"She was willing, but I wasn't. I brought her here on the pretense that we would become intimate, yes, but it was never my intent to actually do so. I was going to trap her here so that I could finally put an end to the madness that's been going on."

The harsh tone in his voice caused all of my thoughts to careen into each other. "What do you mean?"

"I know you haven't been paying attention to what's been going on outside of your own little world, but there have been several terrible incidents across this globe that have kept me very busy, Grace.

"Deaths—hundreds of unnecessary deaths—one after the other, that seem to have no cause. I have been away from you because the stink of burnt flesh and decayed corpses is nothing that I ever want to share with you. I have been in the blackest of moods, seeing needless dead, innocents lives extinguished for reasons that I cannot fathom, in wars that until a week ago did not exist, and I did not want to bring that home to you.

"Isis has knowledge of why these events are happening. I brought her here and was planning on keeping her here until she told me the truth about what is going on. These small events are spread out and seem random and completely unrelated, but I've seen enough of the evil of man to know that when something appears to be too random, it's because it isn't."

"And just how were you going to trap her, Robert?"

"By leaving her in here."

I laughed, his plan so ridiculous it made no sense. "Leave her in your room? Do you honestly expect me to believe that?"

"Yes. Yes, I do, because I vowed never to lie to you ever again, and I have kept that vow."

I wanted to call him a liar, but I couldn't. Instead, I asked him once more how he had expected this Isis person to remain in a room with a wall of windows and a thin wooden door.

"I told you once before that there was another sanctuary in this house. This room, this room is it."

"This room is a sanctuary?" I laughed once more in spite of myself.

"Try to leave," Robert said, holding his arm out and pointing to the door. "You could always try to break the window."

I eyed him suspiciously then turned toward the door, trying once more to open it. Just as it had before, the knob wouldn't budge. The door that had always felt so flimsy and thin for a house so grand was now like a wall of stone. I turned around and headed toward the windows. I knocked on one large pane of glass, smiling with satisfaction when it returned to me a familiar sound. I reached for the handle to slide it open, but it would not move

Knowing that it would take more than just the mere manipulation of a handle to get through the glass, I walked over to the nightstand and grabbed my old lamp. I unplugged it from the wall and coiled the cord around it several times before hurling it toward the far window, closing my eyes when I saw it make contact. The sound of shattering assaulted my ears and I winced, my feet prickling at the familiar crinkle of shards falling, crashing into and onto each other.

Slowly, I opened my eyes, expecting to see the matte view of the outside and instead saw my reflection in the unmarred pane. My lamp lay in pieces on the floor.

"How?" I turned my head to look at Robert, whose face registered only a dim sort of satisfaction.

"I told you. Sanctuary is where one goes to be alone, to be safe. No one can enter without the other's permission, and no one can leave without it either. I was holding Isis' hand so that she could walk in here freely. She suspected the same thing you did—that we were coming here to be intimate—but I would rather burn in hell than be with anyone else but you."

Doubt wouldn't let go of me, and instead prodded me into asking more questions. "Why didn't you tell me any of this before? I'm your wife—you're supposed to tell me everything."

"What could I tell you of the horrors I've seen? How could I tell you of the dark suspicions I've had when your mind was already so troubled with what happened to Janice?"

"And so you'd rather let me think that you didn't want me than be honest with me about what you've been doing? You thought making me feel rejected and ugly was better?"

He was beside me before the last word had left my lips, his hands on my face, holding it like at any moment, I'd crack between his fingers. "You're not ugly—you're not unwanted. My God, Grace, if you only know how much I want to be with you, how hard it's been to stay away from you, knowing that you were sleeping in my bed, waiting for me."

"How could I have known?" I cried, suddenly aware of the stream of moisture that had begun to flow down my face. "It's like some kind of sickness in your family—you don't talk about anything, and when you do, it's never the truth. You say you want to be with me but you never are. You never give in, not even when I'm ready to give you everything."

I pulled myself free from his grasp and returned to the door. "Let me out, Robert."

"No."

I turned around to face him, my eyes wide with incredulity. "No?"

"No."

"Why not?"

"Because right now, the only thing I can think about is what I saw when I entered this room."

"You want me to put on that hideous thing in exchange for me leaving?"

"No. I was speaking about the look in your eyes, the look that told me you wanted me more than anything else in this world. I couldn't care less what you were wearing, Grace. In truth, I much prefer you in your regular clothes than in something that leaves nothing to the imagination."

My words failed me then, because everything that I had feared, every reason that I had come up with as justification for him not wanting to be with me, had just been withered away.

"I like the boxers and the tank tops. I like the old T-shirts and the jeans. And I especially like it when you put on one of my shirts. Those are all you, being who you are. I close my eyes, and I still see you on the bed, wearing my shirt and I can't maintain my solidity."

I blushed at that statement, remembering that at that moment, he truly hadn't.

He approached me, his eyes hooded, his mouth tight between his teeth as he reached for me, his intent clear. "I *do* desire you, Grace. I *do* want you. I *do* want to make love to you. Right now."

His admissions were breaking down the walls of my resistance like a house of cards, and when he lowered his head to press a soft kiss to the corner of my mouth, I had all but given in.

"But we can't."

And just like that, my heart went cold.

# THE LIBERTINE

What is it called when your life has ended but it isn't over? When you dangle between heaven and hell and both reject you because they have found you unworthy of acceptance?

"God, this is freaking purgatory!"

My head lifted to see the pained expression on the face beside me. The boy, whose eyes were rolling into the back of his head from sheer boredom, had taken to voicing his frustrations now, rather than etch them onto the desk in front of him.

Four weeks had passed, and this was the last day of summer school. It was also the longest day of class—an extra three hours long. We had to take our exit exam, to prove that we had indeed learned everything that was required to receive this final credit, and this exam was the culmination of an entire year of lessons crammed into five long, painful weeks.

For the others, painful merely meant the denial of doing what their friends had been up to. For me, it was the knowledge that the end of this day would bring nothing new. There would be no planning, no vacation, no parties. I would pick up my bag and head home, walk into my room and shut out the world.

The only solace I found was in the quiet moments I shared with Matthew, who had figured out that his little dimpled smile was like a balm to my hurt, and so he gifted me with as many of them as he possibly could. And I found it rather strange that while the others were

184

looking forward to their friends waiting outside, their horns blasting their impatience, I was looking forward to going home and changing diapers and preparing bottles of formula.

Mrs. Deovolente put down her pen and then smiled at us. "You've all passed. Congratulations."

One of the other students jumped up and ran toward the window, shouting to his awaiting friends, "I passed! Woo-hoo!"

Celebratory whistles and the blasting of several horns rang in from outside, and I joined in with the others when they smiled and laughed. It was a great feeling, one that I had been starved for, but at the same time, I could not enjoy it as thoroughly as I would have liked. When the bell finally rang, signaling the end of our torture, I picked up my bag and waved a sad goodbye to our teacher.

"Grace, wait," she called out to me.

I turned on a heavy heel and looked at her.

"I know that our last conversation was a bit…uncomfortable, and that I've been kind of avoiding you since then, but now that we're officially no longer teacher and student, I was wondering if perhaps you'd like to do something together—go out for lunch or perhaps dinner?"

This was unexpected. "Mrs. Deovolente, it sounds like you're asking me out on a date," I joked.

She laughed and shook her head. "Oh goodness, no. I just think that perhaps you'd like the conversation. I enjoy talking to you and I thought that you did as well…when the topic isn't so personal, that is."

Recognition of the need for conversation caused my head to bounce once in acceptance. "When?"

"How about tonight? I'll take you out for a celebratory dinner at the Olive Branch."

A month ago, I would've thought that tonight would begin the first night of a postponed honeymoon. Instead, I was going to be eating dinner at some hole in the wall Greek restaurant with my summer school teacher.

"Alright. Are we going to meet there?"

She nodded and then gave me an apologetic smile. "I'd pick you up but my car is in the shop, so I'll be taking the bus."

"No problem," I told her. "I've got my bike."

"Okay then. So, I'll meet you at seven?"

"That's fine."

"See you then!"

I nodded and left, pulling my backpack high up on my shoulders and heading to the bike rack to unlock my bike and head home. But, like a kick in the gut, the only thing that was on the rack was my lock. My bike was long gone.

"Ugh—you pieces of sh-"

I stopped myself before the expletive could escape. "Two bikes in less than a year—this year sucks." I took one last look at the lock and decided to leave it there. I wasn't going to bother with it when there was no point in doing so. There would be no new bike—there wouldn't be any time to ride it.

"Come on, feet," I told myself before starting the trek home.

I knew I had walked nearly three miles when the sound of footsteps behind me caused me to turn around. Lem stood in my shadow, a sheepish look on his face, his shoulders bunched up around his ears as his hands were held out to his sides, as if to say he had no choice.

"You don't have to walk behind me," I muttered.

"I know, but if people saw me walking with you, they might say something and then you'd have to explain it to N'Uriel, because he wouldn't take my word for it."

I frowned at his insinuation, and then shook off the troubling thoughts; my feet pushing me forward once more. "If people saw me walking with you, they'd simply think you'd lost a bet or something."

"Well, it *is* kind of why I'm here," he replied shamefully.

"What?" I stopped and turned around.

"Some of us made a bet as to whether or not you'd stick it out for the full five weeks. I admit that I didn't believe you would, and so

I'm here, stuck on guard duty again for the next few days."

I should have been offended. I had never given up on anything before in my life. Not until Robert. He was the only reason I'd ever found to quit anything. And now, all I felt was a grim sadness that was always there, lurking behind whatever emotion I would shove up to the forefront to mask what I so desperately needed to stay hidden, if only to keep the charade going long enough to keep my friends and family safe.

"Well, I think that if I had known about the bet, I would have wagered against me, too," I admitted. "And since when did angels gamble? Aren't you guys supposed to be able to see the future and all that crap?"

He sucked in his bottom lip as his head tossed from side to side. "Only a select number of us have that ability, and those that do rarely share it with the rest of us. You can guess fairly quickly that those of us that wagered do not possess that ability."

This brought another question to my lips. "How many of you are there? Watching out for me, I mean."

His eyebrows rose and his head ticked as he counted in his head the names of those who had volunteered to look out for me. "There are thirteen of us in total. N'Uriel, Ameila, Lark, Sera, and myself make up the main group that oversee your safety, but then there are others, lesser angels who have no call but who would not see an innocent human be harmed by one of us who does."

"And you're now stuck looking after me for the next few days."

"Yes," he grumbled. "It's not that I do not enjoy it—you are quite a funny creature, very emotive and frank—but I have other pursuits that I will have to put on hold while I am here with you. And, if I may be frank as well, I hold a bit of resentment toward N'Uriel for not seeing to your welfare himself now that things have calmed down for him somewhat."

He started walking ahead of me, and I hurried to keep up. "What do you mean, things have calmed down."

"I'm sure he's told you about the troubles abroad. It's been all over your human news—wars, infighting, political coups. The number of casualties had grown exponentially over the past few weeks, but things are dying down now. The blood lust that once consumed your kind no longer has its place here. It's a rather refreshing piece of news, actually."

As I followed mutely behind Lem, my feet shuffling along the concrete, I tried to figure out why Robert hadn't made some kind of attempt to see me, to talk to me if he was no longer so occupied. That last night at his home, he promised that when he finally had the freedom to do so, he'd come for me and make up for all that he'd done wrong.

I'd wanted to believe him, but when it came to Robert's promises, I was finding them to be thin, veiled and wholly unreliable. It wasn't that he was lying to me; it was more that he simply couldn't live up to everything that he wanted to do and be. And again, that left me feeling shallow and overcome with depression.

"Lem, what do you think of Robert?"

"What do I think of him? I think he's a young angel trying to take on far too much. He feels an overwhelming responsibility to you, and to your family, when in truth the only responsibility he has is to humanity, which I can tell you demands far less than you do."

My feet halted, and I scowled at his back. "Excuse me?"

"Humanity doesn't need our love, Grace. It doesn't need to know we exist and that we are here for it in order for it to continue. You, on the other hand, are a demanding mistress. You need and want and desire everything that you cannot have, and in trying to give that to you, you put a strain on N'Uriel's sense of duty. Had he listened to his call, you'd be dead and he'd be free. Instead, he listened to your thoughts, he listened to your heart, and he chose instead to answer them.

"I do not think he made the wrong choice—what angel wouldn't risk it all for love—but what has loving Robert cost you? What would living without him cost? Nothing. Had the two of you never met, had you never crossed paths, he would have never received his call, and you'd have lived a full, rich life, dying an old woman, and he'd have maintained his ability to heal others, the one thing he truly enjoyed above all others.

"He would have found love with one of his own kind, or several of them if he so wished it. He would not have felt an obligation to remain faithful to them, or to control his needs and his desires while with them the way he has to with you."

He had stopped walking several paces in front of me, his back ramrod straight, his hands shoved into the pockets of his slacks. He wore a sport coat over a light and crisp blue shirt that he had not tucked into the waistband of the dark pants. When he turned to face me, I was awestruck at just how handsome he looked, and I scolded myself silently for that because he shouldn't be. Not to me. And especially not saying what he was saying.

"Angels are meant to be with other angels. We're not meant for toying with humans, or loving them," he said with heavy voice. "And when we do, when we find ourselves falling for them, we suffer ten-fold what any human could. We have to refrain from acting on our instincts, and those of us who have yet to receive our wings have to refrain from the greed of feeling what our bodies refuse to allow."

He walked toward me and tilted his head slightly, his hair falling behind him like a cape shifting open, the slash of red and dark mixing together.

"We cannot touch, we cannot feel, we cannot love. You humans are so breakable, so fragile and yet so willing that it makes it all too easy to destroy you with a single touch, a single thought. For some, the challenge is worth it.

"For others, it's a nightmare, and one that many of us cannot understand. Why put yourself through that kind of misery? Why allow such a thing to happen when there are others who will gladly allow you to allay your stresses, your needs, your wants, your desires on them?

"But I am not one of them. I see what N'Uriel sees in you. Perhaps I see more of it because I know where it comes from. You have your mother's eyes, and your mother's spark, and if I were the one you had chosen, I would never leave your side."

His words did strange things to me, and I struggled to fight them off even as I replayed them over and over in my head. He wasn't speaking out of turn; he wasn't saying anything that was inappropriate or unwelcomed, so why did I feel guilty? Why did I feel like something very wrong was going on here? I needed to direct my mind elsewhere.

"You loved my mother very much, didn't you?" I asked, the squeak in my voice a noticeable annoyance.

"I did more than love her. I desired her. I wanted her more than I wanted my dreams, and when we came together to create our son, it was the culmination of every single one of my desires. The aftermath was less than pleasant, as I learned soon after that she did not view our coupling as anything other than our duty to our kind, but I always held out hope that she'd return to me."

When my breath caught in my throat, I realized that I felt badly for him. He understood—probably better than anyone—how I felt about Robert, but he didn't have a chance to make things right between him and my mother. And, even if he did, I wouldn't want him to. My mother had loved my father. She had loved him with so much conviction that she gave up her entire history to be with him. She would eventually give up her life for that, and that was something that I couldn't see Lem doing for her.

"When my mother died, did you come to the funeral?" I asked suddenly, my mind scouring my memories to see if I could pluck his face from them somehow.

"I could not. The day she lost her divinity was the day she died to me. Ameila was the only one of our kind who had chosen to continue speaking to her, as it had been agreed upon I suppose. Though she should have been censured for that, when I learned why it was she did, I couldn't blame her. I would have done the same."

"Done what?"

Lem's eyes widened before softening as he reached out to stroke the side of my face. "Help Avi bring you into the world."

I turned away from the touch that burned when it should not.

"You would help the woman you love give birth to another man's child?"

"You're not some other man's child, Grace. You have no father. You came from your mother's soul, and not from any union she might have had with anyone else, so yes, I would have done whatever it took to help Avi bring you into this world."

"I have a father. His name is James Shelley."

"I apologize. I did not mean to insult you or your father. I just meant that, biologically, you are a singular creation, unique despite how much you remind me of your mother."

"My dad says that I remind him of her, too." The statement wasn't meant to rub my parents' relationship in his face, but I could tell by how cold it suddenly got that it had. "Lem—look, I'm sorry…"

He shook off the apology. "You needn't concern yourself with how I feel. What happened between your mother and I was something that happened once, and I was the foolish one to believe that it could be something other than duty."

I looked at him quizzically, and I could see the edge of hurt there, right where his irises met the dark curve of his pupils. "You still love her, don't you?"

His lids lowered, his eyes turning into slits at my question before rising and revealing the clear, glassy stare of someone completely unaffected. "No."

"No?" I was shocked by his answer. Someone who spoke of someone else the way he did, who got lost in their description of someone the way that he did could not have been anything but affected, and yet it was like he had become frozen.

"I loved her once, but love doesn't last forever. It's not meant for those who live the life everlasting, who live long enough to see it wither away and turn into resentment. It's meant for those who die, for those who will escape seeing those they love change into something else."

His voice took on a bitter tone, and I couldn't help but feel his anger, his disappointment. Even though inside I still resented my mother's actions, resented what they did to me and Dad, I knew that she loved my father, that they had been meant to love each other; and that in doing so they had broken someone's heart.

"I guess it must suck seeing me, then," I said half-jokingly, starting into a stride that he matched, step for step. "And at the same time, it must be quite cathartic."

"What do you mean by that?" he asked.

"Well, even though you say that you would have helped my mother bring me into this world, it must suck knowing that she wanted to have me with my dad, and cathartic knowing that soon I'll be gone and there won't be anything left to remind you of her."

He stopped, his hand grabbing my arm to deaden my pace. "The last thing I would ever want is to see you gone." There was desperation in his voice, a shaky edge that sliced straight through me, and I saw that he meant every word. He trembled with its truth.

He pulled me toward him, his other hand rising to grip my other arm, holding me immobile against him as he looked down at me, his eyes a study in hot and cold, the glittering gold of one iris contrasting the icy, steely silver of the other. And when they darkened, when they almost disappeared into their darkness, when I felt my breathing stop and my heart shudder inside of me, he lowered his head.

It was the briefest of touches, something that I would have sworn didn't even happen had I not kept my eyes open the entire time staring into his, seeing his reaction, feeling his palms grow hot, his lips turn soft and burning, like bathwater that was on the brink of scalding.

When he pulled away, he said nothing. Instead, he released me, and continued to walk. Silently, I followed. What had just happened? What had just occurred between us? Who was Lem to me but someone from my mother's past? As my street grew nearer, I grew more and more concerned. What if we had been seen? What if this act of betrayal somehow got to Robert? After everything that I had accused him of, I had let this happen—maybe I even wanted it to happen.

Yes. I did want it to happen. I couldn't deny that I found Lem attractive. But more than that, I needed that touch, that contact. And to know that Robert could have returned to me, and didn't—it eased my guilt a bit.

By the time I stood in front of my front door, my nerves were calm, and I even took the liberty of pressing my fingers to my lips, as though they would somehow remind me of what had happened. Lem saw this and I could read his mind almost as surely as he would have read mine if I had let him. He knew why. He knew my intent.

But, if my guilt could be suppressed after a quick glancing touch of lips, what was I to do when he threw my hand aside and crushed his mouth to mine? Where could I hide my guilt when my hand rose to twine in the rich wine of his hair? And when my back pressed up against the door, and I pushed against him, needing to feel that closeness, even if it was a pale imitation of what it was my heart truly wanted, how would I be able to mask the burn of betrayal that I was sure had branded itself across my face?

"Stop," I breathed when I could finally pull away. "This is wrong."

"No it isn't," he whispered harshly against my mouth. "It isn't wrong. I know you want me."

"No," I protested. "No, I don't."

"Yes, you do," he repeated before kissing me again, proving that I did.

I pushed at him, surprised when he moved with little effort. I was panting, my hand running to my hair, pushing it aside before wiping my mouth on the back of it, as though I could somehow wipe away what I had done—what I had let happen.

"Maybe—maybe I wanted the kiss. Maybe I wanted to be reminded what it felt like to be kissed—but it wasn't you that I wanted to kiss me. Maybe that isn't true. Maybe I do want you. But I don't love you; I love Robert."

The transformation in his face was startling, and I pressed my back against the door as he came up against me, his eyes drawn into dark slits, his mouth set in a grim line on a face that had suddenly lost its curves of amusement and now held the harsh angles of someone whose pride had been hurt.

And then it was all gone. The same cheerful expression returned, albeit one that now seemed less genuine, and he sighed the sigh of the defeated. "I apologize for overstepping my bounds, Grace. I can blame no one else but myself."

"I-it's okay, Lem," I said, my voice steady despite the drumming in my heart that was a mixture of excitement and fear.

"I hope this doesn't change our friendship. I would hate to know that my moment of impetuous, wingless emotion has damaged your faith in me."

I shook my head and offered him my hand, a platonic gesture that he understood right away. His hand grabbed mine, gripping it firmly before pumping it up and down. "We're still friends, Lem. Just...not *those* kinds of friends."

To my surprise, he laughed, a carefree sound that made my lips curl up in a smile. "I should be more than content with any type of friendship you give me after my behavior, Grace. Thank you."

"You're welcome," I said before turning around and opening the door. I stepped inside and turned around to thank him for walking me home. He bowed—actually bowed—and said that the pleasure was all his.

"I don't think anyone's ever said that to me before," I commented.

"Well, I'm glad that I could be your first," he replied before sweeping away past the drive and down the street until I lost him in the glare of sunset.

I walked into the house and saw that Dad had fallen asleep on the recliner, a dozing Matthew lying on his chest with his thumb wedged tightly between his pouty lips. I decided not to wake either of them and instead headed upstairs to get ready for dinner with Mrs. Deovolente. I had few things here, having not brought much with me the second time I had returned, but there was no need to dress up for the Olive Branch and so a pair of jeans and a T-shirt would do.

I took a quick shower, and then stood in front of the mirror to brush my wet hair into a slicked back ponytail. My reflection frightened me.

My eyes were bright, glittery, the excitement I had felt from Lem's kiss overpowering the dullness of guilt that I could see lingering in the golden flecks of my brown irises. My lips were slightly puffed, and my cheeks showed the telltale flush of emotions that I should not have been feeling.

"What have I done?" I said to my reflection. "What did I do?" Suddenly, glassy eyes turned watery and red, and the puffiness that had existed in my mouth spread to them, while the redness in my cheeks migrated to my nose and the bitter sting of tears screamed their objection to everything that I had done.

It wasn't so much the kiss…or the other kiss. Or even the *other* kiss. It was the feeling of wanting more of them that hurt. It was the feeling of wanting what came after them that burned.

"This isn't you," I said to myself. "This isn't you. You're not that girl." And I wasn't. I wasn't that girl who would do whatever she could to get what she wanted. I wasn't that person who would betray the person they loved to fulfill a desire. I wasn't that person who would do that…to hurt someone else.

But I just had. I hadn't just betrayed Robert; I'd also betrayed myself and it was far more damaging to my soul than anything else that anyone could do to me. My body had betrayed me just as it had Robert. My mouth, my racing heart, my lungs—only my head had stayed sane, stayed above water, and only it would keep me from falling under the spell of need again.

I needed to get away, and someone was already waiting to help me do that. I splashed cold water on my face and patted it dry before taking one last look at myself, satisfied that if anyone were to ask, I could simply say that I was having a late allergy attack. I cleaned out the crystal lumps that had pooled in the sink and dumped them into the trash, then turned off the light and headed downstairs.

Dad was awake now, Matthew busily drinking down a bottle of formula in his lap.

"Hey, kiddo. I didn't know you had returned."

"And I'm about to leave again," I said hastily. "I'm going out to dinner with my teacher—sort of a congratulatory celebration."

"So you passed?"

I looked at him and felt my eyes bulge at the question. "Duh! Of course I passed!"

"Well then, I suppose that makes it official, doesn't it?"

"What does?"

"Your honeymoon. You've been looking forward to this for weeks."

I rushed to him, my arms clumsily wrapping themselves around him, my body painfully arched away so as to keep from crushing Matthew. "I'm not going anywhere, Dad," I told him with a hiccup. "I'm staying right here with you and Matthew."

Dad chuckled and then gently pushed me away. "You know I'm smarter than that, kiddo. Now, go on. We'll talk a bit more when you return."

I looked at him, his eyes dry, his mouth lifted with a warm, fatherly smile. "All right."

I started to head toward the door when I remembered that my bike had been stolen. "Damn. Dad, my bike was stolen today after school."

"Did you remember to lock it up?"

"Yeah. Whoever took my bike left behind the lock."

Dad muttered a curse and then sighed when he realized that he had just done so in front of Matthew. "The key to Janice's car is hanging up in the kitchen. Why don't you take it?"

"Are you sure?"

"Yes. Take her car."

"Thank you," I said, dropping a kiss onto the top of his head.

"Just drive safe, and stay under the speed limit. I'm not coming to bail you out if you get pulled over for speeding."

I ran to the kitchen and grabbed the keys to the small SUV, then dashed outside. It had been a while since I'd driven—a year, actually—and it took me a few minutes to get used to the feeling of being in front of the steering wheel, but once I put the car into gear, everything just proceeded naturally.

Parking was another story entirely. It took me longer to park in a stall than it did to get to the mall. I had trouble with keeping the car straight, and then I had parked too close to the car beside me, preventing me from being able to open my door. I attempted to reverse into another stall and nearly clipped another car. Finally, realizing how hopeless the situation was, I parked as far away as possible from any cars and objects that might damage—or suffer damage from—the car.

The walk to the restaurant was a long one, and Mrs. Deovolente was waiting by the entrance as I approached, a bouquet of wildflowers in her hand.

"Sorry I'm late," I told her.

"It's just a few minutes past seven. Come on, they have our table ready. These are for you. I thought these would be more acceptable than balloons—less conspicuous as well," she said cheerfully.

I understood her intent right away and thanked her as we walked into the tiny restaurant, the smell of wine and lamb triggering the rumbling in my stomach. We were seated toward a back window, the waiter immediately pouring out two glasses of water with lemon before handing us our menus. As I looked at the specials, the teacher placed hers down onto the table and asked, "So, what did you do between class and here?"

My eyes rose from the dishes on the laminated placard in front of me and answered, "I cheated on my husband."

## NINE LIVES

"You're...m-married?"

I took a sip of my water and nodded.

"F-for how long?" Mrs. Deovolente's voice rose and fell with each syllable, her shock registering in every line on her face.

"Five weeks this past Monday."

"And...and you've already had sex with someone else?" Her jaw hung down past her chin.

The water went down the wrong pipe and I began to choke. When I could manage a few words without another string of coughs, I shook my head violently. "No. No, I've never had sex. Not with anyone."

A puzzled Mrs. Deovolente pushed everything in front of her aside and grabbed my hands. "Grace, are you telling me that you're still a virgin? And you're married?"

"Yes."

"But...why?"

I gave her the only answer that I had. "I love him."

A violent snort came from her delicate nose and it was my turn to stare in shock. "Love is never enough of a reason to get married, Grace. Never. And to be married for five weeks and not ever consummate the marriage? Is...is that why you wanted to know about seducing your boyfriend?"

My embarrassed nod sent her hands flying up in the air. "For the love of God, Grace. Do you realize how ridiculous this sounds? You're eighteen, married, and you're already confessing to cheating on your husband—of five weeks. And on top of that, you're still a virgin. I don't know what to say to you about any of this except who was it?"

I stared at my hands, the rings that branded me as belonging to someone else staring up at me like a pair of knowing eyes. "Someone that I should've never let near me."

In the dim light of the restaurant, Mrs. Deovolente could finally see the distress in my face, and she inched forward to clasp onto my up-turned hands. "You're so confused, aren't you? Oh goodness. Did you *want* to be with that other person?"

Wide eyed and adamant, I shook my head. "I liked the kiss, but I don't want to be with anyone else but Robert. I only want him."

"So why don't you tell him?"

A watery snort left me, and I looked away. "He knows."

"So what's he waiting for?"

My eyes looked into hers, and I saw that she wanted to understand. But would she be able to understand with only pieces of the truth? "We can't be together, Mel. We can't be together the way that I want to—the way he says he wants to."

A glimmer of recognition passed over her and she said softly, "You know, you could always wear a condom."

"It's not that simple. I wish that it was."

The waiter returned then, his pad held out, and I blindly ordered the special, not caring what it was, having forgotten it already. Mrs. Deovolente ordered the same, and when the waiter left with our order, she leaned in, her voice lower, as though she were afraid that someone would hear us in the empty and dark restaurant.

"But it is," she whispered. "It *is* that simple. You can't get pregnant if you use a condom, Grace."

"You don't understand, Mel-"

Her voice grew hard, grating as it registered as low as possible. "Grace—you're the one who doesn't understand. They didn't have protection then, only ways to get rid of it, but…you couldn't get rid of *those* kinds of pregnancies. But it's different now. You can prevent yourself from being impregnated by one of them."

"Wh-what are you talking about?" I stammered.

"I know. I know what Robert is."

I felt the blood drain from my face, from my hands, and I felt incredibly cold as I stared at my teacher from across that small table. I could say nothing. When the waiter arrived with our plate of something that smelled like the back end of a bus, I said nothing.

"Excuse me, but could you have this wrapped up?" the stranger in front of me asked the poor guy, who simply nodded and removed the plates from the table. "Grace, we need to talk. Somewhere else."

"Apparently," I muttered.

When the waiter returned with a bag containing our dinner, Mrs. Deovolente paid for the meal and left a generous tip, and the two of us walked silently outside.

"Over here," I mumbled, pointing across the dark and empty parking lot toward the white car sitting all alone.

"Let's go."

I hurried toward the vehicle, unaware of why, only that whatever it was that this person who had told me to call her Mel, who had given me advice on how to seduce Robert, was, I needed to know more.

Inside the car I fumbled with the keys, finally sticking them inside of the ignition and turning them, hearing the clicking of the starter as it failed to turn the engine over. Twice more I tried, but nothing happened.

"I'm sorry—this is my step-mother's car and it's been sitting in the driveway for a while," I said apologetically.

With one final turn of the key, the engine roared to life, growling at me like a disgruntled lion, angry that I had neglected it. I put the car into gear and began driving, though to where I didn't know. All I knew was that someone needed to start talking and it wasn't going to be me.

"Where am I going?" I asked when I came to the parking lot's exit.

"Turn right and drive," she instructed.

The roads were empty, nothing unusual in this part of Ohio. My fingers itched to turn the radio on, but I knew better than to create any distractions for Mel, who sat staring straight ahead.

"Turn left here," she said, and I turned the wheel, the car pulling onto an unpaved road that got lost in the darkness.

"Who are you?" I asked when I couldn't take the silence anymore.

"Just keep going. A little bit further."

My feet slammed on the brakes when the road disappeared off what I could only guess was a cliff or the top of something that would definitely suck falling off of.

"Well, I guess we'll stop here," she said, unbuckling her seatbelt and turning to face me, her expression far more serious than I had ever seen before.

"Grace, you don't need to know who I am, only what I am. I'm the same thing your father is. I'm a chosen guardian, an Electus Patronus."

"I don't believe you."

She waved my comment away, as if it was inconsequential to what she wanted to say to me. "My charge had me come here to watch over you. Why else would I be teaching your biology class?"

"You said you needed the money," I pointed out.

"I don't need money, Grace. I don't even need that job—I was there for you."

"Why? Why are there all these people spying on me, watching over me, trying to get at me? What the hell is so damn special about me?" I cried out.

"Your birth is one reason," Mel answered. "But more than that, it's what your death will trigger."

"My death? What do you know of it?"

"Grace, you can't die. If you die, then everything that the angels have been doing since the beginning of their existence will be for nothing."

"I don't—I don't understand what you're saying. I'm supposed to die. I'm supposed to die. That was the plan. I'm supposed to die, and then Robert will get to live, and everything will be as it's supposed to be."

Mel's head shook violently from side to side. "No, no it won't. Your death isn't supposed to happen because *you* weren't supposed to happen. But, now that you're here, we can't let you die. We can't let you answer your call."

My voice grew angry. "If I don't die then Robert dies, and if he dies then nothing will matter to me anymore—I'll be just as good as dead."

"Robert is not important to us, Grace. He's replaceable. You are not. There will never be another one like you—human and yet not; angel and yet not. You're the last sign, the last barrier before the beginning of the end."

"What?"

"Grace, you're the daughter of Avi. Do you know what that means?"

"Yeah, that I deserve the title of freak."

"No. Ugh—I started this the wrong way. Let me try again. My name is Melanie Deovolente. I come from a long line of guardians who protected secrets so deep, so dark that to even breathe them to anyone else would result in death. When I turned twenty-one, I chose to take the test to prove my allegiance to my birthright, but it was not to those my family served.

"Instead, I chose to serve those who are considered the outcasts, the undesirables, the ones without calls. It was from them that I learned of the death of a former angel, one who had once held a position so high, so great that she had been feared even by those my family served. That position had remained empty since her punishment and a power struggle began for her seat.

"But her position wasn't one that you could take. It wasn't one that you could steal. It had to be inherited, and when news came that her child, her son hadn't inherited her position as was expected, it was confirmed that she must have had another child. An impossible child; one who did not belong to either world, human or angel, and yet lived in it.

"That child is you. You're the inheritor of her position, Grace."

There was a strange ticking inside of me, the feeling of it acting like a warning, a warning to what she would say next.

"Your mother Avi was the original angel of Death, Grace, the first one, the one created when humanity needed her. She was Death. She *was* Death. You are supposed to take her place, not Robert. Why he received the call is unknown to us, but if you die, if you do not take your place as your mother's successor, then you will trigger something that cannot be undone. It will destroy us all, humans, angels, illegitimates."

"No. No, I don't believe you," I said defiantly. "Robert is Death—my death is going to save *him*. It's going to keep him alive, and he's going to keep my father alive, and my brother, and my friends…"

Mel reached forward, grabbing my shoulders and shaking them roughly. "Grace, if you die, the gates to Heaven and Hell will be left unguarded. If you die, the world will end. Do you understand that? If you die, there will be no Robert left, no father, no brother, no friends."

"But I'm not an angel," I protested. "I can't do what an angel does; I can't do what Robert does. I'm human."

Her eyes widened then with recognition. "You mean you haven't yet turned?"

"No! Who's your angel charge, Mel? Who is it that told you all of this?"

"Oh God. I am…Hell!"

Her eyes widened even further, an almost crazed look spreading across her face before fear finally took over and she lunged toward me. My hands were barely able to protect my face before I felt a violent jolt through my body. The sound of crunching metal and glass shattering all around me was only just a fraction louder than the sound of screaming that could have been mine.

Another rough shake, the feeling of something slamming into me, like a thunderbolt full of steel and iron, before all of the air escaped me and things started spinning. In the darkness, all I could see was the occasional hint of a star as over and over, I was flipped, my body still strapped in, but my head lolling about, my hands swinging to and fro, slicing, cutting, crashing. And then I was upside down.

I could taste blood in my mouth, smell it on my skin. Strands of my hair were stuck to my face, the blood there warm and unending as it dripped onto the ceiling which now lay beneath me. I turned my head, groaning at the shooting pain that rose up to my shoulders, and a wail of despair came out, scratchy and pitiful. My hand flattened against my abdomen, feeling the tears in my shirt.

Mel lay to my side, her neck twisted, her face covered in blood drenched hair. She was motionless, and I was glad for it. Her blouse had torn open, revealing a bloodstained bra that covered a thick, heavy scar. As blood dripped from a large wound just below her throat, I focused on the mottled and webbed flesh, my eyes slowly taking in details that I was sure weren't really there.

As my body slowly grew colder and weaker, my eyes grew weaker as well, and I could have sworn then that the scar started growing more and more defined the longer I stared. It was with a sharp cry of pain that I recognized the tree shaped markings that extended to her navel. It was the same tree that had been burned onto Dad's wall. This one, this marker, had been burned onto her skin.

"What the hell is happening?" I whimpered. "What the hell is going on?"

My hand, still pressed against my belly, fumbled for the seatbelt lock. I pressed it, hearing the telltale click before I slammed onto the ceiling. Dirt and glass rained down around me as I turned over painfully, my head banging on the steering wheel and then the seat before I spied a way out through the shattered windshield. The bent frame of the window demanded that I claw my way through it, and after several tries, I huffed out my victory as my burning and stinging hands met soft, cool soil.

I rested there in the dirt for a while, my face lying against leaves and twigs, not caring about how uncomfortable it was because everything else hurt too damn much. When my breathing had slowed a bit, I stood up, carefully, slowly.

Believing that my injuries were not as severe as I'd originally thought, I straightened, barely noticing the sharp pain in my leg that caused me to hunch over. I limped away from the overturned vehicle, my blood dripping down from my face and landing in loud splashes on the leaves beneath my feet.

"Help," I rasped. "Someone help."

Someone was always watching me—that's what I had been told, at least. "Lem? Ameila? Lark?" I called out every name of every angel I could remember meeting. I called out the names of angels that I had looked up online. I even called out the ones that had been on those ceramic figurines that Janice had collected. None replied. None showed.

And when the noises of the trees that I didn't even know were there began to grow louder than my cries for help, I grew silent. The rustling of leaves and the snapping of branches told me that I was not alone. "Someone is always watching," I whispered.

A loud crunch behind me forced my head to whip around; the bone-rattling pain the motion caused sent me dropping to the ground like a stone. I lay there, unable to move, my body numbing even as the chill of the ground left its imprint on me, the last memory of feeling before the only thing I had left was sound.

"I told you, never to come into my woods again."

The voice, the tinny, hollow voice, was chillingly familiar. "Bala? Bala is that you?"

"You let N'Uriel die. You let him die and I let you live, and now you are back, dying in my woods, just as you should have done."

A pair of black orbs floated above me, darker than the sky, but with a fire in them that glowed in a face that was eerily beautiful in its jade green flesh. White teeth gnashed in a cavernous mouth that opened to show me the level of rage that was held precariously in check.

"Robert's alive, Bala," I gasped, my breathing shallow and pained. "He's alive."

"I don't believe you. He would have told me. He would have let me know somehow."

So, I wasn't the only one he had neglected. "He couldn't. He's been busy—there's so much killing going on, so much death," I explained desperately.

"He would be with you then. He would be following you, watching you. He would be here now. If he were alive, he would be here."

I tried to shake my head, but couldn't. "He isn't here. I haven't seen him in a month."

Green film dropped down over the orbs, a slow, meticulous blink that told me she was processing what I had just revealed to her. When her eyes opened, she smiled at me, a slow, sly, cruel smile that told me she took pleasure in my obvious pain.

"So, he's stopped loving you. He's finally realized how wrong you are for him and has given up on trying to pursue you. Have you given up on him? Have you decided to finally let him go?"

"Does it matter? I'll be dead soon anyway, right?" I barked, unable to keep up the pretense of civility. Not when I felt so trapped. Not when my head was filled with nothing but confusion. My grip on reality had slowly been slipping, and losing it completely was just a hair's breath away.

Bala's keen eyes could see it, and as friendly as she had been to me in the past, knowing that Robert was not here to stop her bolstered the animosity she felt toward me. I would get no help from her, but it wasn't me I was worried for.

Something wrapped around my arm, something I only noticed

because I watched as it rose above me and then behind my head. And then everything began to move; the shade of trees and the sporadic hint of sky began to pass over me as I was dragged through the brush. I closed my eyes and tried to think of Robert, his name, his face, his voice. He would come. He would hear my thoughts and he would come. I knew it. I had to believe it.

"How many times have you died, Grace?" Bala's voice asked, the sound of it like the rattle of the branches as her agitation took control.

"Too many to count," I replied to the dark air, my voice dark with surprising humor.

"Do you think you deserve to live again?"

"I don't know what I deserve anymore," I said to her quietly, my chest burning with every breath. "I'm not deserving of a lot of things, and others are exactly what I deserve. I don't get to choose what happens to me, but it's not about me anymore."

A hiss of acceptance seemed to circle my ears. "So you understand what it means to be one of them. You understand when choice is nothing but a dream, and obligation and duty become iron shoes on your feet that remain hot and never let you forget where you are meant to go with every step you put forward."

I didn't need to tell her yes. I had understood that from the very beginning...even if I didn't understand why. "Where are you taking me?"

"Somewhere I can keep you safe until I have proof that N'Uriel is alive."

"Why do you need proof? Why can't you just believe me?"

"Because you lied to me before. You lied after I gave you sanctuary, after I gave you shelter. You said you would die so that N'Uriel may live. You would lie to save yourself and that is the fatal human flaw that I detest above all others."

"I've never lied to you," I insisted, though I was certain it would fall on deaf ears. "I wouldn't do that to someone I called a friend."

Silence followed, and I simply allowed myself to stew in it, grateful that, if nothing else, the quiet brought no accusations. There were already enough of those in my head.

When at last the sky stopped moving, I turned my head to see where we were. The silver circle that reflected on the still water beside me told me quite clearly that Bala had dragged me back to her tree, the large willow that hung over the water like a paunch. The slender silhouette of a woman appeared before me, her skin a veritable rainbow of vibrant greens and shimmering browns, even in the darkness, and I couldn't help but smile at her unusual beauty.

Though she would have frightened many away with her appearance, she was in no way grotesque in my eyes. Her figure was divine, and her hair hung around her body like a living blanket of flowers and leaves and moss, moving and floating about her, a curtain of life that clung to her skin, covering her where she needed modesty and revealing areas that reminded me she had been a human girl once, a very long time ago. Her eyes reminded me of two jet marbles that had been placed into wide sockets. She stared at me with deep speculation, and I knew she was trying to gauge whether or not it was safe for her to befriend me again.

Her mouth—two smooth, leaf-like markers on her face—pulled into a pout before straightening, repeating this process several times.

"I have decided. I will send you to N'Uriel."

"But you don't know where he is."

She laughed, the sound like wind blowing through the trees, and then her shoulders arched beautifully, in a shrug that was too divine to have had anything to do with her human past. This was all the magic of turning.

"I do not need to know where he is. He will know where you are. He will come, and it will be because of me. A gift; that is what you will be—a gift that I shall be rewarded for," she said before leaving, her departure silent, her absence deafening.

"Some gift," I muttered.

I lay on the ground for what felt like hours, or it could have been minutes. The quiet that surrounded me was eerie, as though every living thing in the forest had disappeared…or run away. There was no wind, and the water in the lake was as still as glass, no sounds of tiny waves lapping at the shore, no faint ripple or drop to be heard. Without the noise of the woods around me, I had now lost every sense except sight, and in the dark, what I could see was of little consequence.

Bala did not return until I was certain that it was past midnight, when my dad would start to worry, when he'd begin his rounds of calling people to see if they knew where I was. If no one had realized that I was missing, Dad would be the one to inform them. And then, knowing him, he'd begin to blame them all for it.

I groaned at this thought and tried to imagine him being more sensible but I couldn't. He was my father, and when it came to me he worried far too much…even when he knew that the time was coming close to when worry would matter very little.

"Grace?"

"Bala?"

"I have returned with your friend."

"Friend? Which friend?" I called out into the darkness.

"The cold one."

"It's me, Stacy."

The sound of her familiar voice was so welcoming, I didn't even flinch when she bent down to look at me and I could see the red stains around her mouth. "My God, Grace, what the hell happened to you?"

"Dinner didn't agree with me," I joked, but my sense of humor was lost on her, her disapproval coming in the form of a deep rumbling within her, one that caused Bala—who stood beside me with her dark eyes dashing between the two of us—to skitter away with a hiss.

"Seriously, what happened, Grace?" Stacy asked once more.

"I don't know. I think I was in a car accident…" My breathing had become so labored the end of my sentence became lost in a wheeze.

"Where?"

I looked down toward my feet and with steady, measured breaths replied, "In that direction. I think the car was pushed off the ledge. Mrs. Deovolente…she's still inside." My voice had lost its ability to emote, the sound of it just a rasp of airy words. But when I paused, I knew Stacy saw the pain that I felt at knowing another person had lost their life because of me.

"I'll go and check. You stay right here."

"Okay," I told her, not pointing out that I couldn't yet move.

She returned shortly, bending down to confirm that Mrs. Deovolente was, indeed, dead. "She looks like she didn't suffer though. Her neck is broken pretty cleanly, but there's a pretty bad injury to her chest. How did you manage to get out alive?"

I looked at her and told her with absolutely no humor, "I was wearing my seatbelt."

"Well, plus one for following the traffic laws, Grace, but what were you doing out alone? And with Mrs. Deovolente on top of that?"

"I wasn't alone. Someone was supposed to be watching me," I pointed out.

"Well, whoever it was should be fired, Grace. You could've been killed. Where the hell is Robert? Why hasn't he arrived yet to take you home?"

"He's…we're…" I couldn't finish the words, but it wasn't because I was too ashamed to admit them. It was because my lungs had finally started to cave in on themselves, and I started sucking on my throat in a desperate bid for air.

I struggled to move my arms, to reach for Stacy, for anyone, but I couldn't move. My body felt like dead weight, and my head began to fill with large spangles of disorganized colors and frantic dots that danced in front of my eyes, hypnotizing me as the lack of oxygen began to cloud my thoughts.

Was this how it ended? Did I simply die of suffocation, with Stacy by my side, her mouth screaming out in a panic? I couldn't hear her, as the buzzing in my ears grew too loud to separate from everything else. It couldn't end this way—I wasn't ready.

"Grace, you hold on—you hold on," I could hear Stacy say to

me, though her voice grew further and further away.

I wasn't ready.

# UNMADE

"She could have been killed. This is your fault."

"I know."

"You promised to keep her safe. You promised to keep her from being hurt. Where were you? Why weren't you with her?"

"You know I cannot tell you that."

"How convenient. My daughter lies dying and all you care about are your secrets."

"Dad…" My lips felt cracked, my mouth dry and dusty. The voices would have been enough to wake me up, but I could feel the tension that extended between the two voices that flanked me, and I wondered at that.

"Grace? Grace, are you awake?"

Dad's voice sounded frantic. God, my guilt was starting to pile up.

"Love, are you alright?"

Great, add another brick to that pile.

"Of course she's not alright! Look at her!"

I allowed my eyes to flicker open, and the faces that greeted me, one lined with guilt and concern, the other lined with concern and anger, were like salves to the pounding in my head that I only now realized existed.

"Stop…fighting…" My throat burned with the effort to speak, and I winced as I tried to swallow down the rest of the sentence before I

212

couldn't talk at all.

"I'm sorry," Robert whispered in my ear, warm lips pressing against my forehead and causing my skin to burn. "You rest. I will not say another word."

"Grace," Dad cut in. "Do need anything? Do you want me to call the doctor?"

"Water," I managed to croak, and a straw was placed against my lips and the cool beads of water reached my parched mouth. I drank greedily until the gurgle of liquid could be heard sloshing inside of me.

Sighing, my gaze shifted from left to right and I saw the familiar hospital setting of chained curtains and an IV pole standing next to me. The beeping of a machine beside me, and the cold, sticky feeling of something on my chest confirmed that I was, indeed, in a hospital room, confined by my own pain and by wires and tubes that shackled me down. "Why am I here?"

"You were in an accident, Grace," Dad told me with as grave a tone as he could manage. "Janice's car was struck from behind, and you-"

"I know about the accident. Why am I *here*, in the hospital?"

Dad's eyes lifted to glare at Robert—a visual slaughter if ever I've seen one—and then lowered once more, his voice thick and filled with pain as he explained.

"Because you were dying. No one could heal you—no one was *around* to heal you. There was no other alternative. The doctors believe your injuries are worse than they are because of the strange… bruising on your body."

I listened to him explain, his words getting lost in my thoughts as I looked at Robert and saw the guilt plastered on his face, his eyes growing dark with it, the downturn of his mouth as each hidden accusation was lobbed by Dad's explanation.

"You weren't there," I whispered. "You didn't come."

"No," he confirmed.

"Then who brought me here?" I knew it couldn't have been Stacy—she was supposed to be dead.

"Llehmai and Lark…after they were informed of your accident."

"What about Melanie? What about Mrs. Deovolente?"

"She didn't make it."

I closed my eyes and moaned in distress at this news; not because this news upset me. I was already upset, and I already knew that she was gone. No, I was disturbed because the list of dead bodies that were caused because of me was growing ever longer.

"Grace, don't blame yourself for her death," Robert said to me, my thoughts obviously free for him to fish through. "This isn't your fault. None of this is your fault."

"She wouldn't have been in the car if I hadn't agreed to go to dinner with her. If I hadn't opened up to her, she wouldn't have felt a need to finish the conversation somewhere else. We wouldn't have been on that road; we would have been eating awful Greek food in a dinky restaurant. She wouldn't be dead if she had been with anyone else."

I tried to sit up but the pain that ricocheted through my body forced a cry from me, and I fell against the pillows, instantly exhausted. "I-I ca-can't stay like this," I panted. "I can't stay here."

"Of course," Robert breathed before placing his hand on my chest, warmth immediately surging into me, centering on my solar plexus and radiating outward. "Stay still."

I tried to, but feeling his touch after so long was like that first taste of water after a year in the dessert. I rose to press myself into his hand, the feeling of my body mending because of his touch alone acting like a cast to my broken heart. A heart that, when looking into his eyes and seeing the overwrought concern and love in them, I realized finally I had shattered on my own.

"I'm sorry," I whispered, before breaking into a sob.

"For what?" he said, lowering his head to mine, his cool forehead resting against my temple.

"For doubting you. For not believing in you."

I felt his head move, shaking in refusal of what I was saying.

214

"You had every reason to doubt me. You felt abandoned, and I did nothing to dissuade you from that. I should have been with you; I should have never left your side. Your father is right—this is my fault."

"It isn't. You weren't there; you couldn't have done anything to prevent this-"

"But I should have been. I should have been there with you."

"No one was there—no one was watching you," Dad spoke up, his ire undeniable. "They all abandoned you, and look at what has come of it."

"No. Llehmai was supposed to be looking after you. He should have seen the danger coming—he would have seen it and prevented it had he been there," Robert remarked, his head lifting above mine to look at my father. "But ultimately, it is my fault."

"Lem was probably still angry," I said softly, knowing what was coming.

"Angry? He is the peacemaker amongst us and is incapable of becoming angry—his patience knows no limits." Robert's eyes delved into mine, and I couldn't keep the truth from him. I wouldn't.

"I think he found it yesterday—I think I helped. Robert-" I took a deep breath and just let the words fall out "-he kissed me, on the way home from class." I didn't wait for a response; my confession was not yet complete. "And then he kissed me again when we got to the house. It...it wasn't a friendly kiss."

Robert's gaze moved to my dad's, his face stony and unmoving. There were no words spoken between the two men, and yet Dad still left the room, obviously uncomfortable with what he knew was about to take place between the two of us.

When the door to the room closed, Robert bent his head down and looked at me, the steel of his eyes cold and hard. He was hurt, and I hated myself for being the cause.

"Did you want him to kiss you, Grace?" he asked in a low voice.

I didn't lie to him. I wouldn't lie to him—I couldn't. "Not at first, but when he kissed me the second time, I did."

"Why?" It was one word that held a million questions within it, but none of the answers were welcome.

"Because…because I needed it. Because I needed to feel wanted. Because I needed to feel desired. Because I needed to feel something other than being alone. I wanted to feel my heart race in my chest. I wanted to forget what it felt like to hurt so much and, God help me, I wanted to hurt you. I wanted you to know what it felt like to hurt, to bleed inside and never know when it was going to end."

The warmth that flowed through Robert's hands had reached the tips of my fingers, and my hands came up instinctively to cover my face, ashamed at what I had done. I couldn't look at him anymore. I couldn't look at his face and see the pain there, see the hurt that I had caused him, even though I had admitted that that was what I wanted. Because it wasn't. I didn't want to hurt him—I loved him. I love him. I was nothing without my love for him, and if I was willing to put that aside for a moment of sadistic and spiteful pleasure, then my love was worthless, and that meant that I was as well.

Strong yet gentle hands pulled mine away, revealing the layers upon layers of guilt that I could no longer hide. I felt the hiccup of grief as I saw the betrayed and heartbroken look on Robert's face, and fully prepared to give up everything, to accept losing him for my faithlessness, I took a deep breath and waited for his rejection.

His mouth turned down, his eyes turning glossy with the damage that I had caused. I had done this to him. I had destroyed the heart of an angel who had loved me and wanted me despite my shortcomings.

"Grace, just shut up," he said before he brought his mouth down hard onto mine, the act so powerful, so filled with meaning that I knew if he were to let me go, I'd still feel it. I'd feel it until I died.

My arms looped around his neck, intent on holding him to me for as long as possible. He in turn scooped me into his, lifting me from the bed as far as the wires would go, crushing me against him, my heart beating so hard and so fast that I was certain it would burst through my chest and dive into his. It was a scattered beat, though, my physical reaction to his touch sending one message while my brain still frightful and wary of his rejection sending another. What if this was not forgiveness? What if this was a farewell?

I could feel him begin to pull away, and I shook my head, pressing my lips even harder against his, not caring if it hurt, not caring if someone walked in on us. I was not going to let him go, not again.

"Grace," he mumbled against my mouth. "I don't want to go—I won't. I just need to look at your injuries. Please."

Reluctantly, I forced myself to release him. He eased me back onto the bed and then pulled the sheets down, revealing my legs that were still horribly bruised, blackened almost to the point of looking dead. But even now, I could see that my skin was changing, lightening, pinking up. Glass lay on the bed on either side of my legs, the shards being pushed out as my flesh mended, torn and sliced tissue coming together as if they had been planning to all along and had simply been waiting for an audience.

Robert grabbed my hands, and I looked down at them for the first time, seeing in the light the crosshatched scarring that lay as evidence to my holding them up against my face. Remembering how difficult it had been to breathe, I pulled down the front end of my hospital gown to see stitches there, their ends pushing up through my skin as the wound that had been sutured healed. Eventually, the tiny fragments of black fell inside of the gown, and I rubbed the spot where they had sat, wondering what had caused the need for them in the first place.

"I can search your memories for you," Robert offered. "May I?"

I nodded, and immediately felt him probing my thoughts, his sifting and searching of the events that took place yesterday bringing things to my eyes that I had not realized I had seen, pushing feelings toward my heart that I had not realized I'd felt.

I could hear the sounds of metal scraping against metal, and glass raining down on me like glittery hail. I could see the frightened eyes of Mel staring at me just moments before she had launched herself at me, my body twisting in the car seat as hers came forward.

There was a burning sharpness in my chest, and then the tumbling and falling had followed, leaving me with nothing but the darkness and smell of blood and smoke and chafed metal. As his thoughts traveled further back, I felt a small sense of panic, and then I felt him stop—and I knew he had arrived at the memory of my kiss with Lem, burned as he had explained, into my mind forever.

My kisses with Lem. And how it felt, how I felt. They were all there, all of them a virtual display case of my crime. There was a chill that seeped into my mind, icy fingers of pain and disappointment that I knew he felt, but he did not linger long over these images of my betrayal.

He didn't have to. Being told about them was one thing—one could easily ignore a spoken confession. But this—this was like being there, like being in my mind as it happened, as I wanted it to happen, and there was no ignoring that. I regretted in that moment allowing him inside, regretted giving him carte blanche to see for himself what had happened because now I felt his pain, and it was tearing me into pieces even as he pushed forward, returning to the moment just before the accident, learning all that I had been told, the impossibility of Mel's story, the suggestion of how we could be together, and my confession to her.

During all of this I held my breath, hovering dangerously on the brink of passing out. Only when I felt his presence inside of my mind ease away did I take that first gasp of air, my nerves needy as I inhaled in short, rapid bursts, waiting for a word, any word from him.

"Your teacher saved your life," he finally said as he looked away from me, unwilling to allow me to see his face this time. "She protected you from something that was coming at you. It didn't come from behind—it came from the driver's side—your side—and she saw it approaching. She threw herself on you to keep you safe."

"Robert-"

"What she told you might not be the truth…or it might be. I cannot say for certain because I do not know. I only know that I have neglected my responsibilities to you and the consequences now lay before me as memories that I have burned into my own mind."

218

I leaned forward and placed my hand on his the hard edge of his back, fearing that he'd pull away—terrified of it.

But he didn't. Instead he leaned into my touch, relaxing against it, and this encouraged me to place my other hand against him, reaching forward to touch the silk of his hair as it faded into the corded muscle that remained tensed in his neck. I squeezed gently, and inched myself closer to him.

"Robert, I-I'm sorry for hurting you."

He spun around, my hands flying away to keep from getting lost in the motion, and when he faced me, there was such a ferocity in his eyes that I backed away. "I hurt myself!" he said with a shudder.

"You did nothing that I did not bring about. You were alone—I left you that way—and you needed the comfort of someone. I should have been that person but I wasn't. I wasn't there to give you what you needed, not affection, not love, not protection, and when it was offered to you by someone else and you accepted it you did so because I allowed it to happen."

"That's not true! I'm your wife—I should have remembered that!"

"You're my wife, but what kind of husband have I been to you?" he said angrily. "I married you and then abandoned you, and now I have to deal with the consequences of you wanting to be with someone else."

"But I don't!" I shouted. "I don't want to be with anyone else! I've only ever wanted to be with you!"

I tried to crawl toward him, but found myself limited by the wires and tube once more. Furious, I grabbed at them, tearing the pads from my chest, and pulling the tube from my arm, not caring as the blood spurted out. I threw myself at him, wrapping my arms around him, climbing into his lap and sobbing with relief when I felt his arms enfold me, his embrace growing tighter and tighter until there was no beginning or ending, just us.

I kissed his face, tracing his jaw with as many tiny pecks as I could, burning the shape of his mouth to memory, feeling the curved edge of his nose as it rubbed against mine. He in turn pressed warm kisses to my eyelids, tickling my lashes with every exhalation, every word he spoke of love, every plea of forgiveness that echoed my own.

His hands cradled my face, and I did the same to his, holding him and needing to feel his smile, see it, see that it was still meant for me, see that it was still mine to have. And when he smiled, when the corners of his mouth turned up and his lips separated to reveal the glistening white behind them, I was giddy knowing that nothing else could make my heart feel more complete.

Except one thing.

"Take me home," I whispered.

Robert didn't need to search my thoughts to know what I meant. He didn't need to hear me say why. He knew why. It was his wish, too.

I know that when Dad came rushing back into the room, following the nurses who had been alerted by the alarms of machines that could no longer detect life attached to them, he would find the room empty. He would see the blood that had spilled from my arm, and he would see the glass on the bed, and the sutures that dotted the sheets, and he would worry. But then he'd know that I was safe.

Probably safer than I had ever been in my entire life.

## THE PROMISE

"I've missed this," I sighed. My fingers weaved into a welcoming hand that stretched across cool sheets, and I brought that hand to my lips, kissing the strong fingers as they curled over mine.

"I've missed you."

I felt the gentle nuzzle against my ear, and the puff of breath against my cheek, and felt the hot prick of tears that threatened to announce my happiness before I could.

The sun was setting in front of us, filling Robert's room with shades of unmatched golds and oranges, slashes of color that were as warm and almost congratulatory in some sense; it felt like the confirmation that the dark moments that we'd shared were seeing their end, just as this day was.

We had found each other when our lives were ripe for change. We had fallen apart when our differences became too much. We had reunited only to find that love cannot thrive on deceit, and then the poison of doubt and mistrust had almost broken us completely, but we had overcome it, all of it, because what we had was far more valuable than love. Much, much more, and as it nestled between us, it was enough. At least for now.

Robert's hand moved down to my hip, and then to my abdomen when he felt the rumble there. "Are you hungry?"

My head jerked to the side. "I'm too happy to be hungry."

I could feel the smile on his lips, and I smiled, too—a full, rich smile that stretched across my face and claimed without uncertainty that I was happy. With him, I felt whole. With him, everything was as it should be, and I marveled at how it was even possible that I had managed to exist without him beside me.

"I was a walking ghost without you near me," Robert confessed to my thoughts. "Every thought I had was of you, and every step I took was a hollow, meaningless one when it wasn't made toward you. Every moment I was away from you was hell for me. Every moment I knew that you were doubting me was agony; I was torn. I wanted to be with you, Grace. I wanted to be wherever you were—I didn't want to be away from you."

My body twisted in his arms until I was facing him, our bodies lying side-by-side, our eyes level with each other. "I know that now. I should've always known it. It was stupid of me not to and selfish of me to expect you to put everything aside just because I can't deal with you not being with me. I acted like a spoiled, selfish brat."

"It wasn't selfish, Grace. There is nothing selfish about wanting to be loved."

"But there is everything selfish in not stopping to think about anyone or anything else because of that love. I hurt you—I accused you of things that were horrible, and I...I don't know how you can even look at me without hating me."

Robert's fingers brushed away a stray tear from the corner of my eye before it solidified as he took in my woebegone expression. "I can't look at you without feeling the need to touch you, hold you, kiss you. I can't look into your eyes and not want to undo all of the wrongs I've done to you. I want to spend forever making up to you the past hurts, and I want to spend forever proving to you that I have never stopped wanting you, loving you, no matter what you did, or thought...or felt."

"But why?" I blubbered. "I accused you of wanting to be with someone else, of not wanting me, and then like the hypocrite I am, I go right around and kiss someone else. How can you not hate me for that? Or at least be angry with me for it?"

The smooth pad of his thumb pressed over my lips, silencing me as he sighed wearily. "I do feel angry. I cannot deny that I would have rather you never kissed another person except me, but I also understand why you did it. You are a human being, with human desires that I cannot understand. If you need to feel that affection from someone else because I've neglected to provide it, I cannot hold that against you. I was the one who gave you little reason to believe that I wanted you—even after saying I did.

"When you left me that night, after I had once again refused to act upon my need for you, all I wanted to do was beg you to return, to come back to me and make to you all the promises a man can make to a woman he loves. But I couldn't because I felt ashamed. I followed you back to your father's home, I watched to make sure you were safe, but after that I couldn't even look at you because to do so would force me to admit that I did not deserve you.

"And with every day that went by without you, every torturous moment, my need for you grew. It grew and expanded and became the only thing I could think of. I was starved for your thoughts, for your smell, your touch. And yet, I refused to succumb to my needs because I couldn't give all of myself to you—not when so much was going on elsewhere.

"It's as though a fountain of black hatred had sprung up and was tainting everyone who came across its poison. I refused to allow the situation to grow out of my control, but it became too much for me. I didn't want to seek the help of those whose sole purpose it was to stop the madness with their own darkness, but I had no choice. I was overwhelmed, and I realized too late that by allowing them in that I had only added to the chaos. I felt that I couldn't return to you—not tainted as I was with my foul decisions.

"In your eyes, I was the healer; I was the one who saved lives. And now, I was doing more than taking them—I was destroying them. How could I return to you with that on my hands?"

He closed his eyes, and I could sense the tension in him, the struggle he had with himself over his decisions, but I knew that this wasn't his fault. He didn't do anything wrong—not in my eyes, at least.

Silver rings flashed as his lids lifted, and they softened as he touched the side of my face, tracing the bow of my lips as his own moved to continue. "You are far more forgiving and understanding than I deserve. You have the countenance of a human, but the soul of an angel far more divine than any of us could ever hope to be.

"It is how I knew when I saw your thoughts, Grace, that you did not initiate it. I know that you would never have. Whatever you felt while it was happening, the one thing you never felt was gladness for it. You might have enjoyed the kiss, but you didn't feel any desire for more. Even in the darkest of places, even in the hopelessness of your shattered faith in me, I knew that you felt only for me."

The blood in my veins began to slow, thickening as I looked into the quicksilver of his eyes and acknowledged that there would be no one else that I could love as much, no one else that I would desire. No one could do with one look what Robert could. Even silent, motionless, he was the key to my senses. He could turn the quiet into a thunderstorm, or the hurricane into the calm. He could make the ice burn, and the fire freeze. He could make the sweetest of emotions seem bitter in comparison to what he made me feel with just that one, scorching gaze.

His pupils dilated, growing wider and nearly swallowing the liquid mercury of his irises as he read my thoughts and saw in them everything that I felt, everything I knew. When he closed the gap between us, his lips finding mine, it was a cataclysmic thing.

I could hear the cracks in my past forming, and feel the beginning of weightlessness as piece by piece they fell away, leaving behind a new shell, one that was stronger, more resilient, fortified by what I saw in his eyes. My arms wound around him, and his around me, our bodies separated by only clothes and air and time.

And in one glorious burst of heat, I was consumed by the silky splendor of him. He had lost his form, dissipating into the fog that smelled sweetly of both heaven and hell, but his presence was still just as substantial as the tickle of that black mist, replacing arms that held me, and hands that caressed me, instead curled around me, over and over until I was sure I would become lost in it.

And even though I couldn't see his eyes or his mouth, couldn't feel his skin, his thoughts were with me. And it was those thoughts, thoughts that caused blushes to burn my skin, that caused my breath to catch in my throat as I fought to keep up with my racing heart, that took me to another place; a place where there were no rules, where there were no laws that prevented us from being together.

It was here that I could lose myself in feeling. It was here that I could embrace the fire that always burned inside of me whenever Robert was in my thoughts and let it completely engulf me. The tantalizing slide of cool mist against the prickly heat of my skin was tormenting just as it was satisfying, the push and pull of it against my human sensitivity unnaturally fulfilling.

Wisps and curls of dark fog danced a ballet with my limbs as I rolled over and over, tangling myself in the sheets and nearly losing my battle with balance on the bed, having almost fallen off twice when I finally lost control over my senses and simply allowed them to feel.

The touch of a hand could be just as light, just as gentle, but it couldn't evoke the feeling of a thousand fingertips the way the simple graze of mist could. Every nerve I possessed, and maybe a million I didn't, seemed to light up at each glancing touch. My body rose and fell against my will, drawn to every spiraling tug of smoke that already knew what would bring me the most pleasure.

I inhaled deeply, taking in what I could, however I could, and allowed the seeking mist to find what it was looking for, what it hunted. And then the part of me that wasn't human, that part of me that was something else entirely seemed to ignite deep within me, having been found by the only one who could, and in too short a time I was gasping for breath, consumed by sensation and satisfaction and…incompletion.

But I was too spent to pay any attention to that part, because this *was* completion.

I was panting, beads of sweat gathering to slide off of my skin, when the mist began to solidify once more around me, replacing smooth, soft cotton with hard muscle. Robert was once more beside me, his chest rising and falling in a frantic dance for breath that he did not need…and yet did. And I danced with him, my own need for breath false somehow, because he was my oxygen. He was my blood. He was my life.

"You," he said between breaths, "are my soul."

I curled up against him, my head resting against his chest, sighing at the silence that greeted me. How odd, I thought to myself, that such a mundane thing, something so many of us took for granted, could elicit both fear and comfort. For me, it was nothing but all encompassing comfort. The absence of a heartbeat was a reminder of what Robert had sacrificed for me—it was a testament to his love. I chided myself for ever forgetting that.

*It is entirely my fault for not being here to remind you.*

I cocked a lone eyebrow up, his voice in my head the first time in so long that it brought a rush of tears to my eyes. "Do it again," I pleaded.

*Do what?*

"That," I cried.

*This?*

"Yes."

*Why?*

I looked at him, puzzled by why he would need a reason. When the blank slate of his eyes told me that he did, I smiled. "Because when you do, I know that it's coming straight from your heart. There's no space, no time for it to get lost in the distance between your lips and my cynical ears. Because when it's in my head, it touches every part of me, and reaches the parts that I swore would never feel anything ever again. Every word that you speak into my thoughts is a promise to me, one that I know now you will never break."

The bed jolted, and I felt myself rolling over onto my back, Robert appearing above me, his hands cradling my face, his body resting lightly atop of mine, floating just enough to keep his weight from crushing me. I wrapped my arms and legs around him and brought him down, smiling when I sunk even deeper into the mattress.

*Grace, my heart, my love—I promise to never leave your side again. I promise to give to you all of me, to love you completely, fully, wholly.*

His words made me feel weightless, boneless, even with him atop of me, and I sighed in contentment. *Robert, there will never be another moment of doubt for me. I will never again question your love for me.*

He smiled, his perfect mouth lifting in revelry of the promise that I had made to him, knowing that it was one that I would never break.

He lowered his head to mine, our lips joining in a kiss that sealed our promises to each other, branded them, and when he lifted away, I didn't hold on for fear that he was leaving me again. Instead, I waited for him to smile, to look down on me and smirk as his gaze traveled to the top of my head and back down again.

"What?" I asked, seeing the glint of amusement in eyes.

"You," he replied, a light laugh touching his lips. "You look thoroughly disheveled."

I squirmed beneath him and leapt off of the bed.

"Isn't that my job?" I heard him call out after me as I ran into the bathroom to see for myself.

My cheeks were flushed a vibrant pink, and my hair was tousled in a way that told stories no one would believe. My lips were swollen, kissed beyond contentment, and my eyes glittered, so full of happiness that I could barely contain the sparkling joy as they fell out in tear after tear, smashing into the sink. This wasn't disheveled.

"You're right," Robert whispered as he came up behind me, his arms slinking around my abdomen, pulling me against him, my head resting against the hard surface of his chest. "This is loved."

"And sweaty," I remarked as I saw the sheen on my face. There was also dried blood crusting at my hairline, and dirt clung to my hair, horrifying me. "God, you must have had your eyes closed the entire time you were…ugh, I feel gross" I mumbled, my embarrassment changing the rosy hue on my skin to something much, much redder. "Is the bed a mess? I bet it's a mess," I lamented, moving to look for myself.

"It's not a mess, and no, my eyes were not closed. I don't care if you smell like sunshine or if you're covered head to toe in peat moss— you are beautiful and you're mine, no matter what you look like or what you're wearing."

I looked down and realized that I was still wearing the hospital gown, and another wave of embarrassment hit me. "I can't believe we did…that while I was dirty and bloody and wearing this stupid gown. I need to take a shower, and I need to get out of this."

Robert nodded and removed his arms from my waist. "I'll go and get you a change of clothes."

He walked away, and as I looked at him, his back facing me through the doorway while he rummaged through my clothes in the drawers, I removed my gown. I stepped into the shower and turned the water on, the blasting stream of hot water massaging muscles that I had not realized were tense, acting like a lubricant on them and easing the tension away, inch by inch, gallon by gallon. The bathroom soon filled with steam, fogging up my vision, leaving me to fumble around for the shampoo bottle.

My hands touched cold tile, and then found the niche where the bottle lay. Only it was empty.

"Robert? Did you use all of the shampoo while I was away?" I asked, knowing that he'd probably answer me silently to maintain my sense of modesty. "Is there a spare bottle under the sink?"

"I have it right here," his voice said from behind me.

"Oh!" I gasped, unable to turn around. "Y-you're in here."

"Yes. Yes I am," he replied, his voice just as shaky.

"Are y-you…are you naked?"

A soft chuckle left him. "Does one ever shower with all of their clothes on?" He was so close, his breath brushed across my shoulder, and I would have bet my life it was hotter than the water that flowed out from the showerheads built into the shower wall.

"Stay still," he said. I felt his fingers begin to massage my scalp, filling my hair with luxurious lather, the familiar scent of my shampoo now taking on a whole new meaning to me. Over the past few weeks, I had contemplated changing my shampoo, but now…

"Don't you dare," Robert threatened, his fingers skimming my shoulders as he gathered up loose strands. "This is the first scent of yours that I can remember. It is you—and I like you just the way you are."

"O-okay," I agreed, closing my eyes and allowing his ministrations.

"Step forward," he said softly, and I walked into the wall of water as it rinsed off the soap from my head. When I was certain that my hair was free of foam, I stepped back and found his hands ready this time with a washcloth and soap. I tried to turn around, but he was ready for that, too. He stopped me, holding me immobile just as soon as the thought had left me.

"Grace…I'm trying to take this as slowly as possible. If you look at me, I might not be able to stop. Please…please stay still."

The quivering in his voice matched the one in my chest as he began to wash me. The last person to wash me had been my dad, and that was a world and a lifetime ago. This moment was…it was everything. I held my body still, just as Robert had requested, and with every soapy glide that removed from me the evidence of last night's tragedy, it left behind a memory that gave me another reason to never want this night to end.

"Step forward," he commanded once more, and I obeyed; only this time, I was not alone. He followed, his arms bringing mine to cross over my chest, and he held me, close to him, but not close enough—not for me. The water that splashed around us, I realized, was meant to distract us, to remind us where we were, what we were doing. We had this moment, but we were not to lose ourselves in it—we could not lose control. Not yet.

As with all good things, so too, did this have to end. Robert's hold on me loosened, and I made my complaint known when he left me completely. I turned off the now cool water, the steam already thinning around me, and was soon swallowed up in the soft embrace of a thick towel. Quickly, vigorously, I was dried and dressed, though not in my staple of boxers and a tank top.

I smiled as Robert slowly pushed up a sleeve on my arm, folding up the end to tighten it and keep it in place. "This is different," I said.

"While I love seeing you in your usual bedtime ensemble, I've had a desire to see you in one of my shirts again for quite some time now. Actually, since the first time you wore my shirt."

I flushed as I remembered his face just a couple of months ago when I'd surprised him, daring to entice him while so many seraphim were under the same roof just meters away.

"No, Grace," he said, a sly smile creeping across his face. "That wasn't the first time you wore my shirt. Remember?"

My eyes widened, and I nodded in understanding. No, that wasn't the first time. The first time had been when we'd met, when I had tried to run away from my problems—from him. He had lent me a shirt, a silky, smooth shirt that felt unlike anything I had ever worn before.

"Whatever happened to that shirt?" I asked.

"It's right here," he answered, walking over to the closet and pulling it out, the gunmetal colored fabric bringing back a flood of memories. I walked over to him and looked at it, and then at him.

Without taking my eyes off of him, I slipped the shirt he had just placed on me, off. I grabbed the other shirt, pulling it off of its hanger and then sliding it over me, relishing the look on his face with each action.

"You're going to kill me," he breathed as he reached for me, his kiss a tempest of what he was feeling—what *we* were feeling.

But suddenly, he let go. His eyes glazing over with something other than the desire I had seen only seconds earlier. "What is it?"

"Trouble," he replied. "There's trouble…lots of it…I've got to go."

And he began to walk away, but then stopped. He turned and his face was stricken, the torment there so palpable, it was my torment as well. "I can't—I can't leave you. I promised."

The blazing fire that had been lit beneath my heart did not cool; it did not waver as I stepped toward him and pressed my forehead to his. "You go. I'm not going anywhere."

Crushing me against him, Robert kissed me, imprinting his taste and feel onto my lips, a silent promise. "I'll send Stacy here to be with you," he said before releasing me.

"Stacy?"

"Yes. She is nearby—I can smell her. She has not let you out of her sight since finding you, and at the moment, I do not trust anyone else to be with you while I am gone."

"Thank you," I said before he kissed me once more, disappearing before either of us could grow used to the contact. "Thank you for that."

*I love you, my Ianthe. I shall return to you to finish what I've started.*

*I love you, my Angelo. I will be waiting.*

# THE RING

I slept, Stacy watching over me nearby, while Robert was away. I hadn't realized how tired I was, or how drained I was emotionally, until I closed my eyes and fell into a fitful sleep that was filled with dark images that did nothing to help free me of the guilt I felt over Mel's death. There were consequences that had to be paid for what had happened.

And when Stacy woke me, her cold hand on my shoulder, gently shaking me into consciousness, I knew that it was now. I rubbed my eyes to remove the haze of slumber and the stricken look on her face was one that acted more like a warning than anything else.

"The police are here. They're at the gate," she said.

"I've got to get dressed," I mumbled, stumbling to the dresser and pulling open a drawer, grabbing the first pair of jeans that lay atop the folded pile inside. Without care, I slipped them on. I hurried into the bathroom and quickly pulled my hairbrush through my tangled mane.

The sound of a buzzing within the house—the button that announced a visitor was at the gate—echoed through the hallway as I headed toward the front door. There, a box sat flush against the wall, and I pressed the largest button there, activating the antiquated speaker that crackled as I asked, "Who is it?"

"Grace? It's Dad. I've got the police with me—they want to ask you some questions. Open the gate."

I felt Stacy's presence, and I turned to look at her. She nodded her head and my finger pushed on the red button that would swing the gates open, allowing this intrusion in.

"I'll be upstairs in Lark's room," Stacy told me. "If you need anything—if anything happens, you tell them you need to go upstairs for a minute and I'll get you out of here."

"Thank you," I mouthed as she disappeared before opening the door, waiting for the headlights to come flashing by.

A police car followed Dad's up the driveway, and both pulled up to the front door. Two uniformed officers stepped out of their vehicle slowly, as though they were timing themselves, waiting for a reaction from me, while Dad seemed to burst through the car, rushing toward me with far more concern than necessary—concern that fed my guilt.

"Grace," he said in a low tone, "you be honest with them, you hear me? Completely and fully *honest* with them."

There was a bulging of my eyes, and then a swallowing of understanding, a nod, and then Dad's arm was around my shoulder, supportive, reassuring as the officers approached. They both appeared to be near Dad's age, though one was obviously younger. His eyes took in the expansive foyer behind me, and the living room even further back, and I saw the appreciative look that crossed over his face before he straightened, masking his features quickly with a look of stony countenance.

The other officer was far less impressed, and immediately launched into his questions, the tone in his voice, and the speed with which he ran down the list telling me that this had been rehearsed, even if only in his head.

"Can you tell us why you left the hospital?" he bit out, without even bothering to explain why he needed to know.

"Because I don't like them," I answered plainly.

"You do realize that, given the nature of Mrs. Deovolente's death, your disappearance makes you appear somehow involved."

I was already irritated with this line of questioning, but my tone didn't betray that. "Of course I was somehow involved. I was the one in the driver's seat. We were both in that accident together."

The officer didn't miss a beat, and he countered with, "And yet you're the only one to survive."

I knew this game. I knew it very well, and stepped into the role quite easily. "Because I was also the only one wearing my seatbelt."

His eyes narrowed. "Why is that? Why *were* you there, on Bellegarde land alone with your teacher? And why did you not take off your seatbelt when she did?"

"We were there because she asked me to drive there—I didn't know it was part of Robert's property. And she had her seatbelt off because she had turned around to talk to me. We were there, talking."

"Talking, huh?" The way he said that made my blood boil, the implication there unwarranted and meant purely to provoke a reaction—one that I was not going to give him. "And you use the name Robert as though you know the family. Do you?"

"Of course," I replied, a smug smile beginning to form on my lips. "This is his house. This is *our* house. He's my husband."

Dad grabbed my arm, tugging me to the side before hissing into my ear, "I didn't mean be *that* honest."

"I'm not going to lie about that. Not anymore," I told him, yanking my arm away and returning my attention back to the officer. "Do you have any more questions?"

"Yes. Where's your husband right now, Mrs. Bellegarde?"

"He's out—he had to run a few errands."

"So, he helped you to leave the hospital, knowing that you had suffered some pretty extensive injuries, judging by the doctor's report, and then left you to…'run a few errands'?"

I felt my nostrils flaring in agitation, but I remained calm, my voice cool as I responded. "As you can see, I'm not as badly injured as originally thought, and I have a pretty high threshold for pain, just in case you'd like to take a look at my medical history and see all of the things I've been through in the past few years. Doctors make mistakes, and my husband knew that I'd rather recuperate at home than in some hospital room."

A flurry of notes was scribbled down as the officer nodded, obviously ticking off items on his mental checklist. When his pen stopped moving, his head rose and he looked at me with a rather ambiguous expression on his face. "The person who found you, the one who called the police, a Mr. Lemhay Fleuric—what is his relation to you and to your…husband?"

"His name is Llehmai, and he's a friend of my husband's family. Why did you want to know?"

The officer looked at his partner, and then back at me before replying, "Because he doesn't exist. Not in our records, not in the state's records, not in any records."

I knew this. Llehmai wouldn't exist in any records because he wasn't human. His life didn't include mingling with humans the way that Lark and Robert did. But how do I explain that to the police?

"He's not from here," was the only thing I could come up with.

"We've gathered as much, but his arrival on the scene of your accident, given how remote the location was, is suspicious. We would like to speak to him—do you know of a way to contact him?"

I looked at the officer and opened my mouth, wanting to tell him no, because I didn't. I was almost certain that even if I did, he wouldn't exactly feel up to speaking to me—or to the police—given what had transpired between us. There was also the issue of him not being there to help stop whatever it was that had happened to Mel and me—where had he gone? Why wasn't he there? Had I upset him that much with my rejection?

My pause seemed to give the officer what he wanted, and I kicked myself for not simply blurting out the truth when it was on the tip of my tongue. "Is he here?"

"Why would he be here?"

"Given your reaction when I brought him up, it seems quite likely that you two have something to hide, and considering how quickly you left the hospital and are now here alone, it only makes sense for me to ask. So—is he? Has he come here to meet you secretly?"

Dad interjected then, his fatherly sensibilities taking over his…well, sense. "Now see here—my daughter's not that kind of girl."

"And just what kind of girl is that, Mr. Shelley?" the other officer asked, his voice sounding rather pinched and agitated compared to the one who stood directly in front of me, the one whose questions had not yet reached their end. "The kind who finds some reason to get married at eighteen?"

"There's nothing wrong with getting married at eighteen," I said firmly. "Are you two married?"

"That's not any of your business," the other officer, the one who seemed eager to step inside and inspect everything, replied.

"Well, neither is it any of yours what kind of girl I am," I snapped.

"Do you know how we can get in touch with this Mr. Fleuric?"

My hair had fallen into my face, and I brushed it aside angrily. "No, I do not. I haven't seen him since late yesterday afternoon. I do not remember him being there at the scene of the accident—I don't remember much about the accident after it happened, but if you want to talk to me about *that* then I'd be more than happy to do so. But if you're going to continue asking me about the person who got me help, as though he had something to do with this simply because he's not in any of *your* records then I'm going to have to stop all of this questioning right here and ask you to leave."

The two officers looked at each other, and then the older one, the one who looked at me with such contempt I could feel it, reached into his pocket and pulled out a small plastic bag. It was the kind that zipped closed, and he held it up in front of me, dangling it as though it were some kind of prize.

"Can you tell us who this belongs to?"

My eyes focused on the object in the bag, the bright metal ring that sat inside familiar to me. "No. No I can't."

"Are you sure?"

There was no hesitation in my nod; I did not recognize the ring.

"That's odd, because it looks remarkably like the one on your finger."

My ring? I looked down at my left hand, the two white gold bands gleaming in the foyer light, screaming their own accusation.

"Mrs. Bellegarde? Where did you get your rings?"

The sound of my attempt to answer, the squeak of a lie that would not be told, was all that I could manage to offer him.

"Those are family heirlooms," Dad broke in, a beaded line of perspiration forming on his forehead as his hand covered mine, effectively hiding the telltale glint that seemed to call out to the mirroring one in the officer's grip.

"Heirlooms? From whose family?" The officer's eyebrow rose slightly, almost mockingly, and I felt a bubble of ire build within me as my mind filled with what I was certain was now running through his head: thoughts that were conspiratorial, dastardly, and above all else…true.

"They're from my husband and my mother's family," I said to him, my chin rising in stubbornness.

"So your husband and your mother are related in some way?"

There was an accusation there that stung, and I bit back the expletive, the unrestrained reaction that I felt it warranted. Instead I nodded, and removed my hand from my father's protection, holding up to the officer's face with an iron determination. "The top ring, my husband gave to me when he proposed to me. You will not find another one like it because it was made especially for him.

"The bottom one my father gave to me; it belonged to my mother and after she died, he saved it to give to me when I got married; it has been in her family for centuries. When I married Robert, he and my mother became related through me. If they look similar then it's merely coincidental, but it's a coincidence that I appreciate.

"These two rings embrace each other, just as I would have wanted my mother to embrace my husband, but she's not here to do that and so this is all I have. If you want to imply that there's something wrong about that, that perhaps my relationship with my husband is something…suspicious, then you're insulting not only me and my husband, but also my mother and I refuse to let you do that. I want you to leave; now."

A moment of silence followed, and the officer's gaze flicked from my hand to my face—once, twice—before lowering his own, the bag dangling by his side as he struggled for something to say.

Rather than wait for any response, I continued. "Now, if you want to ask me if I've ever seen that ring before, I can tell you no. If I may, could I ask where you found it?"

Both officers turned to look at each other, the younger one shrugging his shoulders, obviously unsure of what to do. The one who stood in front of me brought his eyes back to mine and replied, "Inside of you."

My hand flew to the spot on my chest where the stitches had been, and I understood what it was that I had felt in the car. "Inside of me?"

"Yes, inside of you. According to the doctor in the emergency room when you arrived, they could see it and pulled it out while you were unconscious. If this ring doesn't belong to you, and it doesn't belong to Mrs. Deovolente, then it stands to reason that it might belong to whoever hit your car. We need to speak to your husband to find out where he had your ring made—the jeweler might be able to tell us who this ring belongs to. Could you tell us where we may find him?"

Of course I couldn't. I couldn't tell him anything, and once again my pause was enough to embolden the officer, who stepped forward, a slight sneer on his lips beginning to form and chilling the anger inside of me.

"Do you *know* where your husband is?"

"He's with his mother," Dad replied, stepping in front of me and blocking off the officer's approach. "They've been on the outs with each other for a while and are now trying to reconcile their differences."

"He's. With. His. Mother." Doubt made every word its own separate entity, but Dad wouldn't let him to taint anything with it.

"Yes. As you can probably guess, she wasn't too thrilled with him marrying so soon, and to someone he hardly knows. I felt the same way, but I love my daughter and I don't want to lose her, too. It's pretty normal for a child and a parent to disagree—if you have a teenager, then you understand."

A light of recognition seemed to pass through the officer's eyes, and I saw his hard features soften a bit in understanding. Dad had touched a nerve somewhere and Dad knew it. He pounced.

"My son-in-law is a good kid. I'd even say he's a good man. If there is anything he can do to help you find who owns that ring, he will, but right now he's trying to mend his relationship with his mother after realizing how close he came to losing someone else he loves. When he returns, I will have him go directly to the police station to give you the name of his jeweler."

This seemed to appease the officer, and he nodded. He tucked the ring into his pocket, and Dad reached out to shake his hand, patting the officer on the arm before sidling by him and shaking the younger officer's hand as well. The officer's nodded at me, but I refused to give them anything more than an icy stare, allowing daggers to fly at their backs when they turned around to head back to their car.

Dad followed, walking behind them and watching as they drove off, their lights disappearing down the drive and beyond the iron gates and ironic angel statues that fronted the property. When he returned, Dad closed the door behind him and shook his head in disgust.

"I haven't done that in years. I'm surprised I wasn't found out."

"Done what?"

He reached into his pocket and pulled out the small bag, the silver ring still contained within it. "This."

My jaw fell, nearly clipping the floor as I stared at it. "Are you…did you…DAD!!"

"I'm not proud of it, and I wouldn't have done it if I didn't think that this might be useful in some way. And besides, when I left my family all those years ago, I never stopped being what I was. As much as I hate the idea of it, I am still an EP; I still have a loyalty to keeping their secret safe. It's why I never told you that I knew what Robert and Ameila and Lark were; their secret is my duty to protect, even if I don't want to."

He was right, and understanding swept through me as I realized that he'd been faithful to the angels, even if he had left his family behind. He couldn't escape being an electus patronus anymore than I could escape being the daughter of one. Even if he wasn't bound by a family vow sworn centuries ago, he was still be bound by his own vow, by his own conscience.

I hugged him. Fiercely, proudly, lovingly. He was my dad, he was the most firmly rooted part of me, and he was my hero.

"I love you."

"Kiddo, I love you too."

When I released him, he handed the bag over to me and I carefully removed the ring. It was identical to my mom's ring; identical except for the etchings on the side. This one looked as though the etchings were moving, an illusion that was mesmerizing.

"Do you see that?" I breathed, holding the ring up to Dad's eyes. The antiqued engraving on the face of the ring looked like waves, rolling and crashing against its edges. But these weren't static waves, they pushed and pulled, flowing and licking at the surface like black water.

"Put the ring down, Grace," Dad ordered.

"What? But it's just a ring-"

I gasped in shock when Dad's hand slashed through the air, slapping the silver circle from my fingers. The sound of it skating across the wooden floor tailed my surprise, and I stared at Dad with incredulous eyes.

"That ring...it isn't just a ring."

I opened my mouth to object but Dad's eyes narrowed, his furious expression undoing whatever decision I had made. "That ring is a curse."

"A curse?"

"I told you, Grace…remember? I told you that being one of us has its price. This ring belonged to an EP. It's a claim of ownership, a brand that can only be removed upon death. I have one, too." He held up his hand and I saw the pinky ring on his right hand as if for the first time. "You know where that ring came from, don't you?"

I knew. Of course I knew. Images, memories of a scarred tree that had been burned into the chest and belly of my teacher filled my vision. "Yes."

"It came from your teacher, didn't it?"

I nodded. "I didn't know until last night—she told me…she told me what Mom's call was."

I had hoped that Dad knew what I'd learned. I had hoped that he'd be able to deny it or confirm it, something. Instead, he looked at me with baited breath, waiting.

"You don't know, do you?"

When his head shook, when his eyes were as clear as day and held no dishonesty in them, I suddenly felt alone. I couldn't tell Dad that he had been married to Death—not after his reaction to learning about Robert. Dad's faith in my mother had already been shaken and I couldn't destroy what was left. My memories might now be tainted, but his didn't need to be.

"I can't tell you, Dad. I can't tell you what Mel told me. I don't know if I can believe what she said, and now I can't question her, which means it doesn't matter what she told me."

"Grace, if this ring was hers then the angel whom she was bound to—her charge—is a dark one, and she was probably lying to you."

"I realize that now. She told me she had been part of a family like yours—serving the dark ones—but she chose to swear her loyalty to others. Now I see that she was lying."

I felt disgusted.

"Grace, I need to get back to Matthew—I left him with the

Kims-"

"The Kims?" Another shock.

"Yes. Mr. and Mrs. Kim were at the house. They were clearing out some of Stacy's things and had brought over a box for you when the police called. They offered to take Matthew with them while I stayed at the hospital with you. I told them that I'd pick him up tonight so that we could be with Janice—I'm already late."

I looked toward the stairs, wondering if Stacy had heard what he'd said, and then returned my gaze to his, not wanting him to grow suspicious. "I guess you'd better go then."

"I don't want to leave you here, Grace."

"I'll be fine, Dad."

He shook his head and reached for my hand. "No, you won't. I'm not upset that you left with Robert, but I am upset that after removing you from the safety of the hospital, he left you alone again. You're not safe here—not alone."

"She's not alone."

Dad's head rose, and I turned, silently groaning at the voice that spoke behind me. "Lem. I wasn't aware that you were here."

"Me either," I muttered under my breath.

"I apologize for that. Actually, I apologize for a lot of things. I should have been there with you, Grace. If I had, you would not have been injured, and your teacher would still be alive."

"You nearly cost me my daughter," Dad seethed. "Why should I trust that you'll keep her safe this time? Why should I trust you when it was your son who tried to kill me, who killed my wife and our baby? Your negligence nearly cost me Grace. You don't deserve my trust."

"Dad-"

Lem's hand rose to stop me, and he looked at Dad with a pity-ing expression on his face. "James, I know you do not hold me in high esteem, and I do not blame you for it. Humans tend to take out their frustrations by blaming anyone and anything else, but let me remind you that you chose to marry Avi and have children with her, and doing so demands consequences that you cannot deny you were aware of.

"If it hadn't been Samael, it would have been someone else—we cannot shirk our obligations to our call and to our own laws. It doesn't mean we agree with them—or like them—but what you fail to realize is that as much as it was my son who harmed Grace, he was also Avi's son, and she accepted the price she had to pay for loving you."

Everything happened so quickly after that. I saw the thoughts in my dad's eyes—it was as though I could read them there—and I moved, my body blocking the lunging attack that sent Dad racing forward, his fist held back in a kinetic swing that I absorbed in the fleshy plank of my arm, the sound of his shocked and dismayed cry deafening my own.

"Grace! Why—why would you do that?" he asked as he cradled me, my arm lying limply across me while my chest rose up and down with erratic breathing, a lame attempt to control the pain.

"You would-you would have-broken-your-hand," I panted. "You can't just go on hitting angels, Dad. Trust me—I know."

"I don't care if he's an angel—some guys need a good punch to the jaw," Dad growled. "You weren't good enough for Abby and you knew it."

"It's true," Lem conceded with a nonchalant tip of his head. "But no matter how undeserving I might have been, I, at least, am an angel. Regardless of your family's lineage, you were never worthy of being with her—Avi was a Seraph—pure in her existence and untainted by generation. You had no right to be with her, and you know it."

I waited for Dad's reply, but as Lem's words sunk in, Dad's shoulders just…sank. "You're right," he sighed sadly. "I had no right to be with her. Love can make you see past all of the wrong and fool you into believing that everything done in its name is right. If I had had the guts to refuse Sam, she'd be alive today. She would not have sacrificed another person to save her own life. She would not have done what I did."

"Of course not—she was divine. You should feel thankful that no part of you exists in your daughter and that only Avi's blood runs through her veins."

"That's a messed up thing to say," I ground out, "He's my dad—everything that I am is because of him."

"Grace, everything that you are, you are because of Ameila and your mother. Your father has about as much to do with your existence as a fly does to a hurricane."

I felt my mouth pull into a tight line. He was speaking biology, as though that were all that it took to raise a child. Biology could create, but without nurturing, without love, without a foundation, nothing could thrive.

I finally understood why Sam was the way he was. He had a father, he had a mother, but there was nothing else for him. Not from Lem, anyway. Lying there in my father's arms, staring at Lem's stoic face, I found myself feeling sorry for my brother, and for his father. If only Sam had had a dad who could look at him as something more than an obligation. If only Lem had realized just how important being a part of your child's life was.

"Dad, could you let me up?"

Easing me into a sitting position, Dad braced me as I stood, my legs sturdy, even as the pain in my arm sent rockets of stabbing discomfort through me. "You told me you loved my mother. If you had loved her son half as much as you did her, he might have turned into a much better person."

"You don't understand, Grace—how we feel is how we're supposed to feel. If we were meant to love our children, we would."

My head swung from side-to-side in gentle denial. "You keep using that as an excuse to explain away your actions, your feelings, but I know different. You might have a call you have to follow, laws you have to obey, but there is no law that says you have to feel a certain way about anyone. If there were, I'd be forced to hate you because of who you are, but I don't. I don't hate you at all."

"You're human; that's how you're supposed to feel."

"But you just said that my father had nothing to do with my existence," I reminded him. "You can't pick and choose what I am when it's convenient to your needs, Lem. And being what I am, it gives me the ability to see that everything that angels believe about emotions is wrong.

"You don't fall in love with who you're supposed to—love just happens. It's not a definite; it's not something that you plan for, that you see up ahead. When it happens, it catches you by surprise and becomes a part of you, like a scar. It might fade, but it never leaves you, and will remind you for the rest of your life just what caused it."

Lem's mouth surrounded itself in brackets, and he gazed down at me with an almost condescending stare. "What you forget, Grace, is that angels don't scar."

"Yes, you do," I said in retort. "You do scar. You scar in the way most visible. Every time you talk about my mother, you prove it."

An awkward silence took over, and I stood between these two men, two men who had both loved my mother, but only one had had the fortune to be loved back. If nothing else proved to me that love wasn't a path you could deviate from, it was knowing that my mother had fallen in love with my father.

He was everything that she could not have, and yet she could do nothing *but* love him. Being with him had cost her life, something she sacrificed willingly. Angels *could* choose. My mother had chosen my father. Robert had chosen me.

"Grace, I want you to come home with me," Dad said in a low voice behind me.

"I'm staying here, Dad. Robert will return soon. And...I trust Lem. I know you don't—you don't have a reason to—but I have no reason not to. I can't blame him for Sam's actions anymore than I can blame Mom. I blame her for a lot of things, but not that."

"I don't think this is a smart idea, Grace."

"I know you don't, but it's my decision."

With severe reluctance in his eyes, doubt still lingering in lines that puckered his forehead, he nodded. "If that's what you want."

"It is."

"Your arm-"

"Will be fine," I reassured him. "Robert will be back soon, like I said, and he'll heal it."

Dad's eyes suddenly dropped to the floor, scanning the wooden surface quickly. "I need to find that ring."

Lem's head perked up then. "Ring?"

"Yes. It was found with Grace after her *accident*." Dad made that last word sound like an expletive, and I winced at the connotation in it.

"Dad, don't worry about. We'll find it later. You go and get Matthew and see Janice." I used my uninjured arm to turn Dad around and walked with him outside.

"I still don't like this, Grace," he warned. "And after what happened between you two, I would think Robert wouldn't like it either."

I understood his concerns—I had to admit that I shared them—but I knew that Dad wouldn't be able to contain his dislike for Lem, just as Lem wouldn't be able to keep himself from being brutally honest with Dad, and there had already been too much violence between our families.

"It'll be alright," I assured him. "Call me when you get Matthew. And kiss him for me."

Always the father, he found the little girl in me and wrapped me up in his arms, his embrace feeling every bit as strong and protective as I had remembered it all those years ago when he told me that Mom had died. "I will. I love you, kiddo. It doesn't matter what anyone else says— you're my little girl, and I love you."

"I love you too, Dad. Everything inside of me that's good, I got from you—I don't care what anyone else says either."

He let me go, a reluctant and far too beleaguered release, and then walked away, entering his car with a heavy weight bearing down on him that made his leaving much more difficult to bear than anything he'd probably ever done. I could hear his thoughts, as if he were saying them to me out loud.

*Dear God, let her live so that I may see her one last time. Let me be able to say goodbye.*

I swiped away a lone tear as he pulled away. Truth was, I didn't want to say goodbye. I didn't want to see him one last time. I wasn't an angel—I wasn't a human being either—so why did I have to follow either's rules?

## DEPARTURE

I returned to the house to see Lem still standing where I had left him. He gave me the same look he always did, the one that told me how deeply perplexed he was that he couldn't read my thoughts the way Robert could. I closed the door behind me and headed toward the stairs.

"Stacy," I called. "You can come down now; my dad's gone."

"She's not here," Lem informed me casually. "She left as soon as she heard what your father said about her parents. She'll be back though. She didn't realize that the police and your father would be gone so soon."

I bit my lip and frowned. Lem saw this, and immediately knew the reason for my reaction. "You only told your father that you were fine being with me because you thought your friend was here."

My cheeks went scarlet from embarrassment, the truth not needing me to validate it in any way. He smiled and shook his head. "I'm sorry for what happened between us, Grace. It was my fault."

I wanted to let him take the blame for it, but I couldn't. He hadn't really done anything wrong. Not really. "It wasn't entirely your fault. I could've stopped you—I should've stopped you—but I didn't, and the blame lies mostly with me."

"You're wrong on that part," he said softly, his eyes taking on a kinder, gentler light. "You couldn't have stopped me. I was acting on foolish impulse. I did not stop to think about the consequences that you'd be faced with; the guilt that you'd feel over it."

"I've faced my guilt, and I told Robert about what happened."

He nodded. "I know. He was very…charitable about everything."

His tone seemed mocking, and I felt annoyed by this. "He was very understanding, and he even tried to take the blame for it, but I wouldn't let him. He's too good of a person to accept the responsibility for actions he had nothing to do with. And that's not charity, Lem. That's loving someone so much that you want to take the hurt away from them, no matter what it means."

"You're so adorable when you're naïve," he smiled. "He loves you; that is not in dispute. But why he accepted the blame for what we did, and what you felt, had nothing to do with love, and everything to do with trying to keep the peace. Starting a battle with me because I kissed his human girlfriend is no way to keep his life, Grace. Or have you forgotten that he has yet to be handed down a punishment for killing your brother?"

My intake of breath was sharp—razor sharp. "You would hold that over his head?"

"No. I would never do such a thing, but N'Uriel is young, and has been around man for much longer than he's been around his own kind, and the poisonous seeds of man's doubt can stain his intentions with the worst sort of meaning."

"He's over fifteen-hundred years old," I snorted. "You're acting like he just met us or something."

With a grace and elegance that was completely foreign to me, Lem walked toward me and tilted my chin up with a long, lean finger. "And I'm over ten-thousand years old. I've seen the birth of civilizations and watched them burn into ashes. I've seen the creation of species that have given man dreams and nightmares, and seen the extinction of others that have caused much guilt and strife amongst mankind. Your perception of time is localized by your experience and your mortality. My perception travels beyond just years. It travels through light, and sound, and darkness."

He turned away and headed toward the kitchen. I followed him, though I don't know why. I simply felt my feet moving in time with his, shuffling in an ungainly way until I was standing at the kitchen counter with my hands placed atop of it, my palms flat, my fingers splayed. He began to assemble a plate of food in front of me, his movements nimble in ways that I simply could never be.

"Eat," he commanded, just as my stomach began to grumble.

Listening not to him, but to the gurgling deep inside of me, I sat down on one of the stools and picked up a piece of melon he'd wrapped in a slice of ham with my uninjured hand. It tasted…otherworldly.

"You think I'm the devil, don't you?" he asked while he watched me eat.

I shook my head, my mouth too full and too occupied to allow anything else but a guttural murmur. This brought out a chuckle from him, and I smiled, even as I continued chewing.

"I wouldn't blame you if you did. I've been a lot of things to-night—boorish, spiteful, resentful, arrogant, an ass—stop me whenever you're ready-"

This time I laughed, covering my mouth with my hand. "You can keep on going," I said behind my fingers.

"How charitable of you," he replied through white teeth. "Although I do admit I deserve that. You've shown an infinite amount of patience with me, despite my hellish behavior. It would be fitting if you did believe me to be the devil himself."

"You're not that evil," I laughed. "Yeah, you might take advantage of a lonely girl in need of some attention, but that doesn't make you evil; just ballsy."

"Ballsy? Is that one of your human sayings?"

"It's one of *my* sayings—I know a lot of humans who would never let that word pass their lips, let alone admit that they've said it."

He seemed to contemplate this for a bit, and then grinned. "I think I might adopt that word for my own use. At the very least, it'll be a great conversation killer should I ever become involved in another dreaded philosophical debate that forever rages amongst the Seraphim."

I giggled in spite of myself, the image of a circle of antiquated angels sitting around, arguing the logic of humanity and all of its vices, only to be disrupted by an outburst of "ballsy" by Lem, who, if I had to admit it, looked rather good for someone over ten-thousand years old.

"Did that amuse you?"

"Yes, actually," I admitted. "I didn't realize how much I needed that."

"Needed what?" he asked curiously.

"A laugh. I think that's the first time I've laughed in over a month."

"Well, I'm glad I could give you what you need." His eyes darkened on the word "need", and I quickly returned my attention to my plate, thankful for the few remaining morsels of fruit left there to occupy my attention.

And mouth.

"I'm going to walk around the property for a bit," Lem said suddenly. "If you need anything, call out—I'll hear you."

I nodded, never looking up at him, the ease of humor now gone. As soon as he was out of sight, I ran my hands through my hair, squeezing my scalp as I tried to figure out what the hell was wrong with me.

When I closed my eyes I could see Robert's face, his love like a light that filled up every dark corner of my mind. Mouthing his name put every nerve in my body on high alert. They waited in anticipation of his nearness, his embrace, his voice.

But when I opened my eyes, I couldn't get the gold and silver stare of Lem to clear from my vision. It was as though the two conscience images were warring within me, and Lem had won my waking consciousness, while Robert still remained something hidden, something far out of reach.

But that made no sense. I had Robert. I had his love, I had his heart, I had his very life in my hands, and simply imagining any part of my life without him caused my insides to ache. We were so close, so close to finally being together—completely. So why then was Lem still in my head?

Why did he mean something to me when he shouldn't? Why did I keep looking out of the kitchen window to see if he was close to returning? Why did my belly do flips in anticipation of that? I scolded myself, convincing my all too eager mind to believe that it was because I worried for him. Someone was out there who didn't care who was with me, who was near me. He had meant something to my mother, and he was Ameila's friend. This need to see him return was a completely understandable one—I'd feel the same way if it had been Shawn, or Chad, or even Dwayne.

"Grace," his voice broke through my thoughts.

"Yes?" I stood up, trying to look innocent, trying to keep my confusion hidden as I turned to see his frame standing in the hallway that led to the back door.

"Come outside. It's raining."

"You want me to go outside...in the rain?" This didn't seem normal.

"Yes. It's a warm rain, so you won't get sick. Come on—nothing is more enjoyable than a nice walk in the summer rain."

"I never get sick," I replied, unsure of his invitation. "If...if I go out there with you, will you promise..."

He knew where I was heading with this, and he nodded. "I promise to keep things completely platonic while we're in the backyard."

"What about in here?" I cocked a lone eyebrow up, wanting no surprises, no hidden doors for him to find and open up.

"I swear on my wings, nothing will happen in here either," he vowed.

Content and satisfied with his response, I followed him down the hallway, my heart thudding loudly in my chest as we passed Robert—*our*—room. I wasn't doing anything wrong, I told myself over and over again. I was simply going outside to stand in the rain and forget about things for a while. There was nothing wrong with that.

252

Nothing at all.

I wasn't wearing shoes, so when my feet came into contact with the cool, damp, and springy grass, it made my toes automatically curl inwards, sinking ever deeper in the plush green carpet. I stalked to the middle of the large backyard and held my arms out as the rain fell down all around me like little faeries that glimmered in the moonlight.

Droplets gathered on my hair, separate little pearls of water that soon morphed into the dampness that pulled my hair back, making it cling to my skin like webbing. I could feel the beads of water on my lashes, weighing them down and making them feel lush, an impossible feat, even for rain.

"You look so carefree," he murmured as he stood off to the side of me, maintaining a distance that made me feel both comforted and disturbed. "It's as if you've given up all of your concerns to the sky."

"No," I replied, wiping my face with my hands and clearing the blur of moisture from my eyes. "I've just put them on the back burner for now. I can't constantly focus on doom and gloom and still expect to live a normal life. If I want to spend my last days alive that way, I might as well already be dead. I deserve better than that. Robert deserves better than that."

"He's very fortunate to have you."

"I'm the fortunate one," I corrected. "Robert saved my life."

Lem nodded in understanding, his eyes hard and focused on mine, even through the thickening rain.

"Do you ever wish that things were different?"

I looked at him quizzically. "Different? What do you mean?"

"Your circumstances. Do you ever wish that they were different?"

My arms lowered, and I thought about his question. How many nights had I asked myself the same thing? How many nights alone, crying over Robert, crying over what might have been, did I ask myself if I wanted things to be different in any way. My eyes rose to his, and I answered him with a firm, "No."

"No? But look at everything that you've lost—friends, loved ones. Soon you'll have to give yourself over to Robert to die. You would still allow him to take your life?"

There was no hesitation in my response. There could never be one. I was as sure of it as I was my name. "Yes. I wouldn't wish for anything different. Every decision I made brought me to this place. If I hadn't gone to school that first day, I'd probably never have bumped into Robert. He would've never noticed me. I'd have never gotten on that bike with him and learned his secret.

"If Graham had told me he loved me, if he had felt the same way about me that I felt for him, I probably wouldn't have noticed him. I chose my fate, and knowing now what I do, I realize that every choice I made, even the ones that hurt, were the right ones. And while I might not be sure of the choices I'll make in the future—however long it might be—whatever I do choose will be the right one, because each one will be for love and for hope."

"And what kind of hope do you have? You're going to die, Grace," he said, his tone challenging as he approached me, closing the once safe distance between us rather quickly.

"But Robert's going to live," I told him stubbornly. "My hope rests in him. He's going to do what he was meant to do, just as I'm going to do what I was meant to do."

"And you believe that you were meant to die?"

"Yes. I've seen what not following through with one's call can do to your kind. I won't let Robert destroy himself to protect me, not when my life is so meaningless without him in it."

Lem's hands reached for my face, but I pulled back, and they hung there in mid-air, his fingers strained at the emptiness that lay between them. "How…how can you say that your life is meaningless without him in it? How can you measure yourself based on his existence?"

"Because there are some things you just know, Lem. You can't know if you'll ever fall in love, or who you'll fall in love with, but when you do you know it. You know it like you know your own name. You feel it, and it eats at you, consumes you until all that is left is what you feel. And when you meet the reason you exist, the reason you breathe, the reason your heart beats, you know that without them, you cease to exist."

"And what if I tell you that without you, I cease to exist? What would you say to that?"

My head swayed from side to side in quiet denial of his words. "I'd say that you were fooling yourself, that you did not understand what it truly meant to be in love.

"I keep saying that I love Robert. It's not true. I don't love Robert. What I feel for him is something that goes beyond that. Love is a trivial thing compared to what I feel for him. He's every thought in my head, every second of time that passes by, every inch of space that I walk into.

"And, even though when I stand here, and I see you, and I think to myself how much I'd like to kiss you, I realize that the act of kissing you is nothing compared to the thought of kissing Robert. Just the thought of it is enough to wipe out every other memory for me. That's not love, Lem. You don't ever find that with anyone except the person whose soul is the match for your own. Robert's my soul mate, and that continues on long after death."

"That doesn't mean that you just hand yourself over to it. What about your father? Your brother? Your friends? What about them? How selfish is it to put all of their wants aside for one person?"

It hurt, seeing the anguish in Lem's face, seeing his pain. It was as though I was looking at him through someone else's eyes, and every ounce of dismay that lay within him was a cold needle to my heart because despite his words, despite his actions, he'd been a good friend.

"They love me, with as equal devotion and trust as I feel for them, and they know that what I do, it's not just for me, and not just for Robert, but for them as well. I'm a danger to them—the longer I exist, the closer their lives come to ending. I have no obligation to anyone but myself, and it's because of that I've chosen to leave everything behind.

"I'd rather never see my little brother grow up, if it means knowing that he *will*. I'd rather say goodbye to my dad forever and walk away, knowing that he'll live to raise my brother, than live with the knowledge that he's gone.

"So yes, I am selfish. I'm very selfish. I can't accept any harm coming to my family because of me. Too many people have died because of me, and my friends and family have already suffered enough. They don't deserve any of this and I refuse to let anything else happen to them."

"What if I can keep them safe? What if I can keep them from being hurt?"

"Why are you doing this to me?" I asked him softly. "More importantly, why are you doing this to yourself? Do I remind you that much of my mother? She didn't love you either."

I had gone too far. The rain turned cold, icy, tiny shards that were sharp and bitter as they fell on me, slicing my skin and filling the damp air with the scent of my blood.

"She had no choice—but you do. You could love me if you wanted," he said to me darkly.

I ignored the stinging in my arms and held my ground, even as he removed what little distance there was left between us. "But that's just it. I don't want to."

The air around me was bitter with its chill, mirroring the frozen wasteland that I'd turned Lem into. He looked stricken; angry, empty. I felt like crap for doing that to him, but I wouldn't lie to him to make him feel better. I wouldn't do that to someone I called my friend.

And almost as quickly as it had happened, the hard sleet turned soft once more, warming and soothing the stinging slashes on my arms and cheeks. Lem's eyes seemed to widen in surprise, and then a smug, knowing smile crossed over his lips as his gaze was averted, something—someone—now standing behind me.

"N'Uriel, I hope you enjoyed that speech. If ever there was a doubt in your mind where you stood, let it be clear now."

"I never doubted it for a moment, Llehmai," Robert said behind me confidently. "I've always known Grace's heart and her thoughts were one and the same."

"How lovely it must be, knowing that she feels her thoughts are safe with you."

I felt the warm wash of body heat behind me, and Robert slid his arms around my waist, drawing me in, protectively, possessively. "Every part of her is safe with me."

Lem smiled a friendly smile that was incongruent to the rigidity of his body. "As it is with me."

"Thank you for watching over her."

"It was my pleasure. She is full of insight, your Grace is."

"Yes, she is."

Listening to the two of them speak to each other was like watching a tennis match with the sound on mute; the back and forth volley hid the true dialogue, and I yearned to hear what was being said between them. I could almost imagine the inner argument, the accusations of neglect.

Their voices in my head; angry, prideful, possessive. I should have felt smug about it, this silent battle between the two of them over my affections, but I only felt remorse for ever allowing anything to have happened between Lem and me. Even if I somehow managed to live for a million years, I'd never forgive myself for what I had caused.

"Grace, this isn't your fault," Robert whispered against my hair.

"It is," I insisted.

Robert turned me around to face him, the house at his back, and his mouth opened to say something, his eyes brimming with reassurance, but nothing came out. Nothing was able to. There was a flash of white, my eyes felt burned to the back of my skull, and I found myself lying on the ground, my shoulder digging into the wet grass, my head tilted at an odd angle.

I could see white, bright, glowing, hot light, with ghosts of darkness floating inside. My ears were filled with the harsh pinging of something metallic, while my nose was tickled with the smell of smoke. I could feel myself being lifted, feel my body being cradled and adjusted gently, and then passed like a gift to another set of arms whose face hid in that dark ghostly shadow.

There was a strong pain in my abdomen, and my arm, the same arm that I had used to block Dad's attack on Lem, was the only part of me that didn't seem to hurt. I think I opened my mouth to say something—perhaps I was successful and simply couldn't hear myself—no response came to me. A cool hand pressed against my face, and though I could not see to whom it belonged, I felt my body relax and lean into the touch. Cool ribbons of calm seeped into my skin, and my mind grew fuzzy.

"I don't want to sleep," I said. Or, at least I tried to say. "I don't want to sleep—don't make me sleep."

I grew frantic in my thoughts. Sleeping, blacking out, I did not want any of it. I felt myself being lifted once more and placed into a seat. The cool pin-prick of sensation was returning to my arm, as well as the rest of me, my body healing in its usual fashion. Something was pulled over me, and the telltale click of a seatbelt being fastened alerted me to the fact that I could hear again. Or maybe it was just my imagination.

"Grace, you're going to be okay. I'm going to drive you away from here—you're not safe here anymore. I don't know where you'll be safe, actually…"

It was Stacy's voice. Stacy had come back, just as Lem had said she would. I spoke her name, but she didn't respond—maybe I hadn't said it at all. I felt the cool pat of a hand against mine, and then a soft vibration beneath me—the car had been started. Whose car?

"What happened?"

Had I asked that?

"There was some kind of explosion," her voice said to me. I had asked it after all. "It wasn't a normal kind of explosion, like the kind you see on television. This one—it was like everything just got sucked in, like a vacuum on steroids or something. But it made this god-awful sound, and that light…you were looking straight at it."

I had. So that explained why I couldn't see. "Where's Robert?"

"He's okay, Grace. He and Lem are both okay. They've stayed behind to sift through the mess and figure out what happened. Oh, this is going to make the news tomorrow, that's for sure."

"The news?"

"Yes. Your name is going to plastered all over the papers tomorrow, I'm afraid. Everyone will know that you and Robert are married, and that the police came to speak to you about Mrs. Deovolente. It's going to bring up questions…questions about Mr. Branke, and Erica, and even Janice—your dad is going to be fighting off the reporters all wanting to speak to you."

The car was moving smoothly on the road, no alteration in the drive, no sharp turns, no turns at all. "Where are we going?"

"Robert told me to take you to Graham and Lark."

"You know how to find them?"

Silence was my answer for a time, and then the strange, hardened voice that had so often taken over Stacy's usual cheerfulness replied, "She'll find us."

Of course she would. Stacy would only have to call out to Lark and she would respond. We drove on, the quiet filling up time and leaving my mind to wallow in the fuzziness of it all. I was bound to die soon—but obviously not soon enough. Not soon enough for someone.

Who would benefit from my death? What would my death coming days, weeks before it was intended allow for? Death was death, no matter when it happened. The cost of it was endless to those who would be left behind, but if it was meant to occur, then what would rushing it bring?

A sudden jerk and a sharp pulling of the car to the left happened moments before my body slammed to the right, crashing into the door.

"Hold on, Grace," Stacy shrieked, the jerky push pull movement of the car following what I could only assume followed her turning of the wheel, the frantic sound of the engine revving, speed a physical thing that I felt in my sinking into the seat.

"What's going on?" I asked, my hand desperate in its search of something to hold on to even as my eyes struggled against the gray haze that still blocked my sight.

"We're being chased—God!" The screeching of tires, and my body being thrown forward and then back, Stacy's firm hand pressing down on my chest, followed her outcry.

"I'm beginning to really hate these angels," I heard her mutter before I heard the tires fire up against the asphalt, the smell of rubber turning to carbon filling up the interior and stirring a wave of nausea within me. We were flung forward by the release of the brake, and Stacy's whoops and hollers of glee as we sped along the road seemed to echo around us, past us.

I could see blues. Deep, midnight blues as slowly, fraction by minute fraction, spots of gray disappeared. In my head, I could hear wicked laughter. It seemed to exist behind me, and then beside me, and finally above me.

"Stacy, look out!" I shouted, my hand reaching out and grabbing her, pulling her even as the sound of tearing, unbelievable shredding of metal and fabric drowned out my warning.

The car swerved once more, and the gritty, rough surface of something that wasn't the road rumbled beneath us as we were tossed by the driverless steering. I didn't need to see to know that the danger had missed Stacy by inches but had not given up.

"I will not be scared away by you," I heard her growl as she pulled away from me and the car found itself back on the road and in a spin that sent me crashing into the door once more. "I'm not afraid of some goddamn bird," Stacy hissed.

"Hold on, Grace," she ordered, the sound of her foot slamming down onto the gas following her command. I could do nothing but, and as pieces of the picture before me began to form, I was once again thrown forward at the scream of tires grinding to a halt, my body this time prevented from being launched completely out of my seat by the tug-snap of the seatbelt across my chest.

"Hah!" I heard Stacy cheer triumphantly. "Three years of hospital video game duck hunting, you feathered freak!"

There was fire in Stacy's voice, frustration that she directed onto whoever it was she sneered at, her voice so undeniably angry that I could picture the twist in her mouth, and the slant of her brows as she glared at our attacker.

"Come on! Why are you just standing there? Never thought one of my kind would fight back, did you? I'm not afraid of you—I've seen the worst of your kind and I've lived to tell about it so come on!" She was slamming her hand on the steering wheel, the hollow sound of the each blow pinging in my head. How strange this sounded.

A ticking, clicking, growling sound, like the bubbly effervescent warning of a crocodile floated toward us. The blues now included greens and white, and I stared ahead through the spider web cracked windshield that distorted, but did not hide, the figure that stood in front of us, white wings extended outward, honey colored hair draping smoothly over a feminine shoulder.

"Isis," I whispered.

"Who?"

"The angel—her name is Isis."

"Strange name for an ugly little vulture," Stacy cackled.

Isis heard this, heard the insult, and charged, her feet leaving the ground while her body sailed toward us, her wings razor sharp with their intent.

"Oh God," I breathed. "Oh God, oh God, oh God."

I saw the red fury in her eyes, and felt my body pulled, yanked with such a force that I was sure I'd left my soul behind as the car— Robert's car—was torn, bit by bit, sliced with the angry tossing of Isis' wings. A strong arm was gathered beneath mine, and my feet hung above the dirt below. I looked up and saw Lark's eyes staring straight ahead, her wings shaking with emotion. I turned my head and saw Stacy emerge from the ground across from the car, her hands embracing the dirt beneath her, her body hunched over, ready to spring into motion with just the slightest provocation.

*Stacy!*

The thought shot out like a bullet. But it wasn't mine—I hadn't fired.

Stacy's head ticked up, her focus distracted for just a second to acknowledge us, to see that I was alright.

Ice filled me and my blood turned to slush when the white-winged figure emerged from the car, the vehicle flying away from her in feeble pieces. Stacy leapt. Her body was lithe, her face grotesque with dogged determination. She swung her arm and it landed solidly, like a steel beam to a wooden dowel, against the angel's wing, snapping it.

I bit back my foul cry of horror. Stacy had discovered the angel's weak point, and the cry of pain that left Isis aimed itself directly for my already sensitive ears, roaring past them and into my head like a cannon of acid. I writhed in Lark's arms, believing that I'd surely go mad if the sound, the audible torture, did not stop. But it didn't. On and on, it continued, leeching from me every ounce of energy, and when all of it had gone, it borrowed from some unseen source, taking everything until surely there was nothing left.

"Stay with me, Grace," I heard Lark plead. "Fight it, fight the pain."

With what? How did one fight the endless battle without a single weapon at her disposal? And this…this was more than pain. This was beyond what even pain could cause. I felt like a flower being torn from its stem, the violent pluck of each petal a stabbing to my mind.

Outside my suffering, the conception of an argument made itself known.

"Hand her to me."

"I can't. She's my responsibility."

"Your responsibility? Where have you been besides mating with your human lover? You've ignored your call for earthly pleasures Lark—

you have not changed at all from the girl who fumbled through the sky with that disreputable Luca." There was contempt there, in that voice that I knew.

"Do not compare me to that girl I was so long ago, Llehmai—she knew not what was important."

"And you know now, do you? Your brother fights to keep this child alive, at the risk of his own life, and you in turn spend your nights lying in your human's arms without care or concern as to what happens to either of them."

"I care!"

"Then prove it! Hand her to me and help your friend—Isis will destroy her if you do not."

Uncertainty caused tension, and tension caused stiffness that turned strength into weakness. There was a weakness in me for my friends, and this same weakness existed in Lark, who could hear just as I could the shift in the battle that took place within hearing distance. Stacy was strong, but she did not have an unlimited amount of energy—she required to feed; Isis did not.

"Stacy needs you," I moaned. The sound of my words filled the jelly in my head. Isis' shrieks of pain had died down, her attention now focused not on her injured wing but on the noticeable slowing of Stacy's movements. I didn't need to see this to know it, to feel it.

"Take her," Lark finally relented, passing me into welcoming arms before leaving, the swirl of air that followed her tickling my nostrils and reminding me of her goodness, despite what Lem had said.

"I'll keep you safe, Grace," I heard said to me. "I won't let anything happen to you."

We were floating—surely we were floating—when I felt soft lips press against my forehead.

"You…promised."

A laugh that was barely a sound pushed past my consciousness and into my mind. "I promised to keep things platonic in the yard and in the house. You said nothing about in the sky."

I groaned inwardly at my own naiveté, but there was nothing for it. It was a chaste kiss, after all, and I had done nothing to encourage it, but that did nothing to ease my guilt. It must have been noticeable because a sigh passed over my head, brushing aside the hair on my face that had not been swept away by the air as we traveled.

"It wasn't your fault. I just like being near you—allow me that for these precious few moments, please."

What choice did I have? Besides, I had much more important things to worry about—like my friends.

And Robert.

"Where is he?"

"N'Uriel is with his mother—there is much to be done now that their sanctuary has been breached."

Of course. The bright white light, the sucking in of everything around it, the explosion of it all; something—or someone—had violated Robert's room. Entered it without his permission.

"What's going to happen?"

"The fire department and the police are already at the ruins of the house. They've begun a search for you."

My blood, still thick and slow in my veins, simply stopped flowing at his words. "They think I'm dead, don't they?"

I didn't need to see the nod to know that it existed. "My dad—will you tell him the truth? Will Robert tell him the truth, that I'm okay and with you?"

"Ameila is there-"

That wasn't an answer. I frowned and turned my head up to look at him. "Will my dad know that I'm okay? Will they tell him that I'm fine?"

He again repeated his three word reply, "Ameila is there."

Ameila was there, and I wasn't. The police and fire department were looking for me in the rubble of the once beautiful Bellegarde home that sat, guarded by two ironic angel statues. They were searching for me but wouldn't find me because I was here, with Lem. I was here, and they were there, and so was Ameila.

Ameila…

"Oh God, no!" I cried when the hammer of comprehension finally struck. "She can't!"

Ameila was there. But she wasn't there as herself. She was there as me, taking on my form—probably battered, destroyed utterly by the ravages of heat and weight. The police would see—the fire department would see.

My dad…would see.

"Take me back! You can't do that to my dad! You can't do that to him—please!" I sobbed. I writhed and twisted to have him let me go. I begged him to turn around, made promises I shouldn't have in exchange for it, but he held firm and repeated his remorse over the entire affair and maintained that it was for the best.

How could I do this to him? How could any of them do this to him? We had time. We had time and now it was gone, and my dad would be left to mourn when I was still here. He would be left to grieve, and I could not comfort him. I could not tell him that everything was okay, that I wasn't dead—not yet.

"It is already too late," Lem said solemnly, his arms bringing me to him even closer, pinning my arms down at my sides and imprisoning me as my body shook with grief.

Grace Anne Shelley died tonight.

## AT ODDS

I'm dead.

Grace doesn't exist anymore. Who she was, what she did, what she learned, who her friends were—everything that made her who she is was now inconsequential.

Lem had found a place for me to rest, leaning me up against a tree near a fenced-in community garden that was lit up with Christmas lights. The smell of soil and fertilizer burned my nose, and I blamed that for the blurry view my eyes afforded me.

"Grace, can I get you something? Something to eat? Water?"

Eat? Drink? What was that? Why did I need to do that? What would it accomplish? Would eating comfort my father? Would it console my brother, whose tiny cries I could still hear in my head? Would it somehow dull the pain that continued to roll through my mind, tainting every cell with guilt and grief and anger? Of course not. There was nothing that would ease my suffering. I didn't want it to.

"Do you want to talk?" He took a hold of my hand and held it against his heart, the strong, steady rhythm of it an attempt to calm me. All it did was remind me that someone I loved more than my own life believed that my own heart no longer beat.

"Would it make you feel better if I talked? I'll tell you whatever you want to know—ask me anything."

Why? He wouldn't give me the answer I wanted. It was a waste of time to ask. It was a waste of time to breathe.

The sun had risen and was hanging high above us when Robert finally arrived at our location, the onlookers who had come to work in the garden unable to stop staring at the two beautiful creatures who dared to stand and console the woeful lump of a person still curled up against the tree. The silver rings that circled dark centers in Robert's eyes turned from cold and numb to warm and fluid as soon as he saw me. There was no pause, no moment of hesitation on his part—he just took my hand from Lem and held me close to his heart.

His motionless heart.

"I never want to feel like that again," he breathed against my ear. "I never want to see that image again."

His body was shaking, and I wrapped my arms around him to still him, to comfort him, to comfort myself. We were two lone figures surrounded by guilt and loss and blame and endless questions that found no room to separate us. I wasn't letting him go for a second—I wasn't parting from him ever again.

"I'm never—never leaving your side," he whispered harshly, squeezing me even tighter, my breath forced out of my body by his embrace.

"Why? Why did you have to tell my dad that I was dead?" I cried softly.

"They came to our home, Grace," he replied with equal softness. "They dared to come there in search of you. If your father believes you're dead, the safer it'll be for him as well as for you. Doing this bought us time. The whispers of your death have already filled Heath with enough gossip to last for years."

He looked up at Lem and his nostrils flared. "They are also looking for you—they believe you have something to do with Melanie's death. You will have to leave here as well."

"Let me take her, then. You cannot just leave here—it would look suspicious and cast a dark shadow over Grace's life."

Robert shook his head, his hand closing over the back of my head possessively. "She and I will never be apart again."

"How can you fulfill your call if she's always with you? Do you intend on bringing her with you? Do you intend on exposing her to the sights and sounds of the worst kinds of human depravity? Is that what you want for her in her last days?"

"Her days are few and I would rather the world suffer at the hands of evil for a few more days than be without her for another minute."

This was something I couldn't accept. I had already caused way too much hurt and damage, death and…destruction. Hurricane Grace—that should be on my headstone.

I pulled away from him; my head tilting back to look up at his serious face. "Robert, you cannot do that to people. They need you-"

"*I* need *you*," he hissed, cutting me off. "And I'll do whatever it takes to keep you with me for as long as possible."

"Yes, but at what cost?" I said to him, my voice a pitiful sound. "Look at what being together has already taken from us, from other people. If you give up on everything then they win. They win, don't you see that?"

"I can't be away from you anymore," he said, his voice a plea that cracked at my heart, even as it hardened with resolve.

"I don't want to be away from you either—but as much as I say you're mine, you also belong to the world."

Lem's calm, cool voice broke in. "I hate to interrupt, but Grace is right. You cannot put on hold what you're meant to do. The living must die, and their souls must meet their fate. You're the gate keeper and the deliverer of fates, N'Uriel—lives cannot linger when they're not meant to, and souls cannot fester without judgment."

Robert was angry, the truth in Lem's words shattering what hope he'd saved for himself, the hope that we could indeed be with each other without separation. He was always filled with hope, but I had remained cynical and it did not fail me this time. There was no disappointment when he finally nodded in acquiescence. We would part again.

But not now.

Now, I would not let him go for anything. Now was when I needed him the most. "I'm not leaving," he said to me, his thoughts echoing his voice.

"Then don't," I said, my voice challenging, wanting him to prove it. Needing him to prove it. My very life depended on it.

"Well, when it *is* time for you to go, let me know," Lem said with a bored sigh. "But do stay out of trouble—I might not be around the next time your lives are in danger."

"Thank you," Robert ground out, his teeth gnashed together, his lips barely parted.

"Thank you, Lem. For everything," I said to him.

"Anytime," he returned. "I mean that."

"I know."

"Goodbye, Llehmai," Robert said coldly at the departing shadow.

And we were alone. "What happens now?" I asked, wanting to hear from his own lips the truth.

"We have to prepare to leave. When the truth that you survived the implosion spreads, there will be no rest for us. It will be constant, our moving about."

"I can't leave! I can't leave my dad thinking that I'm dead. I sat through a fake funeral—I saw what Stacy's death did to her parents. She did, too! I can't do that to my dad, Robert! I won't!"

"Grace, we have no choice—it's already done."

There were things happening to me, angry, violent things that shook me at the finality in his tone. "No! I'm going—I'm going to tell him myself."

"And then what? What do you think that will accomplish? He knew this time was coming, Grace. Whether it happened now or later, he knew. Telling him that you're not dead will only make the reality of your death much more difficult for him to accept when it finally happens. How will he be able to grieve for you? How will he be able to move on and care for Matthew and Janice if he's filled with some false notion that you'll come back? Do you really want to set him up for that? Give him a false sense of hope?"

It didn't matter what he said to me. I wasn't going to let my dad believe that I was gone. It wasn't right, it wasn't fair, and it wasn't something that I would do.

"Where are we?"

"We're about fifty miles out of Heath."

"Take me back—take me to see my father, Robert."

"Grace, I can't-"

"You mean you won't."

"Yes, that too, but I can't let you go back there. You have to understand how much danger you are in."

He held my arms, pinning them to my sides, as though that alone would be enough to convince me, to force me to concede. His eyes were filled with sadness, but there was no guilt. As short-lived as it was, I despised him in that moment for that.

"I can't do anything *but* understand," I said, my voice low, my eyes averting his gaze.

"I know this is hard, Grace."

"You don't know anything."

"Please…don't be angry with me over this. I don't want us to spend what little time we have left at odds with each other."

When he pulled me toward him, my face resting against the dip in his chest, I didn't struggle. I didn't have the mental space to even try. I was too busy thinking about what it was going to take to see my father again.

The first thing I needed to do was speak to him—he'd hear my voice and he'd know I was alright. He was my dad. He'd know even without hearing my voice that I wasn't dead—he'd know just like Sean knew that Stacy was alive.

"Stacy was fighting with Isis when Lark and Lem showed up. Lark left me to help her."

"Isis chose the wrong person to attack. Even as a human, Stacy was fierce and determined. With everything that her…change has given her, Stacy is a formidable opponent for anyone of my kind."

This was surprising news to me. "What do you mean?"

"She's faster now, obviously, as well as stronger. Her years of training, her knowledge of self-defense and attack—her mind is now sharper and she can utilize everything she's learned much faster, more precisely."

"But Isis can read Stacy's mind—she'd be able to see what Stacy's going to do before she does it."

Robert rested his chin atop my head, and I felt his disagreement. "Stacy's reactions will be completely automatic, defensive, split-second actions that Isis wouldn't be able to keep up with if she could even make them out to begin with. Stacy doesn't think in English."

"What?"

"She doesn't think in English. It's quite normal, actually, for one's thoughts in their head to be in the language that they first learn. They don't realize it, of course, because their thoughts are their own, in their own voice."

"So why wouldn't Isis be able to understand her?"

"Because Isis is like most of living creatures on this planet, divine or otherwise: she's a creature of her environment. She has existed among those who've only spoken one language. Every thought, every notion, every word has been in English, and if it were spoken in anything else it was simply unimportant. It wouldn't take much of an effort for her to learn how to speak another language, but Isis is good for only one thing: destruction. She's not capable of building, of creating, especially knowledge."

"But you understand?"

"Of course. When my mother created me, every ounce of knowledge she possessed was passed into me. What she did not know, I learned, and I continue to do so every day. If I didn't, I'd never have believed it possible to love someone as much as I do you."

"Just not enough to let me see my father," I muttered beneath my breath.

"Grace…"

"How did you feel, Robert, when you learned your mother and your sister believed you had died? How did you feel when you learned that I thought you were gone?"

"It devastated me—my first priority was to reassure you that I was fine, but-"

I cut him off. "You couldn't stay away—why should I?"

He opened his mouth, I felt it. And then it closed, slowly, the pressure atop my head easing. There was a struggle, an inner struggle that I could sense within him.

"Okay."

I pulled my head away to look up at him. "You mean it?"

"Yes. *But*, not now."

"When?" I was urgent, insistent.

"After everything is finalized."

"So, in a day or two?"

"Yes. But it will happen when I say, Grace. I can't let emotion win out on this one—too much is at stake already."

I didn't care if it happened at the snap of his fingers; my father was going to know the truth. But even the knowledge that all that was done wrong would be righted, the fact was that right now, Dad was in pain. He thought I was dead, and there was no one there to comfort him, no one there to make sure that he was eating, that Matthew was being cared for, no one there to make sure that…that he didn't give up.

"Thank you."

"I wish it was more. I hate only being able to give you these tid-bits of promises, Grace."

"It's better than nothing." I tried smiling at him, but it was difficult, even after getting what I wanted. "What's going to happen to Isis?"

"Isis is dead."

272

It was like lightning shot down my spine. "Dead?"

"Yes. Lark and Stacy make a very…efficient team."

"They always did," I said, my smile finally finding its completion.

Something in the back of my head started tap-tap-tapping, an annoying and persistent hint of something that I could not remember. I frowned at the blank screen that kept popping up at each turn, my search for the answer a dead end. "Why can't I remember?"

"Remember what?"

"If I could tell you that, there wouldn't be a problem," I said with mild irritation in my voice. "Look, never mind that right now. Where's Stacy and Lark? What's going to happen to them?"

"They're headed here, to meet us. Stacy is going to travel with us, while Graham and Lark will remain behind."

"You're actually allowing Stacy to come with us?"

"I have no choice. There is no one else who is capable of being with you who desires that you remain alive as much as I do."

I contradicted him. "Lem doesn't want me to die."

"You remaining alive isn't the only thing Lem desires, Grace."

My cheeks burned at the comment. "He has feelings for me, but only because I remind him of my mom."

"You don't remind him of your mother, Grace. He sees in you the same thing I do: someone who loves without question, who is generous and kind, who's forgiving, and who is as stubborn as a donkey in cement. He also sees that you love me, far more than I deserve, and he wants that. All angels do. It's just he wants the feeling—I want the person it comes from."

"But it won't matter soon, will it? It won't matter what either of you two want." There was a hopelessness to my voice that disturbed even me. "It won't matter what any of us want. It's as though even my choices are now being denied to me. It's like they have all along."

"Stacy and Lark will be here very shortly; Graham, too."

The change in subject once more was a welcomed one, and I

sighed away my doubts and my fears, my hurt and my sorrow. "And then what?"

"They'll take you to another home we own, a smaller, unassuming place. I'm going to return to your father. I'll only be gone for a few hours."

"You're not going to tell him that I'm still alive, are you?"

He shook his head. "Not until we're ready to leave."

"So...two days, right?"

"Yes, two days."

Two days. Dad would think I was dead for two days. Would that be long enough to accept it? Would that be long enough for him to doubt anything else he hears after that?

"Is he angry? At you?"

My questions seemed to burden Robert, and I saw that my dad was indeed angry. "He blames me. He isn't wrong. Isis would have never known to find you at our home if I had not brought her there."

The beast that is guilt returned to take another large chunk out of me. "It's my fault. You thought I was at my dad's house. I was the one who walked out on you—I shouldn't have shown up there, dressed...wearing what I was. I'm sure if I had been Isis, and I'd seen that, I'd have been quite pissed off, too."

Robert chuckled, a soft, deep sound in his throat that, despite everything that had happened in the past two days, made me feel warm and bubbly inside. "I do not regret for one moment seeing you in that red outfit. And, I will make you promise me that when we're gone from here, that you will put it on again for me."

My eyes bulged in surprise and embarrassment. "You still have it?"

He nodded, almost a bit too enthusiastically. "It's in my trunk."

"But the trunk was in the house..."

"In my room."

"Yes, but-"

He sighed and rubbed my temple with his thumb before pressing a warm kiss there. "You remember what I said, Grace? About sanctuary?"

"Nothing goes in or out unless you want it to."

"Exactly. Nothing in that room was touched. Nothing. Isis wanted to get in—she couldn't. The house was nothing—it meant nothing. Everything that matters to me was either inside or outside with me. You are the most precious thing in this life to me, and even if everything in that room had been destroyed, you weren't."

"I couldn't see or hear much of anything," I admitted. "I couldn't see anything at all, actually. And everything hurt—but I think I'm getting pretty good at dealing with that by now."

He grumbled, and I shrugged, unable to change those facts for him. "It's the truth, whether we like it or not."

"I don't like it."

Without skipping a beat, I asked, "What did the police and firemen say when they saw that the entire house was destroyed except for one room?"

"They said nothing. Lem filled their heads with what we wanted them to know, leaving them to believe that the room had been the furthest point from the blast origination. It was easy to make them see what we wanted them to see."

Including me dead. "Why did Ameila help you? More importantly, why did you let her?"

This touched on a difficult subject, and he paused for too long. "Did you ask for it?"

"No. She arrived as Stacy was leaving with you. Stacy was given explicit instructions to make sure that no one saw you and to drive until Lark found her. She knew Isis was after you—she knew what she had to do to keep you safe and she was willing to do it."

"And Ameila?"

"My mother did what she always does. She brings closure to those who need it."

"And did she bring closure to you?"

He shook his head. "I cannot forgive her for toying with us the way she has. Her meddling and her scheming have cost you greatly. You did not deserve to be thrust into this life with us. Had we never met, our calls might have never come, and you'd have been free to live your life without fear."

"Until Sam found me," I said softly.

"He would have never done that because there would have been no reason to—I wouldn't have loved you."

I looked at him with sad eyes, and saw deep in those slate rings something that I never wanted to see. It was as though all of his thoughts were there, admitting to me the truth. He regretted coming to Heath. He regretted seeing me. He regretted all of this.

My mind was closed to him, and he knew it. He didn't ask me why, he didn't ask me for entry. And for that I was glad, for now, all he could feel was my pain, and would likely attribute it to my father's grief. How grateful I was to that then, the strange falseness of my death. Without it, I wouldn't have been able to cry without telling him the real reason for it. This way, he was allowed to keep his secret, and I was allowed to feel the guilt of it.

## HOSTILE ENVIRONMENT

The "unassuming" house turned out to be one in a neighborhood similar to my own. The homes were identical for the most part, though much, much older in appearance and wear, each one facing its virtual twin across the street, the only differences being color and layout. The yards were all manicured here, and there were no cars parked out in the driveway. It was tidy, well kept, and left me feeling nervous as we approached the front door like a couple of door-to-door salespeople.

Robert pretended to pull out a key, but the door opened without it, Lark standing behind it with a relieved look on her face. "It's about time you guys got here," she croaked.

"What's wrong?" Robert asked as he ushered me inside, away from the prying eyes of the neighbor across the street.

"Mrs. Culpepper two houses down has been here three times already. She keeps asking me if we're having a house party, and if we are, does our mom know about it. She is so nosy!"

An indelicate sound escaped me at the tone of Lark's voice. It was easy to forget that she was over five centuries old when she whined like the teenager she pretended to be.

"Who's the woman across the street?" I asked, my eyes darting toward the window and seeing that the curtain was drawn open, leaving the living room in full view of the curious stare that I could almost feel directly across from me.

"That's Mrs. Lorimax. If Mrs. Culpepper's nosy, Mrs. Lorimax is the queen of gossip. She's constantly filling everyone's ears with stories about us. Most of them true, of course—we do come in at all hours of the night, we're quiet, we're strangely free from discipline—but it's when she comes over and starts asking questions that I become really annoyed. This entire block needs a hobby, I think."

The curtain across the street closed, and I waited, and grimaced when sure enough, the sound of a door closing, followed by the slow slide of feet across pavement greeted my ears just a few moments before the doorbell rang, a loud, hollow peal that echoed in the small house. Lark groaned, but still walked toward the door and opened it, a false smile plastered on her face, her gaze staring straight ahead blankly.

"Hello Mrs. Lorimax," she said with little enthusiasm.

"W-well, hello Lark," the old woman said with a hint of surprise in her voice. "I didn't realize you'd know who it was—you being blind and all."

Up close, the older woman looked almost ancient. Her skin was covered in fine wrinkles that reminded me of crepe paper. The lines around her eyes and mouth were deeper, turning into veritable canyons whenever she smiled, and even her smile was false in its meaning. Her eyes were a pale color, almost an aquamarine shade that had the inclusions of white cataracts, and her hair was a strange shade of…lilac?

"Mrs. Lorimax, I told you the last time, I'd know you anywhere; that perfume you wear is unique and you're the only person I know who wears it," Lark explained through gritted teeth, her smile never faltering.

The old woman wasn't buying it. "Someone must have told you I was coming. Was it you, Robert? Did you give me away?"

"No, ma'am. Lark is correct—your perfume is one that I can only place on you. It smells like it was made specifically to suit your particular chemistry." At the compliment—was it a compliment?—the woman's smile changed, turning from a rather empty sort of expression to one that was practically beaming.

"You always did know what to say to make a woman feel better, Robert. How lucky your mother is to have a son such as yourself." She finally shifted her focus onto me, as though only now realizing that I was in the room, and her eyes grew beady. "And who are you?"

"I-I"

I didn't know what to tell her. Did I reveal myself to be Robert's wife? His girlfriend? His soon to be next victim?

"This is Grace, Mrs. Lorimax," Robert answered for me.

"Grace, huh? That girl you've been dating? So you've finally decided to bring her around, have you? Too ashamed of where you live or something, Robert? We might be old, but we're still people you know," she chastised before approaching me, walking right past an indignant Lark and taking my hand, patting it with a cold, vein covered hand that looked more like a claw than anything else.

"You are a pretty little thing—odd looking one way, fetching another—and you're all Robert here ever seems to talk about. You're not put off by where he lives, are you? No, you wouldn't be. I don't believe that Robert would ever date someone who cared about things like that."

I looked at Robert's face and saw his sheepish smile, and I suddenly felt quite amused by this. How many times had I felt slightly awkward about my own home and its shabby condition compared to Robert's impressive white colonial? To now be the one on the other end of the stick was different. I couldn't let this Mrs. Lorimax believe that I cared about such things, though.

"I think this house is charming, Mrs. Lorimax. It actually looks a lot like my own," I said to her.

"That's what I thought. Now then, what's the occasion?"

"Excuse me?"

Her hand motioned between Robert and me, going back and forth as though the answer was obvious. "You're here—there has to be some kind of reason."

Sure. Angels are trying to kill me, they just blew up Robert's other house, and we keep getting interrupted before we can have sex.

Robert began coughing, his eyes bulging out, and I felt my face turn red; he had heard my thoughts; my mind was open again.

"I'm here for dinner, Mrs. Lorimax." It was as close to the truth as I could get, and even that was far from it, the guilt that weighed on me from the lie pulling down my smile a notch or two. Luckily, this went unnoticed by the old woman who nodded and began to trod toward the door.

"If you have time, do stop over before you leave," she called out as she walked past Lark, who still held the door open, an impatient frown on her face now having replaced the phony smile. "I want to give you something."

"Mm-okay," I replied, watching her disappear behind the quickly closed door.

"Don't go over there," Lark hissed as soon as she knew Mrs. Lorimax was out of earshot.

"Why?"

"Because when she's got you alone and to herself, she's going start interrogating you like you're a suspect in a presidential assassination plot or something, and you might never leave."

I laughed at this, but Lark didn't seem all that amused. "It's not funny," she grumbled. "She's a holy terror. I hope Stacy comes when it's dark, otherwise Mrs. Lorimax will see her and turn us all in to the CDC."

"You're joking, right?"

Lark's face was as serious as a bleak streak, and I tucked my lips into my mouth to keep my giggle from slipping out.

"I'm not joking. She called the police just two weeks ago when Graham and I were a little too…loud. Graham had to wrap himself in my sheet when the cops burst in—I was so…focused on what we were doing that I didn't even hear them until they were at the bottom of the stairs.

"Mrs. Lorimax told them that he was assaulting me, that he was committing statutory rape! I was very tempted to tell all of them that I'm the older one, and that I was technically robbing the ovary but I didn't. She seemed to think that because I was making so much noise

280

that something was wrong."

Robert's head buried itself into his hand as he shook with unspent laughter. I pressed down on my teeth, biting back my own little outburst. Lark's face went slack when she realized she wasn't going to be getting any sympathy from us.

"Well, Graham should be back any minute now with groceries. I gave him a list, so hopefully he sticks to it."

My lips made a funny, wrinkled line as I tried to imagine Graham grocery shopping. It seemed fairly likely that he'd return with dozens of bags of pretzels and cheese dip instead of vegetables and chicken.

"He's gotten very good at it," Lark interrupted. "Don't discount him just because in the past he's been irresponsible. A lot has changed in him."

"Okay," I said, suddenly feeling tired. "Can I lie down somewhere?"

"Yes, follow me," Robert said before pulling me up the stairs and down a short, narrow hallway. We reached a closed door at the end of the hall, and Robert opened it, leading me into a room that was nearly identical to my old one in its layout, with the exception of the bed—it was larger than the twin I had.

I needed no further invitation and collapsed onto the bed, my head hitting the soft pillows beneath the snow white comforter that covered every inch of it except for the headboard. It wasn't like Robert's other bed, with its pictures of the two of us. This one was plain, almost like the types of beds you bought at the hardware store. I didn't care, though.

My lids were heavy, and my body fatigued. I watched as Robert removed his shirt, laying it across the dresser that faced the foot of the bed, before climbing into the bed beside me, pulling me against him so that my back was pressed up against his abdomen. His cheek rested against my temple, and I sighed with contentment.

It was short-lived, however. The sound of a car arriving, followed by doors slamming, voices booming, and things being jostled around downstairs tore Robert away from me, his eyes focused as his thoughts left a warning in my own. *Stay here until I return.*

I nodded, sitting up and staring after him as he disappeared behind the door, the sound of his movements nonexistent. Violence. That was all I could hear downstairs. Unchecked violence. Three times I was tempted to run downstairs, my worry over Robert and Lark overshadowing any fear I might have had for myself. Each time, a little voice in my head told me to relax, that everything was fine. It had to be fine—who could harm Robert?

The afternoon sun was beating down fiercely through the window, turning the bed unnaturally warm as I waited. Finally, Robert returned, his face bearing a satisfied smile. "Come, there's someone I'd like you to meet."

"Meet? What?" I was confused. More than that, I was annoyed.

"It's alright. It was a misunderstanding. Graham arrived just as he did…you'll understand when you come down."

Despite my doubts, I followed Robert out of the room and down the stairs. Graham was there, busily picking up scattered vegetables and canned goods, while Lark stared angrily. Beside her was a boy. He looked to be no more than ten, a beautiful, red-haired boy with slightly pink cheeks and a rather plump looking mouth.

I bent down to shake his hand when a sort of shiver passed over him, his body blurring before my eyes like ripples over water, and the little boy disappeared, replaced by a man with a rather haunting smile that filled his dark lips and white, sharp teeth. His skin was evanescent, transparent one minute and opaque the next, the effect of it unnerving, and I felt myself take several steps back until Robert's chest blocked my way; he was a wall again.

"Grace, this is Raphael."

There was no further need for explanation or introduction. Looking at him, at the pale gray eyes that flickered and vanished before reappearing again, I knew who he was. His thoughts ran like water all around me, and I drank them in like a wanderer dying of thirst.

He was Raphael, the second angel, the one who healed. He was older than my concept of time could allow and knew the secrets of the world; he knew my secrets, and he smiled at me, a knowing smile that told me he would not share them. I smiled back, feeling as though that simple act had bonded him to me somehow, a friend I didn't know I needed until he lifted a wispy hand to my forehead and placed his palm there, the almost imperceptible contact hitting me like no hit and run driver could.

It was jarring, the feeling of his strength. Though he looked short of substance, he contained within him such an immense power that there was no pretending it didn't exist. It was like being swallowed up by light and still seeing something brighter up ahead. How that was possible, I don't know, but my eyes remained open to what was coming. I saw flashes of faces, pale and inverted in my mind, and images of places that I'd never seen before. There were voices that were foreign, and languages that turned into a symphony of thought that expressed every emotion, every nuance of feeling.

And like a movie beginning to play, I saw the events that had occurred before I had descended the stairs. Graham had arrived with groceries in hand, anxious and proud that he'd done everything in so short a time. He expected to be greeted by an equally pleased Lark, and instead, saw her in the arms of someone else, someone who was striking, tall, and beautiful who held her far too familiarly for his liking. Graham was overcome with the feeling of protection, laced with jealousy and envy all in the same broad stroke and in typical human fashion, lunged toward the perceived threat.

But Raphael was far more attuned to the human emotions of Graham than Graham was to his own, and so simply dissipated into a thin veil of mist, leaving Graham to continue forward, his momentum pushing him toward the short wall that faced the stairs. He crashed into it, stunned and even more enraged. The groceries now scattered on the ground, forgotten. Graham charged once more, his football days coming back to him, only this time he wasn't the quarterback.

Lark was stunned, too stunned to act in time as Graham's arms swung around and then through Raphael's body, the motion causing him to twist around and land on the coffee table, effectively shattering it into dozens of splintered pieces across the living room floor, the wooden surface now dented by the force and weight. Robert appeared and took a hold of Graham before he could launch himself into yet another failed attack, but Graham's voice couldn't be contained, and he threw out epithets that were so unlike him I felt myself gasp, an echo of the one that was emitted by Lark.

Their voices were thoughts in my head, so the sound was richer, the tone giving them more power, more feeling.

"What are you doing?" Lark asked with a mixture of fear and annoyance in her voice. "Since when do you go around attacking people like some kind of animal?"

"He was touching you!" Graham bit back.

"He was hugging me, you idiot!"

"He wasn't just hugging you!"

Behind him, Robert chuckled, amusement at the scene obviously taking precedence to any concern. "You humans are so quick to pass judgment; you refuse to see what's plain before you even when it's pointed out."

"What's there to see?" Graham argued, his chest rising and falling rapidly with building anger.

Robert's eyebrows rose at that question, the answer so obvious that it was almost comical. Graham, finally taking the time to look at Raphael, turned red as he took in the onyx colored hair, the pale gray eyes, and the stubborn chin that was echoed in both Lark and Robert. "Whoa."

"Yes. Whoa is correct. Whoa is definitely appropriate in this instance."

Feeling comfortable with releasing Graham, Robert backed away and watched as Lark approached her husband with mild irritation now skimming the surface of the smile she gave him. "This is my grandfather. He is my mother's father."

"Your…grandfather? But he looks…he looks so young!"

Lark and Robert both looked at each other and their thoughts were clear. *He still sees age as an appearance.*

Raphael turned to Graham and shook his head at his grandchildren's silent words. His mouth opened, but nothing came out. Instead, a wave of thoughts traveled between Graham's green-eyed gaze and the angel's light silver one.

*Your choice in vocabulary is surprising. I would have thought that my granddaughter would be interested in someone with a far larger vocabulary than what you possess. She loves you, despite your flaws, and that is enough for me to not want to see any harm come to you. Be at ease. We are family.*

Graham mumbled a thank you and then began the task of cleaning up the mess he had caused. Raphael turned to Robert and one thought flowed between them.

*Bring me your wife.*

***

When Raphael released my mind, when he backed away and smiled at me, it was with understanding and acceptance. He held his hand out to me, but I backed away, afraid that it would disappear into nothing, much as he had with Graham. My thoughts gave me away again, and he simply reached for what he wanted, taking my hand in his and holding it against his heart like a shield. The intense rush of everything that lay in his head bombarded me, making my knees quake, my heart race in my chest as though it were beating for its very own life.

*You are Avi's child.*

I nodded. There seemed to be no point in answering in any other way.

*You look so much like her. You have her spirit, her will, her heart.*

*She was proud of you. She put into you so much of what was right about her, and I can see that her investment has yielded much. N'Uriel has chosen you, and you have chosen him in return, despite knowing what price such a union will exact. You love him that deeply.*

Again, I nodded. In any other circumstance, it would have meant nothing. But here, with this regal angel standing before me, one whose name I'd known even before I'd met Robert, this response told him everything.

*Then you have my blessing. I will strive to aid you in any way that I can.*

I blinked, surprised by this. What did he mean by aid? But he was gone, vanished into a mist so fine, I only saw it in the remnants of sunlight as it streamed through the window.

"There will be trouble now," Lark groaned as Graham finished putting away the last of the fallen groceries.

"Trouble? What kind of trouble? What do you mean trouble?" he asked, a can of tomato sauce in one hand, a stalk of celery in the other.

"She means that Raphael has never taken a stance on something like this before. The seraphim have always ruled without voice from the oldest. Raphael, Michael, Uriel, and Gabriel, the four fathers of our kind have remained silent since the flood. Everything that mankind has done since then, they've done without interference from them. And yet now, one of them is taking an interest in you—and it is not because you're married to me," Robert said with slow words.

"Then why?" I asked.

"Do you even need to ask?"

Four heads whipped around to see Stacy coming down the stairs, her hands holding onto a towel that she rubbed over her hair. "Your mom was a freaking angel. She conceived you the old fashioned way—with magic and crap—but you were raised like any other girl here in Heath, and now you're married to Mr. Doom and Gloom over there, who's supposed to kill you, and you're okay with all of it. What kind of sane person, angel or otherwise, would do that? This is basically one long, drawn out suicide."

"That was uncalled for," Robert growled.

"No. No, what's uncalled for is Grace being attacked by one of *your* kind. How many times does she have to come close to dying before you realize that?"

My dark angel moved up against Stacy, his body rigid as his rancorous words oozed past his lips into the air. "*Your* kind are the ones who've been ravaging parts of this world, creating havoc in places that have known only calm for centuries. *Your* kind have been nothing but a plague. And seeing what they've done within the past few months alone proves to me that you're all dangerous."

Stacy, unmoved, smirked. "My kind might be dangerous, but I've never tried to kill Grace. You have."

Everyone seemed to move in slow motion: Robert, his wings bursting through his flesh like a dark rose blooming beneath the moon; Stacy, her feet planting firmly onto the floor as her eyes changed from brown to pitch black with flecks of red; Lark, her silky slide through the space between all of us forcing a wedge between her brother and Stacy; Graham, his hands reaching for my shoulders, an attempt to pull me away; and myself, faster than any of them, my body twisting away from hand after hand, until I stood in front of Stacy, ready to protect her with my life if necessary, already shivering as the temperature in the room dropped by several degrees.

"Stop!" I pleaded, my voice mirroring my thoughts as I stared at the hardened steel in Robert's eyes.

"It's okay, Grace," Stacy said with bland encouragement. "He's right. My kind *have* been creating problems elsewhere. I mean, if he wants to judge all of us because of the actions of a few, then he should be willing to be judged himself.

"I mean, it *was* one of *his* kind that killed your mother, Erica and Mr. Branke, and probably Mrs. Deovolente; not to mention put Janice into a coma. It *was* one of *his* kind that attacked us in the car. But

I'm sure he'd say that it was wrong of me to judge *him* for the actions of others. Isn't that right, Robert?"

A flurry of emotions could be seen running across Robert's face, his eyes widening, narrowing, closing, opening, and finally settling into the one emotion that I knew well. Guilt.

"Yes," he said in a low, defeated voice. "I apologize. It was wrong of me."

Warmth began to flow around us again, and I sighed with relief. "Thank you," I mouthed to him, but he didn't want my gratitude.

"However wrong I am, however many wrongs I have committed today by associating you with the actions of others of your kind, it does not erase the fact that those like you have been attacking humans. Their actions will only lead to their extermination."

"You'd kill all of us?"

Stacy's question hung in the air like a knife frozen in freefall. Robert's grim nod was all she needed to buckle; her strength now ebbed to nothing. "Have I made a mistake then? Have I made the wrong choice? I thought that changing into this…this thing would save my life, but if it means that I'm just going to die by your hand then I'd rather have been killed by Sam."

"You can't be serious, Robert!" Lark's voice was cutting, bitter as she glared at her brother. "Stacy has done nothing wrong. Neither has Ambrose. Neither have countless others who've abided by the laws we've set for them. To kill all of them would be murder—a massacre! You'd allow that to happen?"

I suddenly became aware of how difficult this role of Death was for Robert. When the decisions he had to make pitted him against those he loved, decisions he hated himself, yet felt compelled to make based on his loyalty to his kind, it was torture to his soul. He, who had spent his entire life dreaming of healing, was now planning on killing. No. Not killing.

Murdering.

"I have to go," he said in a rush. "Keep her safe."

His order wasn't directed at Lark. It wasn't even directed at Graham.

His eyes were focused, staring hard at the dark eyes that glared back.

Stacy nodded her head.

# DREAM WEAVER

Dinner was quiet, with Lark staring off into nothing, and Stacy standing by the window in the cramped kitchen. Graham and I stood with sandwiches in our hands; the only two people who needed to eat. The sun had set and the dull yellow light that hung above us acted like a filter over our emotions. Stacy had yet to say a word to Lark; this, despite their battling together to dispatch Isis. I still wanted to know what happened, but did not know how to approach the subject without either of them storming off and leaving.

Graham, still sullen over his attack and subsequent failure, mumbled about bread, meat, and cheese between bites. Lark etched patterns into the table, her fingernail slicing through the wood surface like it was skimming water. I'd tried several times to start conversations, but the silence that met me each time was defeating, and after a while, I simply gave up. It felt hollow, consoling myself with a ham and cheese sandwich in a room filled with people all too upset to speak to each other.

Graham was the first to leave, dusting his hands of crumbs and heading wordlessly up the stairs. Lark soon followed, a petulant look on her face. I stared, speechless. Whatever would happen between the two, I knew it would be equally as silent, and I hoped that whatever problems still lay between them could be resolved.

"You're quiet."

My head perked up to look over at Stacy, who was still staring out the window. "No one was talking."

"To us. No one was talking to us, but there was talking going on," she contradicted.

"Well, whatever was being said was something we wouldn't want to hear at any rate. Besides, I tried to get you to talk but you were all stony over there, and I just don't have it in me to try and be cheerful and happy. It's been a really crappy year for me, you know?" I sat in the chair that Lark had vacated and frowned at my sarcastic outburst.

The chair beside me was pulled out, and Stacy sat, her hands on the table now tracing the gouges that Lark's fingernail had made earlier. "It's been a really crappy year for all of us, I think. We've lost a lot: our ignorance, our innocence...our lives. I'm sorry about the whole suicide thing, Grace. I keep thinking that no one understands what I've gone through, but then I remember that you do. You know what's in my head. You know what it's like to feel death always there, right beside you like some kind of freaky shadow that won't go away no matter how dark it is. And I'm not saying that because of Robert."

"I know you're not, Stacy. I only wish that you didn't have to feel like that. That...that place that Sam had you in, locked up in your mind like some kind of bird in a crystal cage...that was my fault. Sam used you to hurt me, and I hate myself for that."

"Don't start blaming yourself for what that creep did," Stacy said, her voice taking on a scathing note. "He's the one who made me sick. He's the one who put me into that coma and messed with my head. Everything that happened to me is his fault. Do you hear me, Grace? *He* did it all. He wanted to hurt you, and he didn't care how he did it, and that's all on him—not on you."

I stared at my hands, studying their lines and bumps in an effort to ignore the denial in my head. If Stacy had not been my friend, if she had not been connected to me in some way, she might have never had to make the choice she did.

"Grace, can you...can you tell me what you saw? When you were inside my head, I mean. I can't remember anything about what happened before I woke up in Dr. Bro's house. I can't remember what was in my head…it's like everything before then is blank."

"I don't know if that's such a good idea, Stacy. Maybe it's a good thing you don't remember anything."

If Stacy could have made the air around us turn as cold as her skin, she would have. "You think I won't be able to handle it?"

"Stacy-"

"That's it, isn't it? You think that I won't be able to deal with what I've seen. I've killed four people, Grace. I've seen the things that they've done to other people. What can you possibly tell me that'll bother me? I just want to know. I want that hole filled."

I couldn't deny Stacy what she wanted, and she deserved to know. I understood what it felt like to have my mind filled with images that weren't my own, memories that did not belong to me. It was the only reason I did not begin immediately. Instead, I stood and filled an empty glass with water from the tap, my stomach queasy, my nerves frayed at the edges.

"Stacy, when I was in your head, I thought it would be like my own. I thought that it would be like some kind of bowl where everything just floated about and I'd be able to fish you out. Instead…instead your mind was one long, crazy hallway. Everything that I saw was meant to keep me from finding you."

I sat back down in my chair and took a swig from the glass. The water tasted metallic. "There was a door behind me, a flower shaped door and it had a ribbon coming out where the doorknob should have been. On my left was a leaf shaped door. It was the first one I opened. It was like walking into a slaughterhouse. There were dead birds everywhere, and feathers and blood. The wings were placed on a table—just the wings—and I saw on the wall a pair of black ones that had been nailed there.

"I couldn't take it, so I left. I followed the doors, one after the other. A bird shaped one; a heart shaped one, then a moon, and then an apple. As I passed each one, I could hear your voice but I didn't know where you were. The last door, the one that faced the other end of the hallway looked like an eye. It looked like Sam's eye. I could hear you behind it; you sounded so frightened. I thought to open it, to find you standing behind it but... this is going to sound weird but when I saw that the handle was a carrot, I stopped."

"A carrot?"

I nodded, the same perplexed disturbance on my forehead mimicking hers. "Right after my mom died, I used to have these dreams that the white rabbit from Alice in Wonderland needed my help. He'd always invite me over for carrot cake just before I'd wake up. I stopped having the dream after, like a week or something, and I didn't dream again until after...well, you know.

"But before you...died, I dreamt of the rabbit again, only this time the dream changed. The rabbit told me he didn't like carrots, and I thought that was the strangest thing. But being inside of your head, it was like it made sense. Being in your mind was like falling into the rabbit hole. And here was that carrot, just begging me to grab it and turn it to get to you, but I knew that you wouldn't be there. I knew it somehow.

"But you were still behind that door so I did the only other thing I could. I tried the center of the door, the pupil of the eye. I could enter it without a problem, but I realized that there was no way I'd be able to get back out, so I grabbed the ribbon from the other end of the hall and thank God it just kept unraveling otherwise I don't know what would've happened.

"I dived into that hole. It was probably the craziest thing I've ever done, but I did it, and when I opened my eyes I was with you. But...you weren't you. You were scared, you weren't like yourself; you looked like one big talking crystal. Everything you said was like hearing it spoken from underwater and then having it echo, and you didn't want to leave, which scared me the most. You were afraid of coming with me and I told you that if you didn't then I would stay with you."

Stacy's face, already pale on its own, seemed to do the impossible and fade even more. "You did not!"

I nodded. "I did. I wasn't going to let you die like that, without your memories, without anyone with you. You're one of my best friends, Stacy. I'd give my life for you!"

There are moments when physical emotion can be uncomfortable. It can be embarrassing and unnecessary, but this wasn't one of them. When Stacy's arms wrapped around me, I more than willingly wrapped my own around her. It didn't matter to me that she was as cold as snow. It didn't matter that hugging her was like embracing a lamppost.

"I always wanted a sister, you know," Stacy sniffed in my ear. "I always wanted one but after five boys and me, my parents were done. When I finally introduced myself to you, I thought that maybe, just maybe we could become friends. I never thought that you'd be the answer to my prayers."

I laughed and dashed away the tears that fell when I pulled away from her. "I never thought I'd ever be friends with anyone but Graham. I never thought about life after this to be honest with you. It's like...it's like I knew that whatever future I wanted, it wasn't going to happen, and so when you and I became friends I didn't want to question it, and I never have. I don't think I could've gotten through any of this without you."

We sat there, our heads bent toward each other like little girls deep in a secret conversation. That is how Lem found us, his entrance so quiet that even Stacy hadn't heard it.

"So you have survived Isis' attack without a single mark. I applaud you, Stacy," he said with an eager smile.

"And why wouldn't I have? Fighting with her was like sparring with my shadow: completely harmless."

"Yes, but while you would have eventually tired, Isis would have been able to continue on. Had Lark not helped you, the likelihood that you would not have escaped with your life is very high."

Stacy snorted and sneered at the insult. "I was tiring, but she was done. Lark was there only to keep me from destroying what was left of her. You angels are pretty fragile creatures, you know."

Soft rumbling filled the small space of the kitchen as the insult tossed between the two supernatural creatures hit its mark. Lem looked ready to kill. Stacy looked ready to feed.

"Hey, Lem, how about we go outside to talk?" I broke in, standing up and grabbing his arm to pull him out through the kitchen door.

"I don't think that's a good idea," Stacy warned.

"I'll be right outside, Stacy. I'll stand right in front of the window so you can see me the entire time, alright?" I didn't wait for an answer, merely maneuvered myself so that I could see plainly the disappointment in her face through the thin pane of glass.

"She is not happy with you right now." Lem seemed pleased with his observation.

"She's not happy with *you* right now. You have really bad timing, Lem, you know that?"

He turned away from me to gaze up into the night sky, the faint trace of light from the street barely grazing over the roof to turn the black dull orange. "I think that I have perfect timing."

"Of course you would. You're here and Robert's not."

"Exactly," he smiled.

"So why *are* you here?"

"Word has spread. Raphael has been to see you."

Lark's words repeated themselves in my head and my shoulders drooped. "Trouble's starting already, isn't it?"

He nodded solemnly, but a smile still lingered beneath his darkened expression. "The support that has been given to you cannot be ignored now. Even with your death so imminent, it still remains a point of contention for my kind to know that someone who many believe should not even exist can wield such influence over those who have the power to crush you."

"I didn't ask for any of it," I reminded him.

"I know. I know that you haven't, Grace. You didn't ask for any of this to occur. There is a good chance that none of this would have happened had Ameila kept her family away."

I bit back a strangled retort, unwilling to let him see the hurt I felt. Hadn't Robert said pretty much the same thing? Instead I let out a cynical laugh, half-swallowed, half-forced. "Yeah, well, you and I both know that my number would have been up regardless."

Lem gave me a speculative glance, his eyes missing nothing. "This isn't the first time you've heard that said, is it? Someone else said the same thing to you already. Who? Lark? Ameila?"

"Is this why you came, Lem? To interrogate me? I have to go back inside before Stacy's patience wears out."

I turned to head toward the kitchen door but his firm grasp on my arm stilled my feet. "It was N'Uriel, wasn't it?"

"He's right. If he and I had never met, none of this would've happened. Janice wouldn't be some vegetable right now. Erica, Mr. Branke…maybe even Mr. Frey would all be alive. And if Mr. Frey was still alive then Mrs. Deovolente would be, too."

"Yes, but then you wouldn't be."

I shrugged. "Would it matter?"

Lem's hand on my arm squeezed roughly, and I flinched as his voice took on an angry tone. "Of course it would matter! This is not the life your mother wanted for you. On the run, hiding, always looking over your shoulder—you should not have to live this way."

"She is the very reason I live this way," I told him icily. "If I had never been born, I'd never have known what it meant to lose not only her, but my memory of her as a person I admired and looked up to.

"I thought my mother was special. I thought she was perfect, but I was wrong, and nothing can compare to having your dreams torn to shreds. Everything I knew about her was a lie, and that lie has cost not only her life, but the lives of others who were innocent."

"You cannot hate her for bringing you into this world, Grace."

"Yes I can! I wouldn't be here. I wouldn't know what it felt like to be responsible for breaking my father's heart. I wouldn't know what it felt like to have to force someone to do something they don't want to do. I wouldn't know what it felt like to lose the people I care about. I wouldn't be here to experience any of those things. She gave me life, but she also condemned me to death. She condemned all of her children to death."

That last line was uttered with a shuddering breath, and I felt my knees buckle, my emotions too heavy now to contain standing up. I sank to the ground and pounded my fists into the soft grass beneath me.

"I don't like to think about Sam as my brother. What he and his partner did to me, what they did to Erica and Mr. Branke...I cannot forgive him or anyone for that. But no matter how much I hate Sam, no matter how much I wished him dead for what he did, it doesn't compare to the fact that our own mother planned out our deaths...even the one she carried inside her..."

My voice wavered and my hands wrapped around my abdomen in sorrow. "Everyone keeps telling me about how wonderful she was, but how wonderful could she have been, knowing that each of her children was going to die because of something she did? You're supposed to love your child, protect them from harm at all costs. You're supposed to do everything in your power to keep them safe. She threw all of us to the wolves."

Lem squatted in front of me, his eyes wide with emotion. "She *was* wonderful. She had no choice in that, Grace. She might have lost her immortality, but she was still an angel with no freedom to choose her own path."

I swatted his hand away when he reached for my face. "That's a lie. She chose to be with my father even though she knew it was wrong."

"How do you know that being with your father was a choice, Grace? How do you know that that was not her path? Because she loved him?"

My mouth opened, and remained so as I tried to come up with some kind of rebuttal, but all I managed to do was cause my lips to crack in the still air. The truth was, I didn't know.

"As much as you like to think you can see what's really going on, Grace, the truth is you can't. You may be the daughter of an angel, but you do not possess the ability to understand what it means to be one. You take for granted your own ability to choose, and so believe that when the actions do not satisfy you that it was a choice that led to that result. But for us, it is not that simple.

"Avi's life was always meant to end as it did. She loved your father, but that was a blessing bestowed upon her, Grace. Had she hated your father, loathed him, she still would have married him. She still would have conceived you, and she still would have died because that was her destiny. She had no choice in the matter."

I didn't want to believe it. He wasn't going to take the guilt away from my mother. She still could have chosen something else.

"No, she couldn't," Lem argued, my emotions allowing my thoughts to slip through. "She couldn't have chosen to go against her path without dying and accomplishing nothing. She was shackled to her destiny; she had no choice in anything. You should be glad that at the very least, she loved you and your father."

A guttural, almost vulgar sound escaped me and I glared at Lem, his silver and gold eyes soft in their hope that I'd understand; that I'd accept what he was telling me.

Fat chance.

"She didn't love us. She knew all of this was going to happen, she knew what this was going to do to my dad and she didn't care. She knew what this was going to do to me and she didn't care. A mother who loves her child doesn't intentionally cause them pain. She doesn't give them the moon and then snatch it away. Only someone who hates you does that, Lem. Only someone who wishes you were never born would do something like that."

I stood up, and watched as Lem's face fell, his emotions plain. "You loved my mom, but she didn't love you. She didn't love you, she didn't love my dad, she didn't love Sam, and she didn't love me. You were played, just like we all were, and just like my dad, you'll defend her because you loved her. Well, I don't and I can't. I wasn't brought up to think of you guys as above the consequences; my dad knew better than that."

"I've upset you."

"No. You haven't. You've enlightened me."

"How so?"

I looked him up and down and lifted a shoulder carelessly. "By admitting that my mother had no choice, and that everything she did, she did because she had to, including being with my dad; it proves to me that you being here has nothing to do with me and everything to do with her."

Something that resembled recognition crossed over his face, and he stood up. "You're jealous."

"What? I am not!" My eyes rolled at his accusation, but my cheeks flared with embarrassed heat.

"You are." He smiled with satisfaction and touched the redness on my face.

I flinched, but he was faster than I was. His hands were on my face, holding me still, and his mouth was on mine in a way that Robert's had never been. I struggled beneath him but there was no use. He wasn't going to let me go. The way his fingers dug into my skin, and the way I could feel the slight tremble in them told me that this was the completion of something he'd been wanting for a long time.

And I realized that it was something that I wanted, too.

But not with him.

"Get your hands off of my wife!"

My face was released swiftly, the blood that returned to my skin reminding me of what had caused this and again, I felt flushed. Lem had moved away, a distance of several meters between us while Robert stood off to the side, the third point in this dangerous triangle.

"N'Uriel…"

Robert raised a hand to silence Lem, and Lem quieted. "You are never, ever to come near Grace again. I should have made this clear from the beginning, but I always assumed you'd respect Grace's feelings. She does not want you, Lem. She's made that point clear to you once already."

"She's human—they're fickle with their wants," Lem replied casually.

"She's always been firm on who it was she wants, Llehmai. She has never once deviated from that. Your attempts to seduce her into thinking otherwise have failed. You will not get another chance." Robert's voice was low, calm, but the threat that had not been uttered still hung in the air, heavy and harsh.

"So be it. I was beginning to tire of these games anyway. I do suggest that you learn to be more aggressive in your lovemaking, N'Uriel—she's as stiff and prudish as a nun, and not the kind I like." Lem was gone before I'd even heard his last word, and I fumed that I had not been able to tell him off.

"Ugh! Why does he affect me like this?" I growled angrily. "I don't want him. You know that I don't, but he makes me so...so mad! He just shows up and he says things and does things that make me...ugh!" I swung at the air, too furious with myself and with what I'd heard to care what I looked like. I turned to look at Robert and saw his amused smile.

"What's so damn funny?"

"You. You're adorable when you're angry." He stepped closer to me and pressed his thumb against the indent between my brows. "Your face puckers up and you look like an imp."

My jaw fell. "A what?"

"An imp. A cute imp. A very, very, attractive imp."

I knew my nostrils were flaring with my dissatisfaction at this pathetic explanation. Robert chuckled and replaced his thumb with his mouth, kissing away the furrow. "He was right, though."

"About what?" I scoffed.

"About the lovemaking part. I've been very neglectful when it comes to doing my husbandly duties."

"I-I...I..."

I stuttered like a dummy, my eyes turning to see Stacy still sitting in the kitchen, her eyes filled with amusement. She had heard everything.

"Yes, she heard everything, and she agrees with me."

"B-b-but I'm not…I'm not turned yet." I don't know why my mouth blurted out something that I knew would hinder what I wanted, what I had been wanting for so long, but it did, and I couldn't pull those words back.

Robert's mouth lowered to kiss the tip of my nose, and I felt my eyes cross as I tried to look into his. He tipped my chin up and then his lips covered mine. This was how Lem had kissed me. This was what I had wanted with Robert. But this was different. This was more. So…so much more.

"Come, wife," he said smiling.

"Where?" I asked breathlessly.

"I'm about to make my dream come true."

"What about mine?" I sulked before he kissed me again.

"Making it come true *is* my dream."

## SUPERNOVA

"Where are we going?"

"Where no one can see us."

I gripped his shoulders with tight fingers. The air was getting colder the higher we flew, and the lights below us had dimmed considerably until they looked like stray flecks of glitter scattering the darkened ground. Pale wisps of clouds wrapped around us until finally they were all I could see. Robert stopped ascending and smiled at me when I gave him a questing look.

"We're here."

I gulped and felt my eyes threaten to leave their sockets. "Here? But there's...there's no bed here."

"We don't need a bed, Grace."

A nervous giggle left me as my knuckles turned white against his shoulders. "I-isn't that how it's normally done, though? On a bed? In a room, with walls and...walls?"

"Yes. For two humans," he replied thickly, his hands at my back moving lower, his grip growing tighter.

I closed my eyes and waited, unsure of what to do now that the one fundamental thing I knew about making love was removed from the equation. When I felt Robert's body shake with laughter, embarrassment burned at my face.

*Are you afraid?*

His voice was warm and hazy in my head, and I nodded. "What

if a plane flies by? What if…what if another angel decides to go…angeling or whatever it is you guys do up here. What if I fall? I don't have wings…I can't fly."

"Shh," he said, pressing a heavy kiss against my forehead. "There are no planes flying here, and no angels will come flying by—I've made sure of it.

"And," he said in a husky tone, "You don't need to have wings. You don't need to be able to fly in order to be near the stars. All you need to do is be with me. Just trust me. Love me, Grace." His hands flitted over my body until the chilled air touched skin that had not been exposed before. My eyes flew open in a gasp when I realized that I was naked.

"Clothes are also not necessary," Robert whispered into my ear.

I looked down at myself and then at him, and then my eyes flew to his, the image that I had seen burned into my mind forever. "You're naked, too," I squeaked.

"Well, it wouldn't have been fair for you to lose your clothes and I remain with mine on now would it?" he said with a soft chuckle. And then his eyes turned dark. It was like watching a storm roll in, quickly and hungrily. My stomach twisted inside of me as my heart began its dance of excitement.

"Are you sure? I-I mean, you've always been so against this."

His hands at my back squeezed, and I yelped. He chuckled. "I've never been against this. You and I being together is the second most important thing I've ever wanted."

My head tilted to the side, my voice tinged with confusion. "The second most important thing? What's the first?"

"Having you love me."

"But I already love you."

"I know."

He smiled just seconds before leaning in to kiss me. The way our lips seemed to meet at just the right angle, with just the right amount of pressure, should have reassured me that what was happening was right, that this was the right time. Instead, all I felt was nervous.

"You're not ready," Robert realized.

"I-I don't know. This is all happening so suddenly and...so differently from how I thought it would that I don't know how to wrap my head around it."

A cold burst of air surrounded us and I shivered. Robert's wings emerged from behind him, slowly, almost like art. Even in the dark, they seemed darker, blacker than any shadow. And like two dark curtains, they closed in around us, sealing us in and blocking out the chill.

"Is that better?"

I nodded.

His skin began to light up, the pale white glow filling up the small space between us and illuminating his face so that I could see every expression, every smile, every crinkle of his eyes.

"You must think I'm such a baby," I mumbled.

"Why would I think that?"

A snort slipped through me at his question. "Really? I whined and complained like a brat about this, even left you because you wouldn't...give it up, and now look at me. We're naked, we're alone, and I'm chickening out."

A tiny puff of mist appeared between us, and I looked down and sighed with a mixture of relief and disappointment when I realized what he was doing. "You don't have to do that."

"You're uncomfortable with our nudity—I don't want to make you feel anything you don't want to."

"I know, but...it's not that I don't like the way you look naked. I...I like seeing you...like that. I just..."

His lids narrowed as he sifted through my thoughts. "You're worried that I don't approve of you."

I nodded sheepishly and shrank inward at his exasperated sigh. "Grace, I know that you'll probably never fully accept the fact that I find you unquestioningly beautiful and attractive, but, for one moment, please believe me when I say that I could never disapprove of you."

Robert shifted, releasing one hand and leaning me back against the folds of his wings while his free hand now began to roam my body. "You forget that your skin was the first I'd ever touched. The way it felt, that first time, it was like every dream I'd ever had came true at exactly the same time."

His fingers trailed up and down my arm, dipping to my armpit and going lower, disappearing into the black smoke. "I don't know what life was like before that moment; not anymore. Every person I've ever come into contact since you gets compared to you, and no one has ever measured up. No one, Grace; not even angels."

"You're just saying that," I told him, my doubt clear.

"You should know by now that I never just say anything. Your skin is like the freckled petal of a lily, soft and delicate, but it smells-" he pressed his nose against my heart "-like every hope I've ever had and every promise I ever wanted to make to myself.

"I want to make love to you, Grace. I want to love you, my wife, my soul mate, my Ianthe. I want to press your freckled, lily skin against mine and feel your heart beat through it. I want to inhale your breaths and hear you whisper my name as I prove to you that there can never be anyone more lovely, more divine, or more sensual to me than you.

"I want you to hear me tell you these words and believe them, not because I say them, not because they come from an angel's lips, but because they're the truth. I would do everything in my power to make you believe me. How can I do that, Grace? Tell me."

"I don't know," I answered truthfully.

Robert brought his hand to my face and stroked my cheek. He lowered his head and kissed my eyes. "You know, angels don't have brown eyes, which makes yours unique."

His fingertips stroked my ear before his mouth found my lobe and he nibbled it. "You've listened to me with these ears. You heard me tell the worst of lies and yet you stayed with me. These ears are precious."

I heard my breath shake when his lips pressed light kisses down my jaw, moving their way to the corner of my mouth and gently licking at the smile I was unable to prevent from forming.

"When you said my name with these lips, it was as if I'd never heard it spoken before, and I never wanted to hear it spoken by anyone else but you. And when you told me you loved me, and that I didn't need to say it back, I was blown away; I'd never been given so much by anyone. You gave me everything in those words, Grace. Everything you had, your trust, your heart, your faith—and I didn't do anything to deserve it."

"You gave me back."

"Huh?"

I laughed softly at his confusion and pulled back so that I could see his face completely. "When I met you, the only thing I wanted to do was disappear. Do you know how frustrating it is, to not only *not* be able to do that but I couldn't even disappear into my own head?"

"Well…yeah, actually, I do," he said, laughing with me.

"I never wanted to be anything but Graham's friend, and when I didn't even have that, I didn't have me. Who I was had been based on my friendship with Graham for pretty much my entire life, and I didn't know that I could be anyone else. But you…you gave me myself. You helped me to be someone on my own, and I didn't think that was possible."

"Is that why you could go to prom after you thought I was dead?"

I was stunned. This was the first time he'd mentioned that, and I could detect a hint of something in his voice; something that sounded a lot like irritation and hurt.

The timing of the question caught me off guard the most, though, but I knew why he asked it: he needed reassurance. He needed confirmation that he was not replaceable.

"I spent a month crying over Graham after he dumped me. I cried every single night after Dad and Janice's wedding when you told me the truth about Sam.

"But when I thought you were dead, I felt the most empty, the most weak I'd ever been. But I was also the most whole I'd ever been, and that's because of you. I couldn't just sit at home and do the same thing, cry until I couldn't move, because I wasn't the same person anymore. I wasn't Grace the freak, unloved and unwanted. I was Grace, who had been loved so much by someone that he gave his life for me.

"That changes everything; that changes how you view life. God, it hurt so much to pretend that I was happy, that I was enjoying myself, but I couldn't waste the time you gave me; I knew that I didn't have much of it. You said that it was what we did when things were at their worst that really mattered—it might not have been what others would have done, but I knew that I couldn't ruin Shawn's prom."

Robert nodded and then smiled. "You didn't want to go with him, but you did anyway because you didn't want to ruin his night."

"Yeah. It wasn't fair to him; he had nothing to do with what had happened with us, or with Sam, and I couldn't have another person be touched by that. You understand…right?"

Again, his head bobbed up and down, and then his mouth was crushing mine, my body now fully supported by his wings as both hands held my head immobile, my mouth opening beneath his. I felt nothing for a moment, because I was so surprised by what was happening. One moment of blank space in my mind and body. And then, the mountain of feeling slammed into me.

My hands that had been simply holding on were now pulling at him, forcing him to pull me in even closer. My fingertips searched for his hair, and I protested when he eased away from me, my lips feeling far more naked than my body did.

"I want you. I want to give you everything," he panted, his breath hot and sweet against my skin.

"I-I don't know what to do," I said meekly.

"Then let me do everything," he replied before his mouth returned to mine.

This time, when the dark hint of smoke crossed over my skin, it was joined by a hand that touched every curve. The gentle grazing against my heart wasn't just mist, it was flesh.

"Your heart is racing."

"Everything's racing," I said, my breaths quickening when Robert's lips pressed against my shoulder.

He chuckled and nodded, his kisses going lower. "Your heart sounds like a freight train. It's distracting."

"What you're doing is distracting," I breathed as the swirl of something wet brushed at my navel.

Robert's mouth found its way back to mine and I couldn't believe how hot his lips were. I wanted to look down again to see if my skin was on fire, but I already knew the answer. *I* was on fire. We both were.

"I want you to tell me to stop if it gets too…scary, or painful."

Robert's voice was a healthy mix of concern and need, and I knew that when I answered him, my voice would sound exactly the same. "I'm not afraid of anything. Nothing you do to me will hurt."

"I love you."

"Show me," I told him.

***

He was right. There had been no need for a bed. I lay on him comfortably, his back facing the city below us, his eyes staring up into the stars. His hand traced patterns on my back, causing shivers to run up and down my spine and reminding me of the moments that led up to this.

My mind replayed over and over again the sweetness of it all, the gentle touch of each finger, the sweeping emotions that never seemed to find an end when I'd finally let go of my fear of falling and allowed it to simply float away from us. Robert's voice had flooded my mind, telling me how I looked, how he'd never felt so free.

My heart still possessed its off-beat rhythm as I recalled each touch that turned my skin into its own storm of feeling. With the cool air wrapping around us, it felt like a war had started between the fire we created within us and nature's need to cool us down. I was almost sure that if I listened close enough, I'd hear the sizzle of steam.

But one moment above all others captured my breath and held it hostage, forbidding anything to surpass its significance. Even Robert, seeing it replay in my mind, seemed unable to contain his emotions, and my skin grew prickly at the heat that he sent into me. "You were so brave," he said with soft reverence.

"Brave?" My voice felt far away, as though I still couldn't believe it was happening to me, and that it was someone else he was speaking to.

"Yes. With all the danger that the two of us being together means, the consequences that we'll face because of this, and the...pain, you didn't show any fear."

"I told you, nothing you'd do would hurt," I said with a secret smile.

"I know, but I understand that for a human, their first time can be...terrifying."

"Where did you hear that?"

His eyes turned down in embarrassment. "Lark."

"You asked your sister for advice?" I shrieked. "Ugh—you know, she's probably laughing right now, thinking of all the different ways you freaked out about this."

"She's the only other person I know who's been with a human, Grace. I had no one else to turn to."

I exhaled in irritation at his explanation. "You could have asked me! I've had sex-ed. I've seen that pie movie like, four times! And besides, when a guy loses his virginity, it's not really...painful."

"That's not what Lark said."

"Well, that's because Lark probably broke Graham in half! I can't believe you'd ask your sister."

The way Robert's feathers ruffled, I knew he was becoming irritated as well, but then my body shifted, and suddenly I groaned at what that movement did between us.

"You know," Robert whispered, his eyes closed, his face pinched as though caught between pain and pleasure, "Being with you makes me understand why the Grigori were willing to give everything up. I didn't know that I could feel hot, cold, fiery, frozen, light, and so heavy all at once."

I swallowed and hushed out as his hands took a hold of my waist and pulled me down. "I felt only you."

I heard fluttering beneath us, and Robert growled, his wings unfurling from behind him to spread wide, covering us and sealing off the light from anything save the steamy glow of his skin. "I'm afraid that you're about to feel only me again."

## FIELD TRIP

We returned back to the unassuming house before the sun rose. Robert shielded my nakedness from invisible eyes with a blanket of mist and carried me into his room where he laid me down and covered me with the white comforter. "Sleep, my angel," he said to me before pressing soft lips against my forehead.

"Where are you going? You're not leaving me again, are you?" I asked in a panic.

"Only for an hour. Stacy is downstairs, and Lark is right across the hall. Everything will be fine. You sleep and when you wake up I will be here."

I nodded, but I knew that doubt was plain on my face as he disappeared. How could he leave me so soon after what had happened between us? This wasn't how it was supposed to be, was it? We were supposed to snuggle, cuddle up to each other and fall asleep in each other's arms, then wake up and begin the cycle all over again.

Instead, I was alone, without my clothes in a strange home, and he was gone. And the last thing I wanted to do was sleep.

I climbed out of the bed and padded to the dresser. It was strange how similar it was to my own; I opened the top drawer, half expecting to see my underwear shoved in there haphazardly. Instead, a neat line of watches filled up the space. I closed the drawer and moved on to the next one. It was filled with tank tops. My tank tops.

I grabbed one and slipped it on. I continued through the rest of the drawers until I was fully dressed, and then headed downstairs. Stacy was still sitting in the kitchen, her body still. "I hear you. Come and sit down."

I pulled up the chair across from her and sat down, my hand swiping at my hair nervously as she looked me up and down, as though she was inspecting me. Did I look different?

"You seem happy."

"I am."

"That's good. I thought you'd be nervous of what was going to happen after."

I didn't need to be nervous. "I know what to expect. I accepted it the minute I agreed to go with Robert. Whatever the consequences are, we're ready to face them."

Stacy's sigh was one that took me by surprise. "You've finally given up then."

I didn't understand her statement. "What do you mean? I've finally gotten what I wanted."

"Yeah, but you've also given the angels who want you dead justification now. It's no longer about them simply not liking you. Now it's a matter of you breaking their laws. You *and* Robert are guilty."

"Stacy…"

"I don't care about what they think, Grace. I'm glad for you. I'm happy that you and Robert are together. But what's going to happen if you two…if there's a…"

I looked at her dark eyes and I could see the thoughts in her head. I knew what she was worried about, and I shook my head. "Don't worry about that, Stacy."

"How can I not worry about it? If you get pregnant, even if those old bats are willing to spare you for the sex part, they won't for the baby part. Lark told me about the Nephilim. She told me about what happened to them and to the people who made them. If you get pregnant, they *will* kill you. And the baby."

"I understand why you're worried, Stacy, but there is no need to worry about that. I can't get pregnant now."

Stacy finally understood, and she sighed with hesitant relief. "Well. At least that's one thing."

My eyes narrowed shrewdly. "What else is there?"

She stood and walked toward the kitchen counter, pulling open a drawer and removing from it a notepad and black marker. She tore the first sheet off of the pad and sat back down. "Tell me again, what you saw. In my head."

"What, we're taking notes now?"

"Yes. I need to know this stuff, and you said you'd help me."

Knowing that I had, and that I really had nothing better to do, I began to relay what I'd seen while inside Stacy's thoughts.

"I saw a hallway. There were doors, one behind me, one in front, and several to my left. There were painted doors to my right that mirrored the actual ones."

"What did the doors look like?"

I told her, describing in order the doors, their shapes, their handles, the contents that I had seen behind them. When I looked down, Stacy had been busily writing everything I had said, listing them individually.

"What did the flower door look like again?" she asked and I tried to explain it to her but found it impossible to do so. Instead, I took the pen from her and drew it.

"That's a lotus. Okay, so we've got a lotus, a leaf. What kind of bird was it?"

I closed my eyes and studied the shape that appeared in my head. "It looked like a hawk or an eagle. That's what it was, an eagle."

"Okay." She stood up and grabbed the pad of paper she'd left on the counter, returning to the table and tearing off another sheet. "So, lotus, leaf, eagle, heart, moon, apple, and eye. Are you sure it was an eye?"

"Yes. It was Sam's eye. Well…his iris, anyway."

Stacy bit her tongue as she wrote down iris on the sheet of paper. She stared at her list and then turned it to face me. "Is this correct?"

I looked at it and nodded. "Yeah."

She frowned and turned the sheet back around. "This is so random. It's like some kind of freaky, hippie fruit salad in my head or something. There's got to be a reason why all of those things were there, right? I mean, it's not like that Sam freak just pulled crap out of a bag—there has to be a reason why I had birds and fruit in my head."

"Maybe there isn't. Maybe there's no reason for it at all. Sam was confused and angry. Hell, *I* was confused and angry. I didn't figure anything out until it was necessary, and even then it was always almost too late."

She sighed and nodded her head. "I'm hungry. It's only been a few days and already my throat burns. I need to feed. When is Robert returning?"

"He said in an hour."

She nodded. "I can wait. I already know where my next meal is—he's not going anywhere."

Her calm demeanor was disturbing, but I still felt the morbid curiosity that led me to ask her who it was.

"He's a bad dude. That's all you need to know."

"Uh-uh, you don't get to just leave it at that. Who is he? What's he done?"

She looked at me, as though trying to decide whether or not I could handle what it was I wanted to know. Sighing, she shrugged, giving in to my curiosity.

"He's a dirty cop. He's killed several people, none of them people that society really cares about, and so people look away. I saw him a few nights ago beating up some prostitute. They found her body in the morning; she died from strangulation.

"He killed her and he's going to kill again if I don't stop him. See, as much as Robert thinks I'm some kind of monster because of what I am, he ignores the fact that the people he's supposed to protect are monsters themselves."

I opened my mouth, knowing the answer I would receive but still needing to say the words. "Can I come with you?"

"Absofreakinglutely not!"

"It's not like I haven't seen people die, Stacy. I mean, I'm like the zombie-horror movie queen. I'm not scared of seeing a little blood."

"No."

"Come on!"

Stacy growled at me, a deep rumbling sound that caused the table to shake. "I. Said. No."

She stood up and began to pace the short distance between the counter and her seat. "I lose it when I smell their blood. I don't know where I am, I don't know who I am. I only know the need to feed. I only know the need to kill…and if you're near me when this is happening, I might confuse you for my meal. I can't take that chance with you, Grace."

"I'll stay far away. I…I just want to see."

"You want to see me kill and eat someone?"

Her question was filled with shock and dismay. I understood what it was she was most afraid of. It was screaming from the sadness in her eyes, the slack gape of her mouth, the sag of her brows. She didn't want me to see her as a killer. No matter how she may describe the act to me, it was still just an imaginary scene in my head. She did not want me to imprint in my mind the image of her as a murderer.

"Stacy, it doesn't matter what you do—you will never be a bad person in my eyes. You're incapable of it."

She rolled her eyes at me. "You don't know what you're talking about."

"I know you." I pushed my chair back and walked over to her. "And I'm not afraid of you. I'm not afraid of what you are, what you do, or why you do it. I know you wouldn't hurt someone you care about. I know you couldn't because that's not you. No matter what you are right now, it doesn't change who you were. You're the same person who wanted to be my friend when no one else would. I trust you."

She gave me one last glare before she sighed in defeat. "Come on. Get on my back."

"Are you serious?"

"If you ask me another question, I'm leaving without you. We have to hurry before Robert gets back and before Lark realizes what's going on."

There was no need to tell me twice. Though she was shorter than I was, she did not bow when I climbed onto her back. I wrapped my arms over her shoulders, and she grabbed them as my legs twined around her waist.

"Don't say a word," was the last warning I received before we were through the kitchen door and over the fence before dawn could expose us.

*** 

"The police station?"

"It's where he works. His shift is ending very soon. He will finish his paperwork and leave for his car in ten minutes."

Stacy's eyes were focused on a red truck that was parked crookedly in front of us. We sat perched in a tree above the large parking structure that stood beside the main police station. "He calls it Lucky. I call it his coffin," she snarled.

"How is this going to happen?"

"You will stay here. I will wait in the back of the cab for him. It'll be quick."

My intake of air startled her, just as her words startled me. "You're going to do it here? *At* the police station?"

"Yes. It's far safer than following him home."

316

I looked down at a black orb that hung beneath what looked like a lamppost. "But there are cameras, Stacy. They'll see you."

She shook her head. "They won' see anything. He parks his truck crookedly so that the camera can't get a decent look inside. That way, he can snort his coke and no one will see. I've watched him, studied his behavior. Here he comes. Stay. Here."

She leapt down from the branch, and slinked her way to the passenger side of the truck. I could hear scraping, and then a snap. She was inside! I hadn't even seen the door open. The sound of keys rattling and a double beep, followed by the flash of lights warned me that the officer Stacy had spoken of was approaching. I pulled my feet up, but leaned forward, my hand grasping onto the trunk of the tree as tightly as I could to get a better view.

The footsteps on the cement floor stopped and then started again, and the officer, still dressed in his uniform, opened his door. I bit my lip, my breath stopping in my chest as slowly, he brought his left foot inside and the door closed. Almost immediately, the vehicle started rocking.

The snarls and the muffled screams soon followed. The officer's face appeared in the windshield, his eyes wide with fear. Even from where I sat, I could see that his eyes were blue, like denim. His hair was short, blonde, and his face was handsome even in its terror. His mouth was pulled taut in a silent scream, and he looked at me, our eyes making contact as Stacy's hand covered the lower half of his face with her hand.

She engulfed part of his neck with her mouth that she'd hinged open, as though her face were cut in half, her teeth extending past her jaw and down her throat. I bit back my scream when I saw the plea in the man's eyes. It was as if his thoughts were there, streaming across them as agony and desperation forced his confession in an effort for release, or comfort.

The windshield grew foggy inside of the cab, as though something were on fire. No, not on fire. Something was very, very cold inside. I could see nothing, only imagine what was going on as the sounds of terror continued to travel softly to me. As though to hint just what it was that was going on inside the vehicle, a spattering of red broke through the haze on the glass. It was soon followed by more, and eventually the vehicle stopped moving.

A hand suddenly appeared on the windshield, the blood smearing into the lines on its palm, and finally disappeared, falling away as the sounds did. I flinched as a sharp pain shot into my hand, and I removed it from the bark of the tree, gasping when I saw the blood smeared there. I pulled out a large splinter and pressed my hand against my mouth to staunch the blood before Stacy returned.

"Now you've seen. Now you know."

"Holy balls; don't do that," I gasped when I turned to see her sitting beside me, dabbing at her mouth with a napkin as though she were merely wiping away some errant red sauce rather than the life of someone who now lay dead in his truck…maybe even in pieces.

"Come on. Let me get you home before anyone notices we've gone."

The red of Stacy's shirt hid the blood that I knew was there, but I couldn't ignore the wet sticky feel of them as once again, I wrapped my hands around her, closing my eyes as we dropped from the tree, hitting the ground softly.

"We walk for a little bit here until we turn that corner near the alley. Don't look at anyone, just look straight ahead," she said in a low voice before she let me down. I straightened my shirt and patted at the gathering of my sweatpants. The morning sun was already warm, and the streets were beginning to fill with cars and people.

With quick steps, Stacy and I walked a straight line toward the alley that lay only a few more meters away. Stacy walked with her head slightly lowered, and I tried to mimic her, wanting to appear casual and uncaring, but in doing so I failed to see where I was heading and collided into a passerby who immediately swung me around to keep me from falling.

Disoriented, I turned my head to see where Stacy had gone.

When I spotted her, the look on her face was one that I could not place. It wasn't fear. It wasn't shock. It wasn't even terror. It was all of the above. My head twisted to look at who was holding me, and my mouth dropped open as unintelligible words spilled out, a rambling sort of nonsense that did nothing to slow the growing anger that filled the dark eyes that stared at me, glowered, seethed.

"You're supposed to be dead," the voice hissed, his tone scathing, his grip on me growing tighter and more painful with every syllable.

"Sean, let her go."

Brother looked up at sister. Recognition flared within him. And then everything passed by in a blur. I felt myself being dragged, then carried, the colors of buildings melting into colors of trees and finally houses. My feet, now firmly on the ground, did nothing to prevent the swaying of dizziness that tipped me forward and then back, pitching like a boat in a storm as I tried to regain my balance.

"Grace, are you alright?" The voice was soothing, calm, even though the frigid fingers that helped to steady me sent icicles shooting into my veins.

"Dr. Bro?"

"What were you doing on the street?" His admonition wasn't directed at me, and I raised my eyes to see Stacy standing in front of me, her hand wrapped possessively around the arm of her brother, who simply stared open-mouthed at the sister he had never believed to be dead.

"She wanted to come," was all Stacy said before she dragged her brother across the street into the house whose door lay open in wait.

"Oh God…we're in trouble," I moaned.

"We all are," Dr. Bro agreed before leading me inside.

## ICE PICK

"Reckless!"

That word kept repeating itself over and over again. In my head, in the air, in my ear. I sat mutely as Robert paced back and forth between Stacy and me, his eyes darting to Sean's, and then returning back to Stacy's, who held her chin up defiantly.

"You want to feed, I understand that. I accept that. I *allow* that. But what I won't tolerate, what I will never accept is you taking my wife along with you. Do you understand the danger you put her in?"

"She wanted to come. She's not a child, Robert. She's seen far worse things with you than anything she saw today."

Her words bore the sting of truth and Robert knew it. Sean, who sat on the sofa with anger rippling through him, said nothing.

"You can't keep her from seeing the world the way it is. Not with what you do, not with what either of you plan on doing. After last night, the two of you are wearing ginormous freaking targets on your foreheads—how much more trouble could she be in coming with me to feed?"

"What if you had made a mistake? What if your prey had escaped and seen her and alerted the rest of the station? Your brother I can deal with, but I cannot manipulate or endanger all of those people," Robert roared.

"Deal with my brother? You're not going to do anything to him!" Stacy's voice was filled with defensive rage.

"He's seen you *and* Grace. He knows the two of you are still alive. What do you expect me to do with him? This wasn't part of the bargain, Stacy. You were to cut off all ties after you were changed. Your old life is dead. Everyone had accepted you as gone."

"I didn't." Sean's voice was like the bell ringing in the silent hallway. The anger that flowed between Stacy and Robert had grown so fever pitched that it had turned into white noise compared to his admission.

"I always knew she was still alive. I even came to you-" he turned his head to look at me "-and told you, but you denied it. But I knew you were lying. I knew it. Why, Stacy? Why would you fake your own death? Why would you do that to Mom, and Dad, and everyone else? Why wouldn't you at least tell me what you were doing?"

"Because she couldn't," Robert answered for her. "She couldn't tell you anything because she was unable to."

"So when you died, you didn't really die. It was fake, right? I mean, it was all planned out so that it would look like you had died, but you're fine. Right? God, Mom and Dad are going to be so freaking happy to see you. They'll be pissed, of course, but still…we've got to tell them."

There was such a hope and optimism in his eyes that it only amplified the pain in Stacy's. "No, Sean. We're not going to tell Mom and Dad anything. They're going to continue to believe that I'm dead."

"But you're fine! Look at you! Healthy, strong, and really fast! You totally beat the cancer! This is like some kind of freaking miracle or something!"

"I'm not fine, Sean," she barked, the solid boom of her voice silencing him immediately. "I'm not okay. I'm not healthy. My God, I'm not even alive! I'm not alive, Sean, do you hear me?" She grabbed her brother's hand and pressed it against her chest. He flinched at first, obviously disturbed by where his hand lay, but it didn't take much for recognition to finally hit him.

Slam into him, actually.

He brought his other hand beside the first, searching. He lowered his ear onto the spot that his hands had warmed, but I knew he'd hear no sound. I almost hoped that he would. He said nothing, but his face drained of blood. Stacy's words could not be refuted anymore, no matter how much he wanted to. He stumbled away from her, tripping over his own feet and landing on the floor.

"What the hell are you?" he said in a panicked voice.

"Sean...oh-pa..."

I knew that word. It meant brother in Korean. I'd heard it spoken before, during happier times. Sean remembered and stricken, he shook his head and then jerked it toward me. "You're not my sister, man. You're not my sister. You're just another freak, like her."

Stacy, not one to continue pleasantries when she knew they wouldn't work, resorted to her usual frankness. "Well fine then, you jerk. I'm not your sister. Why the hell would I want to be related to you anyway? You've always been the weakest one, even when I was sick, you freaking panty, so yeah, I'd rather not be known as your sister. You totally ruined my rep."

It was like a tennis match, as my head and Dr. Bro's turned to Sean to await his reaction. "You're the damn panty! You and your damned ballet classes always forced Dad to rearrange class time for everyone else just so you could attend. You couldn't just pick one thing, could you?

"No, you had to do everything, be little miss goody-two-shoes and kiss Dad's ass so he'd let you get away with always screwing up during practice." He jumped to his feet, his body twisting in such a way that his foot raised over his head and made contact with Stacy's shoulder, causing her to sway but never forcing her feet to move in any direction.

We heard a crack, but Sean hid the pain with a grunt and a shake of his head. He bounced from foot to foot, his hands shaking at his sides deliberately as he glared at his fuming sister. "And another thing: You always had bad form. Dad was always getting on you about that. Your posture sucked—it still does—and all those damn dance classes didn't do jack because you're no freaking twinkle-toes. Your feet are heavy and your moves jerky, clumsy, and to be quite honest, ugly as hell."

Stacy's retaliation was swift, her arm arcing and weaving through the air until it landed solidly in her brother's gut. He grunted before a whoosh of air left his lungs and he fell over onto his knees. "And you always talked too damn much," she said simply.

She stood there, looking down on her brother as he coughed and wheezed, desperate for the oxygen she had forced out of him. After some time, she knelt down in front of him and her head pressed down onto his. I looked at Robert whose emotionless face told me nothing. He was still angry.

I switched my gaze to Dr. Bro, who seemed disappointed and awed at the same time. And finally, my eyes lifted to see Lark and Graham, the two of them standing at the foot of the stairs, Graham's face filled with empathy—he knew what it was like to get his butt kicked by Stacy—while Lark's was filled with sadness.

She had hoped for a reconciliation with Stacy from the very moment their friendship ended, but there was no hope in her eyes now. She did not see the possibility there, and when she heard my thoughts, her shoulders drooped even more. There was no hiding this loss.

"Sean. I know you don't understand. This was the only way I could live." Stacy's voice was barely a whisper, but somehow I could hear her. "I wasn't ready to die. I didn't want to. I was given the opportunity to live and I took it. It meant that I would have to give you and Mom and Dad and everyone else up, but there wasn't much of my life left to live anyway. I wasn't ever going to wake up from that coma. My life was over, Sean. I had to choose between being dead or dying."

"I don't understand. What are you?"

She took a deep, needless breath and whispered to him the truth.

"What the hell is that?"

Rolling her eyes, she answered. He stumbled back on his feet, landing on his behind and scrambling backwards until his back met the wall. His eyes were crazed as he looked at all of us, as though seeing us all for the first time.

In truth, he was.

"Are all of you…are all of you guys zombies, too?" His voice had risen to a pitch that had probably last visited him years ago.

I shook my head at him, knowing that no one else would answer. "Stacy and Dr. Bro are the only ones here who are like that, Sean."

"Then what the hell are you? You're supposed to be dead, too. What the hell are you if you're not like her?"

"I'm a human being, just like you."

"Nu-uh, man. I heard that your dad saw your body. He saw you all burned up and crap. There's no way that you're just like me."

I looked at Robert and saw that he was not going to offer the truth. Lark turned away as well, and Graham held her against his chest, unwilling to part with his wife's secret. I sighed, and decided to reveal my own.

"What my dad saw wasn't me, Sean. It was someone else; someone else made to look like me. My dad's in danger. In fact, pretty much everyone I've ever come into contact with is in danger, and instead of letting anyone else get hurt it was decided that this was the best way to keep people safe. If my dad thinks I'm dead then maybe whoever is trying to hurt me will, too."

"Why would someone want to hurt you? I mean besides the fact that you're a freak?"

I swallowed the insult and forced the words to come out. "Because I'm a freak."

"Grace-"

My hand lifted to silence the voices that had risen in unison to contradict me. "Don't try to argue with me on this. Sean has to know that he's right. They were all right. I'm not like you, Sean. I mean I am, in every way that matters. But I'm also different in a way that matters to someone else, and they don't think I deserve to be alive. They've tried to kill me but that didn't work, so they're going after the people I care about."

"So I was right! You *are* the reason why Stacy kept getting hurt!"

Sean was now standing, his hands balled into fists at his side. I looked at them and knew what he wanted to do. I looked into his eyes and told him silently that I deserved it.

He blinked.

Robert stepped forward and pulled me behind him. "Whatever it is you're thinking about doing, I suggest you change your mind. We haven't decided what we will do with you now that you know about your sister but you could make it very easy for us."

Sean's lips curled in a snarl as he looked at Robert with disgust. "What the hell makes you think I care what you have to say? You and your girlfriend have turned my sister into a monster, man."

"Actually, that's my fault," Dr. Bro corrected. "And I abhor the term monster. Consider us mortality challenged."

"What the hell? You think this is funny?" Sean was quick. His hand grabbed a portrait that was on the wall and flung it at the doctor. His eyes held a glint of triumph as he watched the sharp wooden corners whiz toward the doctor's head. The glint became a dull sheen when Dr. Bro caught the frame between his thumb and middle finger, the sound of the glass and wooden backing sliding against the stone-like surface of his fingertips grating and harsh.

"I don't think that was all that necessary," Dr. Bro said calmly, walking up to Sean and replacing the portrait, straightening it before returning to his original spot. "If you wish to attack me then please, by all means do so. But do not attempt to destroy valuable artwork in the process. We are expendable. History is not."

Sean's mouth dropped at the lackluster response he received, and he decided to take aim at a new target. "So, what the hell are you then? Huh?" His eyes were focused on Lark, and in them there was a new sense of betrayal. He had trusted her. He had trusted her when doubt had fallen on everyone else.

Lark tried to look at him but her own guilt could not allow her to be so brave. "I am not a friend."

"Like I didn't know that," Sean said sulkily. "I thought you were different. Everything you did for my family after Stacy—after we thought Stacy had died…I thought you could be trusted."

Lark's head hung lower. "No one should have trusted me."

"You guys are all freaks, you know that? All of you. I'm telling my parents, I'm gonna call your dad, Grace, and tell him that you lied to him, too. I'm gonna call the news stations and the police station and turn all of you in for being goddamned crazy."

He headed toward the door, his eyes never looking anywhere else but at us. He was inches away from reaching his goal and it was like I could feel the decision being made. Instinct propelled me forward, my feet moving before my thoughts could reach my mind, and I placed myself in front of Sean before Robert's hands could reach him, before Stacy's hands could reach Robert, before Lark could reach any of them.

"Robert, don't!" I cried, pressing myself against Sean, holding him against me despite his protests. "Don't. Please. Don't."

Stacy's fingers were digging into Robert's back, and I saw the ferocity that blazed in her eyes as she glared at him, knowing what his intent was and risking everything to prevent him from doing so. Lark stood with her hand between them, poised to pry them apart before serious damage—damage that went beyond physical—could be done.

Dr. Bro and Graham had remained where they stood, too stunned to have been able to act in any manner, though I was certain that the gum that Graham had been chewing when he came down was now somewhere on the floor.

"Grace, you need to get away from him," Robert said to me slowly, his voice low, the deep timbre of it a warning in itself.

"No. I won't let you hurt him. I won't let you do that to him or Stacy," I said, my head shaking from side to side to emphasize my decision.

"He's going to expose us all, Grace. If your father were here, he'd be the one to do this."

My eyes narrowed into angry slits at his words. "If my father were here he wouldn't be planning my funeral."

"Robert," Lark said softly. "Let him go."

"Let him go," I repeated. "He'll tell the police, he'll tell whoever he wants, but who's going to believe him? Please, Robert. Please. For me."

I saw the tension in Robert's face, the lines of it looking like cliffs of contention where every emotion that ever caused such strain committed suicide, and my heart hurt for him. Everything he was compelled him to end Sean's life, to protect his secret, our secret. And yet here I stood, unwilling to let him do exactly what he had been born to do.

Again.

"I have never asked you to spare someone's life before," I said softly. "I've never asked you to do that because I never thought anyone was worth it. Not even me. But please. I am begging you not to hurt him. He's Stacy's brother. Whatever it is he feels right now, it doesn't erase the fact that he'd never do anything to hurt her."

Stacy stepped back, her hands flying into the air as though she were surrendering to whatever decision Robert made. Lark, too, backed away. The only one who didn't move was me. Instead, my grip on Sean tightened, and though I was certain that I was squeezing him to hard, he said nothing. His eyes were frozen with fear, and his voice had somehow lost its ability to make a sound as he stared at Robert and awaited his fate.

A shimmer of energy seemed to hover over Robert's skin, and he shook with anger. I wanted to close my eyes, afraid that he wouldn't care about my plea; that he wouldn't care about what his decision would mean. But I kept them open because I needed to see. I needed to see the decision form, and when it did, I felt my knees sag in relief.

"Thank you," I sobbed, releasing Sean and throwing myself into Robert's arms, stiff though they were. "Thank you."

"You are the only person who could beg for someone else's life with me, Grace. Don't do it again." His words were dark, but his voice had softened, and he embraced me with far more gentleness than I felt I deserved. He had gone against his call again…and this time it was because I had asked.

Stacy walked past us to her brother, who stood weak-kneed in front of us, his skin pale, his hair straggled, his clothes wrinkled, looking as though he'd been through a nightmare. "You owe Grace your life," she said to him.

"I don't get it."

"Robert was going to kill you, you jerk. I would've tried to stop him, but I know that I can't. You owe Grace your life—she saved you, you idiot. You should thank her."

Sean looked at me, puzzled and still so unsure. "I…I still don't get it. Why the hell would you that? Why did you do that…for me?"

I turned my head in Robert's arms to look at him and told him honestly, "I didn't do it for you. I did it for your sister."

"She saved my life, too," Stacy admitted.

"Mine as well."

"And mine."

Sean looked around the room at everyone who spoke, and I felt the need to argue against it because their lives would have never been in need of saving if it hadn't been for me in the first place, but Robert's thoughts reached mine before my mouth could open.

*Do not contradict us, Grace. We are each alive because of you. Let us keep that belief. Whether you believe them to be true or not does not matter. We do, and that is all that is important.*

Dr. Bro stepped forward, his calm demeanor having never altered once during the fracas. "Sean, if it would help you to better understand your sister's condition, I will gladly speak to you about it in the kitchen."

"How about you go and talk about it in the study," Lark suggested, pointing them to a door behind the stairs that led to a small den.

Sean looked at his sister, and then back at Dr. Bro. For a second, I feared that he'd once again head out the door. But then he nodded and followed the doctor into the other room. Lark closed the door behind them and sighed, pressing her forehead against the door. Graham came down to comfort her but she shrugged him off.

"Next time, open your goddamned mouth and say something instead of just standing there like some kind of ape. He might have taken this a lot better if the captain of the friggen' football team had spoken up in support of his best friend!" She stormed out of the house, the only person to actually leave.

Graham stared, and then turned to look at me. "What the hell was I gonna do? I'm not fast, I'm not strong. And you know that I'm not good at speaking up during times like this. I would've just made things worse."

Stacy clapped Graham on the shoulder, smiling when she saw his knees buckle and his body dip down at the force of the blow. "Self-awareness is a precious gift, Princess. Give her time. She'll come back and understand that you did the only thing you could have. Sometimes a person has to stay out of it in order to help it."

Graham gave Stacy a speculative look. "Are you getting soft?"

"What?"

"You're defending her. You're defending Lark."

Stacy's body stiffened and she sniffed at the suggestion. "No, I'm not."

"I think you are. I think you're starting to realize that you can't stay mad at her forever."

"Wanna bet?"

Graham's mouth sealed shut and I shook my head. "Way to go," I mouthed at him. He shrugged his shoulders at me and bent down to pick up the piece of gum he had dropped.

"I think it would be a good idea if you started to accept the fact that you cannot stay mad at Lark forever, Stacy. The two of you were able to put aside your differences long enough to see me get married, and long enough to defeat Isis, and I'm willing to bet that you might have to do it again at some point.

"Forever is a long time. I don't have that, and I'd like to know that the two of you worked out your differences before it was too late for me to see it happen."

I heard a whine, and then a rumbling groan come from Stacy as she looked at me with guilt ridden eyes. Guilt that I had placed there.

"You're not really going to use that card with me, are you?"

"You bet your ass I am."

She groaned again. "I can't believe this. I never thought I'd ever see the day that you'd use dying as bartering chip."

I tipped my shoulder up in a half-hearted shrug. "I don't have much time left, Stacy. I gotta play whatever card I've got, whatever hand I've got, and I'm going all in when it comes to my friends. You guys became friends because of me. Your friendship fell apart because of me. I don't want to die knowing that you didn't find your way back to each other."

Grumbling beneath her breath, Stacy headed toward the door. "You know, I used to wish that you wouldn't die so that I could see you live to grow and be an old lady with a billion grandbabies or something. Now I wish you'd live so you can't guilt-trip us into doing stuff for you. This is going to suck."

She was gone in a blink, and I hoped that, if nothing else, an attempt was made to begin to right the wrongs that had been committed against our little family.

Robert squeezed me as he heard my thoughts. "Our family."

"I won't let anyone else hurt this family, Robert," I vowed. "We're going to piece it back together and we're going to make everything right. We're going to stop whoever's hurting the people I love and we're going to stop living by rules that were never intended for people like us."

"You sound so sure of yourself."

I remained silent. There was no need to agree with him. I *was* sure. I was positive. Sean was the beginning of the change. Everything else from here on out was going to go my way or I'd die trying.

# THE INHERITANCE

The sun had risen and set again before Lark and Stacy returned, and Sean and Dr. Bro emerged from the den. Lark and Stacy were quiet, but at least they came in through the door together. Sean, matching his sister in mood, followed a rather amused Dr. Bro into the living room, where I sat curled up next to Robert on the couch.

"I think…we've come to an understanding," Dr. Bro said quietly, looking at Sean's pale face and seeing the slight nod that followed his announcement.

Stacy took slow steps to her twin, stopping just a foot away from him, waiting for whatever reaction he might give to her nearness. I held my breath as Sean's hand rose to poke his sister's cheek. His finger met the stony resistance that was her skin, but rather than pull away he pushed.

"I'm not moving," she said to him with a hint of humor in her voice.

"You're very cold. Not as cold as I thought you'd be, but still, you're not like me." He moved his hand to her shoulder and shoved. Hard. "You also feel like you weigh a ton. I always knew you were a fatty."

The mock indignation that came from Stacy's lips, coupled with the gentle shove she gave to him that still sent him sprawling onto the ground, did wonders to lighten up the mood. Lark excused herself to go and find Graham, who had holed himself upstairs since last night. I'd brought him a sandwich and some iced tea, but aside from thanking me for the food, he hadn't said two words to me or Robert.

Dr. Bro approached Robert and looked at him, his eyes never blinking, his face never changing in appearance or expression as he shared with him his thoughts about what was happening with his own kind. The discussion was tense. I knew it by the way the air grew colder despite the heat that I could see reflecting off of the asphalt outside through the window.

Robert sat up straight, his back a ramrod, and his fists clenched into the sofa cushions, easily ripping the fabric and stuffing. He removed his hands and slapped his forehead as though he had just come to recognize the obvious. The sound was like a brick hitting pavement.

"This makes so much more sense. Thank you, Ambrose, for bringing this to my attention."

"Bring what to your attention?" I asked.

"Do you want to tell her or should I?"

Dr. Bro nodded his head and turned to face me. "I just told Robert what it is that I and some of the others of my kind believe is the cause for the attacks against humans. We believe that it's meant to be a diversion, to keep Robert away from you, and to switch the focus from you elsewhere."

"You said something like that before, about Isis," I said to Robert, whose head bobbed down once in confirmation.

"Isis was a troublemaker. She and others like her instigated tiny wars all over the world in order to draw me away from you. Humans fighting other humans for no reason is always something to suspect, but for turned creatures to simply start attacking humans...I had assumed it was their beastly nature returning."

"But it isn't," Dr. Bro confirmed. "When one of my kind decides to break our own covenant and feed directly from the human body, we rarely consume every part of them. We're not gluttonous feeders; our ability to feed is limited to what our human bodies once could contain. But with everything that we've heard through our own sources, the victims of these attacks have been stripped to the bone. The only person who's ever been able to do that in my time is Stacy."

"Y-you don't think that she-" I looked at Robert and he felt my fear, my concern, and his hands took a hold of mine quickly to ease my distress.

"No. I know who her victims are, and she could not have done anything of this magnitude, and certainly not as widespread as it is."

Dr. Bro came to sit beside me, his dark eyes growing darker as the tone in his voice lowered. "I have spoken to someone who has knowledge of every erlking and vampire that exists in this world. There are dozens of new ones, dozens who up until two months ago did not exist."

"Dozens. That's not that many, right? I mean, when I heard the story about Miki and what happened with her, there were hundreds. Dozens aren't bad. And they're not changing people…"

"Grace, they're not like me. They're like Stacy. They were changed while their bodies were riddled with cancer."

I gaped at him. "What? How do you know? I mean, how do you know that?"

"I'm a doctor. I can access the files if I come across their names. I've been given several and all of them were suffering from terminal cancer. Breast cancer, bone cancer, lung cancer. They lived all over the world, came from different backgrounds. The only thing that ties them together is the fact that they were all dying."

"So, what does that have to do with anything?"

"I believe that after Stacy was bitten, the cancer and the virus that makes us what we are somehow spliced themselves together. The cancer's need to feed on flesh made it the perfect platform for the virus to attach itself, and together they've made it nearly impossible for these changelings to satisfy themselves."

I looked over at Stacy and saw that she and Sean were listening intently to our conversation. "So you're saying that the reason Stacy feeds so often is because of the cancer?"

"No, Grace. Stacy *is* capable of satisfying herself, but only for a short period of time. She doesn't need to feed non-stop in order to feel full, and it seems her palate has developed a taste for the blood of those whom society would deem evil. These others, they feed as though their lives depend on it. They don't stop. And...there's one other thing."

He paused and scratched at his arm, the sound of his nails scraping against the hard surface of his skin almost like nails against a chalkboard. I cringed.

"They're only hunting at night."

"What does that mean?"

Sean's question hung in the air, heavy as Stacy began to understand. "It means that they're allergic to the sun. Like the first one."

"Miki," Sean added. "She was the first one, right?"

"So he told you," I remarked, looking at Dr. Bro and wondering what else he had told him.

"Yeah." Sean's face was still. Obviously, I was still persona non grata.

"Miki had a severe allergy to the sun. In humans, it's called Xeroderma Pigmentosa. It is a genetic condition, one that has been purged from our kind hundreds of generations ago."

"So how would these new vampires get it?" Stacy sat down on the coffee table, her face tight with concern.

"The only way is if they were bitten by someone who carries the gene, and I don't mean someone who carried it as a human," Dr. Bro answered grimly.

I looked at Robert, and I saw the deep lines that now bracketed his mouth. "There's no way that could happen, is there? I mean, wasn't that first generation destroyed?"

"Most were. Some had already moved on before the rest were wiped out. It's from them that the current generation of vampires and erlkings exist, but even those second and third generations would not have the ability to pass on any particular genetic structure to their offspring."

"So that means-"

"That means that the first of my kind still lives," Dr. Bro finished for all of us.

"But that's not possible," I argued.

"It isn't," Robert agreed. "I am tied to those who were there, who saw her die and whose visions have become my own. Miki is not alive."

"Are you so sure?"

Lark had returned, her eyes nearly colorless as her feet glided down the stairs, Graham following close at her heels. She looked ethereal, dressed in a simple white gown, her long dark hair hanging loosely down her shoulder. She looked like an angel.

She looked like her mother.

"Are you so sure that Miki is dead? That she died as the visions say she did?"

Robert nodded furiously, angry that his sister would dare questions what he believed to be the truth. "I have seen the events through several eyes, Lark. They do not change, regardless of the perspective."

"Yes, you've seen it through the eyes of Llehmai, Grandmère, Mother, and even Sam. But who was it that killed her? Whose vision did you *not* see?"

Even with the seven of us gathered there, there was no doubt whose vision had been left out. And I felt myself collapse inward as the piles of deceit kept building, layering one atop of the other.

"It always comes back to her, doesn't it?" I whispered.

"What are you trying to imply, Lark?" Robert growled, his arm wrapping around my shoulder and pulling me against him in an effort to comfort me.

"I'm saying that Avi was the one who learned about Miki's illness. She was the one who figured it out, and she was the one who could take away life without actually doing so. What we've seen wasn't what the person who killed her saw, and that's something that we never questioned. Why?"

"Because of what we are. If we cannot trust each other, then how can we expect the humans to?"

Robert's voice stilled as he heard his own words echo around us. "And that's our fatal flaw, isn't it? We trust what we tell each other. It's why I believed Grandmère when she showed me the two outcomes if I chose to come to Heath with Mother or if I remained behind in England as I had planned. It's why I never questioned Mother about Grace.

"Oh God, what a fool I've been."

"You and me both, brother," Lark said softly. "I thought that by keeping Mother's secret about Grace that I was somehow protecting her and you. I didn't understand that I was destroying myself by doing so."

"I want to know," I broke in, "why my mother would've been the one to keep Miki alive?"

My mind was open, my head clear, and only one thought, one memory was allowed to show itself as both Robert and Lark looked at me and realized that there was no point left in hiding the truth.

"You already know," Lark answered first.

"Mrs. Deovolente told you the truth about your mother, Grace." Robert's face was stark. I had one pillar left within me that remained standing. One last pillar of hope. And as he began to speak, I felt it begin to crumble.

"The first circle of angels is the purest of us all. They were created directly from the light of God, to be his own rays of light between Earth and Heaven. But light cannot exist without hands to point them out and eyes to seek them out. Humans needed a way to do this, and so the second circle of angels was born, created from the very marrow of those that came before them.

"Three more circles followed, each from the heart of the one prior, until the numbers were nearing a thousand. Mankind had flowered as a crop, and they spread over the earth in fields. But with the gift of life, human and otherwise, there must also be the price of death.

"Death was the only one who could touch both Heaven and Hell, life and death, good and evil. Death had to be the one who could balance both and never let its darkness or power taint it. Avi was created for that purpose.

"She was also the first female of our kind. Humans never knew she was a woman; they still don't. And, in truth, many angels still do not know. For thousands of years, she existed in two worlds; one where she was adored by those who saw her as the light; the other where she was despised and revered for her darkness. Your mother was Death, Grace."

This wasn't what I wanted to hear. I didn't want to hear this truth, because if it was true then maybe what Mrs. Deovolente said about inheriting the call was also true.

"It isn't," Robert assured me. "I would not have received my call if it were. You are not meant to take her place. You are not meant to take mine."

"Wait-wait-wait-wait-wait. You guys are talking about this stuff like it's all freaking normal and crap. What exactly is this first circle, Heaven and Hell Death crap?" Sean's agitated confusion mirrored my own, and I looked at Robert, waiting for an answer.

"I think we've just let the cat out of the bag."

"There isn't a bag big enough for that cat," I heard Graham snort.

"Sean, Lark and I aren't human. We're not erlkings either." Robert's voice was calm, but he stood with a purpose, and I moved away. The sound of his shirt slicing open, and the ruffling of silken feathers in the still air around him was like the exploding of a cannon compared to the silence that filled the living room.

"You're a vulture?"

Graham hooted. I turned to glare at him and he covered his mouth with his hand, enjoying the fact that he hadn't been the only one to compare Robert to a bird.

"No, Sean. I'm not a vulture, but I do pick on the dead," Robert said darkly.

"Tell me about it," Dr. Bro chuckled.

"Ditto," Stacy added.

"Oh, for the love of—we're angels, Sean," Lark finally informed him, exasperated. "Not birds, not half-bird, half-human hybrids, not super-human mutants, not science experiments gone wrong, and could you *please* stop running through every comic book you've ever read trying to find some kind of alternate explanation?" She grabbed her head and shook it with annoyance.

"You-you were reading my thoughts?" Sean stumbled at the revelation, and Stacy reached out a hand to steady him.

"Thought. I was reading your thought."

"Wow. So, like, if I took you to my girlfriend's house, could you go into her brain and tell me if she's not giving it up because I-"

"Aaaand that's enough of that," Graham interjected, putting himself between his wife and an almost too eager Sean. "Dude, you were just about to ask my wife if she'd spy on your girlfriend. That's a hell no in my book. She's not here to serve you, alright, so back off."

Sean looked at Graham and understood immediately, the hierarchy of high school still having sway apparently. "Alright man, it's cool. Sorry."

Graham nodded, and then turned to look at me sitting on the armrest of the couch. "Look, are we forgetting something here? Robert just revealed that Grace's mom was the big D, and Mrs. Deo-whatever knew. How the hell did she know that?"

"She knew it because she was an EP," I told him before realizing that everyone was now staring at me.

"An extra-terrestrial?" Sean's question brought out a collective groan.

Stacy's eyes rolled in her head, and she took Sean by the arm to drag him to an empty corner, her voice soft, yet not quiet enough to not carry over to us. "Not an ET, you idiot. EP. Electus Patronus. It's like their human guardian, the person who makes sure that their cover doesn't get blown. And speaking of which, where the hell are yours?" She looked at Lark and Robert and her brow wrinkled with confusion. "You guys don't have any. Why?"

Lark sighed. "Angels inherit their EPs. We have a few loyal

friends who've chosen to take on the roles, but we don't have any to inherit."

"Why?"

Lark looked at her brother and waited for his nod of permission to explain why they had no guardians of their own. "Our grandfather is of the first circle. Our grandmère is of the second. EPs come directly from the paternal side of the family, but since there are no EPs for the first circle they have none to hand down. The males of the second circle are the creators of the EP. They found them, humans willing to die to protect the angels, and made them their pets."

"So you can't go and get your own?" Sean asked.

"Hey, I'm an EP. I look after you and protect you," Graham spoke up.

"Well then, that makes me one, too," Stacy said with a proud grin.

"Hey, I want to be one, too! I can kick ass, you know!"

Robert chuckled. "It looks like we inherited some EPs after all, only this time they came from a human."

Lark laughed, the sound full and rich, and soon everyone was joining her. Well…almost everyone. My head was filled with the knowledge that my mother had been what Robert is now. And despite Robert's insistence, I did not believe for a single second that Mrs. Deovolente would tell me the truth about what my mother was and then lie about everything else. There was no reason for it.

My mother was Death. And because of that, she had seen her death, as well as my own. She had done nothing to prevent it, and instead, encouraged it and involved other people including Dad and Ameila, Robert and Lark. I didn't think it was possible, but while the people I loved and cared about laughed around me, enjoying yet another joke about the humor of their situation, I was searing with the raw hatred of the one person who I had spent the past ten years praying would come back.

I closed my eyes and felt the burn of my lids as my thoughts turned dark and vengeful. *I hope you're burning in Hell.*

Two days after my "*death*", my obituary appeared in the local newspaper. Sean had brought it when he came by to visit with Stacy. My senior year photo was there in black and white, framed in a decorative print box that I was certain cost more than Dad should have spent. It called me the beloved daughter of James and Abigail Shelley, and said that I had been survived by a younger brother, Matthew, and a step-mother, Janice.

There was no mention of Robert and Dad still didn't know that I was alive.

Two days after my obituary was printed, they held my funeral. I wanted to attend. Some macabre curiosity made me want to see just how many people *didn't* show up. But, more than I wanted to go, I didn't.

I didn't want to see Dad's face, or see the phony grief on Robert's. I didn't want to see the police officers who would be there, trying to best figure out how to broach the topic of my death once more without insulting or distressing my dad. And more than that, I didn't want to go because I didn't want to face the death that loomed ever ahead.

Robert, Lark, and Graham went. It was meant to be a show of solidarity for Dad, who would no doubt embrace Lark and shed a tear or two with Graham, but who would most likely give Robert the cold shoulder. I watched them pile into Graham's old Buick and drive off, Stacy remaining with me once more, ever the bodyguard.

The night before, Robert had insisted that Stacy feed to prevent any chance of distraction while he was away. The funeral was being held nearly an hour away by car, and while Robert would be able to arrive in half that time, if not less, he did not want there to be a need.

Stacy couldn't help but smirk at the idea of Robert ordering her to actually eat someone, but kept a wise silence and left, returning before dawn to fill her role as best she could. I was still asleep while all of this was happening, too exhausted after too many nights without sleep to stay up and wait for her.

"Lark will be listening for you. If anything comes up, if anything happens, you will call for me." Robert was pushing up the tie he was wearing with the dark gray suit I'd chosen for the funeral—I told him if he was going to be mourning my death, he might as well be doing it in something I picked out—and was looking in the mirror at my reflection as I watched him. "Promise me, Grace. I won't lose you on the day of your funeral."

"I promise." He nodded and turned to press a chaste kiss to my forehead.

"Thank you. I won't stay longer than necessary."

I followed him downstairs where Graham and Lark were waiting, Graham in the same black jacket and dark gray pants he'd worn to Stacy's funeral, while Lark wore a dark navy sheath dress with a black belt. My eyes started to well up with tears.

"What's with the waterworks?" Graham asked as he reached into his pocket to pull out the handkerchief that Lark had most likely placed there.

"It's just…you all look so nice. I'm glad that you're not dressing like bums to my funeral."

Lark couldn't help but smile, her face lighting up at the rather dark humor of the situation, while Graham smiled at the irony. They both hugged me and left, leaving Robert to say his own goodbye.

"I don't understand why you can't tell him-"

"I promise, when the time is right, we will let him know that you're okay."

"Could you…could you at least make sure that he's doing okay?" I asked softly, my hands gripping onto the lapels of Robert's jacket. "I mean, with Janice being in the hospital, and Matthew, and the funeral…I'm scared for him."

"I've been checking on him every day, Grace. He's holding up as best as can be expected, and he's staying strong for Matthew and for Janice. The Kims have been very helpful, especially now that they both share the same suffering. But I will do my best to speak to him so that you may know yourself."

He held me close to him, our bodies touching yet feeling very far apart as what lay ahead wedged itself between us. Robert was going to have to pretend that I was gone. The dress-rehearsal of what was to come.

After he'd left, I sat down with Stacy in the kitchen. I grabbed a piece of toast that had been sitting on a plate next to her and began to slather it with some butter and honey. She looked at it with disgust.

"How can you eat that stuff?"

"The same way you can take a bite out of people."

"Yeah, but I *need* to eat people. You don't need to eat butter. It's totally bad for you."

I looked at her and raised a rather perplexed eyebrow. "What? I'm sitting across the table from someone who eats people, there's a crazed angel out there stalking me, my mother was Death, my husband *is* Death and is destined to kill me, and you're telling me that *butter* is bad for me?"

"Well, since you put it that way, here-" she grabbed the box of butter that sat on the counter "-have a whole pound of it."

I laughed. There really wasn't anything else to do. Her bewildered expression only added to the hilarity of the moment, and she soon found reason enough to laugh herself, and the two of us enjoyed a rare moment together as the friends we once were.

How easy it had been for us when there were no complications other than simply being awkward teenagers. So much had changed over the course of less than a year, and it was hard to believe that we were once so completely innocent of what the world truly held.

"Do you..." I began, but found that I couldn't quite say the words.

"Do I what?"

"Do you ever regret speaking to me? Becoming my friend?" There, I'd said it.

"Of course not! My God, what would my life have been if we

didn't become friends?"

I looked at her and the only word I could come up with was "alive."

"Boring, that's what!"

She obviously had a different idea.

"Grace, I was the only girl in a family of six kids. I went to school, I came home. You took away the monotony and I can't thank you enough for that."

"But look at what's happened because of you knowing me. You got sick again. You had to choose between dying and becoming something that a lot of people call a monster. You dated Graham!"

A lazy toss of her head and a soft chuckle followed. "No one knows for sure if me getting sick again had anything to do with being friends with you. But even if it did, it didn't make me do anything I didn't want to do. I didn't *have* to choose to become what I am, Grace. I know you probably don't agree, but I think that this was how it was supposed to be. I believe one-hundred-percent that everything happens for a reason, and meeting you was just one of the pieces of my life's puzzle falling into place.

"Without you, I'd have never met Lark. Yeah, things between us kinda suck right now, but they're getting better. I'm learning how to forgive because of it. And yeah, I dated Graham, but he's not a bad guy. You liked him too, remember? If nothing else, it's shown me that not everyone's 'perfect guy' is really perfect for everyone.

"He wasn't for you, definitely not for me, but for Lark he's like Prince Freaking Charming. And let's face it, *your* Mr. Right? Yeah, he's definitely not right for me. I might not be alive and all that but I still prefer someone with a bit more beating beneath his chest, if you catch my drift."

She waggled her eyebrows at me, and I couldn't help but laugh at the ridiculousness of it all. "How do you think you'd do with a human boyfriend?" I asked as I stood up to get a glass of water.

"Well," she began, looking thoughtful, "as long as he wasn't some kind of sick, perverted freak, I think it would be safe to say that I wouldn't eat him, and that's as good as I suppose it's gonna to get for me. Besides, I'm only nineteen. I've got what, another eon or so before it'll be acceptable for me to start dating? By then, I'll totally accept that whole cougar thing and maybe I'll find someone who'll accept the whole popsicle vagina thing."

There was water in my mouth.

*Was.*

Now it lay in droplets all over the table…and Stacy.

"Popsicle vagina?" I wheezed.

Stacy's face bore the look of innocence, but I could see the laughter brewing inside of her. Her eyes told me everything and soon, she was guffawing as though her life depended on it. "God, Grace. What did you expect? That turning into a people-eater would somehow delete my vagina or something?"

I shook my head rapidly, but blushed as I realized that what I thought was something far worse. "I knew it wouldn't get *deleted*…just maybe a bit more…dangerous?"

I didn't think her laughing could get any louder, but it did. What was once a guffaw was now a full blown bray. "Dangerous? Really?"

"Well, you remember that movie, where the girl was turned into a vampire and instead of biting them with her teeth she…well, you remember!"

"WHAT?!?!"

That did it. Stacy's laughter went atomic. She began to pound the table, causing the metal legs to curl out beneath it and bending the center until it looked like a four-legged spider. "Oh my God, I can't believe you actually believe the stuff they put in the movies. Oh God, I'm hurting here." She gripped onto her sides as her laughter reverberated throughout her body.

She had a point.

I stood up to get more water and heard the bending of metal as

Stacy righted the table, leaving only a few tell-tale dents. I sat back down and saw that she had placed a sheet of paper on the table in front of her.

"What's that?" I asked, looking over her neat handwriting.

"It's that list you gave me, remember? Of the doors that were in my head? I've been trying to make heads or tails of it but I keep coming up empty. I must have Googled about a billion different combinations but I've come up with nothing."

The doorbell rang, and with a sigh, I stood up to answer it, Stacy at my heels in case anything happened. There was no peephole, and so I had to trust that whoever was on the other side wouldn't leap through and attack. Slowly, I opened the door and felt my jaw unhinge a bit.

"What are you doing here?"

"I thought it was more polite if I rang the doorbell."

I let the door swing open as the figure who stood before me walked in. He looked different. His hair was cut short, the auburn color somehow appearing darker. He wore a rather plain looking shirt over a pair of torn jeans. He looked unkempt and...normal.

"Sure. Come in. You don't need to ask for an invitation," Stacy mumbled, her arms folding over her chest. "Do you think you should be here, Lem? After everything that happened the *last* time you were here?"

"Considering that I'm the only one available to inform you that Isis was Samael's partner and that her death has now removed from you the threat of interference from our kind, then yes."

I felt my breath catch in my throat, and my heart stutter at the news. "Are you for real?"

"Well, I'm not lying. Obviously."

"Yes, yes, I can see that," I said, feeling faint and needing to sit down. Stacy was beside me in a heartbeat, and she kept me from flopping onto the couch like some kind of dying fish.

"I thought that this would be good news," he said, concerned that my reaction wasn't lining up to his imagined one.

"No. No, it is. I just...I guess I didn't think it was possible."

"You didn't think what was possible?"

My eyes rose to his and I frowned. "That Sam would choose a woman as his partner. Even though he wanted me to think differently, he wasn't in control of anything, and I just can't believe that he'd let a woman call all the shots."

"Samael wasn't who you thought he was, Grace."

"What did I know about him to begin with?" I snorted.

"You knew enough to affect him. He was weak and he didn't like having that pointed out to him by one of his own kind, much less a human. But you pointed out every single one of his weaknesses, and you did it knowing what he could do to you."

He took a tentative step toward Stacy and me, but a deep, nearly thunderous sound seemed to rattle within Stacy, and he stepped back. "I can't stay long. I only dropped by to let you know what I've learned."

He turned toward the door, and I heard my voice call out to him to stop. He turned, slowly.

"Yes?"

"Why did it have to be you? Why couldn't Ameila tell me? Or Sera?"

"Because I am no longer welcome amongst them as I have been dropped from my place as a Seraphim."

My gasp was louder—thank God—than Stacy's chuckle. "Why?"

A somber smile passed over his face. "You needn't concern yourself over it, Grace. Just know that you're safe now. The danger of you dying has now passed."

"I never cared about the...danger to myself," I argued before he opened the door. "I only cared about what happened to my friends and family."

He stopped, his hand poised above the doorknob. "The fate of those that have passed was a much better one than what awaits us all when you die."

"Why are you saying that?"

"You know why."

He started to open the door, but I rushed to him, grabbing a hold of his shirt and yanking, the fabric tearing as he turned to face me.

"Tell me why," I pleaded.

"You know why. You know what your mother was."

"Yes, but what does that have to do with anything?"

"You are in the wrong role. You were never meant to be born human. You were never meant to be born mortal. If you had been born as N'Uriel had, it would be *you* receiving the call to be Death. It should have been *you* and not he, but because you have not, and you're the last of Avi's offspring, when you die, the world will soon follow."

My head shook violently. It wasn't true. What Mrs. Deovolente had told me wasn't true; I wasn't going to believe it. "You're lying."

"I wish I were. You were born for a purpose, Grace, but something went wrong and now there is no saving this world. Your birth was supposed to be the beginning of a new age of our kind. Instead, it's triggered the end of all of us."

Everything inside of me seemed to be breaking down. I felt my knees give out, and I collapsed onto them, the hard and sharp burst of pain that shot into me through them doing nothing to shock me out of the stupor I was in.

The last thing I remember hearing before I gave in to the guilt was Lem's rather sardonic laugh. "It's rather ironic, really. You cannot take on your role because of what you are, and yet you'll be the most successful at it, bringing on the death of every living person and creature in this world with one singular act on your part. It's rather remarkable. Imagine, you, the entire reason for the apocalypse. If ever there was a reason to feel guilty, that would be it."

## PIECED

We all live in our own individual worlds, tiny little environments within one large stew of an existence. When your own world falls apart, it's merely absorbed by the one around you, and you soon find yourself completely lost and alone. Even when you're surrounded by people you know, whose faces bear the look of deep concern and worry.

"Grace?"

Their voices call out your name and you fight to respond but you have no will. You succumb to the depression of hopelessness.

"Grace, can you hear me?"

You feel the ground beneath you move. It shakes you with a conviction to unearth you from your premature grave.

"It's like she's not even there."

There is nothing but the shallow feeling of cool suffocation as you allow the dark edges to finally creep over you and take you from the world of consciousness and drown you in a mock world set up to soothe you and placate you as the rest of the world goes on without you.

"I've tried to enter her thoughts but she's shut everyone out. I don't even know if she can hear us speak."

I can hear you speak. I can hear you all speak. It's just pointless to acknowledge it anymore. Asking questions and desiring answers has been my problem since the very beginning. Death. So much death.

"Grace, if you can hear me, blink your eyes. Do something."

What is blinking? What purpose does it serve when your eyes

can't see anyway? Everything I thought about this world is wrong. And everything I thought I had accepted after the fact is also wrong. Everything that I saw with my eyes, in my mind, in my heart, were all wrong.

"She's not blinking, she's barely breathing. She's just staring ahead like some kind of zombie. Should we get a doctor? Should I call Dr. Bro?"

What can the doctor do? He fixes bodies. He can't fix fate.

"No. He wouldn't know what to do. What happened, Stacy? What happened while we were gone?"

When did the air get so cold? How did I end up in Robert's room?

"You let him back in the house?"

"I didn't have a choice! She opened the door and he walked right in. I wasn't going to start a fight with him; that's the last thing she needs!"

Warm hands on my face...

"Grace, love, please just look at me." Silver eyes were staring into mine, but they could see nothing. They would be met with their own reflection.

"She's in shock. What did Llehmai say to her?"

"He told her the same thing that you said before, but then he told her that she was the one who was supposed to have taken over or something, and that if she dies then-"

"Then the world will die, too."

"You knew?"

"No. Not really. I've heard bits and pieces, but...mythology is part truth, part fairytale, and since I received my call, I believed that what I'd heard was the fairytale part. This isn't the first time Grace has heard of this, you know. But she didn't really believe it; she didn't have any reason to until now. None of us did."

"So is it true?"

There was silence. Unnatural, intentional silence.

"It is, isn't it?"

"I cannot say whether or not it's true. If it were true then my receiving the call would have been a mistake, but the call never makes a mistake."

The warm hand was holding my cold one. Everything around me felt like ice. Even the words were tipped with chilled points.

"How do you find out for sure?"

"I have to ascend."

"A-what?"

"Ascend. I have to go up to the first circle and speak to them, ask the first of my kind what is going on. Grace's circumstances are so unique that I'm not certain anyone outside of the first four could be able to explain to me anything without it being tainted by half-truths. My grandfather will accept me there and allow me my questions."

"Wait, you need permission to ask a question?"

Oh Stacy, why so surprised by the levels of restriction?

"I'm not like the others. I came out of a human womb; I've killed one of my own; I've broken too many laws of my kind to count. It doesn't matter what my call is; I'm still at the bottom of the totem pole here; the hierarchy is resolute."

"But one of those dudes is your grandfather, right?"

"It doesn't matter. We can all tie our origins to the first circle in some way, but very few of us have a direct relation to those of the first circle; the punishment for the Grigori helped destroy several generations of angels. Even Llehmai is nearly half-a-dozen generations beyond the first four."

"Well, how long will it take for you to get permission?"

The bed sank beneath me.

"It could be minutes, it could be days. The world is unsettled, and if what Ambrose told me is true, the world is about to be thrown into absolute chaos; what has been going on these past few weeks will seem like heaven compared to what they'll do.

"If the children of Miki are staging a revolt then others might feel induced to do so as well. The creatures that have kept themselves out of human sight in order to maintain their own existence will feel empowered to break the laws we've set for them and this world is not prepared for that. Humans are not prepared for what is truly out there…and it is our fault."

"Your fault?"

"Yes. We created them, we allowed them to remain, we allowed them to reproduce. It's our fault they exist."

"So…when you say 'creatures', you mean what? Things other than me?"

How pivotal, that pause of yours, Robert. You let her hear nothing, and her imagination blooms, setting her up for what we both know will be nothing but shock and terror.

"There's so much out there, Stacy. Angels have been very irresponsible. We're very much like humans in that regard I suppose. We wanted to create things, we wanted to be godlike, and the end result has been nothing but destruction. From the very beginning, we've done nothing but taint this world with our presence.

"Every nightmare a child has ever had, every monster that's ever haunted their dreams is the fault of those like me, who want more than they have a right to."

"What are you saying?"

"I'm saying that it's far better that we didn't exist…you were right when you said that it wasn't one of your kind that was after Grace. The only ones who've ever tried to hurt her have been my own kind. Even I've hurt her. You've done nothing but protect her, and I must admit that I hold some resentment toward you for my own failing in that."

"You didn't fail her. That Lem guy said that that Isis chick was the one who was working with Sam. She's dead now so Grace and her dad will be okay."

Such a warm hand against my face; I wish I could turn into it. I wish I could smile.

"There's always a danger to her. It comes from me. Whatever

the truth is, the fact remains that one of us will die, and the other will suffer as a result. If it turns out that what Llehmai says is true then she'll know nothing *but* pain. She feels such tremendous guilt for the deaths of those she had no hand in, how will she endure being the cause of them? She is fragile, Stacy."

"You don't know her as well as you think if you believe that, Robert. Grace isn't a piece of glass. She's stronger than you think, stronger than all of us. She's risked her life for you, for me, for Graham…she's lived through losing her mother, losing her best friend, losing you. She survived that night in the woods, though how I don't know. She did all of that on her own. If she has to do something, she'll do it, no matter what it costs her."

"And that's what worries me the most. She isn't invincible. For all the parroting of the fact that her mother was Avi, she wasn't when she gave birth to Grace. Her divinity was gone, her powers were gone, her immortality was gone; she was simply Abigail Shelley, and whatever divinity exists inside of Grace is purely residual. Her human frailty can only withstand so much before it succumbs to the strain of the blackness that comes with doing what being Death entails."

"So then fix her."

So sure, Stacy. Always so sure…

"Fix her?"

"Yes. Turn her. Take away her human frailty, or whatever it is you called it."

"I can't."

"What do you mean you can't? She's right here. You're right here. It makes no sense that you keep on putting this off."

"She has to be ready and willing, Stacy, otherwise she'll turn into something horrible."

"Something like me, you mean."

"Yes-no. I don't know."

"Will you still love her, no matter what she becomes?"

"Of course! It's not an issue about whether I'll love her. I'll always love her. I've *always* loved her. It's about whether she will be able to accept herself.

"She never wanted to turn; she never wanted any of this. She's already had all of her choices taken away from her. She has no say in how she lives, or even how she dies. She simply exists because that's all she's allowed, and I do not intend to take even that away from her."

"Well then, start giving her something back, Robert. Give her something. She's dying. She's lying here and she's dying because she doesn't have any hope left. Don't you see that?"

"But I don't know how-"

"Then talk to someone who does!"

"My grandfather...that's who would know."

Stacy's hands flew up in the air, the motion so swift and jerky that the bed shifted. How like her. "Well? What the hell are you still doing here?"

"You're right. I'll go and speak to my grandfather now. Will you..."

"I'm not going anywhere. I don't care if I have to eat Graham; I'm staying right here until you get back."

"Please don't eat my brother-in-law. Not all of him, anyway."

"Go. Hurry up and find out the truth so that we can save your wife."

Kisses. You kiss me as though you already know the answer, and this is goodbye. Is it?

"I will return as quickly as I can, love. Please, please don't give up. We've fought too hard and too long for it to end this way. Have hope. Have hope, Grace."

I have hope.

"He's gonna come back. He's gonna come back and you'll see that everything will be fine."

*Dear God, I hope everything will be fine.*

\*\*\*

"Grace, do you want some soup? I made you the one with the little stars in it. Come on, sit up and let's try and get some of this down."

Liquid warmth, thin and salty; why are you forcing it down my throat?

"She's not eating. It's been two days. She needs to eat, Stacy. I'm running out of ideas here."

"I told you not bring up any of that crappy soup Mrs. Lorimax brought over last night, Graham. It smelled like butt; I mean you didn't even eat it! Throw it out and take the bowl back to her house. Grace'll eat when she's ready. At least she's drinking now. Maybe we can get her to swallow some kind of diet drink or something, you know those meals in a can kinda shakes?"

"Hey, yeah! I'll go and get some. What kind though?"

"What kind does she like?"

"Wow, I don't know. She's never been a milkshake kinda girl."

"Duh, Graham. Does she like chocolate? Vanilla? Strawberry?"

"Oh...strawberry. She really likes strawberry."

"Well then go and get her strawberry. God, Graham, this isn't rocket science."

"Fine! I'll go and get her some strawberry shakes!"

His shuffling feet were the only sounds I heard before the walls shook at the slamming of the door, and then the rumbling of his car's newly restored engine floated up to the windows.

"That car makes more noise than two elephants f...whoa."

The bed dipped down, and I heard the growling even as I felt it vibrate around me.

"Look, I don't know why you're here, but you need to get the hell out."

"I know you don't want me here, but I heard what happened. Did this...is this because of me?"

Lem. Are you feeling guilty now? Because you destroyed my fairytale?

"You're goddamn right this is because of you! God, you're worse than a girl with your big mouth, you know that? What the hell were you thinking anyway, huh? Telling her that crap—why not just blame her for cancer or something; it'd hurt less!"

"I was telling her the truth because what she plans on doing will have the opposite effect that she's hoping for. She won't save anyone's life by dying, Stacy. You know that."

Stacy's body passed over me, and her feet padded lightly on the carpet as she stood in front of the bed, blocking Lem's way to me. "Yeah, well, I don't know anything about any of that. That's an angel thing and I only know what to do about Grace and I'm not gonna let you near her."

So that's why she moved—he'd moved, too.

"I'm not going to hurt her. I won't even touch her if she doesn't want me to. I just want to talk to her."

"No. I promised Robert that I'd keep her safe and I know that she's not safe with you. You're like the absent-minded-angel or something; every time you were supposed to be watching her she got hurt."

"The same thing could be said for N'Uriel."

That wasn't true; not really.

"Look, I get that you've got the hots for her, but she's not into you, okay? She's in love with Robert, and he's in love with her, and they're trying to be happy together, for once, so why don't you just leave them alone and go find someone else."

"I'm trying to be patient here with you, but you should know that I don't owe you any loyalty. Your kind shouldn't exist and no one would miss you if you were exterminated."

Stacy hissed. It was like hearing a snake on a megaphone. "My kind wouldn't exist if it weren't for your kind trying to play God, so who's more to blame, huh?"

I could hear the hard edge in Lem's voice as he responded. "No matter what kind of monster you are now, you are still the raw, imperfect human being underneath, filled with your deceit and your greed for power. Since the moment you humans learned of us, you've tried every trick to get us to give you even a simple taste of our divinity.

"Even the most innocent looking girl can be a temptress looking to lure us in and steal our souls. It doesn't matter if they're peasants or princesses. But you know what? No matter what we do to you, no matter how much power we may give to you, we will always, always be stronger than you because yes, we made you, and we can *un*make you."

"You know, now I understand why that Sam guy was such an asshole: it runs in the family."

Lem's voice was warm and pleasant, despite the jab. "I don't pretend to have loved my son so insulting him really has no effect on me. He was a failure in every way, despite what he was born to be, and I'm glad that he is no longer here to stain the legacy of my kind any longer."

Stacy was disgusted. "Ugh. He was still your son. You could at least act like he mattered, no matter how screwed up he was."

"He was also Grace's brother—have you asked if she's feeling choked up because of his death?"

"She's not exactly in the answering mood, if you haven't noticed."

No. No, I wasn't in the mood.

"Well, maybe I know of a way to get her in the mood."

The contrasting silver and gold eyes that filled my vision seemed pained, as if just seeing me laying here hurt him. "Grace, would you like to see your father?"

My reaction was involuntary. "Dad?"

"Holy balls, she said something." Stacy turned my head so that I was looking at her pale face. "Grace? Are you alright?"

I shook my head; that was the wrong thing to do as a wave of dizziness slammed into me, and I rolled over, falling off the bed. Two sets of hands caught me before I hit the floor, each one tugging for possession.

"Let her go."

"She's not a prize, Stacy."

"Then let—her—go, *Lem*."

My eyes lifted to look between the two of them; they were glaring at each other, like one of those stupid kid games where whoever looked away first was the loser. Lem's face was stoic, while Stacy's showed stubbornness that I was more than familiar with.

"Stop."

"Grace?" Stacy said again with concern.

"Stop arguing."

Stacy's eyes shot daggers at Lem, who leaned back with a smug smile on his face. "I told you I could get her to speak again."

"You cheated is what you did; offer her the only freaking thing she can't have…of course she'd say something."

I pushed both of them away and sat up, another wave of dizziness hitting me before almost instantly disappearing. "I want to see my dad. I want to talk to him. I need to talk to him."

Stacy shook her head defiantly. "That's not a good idea, Grace. Your dad's gonna be majorly pissed off, not only at you, but also at Robert, Ameila, Lark, Graham. He's already pissed off at the world for what he thinks happened."

It was difficult, but I managed to somehow grab a hold of the nightstand and use it as leverage to stand. My legs felt like jelly, my stomach lurching and flinching with its own emptiness, but I fought off the nausea and walked toward the door, passing by a speechless Stacy and a triumphant Lem.

I headed to the bathroom, flipping on the light and turning on the faucet to splash my face with some cold water. I reached for my toothbrush and began to brush my teeth, the mundane act comforting in some strange way. I looked up and saw myself, saw the way the foam formed at the corners of my mouth, the way the toothbrush stuck out like it normally did.

My hair was a mess, and I needed a shower, but overall I didn't look any different. I looked…normal; nothing at all like a girl who held the fate of every single living person in the palm of her hand.

I started to laugh, spitting the foam onto the mirror and speckling my reflection with it. Stacy burst in and looked at me, puzzled.

"Are you okay?"

I nodded and rinsed my mouth. "I'm fine. I'm actually better than fine."

"Are you sure? Because you're laughing like you're about to kill the head cheerleader."

My laughter grew louder. "I already did!"

Lem walked in and looked at Stacy, a wordless conversation passing between them before he looked at me and smiled. "Grace, what are you talking about?"

"Yeah, you didn't kill anyone, Grace."

"Yes, I did. I did. I'm the one who's responsible for all of those deaths; Mr. Branke, Erica, Mrs. Deovolente, Katie, you…I'm responsible for all of you dying—it's who I am.

"I can't escape it. If I die, people will die because of me. If I live, people will die…because of me. And I can't do anything about it. I'm not an angel—I don't have wings, I don't have magical powers, I can't even fly. The only thing I can do is be around people and then wait for them to die."

"Grace, there's a lot more to being Death than that, you know," Lem said softly.

"I know. The thing is, I don't want to know any of it. I've seen what being Death has done to Robert's spirit. I've seen the light in him slowly dim, but I don't have any light in me. Yeah, I can cry crystals every now and then, but that's not going to make me feel better about killing someone. I didn't grow up thinking that one day, I might have to.

"I didn't grow up thinking that one day, I'd hear a voice in my head telling me that the only way that the person I'd fall in love with could live is if I died. If Robert's call is to be Death, and his call tells him that I'm supposed to die, and the voice in my head is telling me that I need to die in order to save his life, then I'm going to listen to that, because if there's one thing I'm absolutely sure about, it's that you don't want me to be responsible for the lives of people if Robert's dead."

"Oh Grace," Stacy murmured, wrapping her arms around my shoulders and pulling me into a cold, hard, yet comforting embrace. "Kinda makes high school seem like a piece of cake, huh?"

"Graham got me through high school. Robert got me through Graham…"

"Well, maybe it's time you started letting Grace get you through the rest of this."

I looked into Stacy's dark eyes and saw the fierce protection and soft, yielding friendship that had always been there. She'd never changed, even after…changing. She'd faced death almost as many times as I had, and she had done it relatively alone. She didn't have an angel who was willing to sacrifice his life in order to see her live. She fought for her life; she fought for every single second of it, even facing down Death himself.

"You're right." She was. She'd done it without being the child of an angel. She'd done it by herself and she did it without breaking the rules.

I didn't have that option. I'd have to break the rules and make up new ones, but that's how I existed.

I laughed again. "I'm one long string of broken rules."

"What?" Lem and Stacy said in unison.

"My entire life is just one big ball of broken rules. My mother broke the rules to have me. Graham broke the rules to be my friend. I broke the rules to be with Robert. I don't know how else to do this without breaking them."

Confused, Stacy looked at Lem and then at me, her brow wrinkling in an odd, almost slow motion kind of way. "What are you talking about? Break what rules? To do what?"

"Get through this. I've been accused of a lot of things, and I may have screwed up a lot, but the one thing I'm not going to be responsible for is the freaking apocalypse. I'm not going to let Robert die, either. I'm not going to let anyone I love die anymore."

"And how are you gonna do that?"

"By finally relying on myself."

Stacy looked almost smug as she folded her arms over her chest and gave Lem a withering glance. "Now that sounds like the Grace I know—stubborn as all hell and not giving up. That's the Korean in you."

The snort wasn't intentional, but once it was out, I didn't regret it. "I'm not Korean, Stacy."

"The hell you aren't! Look, I've been around Koreans all my life. I don't mean my brothers, because let's face it, I don't think most of them are even human; especially Brandon. I'm talking about people like my mom; you know, hard headed, stubborn, kim chi eating, han bok wearing, K-drama watching Koreans, okay? You're Korean.

"Yeah, your mom might not have been up front with the angel thing, but she was stubborn enough to keep her dream of having you alive even *after* she lost her wings, and that's one-hundred-percent Korean, okay? Which means you're Korean; well, half-Korean, anyway."

My eyes watered at her words. "That's probably the best thing anyone's said to me in a really long time."

"Of course it is. I'm your best Korean friend."

"You're my *only* Korean friend," I sniffled.

"Well, now that you've decided that you're going to somehow pull off the impossible, why don't we see about you talking to your father." Lem's smile was beautiful and genuine. I almost felt as if just looking at that smile could fix everything. But it couldn't, and neither could he, no matter what he promised.

"Robert's right. I need to wait. If Isis wasn't Sam's partner, letting Dad or anyone else know that I'm alive only puts them in more danger. I'm not letting that happen anymore. The killing stops now."

I pushed past him and headed down the stairs. I walked into the kitchen and opened the refrigerator.

"You're getting a snack?"

Lem and Stacy were side-by-side in the kitchen doorway, both wearing the same expression. I smiled at them and grabbed a takeout container with chopsticks poking out of the top. "I'm hungry and a girl can't fight the apocalypse on an empty stomach."

# AT ODDS

When Graham came back, his arms carrying several cases of protein shakes, I felt bad. I felt worse when he dropped them all on his feet in shock at seeing me standing in the kitchen eating a box of noodles.

"Jeez, are you okay?"

He shook off the pain and grabbed me in his arms and squeezed me until I think my ears popped. "Holy crap, Grace, don't you ever zombie out on me again, you hear me?"

Laughing softly, I nodded. "I promise."

"I don't like being freaked out like that. I don't like not hearing your smartass comments. And I really don't like being bossed around by Stacy...anymore."

"I'm sorry."

Graham pushed me away, his face hard and frustrated one minute, irritated and annoyed the next. "Stop saying sorry. Hell, if someone told me what that Lemon guy told you, I'd probably freak out, too."

"Yeah, and then you'd go on some kind of food rampage and totally wipe out every grocery store from here to Canton," Stacy quipped before wrinkling her nose. "I...I smell something. I'm gonna go and check it out."

Graham sniffed the air. "What? Did your nose die too? Because I don't smell anything."

"That's because your nose can only smell extra cheese and bean burritos."

364

"Yeah, like you didn't eat two of them every time I took you to the Taco Tower."

"And? You ate six!"

"That's because I needed the energy!"

"For what?!"

"To keep from strangling you! Damn, Stacy, even dead, you're annoying!"

"You didn't think I was annoying when we were making out!"

"Duh! That was the only time you ever stopped insulting me!"

"That's because making out was the only thing you were ever good at!"

The back and forth between the two was yet another thing that I took comfort in. Even if what I knew about myself was different, what I knew about the world and my friends hadn't changed. Stacy and Graham would always butt heads.

"Okay, you guys. I get it, making out with each other was fun, even with burrito breath, but if you keep it up the neighbors are gonna start thinking something's up and chances are they're gonna call the police, and since two of us are supposed to be dead, and Graham's not supposed to be living here..."

Stacy quieted and Graham exhaled hotly. I finished the noodles and tossed the box into the trash. Stacy headed to the kitchen door, her face tilted up, her nostrils sinking in and then expanding as she sniffed the air again.

"I'll be back in half-an-hour. Graham, don't let her out of your sight. And if Lem comes back-"

"He was here? Again?"

"Yeah. But look, he's the reason Grace isn't still the zombie queen of Heath."

"So the creep who made moves on Grace-"

"Snapped her out of it; yeah."

"Hey, can you guys stop talking about me like I'm still catatonic? I'm here—talking, eating, getting ready to punch some people," I reminded them as I positioned myself between them.

"Sorry," they both said sheepishly.

"Sure. Stacy, go check out whatever it is you needed to; I'll be fine and if Lem gets back, I'll tell him thank-you for you."

Stacy nodded and stepped out of the door, disappearing into the darkness.

Graham stared out after her, his mouth held slightly open. "She's gonna eat someone again, isn't she?"

"Yup," I confirmed.

"You know, I never want to hear you complain about what I eat ever again."

I chuckled. "You act like some of the stuff you've eaten isn't as gross."

"Uh-uh. Yeah, I think it's cool and all that Stacy's all super-dead-girl and stuff, but it's not vampire cool. I mean, vampires are sexy! But they're not eating people like they're hamburger! I mean, she's gonna eat someone's face, Grace! Whoa-that totally rhymed."

"Okay, look, I won't complain about your eating again; I promise. But, you've gotta ease up on Stacy. Okay?"

"Why? I mean, yeah, before I always wanted to kill her, but she's already dead! And she can't exactly hurt me, you know? We can finally beat the crap out of each other and not stop!"

My head tossed from side-to-side and my eyes followed. "Seriously? When was the last time you ever hit a girl, Graham?"

"Well...I've only ever kinda, sorta hit you."

"Yeah, so you're not gonna be beating her up now anymore than you did before. You've always tried to avoid getting physical like that; you even let Stacy hurt you just so you wouldn't hurt her."

"If that's what you want to think..."

"Just quit...pointing out the fact that she's dead. She's your friend and she needs your support with this. It's not like what you went through—everything about her life has changed. The only thing that's changed for you is that you can now get laid."

366

"Alright, alright; I'll lay off the dead comments," he sighed.

"Good."

The kitchen door slammed open, and we both turned quickly to see who had just burst in. Stacy stood there, her eyes wide, her face plastered with shock.

"How'd you know?"

Graham's head pulled back in confusion. "Know what?"

"Not you, Princess. You. Grace. How did you know what I wanted to tell Lem?"

"What?" I knew my face mirrored Graham's in confusion because I felt it.

"When I left, you said you'd tell Lem that I said thank-you. How did you know I wanted to thank him?"

I shrugged and felt my mouth twitch. "I didn't. At least, I don't think I did. I guessed."

Stacy shook her head and her features grew serious. "No. You didn't guess. You wouldn't have guessed that I'd want to thank him, not with everything he's done. Graham's right; he's a creep, so there's no reason for me to *want* to thank him.

"So I gotta ask: how did you know?"

My head tilted down and I looked at the floor at her feet. A piece of paper had fallen there and I picked it up as I tried to figure out how to answer her. It seemed to be a natural response to me, her wanting to thank Lem for his help. But if I thought more about it, she had a hard time telling Graham thanks for the things he's done.

Her demonstrations of gratitude tended to be bursts of emotion, rather than simple phrases shared between two people. "Huh," I said upon realizing this.

"What?" Graham asked as he took the paper from my fingers.

"You're right, Stacy. Telling me to tell someone thank-you for you isn't something you would do."

"So how did you know that I was thinking that?"

"I am hell?"

Stacy and I turned around and looked at Graham. His face was puckered up—all of it. The piece of paper in his hands was open and he was staring at it like it was some kind of calculus test.

"All of these pictures on this note, the heart, the eagle, the iris-"

"Iris?" Stacy snatched the paper away from him and huffed. "Well damn, this whole time we thought it was an eye."

"Naw, that's not an eye. An eye's got eyelashes and usually an eyebrow over it or something. This is just the iris part. Or, you know, it could be pupa."

"That's pupil," I corrected. "But you're right. That's not an eye. Wow, I don't know why we didn't realize that before. So what's with the whole hell thing?"

Graham grinned. "Well, if that's an iris, then you've got I, H, M, E, A and two Ls. That means that this spells 'I am hell'. Either that or 'mall hie'; maybe 'all hime'. 'Elm hail'? I don't know; I was pretty good at these when I was a kid, but my brain's farting or something."

"No, no; you're right. This whole time I thought that the doors meant something. But it's not the doors, it's what the doors spell out. And yeah, 'Elm hail just sounds stupid," Stacy agreed.

"See, that's what friends do. We help solve problems," Graham said to me smugly.

"Oh shut-up," Stacy told him with a roll of her eyes. "You helped solve a puzzle you just admitted any kid could figure out. The problem here is what the hell does 'I am hell' even mean? And why was it in my head?"

"Maybe you dated Sam in a past life and he's just reminiscing?"

My eyes bugged at Graham's response. And, of course, I blinked when Stacy's fist pulled back and then snapped forward, landing solidly—almost too solidly—in the center of his gut. He doubled over and clutched her arm, pulling her down as he fell, the whoosh of his breath leaving his body not stopping until his back hit the floor and Stacy lay on top of him.

I braced myself for the retaliation, but this was Graham. He wasn't going to do anything but lay there. Stacy stood up and held out her hand. He took it and let her pull him up, only her strength was still something she wasn't used to and his feet rose several inches off the ground before landing with a solid thud.

"You're getting better," he told her gruffly.

"You're not."

"Yeah, well, all I got with my immortality was beat up."

"I know. That sucks."

Graham nodded. And just like that, the fight was over.

They both turned their attention back to me, picking up exactly where they'd left off.

"Okay, so Sam and that Isis chick were partners, right?" Stacy asked.

"That's what Lem said."

"So if that's the case, what if Sam was talking about Isis? I mean, I don't know what she could do, but she was seriously sick in the head. The things she was saying before Lark and I killed her was crazy."

I pulled out a chair from the kitchen table and sat down, my brain suddenly feeling heavy with thought. "Crazy like what?"

"Crazy like how she could control me, make me do things that I didn't want to do."

"Isn't that what Sam said he couldn't do? The whole zombie-mind-control thing?" Graham noted. "That's what happened with Erica, right? And Mr. Branke?"

"Yeah," I replied. "But, I mean, you saw what Erica and Mr. Branke looked like, Graham. They weren't…there. It's one thing to be inside your head and not able to get out—like Stacy was in her coma—but it's something else when you're basically dead and your body's just doing things because it's being told to."

His eyes lit up with understanding. "Like robots!"

"Exactly," Stacy agreed. "They were like robots!"

"So, if Isis can control a person's mind, that means that the person would have to actually *have* a mind to control. If Erica and Mr.

Branke were...dead when you were kidnapped, Graham, that means that Isis wasn't the one who was helping Sam."

Graham looked disappointed. "Then who was?"

Stacy's head bounced in agreement. "Yeah, who was it? I mean, I'm pretty sure there are tons of psychotic angels out there if I've only met, like, six, and two of them were total nutjobs and one's got serious boundary issues. The ratio of crazy angels to not-so-crazy isn't looking too good if you take Robert out of it because he's pretty much got no choice but to be all deadly-do-right."

I looked at Graham, and together we both looked at Stacy in muted surprise.

"What?" she said at our reaction. "My mom made me take extra math tutoring, alright? Sheesh—it's the only freaking stereotype I live up to...kinda. I'm good with ratios; that's not a crime."

"Do you-"

"No, I don't know how to use an abacus, Graham, so don't even ask the damn question!"

With his lips tucked between his teeth, Graham pulled out another chair and sat down beside me at the table. I smiled at him and then slightly shook my head, focusing on the question that was on everyone's mind.

"I don't know who Sam's partner was. With everything that's happened, I don't really know if I can trust any angel anymore. I knew right away that Isis was bad news; I felt the same way about Sam. But I don't believe for a single minute that Isis was Sam's partner.

"You're right, Stacy. As long as we're not sure, we really can't trust any angel that we don't know. And Graham, if you're really that hungry, go and order a pizza or something."

I looked up at Stacy, her face bearing a look of astonishment.

"What?" I asked, turning my attention to Graham, who looked just as stunned.

"You-you..." Graham stuttered.

"We didn't say anything—nothing at all. You're reading our

minds, Grace."

"What? No, I'm not!"

"My stomach didn't even growl. You totally just read my mind," Graham confirmed.

"Oh dear bananas."

"You're totally reading our minds!"

*Can you hear me?*

I nodded in shock at the sound of Graham's voice, slightly tinny but full and familiar.

*Why'd the rooster cross the road?*

"Because he was stuck in the chicken," I whispered.

"Dude, that's the joke we learned on the seventh grade camping trip! You actually read my mind!"

Stacy whooped and Graham stood up, bringing me along with him and swung me around. "This is totally awesome!"

"Why is that awesome?" I asked, more confused now than I had been just ten seconds before.

"Because now you can totally read those angels' minds and they won't even know it!" Stacy answered for him.

"Well, I was gonna say that you could hear what Lark was thinking when we...you know...and tell me if I need to improve my technique," Graham mumbled.

"Oh-my-God, are you serious?" I blurted out.

"What? I'm still a guy! Immortal but still a guy!"

Stacy groaned and I looked away, too embarrassed for him to continue looking at him. "I think the reading of the angels' minds is a really good idea, but won't they know that I can do that by reading your thoughts?"

"Only if they actually give a damn about us; Sam didn't care about what I was thinking or what I knew. He wasn't beating Graham up to get him to talk. What we think or what we know doesn't matter to whoever it is that's trying to kill you; all that matters is hurting you."

I knew that what she was saying was right, but there was always going to be doubt in my head. Angels have proven time and time again that they're not the pure, good-doing creatures they tell us they are. They've shown me the darkest places they can go to, especially when outcast by-

"Holy crap. Mrs. Deovolente."

The air left me and I was glad that I was sitting down.

"Mrs. Violent? What does this have to do with her?" Graham said out loud.

"She was an EP, remember? She told me before she died that she didn't stay with the angels that her family looked after. She wanted to protect the ones that no one wanted to, the ones who had no calls."

"Okay…what does that have to do with Sam?" The disconnect was plain in Stacy's posture.

"Sam had a call. He'd been an archangel of death for, God, I don't know how long. When you have a call, it's relentless. The voice in your head just keeps going on and on, and if you ignore it, it'll kill you. Whoever is Sam's partner couldn't have had a call."

"Why?" Graham asked, interest forcing his eyes wide open.

"Because whoever it was had to keep Erica alive, pretend that she was psychotic, pretend that she actually gave a damn about Graham for almost a year. And then there's Mr. Branke. He still had to teach. He still had to talk to students and other teachers. And all that time spent hating me and hunting me? When would they ever have the time to answer their call?

"Mrs. Deovolente was Sam's partner's EP. I think…I think that she was trying to warn me about whoever it was and she died because of it."

"So, if whoever she'd been protecting killed her because she was about to tell you the truth, why didn't they just kill you, too?" Stacy's question probably would have left me scrambling for an answer a couple of weeks ago, but today I knew what it was. It was so simple.

"Because they don't want me to die. Sam said so; he said that plans had changed, they didn't want me dead anymore…not physically.

Sam wanted Robert to die first and he wanted me to see it happen. He had Graham and my dad show up because he wanted me to watch them die, too. "

"But why? Why not just snap his fingers and kill you like he did with Erica and Mr. Branke?"

"You don't get it," I said to Graham, his question even easier to solve now that I was starting to see things more clearly. "They were already dead. They weren't alive, which means that Sam wasn't in control at all."

Recognition lit up Stacy's face, and Graham blinked with awareness. "He was being controlled, too."

"Yeah. I didn't get it. I mean, there were times when he was…different, like he actually cared about how I was feeling. And then he was cruel and mean and…cold. And when he kissed me-"

"Whoa-whoa-whoa, hold up. Your brother kissed you?" Graham looked angry and disgusted all at once. I knew how he felt.

"Yeah, but it was weird in a different way than you think. The first time I faced him, he said things that made me think he was attracted to me but he was lying. He lied to me from the moment I met him, and the only time anything ever felt like the truth was when he was hurting me.

"Everything else was a lie. But that last time, it was like, whenever he actually showed that he cared, that was real. I felt it, which is why it felt…weirder than it should have."

"I still can't believe your brother kissed you."

"I didn't know he was my brother at the time, Graham. And it's not like I could have stopped him. You ever try stopping Lark from doing something she wanted?"

Graham quieted and looked away, embarrassed. Stacy squatted and looked up at me. "You know, the more you talk about what happened, the more it seems like Sam wasn't exactly in charge like he—like we—thought."

"No, I don't think he was. He hated me. He hated me so much

that it doesn't make sense that he didn't just kill me when he had the chance. I mean, why not do it at the wedding?"

Stacy's cold hand rested on my knee, and she smirked. "Because that's usually not what people do at weddings."

I groaned. "I know, but angels aren't exactly supposed to be bringing their human girlfriends to weddings either."

"Yeah, but you aren't really human, Grace, and several of the angels that were there already knew that. I mean, Sam did, Ameila did, even Sera and Lem. Yeah, it sucks that they didn't tell you or Robert the truth until you guys were both dying, but that doesn't erase the fact that they knew and didn't see anything wrong with you two being together."

I scratched my head and tried to not show my contempt at her words. "I'm not an angel, Stacy. I don't care if I can read your mind, or cry crystal tears; I'm human."

"Yeah, those are totally the traits of being human," Stacy replied sarcastically.

"Isn't it time you went and ate someone?" I asked, too irritated to care about my tone anymore.

"You know what? You're right. I'm out."

She was gone before I could blink, and Graham whistled. "You think it's a good idea to piss off the people eater?"

"Sure. It's not like she'd eat me—I'm not even *human*, remember."

"Yeah, but I am," he said, swallowing.

# APPOINTMENT

Graham and I were sitting on the sofa, flipping through the billion cable channels on the tiny television set in the living room, when Robert returned. His reaction to seeing me was less painful than Graham's, but no less thrilled.

"Don't ever do that to me again," he breathed into my hair before kissing me and proving that every part of me had awakened.

"I promise." I held him tightly, squeezing him as hard as I could before it started to hurt me.

"Are you guys gonna do it? Like, right here?" Graham asked, annoyed.

Robert's head turned, and though he didn't say anything, I knew that a lot was said. Graham pressed a button on the remote and then stood up, grabbing his keys from the table beside the front door and leaving, his hand raised in a silent goodbye.

"Now that he's gone, we have to talk," Robert said, picking me up and whisking me upstairs to his room.

"Whoa. No one is here. Why can't we talk in the living room?"

"Because I plan on doing a lot more than talk," he said with a slow smile.

"Oh."

Oh!

Robert disappeared in a puff of black smoke that instantly swallowed me, and I shook with anticipation as wisp by wisp, the smoke found every sensitive area that was uncovered on my body and marked them with heat. My shirt began to rise up, and then I felt it tighten on my back as it pulled forward. The mist was filling it up, filling it and growing firm, solid, until I heard the seams tear and then the shirt fell away.

"What are you doing?" I asked when Robert's eyes appeared above mine.

"Trying to keep things from getting boring."

I giggled. "Boring? We've been with each other twice. I don't think boring can happen for at least…two more times."

"Twice?"

"Yeah. That first time and then…after…"

"I don't call that twice, Grace."

"Three, then? That one time in your room; you count that?" I asked, confused.

"No. That night in the sky, that was just one, long moment with you and I want to have millions of them; starting with moment number two."

The torn shirt on the floor was followed by the rest of our clothes, and as we sank into the small bed, I began to laugh.

"What's so funny?"

"I never thought it would be weird, being naked in a bed with you, but after that first time, it is."

"Let me remedy that," he said with a sly smile.

"Oh!" We were rising, and I was turning, my back making contact with what I knew was the ceiling.

"Better?" he asked before kissing me. I nodded and lost myself in everything that followed.

\*\*\*

"So, are we going to talk?"

"I'm sorry. Yes, we're going to talk."

"So…talk."

Robert sighed. "I spoke to my grandfather about you, about us,

376

about everything. I asked so many questions, so many angry questions that I didn't think he'd answer them all."

"But he did."

"Yes. He did. He answered every question I thought to ask, and every question I didn't think to ask."

"And…?"

"And he wants to talk to you. Actually, the first circle wants to talk to you."

"T-to me? Why? Why do they want to talk to me?"

We settled back onto the bed, and Robert pulled the comforter over me before pushing my hair away from my face. "Because of who you are, and what you are."

"Well…when then?"

He grew quiet, and my eyes narrowed. "Robert…they want to see me now, don't they?"

"Yes."

I looked at him, looked at his face, and for the first time, I saw every single thought in his head without touching him. I saw faces, heard voices, felt the depth of every emotion that he contained within him and my mouth fell open as one thought found its way to the front.

"This isn't going to be a short visit, is it? That's why you were in such a rush to make love."

"Grace-"

"I'm not going."

"You have no choice."

"I don't have to do what they want. I'm not an angel."

"Grace, the first four aren't like the rest of us. They control you as much as they do me."

"No, they don't, and I can't believe you're just gonna hand me over to them."

I scrambled out of the bed and began to dress, my eyes blurred by the tears that were beginning to form.

"Don't you see that I have no choice? If I don't take you, they'll come for you, and they don't come for anyone."

"Well too damn bad. I lost you twice; I'm not going to lose you a third time and I don't care what they have to say about it, or what your stupid legends or mythology says about it. I'm not afraid of them and I'm not afraid of your first four either."

"Grace, you don't know what they can do."

I zipped up my jeans and began to pull on some socks. "I've stood up to angels, erlkings, cheerleaders, and vice-principals. I don't care what four antique buzzards can do."

Robert stood up, and I heard my intake of breath as I took in his naked form. It was beautiful and heartbreaking at the same time. He walked over to the closet and pulled out a pair of pants and a simple shirt. As he dressed, I felt disappointed, but I didn't know if it was because he was clothed or because he had agreed to hand me over again, like a package instead of his wife.

*You know that's not true.*

I glared at him as I walked toward the door. "It's true. I understand why it happened before, but I'm not the same person I was when you met me, Robert. I've learned that I'm a lot smarter and a lot stronger than I thought I was, and I'm a hell of a lot more stubborn, too. I know that I don't need a babysitter or a bodyguard. Not anymore.

"If they want to see me, you tell them to make a goddamn appointment because I'm busy trying to find out who's been trying to kill my friends and family."

Robert's eyes lit up. "You've been busy while I've been away."

"You have no idea."

"So you don't believe that Isis was Sam's partner?"

"No. She wanted to kill me. Sam wanted to kill me. But whoever was working with Sam did not. That's why Sam could never actually do it—he was being controlled by his partner."

We walked downstairs, him just a step behind me, and when I landed on the floor I blinked.

The empty living room wasn't so empty anymore.

"Uh…"

Four men stood in a line in front of the door. All of them wore the same thing—band T-shirts with dark jeans and studded black belts—and each one looked at me with interest.

"Uh…"

The one with darkest hair stepped forward, and I recognized him immediately. He smiled, and held out his hand. "Hello."

"H-hello, Raphael."

"I hope that you have time to fit us into your busy schedule of saving the world."

"I-I…"

"Has married life been kind to you?" another voice asked. I turned to it and uttered something incoherent as I recognized the face of the person who had married us.

"She struggles for words, doesn't she Michael?" a third voice asked. This one came from the angel with hair that looked like sun was sitting on top of his head. His eyes were blazing a color that looked almost like white gold, and his skin was deep in shade, like dark coffee. His smile was gleaming and…crooked.

"She does, Uriel. I think we have overwhelmed her with our presence."

"We overwhelm all with our presence," the last voice said in a bored tone. "I see no reason why it should be any different with the half-ling."

"She is not a half-ling, Gabriel," Uriel corrected.

"This is correct," Michael agreed.

"That is yet to be seen," Gabriel responded with the same uncaring voice. "With every day that passes, she becomes more and more divine, but the taint of her origin is growing as well."

Gabriel was the most impressive of the four, with hair that seemed on fire, it was so brilliantly red. He had eyes that looked green one minute, gold the next, and his height was at least two inches above the others. His lips were full, and his nose was sharp, and his chin was square, defining a face that on anyone else would have been ordinary, but on him looked regal.

They all looked regal.

"There is no taint," Robert spoke up.

"You would argue that, N'Uriel, because your birth bears the same stench of falseness," Gabriel said with contempt.

"Now-now, let us not argue about this. We are here to speak to this poor girl. She has been through so much, seen so much, and has had no answers to the questions that creep inside of her. We shall answer her questions, and we shall tell her what we have decided to do." Raphael's instructions seemed to be accepted—if only begrudgingly—and he looked at me with a smile that I couldn't tell if it was genuine or simply the only form of expression he was capable of displaying.

"You're gonna answer my questions?" I asked.

"The questions in your mind, yes. The questions your mouth wishes to ask? No," Gabriel replied with a huff.

"But you just did; answer my question, that is," I pointed out.

Michael and Uriel snickered, and Raphael nodded in amusement. I looked at Robert, who looked mortified at my comment.

"It seems she's more human than angel," Gabriel said stiffly.

"I like it," Raphael announced before taking my hand. Just like it had with Robert that first time, my head began to fill with images and thoughts, like a balloon attached to a fire hose. Robert was at my side instantly as I winced and squirmed, but my hand was firmly locked in the older angel's grip. I fell to my knees in front of him as he looked at me with a peculiar expression on his face.

"You are strange, indeed," he said after letting go, pressing his hand against his chest in awe. "I did not intend for that to happen. I merely wanted to offer you comfort while we spoke."

"It happens," I said with a pained shrug. "Don't worry about it; I've been through worse."

"So we've seen," the other three said in unison.

Raphael backed away as Robert helped me to stand, my knees

quivering with the memory of pain. He eased me onto the couch and sat beside me, taking my hand in his and pressing his other hand against the side of my neck, feeling my pulse and sighing at its rhythm.

"Your concern is touching, N'Uriel. She means so much to you—almost as much as you mean to her. I think that your joining is less a union as it is a *re*union. There seems to be no end and no beginning to you; a rather wonderful thing in such a cynical time.

"But let us focus instead on why we have come to speak to Grace. You, sweet child, have learned some harsh truths over the course of this year. You have felt human heartache and human betrayal. You have felt angelic heartbreak and angelic betrayal. The time will soon come to experience divine heartache and divine betrayal.

"You will take your mother's place, and you will do it without regret. In fact, you will watch lives and worlds end, and you will rejoice because of it."

I shrunk away from his words and actually felt myself shiver. "You're not serious. You're not serious about that. I'll never be happy to kill people! And if I'm doing what my mother did, then that means that Robert won't be, and I won't let that happen. You guys can think and see what you want, but I'm not like you—I'm not an angel. I don't have to follow your rules."

"You think that this is about rules?" Gabriel asked, amused.

"I don't care about your rules anymore," I answered him defiantly. "I stopped giving a damn the minute I learned that my mom was one of you and did this to me on purpose. You guys all think you're these freaking superior creatures, with your wings and your powers, and your pretty faces. You want humans to love you, but more than that you want us to be scared of you.

"But I'm not scared. Not anymore. You and your rules have terrorized my family and my friends, haunted my dad's life for years, and forced me to hurt them. I'm through. I won't let you hurt anyone else I care about anymore. Maybe it's because I'm part angel. But I'm more human, and I still have that choice."

Gabriel smirked. "You think you know everything; typical. Have you never once stopped to ask why the moment you met N'Uriel, who you were began to change?

"I've changed, I know that, and I know it's because of everything that I've been through. Experience does that to people."

"You aren't people, Grace. You aren't even human," Michael said in a smooth, steady voice.

"She is human," Gabriel argued.

"She was *raised* human," Uriel countered.

"I was raised like every other kid here," I reminded them.

"Yes, but you're not like every other kid, are you? The children obviously knew that; they sensed it just as much as you did," Gabriel pointed out with a slight maliciousness that bothered me.

"Okay, so yeah, they knew I was different. But I *look* different, and after my mom died, I *was* different. You guys call yourselves angels, you're supposed to be empathic and crap but you don't understand anything, do you?

"You guys live so far away from people, from human beings, that you don't understand any of them. Try being a kid in school that doesn't look like the other kids. Try being a kid in school that doesn't dress or act like them. Then be the kid who everyone, from the kids in school to their parents, to their teachers blames for the death of her mom."

Gabriel showed no emotion when he spoke next. "But you *are* to blame for her death."

A year ago, even six days ago, this would have broken me. I would have shut down completely at the truth in those words and not even the promise of seeing my dad again would have brought me out. But now I knew better; I knew myself better.

"The only things I can be blamed for are the consequences of my own choices. I choose not to die. I choose not be intimidated by you. I choose not do live by your rules anymore. And I choose not to let who my mother was determine who I become. Whatever happens because of that, I accept responsibility for. But I won't accept the responsibility of my mother's death.

"She made her choice-"

"This is how I prove that you're human," Gabriel sneered. "You still think that what she did was a choice. She had no choice; she had to give birth to you. Do you honestly believe that an angel would willingly choose to put someone through what you have endured?"

My chin rose up and I nodded once, firmly. "You forget that I've already seen what angels would willingly do. I've seen it, and I've survived it."

"And do you ever question why you survived it?" Michael asked, his face sympathetic to the defiance in my voice.

"Of course I do. I ask why every single day."

"The reason you survived is because that is how it was meant to be. You cannot be who you are meant to be without the experiences that you have gone through," Michael said with a proud smile spreading his lips apart. "You met N'Uriel because without him, you would have never known your own kind.

"His entrance into your life was the catalyst to your change. No—not change; reversion. You were born an angel, Grace. You were born one; though your mind forgot, your body never did."

"What the hell does that even mean?"

Raphael looked sympathetic to my confusion and offered in his warm voice an explanation. "It means that everything that you have experienced—the weird bruising, the ability to keep your thoughts from others, the escapes from death—are all traits of an angel. You have been raised human and as a result, your mind has refused to let you reach your full potential. It's like being a bird raised by a cat; you know you're different but you don't know why until you meet others of your own kind."

"Look, I get that you really, really want me to be like my mom because it's the only thing that makes sense to you, but I'm not an angel, okay? Angels don't bleed; they don't get broken bones." I pointed out while Robert nodded his head slowly, as though wanting to agree with me but finding more to disagree with.

"You believe you are human, so your body responds that way. We all have human traits within us, some more than others, because we were fashioned for humanity. When we become so used to it, so attuned to it, we change. You have only known what it is like to be human. You have only known what it means to be the human daughter of a human man.

"It is time you learned what it means to be the divine daughter of the most divine woman."

I looked to Robert, but instead of seeing him, I noticed a mirror on the wall behind him. In it, I saw my reflection. It was exactly as it had always been. My hair was a mess, and my clothes looked second-hand and worn. My forehead was just as wide, my face just as dotted with freckles, my bottom lip still unnaturally larger than my top.

My eyes were still the same shade of boring brown they'd always been, and when I wrinkled my nose, they shrank into crinkled slits. Everything that I had been a year ago, I still was in that mirror. It was what lay behind those eyes that was different.

The person I'd been a year ago knew love, but not hope. I knew what it meant to hurt, but I never knew what it meant to truly die inside. I knew what loss was, but I didn't know what complete abandonment of everything important meant. And, a year ago, my mother was the most perfect person in the world. Now, she was the worst.

"I know what you think. I know what you believe I am and what you think I'm destined to be, but I'm the only one living this life, and I don't want to be the daughter of Avi, or the next Death, or whatever it is you think I'm supposed to be. Right now, I don't even want to be the daughter of Abby, wife of a grocery store manager. I just want to be Grace."

Gabriel's laughter was so sudden and so strangely beautiful that I almost smiled.

Almost.

"Do you really think that just being Grace is going to keep you alive? That it's going to keep your friends and family alive? That it will stop what has been set into motion by your birth?"

"Yes," I said with conviction.

"Then you're completely lost to us."

"I've always been lost to you," I countered. "You think that because you've got wings and you're older than dirt that you somehow know more about me than I do? You weren't the ones who watched your own mother die. You weren't the ones who lived every single day of your life being told that you don't fit in, that you don't belong, that you don't matter.

"You guys sit on top of the world while we look up, hoping for one single glimpse of you, and the whole time you're looking down your noses at us because we're not like you. When was the last time you actually lived with us, huh? When was the last time you actually tried to feel the way we feel and love the way we love?

"You know what? I take it back. I've never been lost to you; you were the ones lost to us. You haven't ever lived the way that we have. You've never known what it feels like to love and lose that love. You don't know what sacrifice is because you've never cared enough about anyone or anything to actually do it."

Uriel came to stand beside Gabriel, his face now filled with concern. "You know what is going to happen if you die."

"I've been told."

"It's not something said to scare you, or frighten you into making a decision. Before your mother's creation, I was tasked with keeping the world balanced. It required the ability to control humans against their will and force them to live lives that would keep them harmonious, especially since they were meant to exist on this earth forever, immortally good and faithful.

"But humans are created with a free will, and my ill-assigned task went against that. I could control behavior, but I could not create emotion that was not there, and humans who've been controlled since birth know no emotion. So I relinquished control and allowed humans to be as they were meant to.

"The emotion that appears most easily is love, and it was like the world had been reborn. The discovery of each other, of want and need, desire and passion came easily afterward. And then the children arrived. Humanity blossomed; we were pleased.

"But then humanity discovered something new. Rage is the emotion that spreads the fastest, and humanity became engulfed in it within months, violence becoming more common than love making. It was a plague, killing nothing but every last ounce of the goodness that had once existed in humanity.

"Taking away their freedom had been our first mistake. Failing to take away their immorality was our second. It was both a failed and a successful experiment for we learned that control would not ensure happiness, and immortality would not ensure balance.

"So Avi was created, and along with her creation came the introduction of humanity's mortality. They took it...badly."

"Naturally," Gabriel sneered.

"Yes. Naturally," Uriel acknowledged. "But when they've never known anything but eternity, to be introduced with the end was like tipping the world upside down; it changed everything for them. The violence that had been seen before was nothing. Now there were consequences; physical, permanent effects of their rage and for many, it became addicting. They attacked each other with renewed vigor and the results were disastrous.

"Avi, with the ability to control the life and death of every single human being, became aware of just how important her role was, how integral she was to the balance of the world when humans began taking more lives than she was. She realized what she needed to do and restored the balance that we had mistakenly disrupted.

"Now that she is gone, you are the key to stability in this world. Humanity grows more and more unstable with each passing day. It is imperative that you take your place among us. The longer you stay away, the closer this world drifts to its destruction."

Robert wrapped his arm around my waist and brought me to his side. "You cannot put that heavy a burden on her."

"It's already a burden on her," Michael said solemnly. "It's been her burden since her birth."

# THE FIRST RING

*N'Uriel, you have a monster in your home.*

Robert stiffened and I blinked. As if by reflex, I turned around and found myself facing Stacy, who was wiping a smear of something dark and red from the corner of her mouth.

"Is this a party of the pretty people?" she asked as her eyes flicked over the four men who stood shoulder to shoulder in front of us.

"You allow her near your wife?" Gabriel asked with a hint of surprise.

"Hell yeah, he allows me near her. He even lets me hold her hand," Stacy sneered before demonstrating just that.

Uriel looked shocked, while Michael merely smiled. "She's harmless; her bloodlust is specific and her loyalty runs deeper than I believe even ours does."

"That's apparent," Gabriel remarked, "since N'Uriel helped to create this monster."

"He didn't *help* create anything," Stacy growled. "And don't ever question his loyalty. His loyalty to creeps like you is the reason why I needed to turn into this in the first place. You guys have the nerve to call me the monster when you let psychos like Sam and Isis exist just because they've got wings and glow in the dark?"

"Sam and Isis existed because they filled a purpose, a necessary purpose that goes beyond what your simple mind can comprehend. And let me remind you that you helped kill Isis."

Stacy's eyes grew darker and she glared, her finger rising to point at him. "After she nearly killed Grace. You guys keep talking about how if Grace dies, that the world will end—yeah, I heard you; I can hear pretty damn well for a *monster*—but none of you did anything to stop people from trying to kill her, did you?"

"It's not our job to interfere," Uriel said plainly.

"No, it's not, but you do it anyway. It's why you're here, right? To interfere?"

The way the four older angels seemed to struggle with an answer, I knew that Stacy was right. She did, too.

"We are here to explain to Grace the truth about what she is."

"Then do it. Tell her," Robert and Stacy both said.

Gabriel broke from the line and opened his hand, a silver circle sitting against his palm. "You see this?" he asked me.

I nodded.

"Do you know what it is?"

"A ring."

He grabbed my left hand and raised it to my face. "Does it look familiar now?"

My eyes flicked back and forth between the rings on my finger and the ring in his hand. "It looks like my mother's."

"It's the first circle. No one but those of the first circle can wear this ring." He tossed his to Stacy. "Put it on."

"I'm not putting that on," she said vehemently.

"Give that to me," Robert grumbled and then placed the ring on his right, ring finger. Almost as soon as the metal touched his skin, it began to glow and Robert's hand became engulfed in a burst of black flames.

Robert gripped his wrist and his mouth opened as a scream of agony left him. I hadn't heard that sound since Halloween, and my entire body began to shake as the pain spread through me. We fell together, his pain my pain.

As we writhed together, Gabriel continued to speak. "Your mother was the most empathic of us all. It is why you feel N'Uriel's pain so completely. She knew what hurt others, what made them weep with sadness and with joy. She felt everything, experienced every emotion even if she didn't know what it was. She was the first of us to feel rage and jealousy.

"She was the first of us to know what being in love felt like. Lust, desire, she felt those for the first time, too. She was the most like humans out of all of us because she lived through their feelings. She was also the most forgiving. She was the most understanding, and because of that, she was the most weak.

"She was tasked with the most significant role this world has ever known. She had control over life and death, the ability to instantly create faith and fear in the palm of her hand. And now look at her daughter—Death, dying in her hand, fear multiplying in her heart, faith slipping away with each agonizing scream."

Stacy was grasping at Robert and me, trying to help, trying to do anything but stand there like statues the way the others were.

But I knew she couldn't do anything to help. I could see it in Robert's eyes, and I could feel it in the way my blood began to boil beneath my skin. Even my head was too filled with fire to hear any thoughts. I could only do one thing that didn't include giving in. I grabbed Robert's hand. The black flames that licked at his skin were shockingly cold, and the glowing ring that still circled his finger felt like ice. I grasped it and pulled, the ring slipping off as if it had never been attached to anything.

Immediately, the screaming stopped. Robert panted, and I could hear my heart in my ears as I began to pant as well, gulping for air that felt like I hadn't been able to taste...ever.

"Jesus, that was awful!" Stacy exclaimed as she grabbed my face to see if I was okay. "Are you hurt? Sore? Do I need to break more wings?"

"No-no, I'm fine." Of course, I wasn't. I knew that. And listening to the floating thoughts that drifted around me, I knew that everyone but Stacy knew that as well. "Can you get me a glass of water?"

"Yeah. Don't move."

She was gone in an instant, and I turned to look at Gabriel who smirked as I felt the thick slide of liquid fall from my nose. I wiped it, knowing what it was and not needing to see the red smear. Instead, I scowled at him.

*You bastard. You knew that would have killed her.*

He shrugged, unapologetic in every way. *One less tainted creature to deal with. You act as if she is worth the same to us as you are. She is not. She can be replaced. They all can.*

At that thought, he winced. I saw it, saw the crease form in his forehead and the lines take shape around his mouth. I smiled. *She can't be replaced. She can't and you know it. There is only one Stacy Kim in this world and she can't ever be replaced. You think you know everything because of who you are but you don't. You don't know what it's like to have friends.*

Gabriel's face continued to change in front of me, and he began to quiver as he held on to his lie. My smile grew wider. *You don't know what it means to have someone choose to be loyal to you for nothing. That's what friends do. You think she can be replaced because she's human, because you don't value us at all, but we're more valuable than you are because I know that I can trust her. I can trust the* monster; *I can't trust you.*

Stacy had returned with the glass of water, and I took it from her with a whispered thanks. She waited and watched as I took several sips, and then took the edge of her T-shirt and wiped my face.

"You look like hell."

"Thanks."

She looked down at Robert and offered him her hand. He took it and stood, her help not necessary but the act proved what I had said about her. Uriel, Raphael, and Michael all nodded in agreement, but Gabriel, looking pale and with no remorse, refused.

"She will betray you in the end. You will see that. She will always be loyal to her kind first."

"I am her kind," I said as I watched his body jerk and twitch with each untruthful word. "I am more her kind than I am yours because I don't treat people the way you do. You wanted to prove to me that I'm Avi's daughter, that I'm really an angel with amnesia, then fine. You've done it. And this angel is telling you to get the hell out of this house."

Michael looked shocked, while Raphael and Uriel both looked hurt. Gabriel, on the other hand, looked pleased. "And why should we?"

"Because you tried to kill my friend, and I don't care who or what you are—I'll kill you before I let another one of my friends get hurt by people like you."

Gabriel's smile was beautiful, as beautiful as any angel's smile should be. "Dying is nothing to be feared. Death is like a caterpillar shedding its cocoon. And that, Grace, is a start."

I knew what they intended on doing before they did it, but still, seeing all four of them disappear in a burst of white haze surprised me. The smoke thinned into nothing the minute Lark walked in, Graham behind her, Sean at his heels looking wary.

"It would be just like them to leave," she huffed.

Stacy was irate. "If those guys are supposed to be the best of your kind, it's amazing there aren't more jerks like Sam running around. Seriously, that Gabriel guy's a total creep."

"Who are you guys talking about?" Sean asked with a completely lost look on his face.

"Don't worry about it. And why are you here?" Stacy looked at her brother with mild irritation and began to speak in Korean, the conversation growing animated and heated very quickly.

Lark nodded her head at things she agreed with, and raised her eyebrows at things that surprised her. I could hear the thoughts in Stacy and Sean's head but they were in Korean as well, and I just threw my hands up in frustration.

"Yeah, I don't understand either," Graham said at my reaction.

"I'm telling him that he's supposed to be helping out our dad. He's gotta take up the slack with the school now that I'm not there," Stacy informed us angrily.

"And I was about to tell her that our dad's selling the school."
Stacy froze. "What?"

Sean's eyes held a great number of emotions, but the most noticeable one was defeat. "He and Mom decided last night that they can't run the school anymore. You were the only one who ever really helped out."

"Yeah, because Mom and Dad let you boys do whatever the hell you wanted. I always got stuck doing chores and work because of you guys, and now none of you want to help out?"

"What do you want us to do, huh? That school was Dad's dream, not ours; not even yours."

The way Stacy's eyes glossed over, and the way her lip trembled, I knew she wanted to cry. Maybe she was…in her own way. What Sean said hurt, but it was the truth. His thoughts said so…now that they were in English, anyway.

"It wasn't my dream. I don't get to have my dream anymore. I don't get to live the life I wanted anymore. But that doesn't mean that I don't want anyone else to either! It's not gonna kill you or your social life to help Dad out a couple of hours a day!"

"Why'd you have to go and turn yourself into this anyway, huh? It's bad enough I've got Mom guilt-tripping me every day because I didn't watch out for you enough. Now I gotta have your ghost doing it, too?"

"I'm not a ghost," Stacy said sadly.

"Yeah, well, it's the only way I'm ever gonna be able to explain why I'm showing up for tonight's shift," he grumbled before turning around and heading toward the door.

Stacy ran after him, stopping him before he'd even moved six inches, and hugged him. "Thank you, opa."

"Yeah-yeah."

He left, and Graham chuckled. "Even dead, you're still the boss."

"It's not funny, Graham," Stacy scolded. "You don't know what it's like, okay? My brothers always got away with murder. They never really had any responsibilities and even when they did, they'd just pass it on to me, or blame me for them not doing it. So when my dad decides that he's gonna close down his school, it's not because I'm the boss. It's because he never was."

Graham stopped laughing. "Sorry."

"Don't worry about it."

"So," Graham started, his cheeks red with embarrassment, "what happened? Who left? Why were they here in the first place?"

Robert spoke for the first time since putting on Gabriel's ring. "They were here to tell Grace more about who she is. But more than that, they showed us something that's even more valuable."

"And what's that? That they're so old even their smoke smells like mothballs?" Stacy said acerbically.

"No. When I put on Gabriel's ring, I could see every thought he ever had while that ring was in his possession. Even thoughts he kept from the others." Lark's eyes widened at his words, and I finally looked at him for the first time since I took off the ring. His mind was like a window, and I looked inside to see the secrets that the ring had kept.

# THE FLOOD

The sound of cries and screams in a memory that doesn't belong to you will always sound hollow. In Robert's mind, the memories that were older than he was sounded like a whisper. But, even as quiet as they were, I could still hear everything as though I was right there, instead of a bystander to a stolen thought.

"Have you told him?"

"Yes. He was the right choice."

Uriel was standing beside Gabriel, his eyes looking down at a man whose shoulders seemed to sink lower and lower with each passing second. The sun was high overhead, and the smell of grass, sweet and green, floated along with hints of something floral.

A bird could be heard singing in a nearby tree, while an axe hitting wood thumped a steady rhythm that joined a whistling that seemed in competition with the bird's song. Together they made for an interesting symphony that felt out of place with the serious tone of the conversation between the two angels.

"It's difficult, this trusting of humans."

"Gabriel, you will see when all of this is done that humanity is worth saving."

"Why do we save them but not our own? I've never thought once to question our orders but I have to now—why are these animals worth more than we are?" Gabriel asked with resentment staining every syllable.

"Because they owe us nothing; we owe them everything. They

are not born to protect us; we're born to protect them. It gives us purpose, Gabriel. It gives us reason. Would you rather we be like them? Making mistake after mistake? Haven't the Grigori taught us what happens when we try?"

Gabriel looked down and kicked at a piece of stone that was jutting out from the ground. It broke off and disappeared, sailing away like a bullet had been shot from the ground. "I do not understand why our brothers and sisters chose to destroy the legacy we have spent centuries to cultivate, but I do know that flawed as they are, they are more valuable to the world than any human being existing now or ever will exist."

Uriel's eyes turned down, disappointment plain in them. "We weren't created to be valuable. We were created to ensure that they—humans—are."

"How valuable can they be? Their weaknesses, their cruelty, their lust for blood and bodies—they've done nothing but destroy what we've built. They've taken the knowledge we've shared with them and used it against each other."

"And that's their right. Humanity has to be allowed to learn and fail. They have to be allowed to be human."

"Humanity will be our downfall, Uriel. I see it. We barely prevented a war from breaking out amongst our own because of these…humans. Saving them now will mean our end later. We should destroy all of them before this happens again."

"And then what would become of Avi? She cannot exist without humanity, and humanity cannot exist without her. Death cannot exist without life, and life can have no purpose without death."

"Avi is more than her purpose. She will exist long after we are gone."

Uriel smiled knowingly. "You love her."

"If you speak of that human condition that blinds one to what they see, then no, I do not. But love in its most divine form…yes, I feel it for her. She may be one of us, one of the first, but she feels more like my child than a sister or a mate."

"You feel a paternal bond to her though she isn't your child. How fickle you are."

"It has nothing to do with being fickle. Avi is special. I think when she was created she was filled with only light. There is no darkness within her; only illumination," Gabriel said wistfully. "She is perfect."

"Perfection is an ideal, not a reality; even among our kind. One day she will disappoint you. Will your love for her still exist when you realize this?"

"She will never disappoint me, Uriel. Avi is incapable of disappointing anyone."

***

Everything was a depressing shade of grey, the skies dark with storm clouds that drenched the world in water that neither felt wet nor dry. It was like a layer of sweat. Sticky, dust coated sweat that clung to my skin and my clothes.

"It has only just begun. The rain will continue for many more days."

"You feel no sorrow for what happens to them, do you Gabriel?"

Gabriel looked at the person who asked, and I swallowed back a whimper. It was my mother. She looked ethereal, peaceful…alive.

"Of course I do. I just don't see how it matters. The Grigori have betrayed our ways, and the humans have betrayed their faith. Why have laws if we do not enforce them?"

"But to take so many lives…to destroy the Grigori because of the actions of a few-"

"Is what we've been told to do. We are not humans. We do not have the choice and if we take it for ourselves we end up like the Grigori and then where would humanity be? We have to be their light, not their darkness."

My mother turned, and I saw what she was looking at. I saw things through her eyes, and it made my heart lurch in my chest. People were busy reinforcing their homes, gathering up their children, and collecting food. It was plain to see that. But, through my mother's eyes, I could see something that I knew they could not: all of them were marked with a black feather on their forehead.

"I do not relish the taking of so many innocents, Gabriel. Look at all of these children—whether their fathers are angels or not, they do not deserve what I must give to them," my mother murmured, though her face remained hard.

"You do not need to have them suffer. Be generous in your task, be merciful. It doesn't matter how you kill them, just that you do it before the rains end," Gabriel told her sternly. "If the world is allowed to continue as it has been, our kind will never be able to walk among the people again."

"I already am unable to do so," my mother lamented. "When the Grigori are destroyed, we will send a new flock of angels to take their place. The world will continue on as it has, and you will return to our circle and never descend again while I remain here; untouched, unspoken to, feared and loathed as though I were Lucifer himself."

Gabriel's voice softened, and he waved his hand across the scene of panicked people. "You are the only one of us who can maintain balance here. Humans would destroy themselves in less than ten generations and then who would be left to fear you?"

"I don't want any of them to fear me."

"If they aren't able to fear you, they won't be able to love you either. And that's what you want, isn't it? You want them to love you."

My mother's face seemed to collapse and she nodded. "Humans feel so much. The love they know is nothing like the love we're born knowing. It's different, deeper almost. It grows and it expands, like a living entity. It dies like one, too. I know death and dying. I am Death. I am eternally dying. But to know the birth of something so incredible, to give birth to love, that would be…well, that would be divine."

Gabriel took my mother's hand and placed it onto her heart. "As long as this beats, you will never have a need for that kind of love. That is a human emotion, with human consequences. You will never know anything more destructive than that and you will never know anything more complete than what exists within you."

"You speak words of kindness when I speak of nothing but my own self. You are a good friend, Gabriel."

"And I always will be one to you, Avi."

"Be my friend now…give me strength as I do this terrible thing."

"I will not leave your side."

With a heavy nod, my mother's shoulders shook and wings the color of the darkest cloud in the sky spread out from her back, sharp and determined toward the furthest areas beside her.

"They've grown lighter," Gabriel commented.

"They continue to lighten as more and more of humanity dies. I fear by the end of this rain that my wings will be whiter than yours."

"It isn't humanity's death that changes their color. It's the death of your spirit. You need to let go of this attachment you have for the humans."

"I can't. I will do what my call tells me but I can't stop feeling for them. I won't."

Gabriel sighed reluctantly. "Then don't. Have this defiance for yourself. If this is the totality of your rebellion, we shall be the better for it."

Wordlessly, my mother descended upon the village. It looked like the sky had lowered to disguise her as she disappeared, but Gabriel's eyes moved, tracking shadows and slight disturbances of air. The crying, the screams all stopped. It seemed even the dropping of rain had become silent as the smell of mud and wet grass changed, souring almost.

Time had not stopped, but life—all life—had, and the stench of it was growing thicker by the second. Gabriel's nose was especially sensitive to its scent, picking up every nuance of the changes in the air. He was seeking a specific scent, one that smelled sweet and deceptively innocent.

He smiled when he found it and puffed with pride as the fog that had hidden my mother now revealed her, exposing her for what she was. She emerged with a pale face streaked with dust and crystal dew, her hands shaking at her sides, her wings even lighter than they had been when they'd appeared. Her shape was rimmed with a pale, golden light, but around that light, almost smothering it, was a darker presence

Her hair was hanging limply around her face, and for a second, it was like looking in a mirror. But then she seemed to fade out, growing less opaque as her body shimmered with a gray, nearly silver mist. Almost as quickly as she thinned out, she reappeared, her face clear, her hair pulled neatly back, looped at the nape of her neck and braided around her forehead, almost like an onyx headband.

"I could not just take the children and leave behind their parents to mourn them. I took them all."

"You did what you needed to."

"Four hundred lights extinguished. This is the smallest of the villages in this area."

"You will need help, then?"

My mother shook her head. "I've already sent out the others. We will not be able to help them all before the flooding begins but the most innocent will be spared the suffering."

"How many will be allowed to survive besides the ark builder?"

"Across the world, only several thousand. They've already been chosen and cannot be harmed. The registrar has already recorded their names."

"That many left alive? I'm surprised. I thought maybe we'd leave behind a dozen or so, but thousands?"

"That is not many, not when compared to the dead; so many…so many dead. So many futures ended by what we've done."

Gabriel's voice rose in pitch as he grasped my mother's shoulders and forced her to look at him. "We did not end their futures; they did. Humans are not infallible."

"And neither are angels, whether of the first circle, the second, the Grigori… These humans, these innocent mothers, fathers, and children aren't dying because they went against what they are; they're dying because we went against what *we* are. Humans didn't implement the law of the Nephilim—we did. Humans have not betrayed their character or their faith; we have.

"I feel their confusion, their hurt, their heartbreak, and the closest our kind has come to feeling anything similar for our own folly has been shame. And so we kill to hide that shame, when instead we should be learning from it," my mother said so passionately, I felt the burn of tears in Gabriel's eyes.

"We are learning from it, my dear one," Gabriel said softly. "With you to remind us, we shall never forget."

"Is it really that simple? Can we save the world and ourselves through chaos and destruction?"

"Yes."

My mother's body grew slack, and she leaned in to rest her head against Gabriel's shoulder. He pulled her to embrace her, and she sighed.

"Peace is the child. Death is the birth."

***

Leaves were floating atop the murky water that churned and bubbled as the winds blew heavily across every surface that the water had not yet touched. The rain had eased only slightly, but the darkness never left. Firelight flickered orange from torches held high by hands belonging to worried parents and children, their voices calling out into the distant darkness for any signs of life.

Gabriel drifted above the fog that settled around the boats. He was watching them with distaste as they moved frantically from one of the tiny boats to the other. Women, sobbing tears that disappeared in the soft rain, carried lifeless babies in their arms. Men who had grown hard through the demands of farm life had broken down, empty shells that were of no use to those who depended on them to survive.

The children were the most affected by what surrounded them. For nearly forty days, they had watched as their mothers, fathers, sisters, brothers, friends, and complete strangers lost the will to live, falling dead around them like the raindrops that kept them from remembering what dry felt like. The eyes of these children, once lively and filled with endless hope and fancy were now empty, flat. They couldn't even cry anymore; inside they were as dead as the bodies that bobbed up every now and again from beneath the watery cemetery.

Children cried, Gabriel thought to himself. They cried and they laughed. But these children did not make a single sound. There was nothing left to be joyful or sorrowful for. It was if they were holes, physical holes in time and life itself, and he had helped to create them.

"You feel for them now, don't you?"

Gabriel turned to see the others. Michael, Uriel, Raphael, and Avi stood wing to wing beside him.

"It's not so much the feeling for them but realizing the failure in our actions. The intent of this flood was to clean the slate and start again. Instead, we have shattered it. What do we build on from here? Centuries upon centuries we've studied them and adapted how *we* behaved because of these miserable creatures.

"Now we have forced them to adapt for us but how can they? The adults are the weakest of them, rigid and unable to change, but we've made their children into the waking dead. Look at them. They show nothing—no emotion, no thought. How will they repair the damage done to this world and to their own humanity?"

"With our help," Uriel said, the others nodding in agreement.

My mother's voice was raspy when she spoke. "There will be more dark times ahead. More deaths. Even ours."

"Dying is inevitable, but we die only when we choose to."

"You will choose to die one day," Michael said to no one in particular.

And no one responded.

Through their silence, the calls for life continued. A large splash could be heard, the rocking of another boat in the darkness causing shadows as small waves disturbed the constant rhythm of ripples that followed every drop of rain that refused to stay in the sky. Another splash, and then another, and then the curve of the underside of the boat made its appearance.

"They have taken to ending their own lives," Raphael said colorlessly. "They are prone to their dramatics, aren't they?"

"They have nothing left to live for," my mother lamented. "We have taken their homes, their food, their children. All that is left to them is faith, and we sit here and refuse to offer even that by way of hope."

Michael uttered a weighed reply. "And would they take it if we were to offer it? They know what caused this, and at this moment the last faces they wish to see are ours. We will be reviled by most of them until we can prove ourselves, and even then many will never forgive us. Generations will die, and we will still be hated and feared, instead of loved."

Uriel bent down and touched a small blanket that floated by, the bloated body of an infant still attached to it. "Today is the last day of rain. Tomorrow the sun will appear, the world will dry, and humanity will recover. We will return to our places above, and we will watch as our children heal the wounds we let be born. The new laws will prevent this from happening again. That is all that we can do."

Gabriel turned away in distaste, but everywhere he looked, the world was covered in bodies. Even the Grigori drifted in death among the corpses. Their wings were stained and wretched, their faces puffy and distorted in disbelief, horror—they had not expected to have suffered the same fate as the humans they had played God over.

These faces were familiar. He had seen these angels as children, watched their wings come, passed along the history of their kind when their calls were finally heard. He had expected to feel the anger, but not the remorse. He didn't even know what it was.

"It is one of the rarest of human feelings," my mother informed him.

"It is detestable," Gabriel muttered.

"I think it is one of the most commendable. It proves that hu-

mans are worthy of redemption. You feeling it proves that you are, too."
She smiled at him and took his hand.

He looked at their clasped hands and felt a surge of warmth reach even the tips of his wings. "You give life to this old angel's heart."

"I will miss you."

"You will miss my bitterness?"

"I will miss *you*. For all your jaded cynicism, I will miss you the most. Uriel, Michael, and Raphael have always been understanding and permissive, but in a way that always made me feel less like I belonged and more like I was tolerated. But you were rigid and firm, and yet always tender. I was never a child, but if I had been, I would have wanted you to be my father."

Gabriel touched the tip of my mother's nose in a gesture that surprised even him. "And if I had had a child, I would have wanted it to be you."

"Sentimental and generous—who would have believed it of our Gabriel," Raphael said with amusement.

"I am capable of many things. Maybe I'll even be capable of forgiveness."

"Lies!" Raphael and Uriel laughed, while my mother giggled in a way that made it clear that she was young, despite her age.

It was a scene that made no sense against the backdrop of death that surrounded them. But they could see beyond it, because they could see what lay ahead. They knew more than the now and they knew the purpose of it all. Anyone looking in would have never understood. But I did.

My eyes closed and reopened to see Robert's face again.

"You saw everything," he said softly to me.

"I did."

"And?"

"And...I think Gabriel is my grandfather."

# THE FOUR LEGS OF KNOWLEDGE

I woke up alone in the middle of the night, knowing that Robert had left to fulfill his call. My stomach was growling for more than just half a takeout container of noodles, and so I found myself in the kitchen with a plate of bacon and eggs in front of me.

Graham, a living bacon detector, was seated across from me, his own plate twice as large and twice as full. "Thanks," he mumbled as he stuffed a strip of bacon into his mouth.

"Ugh, how can you eat that stuff?" Stacy asked as she sat at our side.

"Becujishgood," Graham mumbled.

"But a whole pound of it?"

"What? It's not like I'm gonna get all fat and gross now. If anything, you should be the one watching your weight. Seriously—eating what, a hundred pounds of man meat isn't gonna help you keep your girlish figure."

"Ugh, man meat? Did you really have to say that?" Stacy groaned. "For your information, I've never eaten any man's…meat."

Graham laughed. "I know. I just wanted to get you to say it."

"Creep!"

"Creep eater!"

Lark appeared and took the fourth chair at the table, her eyes darting back and forth between the three of us. "Nothing changes, does it?"

"Nope," I answered.

"Not a chance," Stacy agreed.

"She made bacon," Graham offered.

It was a rare, carefree moment for us, and we took the time to enjoy it as we talked about things that would have probably been taken for granted before. Things like concerts that were happening during the summer and movies that were coming out became reasons to laugh and plan.

"We can drive to Licking to see that new martial arts-zombie movie," Graham suggested.

"I think my days of zombie movies are kinda done," Stacy grunted.

"What? You? Zombie Queen of Heath?" Graham uttered, shocked.

"Yeah, well, I kinda get to live the dream…you know?" Stacy replied.

"Okay, so zombie movies are out of the question," I interjected. "What about vampire movies?"

Groans flooded the table, and I held up my hands in defeat. "Fine! Fine, no horror movies at all!"

A cell phone began to ring and heads turned to see where it was coming from. "That's mine," Stacy said before pushing her hand into the pocket of her jeans and pulling out a small blue cell phone. A folded piece of paper fell out as she answered the call, and I bent down to pick it up.

"Hey, Dr. Bro. No, no she hasn't called. The last time I saw her she was heading to the school. Yeah. Okay; I'll let you know if she does. Yeah—bye."

She closed the phone and then looked at the paper in my hand. "Sorry. Dr. Bro's looking for his wife. Hey, I was gonna ask you about that."

She took the paper from me and opened it up, ironing out the creases with her hands as she spread out the sheet on the table. "I've been thinking about this. We've pretty much agreed that Sam's partner isn't Isis, right?"

Lark's head perked up at the mention of Isis. "Why did that idea even get brought up?"

Stacy's head ticked forward, her lids lowering half a measure in skepticism. "Really?"

"Ahh. I should have known. Lem doesn't know how to keep quiet."

"So we're right? Isis isn't Sam's partner?" I asked.

"No. No, you're wrong. Isis *was* Sam's partner."

"How do you know?" Graham looked at Lark with doubt. "I mean, we thought a lot about it and it doesn't make sense."

"What do you know about angels that would make you think you'd know what does and doesn't make sense," she said with mild irritation.

"What was Isis' call?" Stacy asked icily.

Lark puffed. "What? You know I can't tell you that."

I looked at her and it just happened. I hadn't meant it to, and she knew it, but I had no control over this yet, and I heard her gasp before her mind darkened. But it was too late.

"She was supposed to drive people crazy," I revealed.

"You should have kept your mouth shut!" Lark hissed.

I flinched at her words that filled both my ears and my head, but I bit through the pain and offered nothing but resistance in my face and voice. "I'm not following your rules anymore. Isis had a call, which meant she was *not* Sam's partner. She couldn't have been with a call like hers.

"And I don't need to know everything about angels to know that much. I know what happens when an angel doesn't follow their call—I saw it, I experienced it—and I saw Isis. You did, too. She wasn't showing any signs of being an Innominate. She was just crazy."

"You're wrong about Isis, Grace. I know she was Sam's partner."

"How do you know? Who told you that?" Stacy demanded to know.

Lark held up her right hand and flashed the silver ring that sat on her middle finger. "She did."

"That's *her* ring?" I asked skeptically.

"Yes, this is *her* ring. We're lesser angels, which means I can wear her ring if it ever leaves her possession."

Stacy's eyes lit up. "Whoa! So that's why you took her hand!"

"Ugh, babe! You took her hand?" Graham said, disgusted.

"It wasn't like she was going to use it," Lark said smugly.

"Isn't it wrong to kill angels, though?"

"Yes, but I was fulfilling my call to protect Grace. Besides, I had help," she said, looking at Stacy with a smirk.

"Help? Hah. I did most of the hard work."

"Breaking her wings is hard work?"

"When you don't have wings, can't fly, and can't read her thoughts to know what she's gonna do next, then yeah, it's hard work."

Air spurted through Lark's lips. "Please. She fought like Graham—you could have taken her easily if you'd just fed."

"Well, that's true."

"Hey!" Graham complained.

"And besides, she was too busy rehearsing moves in her head to really pay attention to what you were thinking."

"Kind of like Graham always thinking about food."

"Pretty much."

"For the last damn time, I'm right here. I get it. You guys think I'm an idiot and that the only thing I'm good for is eating and being the goddamn butt of every one of your jokes. Well, I'm not! I've got feelings too, you know. I know I did some crappy stuff, and I know I've got the worst attention span, but that doesn't mean that I'm only good for target practice!" Graham slammed his hand on the table, sending the sheet of paper flying onto the floor.

"Graham, you know we don't think that," I told him.

"You sure act like it!"

"Sorry."

Stacy's apology was the least likely of the three, which is why when it was the first one, Graham didn't accept it. Instead, he stormed out of the kitchen and up the stairs. Lark looked at us and then sighed before following him.

"Alone again, huh?" I chuckled.

"We're not alone."

"Well, no. They're upstairs and Lark can hear us, but-"

Stacy shook her head. "No, I mean we're not alone." She pointed to the front door and I saw what she was looking at. "How the hell is he still alive?" Stacy asked, shoving me to the side and launching herself at him.

Him. He was standing in the doorway, his hair long and loose, a golden sheet of light that spilled over his shoulders and glowed in the dark living room. He was beautiful, the shadows cutting themselves in half on the sharp angles of his face. The one golden eye that glittered in the illumination from the kitchen's overhead light was like a teasing star.

"Stacy, no!" I shouted, grabbing her arm and yanking. My shout turned into a cry of disbelief when she ceased moving forward and instead flew back.

"Oh. My. God."

Stacy landed against the refrigerator, the door buckling from the contact. I looked at my hands, normal looking hands that struggled on a daily basis to open cans of soda, and then looked at Stacy's perplexed expression.

"D-did you just…did you just throw me against the fridge?" she sputtered.

"No!"

"No? Then how the hell did I end up over here?"

"I don't know!"

"Aw hell, he's still here, look out, Grace!" Stacy stood up and ran toward the figure in the living room. Gold and black swirled, caught between shadow and light, and I felt awed and frightened at how my eyes seemed to catch everything, defining the lines inside the blur.

Stacy moved like a ballet dancer, her body lithe and gentle, which made her partner's movements look clunky and spastic in comparison. They coiled around each other, like snakes, but they were so frantic for control that it was like they'd been set on fire.

A lamp toppled over, sofa cushions went tumbling like square wheels across the floor. The mirror that was on the wall crashed to the ground, shattering into endless miniature reflections. I dodged a picture frame, my face whizzing by so quickly, it looked like I was laughing.

"Stacy, stop," I whispered.

"Hell no," she growled. "He's supposed to be dead! I saw him die! You did, too!" She pulled back her arm and sent her fist sailing forward, just missing his jaw and landing on his neck. The sound of one solid mass of flesh hitting another shook the house, and I winced as the windows rattled, threatening to shatter at any second.

"It's not him."

"What the hell do you mean it's not him?" Stacy shrieked from her position on top of the blond intruder. They were lying on the ground, her knees pinning him down, her fingers digging into his throat.

"She means it's not him."

Llehmai pulled Stacy's hands from around his neck and stood, pulling her up along with him.

Stacy's eyes opened wide as she looked at Lem, recognition finally taking hold of her. "Why the *hell* is your hair blond? And long?"

"Because it is."

"Dude, I was gonna *kill* you! What the hell is up with your family, huh? You guys have some kind of death wish or something?"

Lem chuckled. "*You* kill *me?*"

"She'd have help." Lark was at my side, with Graham standing beside her, two pillars of protection that I simply did not need.

"No one is gonna kill anyone here," I said, stepping around them and placing myself at the center of the triangle that had formed. "Lem's obviously made a pretty bad choice in hair style, but he's not

Sam. And he's not trying to kill me."

My head snapped toward the door at a noise that sounded like it was booming through loudspeakers.

"Oh no, the old bat's awake," Lark groaned before disappearing in a blur of movement, the living room returning to its original state before our eyes. Only the mirror was missing.

She didn't look at him, but I knew who she was speaking to when a flurry of unspoken words floated in the air.

*You have to leave. Hide, dissipate, die—I do not care. Just do not interfere.*

The doorbell rang, and instantly, I was alone with Lark and Graham.

Lark opened the door and spoke quietly with the old woman who stood on the outside. I backed away into the shadows, pulling Graham with me, and listened as Lark lied about the noises that had carried across the street.

"I thought someone was fighting in here," Mrs. Lorimax said, her head poking past the door to scan the living room for signs that her suspicions were correct.

"No, no fighting going on here," Lark laughed stiffly. "I'm just working on a routine for my dance class and I think I got a little too excited."

"Those new dances you kids do are too jerky, too sexual. I don't understand parents today who let their children listen to that kind of music. It only leads to two things: fornicating and baby making."

Graham began to choke and I pressed my hand over his mouth. *Shh! She'll hear you!*

He stilled. *You're in my head. Holy cheese balls, you're in my head!*

I removed my hand and pressed it against a throb that appeared at my temple. *I know. I wasn't sure if I could do it or not.*

*Well, you're doing it! Wow, this is so awesome. Now I can talk to you while I'm eating, like I do with Lark.*

"Where's your mother? She isn't letting you stay up this late, is she?" I heard Mrs. Lorimax asked loudly.

"She's at a function, Mrs. Lorimax. And it's summer—kids always stay up late during the summer."

I heard a huff, and then the sound of something wet hitting the floor. A mumbled curse followed. I knew Graham only heard this. But I heard something else. It was whisper soft, like a baby exhaling in his sleep. I moved away from Graham as the sound became more distinct.

It was a struggle. A silent one. I probably didn't move as quickly as it felt I did, but I moved fast enough to see that Mrs. Lorimax and Lark weren't alone.

Mrs. Lorimax was on the ground, something dark spilling from her head. Lark's arms were pinned behind her by someone I'd never seen before, while another person, someone taller than anyone else I'd ever known, held his hands against her back, pushing down on her even as the one who held her arms pulled her back.

"What the hell are you doing?" I cried out.

I ran toward Lark.

*NO! Go back inside! Get inside, now!*

The front door slammed against a wall, and I saw Graham charge. The tall stranger let go of Lark and caught Graham by his head. I wedged myself between them and shoved against Graham with one hand, my other pushing up against his attacker's chin.

I heard a snap and a tearing sound, and for a second I looked at Graham in horror. But he fell back, his eyes filled with shock as the tall attacker fell in the opposite direction. I turned to watch him stumble and fall, and bit back a scream.

His head was gone.

"Oh God, oh God, oh God."

Graham grabbed my hand and pulled me away. Lark roared and her wings burst free, knocking her captor to the ground. I gulped when I saw that he was armless.

Stacy appeared and threw herself onto him, her hands grabbing and tearing until only pieces remained. Lark had already done the same to the headless attacker, the street now covered in dark masses of flesh that did not bleed.

"Are you okay?" I asked her.

"Yeah. I'm fine. They weren't going to hurt me; they couldn't have. And are you *insane*? I told you to get inside! What the hell made you think you could save me anyway?"

"I wasn't gonna save you; I was trying to help you. Who-what were they?"

"They're vampires," Stacy said with disgust.

"Vampires? But, aren't they supposed to, like, bleed all over the place or something?" Graham asked as he bent down to inspect one of the pieces that had fallen by his feet.

I moved toward Mrs. Lorimax and knelt down. Her eyes were closed, and I couldn't see any movement of her chest. "Mrs. Lorimax? Mrs. Lorimax, can you hear me?"

I bent my ear to her mouth, listening for even the slightest hint of a breath. It was faint, but it was there, and I turned her over. It had been almost two years since I'd learned CPR but I didn't know what else to do. I began to pump on her chest, counting each compression before blowing into her mouth, each time hoping that she'd blow back, or make a sound, or move.

I didn't really care what she did, as long as she didn't stop.

"Grace, you've gotta stop."

"What? No. I'm not gonna let her die."

Stacy eased up beside me and put her hands over mine. "She's already dead."

"No, she's not," I insisted. I flicked her hands away and continued to press against the old woman's chest. "She's not dead. She's not."

A light across the street flicked on. I could hear clothes rustling, and feet slipping into shoes, and I tried even harder to revive Mrs. Lorimax. "Come on. Come on, you can do it," I said between breaths. "Don't die on me. Don't die. I won't let you die."

"Grace, we've got to go," Lark said, tugging on my arm. "The neighbors are coming and I can't lie away three bodies on my front lawn."

"Then clean it up!" I shouted, pulling my arm away from her. "I'm not leaving her to die here on the ground. I'm not letting that happen again, okay!"

Stacy looked at me, and then at Lark. And then she began to move. Lark followed, while Graham crawled over to me and pushed me aside. "Here, let me do it," he said, taking over. "I got an A in this, remember? You got a C."

I held the woman's hand, squeezing it in encouragement. "Come on. We need nosy old ladies like you around to keep us in line. You're not gonna die today. You're not gonna die."

"Oh my goodness, is that Tilly?" a frightened voice asked. I looked up to see Mrs. Culpepper standing on the sidewalk, her hands clutching at her robe. "What happened here?"

"She fell," Stacy answered quickly. "She fell and hit her head. I've called 911 already; they're on their way."

"Oh goodness, she's always been clumsy; especially after that stroke she had last year."

I didn't notice when the ambulance arrived, or when Graham moved aside to let a paramedic take over the CPR. I continued to hold Mrs. Lorimax's hand, speaking into her ear, her thoughts. I really don't know when my mouth stopped moving and when my mind took over, but I knew that I couldn't stop talking to her. It felt like my only real tie to whatever was left of the life inside her.

Because no matter what Stacy said, I knew she wasn't dead yet. I hadn't heard her breathe on her own yet, and I didn't know if she had a pulse or not, but I knew that she was still alive.

"Are you family?"

I looked at the paramedic and answered him honestly.

"You can't come in the ambulance unless you're a family member," he informed me.

"Yeah, I know," I said quietly. "Is she going to be okay?"

He shrugged. "It's hard to say with the older ones. If she doesn't start breathing on her own, she won't last the morning."

Mrs. Lorimax had a clear, triangular-shaped plastic cap over her mouth, a woman busy squeezing a bag of air every few seconds while the paramedic who'd spoken to me was checking her pulse. He was looking at his watch, and I could hear him counting in his head, hear his thoughts as he doubted that any of our efforts was going to be worth it.

A crowd had gathered, faces I didn't recognize, worried expressions covering all of them. They spoke quietly amongst themselves, but it wasn't what they said that I heard the loudest. Instead, it was what they didn't say.

*That family has always been weird.*

*It's not normal for them to be alone so often at that age.*

*That's what the old hag gets for sticking her nose into other people's business.*

It was overwhelming, the ambush of thoughts. I forced my eyes closed, squeezing them shut and trying to concentrate on the woman whose hand I still clutched in mine, but the voices grew louder and louder, more of them joining in as more people arrived.

"Let go, Grace."

"Grace, let go."

*Why is she holding onto her hand?*

*Does she even know Tilly?*

"Grace, you have to let go."

*Why isn't she letting go of that woman?*

*Someone's gonna have to tear her away; it's like she's obsessed or something!*

"She's breathing!"

Two words; not nearly as loud as the voices in my head, but still loud enough to get me to open my eyes. "She's what?"

"She's breathing!" the paramedic exclaimed. I looked at Mrs. Lorimax and saw that her eyes were open. She was looking at me, and she squeezed my hand. It was a weak squeeze, but it was more than she'd given me in the last half-hour.

"Hey," I said to her. "Welcome back."

*My head...hurts so much.*

"The paramedics are going to take you to the hospital now, okay?"

She blinked. *Who's going to take care of my babies?*

"Everything will be fine, Mrs. Lorimax, I promise. You just get better," I whispered before I moved aside to let the paramedics work on getting her into the ambulance.

I let go of her hand and watched as quickly, with a precision that came from years of repeating the same procedures over and over, the paramedics had an IV in her arm, a board beneath her, and a silver blanket covering her body. She disappeared into the back of the ambulance, one paramedic following, while the other ran to the front, turning the siren on and driving away.

The crowd dispersed as soon as the flashing red lights could no longer be seen, and in just a matter of minutes, Lark, Stacy, Graham and I were alone again on the street. I walked over to Mrs. Lorimax's house and found the door open.

"She said she had babies in here," I said out loud, knowing that I'd been followed.

"Babies? You mean like old lady babies? The four-legged meowing kind? Or the kidnapped and put in freezers for soup and knitting kind?" Graham asked with a shiver in his voice.

"I thought we agreed no more horror movies," Stacy commented as we walked into the living room of cluttered home.

"You kinda don't ever get rid of those images, Stacy."

"I told you to close your eyes. It's your fault. I told you, Cheerleaders vs. Sharks or Grandma Gore-fest; you chose gore."

"That's because I thought the last thing you wanted to see were half-naked cheerleaders fighting fish!"

"Well then, that's your fault."

I turned around and fumed. "Could you two quit it? Just once?"

"Sorry," they both said bashfully.

Lark bent down and picked up a bowl with a picture of a fish glazed on it. "She's got cats."

"Cats. With a 's'. Great," I said before clicking my tongue. "Here kitty-kitty."

"What, you don't like cats?" Stacy asked, pushing a sofa away from the wall with her finger before returning it back to its original place.

"I've never owned one. My dad's allergic to them."

Lark let out a guffaw. "With all of the singing cat albums he's got, and he's allergic to them?"

"Yeah. He breaks out into a pretty bad rash whenever he's around cats."

"What about a dog? We had a dog when I was twelve but it ran away. I think it got tired of my mom trying to feed it leftover kim chi stew."

I shook my head. "My mom was allergic to dogs."

"Your mother was an angel—she wasn't allergic to anything," Graham reminded me.

From the corner of my eye I saw movement near the kitchen. "I think one of the cats is in there."

The four of us walked quietly to the small area and each one of us gasped. There wasn't one cat. There weren't even two or four cats. The entire kitchen floor was covered in cats.

"How many?" Stacy asked.

"Ten here," Lark said with a shudder.

"Here?" Graham gulped.

"There are more upstairs," Lark continued. "I can hear their feet."

"But…they can't see you, right?" Stacy asked, bending down to pet a small calico that shrank away from her strange touch and smell.

"No, they can't." And, as if to demonstrate, Lark walked directly into the middle of the group of cats that sat on the floor. None of them moved. She knelt down to pet the same calico but this time the animal remained still, as though she wasn't even there.

"You think that's why you never had a pet, Grace? Your mom didn't want you to be disappointed when you were ignored?"

I thought about that for a minute before realizing that I'd never actually wanted one. "I'm pretty sure if I wanted a dog, my dad would have found a way to get one."

"Go on, Grace. See if the cats can see you?" Stacy suggested.

"What? Isn't it pretty much a given now that they can't?"

"Well...no. I mean, this whole you-being-an-angel thing makes sense sometimes but other times it doesn't. You can read my mind but you can't fly. You get hurt, you bleed, but you're starting to get really strong. And I mean *really* strong. What if, you know, animals like you? What if you end up being some kind of meerkat messiah?"

My jaw dropped along with my shoulders in disbelief. "Are you serious?"

"What? Pet the stupid cat!"

"Fine!"

I shoved my way to the calico and bent down. Up close, the cat looked more like a kitten. Its eyes were different colors, one a rich gold, the other a light blue, and it had black, tan, and orange splotches all along its white fur. Its tail was fluffy white, with a black tip.

"Hey, kitty," I said softly. My hand reached out slowly, gently, and I touched its head. The cat didn't move. It wasn't even looking at me. I pulled my hand back. "Well, there you g-"

The cat's paw lashed out and caught my hand, pulling it in with its claws and then...

"Is it...is it licking your hand?"

I flinched at the friction that came from the cat's tongue. "Is that what it's doing? It feels more like it's trying to skin me alive."

"Cat's don't lick people. I mean, seriously. That cat likes you, Grace."

"Well," Graham clapped, "I guess that answers the question

about whether or not animals can see you."

"It's one cat," Lark said skeptically. "Some cats aren't cats, if you get my meaning."

Stacy grabbed me and dragged me closer to the army of cats on the floor. "Stick your hand out."

I did as she instructed and struggled against her hold when one by one, the cats surrounded my extended hand and began to lick it and rub the sides of their faces against it.

"Okay, okay, stop! Cats can see me, cats can see me! They're going to lick my hand off!" I squealed as I pulled my hand away.

"So what? What does this mean?" Graham looked at Lark and waited for her to answer.

She looked confused. "I don't know what it means."

"It means I've gotta find the cat food," I muttered as the room began to fill with more cats, their meows filling up whatever silence had been left between the four of us.

## BACKWARDS

Robert was pacing the living room, one hand gripping the back of his neck in frustration. "What were you guys thinking? Starting a fight in the front yard? The two of you are supposed to be dead and now half the neighborhood has seen you!"

"Lark was being attacked," I pointed out.

"By two vampires. What were they going to do to her?"

Stacy growled. "They were doing plenty!"

"And they'd have no reason to do anything at all if you hadn't been fighting with Lem in the living room at three in the morning!" he growled back. "Attacking an angel isn't something that will keep you alive, and it certainly won't help to keep Grace safe."

"He changed his hair to look like Sam. He knew what kind of reaction he'd get, and I'm not going to apologize for what I did. You would have done the same thing. And where the hell were you anyway, huh? She's *your* wife, but you're never here!"

"I wasn't here because I was out answering my call! And I wouldn't have attacked Llehmai because I would have known who he was. Lark didn't attack him because she knew that as well. Didn't you stop to think about that? Her call is to protect Grace—she wouldn't have let Sam into this house."

I rubbed my eyes and exhaled at the rebounding arguments. "You guys need to stop already. Just stop. Mrs. Lorimax is in the hospital and no one is asking why. No one is asking why those…whatever they were attacked her and Lark."

420

"They were told to," Lark said coldly.

"What?" I looked at her with alarm. "I didn't hear that."

"That's because you couldn't. Those vampires weren't like the ones that are allowed to exist. They didn't think; their minds were dead. All that was left was what they were told to do and even that was buried. You would have only known it was there if you were looking for it."

I frowned. "And you were looking for it?"

She nodded. "When you can't hear a single thought coming from something that's attacking you, that's a bad sign. Whoever was controlling Erica knew that. That's why her head was constantly filled with rage and hatred over you. But those things…they were made by someone who thought that only you'd be listening."

"Grace-"

"Wait, their minds were dead? They were just trying to kill?"

"Grace-"

"Dammit, Robert, I'm trying to get some answers here!"

"Mrs. Lorimax is gone."

Robert's words were chilling. They were silencing. They were destructive.

"She was alive. She was fine," I whimpered.

"She was old, and it was her time," Robert said in a soft, soothing voice.

"No. No, it wasn't her time. I know it wasn't her time; I felt it."

He kneeled onto the floor in front of me and brought my hands down to my lap. "What you felt was her reluctance to go."

Snatching my hands away, I squirmed off of the sofa and toward the opposite wall. "Those vampires killed Mrs. Lorimax and you're worried about the neighbors seeing my face. What the hell is wrong with you?"

"I'm worried about people recognizing you as the girl whose face has been plastered in the papers all over Ohio for the past year and wondering why you're here, alive, when your obituary was just in the paper.

"I'm trying to keep you safe, Grace. Can't you see that?"

There was a tiny part of me that did. It accepted that he loved me and didn't want to see me hurt. But it was too small to stop the part of me that was tired of running, tired of hiding, tired of secrets.

I walked toward the kitchen and reached into the cupboard for a glass. I opened the refrigerator and pulled out a pitcher of lemonade and poured it into the glass and then took a long swig. I looked down at my feet and saw the piece of paper that had been in Stacy's pocket, and I bent down to pick it up.

"You know, the more people tell me that I'm not what I think I am, and that I'm something else, the more I have to ask why I need to be kept safe? If I'm an angel like Gabriel and Michael say I am, then I'm a lot stronger than everyone else thought. If I'm not an angel, or not a whole one, then I'm still different enough to not exactly break like glass.

"I've survived a car exploding, a car running me down, being strangled, stabbed, and blown up. Don't you think that I'm not as fragile as you thought I was?"

"I know that you're stronger than any of us gave you credit for, but you still have a human heart, Grace. That's not something that I or anyone else can ignore."

I put my hand on his chest and gave a sort of half-smile. "You're attached to my heart, aren't you?"

"It's the only one that beats just for me; I'm more than attached."

I wrapped my arms around his neck and held him against me, his arms closing around my back and bringing me in close. I inhaled the smell of smoke and grass and leather that always seemed to be a part of him. At least the angel thing hadn't changed my ability to smell things. I would have hated smelling something different about him.

*You've noticed a lot of changes in you.* His voice was rich and full in my mind.

*I don't like it when everyone's thoughts cram into my head at the same time. I don't know why it happened, if I did something to cause it, or if it's normal, but it's like being in a crowd and everyone's got megaphones all pointed at me.*

He sighed and brushed the back of my head with his hand. *That is normal. You will learn to tune it out so that it's more of a soft hum.*

*If there's time*, I thought.

He turned me around so that my back was up against the kitchen counter, the light directly in my eyes. *I thought you weren't going to give in to it? I thought you were going to fight this.*

I nodded. *I am. I meant if there's time after our honeymoon.*

He chuckled. *You want to go on a honeymoon?*

My shoulders hitched up. *Well we didn't have one, remember? We were going to take one after summer school but then...*

*Then I screwed up.* Robert's words brought a smile to my lips.

*We both did. But that's over. I'm not planning on dying anytime soon and I'm not letting you die either. I have a good a feeling about us, about this. We're going to be okay.*

He bent his head to kiss me, and I brought my hand up to hold his head. My eyes darted up briefly, seeing that I was still holding Stacy's notes, and I froze.

"Grace?" Robert looked at me, feeling my sudden chill and taking it into himself. "What's wrong, love?"

He turned his head, seeing what I was staring at, my hand beginning to shake. Stacy's paper was backwards but with the light hitting its front, Stacy's crisp and clear writing showed through easily.

"I AM HELL" it had said.

Now, backwards, it spelled a name.

"LLEHMAI" I breathed.

Robert let me go and was gone, leaving me tumbling, reaching for the table to keep me from falling. Lark appeared in the kitchen for a split second, but my thoughts had already reached her and she was gone, too. Stacy and Graham ran to me, chaos running through their thoughts as they both looked at each other and me, not knowing how to ask what had just happened.

"It was Lem," I breathed. "Lem was Sam's partner." I showed

them what I had seen, and let Graham snatch the paper from my hands as he held it up to the light. I could feel his fury; see the dark images that formed in his mind.

Stacy vibrated with rage. "That jackhole. Oh, I hope Lark and Robert tear him into more than just two pieces. I hope they save some for me."

"I'm going to find them," Graham said before he started running.

"What the hell are you gonna do, huh? What the hell do you think you're gonna do to him?" I shouted angrily, grabbing his arm before he could leave the kitchen. "Did you forget that he beat you into a vegetable? Or that he killed Erica and Mr. Branke? How about the fact that he was controlling his own son!"

"Of course I didn't forget! But what am I supposed to do? I can't do anything! I'm not strong like Stacy. I can't read minds like Lark. I can't kill people with a freaking thought like Robert. The only thing I'm good for is eating cold pizza and acting like an idiot!" He slammed his fist into the refrigerator. It was so damaged from me throwing Stacy into it that it couldn't take anymore abuse and its door fell off its hinge.

"Well damn," he grunted.

"Way to go, Princess. You showed that fridge who's boss," Stacy snarked.

The kitchen door flew open and Robert stood there, my dad clinging to his side, his hair wild, his eyes wide and filled with uncertainty. Lark appeared behind them, Matthew in her arms, his eyes closed as he snuggled against her chest.

"Dad!"

"G-Grace?" He let go of Robert and took a tentative step toward me. That one was followed by another, and then another, and then all I could see was Dad's shirt.

"Oh God, baby. Oh God."

He was sobbing, his whole body shaking with the rawest emotion I've ever felt come through him. His hands clawed at my back, pulling me close, closer. He squeezed, hugged, grasped, and in between he hiccupped, gasped, bawled, roared.

"You're alive. You're alive. This isn't possible; this can't be happening," he rasped into my hair before pulling away suddenly, taking a hold of my head and holding me still so that he could examine my face.

He looked at my eyes, his own red and bloodshot. I could see the days, hours, minutes, seconds of grieving in the tiny red veins that crisscrossed the whites of his eyes, netting in every moment of sorrow and holding them there.

But as each tear slipped through, I saw some of the darkness that lived behind his eyes begin to disappear. "You're really here."

I nodded, my vision blurring as tears distorted his face. "I'm here. It's really me."

Again I found myself breathing in his shirt, inhaling the scent of baby powder, the plain white bar of soap he'd always used, the laundry detergent that we bought in bulk because it cost less. I held onto him and felt something inside of me creak, like a faucet being turned or an old door being pushed.

I blinked, inhaled, and then burst open. Every second of guilt I felt for deceiving him came back in a rush of tears and garbled words that got lost in spit and puffy lips. I apologized, but I don't think he understood what I was saying. I don't think *I* even understood what I was saying, I was such a mess.

And then I was let go just as suddenly as I'd been grabbed. Dad turned around. "You son of a bitch! You knew she was alive this whole time and you let me think she was dead!" He flew forward, and I could see his intent in the angry thoughts that shot out of him, thoughts that I knew he intended for Robert to see.

"No, Dad!" I shouted before somehow moving around him and blocking his path. "Don't!"

"Get out of my way, Grace. This is between me and Robert."

"No, this isn't! This is between you and me. Robert was only doing this to protect me. I could have told you that I was alive—I had the opportunity to—but I didn't."

"What? Why would you do that to me, Grace? Why would you put me through that, knowing what I've been through, knowing what I'm going through?"

The tiny plinking of tears hitting the linoleum floor were like tiny bells, hinting at something that he did not yet know. He looked down at his feet and his shoes crunched against the shattered shards. "You…you move very fast.

"You moved too fast."

"I'm gonna go and put him upstairs in Mom's room," Lark said to Dad before leaving us. "I'll go back and get your things. Graham, come with me."

"But I wanna hear-"

"Come. With. Me…NOW."

Graham grumbled, but followed obediently.

I turned my head to see if Stacy was still around but she was gone, taking the opportunity to leave when she had it. *I hope she doesn't go searching for him.*

*She's hiding upstairs,* Robert's thoughts revealed.

I sighed, and then returned my attention to Dad. "There's a lot that you need to know."

"That's apparent."

"I…I talked to Gabriel."

"That stuck-up winged bastard? What did he have to say?"

"He said…he said that I'm not human. He and the others-"

"The others?" Dad looked at Robert, who stood behind me knowing how much I needed his support. "She spoke to all of them? The four?"

Robert nodded. "I asked for their help. She found out what Avi was-"

"Who told her? Was it you?"

"It was Mel," I answered. "Mrs. Deovolente told me before she died. I didn't really believe her but then Lem said it was true, and I guess

I took it badly."

"She took it more than badly," Robert corrected. "She became catatonic with shock. I don't think she realizes just how scared we all were when that happened. I went to speak to my grandfather and ask him for help."

"And they decided to come and speak to her," Dad finished for him.

"They believe that she's not human at all. I wanted to turn her, but they told me it's impossible since she's already divine."

Dad looked at me and exhaled as though a weight that had rested on his chest for a long time had suddenly been lifted. "The minute Ameila said that she had helped your mother conceive you, I've been worried that you wouldn't be accepted. If even Gabriel says you're one of them then that means you're safe."

"She's not," Robert said in a gravelly voice. "Llehmai is the one who's been trying to kill her."

"Llehmai? That's not possible," Dad argued. "Why do you think it was him? Ameila told me that the evidence pointed to Isis."

"Before Stacy died, Lark and I helped Grace search through her thoughts. What she saw was chaos and destruction. Stacy's mind had been attacked, and her attacker had left behind clues as to who he was."

Robert showed Dad Stacy's notes and I saw Dad's eyes roam the sheet, his forehead wrinkling with confusion. Then Robert turned the sheet over, and raised it up toward the light. Dad gasped and recognition hit him with the same ferocity and fear that had slammed into all of us.

"Is that why you just came and snatched me and my son? Because of this?"

"Yes. He is one of the Seraphim who've offered to protect you, but you see how that's not possible any longer."

Dad's head tossed from side to side. "I don't get it, though. He could have killed Grace whenever he wanted to. He's been alone with her so many times, if he hasn't killed her by now, he's probably the most incompetent angel in your history."

"I don't think he wants to kill me," I said matter-of-factly. "Not anymore, anyway."

"Why not?" Dad asked.

"Grace, do not give him the benefit of the doubt after everything he's done," Robert advised.

"I'm not giving him the benefit of the doubt. I'm looking at the facts and seeing them for what they are. Dad's right; he could have killed me at least half a dozen times already, but he didn't. I don't know what he wants from me, but it's not me dead."

## THE DANGER IN TRUST

"Where are you taking us?" I asked as Robert moved in a blur of speed. He stilled long enough to hand me an overstuffed backpack.

"To the only place I know of right now where you'll be safe."

"And we're all going? My dad, Matthew, and me?"

The blur returned. *Yes. I understand why you believe that Llehmai doesn't want to kill you, but he allowed his son to try multiple times. He encouraged it. He condoned it. He is a danger to you and to those you love.*

"But what about Janice?"

*She will be moved*

"Moved? You can't just move a person in a coma, Robert. She's attached to all kinds of wires, and she's got all kinds of doctors looking after her. People will notice that she's gone. My *dad* will notice that she's gone."

*Trust me on this, please.*

I huffed. "What about Graham? And Stacy? Lark? And what about you?"

*Graham will go wherever Lark goes, and Lark's call, now more than ever, demands that she be with you. Stacy can take care of herself, but she will know where you will be.*

"What about you? Are you coming with us?"

He stopped once again and looked at me. "I will be looking for Llehmai."

"But what if something happens to you? What if something happens to me? What if the call comes back? You promised that you would stay with me, Robert. Remember? If something happens to you, I'm not strong enough to deal with it again. I'm not. I don't care who says I'm an angel—you're the only reason I'm alive."

He kissed me. His lips were sweet and soft, but I've had enough of his kisses to know that this was the kind of kiss he gave to calm me, and I...

Oh hell, I wanted more of it.

"Mmph-Gr-"

I dropped the backpack on the floor and placed my hands on his head. I held him still—surprising the both of us that I could. I let the kiss deepen. I let it become the kind of kiss that didn't care about calming you. It wasn't meant to calm. It was meant to excite and build heat and fire and need.

And I needed. I needed so much and I wasn't sure if I'd ever feel satisfied. I needed to smell him, to touch the warmth beneath his skin, feel the power that threatened behind his eyes. Everything that made him who he was, even the flaws—especially the flaws—was everything I needed.

So I let him go.

"Why?" he panted against my mouth as my hands lowered to the tops of his shoulders.

"Because I have you. I already have you. Even if you're a million miles away, you're still here with me."

His eyes sparkled, his smile growing wider with each breath that mingled with mine. "Of course you have me. You own me body and soul."

"I don't want to own you, Robert. I just want to love you."

"Well, you do that perfectly."

"At least I do something well," I laughed softly.

"You do many things well; some things better than well," he said thickly.

A cough at the door silenced our exchange, and I turned around to see Dad standing there, a suitcase in one hand, the baby carrier in the other where a red-faced Matthew lay strapped in, his mouth opened in a silent cry.

"I'm sorry—I'm interrupting, I know, but I've got a tired and hungry four-month-old and no formula to feed him."

Robert nodded and then bent down to retrieve my backpack. I took it from him and looped my arms into it, tightening the straps to my back. "I guess it's time we got going."

"I'll see about getting the formula," Robert said before disappearing.

"You've had to say goodbye to him a great deal, haven't you?"

I looked at Dad's sympathetic face and nodded. "I knew it wasn't going to be easy when we started this."

"It never is, kiddo. It doesn't matter who you're with," he said comfortingly. "It's even more difficult in your situation, but you've managed to handle it a lot better than I did with your mom."

"You knew what Mom was when you met her…didn't you?"

He struggled with a reply, but finally managed to answer. "It's hard to be what I was, come from the family that I did, and not know."

"Llehmai told me that meeting you was part of her plan."

"Yes. She told me the truth after you were born. I didn't care; I loved her. I loved her so much, but seeing you and Robert together, I realize that I didn't love her as much as she loved me."

"Why?"

"Because of how strongly you're fighting to keep what you and Robert have. I didn't fight at all. I accepted what was going to happen. I accepted it and when it happened, I was prepared for it. If you truly love someone, you're never prepared to let them go. You do it, but you're never ready, never able to accept it.

"I loved your mom—I *love* your mom—but I don't think I loved her as much as she loved me. I don't think it's possible to love an angel more than they love you. It's why I'm glad I met Janice. Loving her always feels equal; I never feel like I'm coming up short with her. Maybe that's why I…I feel more lost without her around."

It was hard to hear these words about Mom spoken by my dad, but at the same time they offered me a window into his head that I didn't want to look in unless he offered it. I always thought that my mother was his greatest love, that Janice was just filling a role left vacant by my mom's death. Instead I realized that Janice had filled a role that my mother never held.

Dad, seeing how his words had affected me, put down the suitcase and clasped me in an awkward hip-to-hip embrace. "Your mother was my best friend, Grace. I talked to her every single day we were together; we were everything to each other: family, friend, husband and wife. I would have been more than grateful to have spent every last moment alive with her but she and I both knew that was never going to happen."

"Do you ever regret it? Being with Mom?"

He clutched me closer to him, and I felt his head shake. "Not for a single moment. Even after all of this, I'd do it all over again. Without her, I wouldn't have you, and if I didn't have you, I wouldn't have Janice, and Matthew. God, promise me you'll never pull a stunt like that again, Grace. Don't ever, ever make me believe that you're dead when you're not."

"I didn't mean to," I swore.

"I know. I know you didn't. But…when I saw your body, or what looked like your body, I-"

"Dad, don't. I wish you never had to see that, and if I could have stopped it, I would have. I hated it, I hated doing that to you and I promise that it'll never, ever happen again."

"Good. You might be married, and you might be able to throw me across the room, but I'm still your father, and I can still send you to your room," he said lightly.

Robert returned, his arms full of cans of different varieties of formula, his face frozen in confusion. "I didn't know which one to get. There were so many—how do you choose? Do all human babies require so many options?"

Dad laughed and reached for a blue and white can with the image of a blue duck on the bottom. "This is the one we give him."

Robert nodded and disappeared again.

"Is he going to buy every single can in the store?" Dad asked.

"Knowing him, yes."

"Here, hold onto Matthew while I go make him a bottle."

He left and I reached in to unbuckle the still quietly bawling baby. His cheeks had grown chubbier since I'd last seen him, but then again it could just have puffed up from the contained crying. "Sh-sh, Matthew. Dad's coming back with your breakfast."

Almost instantly, he quieted. "Missed me that much, eh?" I chuckled. "Well, I missed you, too." I kissed the soft cap of hair on his head and looked into chubby face. "You've gotten heavy. Maybe you don't need that bottle after all."

He squealed and blew out his bottom lip as though he understood. I tugged at it and laughed when he grunted in complaint. I patted his bottom to see if his diaper needed to be changed, and smiled in satisfaction when I found it dry.

"I guess you're saving all of it up for your brother-in-law, huh?"

Dad returned, a full bottle in his hand. "Okay, it's breakfast time."

I handed Matthew over and watched as he practically inhaled the nipple into his mouth, greedily gulping down the milk, each swallow amplified by his hunger.

"Jeez, Dad, when did he last eat?"

"Around nine last night. He's been going the whole night without getting up so when he wakes up in the morning he always acts like he's starving," Dad said as he fed the baby.

"You used to complain all the time about how I never slept at all," I remembered.

"That's because you didn't. Your mother stayed up with you all night with you when you were a baby so that I could get some sleep, but there were times when she'd be so exhausted I'd stay up with you. You were like an owl, always looking around, curious about what was going on. Those big, brown eyes of yours never missed anything. Whenever your mother would put a new toy in your crib, or change the curtains at the window, you'd just stare at them."

The sound of a burp interrupted us and we both looked down. Matthew had finished the entire bottle and was now fast asleep. "He burps himself?" I asked, amused.

"Yes. I think it's the only thing I can really claim."

I giggled. "He looks like a miniature you, Dad; I don't know why you'd say something like that."

"Probably because I see so much of his mother in him, just like I see your mother in you," he said sadly, stroking the baby's hair and then turning his hand to my face, cupping my chin.

"You know, I've never seen any part of Mom in me. I always saw you."

"That's a pretty generous thing to say, considering that more than one person has commented on how much you look like your mother."

"The only person who's ever really said I look like Mom was Lem, and I'm not really interested in remembering anything he's told me."

Dad smiled faintly, nodding in understanding. "Well, let me tell you that you do look like Abigail in some ways. It's not as striking a similarity as Lark and Ameila, but there are moments when you smile that I swear I'm looking at your mother."

"Thanks," I said halfheartedly. Being compared to my mother used to be the greatest compliment I'd ever received from him. Now, it was tainted.

"Do you know where they're taking us?" Dad asked, sensing a need for a subject change as he bent down to put Matthew back in his carrier.

"No," I said quietly. "He just said that it's with someone he trusted."

434

"Well, I'm just glad that we'll be together."

Lark's face appeared in the doorway. "It's time. Robert said he'd meet us there."

"Are we driving?" I asked.

"Yes and no. Your father and Matthew will be going with me. You'll be riding with Graham."

"Does he know where we're going?"

"No. I'll give him directions as he drives, but he won't know anything until we get there."

"But won't Lem know? Won't he just follow us?"

She shook her head. "He knows that we know. When news of this reaches the Seraphim and the first circle, he will be banished; he thinks he can outrun them but he should know better who he's up against."

Dad grunted, standing up and grabbing the infant carrier. "Banished? You mean all they'll do is strip him of his divinity, after what he's done to my family?"

"His divinity, his beauty... It's the standard punishment for his crimes, you know that, James."

"But I don't get it," I said with reluctance. "He didn't do anything that was worse than what Sam did; why is he being punished when Sam wasn't? I mean, they actually *made* Sam better! Why would they punish Lem and not him?"

Lark exhaled in dissatisfaction that mimicked mine. "Because Sam never abused his position, while Llehmai has."

"You don't sound convinced," Dad noticed.

"That's because I'm not," she said simply.

"Hey, are you guys coming or not?" Graham called out from the bottom of the stairs.

Dad lowered to grab a hold of his suitcase and then looked at me. "Let's go, Grace. We can complain about this later."

He kissed my forehead and then turned to face Lark. "I don't know how you're going to do this, but Matthew and I are ready."

"You'll put your suitcase in the car and carry the baby."

Dad's eyebrows rose at such a simple explanation, and then followed Lark down the stairs. I took one last look at the room and tried hard not to feel sad. This was the third home I'd said goodbye to in less than three months, and I wasn't exactly pleased with the trend.

I closed the door behind me and took the steps down to where Graham was waiting. He offered me one of his signature smiles and then punched me in my arm.

"Ow! Holy-what the-" He grabbed his fist and looked at me in shock.

"What?" I asked, stunned, reaching for his hand to inspect it for damage.

He held it up. "Gotcha," he laughed.

"Oh, you dork!"

"Come on Frank," he joked. "Let's get going before my wife starts to get the wrong idea."

"I don't think she'd ever get the wrong idea with you," I chuckled.

We walked outside, early morning sun already brightly lighting the street and the houses. There was a dark stain on the cement and I was reminded of Mrs. Lorimax's cats.

"I'm gonna go and check on them really quickly," I told Graham before crossing the street.

"You really think that's a good idea?" he called out. "She's dead. Can't you just call the Humane Society or something?"

"I promised her they'd be okay; I'm just going to check if they have enough food and water until someone comes to get them."

"Well, hurry up. I don't like getting yelled at by my wife; especially when she's not even here."

The front door was still unlocked, and I walked in, calling for the cats as I shut the door.

They were all lounging on the sofas and the carpet in the living room, meowing at me for interrupting their morning nap. "Sorry," I told them.

I reached out to pet one of them, its warm, soft head tilting up to accept my touch. The soft vibration of its purring and the mewls of the other cats around made me smile, reminding me of my dad and his strange love of themed music using those very sounds. I suppose it was this reaction that left me feeling at ease.

Because I forgot that they normally can't see or sense the presence of an angel.

Which is why I didn't realize that I wasn't alone until it was too late.

# THE TRUST IN DOUBT

*You should have let things be. Everything that was done was done for you. I risked everything I am for you. I broke the rules, the laws of my kind for you. I've done more for you than I did for anyone else—even your mother. I would do anything for you and you had to go and ruin everything.*

You know, I don't think angels are supposed to have headaches. They're not supposed to have bloody noses, either. But I had both; I could feel the stickiness clinging to my upper lip and smell the metallic tang of blood, while my head felt like a church bell.

*I'm sorry for that. There was no other way to subdue you. That and you struggled more than I expected. You're strong, but your human weaknesses are still present.*

I tried to open my eyes, but they felt like they were glued shut. My mouth was dry, my tongue heavy in my mouth. It hurt to think.

*You'll feel better soon. Your body heals faster because of what you are. You know that, don't you?*

I didn't intend to, but my head fell forward in a nod. My body didn't move, though. I was sitting upright, but not necessarily in a chair. My hands, I could tell, were at my side. I was clutching onto the bottom of my wooden seat, my feet balanced on a bar. I was on a stool. Well, if I fell, I wouldn't hurt for too long.

*Don't get too confident. You can still die. In fact, you are more susceptible to dying than a human being. It's in your make up. It's who you are.*

A hand touched my hair, fingers running through it and tugging slightly. *She had hair that was so smooth, like dark water. Your hair is thick*

438

*like tar.*

I coughed, my lips cracking as they opened to allow the action. "I get my hair from my dad."

His voice was harsh and piercing in my mind, and I flinched as it filled every corner that I'd left opened. *You have no father. You are the sum of only one person, who wasted her love and her devotion on someone who admits to loving a human more.*

"Y-you were listening to me talk to my dad."

*How can you continue to call him that?*

"Because that's what he is," I wheezed. "He loves me, no matter what I do or say. That's what fathers do. They love their children no matter what kind of mistakes they make, and I've made some pretty big ones."

*You say this to attack my own lack of remorse over my son. But no mistake you have made can equal the failures of his, so to compare the two of you in some misdirected attempt to make me feel inferior to James Shelley is foolish and futile.*

"You couldn't ever measure up to my dad. He might be human, but he's never failed me as a father the way you did to Sam. And Sam never failed. But you already knew that."

Lem's voice boomed, bouncing and amplifying quickly, telling me that we were in a small room. "He failed at everything. He was weak, he was incompetent. His hatred of humans was so strong that he couldn't even charm them; I had to do it for him."

"You changed your look before, didn't you?" I asked, noticing that my throat was growing less itchy.

*What do you mean by that? Don't be obtuse, Grace.* He was back to thinking. He knew I was gathering clues.

"No, no, you have; I'm not being obtuse. My friends told me, but I didn't pay attention to it. They said that Erica had a boyfriend; a blond, tall, handsome boyfriend. I think if I hadn't known deep down who Sam was, I would have thought it was him. But I didn't, because I knew it couldn't have been. He couldn't show anyone affection. But you…you've shown more affection than you should have.

"That's how you got to Erica, isn't it? You made yourself look like Sam so that other people would think it was him, and then you hurt her."

*I didn't hurt that girl.*

"You tricked her into thinking you were Sam. You made everyone think that you were him and then you attacked her. You turned her into a zombie!"

*I didn't hurt her. Even after learning about what she wanted to do to you with that human boy, the one who married Lark, I did nothing to her.*

My stomach clenched at his statement. "You knew about that?"

*Of course. I know everything about your life.*

"What-what the hell? What were you doing? Were you…were you stalking me? Do you know how creepy that is?"

*Stalking you? I was protecting you.*

I huffed. "Protecting me? *You* were protecting *me*? Now I know why Sam couldn't do anything right—he had a pretty damn lousy example to follow."

I felt tight fingers on my shoulders, digging through my shirt and into my skin, and I cried out at the pain. *Who do you think kept you safe before N'Uriel arrived into your life? Who do you think kept you out of Samael's sights for so long?*

"You sure didn't seem all that willing to protect me at that wedding," I sneered.

*I couldn't do that without bringing suspicion to all of us. You have every single angel focusing their thoughts on you.*

*What Avi did to bring you into this world, her sacrifices, her death, has left us with a void that we are unable to fill on our own. You are the reason for that and to draw any further attention to you would have made you an even bigger target.*

"Oh please, like you give a damn about that. The truth is you're doing this because of my mom. She didn't love you and you're trying to prove to the world that she made the wrong choice."

His fingers loosened, and I could hear him stumble backwards, even falling. He wasn't on a carpeted floor—I could hear the scraping of his wings. I stretched my foot down and felt the give of something beneath my boot.

Dirt. Small room, dirt floor, somewhere he didn't want anyone to recognize… "You brought me to your sanctuary." It wasn't a question, because I already knew the answer. I don't know how, I just did. It made sense.

The air around me vibrated with emotion. It was chilled, yet smelled like burnt hair. I could hear the back and forth sawing of something, a grating sound that pierced my ears and caused my already closed eyes to tighten.

He was crying, and if I could have seen it, it probably would have been the kind of crying that Stacy called "ugly crying"; the kind that contorted your face into grotesque shapes, reddening it, puffing it up until you looked like a smashed apple.

"Did I say something wrong? Lem?"

*You said you made mistakes. What kind of mistakes?*

His thoughts were shaky, as if the vibrations in the air affected everything on the inside of him, too. This affected me for some reason and I felt compelled to answer him, even though everything inside of me that possessed any sense left screamed against it.

"I-I lied to my dad. I lied to him about Robert. I lied about Stacy. And I let him believe I was dead. I broke his heart and put him through hell-"

*You don't know what hell is like!*

I straightened up, my back turning stiff instantly at his insinuation. "No. But you do, right? Because you are hell? *I am hell*—Llehmai. That's your name. You were the one who put Stacy into that coma. You trapped her inside of her own mind."

*You have your mother's heart but you do not have her head; you are not as intelligent as she was,*

441

I don't know why, but that made me angry. "I know that. I know I'm not as smart as she was. She was a freaking angel. I got a B in English and flunked Biology and had to go to summer school. I don't know a billion languages and definitely don't know everything about angels because I'm *not* an angel.

"But I know what I saw in Stacy's head. I saw the room with the birds. Sam didn't hate Robert; he hated me. What I saw in that room was done by someone who hated him, and the only person I know who has a reason to hate him is you."

*Why would I hate N'Uriel? What does he have that I do not?*

"Me."

He laughed, both out loud and in my head, the stereo of the sound filling up the small space quickly. *I never thought you, of all people, could be so conceited.*

That stung. "Well? Am I wrong? Tell me that you don't hate the fact that I chose Robert over you the same way my mom chose my dad over you."

I heard a high pitched whistle before the cracking of wood and then the sound of crunching as my head hit the ground.

*I don't hate N'Uriel because you chose him. I don't hate him at all. I hate myself for never making myself known to you. If I had, you would have chosen me instead. I would have made you happy. I would have done everything to make you happy.*

I groaned as the throbbing in the back of my head moved forward. "Is that what this is? Stalking me, kidnapping me is you making me happy? What's next, huh? Are you gonna feed me to some vampires and call that foreplay?"

*I...I'm sorry. I am angry and I am directing it toward you.*

"You think? Ow...if I didn't have a concussion before, I will now."

Hands that were firm and gentle slid beneath me, and I inhaled almost automatically, the burnt hair scent stronger now. He lifted me and placed me into his lap, my head falling into the crook of his arms, my legs hanging over his thigh. My leg brushed against the thick stiffness of his wings and I shivered at how rough they felt, even through my jeans.

"Why can't I open my eyes?" I asked.

*Your eyes are open.*

I felt myself blink, but everything was black. "What are you doing to me? Why can't I see anything?"

He sighed. *I'm making you see nothing but darkness,*

"Why? Are you scared I'm gonna see your face? Because I know what you look like already. I've seen it up close, remember?"

I felt his head shake, the motion causing his wings to rub my leg. *It's because your sister-in-law has the ability to see what you see and I cannot risk having her see where we are.*

"Can't she just dig into your head?" I asked through gritted teeth; his body wasn't as giving as Robert's was while holding me. It felt like I was lying on a rock.

*She can only see what I want her to see. She knows this. She knows trying to find you through me will get her nowhere. And as long as you are here, no one will find you. No one.*

My heart slowed down. I didn't need him to explain what he meant by that. What I needed was to somehow un-hear it. I wanted to have it be erased from my mind, blacked out like he'd blacked out my vision.

"You don't know what you're doing," I whimpered.

*You know that I do. You know that I know exactly what I'm doing.*

"Why? Why are you doing this to me? Why are you doing this to Robert?"

*Because I cannot lose your mother again.*

I raised my head and turned toward his voice. "You can't lose her again. She's gone. She's been gone for eleven years."

*You don't understand. You are the only proof left that she existed.*

"But I don't plan on dying. I told you-"

*You told me a fairytale. What makes you think you can outwit the call? It will take either your life or N'Uriel's soon. If it takes yours, the world will fall apart. You are the irreplaceable one, not him.*

"Yeah, I keep hearing that, but news flash: I'm not Death. I don't hold the keys or whatever the hell you think I do to the freaking balance of this world. If my mother wanted me to take over for her, why didn't she tell me so herself? You know why? Because she knew that I couldn't do what she did. I don't have it in me to kill people; I'm not that strong." '

He laughed sarcastically. *You think you're not that strong? You defeated my son.*

My arms flew up in the air in exasperation. "I didn't do anything, okay! I don't know what happened that night. I had some kind of freaky epiphany and stabbed him in his eyes; that was it. I didn't stop him; someone else did. Maybe it was you, maybe it was someone else, but it wasn't me."

Angry and tired of having to repeat myself, I shoved against his chest, the force causing me to roll away. My face fell into the dirt and I inhaled some of it, coughing and choking on the dust. A strong hand rapped me on my back, but I shook it off. "Get away from me."

"Grace. You can close your mind to me but you can't stop me from speaking."

I crawled across the ground until I hit a wall. I scrambled to place the wall against my back and brought my knees up to my chest. "I don't care if you talk until your tongue rots and falls off. I just don't want you touching me anymore."

"Fine, I'll stay away," he said gruffly before his voice turned remorseful. "I know you think that I was Samael's partner."

"I don't think it. I know it."

"And you are right."

I jerked at his confession. "Y-you're admitting it?"

"I did seduce that girl, Erica, yes, but I did it for my son. Contrary to what you think, I did care for him."

I hoped he could see me roll my eyes at that. I hoped I was actually rolling my eyes. "You did it for him? Because you cared about him? Like I'm going to believe that."

"You don't have to, but it is the truth. I have never lied to you and I never will. That's not something you can say about N'Uriel, now is it?"

"Robert's lies weren't meant to hurt me."

Lem chuckled. "Yes. One never truly intends to harm another when they lie, and yet they always do."

"Your son never told a lie that he didn't mean to hurt someone."

"This is true. You think I was a terrible father; you're right. He asked me for my help; he'd never done that before and I was too surprised to say no. He said he needed me to make her see him as someone good. He said she only saw evil in him."

"She obviously knew her kind," I sniped.

"Perhaps. I admit that I wasn't concerned. I did this thing for him and unwittingly became a part of his plan. By the time I found out why he needed me to get her to trust him, it was too late. She was dead in every way that mattered."

My voice was loud when I threw out my accusation. "It's your fault! You made her act like a zombie. You made her hurt my friends; you made her hurt me-"

"I never did any of that. I told you, I've been protecting you. I tried to stop him. I tried to make him see you as someone else. I wouldn't have done anything that I knew would end up hurting you."

I buried my head in my arms, feeling the strain in my neck and my back as I mumbled to him from beneath my partial shelter, "Everything you did ended up hurting me."

I heard his muffled movements, and I looked up, seeing nothing, my head shaking violently from side to side. "Don't come any closer. I don't want you near me."

"You'll have to let me near you one day," he said softly, almost hopefully.

"That'll never happen. Robert's going to kill you when he finds you; you realize that, right?"

"He won't find me. He won't find you, either."

I scrambled to my feet and tried to point my body in his direction. I threw out my arm; my finger pointing at what I hoped was his face. "Then you don't know Robert. He came back from the dead for me. He'll find me no matter where we are."

Lem's laughter was hollow, as if he doubted what he wanted to say even before the words left his lips. "No one will find you here until it's too late."

"If anything happens to Robert while I'm here, I promise you, I'll kill you myself."

"I thought you weren't strong enough to kill anyone," he said lightly.

I turned my head, knowing now where he stood. I walked toward him, feeling his presence, smelling that same burnt scent, until I was within inches of him. I raised my head until I knew I was looking directly at him. Even if I couldn't see him, even if he looked away, he and I knew that what I had to say wasn't going to be wasted on empty spaces between us.

"If Robert's call to kill me returns and he refuses to answer it, he will die, and he won't die alone. You know what your son planned. You saw what he wanted. Keeping me here finishes what he started. And if you do that, if anyone I love is hurt because of you, I swear on my love for Robert, I *will* kill you. I will find the most painful, awful way to do it and I will.

"I will never love you, I will never want you, I will never forgive you. If you kill my heart, there will be nothing left for you."

"That's a risk I'm going to take, Grace."

## DOUBT IN CIRCLES

My stomach gurgled for the thirteenth time. I knew it was the thirteenth because counting each one helped to keep me from focusing on the quiet. It's scary, what complete darkness and silence can do to a mind. You start to imagine things, hear things that aren't really there. You even start to feel things that aren't there.

So when my stomach growled that first time, I giggled. It was such a welcomed sound. I put my hands over my waist to feel it the next time it came. When it did, I hugged it to myself. It was sound and motion that were real. I was alone—I'd been alone for a while judging by how many times I'd replayed Rocky Horror in my head—and my body was finally starting to recognize this.

So of course, when you're hungry and you haven't eaten in a while and you don't have any options available, your mind begins to run through a virtual buffet of food. Hamburgers, hams, salads, pasta… I began to picture different pies and cakes…

"Ugh, I'd kill for some of Dad's egg-in-a-hole," I groaned.

I could smell the butter, hear the sizzle of eggs. My stomach grumbled again.

"I'd eat them with a full plate of bacon," I said out loud. "And a glass of iced tea. Oh God, a pitcher of it." My mouth was dry. I didn't realize how dry it was until the image of a frosty glass of tea made me cough.

"Ugh. I'd drink coffee right now if it I had to."

I stood up and began probably my fourth lap around the small room. I was dizzy, but that wasn't anything new. The room had no corners, and the floor dipped a little at one end. There was no door, but then again I didn't expect there to be. The walls were soft, made of dirt, and they crumbled whenever my nails dug in a little too deeply.

"Like chocolate cake," I mumbled.

I stopped walking and my shoulders sank. "Ugh…I'm starting to act like Graham."

I shoved my hands into my pockets and started walking again. I needed to think about something other than food.

"God, why is this happening? I don't care about what happens to me. I don't. But Dad's probably never going to let me out of the house again after this, and Robert…"

I broke down, stumbling over my own feet and hitting the dirt hard.

Everything seemed to jiggle loose inside of me. Every thought I'd ever had about him, every feeling, every wish and hope scattered like glitter in front of me. And even blind, I could see them. Every sparkle that I'd seen in his eyes, every bright spot he added to my life that I thought would always be dark. Robert had told me once that I had completed him.

I always thought that was sweet, but wrong, because I couldn't complete him when he made up all of me. But I knew that I was wrong. I closed my eyes and imagined him there, beside me.

"You know you and I are two halves of the same whole," he'd say to me while stroking my face with his thumb. He would know how comforted that would make me feel and then he'd kiss my forehead, and tell me that he loved me.

"I love you," I'd say back to him, and he'd smile and say that he knew that.

He must be going crazy with worry. His head must be filled with so many dark images. He's seen the worst in people—his imagination wouldn't give him a break.

"Ugh, even if Robert's okay, I'm still gonna kill you, Lem," I hissed, hitting the dirt with my fist. "He's never done anything to you. He's never done anything to anyone."

"Whoa." My fist had sunk into the ground several inches. It was like I'd punched jelly instead of dirt.

I pulled my hand out and frowned at the gritty feeling against my skin. "Great. I'm gonna look like a catfish when this is all over."

Pushing myself back, I sat against the wall again and tried to focus on something other than food and Robert. I needed to think.

Lem admitted to being Sam's partner. I knew that already. But it didn't…mesh. Sam was pleased with his partner's work, but when Lem's name was mentioned, he seemed…upset. He said the plan had changed. Of course it changed—I wasn't supposed to die anymore.

But Sam wouldn't have gone along willingly with that. Not unless he feared what disagreement would mean. He loved hating me. He loved the idea of killing me; looking in his face when he believed that I was dying, I saw the only real joy he'd ever expressed.

If what Llehmai said was true, if he had been looking out for me for years, if he had been protecting me then that must have pissed Sam off. "There's no way Sam would have agreed to work with Lem if he knew that."

But why did Sam ask for his help? "Stupid, he wanted a way in to Erica."

I slapped my forehead. "God, I'm so stupid. If Lem knew who I was then of course he did, too." I continued to slap my forehead. "Stupid-stupid-stupid. He knew who I was the whole time. He just didn't kill me until he knew I had a reason to live. He wanted to make it hurt. He knew…"

"Ugh!" I kicked the ground and screamed in frustration.

"He was waiting for me to meet Robert. He knew what was going to happen; he waited for it to happen! Every freaking thing about him is a lie! What's next? He's not really my brother?"

My head hurt, but I couldn't stop. Sam wanted me dead; Isis wanted me dead. Hell, I'm pretty sure even Gabriel wants me dead. But

Lem doesn't. Unless… "Unless he wants me to starve to death," I mumbled when my stomach let out another growl.

This back and forth was mind numbing. Lark said she knew Isis was Sam's partner. She didn't believe that it was Lem because of what she saw from Isis' ring.

"Why didn't I ask to see that ring?"

"See what ring?"

Lem's voice, after hearing nothing but my own for hours, was like hearing a gunshot.

My head snapped back and hit the wall behind me. I yelped in pain and grabbed my head. "Where the hell have you been?" I grunted.

"I went to get you something to eat. Your mind and body isn't ready to accept the fact that you're an angel so you must eat."

"I'm not hungry," I lied. And of course he knew I was lying. Even if he couldn't sense it, even if he couldn't hear the defiance in my voice, he knew by the almost thunderous rumble that erupted from within me. "Traitor," I said to my belly.

He chuckled. "I know you like burgers so I got you two, plus an order of fries and one of those incredibly large cups of soda."

The crinkle of the package and the smell of fried potatoes made my stomach turn over in anticipation.

"I'll help you."

"I don't want your help."

"Have you ever eaten blindly before?" His voice was almost mocking in its tone.

"I'm only blind because of you," I reminded him.

"And that's for your own good."

"You mean that's for *your* own good."

He grabbed my hand and placed the side of the cup against it. "Drink something. You're delirious."

A part of me wanted to throw it at him—I gripped onto his hand and knew where exactly he was—but a bigger part of me wanted to drink every single last drop of soda in the cup and then suck on the ice cubes until my mouth was numb and my teeth hurt. I took the cup from him and through trial and error, found the straw sticking out of it.

"I know you like the strawberry one, but they only had cherry," Lem said casually, as though we did this kind of thing all the time.

I took a deep gulp and sighed with satisfaction. "It's wet. I don't care if it tastes like celery."

The sound of a wrapper being opened up and the smell of bread and meat and cheese were almost as good as Christmas. And when he held the burger to my mouth, and I took a bite, I moaned. "Oh God, that tastes like heaven."

More crinkling, and a bag of fries was placed in my lap. I sat there in silence—well, as silent as I could get, what with the completely inappropriate noises I was making while eating—and consumed the food that probably would have tasted like dirt if I hadn't been so hungry. Every bite, every sip, every swallow made me appreciate how sometimes the simplest of things really were the greatest.

"That was...ladylike."

I'd burped. No. No, what came out of me after the final guzzle of cherry-flavored soda was more like a cross between a frog's croak and the bark of an overgrown donkey-dog hybrid.

"Excuse me," I said before bursting out laughing.

It felt good to laugh, despite my company. And I didn't care that I was the only one doing it. I didn't care if he didn't understand why I was laughing. I didn't care that he was probably looking at me like I was losing my mind. I'd been wound up so tight, I felt like a spring.

As though my body knew how much I needed it, another rolling belch slipped out. "Oh, Graham would have been proud of that one," I said between what breaths I could catch, my laughter almost uncontrollable now.

I held my stomach to prevent the pain I knew was coming from crippling me too much, and I fell over.

"You can find it in you to laugh despite being here with me?"

"I think I laugh *in* spite of being here with you," I corrected between giggles. "If you keep quiet, I might be able to forget about you completely and pretend that my friends are here instead."

"I do recall N'Uriel speaking to you about uncharitable moments."

I lashed out with my feet before hurrying to stand, all sense of humor lost; now replaced with undeniable anger. "You listened to us? You spied on us?"

"I told you; I've been looking out for you, watching over you."

I shook my head, my hands clenching into tight balls against my side. "No. You said you did that until Robert arrived. The watching out part stopped the minute you started listening to our private conversations."

"Don't you understand, Grace, that there really is no such thing as a private conversation? The truth will come out one way or the other; especially with our kind."

"What are you talking about? I know that you guys can keep secrets; you wouldn't have been able to have gotten away with half the stuff you pulled if you couldn't. Robert didn't know about my mom because all of you kept it from him."

Lem laughed, the kind of laugh Sam had made when he knew I was talking about something I didn't know anything about. "I told you that the truth would come out one way or the other. It doesn't mean that a secret can't be kept for a time. You know this. You've seen the proof yourself."

"I haven't seen a damn thing. I haven't seen a goddamn thing. People keep telling me things as if I already know what it means. It's like you guys can't see who I am. You only see my mom, or you dream you see her. Whatever it is, it's not real, okay? I'm not my mother. I'll never be her no matter what you want or think or do."

"I see your mother in you, I won't lie. It's hard for any one of us to look at you and not see her. But I'm telling you that you've seen the proof yourself. Not your mother, not a dream of your mother, but you."

He grabbed my hand, fighting me to open my fist. "If you do

not open your hand I might break your fingers," he warned.

"Then break them! I don't care! I'm not going to do anything you want, you creep!"

I struggled, but he was stronger than me no matter what I might have been. He opened my hand and placed something warm against my palm. "You now have every single secret I've ever had in the palm of your hand."

I heard him move away, his feet intentionally dragging against the floor so that I knew he wasn't near me anymore. I contemplated throwing whatever he had placed in my hand at him. I told myself that I didn't care what it was, or what kind of secrets it held. He'd kidnapped me, hurt my friends, and was willing to do a lot more to get what he wanted. There was no reason to give him what he wanted.

I squeezed my hand around it, fumbling with my fingers until I felt one slip into it. I knew right away that it was a ring—his ring. "I don't get it."

"What don't you get? Everything that I've ever kept from anyone since the moment I received my wings has been etched into that ring's very make up."

The large circle spun around on my finger easily, slightly heavy, thick, but nothing particularly special from what I could tell. It probably looked as plain as my mother's ring, but aside from its sentimental value, there was nothing interesting about either of them.

"Great. So everything that proves you to be the jerk I know you are is on this ring."

His voice grew unsteady. "You can't see anything?"

"Of course I can't see anything; I'm wearing my mother's ring; I'm wearing Robert's ring. I've never seen anything just by wearing them. Why would I see anything from yours? I'm not an angel—not enough of one, anyway."

I held my hand out, wanting him to take the ring back. His hand pushed my fingers toward my palm and then my hand to my chest. "Keep it. One day you'll know the truth about me."

"I still don't get it. What does giving me your ring have to do with anything?"

"When you and your teacher were attacked, a ring was found."

I nodded. "Yeah, in my chest."

"Do you know where it is now?"

I had to stop and think. And then I laughed. "My dad stole it."

It was like I could hear the brakes on his brain being slammed. "Your dad stole the ring?"

"Yes. He took it from the police officer who had it. You were there."

"Wow…"

"Yeah. I thought the exact same thing when he told me what he did."

He grunted in response.

"Why do you care about that ring anyway?"

"Because it's the only thing that will prove that I'm not the bad guy."

How strange, to laugh the way I did when he said that. It sounded like something inside of me had snapped, and all the crazy that existed in me just came out all at once.

"You're not the bad guy? *You're* not the bad guy? If you're not the bad guy then why the hell am I stuck in an oversized grave?" I shouted. "If you're not the bad guy, then why did you help your psychotic son try to kill me?"

This time he shouted back. "I didn't try to help him kill you. I tried to stop him—"

"How?"

He stopped. And then his voice grew soft. "By making him see you as someone to desire."

A ripple of disgust ran through me. "I knew it was you. I knew it."

"I'm sorry."

"You're sorry? You were there, the whole time—you saw what

454

he did, you knew what he was going to do—and you didn't do anything to help."

"I told you, I tried to stop him-"

I threw the ring in the direction of his voice and hissed. "You tried to protect yourself and your secrets. Well I don't want to know any of them. You watched your son attack me and then you made him…ugh, you made him do things that I can't even…I hate you, Llehmai. I hate you. You and my mother deserved each other and I don't know why the hell she never realized that."

"Even in her most fiery of moments, Avi never once told me she hated me."

"I don't care."

"She was very conservative with her affection toward me."

"I said I don't care."

"The more that I think about it, the more I realize that perhaps the reason for that was because she never felt anything for me at all."

"For the last goddamn time, I-don't-care!"

"But you do. You care. You wouldn't be able to hate me if you didn't. Your mother was indifferent to me. She was indifferent to most of us thanks to millennia of killing *for* us. But you aren't. You're incapable of being indifferent. You even feel remorse for Samael."

Ugh. I hated him. I hated him for his plans, for his thoughts, for what he's done.

But mostly I hated him for being right.

Because he was right: I did feel remorse over Sam's death. Everyone who died because of this didn't have to. I know I wished it, I know I had hoped beyond all reason that Sam would die. But when he did it didn't make me feel better. It didn't give me the sense of relief that I had expected.

Instead I felt like I'd just taken Sam's place.

Or maybe…

Maybe I'd just taken mine.

## GRAVE IMPORTANCE

I smelled. It's an unspoken rule that if you can smell your own funk, you stink pretty badly, and I was covering my nose at the odor that seeped out of me.

"How long have I been here?"

"Almost a week. Why?"

A week? Was that all it took to turn into a she-beast? "I need a bath."

"I can clean you if you want."

I shuddered. "I said I need a bath, not to be molested."

"If it's any consolation to you, I think you look just fine."

"I don't care how I look to you. I don't care how I look period. I just smell…this whole place smells."

"I'm sorry. I've never had to take care of someone like you before."

I tried to run my fingers through my hair to bring some kind of order to its chaos but they got stuck. "You call this being taken cared of? I've spent the past week living in a hole. I'm stuck on this side because I've used the other side as a toilet; I *smell* like a toilet. I've spent so much time talking to myself that I'm pretty sure I'm ready to be committed to some psychiatric hospital."

"You're being dramatic. I didn't expect that."

"Well, maybe I'm being dramatic because I'm stuck. In. A. HOLE!"

I shook my head and groaned when the sound of things falling out of it bounced around me. "I've probably got trees and things-"

I stopped. "You know, I really, really want to take a bath."

"I don't know how to help you with that."

Why did I assume that this was going to be easy?

"I need to take a bath. I feel gross, I smell like roadkill. You need to get me hot water, some soap, a washcloth. I don't need a tub, but I need lots of hot water." I waited for him to respond. When he didn't, I almost felt like crying.

I needed him to do this. I needed him to believe me.

"Fine."

He left—I only know this because the smell of burnt hair was gone again—and I waited. I didn't know how long it would take for him to get me what I'd asked for. It seemed to always take him hours just to pick up a crappy burger and fries.

"Maybe that's on purpose," I said to myself before grabbing my head with both hands and groaning in embarrassment. "And there I go talking to myself again."

I stood up and began to pace. I counted ten steps before turning around and returning to the wall. I did this over and over, never going over ten.

"You know where to stop."

Lem's voice never just eased into the silence, and I almost lost my count. "Damn you; why can't you just...talk like a normal person."

"Because I'm not a person; I'm an angel. I have your hot water, your soap, your washcloth, and some clean clothes. They're five steps behind you."

"Now I want some privacy."

He laughed. "Why? You can't see me watching."

"I can feel you watching. I can smell you."

"Fine. I'll give you twenty minutes."

"Thank you."

I felt a hand against my cheek and I flinched. He felt it, too.

"Goodbye, Grace."

I waited until I was certain he was gone. And then I hurried to the water. "Ugh, I don't want to waste you, but I have to." It was in what felt like a large pot, and I heaved it over. The smell of the water turning the dirt floor and walls to mud reminded me of rain and wet moss. I sank to my knees and began to dig. I'd felt something in my hair, something that wasn't dirt.

It was a plant. Well, part of a plant. I knew that I didn't bring it with me, which meant that it had already been here, and if it had already been here then there must be more. I needed to find it. Or at least find the roots.

I knew I couldn't talk out loud anymore. I didn't know where Lem was, but if he could still control what I saw from outside, then he could hear what was going on, and I couldn't risk that.

My fingers clawed at the wet soil. I dug quickly, scraping and pulling out small rocks. I kept count in my head the seconds and the minutes that had passed since Lem had gone. I'd reached thirteen when my fingers brushed up against something wiry and cool.

This time my digging grew frantic. I didn't want to hurt the root, but I also didn't want to be so careful that I ran out of time. When I'd uncovered enough to hold on to, I grabbed it and closed my eyes.

*Bala…I don't know if you'll hear this. I don't know if you can. I don't know if you want to. But I need your help. I need your help, please. Please, Bala…*

I continued to count the seconds and the minutes. If Bala didn't respond, I'd have to hurry up and cover the hole.

And I'd be muddy.

"I don't want to spend the rest of my life in here covered in mud," I groaned.

I had two minutes left. The dirt was cold and soft, but all I focused on was that root. Each fragile tip, each little branch felt like my last hope. One minute, forty-five seconds. I let the root go and began to push the dirt back.

The hole was filled, and the mud had already dried into a thick crust on my arms when I heard Lem return.

"You don't look clean."

"You think? I had an accident," I explained, the lie already so deeply ingrained it came out without a single thought.

"An accident?"

My head rocked forward roughly. "Yes, an accident. I'm blind, trying to bathe out of a pot, in a hole in the ground. Have you ever tried to do that?"

"I can honestly say that I have not."

I scratched at the dried mud on my arm, my skin growing tight and itchy. "Why can't I see? I thought when someone was in this place that they couldn't be disturbed, or bothered."

"That's usually true. But this isn't my sanctuary. I'm mere-ly…borrowing it."

"How do you *borrow* one of those?"

"I wouldn't answer that question even if we weren't here."

My teeth began to grind against each other at his reply. Instead of saying what I wanted to, instead of repeating to him all of the best cuss words I'd ever hear come out of Stacy's mouth, I turned away from him.

"Would you like me to bring you more hot water?"

I moved toward the wall and leaned against it, inhaling the cool air that seemed to flow through it. "I just want you to leave me alone."

"Are you hungry?"

"Just…just go. Please."

"You're angry at me because I won't tell you."

I slammed my palm against the wall, feeling the soft dirt spill to my feet. "I'm angry because I even have to ask the question."

"I'll leave you alone for a while. I'll return with some food. Something different, perhaps?"

"Whatever."

The minute I knew he was gone, I screamed. It wasn't the kind of scream I'm proud of. There were some things said during that scream that made me cringe, but I had to say them; I didn't know what else to do.

I hit the wall again. I kept doing it, ignoring the pain, the burning; needing to feel something other than hopelessness. The dirt continued to fall at my feet, and I began to wish that it would just bury me. Lem was going to win; I wasn't going to get out. Everything I thought I could do because I'd finally accepted who I was nothing but a lie used to make myself feel better now.

I hit the wall again.

No.

The wall hit me.

I was shoved to the ground by a wall of dirt. It grew, weighing down on me, heavy and cold. I was being buried, just like I'd wanted. I struggled against the weight, but the dirt kept falling, covering my legs and my chest, slipping and sliding to my neck. I took a deep breath and felt the dirt pour over my head.

Remember as a little kid, when you'd pull your blanket over your head thinking it would protect you from everything? It didn't matter how scary the world was outside; inside that blanket, you were safe. Well, as strange as it might sound, I felt safe in this accidental grave.

Even if I couldn't breathe, even if it seemed darker, even if my body was being crushed beneath who knows how many pounds of dirt, I felt safe. It felt like my mind was clear.

I exhaled, knowing that it would probably be the last time it happened, and felt the dirt settle into the indentation created in my chest and stomach. *I wish I could have told you...I wish we could have told you.*

When the pressure of holding my breath finally became too much, I opened my mouth and inhaled. The dirt fell into my mouth, smooth and gritty at the same time. The taste of dirt is one you never forget, and will remember for the rest of your life—if you last that long—reminded by just a hint of its smell. It's clean, musty.

Eating dirt isn't really as bad as it sounds. It's when that dirt turns to a gummy paste in your mouth that you realize you're choking. It sticks to everything; your teeth, the sides of your mouth, the back of your throat. You feel it getting thicker, almost as if it's growing in your mouth. And when it fills it completely, you do what comes naturally, instinctually: you breathe through your nose.

And when that happens, you know it's over. You don't have to think about it anymore. You just prepare yourself, try not to panic, try not to make it worse than it already is.

So this is where I was. I'd accepted death a long time ago and then rejected it, and now had no choice but to accept it again. This was much more difficult than I thought it would be. Gagging, clawing at my throat, feeling my lungs stretch and fill with useless sludge took over everything.

My hand pulled away from my body, surprising me. Maybe this was why I'd failed biology; was this normal when you die? Did your body jerk and do things you didn't tell it to? Did you start to hallucinate and see things when you knew you couldn't?

If so, then I was very close to being dead. Because my shoulders were straining; both of my arms had snapped over my head, past my head, behind me. I felt stretched, pulled.

My fingers were numb. What little of my brain was left working told me that this particular numbness wasn't the kind that came when your nerves were dying. This type of numbness came when you'd cut off the blood supply.

Something tight was around my wrist; something that felt like rope. It wasn't rope.

Roots!

Bala!

*Bala! Oh my God, Bala, you found me!*

I needed to breathe; my chest was burning and felt like at any second, it was going to explode. Oh dear God. *Wait! Bala, wait, if you take me out, the sanctuary will explode!*

The pulling continued, faster it seemed. I felt frantic as the two ends warred within me. Dying through suffocation or dying by being blown up because I was leaving both sounded pretty bad. I'd already survived being blown up, but I really didn't want to die because I had a Graham-sized appetite for dirt.

My heart was racing so fast it seemed like it was screaming. There was almost nothing left for it to pump. I'd finally found hope, but hope couldn't keep a heart beating.

"Oh yes it can."

Hands, strong hands that I knew so well, as though they'd been part of my very first memory, were grabbing onto mine. Hands began to pound on me, beating on my back, holding my face, forcing my mouth open.

I was vomiting. Someone had shoved a finger down my throat and I was puking up what felt like last year's Thanksgiving dinner. My body was wracked with rough, violent heaving.

"That's a good girl. Throw it all up," someone said encouragingly into my ear.

"She needs water. Get her some water, dammit."

Cold, fresh water splashed on my face and was brushed against my lips. I gulped the liquid, my mouth open like a fish. The water felt unnatural, almost as if nothing could feel that good. And then I threw up again.

"She expels things from her like a bird would to feed its young. Only she's not feeding her young."

"That's because she has no...young, or whatever. And get the hell away from me, you freaky Ficus!"

Graham!

"You're funny. And very attractive. If Lark ever tires of you, I could make use of you."

"Okay, the plant just made a pass at me—get it away!"

"Oh God, Princess, she's not a plant."

Stacy!

"She's got roots! She's got leaves and flowers growing on her skin! And she's—oh my God, she's naked! Hey…ow!"

"Idiot. Grace, Grace how are you feeling?"

I turned my head to her voice, and slowly opened my eyes. Everything was still dark. "I feel like crap."

"Of course you feel like crap. Bala here just dragged you out from about fifty-feet of dirt. Oh, and you smell like a-"

"That's enough, Stacy. She's been through a great deal. Let her catch her breath, please."

I threw myself in the direction of that voice. To hear it, to hear it so close to my heart, I knew I wouldn't be able to contain my emotions. I burst into tears as my arms clasped onto him, squeezing him and holding him as tightly as I could to me. I couldn't smell anything but dirt, but I knew it was him.

"It's me, love. It's me. I'm here; you're safe."

"Don't leave me again," I sobbed. "Don't ever-"

"Shh. I promise, I promise. I'm not going anywhere." The hand that stroked my hair was so gentle, it only made me sob harder.

"God…what did he do to her?" Graham asked angrily.

"Does it matter what he did? Look at her; she's shaking like a fault line!"

Bala's strange voice floated over the both of theirs. "She just won't die. Even buried she rises."

"You need to return to your tree, Bala. You're weakening; your petals are falling."

"You remember what you promised, N'Uriel."

"Yes, I remember."

The ground shook beneath us, and I heard Graham whistle. "Whoa. She just…she just sank into the ground. Where's she going?"

"Back to her tree," Robert said grimly.

"Her tree? But she went underground."

"She's a nymph, Graham. She's physically tied to a tree and usually can only travel as far as her roots stretch."

"Usually? What do you mean by usually?" Graham sounded genuinely frightened.

"Bala's had nothing but time to figure out how to leave the confines of her tree. She learned she can move from tree to tree for a short period of time through their roots as long as they're touching each other. The longer she remains away from her tree, however, the weaker she becomes."

"So...the plant used other plants to dig Grace out?"

"She's not a plant. She's a nymph; God, Graham, pay attention!"

I heard a grunt, and then a huff. "I don't want to pay attention to that! My best friend's spent the past week buried beneath, like, a hundred graves!"

Graves? I laughed. I couldn't help it; the sound just came out and the motion's already so similar to sobbing, there really was no change.

"She's cracked. She's finally cracked."

Something wet and soft began to wipe at my face, gently rubbing over my eyes. "Open your eyes, Grace."

"It won't work. I can't see. He's doing it," I mumbled.

"Open them. Trust me and open them."

I scrunched my face up, suddenly afraid. I hadn't seen anything that wasn't behind my lids for a week. I didn't know what light would feel like, or what seeing faces that weren't frozen in place from a memory would do. Everything that I'd wanted was suddenly waiting for me and I couldn't let myself have them.

"What's wrong, Grace?" Stacy asked, her cold hand rubbing mine.

"Yeah, what's wrong with her?" Graham added.

"She's been blind for the entire time that Lem's had her," Robert explained, his voice rigidly calm despite the anger I felt rippling deep within him. "He refused to let her see his face and where she was."

"Come on, Grace. Open your eyes."

"Come on, Frank. You know you want to look at my handsome

face."

"It's not that handsome," I murmured before relaxing and allowing my lids to rise millimeter by millimeter.

Light hurts. It's painful, especially when you've only seen darkness for a while. Every second of darkness means one more spent adjusting to the burn that happens when it retreats. Instantly, my eyes filled with tears. They acted like a filter to the light, but I closed my eyes anyway.

"Take your time. It doesn't have to happen right away," Robert said encouragingly.

It took several blinks, but I managed to get my eyes open just enough to see Stacy's dark eyes and Graham's light green ones forming a straight line of concern for me. Stacy's darkened when she could see the recognition in my face, while Graham's lightened.

"Hey, you."

"Hey," I squeaked.

A hand cupped my chin and gently pulled my head inward, and I felt a shuddering sort of whimper attack my chest when two silver rings filled with more light and joy than anyone had a right to locked on to my eyes.

"I see you," I breathed.

"And I see you," he said back before bending down, his mouth not quite covering mine, but not quite avoiding it either.

"Did Lem stop? Did he stop with the blinding thing?" Graham asked.

"He stopped the minute he realized she wasn't where he'd left her," Robert answered.

"Does Lark know where he is yet?" Stacy demanded, her fingers cracking as she opened and closed her fists. "Because I really, really want to hurt this creep."

"Lark's relying on the sight of others to help her find him but he's using his ability to change what people see to his advantage. If Grace hadn't tried to contact Bala, she would still be down there."

I needed to sit up. I needed to see where "there" was.

"Grace, don't—not yet!"

My eyes closed and then opened wide, allowing for everything that was in view when I sat up and looked around. Headstones lined the grassy area that surrounded us. Old trees bowed over some of them, shading them and hiding the names etched onto the old, weathered rock.

But I didn't need to know the names to know where we were. I turned around and stared at the one stone that I'd know, blind or not. "Abigail Shelley…loving mother and wife…

"There's a sanctuary under my mother's grave."

Robert shook his head. "You weren't in a sanctuary, Grace. There's no way you would have been able to leave if you'd been in one; you know that."

"I know that. He said that it wasn't his, though. He said it was borrowed."

"You can't 'borrow' an angel's sanctuary, Grace. The only way you can enter one that isn't your own is if the sanctuary's owner is with you."

"So it was his then, and he was lying," Graham argued.

"This isn't Lem's sanctuary," Robert corrected. "And this isn't Sam's either."

"Who cares if it's not Sam's?" Stacy snapped.

"We're linked by our descendents, Stacy. Lem could use Sam's sanctuary, and vice versa. I've been to both."

"So, who's related to Lem then? Maybe it's his dad's. Or his mom's."

"That doesn't answer the question on how Grace could have left without the ground beneath us imploding and taking half of this cemetery with it." Robert was agitated, as though the answer was right in front of him and he just couldn't see it.

But I could. Because it was right in front of me, too.

"It's my mother's."

All three of them responded with the same one word question. "What?"

"That's why he wouldn't tell me. He didn't want to tell me that we were in my mom's sanctuary because he'd have to tell me how we could get in there. Oh my God, we got in because of me. I could have left any time I wanted. It's my fault I was in there for so long." I shoved my hands into my hair, and groaned in dismay when they became stuck in the mud and tangles.

"This isn't your fault, Grace," Robert insisted.

"Yeah—you didn't know," Graham agreed.

"Lark's here," Stacy announced before leaving.

I yanked at my hands and winced when they came free, pulling out some hair in the process. I looked at my arms and my hands and then looked up into Robert's eyes. I could see my reflection in them and I shrieked.

"Why didn't you tell me I looked like a hag!"

"Because you don't," Robert insisted. "Yes, you're dirty. Yes, you're exhausted. But underneath all of it you're still Grace. You're still my wife."

"I never thought I'd be so happy to hear myself being called that before," I said in a half-laugh, half-sob.

"Well, get used to it...wife."

Lark approached tentatively, her face showing nothing but regret. "I'm sorry."

Well...

"Whoa."

*Lark, when have you ever apologized to me for something?*

"I should have taken you instead. I shouldn't have let you go with Graham. It's my call to protect you. I'm supposed to keep you safe and I didn't. I failed. I failed at my call and I'm sorry."

Seeing Lark look so weak, so broken and imperfect, it was like being in a fog. I looked at my friends faces, I looked at Robert's face; they were all frozen, as though blinded by what had happened. It was as if all of us had spent the past seven days in the dark, and with our first glimpse in the light, we were seeing things we didn't want to see.

And what did I not want to see?

I looked down again at my hands, and it was right there, stuck to my finger by a clump of dried mud. It was Lem's ring, probably finding its way onto my hand after digging through the mud.

*You now have every single secret I've ever had in the palm of your hand.*

"I need someone to wear this ring," I blurted.

Robert looked at it and then reached for it.

"No!" I clutched my hand to my chest and shook my head. "Not you. Not after what happened with Gabriel's ring. I don't want you going through that again."

"Well then, who?"

I looked at Lark, who looked at Robert, who fumed. "Fine."

I exhaled with relief. Ameila was the only Seraphim I trusted, the only one who could wear Lem's ring and not be hurt by its designation.

"So where is she?"

Lark answered when Robert refused. "She's at the hospital. She's taken Janice's place there so that we can keep Janice safe."

I nodded. "Well, this is important. Lem said he wasn't Sam's partner. I don't believe him...but the truth is here, and we need to find out what it is before someone else gets hurt or worse."

"Let's go," Robert said gravely.

"C-can I take a shower first?" I asked sheepishly.

# DUALITY

The ICU currently smelled like boiled meat. At least, that's what Graham said when we walked in.

"That's just the bed pan smell," Stacy said casually as we were led down a hallway with glass for walls.

The nurse who had offered to show us where "Janice" was stopped in front of a curtained doorway. "She's in there. Your father's in there with her," he said with a wan smile.

"Thank you," I said before pushing aside the curtain and stepping into the large room filled with off-white machines, chairs, and an occupied hospital bed.

Dad was sitting in a chair in the corner; his head held in his hands, his shoulders slumped forward in obvious defeat. He didn't hear us enter. Instead, he was told by a single thought, and when he looked up and saw my face matching the voice that told him that I was okay, it was like watching the years wind back, the aged lines on his face disappearing with gladness and relief.

"Oh thank God," he let out, his hands finding me, pulling me into his desperate embrace and squeezing hard, cutting off my ability to breathe for just a moment. "Where was she?" he asked into my hair.

"Llehmai had her in Avi's sanctuary," Lark answered gruffly.

Dad didn't react at all. He just continued to hold me, his breathing slowing down as he grew more and more sure that I was actually there. He touched my head, my shoulders, my ears. He held my face and looked into my eyes, not blinking, not breathing. He pushed my head against his shoulder again and sighed after inhaling my hair.

"We need to speak to Ameila," I whispered into his ear, knowing that we didn't have much time.

"Ameila? Oh." He looked up and then toward the curtained doorway. "You won't find any privacy here."

"I won't need privacy," I told him before easing away and then turning to the still form that lay in the bed. It looked like Janice. To anyone who didn't know the truth, it *was* Janice. Ameila had perfected her role as comatose woman, with the pale skin and the dull hair.

The machines attached to her were quiet, the numbers probably telling someone who understood them exactly what they were expecting. Through the soft pump of air and the even softer beeps, I felt her push of thoughts.

*You have returned safely. I am glad.*

It was strange, seeing Janice's face while hearing Ameila's voice, especially after everything that Ameila had done. I trusted Janice. Even though this was my idea, I wasn't sure I could trust Ameila. But I had no choice. *I need your help.*

*Slip the ring on my finger; I already know what to do. Hold my hand; let the memories slip into you. But...are you sure you are prepared for what might be contained in his ring? You've already seen some the worst of what we're capable of, but these are the memories of someone you trusted. What you learn might be worse than even that.*

I looked at the serene face of my step-mother and knew that it didn't matter whether I was prepared or not; the worst was already happening.

*I understand.*

*Alright.*

Lem's ring was heavy in my pocket. I removed it and then slipped the ring onto the middle finger of her left hand. The images began almost immediately.

***

"He will serve an important purpose when he receives his call."

"We all do."

"Avi, can you not see it? Feel."

I could see Lem's hand reach for my mother's. He pulled it to her belly, which was round and full. "He will have a great role in the future of all of us."

"The role he will serve will be no more important than any other that we fill. We cannot keep believing that we are somehow better than anyone else. We are not unique or individual, Llehmai. He will do what he has born to do, nothing more."

This surprised me. I didn't remember much of my mother, but I knew that she'd never sounded so...cold. And by the way I could feel his skin harden around his mouth, I knew he felt the same.

"This is our son, Avi."

"Yes, the son we had to have."

I felt the pinch in Lem's chest at the tone in my mother's voice. "You hate what we had to do that much?"

"It isn't hate. It is sadness over not being able to say that he was conceived out of love."

"But he was!"

My mother removed her hand from Lem's grip and floated away from him. "You know those feelings are unnecessary. I already feel a genuine love for you, but I cannot be *in* love with you. It serves no purpose to either of us. We are not here to be lovers. We were not created to love each other. We were created to love them, humans, and by confusing the emotions we feel through them with the sense of duty and responsibility we have within us, we only set ourselves up to fail as both angels and as lovers."

Lem's body ran cold with hurt and dismay. He looked at my mother through the rose-tinted glasses that I thought only humans were aware of. He saw her as beautiful, perfect, and everything that an angel was supposed to be. But she was also changing. He made a mental note of it; she was becoming more and more like her mentor.

"Gabriel's cynicism is turning you cold, Avi."

My mother smiled as though it was expected, automatic. "His cynicism is toward the humans. Mine is toward our own kind. I would hardly think that makes me cold. I think it makes me a better angel."

"You think caring more for the humans you kill than for your own kind makes you a better angel?

"Yes. You forget; we aren't here for ourselves; we are here for them. Wanting to be here for ourselves is what caused the flood."

"You think I don't know that?"

My mother's voice, loud and violently angry, shocked me when she snarled. "Yes; I believe you don't know that. You weren't there. You did not see what I saw, do what I did. You were created in a time when people had already forgotten what had happened and why. They had already forgotten when the world was one ocean, and it was made of the dead.

"Until you have seen half of our kind decaying because of their selfishness and their greed for power, you don't know anything."

Standing away from her, Lem's eyes took in everything about her. She was very pregnant. It looked like she was only a few weeks away from giving birth. All angels glowed, but she seemed to radiate a much deeper light, one that felt all too familiar.

"I know that I did not exist then, but it is hard to not know what happened when they consume your thoughts. You bear so much of that weight alone; let me help you."

My mother shook her head. "I do not need your help, Llehmai."

"You will one day."

"I know."

\*\*\*

"How could you let her do this?"

Sam.

Even through his father's eyes, Sam was perfection. There was no hint to the malice that skirted just beneath the surface of his golden smile.

"You seem to forget that Avi outranks me; I didn't *let* her do anything. I've expressed my disapproval but she will do what she wishes."

Lem was staring out across a watery surface. It was evening, and the reflection of stars could be seen glittering from both above and below. Lem sighed at the sight.

"Then you know what I will do."

"You say that as though it is not something that you've wanted to do for a while."

Sam's laughter was too full of glee to have been anything but genuine at his father's comment. "I've wanted to kill her, yes. But unlike her, I know my place. As evil as you think I am, I've always obeyed the laws."

"It's not the laws that matter to you. You have not forgiven her for what happened to Miki."

Sam's laughter died away. "I haven't forgiven any of you."

Lem's vision narrowed, his body tightening in reaction to Sam's simple statement. "She is your mother."

"And you're my father, and both of you worked together to deny me the type of happiness that you were unable to find with each other. Your selfishness killed the only thing in this world I ever cared about, and I will never stop hating you for that."

\*\*\*

The little girl crying on the steps of the empty school made his heart burn. He had watched her all day, from the moment she awoke to the moment she finally gave up waiting and sank to the ground, the dress she wore stained, torn, and unrecognizable.

How cruel these human children were. They'd mocked her, teased her, and she kept her chin up throughout it all. But it was when her last pillar of support left that her spirit broke and she was forced to look at the damage that had been done to her.

One of the human children, a boy named Tomas, had called her a dog in a dress. The little girl had said nothing, but Lem had felt the pain that turned over and over in her chest. When Tomas' friend Harrison came back with a slur that was so offensive even Tomas gasped in shock, the girl's chin stuck out in defiance of it, but he could see the tremble in her knees as she fought against the hurt of it.

All throughout the morning, she'd listened to the jabs and the barbs thrown her way, and she handled them like a soldier would gunfire. It was what happened on the playground that nearly caused him to react to their heinous behavior.

As soon as some of the chaperones had turned their backs on them, a few of the girls gathered in a circle around her, like a pack of hungry lions. They kept quiet, but they didn't remain still. They pulled at her dress, a soft blue confection that had little flowers stitched in white thread all over it. One girl pulled at a sleeve so hard, it tore.

The little girl remained quiet even as the others pinched and tugged, ripped and tore, until part of the dress hung in the dirt, covering one worn leather shoe with the stained and tattered edge of a hem. When the bell rang, the others scattered, leaving her standing there alone.

"Grace? Grace Shelley, what in the world did you do to your dress? We're taking photos in ten minutes! Oh, why does it always have to be you?" a teacher complained, grabbing her by her arm in a way that caused the little girl to flinch. "All of the other girls kept themselves pretty. You're going to have to stand in the back of the class today."

The little girl nodded, blinking rapidly to fight back the threat of tears. "Okay, Mrs. Mackey."

"Honestly, I don't understand why you just can't be like everyone else. No one causes as much trouble as you do."

"It wasn't her fault," a little boy shouted as he ran up to them. "I saw it. Michaela, Shannon, Tanya tore her dress."

474

"You saw this happen and you didn't do anything?" the teacher asked with skepticism.

"I was getting chewed out by Mr. Duncan! I told him what was going on but he didn't do anything."

"I doubt Mr. Duncan would have done nothing if someone was harassing Grace."

"All of you guys do nothing about it!"

"If you raise your tone with me again, Mr. Hasselbeck, I will call your parents."

"It's okay, Graham," the little girl said softly to her friend. "I'll just stand in the back."

"Then I'm gonna stand in the back, too."

The teacher looked at the defiant boy's face and shrugged. "You were going to be in the back anyway; you're taller than the other kids."

She dragged the two children with her toward their classroom, stepping on the strip of the little girl's dress on the way and tearing it even more. She cursed under her breath at the sound of the fabric tearing and glared at the little girl, as if she had done something wrong.

*Ugh, why can't you just be normal like everyone else? Damn mongrel, I can't stand seeing your face; you should have died with your mother.* Her thoughts were icy in Lem's mind, and he shook with quiet rage.

His vision drew in to tiny pinpoints of light and colors and he growled slightly. He moved closer to the teacher, so close he could see the line where her makeup split her face from her neck. He grazed over her shoulder, and she shivered, looking around as though she knew he was there, but she couldn't see him.

*You can't stand seeing her face. Let's see how you like seeing the things you fear the most every time you* don't *see her.*

The woman blinked as the words pinged inside her head. She looked down at the ground and screamed, jumping back and flailing her arms. The children beside her stepped out of her way, and she fell, crawling to a far wall and running her hands into her hair and scratching at her arms and face.

The little girl, undaunted by the sudden shift in behavior, stepped toward the teacher and took a hold of her hand. The woman looked up at her face and flinched. The girl knew why, but she didn't react the same way the teacher did. "It's gonna be okay, Mrs. Mackey," she said in a soft voice.

The teacher looked away and screamed, shaking her head. "They're everywhere. They're all over me."

"Nothing is on you. Graham, go get help. See, Mrs. Mackey, Graham's gonna get help and you'll be okay."

The boy took one look at his teacher lying on the ground, and at his friend kneeling beside her, holding onto her hand and took off in the opposite direction even as the rest of the classroom crowded around them to watch in morbid fascination.

The woman looked once more at the little girl and shut her eyes. "I don't want to see anything anymore."

With a gentle hand, the girl cradled her teacher's face. "I know what that's like. It's gonna be okay."

Once help arrived, the rumors and stories spread like a cancer among the children. Truth wasn't important: sensationalism was. The history of the little girl turned a child helping a teacher into a child harming her. The ridicule she'd endured that morning was nothing compared to what she endured the rest of the day.

The jeers, the hair pulling, the accusations and innuendos made Lem seethe. He wanted to snap the necks of every single child who'd dared to turn her kind act into something worth hating. Was there no solace to be had by humanity for someone who was different?

At the end of the school day, as everyone went home, on buses with friends, in cars with parents who showed up on time, Grace stood apart from everyone else. Only one person remained, standing beside her protectively. With him beside her, she seemed to glow, content and complete.

But the minute his mother arrived and he left, the change was instantaneous. The light within her disappeared, her strength floating away as she sank to the ground. She was alone and exposed. No teachers came to check on her; no one seemed to care, and this angered him.

Every single tear that fell from her eyes onto the ground stained the concrete a dark grey. She sniffed, and then looked up. For a moment, he swore she was looking directly at him. Then he heard the quiet rumble of an engine growing louder and turned to see her father's car approach.

It stopped abruptly in front of her, her father rushing out to her and picking her up, apologies slipping out of his mouth as he hugged her to his chest. "I'm late, I'm sorry. I tried to get Ivy to pick you up but she said she had to take Graham to the dentist. Are you okay? What happened to your dress?"

"I fell," the little girl lied through a slight pinching of her face.

"You fell? From what, a moving jungle gym? Kiddo, tell me what happened."

"Nothing, Dad. I fell down, that's all. Can we go home now?"

"Yeah, I'm sorry kiddo. Come on. Hey, how about hamburgers for dinner?"

"Sounds good."

Lem watched the two climb into the car and drive away, choosing not to follow them and instead walking toward lightening spot on the concrete. He bent down and ran his finger across the moisture, smiling when the only grit he felt came from the concrete itself.

*Soon. It'll come soon.*

***

Erica Hamilton looked uncomfortable, almost insecure. "I don't know why I feel so nervous around you."

"I don't either. If you want, I can take you back home."

"No, no I want to be here with you. It's just...the first time we went out, you seemed so cold and distant. And now, it's like you're a completely different person. Was it me? Did I do something weird that day?"

Lem looked up at his surroundings. They were in a restaurant, something small and cozy, with framed mirrors of different sizes and shapes lining the walls. He could smell every dish, every perfume, every shampoo. He caught his reflection in an oval mirror across the room and sighed.

He knew what he looked like. He also knew that everyone sitting around him was seeing someone else. How easy it was, he thought, to fool them into believing he was someone else. Their minds were so simple to trick, their desires so easy to please.

His gaze returned to Erica's. "I think I was just nervous. You are so beautiful and it's hard to really be myself around you."

Erica's laugh sounded so sweet, so innocent that I doubted it was hers. "I'm beautiful? You're like this god or something. Every girl, every *woman* in this place is looking at you and wishing they were me. They wish they were sitting here right now, with you looking at me the way you are."

Lem laughed, an easygoing laugh that would have made anyone feel special. I knew that laugh; I knew I was right. But Lem's thoughts betrayed what he said to her. He downplayed his effect, but he knew she was right, if only partially. Most of the women did wish they were sitting in her seat, but they didn't want to be her. They wanted to be themselves with him admiring them.

They weren't deluded enough to want to be that age again, when nothing seemed important until it was too late. They had the confidence that Erica lacked, a confidence that she envied. Erica knew she was beautiful, but even more so, she knew that it wasn't enough.

"I don't know what I did to find someone like you, but whatever it was, I'll do it again," Erica sighed.

*** 

Lem was staring into eyes that looked almost maniacal. The face

478

they were settled in was frozen in a laugh that made even Lem's skin crawl.

"Why are you trying to hurt Grace, Isis?"

The angel cackled. "Why do you care? She's nothing; she's less than nothing. Insignificant little speck of human waste to be burned from the world."

Lem looked down and his hand came into view. It was wrapped around Isis' throat. He laughed and let go. "If she were so insignificant, you wouldn't be trying to kill her."

"Samael told me what she means to you. Do you think I don't see how much you want her?" Isis sneered. "You're lusting after the daughter because you couldn't have the mother; do you realize how pathetic that is? Especially for an angel?"

"You don't know what I want from her. You only know what Sam's told you, and his mind was too clouded with rage to know anything but his own delusion-filled call. Why are *you* trying to hurt her."

"As if I would tell you."

"You know I know how to find out."

Isis raised her right hand and wiggled her fingers in Lem's face. "The truth is never the truth until all the lies have been removed."

Lem grunted as a hard and heavy kick landed in his chest, Isis pulling her legs up between them, tucking her head down to roll away from him. Lem's vision flashed with the ceiling of a white room. He crashed into a large object before rising to his feet and glaring at the pixie-like angel who smiled at him from her perch atop a bed.

My bed.

"You know they will kill you, right? Her friends are loyal and N'Uriel will do everything in his power to keep her safe. He has more power than you and I combined and he will use that power to destroy you until you're not even a memory."

Isis laughed. "You and I both know that his power is only temporary. His existence is as much a mistake as hers is. When they are both gone, we will have control of the world again."

"You're an imbecile if you think that will happen. We only had one second chance after what the Grigori did; throwing off the balance of this world will sentence all of us to death. _All_ of us; not just the humans."

"And you believe this? How many times have we been told that story? How many of us were even there? You weren't. I wasn't. The way I see it, thousands of years of fear has done nothing but keep us from fulfilling our true roles.

"I can make a human mind explode into chaos with a single thought. I can make the most beloved of mothers turn against her children, like a monster from someone's nightmare. But I can't even blink insanity into someone's mind without permission so long as they exist. Once N'Uriel and his whore are gone, I'll be a god."

"You will leave Grace alone, Isis. I don't care about what you do to N'Uriel. I don't care about anything but keeping Grace safe."

"Well then, maybe you should have stopped us before N'Uriel killed Sam because there's nothing that can be done for her now. She's going to die, Llehmai. The dark ones are coming for her. They're bringing their children with them and they're going to kill her. She's going to die and she'll do it knowing the truth about you."

"What truth?"

"That you did nothing to save her mother's life. You watched Samael kill her. You watched your son kill his mother and you let her daughter see it. She will know what you did, and she will never forgive you. You might be content to settle for her friendship like you did with Avi, but after this, you won't even have that. She will hate you. She will hate you with her very last dying breath and you will live just long enough to hear them."

Isis' laugh was cold and critical. She faded into a white mist that drifted out of the window like smoke. Lem watched it, saying nothing, hearing only the beating of the heart within his chest, the only real tie he had to the humanity that my mother gave up everything for.

_I promised to look after her. I promised to keep her safe from Samael_ *until it was time. I promised to love her. I did everything that you asked, Avi. I just didn't think that the potential of losing her would hurt more than losing you did. And you knew it, too. You knew it would and you still let me make that promise.*

He roared, the sound rattling the walls and the window, my mirror cracking from the sound of it. Through his eyes, everything looked red. The white walls now looked like they were covered in blood. Everything was tainted with crimson and rage.

Lem turned, seeing the split reflection of himself in the cracked mirror. Each sliver of his face showed a different side of him. The cold side that had been able to stand by and watch as the angel he loved died on an empty road eleven years ago contrasted with the warm side that made it so easy to love those he couldn't have.

His eyes flicked down to the ground where they spied something I'd missed: a photo. Or, what's left of a photo. Two faces joined together like one, but only their eyes could be seen. Lem's eyes saw more in those eyes than anyone human could. While he was sure that the missing pieces contained smiles, the message hidden in the eyes was clear: happiness didn't live here.

*Our son was right; you were selfish and Grace will end up paying the price for that. I forgave you for not loving me. I forgave you for loving a human. I even forgave you for dying. But I won't forgive you for this.*

\*\*\*

He was looking at me; looking at my face, pinched in distress as I railed against him in the dark. The smell of earth and moisture couldn't drown out the scent of my hair, he noted. He held his hand out to me, his fingers flexing just to the point of impossibility before he drew them back into a fist.

*I'd give everything up for you to trust me. I know you won't love me. I know you probably feel nothing but hate for me now. But...*

He looked away, his gut filled with emotions he hadn't felt in a long time. It embarrassed him, the disappointment that bubbled with the simple joy inside of him. As much as he had criticized Samael for being a failure, he was every bit as much a failure as his son.

Samael failed because he couldn't trust anyone.

And neither did he. Even now, he couldn't trust the sleeping girl just feet away from him. She was as much a threat to him as she was to his son, despite her weakness and her innocence.

But she wasn't as innocent as she appeared, he noted.

She'd hurt them. She had brought down an archangel of death, and she'd done that without knowing what she was or who she was meant to be. If she could do that as a human, what could she do when she reached her full potential?

Isis' words came back to haunt him. When Grace learned the truth, she *would* hate him, and Isis knew that it would kill him. His feelings for her went too deep, too far.

*I don't know what to do, Avi. I don't know what to do. I've never not known what to do before and it's killing me.*

He brought his hand to his face, his glow glinting off the silver ring around his finger. Distorted and dull, he could see his face, see the doubt, see the distrust. He was glad that the darkness prevented me from seeing his face, because he didn't want to see it himself.

Finally I said something that made him approach me. He took my hand and despite my complaints, forced the silver circle into my palm. Every word that came out from him, from me, seemed meaningless the moment he'd let go of the one thing that kept who he was a secret from everyone else.

*I don't know what I'm doing anymore. I've just handed your daughter my life, Avi. It's every important moment, every dark second, every feeling of wanting… I'm giving her control and it terrifies me. I've never been terrified before. Please don't let me have made a mistake.*

He watched me throw his ring and I could hear his heart shudder to a stop.

*Please.*

# THE SEATS

The quiet in the room was the first thing I noticed the moment I let go. It was as if sound had died along with the belief that Lem had been Sam's partner. Losing that one piece of information felt like I'd lost a lifetime of knowledge. How could I have been so sure and yet so wrong?

"It might not be wrong," Robert said in a hushed tone. "You might still be right."

"But I'm not.

Truth can come on slowly like a cold, or it can slam you into you like being hit by a car. I knew what that felt like; that's what this felt like.

"So what? Lem's *not* the guy who screwed with my head?" Stacy asked angrily. "What kind of crap game is this, huh? Why would someone put all those things in my head and make us believe it was him?"

Dad's head jerked to Stacy's voice, his jaw falling open in shock. "You're alive..."

Stacy looked at Dad and somehow managed to grow even paler. "Uh...hi, Mr. Shelley."

Dad's brows crimped into furrows over his eyes as he touched Stacy's arm, unsure if she was real or not. "How are you alive?"

"You don't really want to know the answer to that question, Mr. Shelley," Stacy said quietly.

"You're probably right. There's a lot I don't want to know right now."

Stacy nodded and then returned her attention to me. "So what? Why did this happen? Why make us believe that Lem's the guy who was screwing around with us? Why make us think that he was trying to kill you?"

"Because we'd believe it," I answered quietly. "Whoever did it knew that we'd believe it. We wanted to find out who did it so badly, and it made sense."

"Yes, but if they wanted us to believe that it was Llehmai who did it, then why does Isis' ring show that she was Sam's partner?" Lark held a ring between her thumb and index finger. "This isn't Isis' ring."

I nodded and then turned to look at Dad. "You remember the ring you stole from the cops, Dad? When they came to Robert's house after what happened to Mrs. Deovolente?"

Dad nodded. "Yeah, what about it?"

"We need it. Where is it?"

"It's back at the house. I put it in the first aid kit."

I looked at Graham and Lark. "You remember where the kit is, right?"

Graham nodded, and Lark disappeared.

"If the ring that Isis had on her wasn't real, then maybe Lem's ring isn't real either," Stacy said hopefully.

*Llehmai's ring is his. I'm the one who gave it to him.*

Ameila's thoughts were meant for Stacy, but I heard them, and I didn't hide that fact. "You gave him that ring?"

*Llehmai had no family. He was one of the last to be created, not born, and so there was no one to ascend with him. I chose to go because I could. I was given the ring to give to him. I engraved the ring with its inscription.*

I looked down and removed the ring from Janice's finger and held it up to the light, seeing the engraved words sparkling in the fluorescence. *Dum spiramus tuebimur.*

"What does it mean?"

"While we breathe, we shall defend," Robert answered.

"So maybe he faked it," Stacy argued. "I mean, I can buy a twenty dollar ring at Juno's and have it engraved for five bucks."

*The ring remembers me holding it. No one can fake that. It cannot fake a memory of me holding it without me knowing.*

Lark returned, her eyes wide, her mouth hanging slightly open. She held a baggie in her hand; Dad hadn't even tried to remove the ring from it.

"Is this really Isis' ring?" she asked nervously.

Robert's face was stoic. "If Isis was the one who attacked Grace, then it's got to be hers."

"So is that the story? That Isis was the one who killed Mrs. Deovolente?" Graham asked.

"There's only one way to find out," Lark said as she opened the bag and slipped the ring on her finger.

We stood there, Stacy, Robert, Graham, Dad, and I, watching Lark's eyes shake, her face and her mouth grow tight and then slacken. To anyone coming in, it looked like we were standing around Janice's bed in solemn solidarity. They didn't know that what Lark was seeing would destroy the peace of mind of everyone there.

"Oh my God." Lark regained focus and looked at us. "Grace..."

"What?"

Robert shook his head in short twitches, denial slipping out of him like hiccups. "No. Don't tell her. Don't tell her, Lark. Don't say a word."

"What?" I asked again, trying to see what they both saw and finding only darkness.

Stacy grabbed Lark's arm and shook her. "What the hell did you see?"

Lark's eyes were cold, flat, and defiant as she turned to face Stacy. "Grace's death."

"Well, it's wrong," I said adamantly. "I told you, I'm not dying. I'm not giving up anymore. And besides, Isis is dead. Whatever she tried to do is over."

"Grace, you don't understand," Lark said softly. "Isis wasn't Sam's partner. Sam didn't have a partner; he was part of a plan. He and Isis were working for someone else."

"Who?"

Lark and Robert looked at each other, and then both turned their gazes toward me. Lark's mouth moved, but the words didn't come from her. They came from Robert. "Our grandfather."

The room blasted with cold air, a hurricane that was hell bent on destruction as the curtains fronting the entrance of the room began tearing at their grommets, the metallic silver rings clanging onto the floor. The machines in the room began to beep wildly before sparks shot out from them in bright arcs. A nurse ran in, tripping on the curtain and nearly falling on her face.

But I was there. She fell into my arms and I didn't sway at the contact, despite her being at least half a foot taller than me and about fifty pounds heavier. Instead, I felt rooted to the ground, unmovable and unbending. I was just as stunned as she was, but she didn't pause to question why. She was there for a reason that went beyond being shocked. She rushed to the now smoking machines and began pulling at cords and jamming at buttons, trying to stop the strange squealing that now came out of the overheated and confused devices.

Another nurse ran in, followed by a doctor. I felt a hand grab my arm and tug me away as the bed crowded with people concerned over the false Janice. I could hear the faint sounds of crackling, and I ducked just moments before everything that was made of glass shattered, raining down onto the floor and onto us like rain.

Or like tears.

Because what traveled throughout the room wasn't just disbelief, it was pain, disappointment, grief...

"Grace, come on," Dad said to me, picking me up and pulling me out of the room.

"What about-"

"Don't worry about her. She knows what she has to do," Lark

whispered into my ear as I felt my body being dragged further and further away from the room.

That's what worried me the most.

"What…what else did you see? What did you see on that ring, Lark?" I asked as my feet moved, one after the other, out of the hospital and into the parking garage.

"I can't tell you that, Grace."

"Then don't say it. Show it." I forced my feet to stop moving, and I stared her down.

She looked around, the darkness of the garage cut only with a few dull yellow swaths of light, and then her eyes narrowed.

*I won't show you that. I won't show you your death. No one will.*

My jaw locked and my eyelids lowered as I felt the anger in me begin to rise. "What's on that ring is important to me. I need to see what's on it."

"No, you don't," Robert insisted.

"Yes, I do. God, why can't you see that this is my life? Everyone keeps telling me what I am, what I'm supposed to be, what I'm supposed to do, *when* and *how* I'm supposed to die. I'm through with it. I'm taking control of my life. Now show me what the hell is on that ring."

Lark shook her head and then evaporated into a cloud of white.

"Coward!" I shouted.

"Why can't she see what's on that ring?" Stacy demanded to know.

"Yeah," Graham agreed.

"Because she'll try and change what happens and she can't do that anymore."

"Why? Why can't I?"

Robert looked at me and his eyes watered as he answered, "Because it's your fate. It's the same thing I see when I look at you. I told you, I've seen your death. I've seen it and now I know that I'm not the only one. This isn't something you can change, Grace."

"The hell it's not," Graham barked. "We just gotta know the time and the place and we'll avoid it."

Robert laughed. "You really think it's that simple?"

"Yeah, I think it's that simple. If she's supposed to die on a Tuesday in a mall, we stay at home. What's so difficult about that? You know when it's supposed to happen so why not?"

"Because I'm Death, and I am unavoidable," Robert said simply. "Grace's death, the one she's meant to have, will happen no matter where she's at when it's the right time. You can't run from that. You can't hide from that. No one can. And trying to will only make things worse for everyone around."

I began to walk away from them, their words sounding more and more like the death sentence I'd rid myself of just days ago. I didn't want to hear it. I didn't want to hear them confirm that I was going to die.

"Grace, wait." Stacy fell into step with me, her footsteps quiet while mine dragged like bricks against the pavement.

"I don't care what's on that ring, Stacy," I told her fiercely. "I don't care what anyone has to say about it; I'm not dying. Not by their rules, anyway."

"Of course you won't. You're too stubborn to do things the way they're supposed to be done," she said casually.

I stopped walking and turned to look at her. "God, Stacy, do you realize what's going on? Robert and Lark's grandfather has been trying to kill me."

"A lot of freaking angels are trying to kill you, Grace. A lot of them."

"Yeah, but none of them succeeded. Someone has always been in the way. My mother, Lem, Robert, Mrs. Deovolente... And it was always someone else, someone expendable, someone to doubt that did it. No one would ever doubt him; no one would ever suspect him-"

I looked over at Robert, and my eyes grew wide with a revelation. "He could come and go as he pleased and no one would think anything of it. He could leave notes and no one would think anything of it. He could enter a family's sanctuary with someone else and leave them there to try and escape and no one would suspect anything.

"Did Lem have a call, Robert?"

"Yes. Yes, he did," Robert answered, taking quick steps toward me.

"Tell me what it is."

"Grace, you know-"

"Tell me what his call is. This isn't the time to be anal about the rules. Right now, there are no rules. What is Lem's call?"

Robert stopped in front of me, the struggle he had playing out in the tiny twitches in his lips, his eyes, even the curves of his nose.

"He's makes people fall in love."

"How?"

"By making them see people the way they need to. Why does any of this matter, Grace?"

I nodded, moving toward him and taking a hold of his face. "Because Lem wanted me to love him, and he could have done that by making me think that he was you, but he didn't. If I'd known that, I would have never believed that he was the one who'd hurt Stacy.

"Your grandfather knew that you wouldn't tell me. He knew; that's why he could blame everything on Lem. He knew I'd be stupid enough to believe him."

"You weren't stupid to believe it, Grace. We all believed it."

Robert's voice was clear and echoed in the cement garage as he spoke, but from behind me I could hear something, a sound that didn't fit. I looked at Stacy and saw that she heard it, too. My hands dropped from Robert's face and I turned, instinctively shoving him out of the way as a blur of red and white charged toward us.

Stacy's snarl and Robert's grunt didn't mask the whirring sound that preceded the crashing of bodies. I saw white eyes with red pinpoints before I felt myself being slammed onto the ground, hot and cold breaths covering my face.

Bright red hair glowed almost orange in the yellow light, and I caught a glimpse of a scarred face before hands that felt more like claws began to scratch at my neck and my abdomen. My hands flew up to protect me while my legs kicked reflexively.

Stacy flashed by, her hands scratching at my attacker whose breath came out in an ascending wail as she threw the person off of me. "Get up," she said before turning her back to me.

I jumped to my feet somewhat unsteadily and felt more hands grab at me. I spun around, my hands clenching into balls to attack and yelped when I saw Robert's face. "Come on," he said before pulling me away.

"Wait! What about Graham!" I shouted, turning my head around and looking for him and finding nothing.

"Either get her the hell out of here or help me out," Stacy complained loudly from a dark corner before rolling toward us, a ball of white, red, and black. I jumped back as a claw lashed out at my feet.

Robert let me go and reached down with a strong hand, taking the red-haired assailant by its head and rising, floating above the ground. I saw that my attacker was a woman with a mouth that was so riddled with scars it looked like she'd been doused in wax and left to harden. Her teeth weren't smooth and straight; they weren't even fangs. They were jagged, like a saw, with no breaks between them. It was like one long tooth on her top and bottom jaw.

She screamed an awful, grating sound that felt like scratches in my head. "Let me go black one!"

"Not a chance. Who sent you?"

"No one sent me. I only know that she has to die!"

"Why are you asking it questions? Kill it!" Stacy spat.

"Demon," my attacker spat back.

"Demon? I'll show you demon, you period-headed b-"

"Stacy, that's enough," Robert said calmly.

"No it isn't! She just attacked Grace! Either kill it or let me eat it."

490

The rumbling sound of an engine, coupled with the squeal of tires silenced the argument as Graham arrived, his car's newly rebuilt engine roaring hungrily. "Get in," he ordered to me.

"Go," Robert agreed, with Stacy nodding beside him.

I jumped into the passenger seat and held on as he tore through the garage, the scene between the angel, the erlking, and the…I don't know what, faded behind us. Graham turned the wheel, the car moving on to the lower floors, repeating this until we were out onto the street.

I didn't know what time it was. The sky was still bright, but traffic was scarce. I didn't even know what day it was. I looked at Graham, his eyes almost glued open in a shocked expression, and I frowned.

"I don't know where we're going," he mumbled.

"Just drive," I said before turning to look back out of the window. "It doesn't matter where we go. This is gonna follow us."

"So it really wasn't Lem…it really is Lark's grandfather that's trying to kill you."

"Yeah," I said quietly. "Who knows; it might be all of them."

"I should have taken care of that red-headed jerkface when I had the chance."

"What the hell do you think you would've been able to do, Graham? You're not an angel. You're not even one of those things that get made when you're turned without permission. You don't have the kind of strength or skill that you need to fight an angel.

"But even if you did, he's one of the first angels to exist. How are you supposed to get rid of one of the most powerful and important angels in not only our world but theirs?"

The car hurtled to a stop, tired screeching behind us and horns honking as angry drivers tried to avoid hitting us. "Dammit, Grace, I already feel inadequate and useless. I don't need you reminding me that I'm not as good at anything as you are, or as Robert is, or hell, even Stacy is. I'm not fast, I'm not strong, I'm not even smart."

"You're smart, Graham!"

He slammed his hands against the steering wheel angrily. "Don't patronize me. Don't tell me I'm something when you know I'm not. You didn't like it when I did it to you."

I sighed and reached over, covering his tightened grip on the wheel with my own hand. "I think you're one of the smartest people I know. You don't have to know how to complete complex math sequences or speak French fluently to be intelligent. Lark wouldn't have fallen in love with an idiot."

I watched him, watched his head lower, his shoulders sink, and then felt his forehead touch the back of my hand. "What if she made a mistake?"

"She didn't make a mistake. She knew that you were the one for her the moment she met you. It's one of those things that are a given, like lightning in a storm or…or cheese in a burger."

"Heh," he snorted. "Cheese in a burger."

"It's true. I knew when we first met that I would love you for the rest of my life. How could anyone not love you? You're cute, you're funny, you're heroic. Loving you is the most expected thing in the world."

"So's loving you, you know."

I shook my head. "It defies logic to love me. Look at everything that's happened because of me. Look at what I do at the first sign of trouble. People get hurt, people die, and I run."

"You're not running, Grace. You're trying to survive. There's nothing wrong with that."

"There's everything wrong with it if surviving means someone else doesn't. We need to go back. We need to go back and help Stacy and Robert."

"We don't need to go back. They can take care of themselves."

"Yes, and so can I," I insisted.

"Not yet you can't. Lark told me that you're changing, your body is remembering what it's supposed to be, but your mind is still human and you-"

He was cut off when the car began to rock, shifting and swaying from side to side. We both turned to look out of our windows, and he bit out a curse while I inhaled as we both realized that we weren't on the street anymore.

I rolled down the window and stuck my head outside, gasping when I saw the creature that held us suspended in the air. It looked like an angel on steroids, muscles rippling and bulging beneath tight skin. There were no veins pulsing anywhere—of course there weren't—but you could see sheer power almost vibrating through him, like heat shimmering over hot asphalt. He looked down at me and smiled evilly, the stoniness of his face almost cracking, the fascinatingly terrifying features looking so much like a gargoyle that I was certain that's what he was.

And then he let go.

A voice shouted, "Grace!"

I felt myself being yanked, my head slamming into something soft and yielding before the roof caved in and the bottom of the car gave out.

It was almost comforting, the sound of crunching metal and shattering glass. I'd heard it so many times by now that it was almost like an old friend.

But this time, I knew something that the car did not, something that was now instinctual, a part of me. This time, I could protect myself. I grabbed onto Graham and wrapped my arms around him. His hands clasped around my back and together we curled into a ball as the doors, the roof, the front and the rear of the car curled around us like some kind of metal flower, the petals growing unbelievably hot from the friction.

Through the screeching and the scraping, I could hear the screams of people who watched, stunned, at what was happening. I could hear their thoughts, the incredulousness, the shock. What they were seeing happening in front of them couldn't be real. They did not just see some winged giant pick up a car and then drop it from over a hundred feet. Things like that didn't happen in Ohio.

"Are we dead?" Graham whispered.

"No," I answered.

"We should be though, right?"

"I don't know. God, I wish that thing would leave already! I don't know how much longer I can do this."

The pounding on the car stopped, the screams turning into exclamations of awe. "He's gone."

"Who's gone?"

"The thing who did this."

"How do you know that?"

"Because everyone outside said so," I answered matter-of-factly.

"You can hear what the people outside are saying?"

"And thinking. He's gone. Hold on."

I loosened my grip on him, my arms only able to move millimeters away. Slowly, I pushed against the pressure on my back.

"Whoa," Graham murmured as he heard the creaking of folded steel. "Are you doing that?"

"Shh. I need to concentrate."

"Why? This isn't origami!"

My fingers touched the still warm metal, feeling it, gauging it. And then, like I'd always known I could do it, I shoved roughly against it. An explosion of sound and sparks scattered around and onto us. From outside, the screams and the cries for help grew louder, more frantic. I could hear sirens.

"Whatever the hell it is you're doing, you'd better do it faster; the police can't see you alive," Graham warned.

I shoved against the steel once more, this time cracks of light cutting through. One last push and a seam split in the metal, creating an opening that was just big enough for Graham to squeeze through.

"Uh-uh. You're going," he said, as if my thoughts had been spoken out loud.

"No, you first," I insisted. "I don't know if the car will collapse on you if I escape."

"I'm indestructible, remember? You're supposed to be dead. Dead people can't be found alive in cars. Go. Get out of here and run, Grace. Please."

In the little light we had, I saw the desperate expression on his face and my heart burned. "I can't leave you."

"You're not. Trust me; I'll be okay. Go."

I hugged him, kissed his cheek, and then climbed out of the hole I'd created. In the dull light of the street, I could see people standing in a crowded circle around the car. They gasped when they saw me, and backed away when I jumped down and ran through them, not knowing where I was going but only that I was moving very fast.

I looked over my shoulder and saw the crowd converge on the car, shouts of encouragement and cheers following shortly afterward.

The flashes of red, blue, and white faded as the police arrived and I left. I didn't know where I was. I didn't know where I was going. I only knew that I'd just abandoned my best friend.

I stopped moving.

"What am I doing? I can't let Graham face this alone."

I turned around and started to run back before I skidded to a halt, a wall appearing in front of me.

"Robert!"

Strong arms, strong, shaking arms grabbed a hold of me and clutched me tightly to a chest that would have been slammed from the inside if it could. "Come on, Graham will be fine. We need to get you out of the open."

He scooped me up and leapt, my body once more rising into the sky only this time I wasn't going to drop down. I wrapped my fingers around his neck and tried to reassure myself that what he'd said was true; that Graham would be fine.

"Trust me, Grace. He will be fine."

"Who was that? *What* was that?" I asked, my mind bringing up the image of the gigantic angel.

"That was Bane. He's a throne."

"A throne? But aren't those the ones that give out the punishments?"

"Yes," he answered gravely. "Their call is to follow the orders of the seraphim."

"So one of the seraphim is trying to kill me now?" I asked almost hysterically.

"The angels of the first circle *are* Seraphim. They are everything."

"And that...thing at the hospital; what was it?"

"Not a what, a who."

"Okay, who was it?"

"That was Lamia. Think of her as a younger, more human, more *alive* Miki."

"Alive... So Miki really is gone."

Robert's head fell once. "Yes."

"Then that means that those...those vampires that killed Mrs. Lorimax came from her, from Lamia."

He grew quiet and cold. I dared to ask why, and I dared him to answer.

"She's infected dozens of people, created a small army to come after you."

"But why? Did your grandfather do this, too?"

"No. This is something she did on her own."

"Why?"

"Because she knows what's happening, Grace. I told you, chaos is starting to take over. Every single creature that exists on this earth that doesn't have the freedom to live the way they want to, that have had to hide who and what they are because humans have always been deemed more important know what's going on. They know about you."

"How? How do they know about me? How can they know about me when I don't even know?"

We started to descend, and our feet touched the ground before he answered.

"They found out because they sense you. They sense you in a way that they never sensed me."

His words were simple and yet…and yet they were the most complicated and most earth shattering words I'd ever heard because that meant only one thing.

Everything that Gabriel, Lem, Michael, Uriel, and even Raphael said was true. Robert wasn't Death.

I was.

# FOR SHADOW

The small house we stood in front of was charming, perfect. It had a dark red front door, cream siding, and white shutters around white trimmed windows. It was surrounded by a green lawn that was immaculately kept, and a white, picket fence that blended in with the rest of the idyllic scenery that surrounded it.

This was what I imagined heaven to look like.

"This is Ambrose's home," Robert informed me before turning the knob and opening the red door.

"Ambrose? Dr. Bro?"

"Yes."

"This is where you were going to take me before Lem kidnapped me."

"Yes."

"Why Ambrose?"

Robert closed the door behind us as we entered a parlor that was bright and cheerful, the walls glistening with gold and cream striped wallpaper. "Because he knows his kind, and his wife knows everything else."

"I've never met his wife, although I guess I am curious to know what kind of woman marries an erlking," I said, looking around. The furniture that filled the room was antique looking, with floral fabric covering the seats and dark, polished wood curving and bowing to make graceful arches where arms would rest and backs would lean. "I'm going to guess she did the decorating."

"What makes you say that?"

I pointed to the furniture. "Because Dr. Bro wouldn't choose sofas like that."

He laughed and then led me into the dining room and finally what I assumed was the family room. This room was cozy, with large tan sofas and ottomans spread around. There was no television, no stereo, but a piano did sit in a far corner while a harp stood beside it.

"There you are. I was wondering when you'd get here. I hope everything went alright with your visit. Are you hungry? I just made a nice pot of chicken and dumplings from scratch."

My lower jaw hung down in shock. The woman who stood before us wore a beaming smile in her plump face, her bright eyes twinkling with an obvious joy at seeing me.

"Oh you poor thing, you've got holes in your clothes. Well, it's a good thing we've got your bag of things upstairs. Come on; let's get you changed before you eat supper."

I stuttered looking at her, my words wanting to come out, but unable to.

Robert did his best to make up for it. "Thank you, Vanessa, for your hospitality."

"Oh please," she said with a wave of her hand. "I've known about Grace for years. She's always been a good girl, just like her mother; what kind of registrar would I be if I didn't want to help her?"

"You-I...I..." I watched as she headed toward a small staircase, Robert picking me up since my feet weren't moving on their own.

"Stacy told me that you would react this way," Robert chuckled. "I didn't believe her. I owe her about a million dollars now."

"She knew? Wait, of course she knew; she's been staying here. Did Graham know?"

Robert nodded as he reached the top of the landing, setting me down and taking my hand, half-dragging me down the hallway. "He only found out after you were taken. He took it about the same way you did."

"She's Mrs. Mayhew! She's the registrar! What is she doing being married to an erlking?" I hissed.

"You can tell her," Mrs. Mayhew said, stopping in front of the last door at the end of the hallway. "I have no secrets. Avi's ring looks lovely on you, by the way."

I choked.

"Grace, Vanessa isn't just the registrar. She's also your mother's wing-bringer."

"No she isn't."

"Oh yes I am," the woman said stubbornly while opening the door.

I walked into the small room that held only a bed, a chest of drawers, and a nightstand. "I don't believe you," I told her as I sat on the edge of the bed, the coverlet downy and soft beneath me.

"Believe it or not, I knew your mother before she became what she was. I saw her birth."

"Well, I saw her death," I said acidly.

"And that is how it was supposed to be."

"Wha-"

She came forward toward me and touched my hand, sitting beside me. This alone was enough to quiet me, because her smile faded as she did so. "You know what your mother was. You know *who* she was. And so you know how important she was to all of our worlds.

"When she was born, she came out of the light, like night falling out of a star. She wasn't a child when she appeared; she was a grown woman with awareness of everything: every second of history, ever word ever spoken, every language ever given to the world's people was hers.

"I was there, with my two young children, searching for roots to eat. We watched her, heard her speak. It was like a gift that could not be taken away, it traveled so deeply into my head and my heart.

"And then Avi looked at me. She saw me, saw my children, and with the most beautiful smile I'd ever seen, she came to me and my children. She opened her arms to them and my children went with no fear."

She paused, her breath fumbling in her throat. She touched her eyes with shaky hands and then exhaled. There was a struggle within her, I could feel it, sense it, but I didn't want to search her thoughts to try to understand what it was. She was going to explain it when she was ready; I had to be patient. Her head lifted and she looked at me curiously. I blushed when I realized that while I hadn't gone searching through her thoughts, I didn't exactly stop from sharing mine.

She sighed. "It's alright. I appreciate your patience, but I will finish. It's just…been a while since I spoke about this."

Her lower lip jutted forward and her face expression grew more pinched as she continued. "In her arms, my babies, my sweet, innocent children died; my son was only three…my daughter, one. Your mother seemed stunned at what had happened, unaware that she could kill so easily, or that her first deaths would be of those too young to be guilty of any sin.

"She apologized, begged me for my forgiveness but I wasn't about to forgive her for taking what mattered the most in this world from me. I attacked her. I tried to kill her like one could kill an animal. When that failed, I tried to kill myself now that I knew that death was possible for us.

"And then she began to scream. She was looking at me, looking at the pain in my heart and my eagerness to die alongside my children and she began to change. She grew wings, like a bird hatching from an egg, and they were black as my heart was for her right then.

"Four others appeared like storm clouds at the sound of her screams. They surrounded her, protected her like brothers, or fathers would. The one named Gabriel told me that my children's deaths were a blessing for me. He was cruel with his words, telling me to be grateful that my children were gone. I spat in his face. I cursed him with the same fate he would wish upon his worst enemy.

"But then the one named Raphael approached me and said that because of my loss, because of this *noble* sacrifice that I had been forced

501

to make, I would be rewarded handsomely. And what was my reward? Eternal life; forever spent mourning my children, as if never dying, never being able to join them was a gift."

She sighed, her sadness weighing the bed down even more than her body did. "I hated them; I hated them all. But I hated Avi more than the others. I begged her to kill me like she did my children. I begged her to end my suffering, to let me leave this world so that I did not have to endure it without my children, but she refused. So I tried to do it myself.

"I slit my throat in the same way one would an animal. I consumed the poison the farmers would leave to kill the rats. I leapt from cliffs to drown in rivers below like the sickly sheep would do. I set myself on fire in front of her, because she would not do allow me my one wish. She was Death, and so she would be my end. And do you know what she told me? She said that death isn't always the end. She told me that one day, death would be my-"

"Savior," I finished for her. "She said the same thing to me before she died."

She nodded. "She was right. My children died quickly, peacefully. In six months, my village was overrun with a plague. I watched children suffer and mothers grieve. In a dozen years, I watched fires destroy what was left. Everything that had ever existed in my world was gone.

"Centuries passed and I learned, finally, the meaning of time as around me things changed. I watched angels and mankind fight for power. I watched the earth become swallowed by water. I watched disease and war and religion and evil wash over the earth and destroy civilization over and over again.

"But I survived. I survived everything and I kept record of it all. It is what I'm meant to do. I keep the names of those who would have been forgotten from being lost. If not for that, you would have never heard about my son Andru or my daughter Alle. Through me, they survive. Through me, their existence will never be doubted.

502

"That is how it's supposed to be; just as it is with you. The harshness of this world is what strengthens us; it's what makes us who we are. I was nothing but the wife of a poor butcher before your mother arrived. It was a life I would have accepted because I didn't know any better.

"You were also headed for an ordinary existence, a life that you would have accepted because you didn't know anything different. But those lives weren't for us. My life, the one I live with Ambrose, where every child that passes through the doors at Heath is mine—that's what I'm meant for."

"And me? What am I meant for?"

Her effervescent smile returned at my question. "You're meant to have the one thing your mother could not, being what she was."

"And that is…"

"Life."

"She had a life. She had a life with me and my dad. And that completely goes against the whole me-dying part."

"You don't get it right now, but you will. In the end, you will. Your mother was right."

She stood up and took the four steps between the bed and the door. She looked at Robert and then turned to look back at me. "Come down when you're ready for dinner. Don't worry about any of those toilet angels coming to bother you here. They know better."

"Toilet angels?" I asked, confused.

"Well, they like to call themselves thrones, but after several thousand years of knowing them, the only thrones they resemble are the ones you sit on after a bad bowl of chili. Speaking of which, we're having that for dinner tomorrow." She left, and I grunted in response.

My eyes moved to focus on Robert, whose shoulders were bouncing up and down with muted laughter. "Why won't the thrones bother us here?"

"Because when Vanessa was turned, that's when our history's human documentation started. She took record of every angel, every human, every creature' ever created. You know how EPs have their family tree that follows them everywhere?"

He waited for my nod. "She is our family tree. She's a living record showing the roots, the branches, the leaves and the fruit. Without her, we are orphans to our own history."

While I processed this, he came to sit beside me on the bed. "I trust Vanessa to keep you safe; at least for now. When my grandfather decides to stop using others to attack you and come for you himself, you won't be safe anywhere; and no one will be safe with you."

I already knew that. I didn't need him or anyone else telling me that I was a threat to everyone I ever cared about…and now to everyone, period.

"We'll stay the night. I don't want to be here longer than that; Mrs. Mayhew and Dr. Bro don't need me destroying the life they've built together."

"Grace, they're helping because they want to."

"I know, but helping me, being friends with me, caring for me…loving me means putting everyone in danger. I don't know what your grandfather wants with me. I don't know if he wants me dead or alive, but I know he doesn't care who he has to get rid of to get to me.

"That's why I'm not running away from this. I just want some time with the people I love…I want one more day."

"Grace-"

I pressed my fingers against his lips and shook my head. *I'm not giving up. I promise you, I have more to live for now than I ever did before, and I'm not going to lose any of that for anyone. I just want one day without worrying about it, without thinking about it. I want to be around my friends, my family, and you.*

*I want to laugh and sing. I want to dance and eat. I want to smile and kiss you until I can't breathe.*

Robert grabbed my wrist and pulled my hand down. His eyes grew wet, hot, and he leaned in, his intent clear and his motives obvious. And I wanted everything he was going to give, everything he was going to share.

## PRIVATE UNIVERSE

His kiss was sweet and soft initially. The warmth in his lips was soothing, like the morning sun after a storm. I let it wash through me, erasing so much of the hard edge that I had felt forming around me from the moment I'd learned about what I was.

I didn't close my eyes. I wasn't going to close my eyes anymore, I realized. Looking at him was like a revelation, a cure for every ache. He smiled at my thoughts and touched my face with the back of his hand, grazing my skin so gently I had to question whether his hand was even there. Or, maybe it was the other way around; maybe I wasn't really there, just the ghost of me.

With his free hand, he waved at the door, which closed obediently. His fingers trailed down my throat and skimmed my pulse before he let his lips tattoo a warm line from my jaw to my shoulder. I couldn't help but smile at that one simple act.

"I think it's time we got rid of this shirt," he said, looking at the singed and stained garment that covered me. I looked down and felt my cheeks redden when I realized just how badly the attack in the car had damaged my clothes.

There were holes of varying sizes on my chest revealing the shirt that lay beneath it. Parts of the shirt were charred beneath my armpit. I could feel the hard edges on my back and after inhaling, I could smell the burned cotton. "I didn't realize the car had gotten that hot. I'm surprised I didn't get burned, too."

Robert said nothing at that, his hands finding the edge of my shirt and lifting, my arms rising to allow him to lift the top over my head. Beneath it was a simple white tank top, the same thing I'd been wearing to bed since I could remember. He looked at it and smiled.

"When we've spent a hundred years together, I will still find this to be the most charming thing I've ever seen."

"And what happens after a hundred and one years?" I asked lazily as his fingertips ran up and down my bare arms, sending miniature waves of sensation pulsing to my stomach.

"You'll wear my shirts for the next hundred. And then nothing at all."

"Nothing?" I gulped.

He lowered his head and licked the inside of my arm and the crease of my elbow. "Yes. I figure it'll take at least two centuries before you feel comfortable enough to sleep naked with me."

"That's an optimistic number," I said, half-laughing, half-gasping.

"It is, isn't it? But I have faith in you, Grace."

He stopped doing what he was doing to straighten, taking my face in his hands and holding me still, his eyes clear and sparkling, his voice steady and firm. "I have faith in you, Grace. I don't know if I've ever told you that. I always thought it, I always felt it, but I want you to hear it.

"I have faith in you. I believe in you."

I blinked back tears that had no source; they just appeared. His face blurred, his features warping and expanding in exaggerated shapes, and I hiccuped at the effect. How could he do that to me? How could he just say something as simple as that he had faith in me and turn me into a fountain?

And I knew why.

"No one's ever said that to me before. Ever."

His mouth made a funny curl in my vision as he smiled, his thumb brushing against my eyes to wipe away the tears that clung desperately to my lashes. "That's because we're all idiots, every last one of us. Having faith in you is the most natural thing in the world."

I shook my head in disagreement. "No. No, loving you is the most natural thing in the world."

He chuckled, taking a stray strip of my hair between his fingers and rubbing it. "That's funny. You seemed to find it much easier to get mad at me in the beginning. I still remember you yelling at me on the side of the road, like a little terror."

"Well, you'd just dumped chili all over me," I told him, my hand diving into his hair and rubbing back and forth, causing the slight curls to tighten.

He leaned back, his mouth popping open in mock shock. "I did not! You bumped into me!"

"Wrong again! I was pushed," I laughed.

"Sure," he laughed back. "You don't have to lie; you can be honest and admit that you were so drawn to my angelic charm that you couldn't help yourself."

"Oh!" I scoffed. "Angelic charm? You couldn't say anything but 'so we meet again', like those were the only words in your head!"

"There were other words in my head, but you would have probably punched me if I'd said them. Or eaten me. Now that I think about it, I probably should have said them…you eating me sounds rather exciting."

I shoved his shoulder playfully and gasped when his sleeve separated from his shoulder. "Oh no! I'm sorry!" I tugged on the torn seams, trying fruitlessly to put them back together.

He looked at the damage I'd caused, inspecting the seam to see just how bad the repair job would be and then, without a word tore the sleeve off completely. He turned to the other side and repeated the action, throwing both sleeves onto the floor and smiling at the result. "There. Even."

I laughed. I'd never seen him look that way before. He'd always tried to look the part that he played: perfect and contained, calm and cool, handsome in ways that could only come from something divine. But here he was, his hair tousled, threads poking out and hanging from his torn shirt, his eyes wild with amusement, and his mouth half-open in a crooked, less than perfect smile.

He looked free, and happy.

He'd never looked better than he did then. Not divine, not angelic, not perfect. Everything that made him so attractive to everyone else was nothing compared to the fading worry that caused tiny creases around his eyes and mouth and the slouch in his shoulders.

I moved closer to him and, one by one, undid the buttons on his shirt, kissing his chin for each one. He eased his body so that I could push the remnant of his shirt off, my breath catching in my throat at what I saw beneath the fabric. His shoulder was bruised.

The color brought the tears back to my eyes and I looked up at him and in the haze he smiled, bringing one of my hands to his mouth to kiss the pads of my fingertips. I smiled back and kissed the dark purple section of his skin before pressing my cheek against it, feeling the slight coolness to it.

Unspoken thoughts traveled between us as we both stood and, slowly, we undressed each other, the soft lamplight working with us to hide the other bruises we found on each other. Hands had never been more necessarily slow or gentle. It was like every reveal was a communion, and every brush of air against our skin a blessing.

We were generous in our attention to each other, each nuance of softness and hardness, each curve and angle that existed only because the other did. Finding the weaknesses of each other became a game and we both cheered the other on to win. On our feet, we were each other's strength but what we needed was more than physical strength. We collapsed, tumbling onto the bed.

I leaned back into the soft pillow and cover, feeling the weight of him and the heaviness of his gaze. The bed was small, but we didn't need much space. This wasn't about trying to conquer each other or consume each other.

This was about becoming each other. I wanted his cold heart to beat again, and so it did when pressed against mine, the echo of each beat filling his chest and giving it life. We didn't let anything come between us for those careful, quiet moments between us. Even breathing seemed to cease.

Skin to skin, thought to thought, we were together. We shared every dream we'd ever had for the future, every wish ever asked and never granted, vowing to make it come true somehow for the other. We laughed about the silliest things, and we sighed at the most pleasurable.

There were tears, but not the kind shed out of sadness. We let sorrow stay behind this time. Our hands fit against each other, his heart line never ending, mine never reaching the end of my palm, but together it didn't matter. My pulse proved that to the both of us, and the heat that bubbled up when he kissed that line, traced it with his tongue, told the world that nothing that was said by anyone else about us mattered.

We were more than what we'd been told.

We knew it by the way a simple look turned sweat into steam. We knew it by the way a graze of hair against skin turned solid steel to liquid mercury. We knew it by the way life and death joined together in every way possible, the connections being made from head to toe and beyond.

We became weightless, boneless, guiltless, and lost to everyone and no one who'd ever tried to find us. I could feel myself lose who I was, only to find myself again in a rush of scent, sight, touch, and sound. Every part of who I was felt him with me, around me, inside me. Every thought that dared to be formed had no real ending or beginning that didn't include him.

And I was right. There was no need to breathe, because he was every breath. I couldn't feel the need for anything anymore. Blood didn't exist, hunger didn't exist, need didn't exist. This went beyond desire and passion. This was the moment of everything. This was everything.

I shouted. I shouted at the beauty of it, the oneness of it, the peace of it. I felt no need to remain quiet; I felt no fear that the world would hear me because every emotion that lived and died in that shout would only be heard by Robert. We were shouting together, hearing together.

Existing together.

Robert N'Uriel Bellegarde and Grace Anne Bellegarde weren't two people lost in a moment. We weren't angel and human, destined to fail in our attempts to combine our two worlds into one. We weren't even two souls destined to be together who'd found each other.

We were the same person.

We were the same soul, the same angel, the same human.

I was him, he was me, forged together like the stones in my ring, his ring, bound in an endless circle that started at each other and knew no end.

Together we were the fire that burned skin and scorched hair and scarred memories. Together we were the sun that gave life. Together we were the moon that gave birth to dreams. Together we were stars that welcomed wishes.

We weren't in heaven. We *were* heaven.

As the human sun rose in the sky, filling up the room with its light, we forced it back out with our own. There was no room for it here, no need for it. Not yet, anyway.

Not until we'd both shattered into a million pieces of each other, too scattered and too lost to do anything but leave enough of me in him and him in me to never fully be apart again. This was what completion really was. Coming apart and still being together.

"I want to tell you I love you. I want to tell you that I feel for you something unending and more powerful than anything divine. But I can't, because what I feel is so much more," he whispered against my mouth, his breath hot, smoky.

I kissed his pursed lips and smiled. "Then don't tell me anything. I already know everything that you think, everything that you feel. For the first time, there's nothing hidden between us."

He looked into my eyes and smiled. "Nothing hidden between us at all."

We kissed, our mouths fusing in the physical way that was different from what we'd just experienced, but just as fulfilling and rich. This was the moment when I felt the acceptance that I'd always longed for but never really achieved.

Because I'd always been searching for it from everyone else when all I really needed was to accept myself for who I was. Only I hadn't known who I was until right then. Who I was had never been more clear, more obvious, more blatant. It was as if it had been written down the whole time and I'd just never realized it, even when it was right in front of my face.

"Are you sure about this?" Robert asked, concern and pride mixing to change the tone of his voice.

"I've never been more sure of anything in my life," I answered firmly.

"When do you want to tell your dad? Graham? Lark?"

I closed my eyes, the first time I'd done it in what was probably hours. "Later. The time isn't right."

"Okay."

"Are they here?" I asked, opening my eyes and seeing his bemused expression.

"Oh yes, and already complaining that we're spending too much time together."

I giggled and caressed his face. "There's no such thing."

"No, no there isn't."

"Do you want to go downstairs now? Spend that time with them that you wanted?"

I had to think about that for a minute, and then shook my head. "Not yet. I want to stay here with you a little while longer. I don't know when we'll have this kind of peace again."

He rested his head against my chest, his ear pressed against my heart. He was quiet, in both ways, and I stroked his hair, enjoying the silence between us. I inhaled, the smell of everything that had happened between us a strange perfume that I never wanted to forget. It was the scent of us, the scent of letting go, the scent of change.

I laid my hand flat against his back, covering a small bruise I found there and ignored what it meant.

We'd spoken of three-hundred years together and I was going to believe in it. I was going to hold onto that number until the very end, because I knew that covering that bruise, in my palm, lay another bruise, one that was darker than any I'd had before, one that had just appeared, and one that I could never show him.

Three-hundred years.

But first, I had to fight for the next three-hundred minutes.

# FAMILY

Glasses clinked against each other around the crowded table.
The thunk of glass against plastic followed, and laughter made up for the
rest as I watched the faces of everyone I loved filled with love and
amusement.

Ambrose and Vanessa Mayhew sat beside each other, their
shoulders touching, their body language telling everyone in the room
that they were in love and had been for a very long time. Even though
they couldn't share their thoughts the way that Robert and I could, they
still found a way to speak to each other without anyone knowing what
they were saying. They had their own language, one that they spoke with
looks and touches.

Graham sat next to Mrs. Mayhew with Lark seated in his lap.
She had an arm draped around his neck while the other hand raised a
glass to me, her smile more genuine than I'd ever seen before. I was surprised at how easily Lark laughed, the things that she would have
normally criticized for being too human, too simple were now amusing
to her, pleasing.

Beside them, Stacy sat with Matthew in her lap; his face
crunched up in frustration at the constant jiggling his bottle was going
through. He was growing so quickly, his cheeks puffed up with a healthy
pink, while his legs were so long they dangled over her arm. He didn't
care that she was cold and hard like rock. All he wanted was his bottle.

Stacy seemed content, more content than I'd seen in days. She
smiled and laughed, and even gave Graham a compliment, which no one

took to be shocking. She kissed Matthew's head, cooing and singing a lullaby that sounded both foreign and familiar to me.

"Your mom used to sing that to you when you were a baby," Dad said to me softly when she'd begun. He sat between Stacy and me, his hand clasped tightly over mine, his eyes watering as he laughed at something Graham said. I hadn't noticed it at the hospital but his hair was graying at the sides, which should have made him look older but to me, it didn't change a thing. The wrinkles at the corners of his eyes made his smile appear warmer, and the lines around his mouth looked like a hug, one that I never wanted more than right then.

Robert sat on the other side of me, his right arm resting at my back while his left hand held a glass in the air, the contents spilling onto the table as he, too, laughed at Graham's comment. To see him like that and compare him to the angel I'd met almost a year ago was like comparing an empty garden to one filled with flowers. He looked full, happy. And it did something to me, knowing that it was partly because of me.

There were no empty chairs at the table, even though the presence of the two people who should have been there hung heavily over our heads, but we said nothing about it, even though we all felt it. Janice was hidden away, in a hospital out of state under a name that even I did not know. Her condition hadn't improved, but it hadn't grown worse either; that was enough for us.

As for Ameila…she remained in her false coma, though her thoughts were shared by Lark, who did so quietly and to the annoyance of her brother whenever something was said that amused her. To anyone else, talking the way we were with her probably sounded unnatural and weird, but after a while it was no different than having someone on the phone, listening in.

But despite the absences, despite the uncertainty of the future that lay just outside the front door, things inside were perfect. Dad, after finally hearing the full story of what happened to me after Lem had kidnapped me, had made me egg-in-a-hole for breakfast. I even managed to eat a whole one before Graham devoured the rest.

Lark still refused to show me what was on the real ring that had belonged to Isis, but she did tell me that Lem had been telling me the truth about not being Sam's partner. Of course, this didn't make up for the kidnapping or trying to keep me and Robert apart, but I found myself feeling less hateful toward him; maybe even a little forgiving.

Robert didn't feel the same way.

"Now who's being uncharitable," I kidded when he made it clear that the moment he saw Lem, he'd tear him in two like he did his son.

"I always knew you were the real angel," he replied with no sarcasm.

It was easy to believe that now, and I didn't contradict him like I normally would have. I didn't need to anymore, which only made him happier. This was how it always should have been, I told myself. It was easier, and it felt more right than holding on to my insecurity did.

The afternoon was spent watching Rocky Horror, and I laughed when Dad began singing the songs, forgoing his usual meows and actually reciting the lyrics.

"Well, I've heard them enough; I think it's only time," he said with a shrug.

We ate sandwiches and drank lemonade, played board games and sang along to the oldies station that was Dr. Bro's favorite. Mrs. Mayhew started on the chili and Graham and I went into the kitchen with her to help, while Robert and Dad sat at the kitchen table talking, strangely enough, about football. Stacy and Dr. Bro were talking on the sofa, while Matthew slept soundly in his stroller.

It was as normal a scene as anyone could imagine. No one looking into the window would have guessed at who we all really were, or what we really were. And that was how we wanted it. Hiding in plain sight, Robert had called it. I called it living.

Dinner was a loud and raucous affair, and I'd never remembered feeling so content and so fortunate. Everyone passed Matthew around, and when Mrs. Mayhew took him into her arms, I saw that the sadness that had possessed her the evening before was gone, replaced with a sort of gratefulness that I knew only came with time.

It was nearly midnight when Dad went upstairs to the other guest bedroom with Matthew. He made me promise to still be here when he woke up, and I nodded, kissing his cheek and then kissing Matthew's head before watching them leave.

Stacy stretched out on one of the sofas in the family room, and Graham stretched out on the other one, Lark squeezing in beside him, half-floating off the side since he took up most of the room. They weren't going to sleep; Stacy didn't sleep anymore, and Graham didn't want his dreams to progress into something more real, a concern that made me spit out the water in my mouth the minute he voiced it.

I helped Dr. Bro clean the kitchen while Mrs. Mayhew took a shower, and Robert patrolled the house, always keeping in contact with me through his thoughts, some that made me sputter mid-answer to one of the doctor's questions.

"Was 'Nessa's chili too spicy?" the doctor asked as he saw my red face.

"No, no, it wasn't spicy at all," I answered truthfully while silently cursing Robert and his suddenly lewd mind.

I dried the last dish and he put it into the cupboard, and then he turned around to face me with inquisitive eyes. "You haven't asked how my wife and I met. Stacy asked me almost as soon as she arrived; it was Graham's first question. But you...you don't seem interested. Why?"

I hung the towel over the side of the sink and let the right side of my mouth curl up into a smirk. "Because I think you've been asked that question more times than you like, and that the answer shouldn't be one that you dread telling, which it's probably starting to become."

He perked up at my response and smiled, his teeth glistening in the bright florescent light. "It's funny you said that, because I was just telling 'Nessa the other day that I didn't really like having to explain over and over again why someone like her is with someone like me."

"I think the two of you are cute together, and I don't really care how you met. You're happy and that's what's important, right?"

His head bobbed up and down in agreement. "We are happy. It wasn't always that way, but we made it work."

"I don't think anyone can always be happy. I think we need those moments when everything is screwed up just so we remember why being happy is important and we learn to appreciate every single moment we have. It's even more important when you don't have the guarantee of living forever."

"And you think that applies especially to you."

My eyebrows lifted and my mouth went slack at my lack of an answer. Instead, I looked into the family room at the bodies of my friends. Lark and Graham had forever. They were going to have many rough times, I knew that for a fact, but they were going to have much more time spent loving each other and being grateful for each other and they knew it.

Stacy…if Dr. Bro could find love and happiness, then there was no reason to doubt Stacy's chance at finding that, too. Especially now that she knew that she wasn't going to die. She had infinity to find the one person who would make everything in her life make sense.

The sliding door off to the side of the family room opened, and Robert walked in, his face brightening as he saw my face and my own reaction. I knew I had an answer then for Dr. Bro, and I gave it to him without saying a word.

I walked into Robert's outstretched arms and pressed my forehead to his, sharing our thoughts, the good and the bad. This was bliss, and everyone knew that bliss never lasted forever.

Robert looked up suddenly, Lark appearing by our side almost instantaneously, with Dr. Bro and Stacy arriving less than a second later.

Mrs. Mayhew was at the foot of the stairs, her face ashen, her eyes wide.

"So many…so many new ones," she whispered.

Robert and Lark exchanged glances before she was back at Graham's side, shaking him awake—he'd decided to fall asleep after all.

"So many new what?" I asked, unable to hear a single thought even though I knew that a conversation heavy with information was being held right in front of me.

"Monsters, creatures, the un-turned," Mrs. Mayhew said faintly. "Almost two hundred of them all made within the hour. Oh dear, this isn't good. This isn't good, Robert. They're not the harmless kind."

Dr. Bro took his wife's arm and led her to one of the oversized ottomans. "Sit, 'Nessa. Sit and catch your breath."

She shook her head. "I don't need to catch my breath, Ambrose. I need to get moving. We need to stop him. They're all being made here, just a dozen or so miles from away. They're coming here, Robert."

"Is it my grandfather?" Robert looked at Mrs. Mayhew with as cold a gaze as I'd ever seen from him. She didn't have to nod for him to know what the answer was.

Stacy pulled her hair into a ponytail. "Well, I wasn't planning on feeding until the morning, but I'm gonna do it now. If there are two-hundred creeps coming this way, I'm gonna need my strength."

I grabbed her arm before she could leave. "No, Stacy. This isn't your fight."

She pulled my hand away and jabbed her finger into my chest. "Listen, I've been pissed off one too many times by this guy and now he's turning people in my neighborhood into…well, who knows what he's turning them into, but it's not because they asked for it."

"I don't want him to kill you!"

"I'm already dead! He took away my family, he took away my future, and now he's doing it to innocent people and you can't tell me that I don't have a right to stop that."

"God, Stacey, you still got your family. Sean knows you're alive. Do you want him to lose you twice? Ask my dad what that feels like if you think Sean can handle it."

Her jaw clenched, her breathing growing rapid and hard, like one of those trains you see in the mall during Christmas. Huffing and puffing, she headed toward the door.

"Stacy…please."

She stilled, and stubbornly turned around. "I'm going, Grace. But I won't go without you. We do this together or none of us do it."

It was as good a compromise as I was going to get, so I lowered my head in acceptance. "Good. I'm going to feed. I'll be back in an hour," she said before disappearing out the door.

"Ugh, what did I do?" I groaned.

"Nothing. You were trying to be a good friend," Dr. Bro said with the tone that sounded a lot like my dad's.

"A good friend doesn't let one of their best friends get involved in something that could kill them."

"You're right, but a good friend also doesn't doubt a friend's ability to help, either."

Mrs. Mayhew headed to the kitchen, kneeling down in front of the sink and pulling open the curtains that covered the pipes below. She climbed in, far deeper than it looked possible, before emerging with a large book in her hands.

"This is it," she exclaimed with a humph.

"What is it?" I asked as I took in the dusty cover and the innumerable pages.

"Every creature, every angel, and every rightfully turned human to live in Ohio has their name in this book."

"Are you gonna add another two hundred names?" It didn't look possible to add even one more name in the already straining book.

"They're already in there," she said, bored. "Their names, their designation, their maker have already been documented and cataloged. The book keeps record of every name that passes through my thoughts."

"So what are you going to do with it?"

She opened the book, which seemed to settle on its own at a specific page. "I'm preparing it."

"For what?"

The question wasn't much of one, but the answer…that was a

different story.

"To be destroyed."

My mouth fell, but I appeared to be the only one who looked shocked by what she'd said. "If that book contains what you say it does, then why do you want to destroy it?"

Grim faced and without any sarcasm, she replied, "Because by this time tomorrow, most of these names will no longer exist in this book."

I looked at Robert, at every face that I could see, and I knew that this wasn't an exaggeration. "All those people?"

Mrs. Mayhew put the book on the kitchen counter and then touched a hand to her hair, smoothing it out before walking toward the front door and opening the closet there and retrieving a jacket.

"Come on, Ambrose," she said with a renewed vigor. "Let's get started."

"Started? Where are you going? You're just going to leave that book there? Out in the open like that?" I asked, panicked.

"Yes. The counter's marble, so no damage will be done to the house," she answered with a shrug. "Oh, and I'm going to get you some help from those we can trust."

"How? How do you know who we can and can't trust?"

This time she smiled, the warmth of it reaching me despite the distance between us. "Because I'm the registrar, silly." And then she and Dr. Bro were out the door, disappearing like Stacy to who knows where.

"What are we going to do, Robert?" I asked, still facing the door.

"We're going to pretend that the world outside will wait for us. We're going upstairs, we're going to forget everything for a few hours except that we love each other, and you're going to keep your promise to your dad that you'll be here in the morning when he wakes up."

"Is that it? Is that all we're going to do?"

He picked me up and stepped quietly toward the stairs, allowing me a glimpse of Lark and Graham snuggling, Graham oblivious to everything except his wife's presence. "If you mean rather than get worked up over the inevitable, I'm taking you to bed then yes. If you're wondering if all we're going to do is go to bed then no."

I flushed at his words and buried my face in the crook of his neck, trying hard to keep both my anxiety and my excitement from bursting out into what would have most likely been an unattractive squeal.

"Make the most of it," I heard Lark say from the nest she made in Graham's arms.

# THE LAST TALK

We didn't sleep. I don't think anyone really did except for Dad and Matthew.

Robert and I spent most of the night talking, laughing, crying...wishing. When the sun rose and the sounds of movement in the house became too loud to ignore, we finally said goodbye to our peace and walked together downstairs for breakfast.

"Good-morning, you two," Dad said as he stood in front of the stove. "I'm making pancakes and ham for breakfast. Matthew's ready for a change, I think—could you help me out, Robert?"

Robert looked at me and then at Dad, and finally at a pinched-face Matthew. "Uh...I don't-I don't know-"

"Oh, everything's in the diaper bag upstairs. He's made a mess—I can smell him from here—so you might have to bathe him."

The look on Robert's face showed one of fear and uncertainty, and I laughed because I'd never seen him look that way before. "Go on," I told him. "He likes powder on his bottom after a changing, too."

"You're enjoying this," he said with mild annoyance.

"Actually, yes."

"Why?"

"Because considering how long you've been alive, seeing you look so petrified over something as simple as cleaning a baby is pretty funny."

His mouth puckered as his annoyance grew more pronounced, but he walked over to Matthew's carrier and picked up the baby, holding him out at arm's length when he inhaled the smell that Dad had warned him about, his nose wrinkling as a result. "This should be considered cruel and inhumane," he noted.

"Well, you're not human so just hold your breath," I laughed.

With their confusion-filled eyes locked onto one another, Robert took Matthew upstairs to be changed.

I peeked in on Graham and Lark and saw the sofa they'd been asleep on was empty.

"They're in the bathroom," Dad said with obvious disapproval.

I smiled at that, knowing that he'd probably spoken of Robert and me in the same tone to Graham. "Want me to carry that plate of pancakes to the dining table?"

"Yes, and the syrup."

I carried the overlarge plate filled with fluffy disks to the dining room where an even larger plate already sat. "Dad?"

"What?"

"Which one is Graham's?"

"The one in your hand."

Nodding, I placed the plate in front of the chair Graham had sat in last night and then returned to the kitchen. "You know, he probably doesn't need to eat as much as he does. I don't know if the turned can gain weight but if they can he's gonna end up causing sink holes."

Dad lifted a ham steak off a skillet and put it onto another plate already stacked with browned pieces of pork. "The turned stay relatively the same. Graham could eat an entire cow and not gain a single pound."

"Does he even *need* to eat?"

"He won't starve, but he's still human in here-" he pointed to his head "-so he'll still feel hungry when he normally would."

"Which for him means all the time."

Dad laughed. "He wasn't always like that, you know. The two of you used to be pretty picky eaters."

"Pictures or it didn't happen," I said with a smile before taking the plate of ham into the dining room.

524

Dad followed behind with a pitcher of orange juice and a roll of paper towels. "I think Richard caught it on video. You two wouldn't even eat hot dogs as kids."

"Well, I still don't eat them."

"Yes, and Graham eats enough of them for both of you."

Dad put down the roll of paper and then took my free hand. He reached for the plate and set it down before grabbing my other hand, turning me so that I was facing him.

"Grace, thank you."

"For?"

"For being here. I know what's happening. I know that you wanted to leave last night and the fact that you stayed, that you kept your promise makes me feel so proud, Grace. Your mother would be so proud of you right now-"

"Dad."

"Listen to me," he interrupted. "I know that you don't want to hear about your mom, that you're mad at her for what happened, what she, what *we* didn't tell you, but no matter what, she never wanted to hurt you. She loved you more than anything, more than anyone, and she gave you so much of herself. I see it in you. It's why you are the way you are. You might not care right now, but you will."

"I-"

"No. Don't say anything. I might never get another chance at this so let me finish while I still remember the words in my head."

His fingers on my left hand touched my mother's ring; he pinched it and turned it, looking down at his actions before returning his gaze to mine. "No matter what you do today, no matter what happens, you remember who you are. And I'm not talking about what they say you are; I'm talking about the person you are.

"You have more good in you than anyone I've ever known. You're generous and patient, forgiving and stubborn in more good ways than bad. You remember that. You remember what kind of person risked getting sick to sneak Graham chicken soup when he had the chicken pox. You remember what kind of person called up the woman she couldn't stand to made amends so that she could make her old man happy."

He choked up, his voice cracking like glass. He reached out to me, grasping my two hands in one of his, while using the other to hold my chin. "You remember the person who sacrificed herself to save her family and friends, and most importantly you remember what kind of person forgave a stupid old man for keeping secrets from the person who matters the most to him in the world."

It was violent, the way he yanked at me to hold me in his arms. The movement was so quick, the action so rough and jolting that I couldn't brace myself for it, even with the abilities I was discovering I had. It hurt, the crushing of arms against my back, the digging of a chin into the top of my head.

But through the pain I felt the weight of my father's grief, his remorse, his friendship, his love. This might be the last time we spoke, the last time we held each other's heart against our own. He was my father, but more than that he was my dad, and through every fight, every disagreement, every lie, every secret, he'd always been that person.

This wasn't a goodbye. I'd vowed that there wouldn't be one. But the heaviness of reality made it feel like one, more so than any other we'd ever had.

"I love you, Dad."

"I know. I know that more than anything, kiddo."

He squeezed me one more time before letting me go and swallowing down whatever else he was going to say. He wiped his hands on his pants and then held them out to the table. "Well...ready to eat?"

"I am!"

Graham arrived with his appetite, while Lark arrived with a smile. He sat down in front of the plate filled with pancakes, his hand poised over his fork, waiting for a sign that it would be okay to eat.

I sat down in the same seat I'd occupied for dinner, grinning when Robert returned from upstairs, his face still pinched up in disgust, his skin impossibly green while Matthew gurgled in his arms, content and clean. "You okay?"

"This...this kid's not human."

Dad laughed and reached for the baby. "Oh believe me, he's human."

"I refuse to believe it. I refuse to believe that what came out of that...that tiny person is what comes out of other babies. Nothing that smells that bad, or looks that foul could possibly be human," Robert insisted as he sat next to me.

"I don't know about that," Graham argued. "I've seen some things in the locker room before and after games that would make you think aliens had landed or something."

"Is it a human thing to discuss feces at the breakfast table?" Lark asked baldly.

"Apparently not, since Robert's the one who brought it up," Graham replied, eyeing the plates on the breakfast table and then the empty chairs around it. "Hey, where is everyone anyway?"

"I'm here," Stacy answered, her hair wrapped in a towel.

"Where'd you take a shower?" I asked.

"Dr. Bro's bathroom."

"So where are they?"

"I don't know. I just didn't want to wait for the six-foot-high club over here to hurry up and get out of the bathroom so I used the doc's."

Stacy sat down and looked at the food on the table with a strange longing. "It looks so good...and at the same time it makes me want to throw up my dinner."

"See, gross table discussions aren't being brought up by humans," Graham pointed out. "So can we eat already?"

"Go ahead," Dad insisted, pulling a bottle from his pocket and sticking the nipple into Matthew's mouth.

Graham didn't need to be told twice, and began to scarf down his pile of pancakes, finding a rhythm that allowed him to take bites of ham, gulps of orange juice, and still answer questions without once having his mouth empty of food.

"So, tell me what your plan is," Dad said calmly.

"Whose plan?"

Lark picked up a fork and began pushing at the tines with her finger, the points moving back and forth like jelly. "He means Grace's, although everyone seems to have a plan of their own right now."

I took a pancake and a piece of ham for myself and spoke between bites. "According to Mrs. Mayhew, there are a lot of people coming this way to get me. We can't let them hurt anyone before they get here, and we definitely can't let them get here, so right now the only thing I can think of doing is stopping them."

"Yes, but how?" Dad wanted to know.

"I don't know," I answered truthfully.

"They want Grace," Lark said flatly. "They've all been told that if they want to go back to being normal, they have to kill her. The ones who don't want to go back to being humans have been told the opposite. Basically whatever they want to hear in order to do it, that's what they've been told."

"How many?"

Lark closed her eyes, her head tilting forward slightly before cocking to the side. "Too many…Vanessa would have a more accurate number. I can only guess at two hundred, but more are being turned every hour."

"This is your grandfather doing this, right? So why aren't we stopping him first?" Graham asked, his plate empty.

"Because he's not just my grandfather," Lark answered, exasperated. "He's one of the first four. That means that the minute he feels threatened, he'll ascend and then no one will be able to get him."

"So what? He keeps on turning people and we kill them?"

"What's this *we* business," I asked, annoyed. "Since when did you become a vigilante?"

"Since my best friend became someone's extra credit."

"You can't actually be considering letting him come along?" I looked at Lark, her eyes still closed.

"I can't force him to stay out of this anymore than you can, and I won't try to either. If he wants to help then I'm going to let him."

My eyes flicked to Graham, who listened intently for my argument. *Graham can't fight against them. He's not strong, he's not fast. All he has is the ability to heal. That's not going to get him very far with whatever the hell is out there.*

"Hey, none of that thinky-talky thing," Graham chastised. "I know when you guys are doing it because everything gets really quiet even though it still feels like you guys are arguing. I don't care if you think I can't do anything. Not doing anything is only gonna drive me crazy."

"You'll be staying here with me, Graham. I'm going to need someone to talk to so that *I* don't go crazy," Dad informed him.

"So wait, now I'm the babysitter?"

"Graham..." Dad growled.

"Mr. Shelley, I don't mean to offend you-"

"Oh no, you don't *mean* to offend me by insinuating that I need a babysitter."

"It's just...you've got a baby to take care of. I don't wanna sit here and change diapers when I could be out there kicking butt!"

"I won't just be sitting changing diapers," Dad corrected him. "I'll be working, too."

"Working?" I asked, confused.

"Grace, you already know what'll happen if they get to you. EPs don't want that to happen anymore than the angels do. We are raised to do nothing but protect them from exposure. We are their alibis and their enablers. If there's no need to do that anymore then there's no reason for us and whatever protections *we* might have had will be gone.

"So, I'll be working with my sister to get what help out to you that I can."

This bothered me. "And what did she ask for in return? Is she gonna demand that you hand over Matthew in exchange for her help?"

"No. She doesn't want anything. Being an EP, looking out after her angel charge is all she has. She would give up everything to protect that, to protect her way of life."

I was skeptical of that. "Dad, I don't know if I like the idea of you working with her…or any of the EPs who do what your family does."

"Well, whether you like it or not, kiddo, it's what has to be done. Even if your mother wasn't who she was, that doesn't change what I was and what I did. There are hundreds of innocent EPs out there who will suffer the same fate if we abandon them."

"Fine. But you make sure she knows that if she demands custody of Matthew again, I'll knock her out," I warned.

"I promise," Dad chuckled.

"That still doesn't sound like something I wanna do," Graham huffed. "I'm not going to stay here."

"And how are you gonna get anywhere; fly?" Robert asked sardonically.

"I'll take him wherever I go," Lark answered protectively.

"Fine. Let him be your burden."

"He is no more a burden to me as Grace is to you."

"Grace cannot fly, but she has discovered the ability to move rather quickly," Robert informed her. "And she's strong; stronger than Graham, maybe even stronger than Stacy. She's the only reason you're not sitting next to a cup of Graham juice right now—she protected him from Bane.

"And I agree with her: Graham should stay here."

"I'm not saying he shouldn't stay here. I'm saying I won't force him to stay here." Lark looked at Graham, who grunted in protest. "I know you want to come, but I can't protect Grace if I'm worrying about you."

"You act like I don't know my own limitations. I know I can't do any of the things you can do, but don't forget that I've studied offensive and defensive plays for four years. I know what it takes to avoid getting sacked. Most of these things coming this way are still human up here-" he jabbed his index finger against his head "-which means I'm much better at understanding them and what they're gonna do than you are."

"He's got a point."

Five heads turned to look at Stacy, our faces all mirroring the same shock.

"I've been in this body for months now and I'm still learning about all the things I can do. I still think I have human limitations and when I expect something to happen and it doesn't, it throws me off.

"These turned people are only hours, maybe days old, right? That means they won't be doing anything the way that someone like Dr. Bro would. Graham's right: while they're still new and unsure of themselves, he's got the advantage."

"What about the vampires? What about them? They're mindless; they're not thinking like humans; they're not thinking at all. How's he gonna stop them?" I wanted to know.

"How about you let me take care of that," she responded, her tone so sure, I struggled to fight the death of doubt in me.

"So what? You're gonna fight off a dozen or more monsters by yourself? That's gonna make me feel better?"

Stacy sat up in her chair and leaned over the table to glare at me. "Well I don't know; does it? Does it make you feel better knowing that no matter what happens, by this time tomorrow, there's a good chance that hundreds of people will be dead?

"Because that's the reality here, Grace; Graham wants to help and he can. He knows how to do it without killing anyone, and you said it yourself that you don't want anyone else dying because of you."

"And that includes him!" I shouted. "Graham, I love you, but this isn't a game. You don't get four quarters and a half-time show here."

"Why can't you trust me to make the right decision for myself?" Graham barked, his face filled with more disappointment than anger. "I screwed up before—especially with you—but isn't the whole point of screwing up so that we can learn from our mistakes? Well, how the hell am I gonna prove that I've learned anything if you won't let me?

"I'm not just doing this for you, you know. I'm doing it for me, too, as well as for Lark and my parents. Hell, we should be doing this for everyone because they don't deserve what's gonna happen if we don't."

"Fine! Fine, do what you want. Just…just don't die, because I might have to kill you if that happens."

It wasn't a very good threat—at least to me—but it made everyone else laugh nervously; the kind of laugh you only hear when something is far more true than funny.

"So that's it, then. Graham's going and I'm staying. Where's Ambrose and his wife?" Dad was patting Matthew on the back, trying to burp him.

"They'll meet us when it's time," Lark answered quietly.

"Meet where?"

"Some of the turned are heading to your house, while others are going to the school. The rest will be waiting at the retreat. They're looking to pick off the weakest ones first-"

"Which means me," Graham finished for her.

"Well, they don't know who's weak and who isn't. They're confused and scared, and only know that they need to kill Grace. They don't know what she is; only what Robert and I are."

"And they won't expect Graham to be what he is. Their ignorance of what it means to be turned, what it means to have angels want to help you instead of hurt you makes them weak. You all will have the advantage on them in that area," Dad added.

"So we head to your house first, Grace," Stacy confirmed.

"I guess so."

Everyone stood up, looking at each other for the last time with eyes as innocent as they'd ever be; our hopes and our fears warring with one another in our faces as we tried to present a brave front.

Stacy's mind was filled with thoughts of her family. She

thought of her parents, of how hard they'd worked for the life they'd led, and how her failure would destroy that. She worried over her brothers, fearing that they would fail to help when they were needed the most. There were thoughts and feelings of guilt within her that she would never be able to rid herself of and already she felt their weight.

Lark and Graham stood side-by-side, their hands clasped so tightly that the world splitting in two probably wouldn't tear them apart. They were promising each other a vacation when all of this was over. Lark would take him to see where she was born, and he would take her to see the monument dedicated to the greatest football player there ever was.

Dad was looking at Matthew and seeing in his face every dream a father has for a son. Every hope he'd ever had before I was born, every hope he'd held onto with desperation could now finally be let loose and I didn't want to disappoint him.

But when Dad looked up at me, his thoughts shifted and I blinked away tears when I saw that his hopes for me had been much greater…and he didn't feel one ounce of disappointment. Instead, what he felt was pride. He was proud of me, of what I was doing and what I was trying to do.

Robert was no less proud. His mind wasn't cluttered with memories and promises. There were no plans being made and no hopes being shared. Instead, he only allowed one thought to exist, one thought to be heard, and that was how much he loved me. It was more than enough.

These were the people who made up my family. They were everything to me. Every branch, every leaf, every crooked knot and twisted root that made me who I am was standing right in front of me, supporting me and fighting with me for an uncertain future, but one that they only wanted if I was a part of it.

I had never imagined having so much. This was what mattered. Not popularity, not acceptance, not beauty, not money. And I was ready to die for it.

"Let's go."

# THE ROAD TO PERDITION

It was decided without a single word being spoken that we would head to my house separately.

Stacy would go on foot—the fastest way for her to travel—and try to lure whatever was waiting there for us out. She took Dad to the side and spoke to him quietly, handing him something small before leaving, her head lowered, her mood darker than it had ever been. I had refused to listen to their conversation, but I couldn't fight the curiosity within me.

"What did she give you?" I asked.

"It's a letter for her brother. She asked me to give it to him in case she doesn't return."

"She will, though…right?"

"I don't know. "

"We're leaving," Lark announced, her voice sounding gritty, as though she was hardening herself for what she was set to face.

She'd said "we're", and she was right. She and Graham were leaving at the same time, but Graham was leaving in Dr. Bro's car, a tiny little thing that made Graham look like a giant.

"Stacy—has she come across any trouble yet?" I asked as I walked them out of the house.

"No. She's almost there; I don't want to leave her alone. There will be more than she can handle."

She grabbed Graham by his shirt and tugged, the fabric tearing as he fell toward her. She kissed him, fully, roughly, and then she was gone.

"I gotta go," Graham stuttered, half-breathless, half-energized. He climbed into the car and turned the key that sat in the ignition. It purred when it started, like an overgrown metal cat.

Dad would have been pleased.

Graham jumped out of the car and wrapped his arms around me, squeezing me without saying a word before returning to the car and driving off, the tiny car zipping down the street at a much faster speed than I expected.

I went back inside the house and gave one last look at everything there. It wasn't my house, and nothing here was familiar to me in any way, but if I returned I knew that the way I saw things would be different. Life would be different.

Would a book look like a book when I'd just experienced the most unbelievable story? Would the comfort of a couch really exist after today? I didn't know anything but the world right now, the world the way my eyes had always seen them. I'd seen death. I'd seen heartbreak. I'd seen betrayal and forgiveness. But I didn't know what to expect now.

And then there was always the possibility that I'd never see any of this again. Nothing as mundane as a table with a plate of half-eaten food or a spit-up rag hanging off the back of a chair. I'd come to terms with that a long time ago, but it didn't make it any less difficult.

"Dad," I called out softly.

"I'm here, Grace."

He was holding Matthew close to his chest. I walked toward him and held out my arms, taking the baby into them and cuddling him, breathing in the scent of baby powder and something sweet. "You be good, little man. I'll see you in a little while."

It sounded so simple, so ordinary that I couldn't help but giggle at the absurdity of it. I was speaking to him like I was going to the store or something.

"He'll be fine. We both will."

Dad's face was relaxed, the lines and crevices that framed his mouth and his eyes thinner and shallower than they'd ever been. He looked…proud. There was no fear or reservation like I expected. Either he was genuinely feeling it or his past as an EP was coming back.

"When is your sister coming?"

"She and some of the others will be here in a few minutes. Jessica never left Ohio; she probably knew what was coming and knew that eventually I'd call. It's funny."

"What?"

"She doesn't consider you a part of our family, but her very survival depends on you and your devotion to us."

"To you and Matthew; not her."

"I know, kiddo."

"So, is this the part where we do the whole goodbye thing?" I asked, strangely embarrassed all of a sudden.

"No. I wouldn't be able to let you go if it was a goodbye; you're not going to tell me goodbye ever again. Instead, just tell me the same thing you told Matthew; minus the little man part."

I laughed softly, handing the baby back and then giving Dad the biggest smile I could manage. He deserved to see that before watching me leave. "I'll see you later, Dad."

He returned my smile, width for width, hope for hope. "Don't be late. I'm going to make chicken lasagna for dinner."

"My favorite," I whispered.

"Robert, may I speak to you for a minute?"

I hadn't noticed Robert's presence, but he placed his hand on my back and kissed my head before walking away with Dad toward the kitchen. I closed my mind off to their voices, choosing not to hear the conversation that was going on between them. If it was one of those chats that started and ended with "you take care of my daughter or else", I was definitely better off not hearing any of it.

I took one step outside the small house that had brought my family closer than it'd ever been before, and waited. It's not goodbye. Goodbyes were final. Goodbyes were the words spoken by those giving up on ever seeing anyone or anything they cared about again.

"See you later, house," I breathed.

***

We were on Robert's motorcycle.

"They will expect us to arrive from the sky. Their heads are just as full of stereotypes about angels as yours was when we first met," Robert explained as he put the helmet on my head, clipping the strap beneath my chin.

"I didn't really know much of anything about angels," I replied honestly. "The only thing I thought was that you had wings and wore togas."

He laughed, pushing the visor on the helmet down and climbing onto the black beast that had taken me for my first real ride. "Togas? I was wearing a pair of pants and a rather expensive shirt when we first met."

"I know," I answered, my voice muffled.

"And I didn't have wings."

"I know that, too."

The roar of the engine startled me, the vibrating between my legs teasing them, and my legs responded by clenching against the black, metal frame. It was just as terrifying and exciting as the first time, and just like it was then, I didn't know where I'd end up, only that it was where I needed to go.

We didn't need wings to fly. The motorcycle flew on the road, Robert throttling it so fast that it floated above the pavement. Black against black, Robert dressed to match; I was the only thing that stuck out in my white T-shirt and dark blue jeans. It was the only way to know for sure that what had just blown by wasn't just a shadow but something real.

And my arms wrapped around Robert's waist, my head resting against his back, my thoughts filled with his told *me* that he was real. It didn't matter how close we were, or how intimate we'd been—I needed to know that. It was the human side of me.

Acknowledging this, that there really were two parts to me, didn't feel new. I'd accepted it the minute I protected Graham from Bane's attack. But it gave me something that I don't think I expected. I felt...brave.

Hitting the pavement didn't require bravery.

It required an ability to handle sudden pain and swallow fear.

So when it felt like a house crashed into me, when the back tire of the motorcycle burned against my thigh and peeled away the top layer of skin, and I saw sky and asphalt rotate in my line of vision until I landed in weeds and trash, I did just that. I didn't scream. I didn't cry out or focus on the incredible pain that shot out like firecrackers beneath my skin.

Instead I took deep, steady breaths and listened for the crunching of bones as I slowly tried to get up. There was a crack in the visor of the helmet, and I tugged at the strap and pulled it off my head, breathing in the scent of burnt rubber and spilled fluids.

"Robert?" I called out.

A blur. That's all I saw.

Fingers gripped into my shirt and shoulder as my feet left the ground. I couldn't see who was holding me, only the shadow they created above the pavement.

"I know it's you, Bane," I said half-panicked.

His voice was soft and delicate, almost absurdly so when he responded. "My name is not for you to speak."

"Why not?"

"Nephilim do not speak to the divine."

"I'm not Nephilim. I'm one of you."

"That is not possible. You are not divine. You are an abomination, a black mark upon us."

The ground was growing farther and farther away, and his thoughts were focused on one thing: dropping me.

"Don't do it! Don't do it, Bane!" I pleaded. "Put me down. You don't have to do it; I'm not what you think I am."

His ascent stopped. It actually stopped. We dangled in the air for what was probably only seconds before slowly descending, my feet finding the ground, my toes curling into my boots at the solidity.

"Thank you," I said tentatively before stepping away the second his fingers loosened before tumbling to the ground when an explosion sounded, the sky filling with light that made the morning sun seem like night.

Bane, unmoved and unconcerned by it, stared at me, confused and angry, his thoughts still focused on dropping me but now…now they warred with the fact that he hadn't.

"Grace!"

Robert grabbed me, pulled me to my feet before shoving me behind him as he faced the gigantic angel standing in front of us. "Stay away, Bane."

"I don't take orders from you, N'Uriel."

"Well then you'll die like Azor just did," Robert said firmly.

"You killed Azor?" Bane asked, his face falling, almost like a child's would after losing a favorite toy.

"I'll kill anyone and anything trying to hurt Grace," Robert promised. "She is my reason for living. I won't let you take that away from me."

"It is what I am. I have no other purpose than to punish. You cannot kill me for doing what I was created for."

"I will, and I'll do it with no remorse. You stay away from us."

"I do not take orders from you," Bane repeated, this time stepping toward.

"This is your last chance," Robert warned, his body growing rigid as the air grew colder.

Bane did not look at me. He didn't even notice me. He was too busy staring Robert down, the battle of wills threatening to turn from simply staring each other down to tearing each other apart. "I. Do. Not.

Take. Orders. From. You."

I stepped in front of Robert, putting my hands out and touching Bane's grotesquely large chest with my palms, pushing and yet not because I couldn't. He wasn't a wall; he was the house.

"You don't take orders from Robert because you can't. But you can from me. Right?"

Bane looked like every thought in the world had suddenly exploded in his head. His eyes bulged, his lips curled back over his teeth in rage and confusion. His nostrils—already the size of grapes—flared; hot air blowing out from them onto my face.

"I was told that I'm part of the first circle. If that's true then you have to listen to me. Stop."

Bane did just that. Everything stopped, like a switch had been flipped and his power had been cut off.

"You went away because you had to, didn't you? When you were attacking my friend's car?" I asked, stepping closer.

"Yes."

"You went away because I wanted you to."

"Yes."

"And you put me down because I told you to, right?"

"Yes."

"Then tell me who told you to kill me."

"Gabriel."

This wasn't a surprise.

"Bane, I want you to stop trying to kill me, okay?"

"I cannot. I was given an order and I have to follow it. It is my call, it is my duty."

I looked at him, his face so unnaturally large that every feature was exaggerated in its distortion, and I felt sorry for him. He couldn't help what he was doing. He didn't want to die anymore than I did.

I moved my hand away from his chest and brought it to his face. It was hot, instinct and duty pulsing inside him like blood would. *I promise I won't make you go against your call. I just need you to listen to me.*

I felt Robert shuffle behind me, desperately trying to hear the thoughts I was sharing with Bane, but I wasn't about to let that happen. Bane wasn't evil. He didn't have any ulterior motives like Sam and Isis did. He wasn't even keeping secrets the way Lem was. He deserved to be trusted, and he needed to know that he could trust in return.

And keeping Robert out was the only way I knew how to do that.

Bane left after hearing what I'd had to say, but the chill that Robert had created remained. He was angry with me. He was more than angry. He felt betrayed.

"You struck a deal with him," he accused.

"What I said to him doesn't matter right now."

"It matters when he still plans on killing you. I could see that as clearly as if he'd said it."

"Yes, but it doesn't matter *right now*. We have to get to the house."

"Grace-"

I spun around on my heel and glared at him, suddenly angry that he was questioning me when it was my life that was in jeopardy here, not his.

"If you want to stay here and argue then go ahead and do that; be stubborn. I'm going to help your sister and my best friends. They're facing who knows what because of me and I'm not there to help, so excuse me if the only thing I'm worried about right now is whether or not they're okay."

It hurt to see his face change from angry to disappointed, but I didn't have time to dwell on it. I didn't have time to feel any guilt or even any remorse. He would have simply have to understand, the way I had to understand.

"I'm sorry."

"Don't apologize—you're always apologizing, the way I'm always apologizing, and right now there's no room for it. We just have to...do. We have to do what we need to."

His expression was one of distaste, but he was giving in. He moved quickly, lifting me and cradling me in his arms as he ran, pushing off into the sky just as the sound of sirens reached us.

"Azor…was that another throne?"

Robert nodded. "He was Bane's…companion."

"Companion? His friend companion or his-"

"They were lovers."

"Oh."

"You sound surprised."

I nodded. "I am. I didn't think…"

"You didn't think what?"

"I didn't think something like that could want or love anything. He seems so cold, lifeless…even his reaction when you told him that you'd killed Azor seemed like it came up short, especially if that was his lover."

It was easy to see the sadness in Robert's face, even when he tried to appear stoic. It was in his eyes—they always said more than even his thoughts allowed.

"Thrones don't have the ability to really feel anything. They were all created to do nothing but punish others—they couldn't have the ability to love or feel remorse. What you saw in Bane was as deep as his feelings allow."

Now I understood the sadness in Robert's eyes. He knew what it had felt like to not feel anything, and then to be bombarded by it because of me. And despite the pain and heartache he'd suffered, he wouldn't have given it up for anything.

"You always were able to understand me better than I could," he laughed softly before pushing aside my hair with his nose and nuzzling a kiss to my temple.

"I'm supposed to be your better half; of course I understand you better," I kidded.

I looked down and saw familiar streets of my neighborhood. Summer was almost over; kids were out enjoying their last days of freedom.

"It's a good thing none of the kids here like to fly kites," Robert joked.

"It's kinda dangerous to fly kites in a neighborhood with power lines over every house," I pointed out.

"So is getting on a motorcycle with a complete stranger."

"I knew you weren't dangerous," I said unconvincingly.

"That, my love, is a lie." We laughed, a final moment of freedom before my street came into view and my house, familiar and comforting in its rundown appearance, welcomed my eyes.

We approached it like a solitary storm cloud, Robert's misting camouflaging our arrival. My bedroom window was open, and I climbed in, the quiet that existed there completely unnatural and eerie. I called out for anyone, certain that Lark and the others had already arrived—I could feel them—but even after Robert drifted in, his arrival far more graceful and fluid, I received no response.

"They're not here," I noted out loud.

"They were drawn out," Robert said, moving blindingly fast around me and out the bedroom door. I ran after him, finding him in the living room, my voice cracking at the mess that lay there.

Every piece of furniture looked like it had been hacked to pieces. The photos that had rested on the walls and on the shelves were on the floor, frameless and shredded. Dad's Christmas albums were in pieces as well.

"What happened? Did something blow up in here?" I asked, hearing my boots crunch against debris and not caring as I bent down to pick up the only album cover that had not been destroyed: the cat carols.

"No. They weren't even here. They never came inside." He looked away and then the door flew open, and he was gone. I ran to the door and then I heard it. Everyone heard it.

The commotion next door was louder than anything that should have existed in any neighborhood. Oh God…they weren't drawn there. Only one person had been drawn there—the other two followed.

"Graham!" I shouted, rushing toward the house.

Something had forced him to run home. And I knew what it was. The white truck parked in front of the garage was screaming it.

Richard had finally come home.

And so had the first wave of the turned.

I didn't care if an audience was crowding around on the street, or if the police and fire department were on their way. My best friend was in this house, fighting to save his dad. After everything he'd done to help save mine, nothing else mattered but making sure he succeeded.

I ran into the open door, hearing it slam shut behind me, cutting off the world.

# FALLING FROM GRACE

There's a certain smell that one associates with hopelessness. It's stale and heavy, like a moldy, wet towel. It clings to you the moment you inhale, and you can't shrug it off.

That smell used to exist in Graham's home. It had taken weeks to air out but eventually it left. The residue had finally been wiped clean when Lark and Graham began spending most of their time together in this house. Happiness and love finally had taken back control and it had showed.

And even now, with the stench of mutation and death, I could still feel the hope that existed here. The trouble was, hope can be had by anything. It doesn't matter if you're good or evil, you still hope for things, and I could hear the thoughts of things inside...and they were evil.

The living room was a warzone. It was even more destroyed than my own. I could hear the violence taking place in every room. I could see Robert in the kitchen, his hands on the head of a creature that looked half-human, half-rabid dog. It foamed at the mouth and screamed as its hands, with fingers that looked like the pads on a dog's paw, tried desperately to grab Robert and tear him away.

I rushed forward and then stopped because I didn't know what to do. How could I help Robert? I didn't know how to fight, and I didn't know if this...person was even worth fighting. I looked into its eyes, large and gray like dishwater, and saw recognition there.

My face had been burned into its mind, and it believed hopelessly that destroying me would return it to its former life, a life that I realized I would have done anything to regain if it'd been me.

But it *was* me. My life had been hijacked just as much as this person's. Everything was dependent upon me surviving. I didn't want to die. I didn't want to die.

"Graaaahhh!"

Rough hands were around my throat, and I fell—hard—onto the wooden floor. I heard a crack but didn't know if it was bone or the floor that made that sound. Hot, moist breath that smelled like roadkill swallowed all breathable air around me, while foamy saliva dribbled onto my face, burning my skin.

I couldn't see any eyes; I could only see that cavernous mouth hovering above me, coming closer and closer, blocking out the light. The inside of that mouth looked like corrugated cardboard, the teeth lined lips that looked like wet sponge blackened with gray points.

This wasn't my plan. I wasn't going to be taken out by a giant mouth. I planted my feet on the ground and pushed, my body lifting the creature just enough to fling myself to the side. The two of us rolled across the living room floor, crashing into overturned tables and destroyed sofas. Broken furniture stabbed my back, my arms, and my face while shattered glass and porcelain sliced into my clothes, jabbing into me like dozens of bee stings.

We both grunted, like desperate animals, each one fighting for the dominant top position. I knew what would happen if I lost this fight, but my attacker didn't. It and every creature like it were fighting for a lie, and in this case, the lie was far more powerful than the truth. So powerful that I found myself on my back again, my neck pinned down by those hands once more, my head cracking against the floor and sending spangles to my eyes.

I brought my hands up to the creature's face, its overly large jaw still hanging open above me, and shoved. It barely moved; my fingers unable to find any traction in the wet, slobbery fur that covered it. I brought my feet up against my chest and kicked but the creature was slippery, its body covered in some kind of slime that caused my feet to lose their grip and just slide down its torso. And the more I tried, the more gunked up my boots became.

The hands circling my throat were squeezing, pressing against my windpipe and forcing me to both gag and choke at the same time, my eyes closing in reflex. This was a mistake.

The mouth, wide and open and dripping with saliva closed the moment I couldn't see. Its teeth clamped down with hesitation, surprising me, but even in that hesitation, each pierce of its teeth burned as the saliva entered my skin. I screamed in pain, the only time I made a sound that wasn't guttural. The minute the cry of my voice left me, the pressure against my head lessened.

My scream was replaced by shrieks that weren't my own, and as the pressure around my neck disappeared, my eyes opened in relief. I could see Robert from the corner of my eye, his face frantic as he heard my thoughts and found himself unable to help me, his attacker now joined by two others.

It was my turn to feel frantic. I called out for him, but a body blocked the doorway and Robert disappeared. I wanted to call out to him, but inside I knew that I would only distract him further, and what he needed wasn't distraction—he needed reassurance that I was okay.

I heard a whimper and turned my head. That was when I saw the creature that had attacked me, its body curled up in a corner, cowering from fear.

From where I lay, I could take in its appearance completely, safely. Its head was almost plantlike, rounded and capped like a mushroom, what I thought had been fur merely a gray velvet cover. The rest of its body was dark and brown, glimmering with slime. Small, white dots marked its body like a trail that showed you where arms and legs were. Its feet were circular in shape, two stumps that didn't look solid at all. It was shaking, more afraid than I was, and immediately my mind opened to its thoughts.

I whimpered at what I heard and saw.

But not out of fear.

Out of sadness.

What had attacked me with such power hid beneath a grotesque shell—a girl; a young girl who'd been tormented and abused and thrown to the wolves like trash. Everything in her life had been pain and suffering, and yet, despite the bleakness of the future that lay ahead of her as a human, she wanted it. She wanted it so badly that she'd try to kill a complete stranger.

She had been led to believe that I was something horrific, something evil and the reason for all of her suffering, both past and present. It, coupled with her desire to be human again, bred in her an incredible resentment.

This resentment had altered my appearance in her mind, turning me into a monster in her eyes. It was only my scream that cleared away the fog of anger and allowed her to truly see me for what I was. Only she hadn't expected me to look like me, another girl who'd once felt just as desperate, just as alone. And now…now she felt she had nothing because in her head, killing me would be like killing herself.

"You don't have to do this," I said softly. She couldn't hear me over her weeping.

*You don't have to do this.*

Her head flew up and finally I saw her eyes. They were white, fully white orbs in her dark, featureless face. "You speak like he does," she said in a voice that sounded like it came through water.

"I've had practice," I said half-heartedly.

"He told me if I killed you that he'd make me normal again. He said that you were the reason I look like this."

I didn't have to ask who "he" was. I'd already seen his face in her memories, heard his voice and felt his presence. He'd left a mark on her that ran deeper than anything she bore on the outside. He'd taken a fragile girl and broken her when he should have helped solidify her.

"I wish I could tell you that what he said was true, that you could be turned back into what you used to be but that's impossible, whether I'm dead or not."

"He said he was an angel, and that he couldn't lie. He said that killing you is the only way to be normal. You don't understand how much I want that."

I crawled over to her, slipping in the trail of slime she'd left, and put my hands on her knees, her name spilling out the moment it became known to me. "I understand that more than anyone, Patricia. I used to want to be normal, too."

"You don't look like anything's wrong with you," she said almost snidely.

"Yeah, well, to the kids at my school, everything was wrong with me. I didn't look right, I didn't dress right, I didn't have the right kind of family, I didn't have the right kind of past. We suck as people sometimes because we make others feel like crap—like how you felt and how I felt—but you know what? Being normal for someone else isn't being normal.

"Do you really want to be like all those girls who made fun of you? Who only felt normal because they picked on you? Do you really want to be with a guy who wouldn't accept you for who you are just so you can say you're with someone?"

"Who's gonna accept me like this?" Patricia cried out in a burst of noise and slime. "Who's gonna want a girl who looks like snot? Who's gonna even be able to look at me like this? You can't even look at me, I'm so ugly."

I wanted to argue against everything she'd said, but the fight in the kitchen stole away my attention. I fought against the need to stay with her and the need to help Robert. My mind filled with images that were his, but my heart hurt with the grief and the sorrow that were hers.

"You have to kill me."

My eyes widened in shock. "What?"

Patricia stood up. She was taller than I was, her head disk shaped like a mushroom, with a rounded point at the top. Her white eyes were focused on me, her unnatural mouth turned down, altering the shape of her head as she spoke.

"You have to kill me. I don't know what's true or not. I don't know what's real or not. Two days ago I thought my life was over; I was ready to kill myself. Ten minutes ago, I was ready to kill you. This is all I know now. Killing you is the only thought I can hold onto for more than a few minutes. It's all I'm *allowed* to know."

I shook my head. "You don't want to kill me."

"You're right. I don't want to kill you, but I will. I will if you don't kill me first. If what you said is true, if killing you doesn't turn me back into a human being then I'm dead anyway."

A body flew past me, crashing into an overturned chair. It was twisted, broken in ways that seemed impossible. Patricia screamed, the kind of scream that came from terror that began deep within you. She had been prepared to die—she had begged me to kill her—but seeing the results of death was more than she could handle.

"It's okay; it's okay," I comforted.

"That's gonna be me. That's gonna be me next. Oh God, that looks like it hurt."

I approached her, blocking her view of the body with my own. "That doesn't have to be you. You don't have to die."

"There is no choice left for me." She said this so quietly, I probably wouldn't have heard it if she hadn't thought it at the same time. The despair in every word weighed them down like sludge. She sighed.

And then she was on me again.

This time, her hands were less hesitant, her body moving with more assuredness. She was pressing down on my throat, squeezing, twisting. I grabbed at her wrists, struggling with her strength and my sudden lack of it. She pinned my down my legs, the slime that oozed from her skin acting like a glue that sealed me in place.

Her body was shaking, adrenaline pumping through her as she realized she was close to completing what she'd set out to do. But adrenaline was coursing through my veins, too. It was pulsing, a hard beat that was louder than any thought she had of victory and hope. She wanted me to die.

But she didn't want that as much as I wanted to live.

I roared, a genuine, guttural, animalistic sound, and tore my legs up off the floor, my jeans remaining behind. I raised my hand into a fist and punched the side of her head. Even without being able to see it, I knew that I'd hit her ear. She screamed, and grabbed her head with her hands, freeing my neck.

I brought my head up and smashed it into hers. It did nothing but hit soft flesh. I took my other hand and brought it beneath her jaw, my fingers finding her narrow neck and squeezing. She began to cough, and I allowed my other hand to join its twin as I continued to squeeze.

A strange, sickening feeling came over me as my fingers dug into the slimy, giving skin of Patricia's changed body. It was like walking through a sticky rain, every drop that fell spreading out like webbing and drawing in every inhibition, every ounce of hesitation so that all that was left was the desire to finish what I'd started.

My strength suddenly renewed, I pushed up with just my shoulders and rolled until she was on her back. I could see the underside of her jaw, the same, gill-like panels that lined the bottom of a mushroom cap. I continued to squeeze, and I watched as those gills expanded and collapsed weakly.

Each compression of my hands brought on a euphoric high and an almost immediate low of guilt and shame. Patricia's dark brown skin was turning gray, the white spots that marked her limbs fading slightly.

Her disk-shaped head lowered, covering my hands, hiding the act of strangulation, and leaving me with the sight of her eyes, eyes that even in their blankness showed gratitude. But beyond that, in the glossiness of those eyes I saw myself.

I saw two selves, actually.

There was me, wanting to die, wanting to be free of every ounce of pain, every prick of loneliness, every tear drop filled with hatred of myself and everyone who'd ever made me feel like I wasn't good enough. I'd tasted life, I'd grasped love in my hands only to have it leave me for something better, something that was worth more than I ever could imagine.

But that me had struggled to survive despite the possibility of never knowing happiness again. That me had wanted to live because even in the deepest and darkest moments, where my fears became reality and the lies became truths, there was still hope. There was still promise. There was still a life that was meant for me, no matter how bleak.

And then I saw the me that Patricia saw: I was the killer. I was the destroyer of lives and futures. I was the cruel and mocking person who inflicted nothing but pain with lies and those very same truths that could destroy a lifetime of belief. Everything that was good was gone, or it was too deeply buried beneath the blackness of what I was to be seen.

I held between my fingers the path to the end or to the beginning. I could be cruel or I could be kind. I could make it end now, or I could extend the suffering until the very last moment. This was the power of being what I was.

"Death isn't always the end, Grace."

"You don't have it in you to kill me, Grace."

"Don't turn away from Death, Grace."

"Grace."

"Sam."

"Grace."

"Robert."

"Grace."

"Mom…"

I let go.

I threw my hands back and scrambled off of the girl, continuing to move backwards until I met resistance from a wall. I watched as she coughed, her hands coming up to her throat to rub away the pain and the tightness that I had caused. She sat up and turned her head to look at me, confusion pouring out of her like the ooze that puddle on the floor beneath her.

"Why?" she asked in a scratchy voice.

"I can't. I can't do it. I can't be her."

"Who?"

"I can't be my mom; I can't do what she did. I don't care how much you want to die, or what you do to me. You can't make me kill you; you don't deserve to die."

"It's not up to you to decide who deserves to live and who deserves to die," she shouted.

"Yes it is," I shouted back. And then I straightened, realizing that by *not* killing her, I had proven that. I'd done exactly what had been planned. It didn't matter what the outcome was—all that mattered was that I make the choice. "Oh my God."

I moved away from her and ran into the kitchen. Robert was twisting the head of a final assailant, the snapping and cracking of bones and skin only emphasized by the pounding that took place above him. He looked up at me and relief took over the hard edge that had enveloped him.

"Grace," he breathed, his eyes giving me a once over before he pulled me into his arms. "You can't let them live. They won't stop trying to kill you. They don't know how. They have no hope left but in your death."

"I can't kill her, Robert. She hasn't done anything wrong."

He pulled away and looked down at me. "She tried to kill you!"

"She tried to save herself! There's a difference!"

"There is no difference!"

"If there isn't then I deserve to die just as much as she does."

"For what?"

"For Sam," I answered.

"For Sam? What are you talking about? That's not the same thing."

"Yes it is. It's exactly the same thing, only now I'm in Sam's place. She's me, trying to survive, and I'm him, fulfilling someone's plan."

Robert yanked me toward and then pushed me behind him as

554

Patricia appeared in the kitchen doorway. "I can kill you in an instant," he warned.

"Then do it," she dared. "I'm not afraid of dying. I don't have anything to live for."

"You have everything to live for," I argued, stepping around Robert and looking at her for the girl she was, seeing the human beneath the monster.

A sprinkle of dust fell from the ceiling as she opened her mouth to respond. We all looked up, but only Robert and I moved away quickly enough to miss the ceiling collapsing, falling onto a stunned and too slow Patricia. A cloud of dust filled the kitchen, covering everything in a layer of pulverized drywall.

Stacy was poised on all fours, her jaw unnaturally long, as though it had been stretched out, while her teeth were bared, white and shining. She was snarling, hissing like a cat, her eyes focused on a man who was crouched in front of her. He was naked, and all I could see was his back.

"Stacy! It's not-"

"It's not human anymore, Grace," she said in a voice that didn't sound like hers.

As if to prove her right, the man turned and I froze. Everything about him was normal, right. He would have been attractive to anyone looking in. That is until they realized that his face was upside-down.

"Don't you like my frown turned upside down?" he sneered at me before Stacy pounced, her jaw now long enough to encircle his throat completely. In a singular moment that exemplified everything that was necessary and wrong, Stacy bit off the man's head.

I'd seen her eat before. I'd seen her fight for her life. But this was the first time that I'd seen her kill. Everything before that was nothing compared to this. She was quick, efficient, and she didn't hesitate before or after she was done. This was what she was—a killer. And I never felt more thankful that she was my friend.

"Lark's finishing off another one up in the spare bedroom," Stacy said before realizing where she was. "Damn. You guys alright?"

"We're fine now," Robert said with no hint of distaste at what had just happened. He looked…grateful. "How many total?"

Stacy looked at the corpse that lay at her feet. "With this one: four for me. Lark's last one will make ten. You?"

"Three for me, one for Grace."

"You took one out?" she asked, surprised.

"Actually…I think *you* did," I said remorsefully.

"I did? How?"

"By dropping," Robert answered flatly. "We need to go. This is only a small sample of what's out there and we're lucky it was contained to the house and no one was hurt."

Stacy looked at me and then at Robert, and I saw what she'd seen, and knew that Robert was wrong.

I ran past her, ignoring Robert's call for me, and took the stairs two at a time. The floor in the master bedroom was what had collapsed into the kitchen, and the remains of bodies littered the hall leading up the spare room in the back. Graham's bedroom door was closed.

I reached for the knob, my hand shaking, my lip quivering as I felt the death that hung just behind the door. My fingers covered the aged brass, and I turned the knob, pushing the door gently, holding my breath as I stepped in, my heart already feeling like it had fallen through the floor.

There was blood everywhere. Instantly my mind flashed back to the room in Stacy's mind. Only this time it was real. Feathers sat atop the skin that had formed on the drying, bloody pools, and I sniffed, biting back a soft cry.

Feet poked out from behind the bed, a missing shoe revealing a blood-stained sock that covered obviously broken toes.

"Graham?" I whispered, stepping in carefully, avoiding the blood and trying not to see the carnage that had caused it.

"He's gone, Grace," his voice answered weakly. "I didn't get here fast enough. I couldn't save him."

Graham was leaning over the body of his father, the battered and bruised Richard lying lifelessly in his son's arms. Graham looked pale and lost. It was the first time I'd ever seen him so vulnerable, like a little boy who'd just lost his hero.

"I didn't even get to tell him goodbye, or that I loved him, even if he was a drunk. I didn't get to tell him anything."

"He already knew how you felt," I said to him softly. "He knew you loved him no matter what."

"No he didn't," Graham argued. "He thought I was ashamed of him, that I hated him."

I bent down and put my hands beneath his chin, pulling his head up to look at me. "He was angry, he was drunk, but he never believed that you were ashamed of him or hated him."

"How do you know that?"

I blinked. "Because he came here to see you. Your dad wouldn't have bothered if he knew you didn't care; you know that."

"Grace…"

I looked up to see Robert, Stacy, and Lark standing in the doorway.

"We have to go. The school is being swarmed by dozens of the turned. There's still staff on campus."

"We can't leave him like this," I argued.

"I'll stay here with him," Stacy spoke up. "We'll meet you at the retreat."

"I can't let you stay here with him," Lark argued. "He's *my* husband."

Stacy pushed forward and knelt beside Graham. "I can't fight as long as you can—not like this, not until I feed—but I can stay and protect Graham in case anymore of those things come here. You need to get to the school and stop those things from hurting anyone else."

"I'm not leaving him here!" Lark protested.

"Go, Lark," Graham told her, his voice cracking. "The police are probably already on their way. I have to be here when they get here to let them know that Dad didn't do this. I can't let them think that he's just a drunk nobody."

"The police can suck it," Stacy snapped. "I'm gonna try and clear out the bodies and move them to the basement. Robert, Grace—go. We'll meet you at the retreat."

"Go, Grace," Graham agreed, although his voice was unbearably hardened. "You can't help me here. None of you can. You need to go. Just...just go."

Robert didn't wait for me to argue again. He grabbed me and then we were gone, out of the house and in the sky, the ground, the death, the end of Graham's family behind us.

"This is going to change him," I said coldly.

"This is going to change all of us," Robert replied knowingly.

I turned my head to see Lark floating behind us, her face stoic but her eyes glossing over, letting tears fall that she had been unable to shed back at the house. She knew, too, that the changes were coming. The trouble was that none of us knew what those changes were.

# BIRD SONG

The chaos that we'd feared had already begun. There were police cars parked haphazardly in the lot; officers crouched behind their vehicles with their guns pointed at indescribable creatures who mocked their threats.

Screams—horrific, terrifying screams that I heard in my thoughts and in my nightmares were as loud as if they were being sounded directly in my ears. I winced at the pain that caused them, the fear that provoked them, and I struggled against Robert as we landed behind the school.

Almost immediately I ran, heading toward the doors that looked like they'd been pried open by dozens of crowbars. The hallway just beyond those doors echoed with cries for help, for mercy...for death. Robert moved automatically, brushing past me and heading toward the sounds.

I followed tentatively, unable to move as quickly and decidedly as he could. Lark was directly behind me and her thoughts were my instruction, and I followed them precisely.

*Don't speak. Don't call out for anyone. The turned cannot hear your thoughts so use that to your advantage. There are others here—you know what I mean—they will be hiding in the dark, in the shadows where it's safe, and attack you when your back is turned. Stay in the light, stay where there's always a window and a door near you. Don't fall into the shadows.*

The door to the bathroom where I'd had my first encounter

with Erica almost a year ago was open. I looked at Lark and she nodded before heading inside. She returned quickly, her face pale. "I can't do anything for anyone in there. Let's move on."

I watched her walk away, her shoulders stiffening as she skulked toward another door. I was about to ask her what she heard when she jumped, her hands and her feet clinging to the ceiling as the door blew open and a bloodied, snarling beast rushed out.

It skidded to a stop and turned its grotesque head toward me. Its face was covered with eyes, dozens of them that blinked at different times, making for an even more disturbing image. "You!" it growled.

It built up to a charge, but it never got to let itself loose. Lark dropped down onto it and without any ceremony, tore its head from its body.

I turned away, disgusted. "Does it have to be like this?"

"When your abilities finally kick in, you can kill them however you want. Right now, I don't have the time or the patience to be nice or neat about it," Lark said stiffly.

"Where'd Robert go?" I asked, my eyes darting down the hallway and finding it empty.

She was quiet, her eyes seeing nothing and yet seeing everything. "He's doing what he's got to do."

"What he's..." I looked away, my heart sinking. I knew what he was doing. The damage done here was too great to undo, and I had been naïve enough to believe that we could have prevented all of it.

"Grace, now's not the time to start feeling sorry for yourself; come on. We have to find the rest of them. There are at least a dozen more here; I can hear them, smell them."

Lark methodically began to open doors and charge into classrooms and offices. Screams and cries almost immediately followed. Sometimes a teacher would appear, sometimes two. It was so close to the beginning of school that everyone was in their classrooms preparing for the new year. Each time a familiar face would appear, dazed, in shock, or completely terrified, I'd speak as calmly as I could to them and then send them out the way we'd come in.

It was the safest route I knew because Lark had removed all of the threats already. I could hear their thoughts, feel their relief when they spotted the outside. But the moment they left the school, I lost them; I couldn't hear them, sense them. If they'd made it to safety of if I'd sent them straight to hell was unknown to me. I only knew they were gone.

Halfway down the hall, the screams were fading. Lark burst into a classroom, disappearing for no more than a second before flying backwards into a wall of lockers, crumpling them as though they were nothing but paper. I ducked, covering my head with my arms when a winged monster flew into her, its fists large and closed taking alternating blows to her head.

The lights in the hallway stuttered out and I saw the orange glow that surrounded it. I realized that this wasn't a monster at all. This was another angel.

"Hey!" I shouted as I lowered my arms.

With a grunt, it turned its head toward me, revealing large eyes the color of sea glass; foggy and pale green in color. It smiled, showing no teeth, the corners of its mouth lifting up to the crease of its eyes. *Grace...*

"Aaah!" I shrieked at the voice in my head, the way it burned, stabbed, and throbbed—it was everything that was pain. I began to back away, as though distance would help relieve the suffering.

*Wait.*

I felt my knees begin to buckle but I fought against falling. That was all I could give, though. I wasn't strong enough to keep moving. Two words, two single words had immobilized me. This wasn't good, especially if it was stronger than Lark.

*You're stronger than he is. You know how to stop him, just like you did the other one.*

Lark's thoughts in my head rang out, sharp and clear despite the fog of pain.

Of course I knew how. This wasn't just another angel, who only took orders from their call. This was a throne, whose call was to obey me.

"Put her down; stop hitting her," I commanded behind a grimace. My legs were quaking and the tips of my fingers were numb from straining against the pain in the rest of my body, but I was not going to let any of that show. "Put her down. You know you have to listen to me; you can feel it."

The throne looked at me, its face showing nothing but shock as it reluctantly did as I ordered. Lark fell to the ground, her body shaking from the sudden release.

"Now, come here," I gasped as it began to argue with me silently, each word cutting and slicing into my mind. "You can fight it but you won't win. I'm in control now."

*You lie.*

I nearly crumpled; each syllable was like being punched in the head. I had to stop it. "You won't think another word. You will only speak out loud. If you can't, then you will only respond by nodding or shaking your head. Is that clear?"

The angel nodded, although each bounce of its head was preceded with a roar.

"Good. I want you to find all of the monsters that are hiding in the dark and I want you to destroy them. Don't touch any humans; leave the humans alone. Protect them if you can, but do not do anything that might hurt them."

The angel growled at me, its eyes growing dark as its pupils widened. But it nodded and then turned around, running toward the stairs and disappearing. I hurried to Lark, who seemed dazed and in disbelief.

"Are you okay?" I asked as I took in her disheveled hair and strangely unmarred skin.

"I'll be fine. Zarus doesn't have permission to punish me so he couldn't really do anything; he just caught me off guard."

"Zarus? Really? Thomas too boring a name?" I quipped. "It's

strange; these thrones guys are huge. They're like the monsters that we see in those really crappy movies, you know? But they're not as scary as they look; not really."

"Well, nothing is scary when you can control them with a single word," Lark pointed out blandly. "Enough talking; we've got work to do."

She dashed ahead, finding classroom after classroom empty. I followed and listened as she did, my head held high, tilted slightly toward each hint of sound. I mimicked her as best I could, but each time she moved forward I could see where I fell short. She knew what she was doing – she'd done this before – but I wasn't so sure of myself.

I was so busy trying to listen for anything that sounded like someone in trouble that I tripped over my own feet. I fell, landing on my elbow and yelping, the cry carrying down the hallway and distorting the further away it got.

"Are you okay?" Lark called out, never stopping to look back.

"I'm fine," I groaned. "I just need to…pay attention."

I stood up and saw that my fall had torn the sleeve on my shirt. I ran to catch up to Lark, who was near the end of the hallway. She was frozen in front of an open classroom door—the first time she seemed unsure of what to do. She turned to face me, her eyes closed, her hands held out with her head shaking from side-to-side.

"Don't. Don't come any closer, Grace," she warned.

"Why? What's in there?"

"You don't want to see this."

Never tell someone as stubborn as I am that I don't want something.

I shoved my way forward, surprising Lark—and possibly myself—with my strength and determination and looked into the classroom, my feet locking in place the moment I saw what she didn't want me to see.

"Oh God…"

It was Madame Hidani's class. Or what *was* Madame Hidani's

class.

The windows had been blown out, and all of the French art posters that were on the wall were shredded and spattered with blood. The desks had all been overturned and piled up in the center of the classroom.

And they'd been set on fire.

"Madame Hidani?" I called out.

I heard her respond, but it wasn't her voice that came out. Instead, I heard her thoughts. They were peppered with pain and fear, but my voice, the sound of it calling for her, acted like a balm.

*He took my legs. He took my legs, Grace.*

I ran around the classroom but I couldn't find her. "Where are you?"

*He buried me.*

"Buried?"

My eyes couldn't see what my head was saying. She was buried, but how? And where?

"Grace, over there," Lark whispered, her eyes staring at the burning pile of desks.

"No..."

Lark clapped her hands, and like a candle that had been blown out, the flames disappeared behind an explosion of smoke. Together we tossed charred desk after charred desk to the side until we reached the broken and blistered body of my French teacher. She was weak and pale, her eyes staring out through wide pupils.

There was no blood, but there should have been. There should have been because she was right—her legs were missing.

"Who did this?" I asked as I knelt down beside her. "Who did it?"

"That's not important right now, Grace," Lark said softly. "She needs your help."

"My help? I don't...I don't understand. What can I do to help her?"

564

Lark took my hand and placed it onto Madame Hidani's chest. *She needs you to help end her suffering.*

I tore my hand away and stared through shocked eyes at the beautiful angel who looked at me as though she was surprised by my reaction. "You're crazy. You're out of your mind if you think I'm gonna-"

"She's in pain, Grace. She's going into shock and if you don't help her she's going to die a very painful death; your mother would have-"

"I'm not my mother and I never will be! I can't do what she did. I *won't*."

I fell beside Madame Hidani and held her head so that I could look into her eyes. "I'm going to get you help. I promise—you're not going to die."

"You can't make that kind of promise, Grace," Lark warned. She grabbed my arm, yanking it before stopping, her eyes locked on her hand. "Your elbow…it's black."

I looked down and saw the dark webbed bruising that covered the joint like a patch. "I know."

"You *know*? What do you mean, you *know*? Does Robert know?"

I tugged at the sleeve of my shirt, trying desperately to cover the slowly spreading blackness. "Yes."

Lark's face filled with panic. "What about Robert? Has the brui-"

She couldn't finish. She already knew the answer; the curse of the Innominate had returned.

"Oh Grace. I'm sorry. I thought…"

I shook my head and returned my focus to my injured teacher. "It doesn't matter what any of us thought. What matters is that we end this and we end it now. Help me pick her up."

"She's in shock, Grace. She can't be moved."

"She can't stay here either. Whoever got to her might still be out

565

there."

*It was Salsa. Salsa did this to me.*

In any other situation, in any other life, those words would have made me laugh. Instead, I didn't know whether to cry or simply give up.

"Shawn? Shawn did this to you?"

*He's not himself anymore. He's different. He's dangerous. You have to leave before he comes back.*

"He's not half as dangerous as I am," Lark said with a growl before turning on her heel and rushing out of the room.

"Lark! Wait!" I called out but she was gone. I slipped my arms beneath my teacher's body and lifted. I was prepared to strain and grunt with the struggle but she seemed to float up without any effort, as though she weighed less than a baby.

"I'm going to put you someplace safe."

*I'm going to die, aren't I?*

"No," I answered with more certainty than I think I was allowed. "No, you're not going to die. You're going to be fine. You're going to be more than fine."

*I don't want to die, Grace. I don't do dying well.*

I ran out of the classroom, sensing more than hearing the footsteps that were heading toward me from the end of the hallway. Robert was approaching, his face emotionless, his eyes focused on the injured woman in my arms. He wanted her.

"No. No, you can't have her," I said before turning around and running in the opposite direction.

I knew he would follow, but I didn't care. All I could see was the wall of police officers and paramedics standing outside the school. I moved as quickly as I could, faster than I think anyone believed possible, and didn't stop until I felt the sun on my skin and hands at my side, reaching and grabbing for Madame Hidani, whose thoughts had grown quiet.

"Help her," I said to the paramedic who began working on her the minute she was on the ground. "Help her, please."

"Are you alone? Is there anyone else in the school?" a police officer asked as a pinpoint of light passed from one eye to the other. "Are you okay? Are you hurt? Are there any more people in there? Do you know what's going on?"

"I...I can't..."

I backed up, pulling away from the groping and grasping hands, shaking my head as I avoided the gazes of the curious, the fearful, the worried.

"Wait!" one of them called out. "Don't go back in there!"

But it was too late. I was already inside.

Robert's hands now replaced those of the officers outside, but it was harder to face him than it was the others.

"Why didn't you let me help?" he asked softly.

"Because the kind of help you want to give wasn't the kind of help she needs."

"Grace, I know you care about her, but she's not going to survive her injuries. I could have made the pain go away. I could have ended her suffering."

I forced myself to look at him, forced myself to confront his words. "Why does it always come to that? Ending someone's suffering means ending their life? What if they don't want to die?"

"No one wants to die, Grace. Even those begging for it don't want it."

"But she wasn't begging for it. She told me she doesn't want to die. If she can tell me that through all that pain then why can't you respect that?"

"Because that's not what I am!" he snapped.

"No, it's not—it's what *I* am," I barked back.

His face crumbled instantly with remorse over his tone.

"I'm sorry. I didn't mean to speak to you like that."

"I know. You can't help it..."

He nodded and then looked down at my arm, noticing the same bruising that Lark had. "It's moving faster this time," he said softly, his thumb stroking the darker webbed lines that ran up my forearm, peeking slightly past the end of the sleeve at my wrist, like feelers.

"We have to hurry," I murmured, seeing the same darkness covering his entire left hand.

"Grace, you know that there's nothing we can do to fight this-"

"There's everything we can do," I argued stubbornly. "I'm not giving up; not this time."

I began stomping down the hallway, listening to Robert call out after me but not responding. I headed up the stairs, ignoring the rush of teachers and faculty that ran past me hysterically.

"Grace-"

The second floor of the school was covered with sheets of bloodstained paper that lay scattered between tumbled lockers and beneath shattered glass. Screams and sounds of shuffling feet bounced off the bare walls as more people ran toward the stairs in a mad dash for their lives.

Lark could be seen flitting from one classroom to another, sending people rushing out as the sounds of a struggle and then the unmistakable tearing of flesh and breaking of bones that followed answered any question as to what was happening.

"Shawn?" I heard her call out, her voice and her thoughts acting like a loudspeaker throughout the school. "I know you're in here. I can hear your crappy jokes in my head."

"She's going to kill him," I worried as I ran toward the taunting thoughts.

"She has to," Robert reminded, his body floating beside me as I reached the math class I'd had my freshman year.

"No, she doesn't."

"I told you, Grace-"

"I know what you told me. I know. But this is Shawn. This is Salsa; he's our friend—he's *my* friend."

Robert grabbed me, stopping me from going any further and forcing me to look at him. "He *was* our friend, Grace. What he is now is

568

something completely different, something dangerous and desperate. Those two things will erase any ties our friendship might have formed."

"I don't believe you," I said defiantly before pulling away. "That girl in Graham's house…she didn't want to hurt me. She wouldn't have, either."

"You don't know that."

"I did; I *do*. I could hear her thoughts like you can hear mine. She wanted to go back to normal, but not if normal meant being a killer."

"Shawn's already hurt one person; he'll never be normal after that. No one who survives today will."

I frowned at the finality of his words. "I don't believe that. Not anymore. Normal isn't something that's permanent. Normal changes—I'm proof of that."

"But you're different, Grace; you know that."

"I know. I know I'm different. But so is everyone else. Everyone is different and everyone is exactly the same, and I'm done trying to figure it all out because none of it matters! I'm not going to give up on my friends just because they're different. They didn't give up on me."

Robert's face grew serious—ferociously so—before softening, conceding. "You're right."

He disappeared, moving so quickly I didn't even see him leave.

"Robert?" I called out, listening for him in the sudden silence. "Lark?"

Nothing.

And then came the screams as several teachers burst out of a classroom, their faces covered in blood. I didn't know if it was theirs or not; I could only see the terror in their eyes as they rushed past me, escape their only concern.

Lark emerged, furious, her feet floating inches off the ground as she glowed a bright red in the dim hallway. Her thoughts were just as angry.

*You think this is how to save us—save everyone—by sparing him?*

*He's trying to kill Grace, and he doesn't care who he hurts to get to her.*

Robert appeared, his hand gripping a limp body, his own floating above the ground as well. *He's scared. He's been turned against his will and thrown into our world without any explanation and with the lies of our grandfather in his head. We failed to protect him as a human—we can't just give up now that he's not one any longer.*

Lark's hand flew out in an exaggerated point. *Did you see what he did? Did you see what he did to that woman?*

*Yes. Did you see what our grandfather did to him?* Robert lifted the body up, and I felt my teeth clench over my lips, a poor attempt to stifle the cry that demanded to come out.

Shawn—or what had once been Shawn—looked like he'd been turned inside-out. He had no eyes, no mouth…no face.

And yet, I knew it was him. I knew it. I could feel it. Sense it. Even without the abilities that I was slowly accepting, I would have known it was Shawn—the carefree spirit that existed in him couldn't be ignored.

*He can't exist the way he is. He's not like the others, who can pass for normal in this world. Look at him—what kind of life are you giving him by letting him live? What kind of future are you giving anyone by letting him live?*

Lark's thoughts rang with truth, and it was hard to ignore that. But Robert did.

*The human world might reject him, but ours shouldn't, especially when we're the reason for this. He'll never live the life he might have had, but we owe it to him to at least give him a chance. When did we stop being angels and start being demons?*

*When we forgot that evil can exist in our kind just as much as it can in humans,* Lark responded, her thoughts cold.

*You never forgot. Not after Luca.*

Lark nodded at Robert's quiet statement. *And I never will. Luca's death should have been taken as a warning of what was coming. Instead, we all took it as a warning against ourselves.*

She turned her attention to me, saw my anxiousness mixed with fear and concern, and frowned. "We're not going to kill him...yet. I only hope you understand the risk to everyone else by doing this."

My voice was just as serious when I replied, "There's no risk involved when it means saving not only the life of someone you care about, but also your own soul."

Robert hefted Shawn's body over his shoulder effortlessly. "Zarus has returned to join the others. He's destroyed everything that isn't human; the damage that has been done today cannot be undone by our kind."

"No, but it can be by ours," a woman said in a loud, booming voice.

I turned to look at her, frowning slightly when I recognized her as Dad's sister.

"What are you doing here?" I demanded to know.

"This is what we do," she answered simply. "You make messes, and we clean them up."

She walked casually over to Robert's side and looked up at Shawn's grotesque features. "This...this we can't fix. But we know how to make problems like this go away."

This confused me. "What do you mean by that?"

"We keep the secrets of your kind. We protect you. We defend you because we are the chosen; we are electus patronus."

Around her, more faces appeared. They belonged to individuals dressed as police officers, paramedics, fire fighters...

"What are you going to do?" I asked nervously.

"What we always do. The survivors will be treated, their accounts taken, and then the records destroyed. There will be no trace of anything evil happening here. The dead will be explained, and their families, as well as those that have been injured, will be compensated."

One-by-one, the people filed past us, inspecting, cleaning, moving like machines. Even though I couldn't imagine where to begin or how, they did it wordlessly. They knew exactly what to do, and they did it with military precision. They'd prepared for this.

*That's what EPs of the dark ones are supposed to do. It's because of them that humanity remains virtually ignorant of the dark side of our world.*

"Well, they do it pretty damn well," I remarked at Robert's thoughts.

*Sometimes too well.*

We only watched for a few minutes the movements of the electus patronus before Robert notified us that we had to go; this battle was over, but the real fight hadn't even begun.

"Before you leave, I have to tell you-" Jessica took a hold of my arm, her fingers wrapped tightly around my elbow "-your father does not know what you are going to do, but we do."

"What do you mean you know what I'm going to do? I don't even know what I'm going to do."

Jessica's eyes flicked over to Robert's, who hissed at the thoughts that filled her mind. "There is nothing wrong with being selfish; nothing. Embrace what you are."

"Why...why do you suddenly care about what happens to me?"

"We've always cared. You just never needed our help until now."

"I never needed your help? Are you kidding me? What about all those times I almost died?"

Jessica snickered. "Is that all? Despite what you may think, you were never in any danger."

"What?" I asked, incredulously.

Her smile faded and her voice lowered as she repeated, "You were never in any danger; not until you and Robert finally met, that is."

## BLACK HALO

Robert was quiet on the short flight to the field. Shawn's body was draped over his back, still unconscious; still grotesque.

I held on to Lark's neck, feeling my weight, knowing that she felt it, too. She was silent, her thoughts closed off to me.

How strange to be able to read minds and yet not hear a single word. The quiet only made what was coming that much more dreadful. Jessica's last words to me before we'd left her to clean up after us weren't enough to keep me from feeling alone.

"Your mother was right."

Four little words have never seemed so painless and yet so painful at the same time. She wasn't right. No one who could put their daughter through so much pain could ever be right.

*Hold on!*

The shattering of one's thoughts by a command so harsh and demanding literally felt like being glass. A jolt ran through me, straight from Lark's body, as we tumbled from the sky to the ground. Lark landed first, using her body to shield me from the impact of the fall, the grass turning into walls of dirt as we sank into the ground, not by inches, but by feet.

I felt like I'd been sucker-punched, and a part of me thought for a second that Erica was still alive and here, but there was no time to dwell on that or even to catch my breath; Lark pushed me up out of the hole we were in and immediately put me against her back.

*Stay by my side.* Her wings were out and she tucked me between them, blocking my view of what was around us with white fluff.

*What's going on?*

*He is here, my grandfather. So are the others.*

I couldn't see anything; only trust her thoughts as we moved swiftly over the ground, the sound of fighting slashing through the visions that burst through like explosive slideshows, bloody scenes that made my skin turn clammy and my heart race to catch up.

A shadow appeared overhead, and I looked up. A face broke through the gap in the wings and a mischievous grin filled a face that was unfamiliar to me.

"'Allo, little witch. Let's have a little fun w'ya!"

A small hand appeared and grabbed at my hair. I struggled but the strength that was attached to that hand was unlike anything I'd ever felt before. Lark's wings tried desperately to clamp onto me, but there was no fighting this creature's need.

"Lark!" I screamed, but she was unable to do anything but watch, horrified. Her arms and her legs were held immobile by matching imps, their bodies small but their strength immeasurable. Even her wings were being forced closed.

"Stop fussing and stay still," the small creature said as it dragged me across the ground toward a slight clearing in the chaos. "It'll be over soon. Raphael's quick when he wants to be."

I wasn't about to listen; not to him.

My hands reached down and grabbed one of the spindly little legs that pushed his tiny body along. I closed my eyes and braced myself, saying a quiet apology before I twisted, the sound of snapping and the sharp cry of pain followed. Immediately the pressure against my head eased and I stopped moving.

I jumped up and began to run in the opposite direction, back toward Lark, who seemed swallowed up now by replicas of the creature that had taken a hold of me. All around me fights took place between winged angels and creatures that looked like they'd fallen out of some kind of fairy tale book.

There were faces I didn't recognize, and then faces of those I did. Some of the guests that had been at Hannah's wedding were here, fighting. Strange winged creatures were appearing and disappearing in puffs of smoke as they avoided blows by what looked like giants with arms the size of tree trunks.

I saw Graham run between two wolf-like figures, his arm crooked against his chest, an invisible football in his hand. I wanted to cheer him on at the same time I wanted to tell him to find somewhere safe to hide. But even as he dodged snarling, jaw-snapping creatures who were trying to kill him, I could see others who were helping him, taking advantage of his actions and picking off his attackers one-by-one.

There was death and dying happening all around me, the bodies of those that *could* die littering the ground with their blood and their filth, while the bodies of those who had already been dead and were just existing in pieces shook and shivered on the ground, nothing now but nerves and hatred.

But what horrified me wasn't that. It was seeing angel against angel, over and over again all around me. Wings were wrapped around bodies like shields, while others were held high, swinging back and forth like giant blades that made slicing sounds with each arc in the air.

Those that I knew were fighting to keep me alive were outnumbered by those who wished me dead, and the outcome seemed plain to me.

The ground began to rumble, the sky crackling with angry white lines as storm clouds that had no purpose other than to disguise the hell being created right here in the middle of Heath crept in. It seemed like the thunder that boomed out went directly through me, my body shaking, my feet wobbling despite my boots.

I looked ahead, charging toward Lark even as she disappeared beneath a mountain of imps. And then the ground erupted, the red-fleshed creatures being tossed into the air like lava spewed from a fiery volcano, while Lark rose up, her white wings acting like a cap of snow as the peak rose up with her.

"Are you kidding me?" I shouted when she stood up, her face showing nothing but smug satisfaction.

"Vanessa came through!" she called back before leaping down, her wings fluttering open behind her.

The small mountain that had formed beneath her now burst open, a writhing mass of roots and vines emerging from the top. The ends twitched and twirled, grabbing outward—no, not grabbing, opening—and from its center emerged a silhouette of a woman who was as beautiful as she was terrifying.

She looked like Bala, with jet black eyes and skin the color of new leaves, but her hair wasn't made of the same moss that Bala's hair was. Instead, thin replicas of the vines that swirled around her curled and wiggled like tiny snakes. They stretched to accommodate her nude body, covering as much as they were revealing.

"Who is that?" I asked as Lark reached my side, her wings moving to shroud me.

"That's Ampy. She's kind of like a hormonal version of Bala."

"A hormonal-"

I stopped speaking as Ampy moved, her body carried by the dozens of vines that slithered beneath her. Her hands, attached to long, lithe arms pointed gracefully at the red little demons that charged toward her, angry that their attack had been thwarted. From her fingertips, tiny wisps of green shot out, floating in the air and growing, increasing in length and width until they resembled faceless snakes.

One by one, those vines found a target, coiling around each one tighter and tighter until tiny pops could be heard. I cringed and looked away, my eyes widening as a strange scene took place just feet in front of me.

A monster with a horse-like face—an exact replica of the erlking that had tried to kill me in the woods the night of Janice and Dad's wedding—was fighting hand-to-hand with what looked like its twin. Their hands were covered in long, course-looking hair, and each swipe at each other was oddly beautiful to see, the flowing waves of alternating colors contrasting greatly with the ugliness of their overly long jaws, and the blood targets that red-rimmed eyes reminded me of.

But even though they looked so similar, one was smaller than the other. The larger one seemed more comfortable with its body, much more attuned to what it was. It moved quickly, its body changing to fit the need—a sharp-clawed paw, a long, thick tail, a sharper-toothed jaw—and when it attacked it did so with excellence.

But the smaller one was faster, sharper. Its reactions were so precise that I almost didn't care what side it was fighting for—I wanted it to win just to see how it would do it.

The larger erlking crouched, its large ears twitching at every sound around it. Its eyes were unblinking, staring purposefully at its smaller opponent with such deep concentration that even when dirt from a battle taking place just half a foot away flew into its face, it didn't flinch. And then, without any warning it sprung, the motion chock full with such energy, I felt the ground vibrate with it. But the smaller one had anticipated it, anticipated such a charged and forceful attack, and merely stepped aside, appearing almost bored by the maneuver.

My jaw fell open.

"That's Stacy!" I shouted.

Lark didn't respond. She simply leapt into action, her body so quick that I didn't know where she ended up until I heard the sickening thud of the larger erlking's body falling dead beside me.

She stood beside Stacy, her shoulders held back with pride as she looked at Stacy, whose hands held in them things I didn't want to recognize. Lark's eyes found mine and dilated to near black.

*Look out!*

I didn't have time to react. All I heard was the air giving up its place in my lungs.

The ground and I became intimate, the feel of dirt and grass in my face a sort of baptism. Immediately, I was turned over, the darkening sky enhancing the red glow that surrounded the face that looked down at me with a strange glee.

"I didn't think it would happen this easily," the voice said with malice tinged joy.

"What would happen; that you'd end up in the mud where you belonged?" I cracked.

Raphael grinned. "The coming of your end. Your very existence in this life and the next will be wiped clean; despite what you see, you are a nobody to these pathetic creatures. They are not fighting for you; they are fighting for themselves. They don't care about you; to them, you are nothing; to the world, you will soon be nothing."

His hands dug into my shoulder, and he lifted me up, holding me high so that I could see the destruction going on around me, but it wasn't what I feared. We were winning. Mrs. Mayhew was standing in a clear circle, a clipboard in her hand, a pen ticking off names left and right, a smile going up with one tick, a sad little frown with another.

Dozens of holes had been dug into the ground, with roots and vines strategically pulling creatures into them, the sounds of muffled terror erupting from the darkness. I didn't want to, but against my will I could see and hear the thoughts of each one of them before their minds turned black with death.

Raphael sneered. "You see? Despite what you have been told, you can do nothing for them. You cannot bring them peace—you are not your mother's child. You are weak in every way imaginable: weak in the mind, weak in the heart, and weak in the spirit. It is as though Avi took every flaw that existed in her creation and magnified it in you."

He threw me down. I was unprepared for this and landed awkwardly, my leg bending in a way it was never meant to and the resulting snap seemed to signal a blanketing quiet over the field of death and destruction.

From that silence, I heard the cries and the thoughts of those that mattered most as they moved to reach us, though every word, every thought, every action sounded like it was being played at one-tenth the normal speed. In the time it took for Raphael to take me down, lift me, and then drop me, less than a few seconds had passed. His words, what I had seen, time seemed to have slowed down just for that moment, and I saw his smile at my recognition.

Beside him appeared the other three: Michael, Uriel, and finally, Gabriel.

"Time passes so quickly for most creatures," Uriel said in a bored tone. "Humans, animals, even angels fail to appreciate just how malleable it is."

Raphael nodded. "For us, for the four who existed before even man, time refuses to obey its own principles. You merely experience it because we allow you to; the others experience time as it should be and know no difference. It is why I will be able to kill you before they even hear my thoughts."

"Why are you letting him do this?" I cried out to the stoic faces that flanked Raphael. "Why aren't you stopping him? Michael—Robert called you his friend; why aren't you stopped Raphael? Why would you do this to us?"

Michael and Uriel said nothing, but Gabriel broke his silence.

"Why would we stop him?"

"Because you're angels! Because you're supposed to care about humans! Because you're supposed to care, period! Because you cared about my mom!"

Gabriel's voice thickened as he sneered. "Your mother betrayed us...for humans. She was born into our fold, given everything she could ever desire, and she left it to marry a human and give birth to you. She broke the circle—she broke us. It is *because* I care for her that I do this."

"Did you honestly think that you'd be able to stop us?" Raphael laughed. "Did you honestly believe that your *love* and your *friends* would somehow give you the advantage over tens of thousands of years of knowledge and power? Your mother was a traitor, and it is time that those she betrayed us for suffer the consequences."

I stood up on my good leg and hobbled toward them, my eyes darting from one to the other, trying to understand. "Why do you want to destroy the world so much? Why do you hate us?"

"Destroy it? We don't want to destroy it. Why destroy what you want to control?"

I snorted. "You want to control the world? And how are you supposed to do that? The world isn't yours to control. The world belongs to humans, not to angels. Humans are the ones whom the animals see and respect. Humans are the ones that were given the choice to choose their own destinies and not suffer the complete rejection of their own kind for it."

He was beside me in a heartbeat, his head level with mine as he stooped to look me in the eyes, the last remaining light glimmering in the hatred that turned his pupils an impossible black. "And that has been the problem from the very beginning. Humanity is a virus. For tens of thousands of years we have watched mankind eat each other alive. They were given freedom and they used it to hate and create suffering like nothing ever known."

"That's funny, because I seem to recall a story about how angels were the reason for the single most destructive act this world has ever known," I pointed out smugly.

Uriel snarled. "Humans caused that. If not for humans and their incessant breeding, there would have never been a need for the Grigori. Without humans, the there would have been no Nephilim, or the desire to create them, and with no Nephilim, the flood would have never been deemed necessary.

"Do you think that it was easy to warn the humans but not my own kind? To allow those wretches to live while my brothers and sisters, my own child died beneath the waters?"

"You said that humanity was worth saving, remember?" I reminded him.

580

"Yes. And it was; for *us* to control. Who do you think created your history? Who do you think gave you stories to tell? We created the dreams, the heroes, the nymphs-"

"Nymphs? That was you? You did that to Bala? To the others?" I exclaimed in shock.

"Of course it was! Do you think anyone else capable of creating something so fantastical? Humans have no sense of creativity or imagination. Everything you've ever dreamed of came from us, and then you demand us fulfill them!"

Raphael's voice rose above Uriel's. "We have long been at the beck and call of humanity but no more! Angels will return to the top of the hierarchy of this world; the first circle will once again be the leaders of man and man will return to being the lesser creatures they were meant to be."

I looked behind me and saw the fear in Robert's face despite the slowness of his movement. "You're not doing this for angels. None of you are! You're doing this for yourself! Look at what you're doing to your own kind; look at what you're doing to your own grandson!"

"My grandson?" Raphael laughed. "He is no more my grandson than you are your father's daughter. His life is no more valuable to me than yours. He is a cancer, a plague that has been unjustly awarded the most coveted of roles. But...that will change. Time, as I have said, is ours to control."

My face pinched with confusion at his words. "What do you mean by that?"

My eyes were still locked on Robert's face, but even as he seemed frozen in place, his features were changing as quickly as a breath is taken. His eyes turned from a deep silver to black in an instant; dark orbs that stared determinedly at me. His skin darkened to a brilliant onyx, his suddenly blue glow reflecting off of it like a kind of ethereal bruise.

He had looked this way once before, and my heart convulsed when I remembered what had happened as a result. But this time, things were different. His wings began to creep out of him slowly, but not like the wings I was used to. Instead, they emerged like blackened claws from his back; sharp, pointed, and eerily beautiful.

"You see? Even if you had somehow succeeded in delaying us, you would never have succeeded in delaying his fate. Only we control that."

I shook my head, tears forming and falling from my eyes as I fought the blur that distorted everything. "No. You won't hurt him. I won't let you."

"Ahh…but you can't stop him from hurting others." This was said so sweetly I almost didn't catch it.

But then I saw Robert's attention turn to something else; or someone else as time returned to normal. Two figures were moving toward him, their faces filled with concern, their thoughts unrelenting in their wish to help him.

Graham and Stacy, her face still somewhat distorted though her body had returned to normal; both had their hands held up in supplication; their voices were calm and subtle.

"Easy, Robert. Easy," Stacy told him. "It's us, your friends, remember? Stacy? Graham?"

"Yeah. I'm your brother-in-law; we're buds!" Graham added.

Stacy's movements grew more stealthy, her limbs lengthening to prepare for anything. Her eyes darted to Lark's, who stood behind her brother, her arms and her wings ready to react at a single thought. And, it seemed, Robert thought it.

Lark moved, her wings closing over her brother like a cape, her face disappearing behind the wall of white and the erasure of black. I limped forward, the words in my throat being stolen away by the laughter that boomed behind me.

"It is too late. It is all too late! You can stop nothing!" Uriel mused.

The struggling form of Lark and her shuttered wings were just a few feet away from me; I could almost smell the powdery scent of the white feathers that fluttered from the struggle taking place beneath them. And then a piercing, bone shattering scream broke out. Lark's wings flew open in a burst of feathers and light. She fell backwards as one wing hung limply to her side, bent and broken, while the other...

The other wing lay on the ground, separate from her body which now bore a charred stump. She clutched at the stump with a mangled hand, her eyes seeing what ours did. She cried out, her thoughts almost as loud as her voice to get away, but Graham had already seen enough, and Stacy could not disobey her own nature.

Together, the two of them sprang toward Robert angrily.

I saw his face, saw the dark sneer form on his lips, and knew that this was not going to end well.

"No!"

*No!*

Momentum is often thought of as something physical; but it also something emotional. You feel it within you, like a battering ram that is pushing forward toward its destination. It does not want to stop, doesn't know how to stop, until it bursts down the doors that were never meant to be closed.

That is what brought me to this place, where the lives of my friends and the soul of the person I loved the most mattered more than the promise I'd made to myself. There was no compromise, no time for consideration or thought. Every increment of time was precious and could not be wasted. And, I suppose, even if I had wanted to hesitate...I couldn't.

Because momentum is destiny. You can do nothing to stop it, nothing to avoid it. You simply struggle to ignore it, force yourself to endure the pain that is the delaying of it until your feet and your conscience give in and you find yourself hurtling toward the end of the world.

And this was my destiny. It had been from the very beginning.

I moved past Graham with awkward speed, seeing his confused expression and hearing his gasps of fear. I pushed him aside as I bit through the pain that shot through my body with every jerk of my broken leg. His body gave like water to my dedicated intrusion and I shoved even harder, watching him fall to the ground in muted shock. There was no time to apologize or explain; he would just have to understand that this was for the best.

Stacy's face was frozen in outrage as she watched me pass her by. The length of her jaw had not returned to normal, and she still bore a slight reddish hue around the dark brown of her eyes, but I knew her thoughts, knew her voice, and it was to her that I mouthed a farewell to. I had just enough strength in me to throw her back as she reached for my arm.

Momentum is what kept Robert moving as well, his own fate tied to mine. His mouth was open in a roar, a dark cave of what had once been filled with kind words now only filled with rage. There was no room in him for love any longer; Raphael had made sure that Robert would not recognize me when he sped up the effects of the Innominate.

It took everything I had not to break down as I took in the shadowed remains of the angel who'd shown me how to accept who I was and what I was. This was for him as much as it was for me. I said nothing, thought nothing as finally we collided.

My hands reached out to him, hopelessly wanting once more to touch the unmoving spot beneath his chest, a final reminder of what he had given up for me. His wings, once beautiful, glossy arcs of ebony feathers, were now daggers that he drove straight toward me.

And into me.

The crushing, crunching sound of flesh and bone seemed to signal a halt to everything else around us. Everything that had eyes and could see had locked onto me, and not even the sound of breathing could be heard over my own pained gasps.

I looked down, my hands gripping onto the blackened spines that jutted through my chest and abdomen. I reached behind me and felt the tips poking through, the stickiness of blood running down my back and soaking my clothes. I coughed involuntarily, and watched as red foam spilled past my lips, dripping onto the black and deepening in color.

"Grace?"

My head lifted at the sound of Robert's voice. I felt a jolt and then a slow, wet pull as his wings retreated, disappearing into his back that grew lighter with each passing second. A gush of warmth spilled out of me, flowing quickly and purposefully down my body and onto the ground.

Robert's eyes had already cleared, his face now marked with the webbing that I was so familiar with as his voice regained the emotion that I believed had died.

"Oh God, Grace—what have I done?" he cried out as I collapsed into his arms. His hands moved to cover the holes that his wings had left, but there were too many. "I'm going to heal you."

I tried to shake my head, finding myself only capable of moving it just a fraction. *No. Don't.*

"What? You can't ask me not to."

A heavy, pressing weight seemed to have found one side of my chest, while a pulsing, drowning crush seemed to appear on the other. *Look...look at your hands.*

His eyes dropped quickly to see that black no longer showed through the blood that covered them. "That means nothing to me. I don't care about myself, Grace; I only care about you. You should have done the same! You promised me that you would live, remember? You promised *us*. My God, you're-"

Weakly, I raised my fingers to his lips. *Shh. There was no fighting this. I was stupid to think that I knew better.*

His eyes grew glassy, his voice cracked. "You can't leave me, Grace. You can't. You promised you wouldn't..."

My fingers dragged down his chin and finally found the spot I had been looking for. The silence, the unmoving flesh beneath the soiled and bloodied shirt he wore had always been a strange comfort just as it had always been a stinging reminder of what love demanded as payment.

I had never had a problem paying that price. It was well worth it.

Breathing suddenly became an impossibility; my body convulsed as my lungs collapsed under the weight of so much damage to them. My heart stuttered and skipped, tumbling in the open cavity that was my chest and I did nothing to will it to fight. Instead, I only struggled to keep my eyes open and my vision clear long enough to look into the silver rings that encircled the endless love that had always existed in his eyes and found, through the numbness, the pain, the fire, the ice, life, and death, the strength to say...

*Goodbye...*

# AVI

I am born. Is this what man experiences at birth as well; this sudden and strange need to feel the light on one's flesh and the sweet air in one's chest? Is this what life is? It is no wonder that I feel a need to hold on to it with both hands and cling to it like a star clings to the sky.

A scratching sound whispered to my right, and I looked between the leaves and branches of bushes that tried to hide its secrets behind them. Humans! Human children! They are beautiful in their preciousness. What is it that makes them so sweet to look at? I felt a yearning to touch them, and without thought they came to me, eager to do the same.

I hurried to their sweet sides and gathered them in my arms, feeling the warmth beneath their skin like a dawn that I had yet to experience. This was happiness; I was certain of it. To smell their sweetness and hear their breaths-

"Why are you not breathing?" I asked when I felt their stillness.

"My babies!" a shriek sounded.

Death. Humans know it the moment it arrives. And it has touched them—*I* have touched them.

"They are not moving! They are not breathing! What did you do to them?" their mother demanded to know.

"I...I believe I have ended their lives."

"Ended? Ended?"

She was as horrified as she was confused, but she knew that end did not mean anything different than when it is used to speak of animals.

"I did not mean to do it, and they did not suffer."

"Suffer?" This word seemed to spark a fire within her, and she began to weep tears, thick like jewels.

"I am...I am sorry," I said in supplication. "I did not know that this would happen. I only wanted to hug them."

"You...you ended them! You killed them!" The mother's cries were like thorns in my chest, pricks that spread through my body, burning, feeding until it formed a circle of fire at my back.

I cried out, hearing for the first time my own pain. This task that I had been born for, this unyielding need to fulfill cannot be mine. Nothing this destructive to one's soul could be a blessing. It was unbearable, unforgiveable. And it was consuming. It ate at me, destroying faith and renewing it as my divine body was rendered to pieces, two dark protrusions emerging from my torn flesh like arms that reached toward the sky.

*We are here, new one. We are here to guide you.*

How strange and brilliant a sound, those words that filled my tortured mind. *Is this what it means to be joined in thought?*

"We have confirmation that she can think—can she speak?"

"If by speak you mean open my mouth, then yes, I can," I replied.

I saw them, the four who came before me. They watched me curiously while keeping their thoughts quiet, sharing them only with each other. Was I so different? Was I so unique?

"You are everything that is different," said one whose face was so gloriously dour, I will never allow it to leave my memory.

"Then different is exactly what I want to be," I said firmly.

"We cannot call you that, for that is not your name. You are to be called-"

"Avi, I know. It sings in my veins," I finished for him, my eyes focusing on the frightened mother who hid once more in the bushes, unwilling to leave so long as the bodies of her children remained.

"I am Gabriel."

The others surrounded him, their faces each bearing looks that ranged from pleased to bored.

Gabriel turned to them and held out his hands in introduction. "This is Michael, Raphael and Uriel. We are the first four, the inner circle, the-"

"I get it. You are the leaders and I am to be the tail on the beast."

The one named Uriel laughed, a strange sound that I'm certain would not resemble any laugh I would hear again. "You are different in ways that defy the very makeup of our kind. If there can be a word to describe you, it would be…obstinate."

"Yes. That is it," agreed the one named Michael. "Obstinate would be a perfect word, judging by her thoughts and her actions."

"What about defiant? Or selfish?" asked the one named Uriel. "Selfish?"

"Yes," Raphael said with authority. "You've taken the lives of these children, but you've left their mother to suffer."

He turned to the woman and spoke to her quietly. She grew angry, violent, but he did not seem fazed by her reactions. He whispered to her gently that her sacrifices were not wasted, and that she would never fear the same fate as her children.

Raphael took her in his arms, his voice calming her. "You are the first of your kind to be blessed this way. It is an honor that we will never forget."

She was the first wing-bringer and so, the first turned. She was the mother to loss and to creation and I owed her everything.

"You owe her nothing," Raphael said, dropping the woman's limp body on the ground. "She has been repaid; immortality will be hers forever. That is more than can be said for the rest of the world. You have a duty to fulfill. Your calling is to end the reign of immortal men. Why do you delay answering it?"

"How can this be what I am meant to do? Look at these faces," I demanded, dropping to my knees to cradle the dead children at my feet.

"Children grow up to be faceless. You have seen this—you were born with this knowledge. A child's death does not erase this fact."

"Leave her be, Raphael," Gabriel ordered. "She has seen what we've seen, yes, but until she experiences the sins of man herself, she will never understand."

"Then let her start understanding now," Raphael announced.

My body shook with understanding and obedience. This...calling, as Uriel described it, now took over the song that sang in me. Man must learn to fear death, it said, the words finding a rhythm that pulsed with the strange thumping in my chest.

"A reminder," Michael said with melancholy at my thoughts, "of what it means to exist. You are the first of us to have one. Consider it a gift."

"You do not have them?" I asked, amazed at this news that had not been revealed to me.

"There was never a need; we are not man's keepers," Gabriel said with a haughty sniff.

I brought my hand to my chest, feeling the strength of each beat. A fluttering began above my head, a sound that I was unfamiliar with even as each wave caused my body to push back and forth.

"Black...I should have known."

I looked up at Gabriel's comment and saw that his eyes were drawn to what flapped behind me. "I have black wings," I said in awe.

"They are glorious."

"But why?"

"Because you are meant to do the most sinful of acts—so sinful in fact that we are incapable of doing it—and we must never be allowed to forget just how different from us you truly are."

"As if her being female would simply slip past our thoughts," Michael quipped.

Uriel groaned. "Enough—we have an eternity to discuss the differences between us. Mankind cannot wait. Their eyes need to be opened and we finally have a way of doing that."

***

*I do not wish to be a mother. There are others that can bear children; why must it be me? Why can't God simply create more angels if there aren't enough of us?*

Gabriel looked at me with sadness in his eyes. *There will be no more angels created by God; not after the flood. He has left us to our own end.*

The ocean water was warm against my feet as I bathed them in their blue waves. We had come to bask in the beauty of the sea before the winter came over the earth once more and my calling pulled me away from the serenity that was simple comfort.

*The numbers make no sense then. We are allowed only one child. If we are ever to experience another flood, we will have too few left to have any effect on this world. Humanity needs us.*

The water fizzed as Gabriel placed his hands beneath its surface. "Humanity needs you. It does not need me or any of the others. We've long since outlived our purpose here."

"Is it safe to speak so freely?" I asked, surprised by his voice.

"What is there to keep secret? Who is there to fear? We are the first four. Well…five. There is only one way to remove us from power and since neither I, nor the others feel so inclined, we are able to speak as we wish."

"But you don't," I reminded. "You tell me things you do not share with the others."

"That is because you are different, my dear. There will come a time when you will find in us a reason to be distrustful and I want you to know that you can always, always trust me."

"That trust might be tested one day," I said softly.

"As all trust is," he returned. "But *mine* will never fail you."

*** 

*We have a strange friendship, you and I, Ameila. It is too similar to those that the humans share.*

Ameila was holding her son to her chest, his dark hair sitting atop his tiny head like a cloud of midnight. There was an ache in me as I looked at him, and at her. There was such an affection between them that I was a stranger to.

*When it comes to friendship, there has never been one for me except with you. You should know our kind holds no compassion for each other.*

I laughed at her words and nodded in agreement. *We are enigmas to our kind. Gabriel seems to think that what you and I share is unnatural.*

*Of course the old lion would think that while ignoring his friendship with you. He has never been one to accept and acknowledge his own hypocrisy. But the others have followed your lead, or have you failed to notice the changes in my father's behavior as of late?*

At this I nodded. *Perhaps it is because he is now a grandfather?*

Ameila's smile faded. *He does not accept N'Uriel as his own. I did not expect him to. He has, however, become quite attentive to me. I believe that when the time comes for me to find a mate and bear a child in the usual manner that he will be a most doting grandfather.*

My lips pursed in distaste for her words. *That is unfair to N'Uriel.*

*Unfair or not, it is the way of it. But it comes with a price—you and I both know this. We do not have children to encourage interaction with their grandparents; we have children to change the world.*

My thoughts drifted on their own to my son and I sighed. *If only we could choose their destinies before we gave birth to them, rather than having their destinies be laid out before they are even a thought in our minds.*

*We have too few choices as it is, and those we take for ourselves always end up hurting the innocent.*

The burn in my heart was almost unbearable. How humans tolerated it with so much despair in their lives was, to me, a miracle in itself, if I could barely keep the signs of it to myself. *Especially our children.*

Ameila placed her son on the straw mattress, her hand gently covering his head to shield his thoughts from what she was about to say.

"A parent, whether human or divine, will always hurt their children; especially during acts which are best for them. There is nothing we can do to prevent that once we choose to have them; we choose to bring them into a world where even amongst their own kind they will be vilified for their differences."

"And they will be the stronger for it," I said stiffly.

"You can never know that for certain. What we would do is not what our children would do. You know this better than anyone."

My mouth stilled at her words. She was correct, her wisdom never failing.

"I did not mean to offend you, my friend. But…you know that one day our children will face the consequences of their births, and the choices that we would have them make may very well be the choices they choose not to."

*We have many years of planning left to ensure that they do.*

"Yes, but we also have the same amount of years to ensure that they don't."

*Have you changed your mind then?*

Ameila's smile, always serene, always beautiful, appeared on her lovely face as she shook her head. "After speaking with my mother, and seeing the joy brought to my son's life, I cannot want anything else."

*Even though they will hate us when they learn of the truth?*

She paused, sadness crossing over her face for a brief moment before her smile returned. "Yes."

*Then we proceed as planned.*

\*\*\*

"Are you sure about this?"

"More sure than I've ever been in my life."

"Okay then. I'll go and put the bag in the car."

I reached for his hand, grabbing it firmly. "I love you, James. You are going to make a great father."

His eyes lit up at my words, his smile spreading so widely I could not help but do the same despite the pain in my belly.

"And I love you. Thank you for allowing me to be a father to our child," he said in return. "Now, let me go put that bag in the car, otherwise I'll forget and then you'll never let me hear the end of it."

"That is true," I laughed before grimacing as a rivulet of pain shot from my abdomen to my leg.

This was far different than the last birth I'd experienced. There had only been one moment of pain, a signal that it was time to release Samael to the world and then it was done: my womb split to allow his exit and then returned to normal, as though he'd never spent even an hour within me.

But with my Grace, every breath I took felt like I had just told an inexcusable lie. I tried to stand, a need to not feel so helpless taking hold, but lightning shot through me and I fell. This human body I had accepted broke too easily against the glass coffee table that stood in my way.

My wrist met glass, the two joining to release my human blood.

"Abby? Oh God, why did you move? That's it; I'm calling for an ambulance," James cried out. He ran to the kitchen, my bag still in his hand, his voice panicked as he fumbled with the small buttons that lined the phone's face.

My poor James; worried over nothing. It wasn't time yet. We still had many years to go before that day came.

"Wrap it up? O-okay!"

He was back at my side, tearing off a piece of his shirt to tie my wrist with. "I've gotta wrap up the cut."

"And then what?" I asked calmly, watching the bright red liquid pump out of my arm.

"And then—oh, I don't know!"

He dropped my hand and hurried back to the phone, his eyes showing fear and panic. "What do I do after it's wrapped up?" he asked hurriedly into the phone.

He nodded, looking at me the entire time. "Uh-huh. And then what? But she's pregnant—um…forty-one weeks. Yeah…yeah. Is she in labor? Yes!"

While he nervously chattered, I grabbed the torn piece of shirt and did my best to tie off my wrist and stop the bleeding. By now, the front of my dress was soaked with blood, and I could feel a strange lightness in my head.

Inside me I felt a fluttering. "Shh, my little love," I whispered to my belly. "Now is not the time to panic."

But my daughter wasn't about to listen. She was going to be as defiant and as stubborn as I was, and I knew that I didn't want her any other way. "Okay, fine. Do what you want, but promise me you won't make this hard on your father."

A sharp, searing pain crossed over the tightening in my belly in response, and I grabbed at it, sensing the heat that radiated from it. "This is *not* how you keep from worrying your father," I whispered as I bit back a groan.

"The ambulance is coming, honey!" James rushed, breathless from his concern and his explanation to the operator. "They'll be here in a few minutes."

"That's…good," I breathed.

"Abby? Ab…"

James' voice grew faint. I saw strange dots…

\*\*\*

"Mommy's asleep. You wore her out. I suggest you not cry any more so that she can sleep a bit longer."

I opened my eyes and saw them, the two of them, rocking in a wooden chair beside the bed. Father and daughter, cuddled up together, made for the most peaceful image I'd seen in a long time. It was one that gave me hope.

"Go back to sleep, Abby. I've got her."

"I can sleep when I'm dead. I want to hold her," I argued before stopping, my breath catching in my throat with a sudden worry. "Is she alright? Is something wrong with her?"

"Nothing is wrong," James said with a soft laugh. "She's perfect. Two eyes, a nose, a mouth, ten toes, and eleven fingers."

"Eleven?" I choked, reaching for the tiny pink bundle and pulling open the blankets to inspect my daughter's small hands, counting quickly; one, two...

"I'm joking, Abby! She's fine. She's perfect, like I said!"

I blinked as I saw that each tiny hand bore five little fingers. "She is perfect," I breathed with relief. "When...when did she come?"

"Yesterday. You fainted before the ambulance arrived and I...I panicked. I think I might have angered the paramedics and some of the doctors in the emergency room."

"Well," I chuckled, "hopefully we won't have to revisit that emergency room for a while so that they forget who you are. Did they have any trouble...getting her out?"

"No. There were no problems, no complications. Aside from you not being able to see it, everything went exactly as it should have. She came out healthy; she cried and I cried...I think even the doctor who hates me cried."

My eyes welled up. "So she's all right?"

"Yes."

I looked back down at our daughter, at her closed eyes and her pursed lips, full and pink, and I felt my heart swell. And, despite reassurances otherwise, I inspected my child, looking for any sign that something was wrong or different.

All I found was the hospital tag that was attached to her ankle, with names and numbers that labeled her as mine. Against my wrist was a matching band. It was the first, real piece of confirmation that she was, indeed, mine.

It was the only confirmation I would get when I remembered too late that I could not hear the thoughts in her head. We had shared a bond while she was within me, but it was one that I knew existed between all pregnant women and their children and nothing unique to me. But I had to admit that I had hoped that upon her birth, we would be able to speak like an angel mother and child would.

*But you're not an angel any longer,* I reminded myself.

"Is something wrong?"

I swaddled the baby in the pink blanket once more and shook my head. "Nothing is wrong. Grace is everything I imagined she would be and more."

"So you've decided for certain that her name is Grace?"

I nodded. "This world will be a better place because of her."

"This world is a better place because of her mother."

"Maybe once, a long time ago, that was true. Now they have her."

"Well, I have you both, and my world is perfect, so I suppose you're right. Hey, how's your wrist? They wrapped it up before they put you in the ambulance but I don't recall them checking it since."

"That's not important right now," I said with a shrug, handing Grace to him quickly. "Here. I think I'll take your advice and get some rest while I can."

"Okay."

Even without the pain that came with lying, I still felt the sting of guilt as I hid my hand beneath my pillow. And yet I still reasoned with myself that it was all for the best.

\*\*\*

*You do not understand what you are risking, Avi.*

"My name is Abby, now; I stopped being Avi years ago. And I

understand fully what I am risking, but it is a risk I have to take."

It's Valentine's Day. Only a few hours left.

*What if she doesn't make it out of the car? What if she stops you from dying before she can stop herself?*

"That won't happen. You won't let it."

*You seem so sure of that. Why should I help her; or you for that matter?*

"Because you know that this was how it is meant to be. You've seen it yourself. And because you love us."

Gabriel's face softened, his eyes sparkling in the remnants of night before the sun broached the horizon. *That I do. It is hard to pretend otherwise, but I do because I know to betray that would put you and every-thing that you have planned in jeopardy.*

"Do the others know? Do they suspect anything?"

*They only know that I come to bid a former pupil farewell. I have kept my resentment of you below excessive. I cannot pretend to hate you, but I can pretend successfully to despise your decisions.*

"And my child."

*Yes, and Grace. I dread the day when I must make her believe it, too. She will never know the truth about me.*

I put my hands on either side of his face and held them there. It had been a long while since I could force him to do what I wanted, but today I knew that whatever I wanted, he would do.

"She will know the truth about you, Gabriel. I will make sure of that."

*Yes, but will she know why you've done all of this? Or will she only live with the lie we will tell her?*

I heard some stirring upstairs and quieted my words. *She will learn the truth eventually: that the apocalypse that she is to be blamed for had already begun the moment Uriel warned Noah of the flood, and that the only way to stop it is to destroy the four who started it-*

*Four?*

*Yes...I will be gone by then, remember?*

*I forgot. I apologize.*

598

*Do not apologize to me, Gabriel. I am complicit in this as much as anyone. The killing that I did—the deaths that I caused covered this world in just as much evil as Raphael and Uriel's lies did; but she cannot know any of this until after she's made her choice. She cannot know what we've done. She must choose this life and she must do so out of love.*

*And what if she does not die the way she is meant to? What if Ameila's son does not return and she is destroyed by your son?*

A cloud of darkness hovered over my eyes as the doubt that I had once possessed returned. *Then she will be a part of the destruction of this world and we will have failed. But I do not believe that will happen; Ameila vowed that she would return. Grace and N'Uriel are destined to be together; night and day, life and death. It is more than we both had hoped for.*

*My only concern is that N'Uriel will falter. Whether by his own hand or by Ameila's soft heart, the chance that one of them will stop Grace from doing what she must is great. It is why, despite my friendship with Ameila, I've put all of my faith in you and Grace. She will be the one to succeed.*

*And if she doesn't?*

I turned my head to look at him. "Then you must make sure that she does. Whatever it takes. Don't let the choice be taken from her, Gabriel—I raised her as a human child to believe in human choices and free will. She must be allowed to make her own decision."

Gabriel's hand came up to cover mine, his fatherly concern plain. *Have you considered that maybe, just maybe she will simply die? That she has been raised as a human child because she is, in fact, human?*

My head tossed from side to side in disagreement. I pulled my hands away and turned them over, my wrists pointing up for the both of us to see. *Before she was born, I fell on a glass table, shattering it. I cut myself so badly in that fall that I fainted from the blood loss. When I awoke, the wound was gone.*

*And you believe that Grace did this while still inside you?*

I nodded. *She was fighting for her survival as much as she was mine. The light within her protects her, even when her mind fights against it. When her mortal body is finally gone and she has accepted fully what she is, she will have the ability to do far more than heal a laceration.*

*I believe you.* His thoughts covered my mind, comforting it with his faith.

My heart grew heavy when I heard more than just stirring upstairs. *James is awake. I have this one last morning with him before it is all over. I don't know how I will be able to tell him goodbye when he leaves for work.*

Gabriel's smile grew somber. *You will tell him the same way you told me, and you will do it with love. Thank you for allowing me this time with you. Thank you for giving me your last night*

*Thank you for being my guide, my mentor, and the father I always needed. We shall see each other soon.*

*We shall, Avi. We shall.*

## GRACE OF DAY

My eyes opened.

The world had not changed. It had not fallen apart. It had not crumbled.

I was almost disappointed, but it is hard to find disappointment when you're lying in the arms of the person whose face was clear of any darkness.

"Grace?"

"Dear God, is she alive?"

"She's breathing. She's breathing!"

"Grace, can you hear me? Love, can you hear my voice?"

*Yes.*

"She's alive!" Robert cried out with joy, his body crushing me against him in an embrace that neither felt like too much or not enough. Being able to breathe him in, hear is voice, was heavenly.

 "Impossible!"

Not impossible.

Dozens of hands suddenly fought for control of my body—I felt them and the desperation that bled from beneath dirty fingernails and skin. I felt the air's layers of crisp chilliness and suffocating heat. There were dozens—no—hundreds of creatures breathing around me, each exhalation one of anticipation laced fear or hope. The news that I had died, and that Robert had killed me, had traveled as quickly as a thought could.

Those thoughts were in my head, all of them, clashing with despair and joy from one mind to the next. And now, those thoughts were joined by confusion, elation, disappointment, and most important-ly…fear.

They knew, just as I was beginning to realize, that a change was taking place within me.

"Let her go!" Stacy shouted. "Dammit, let her go you creeps!"

I heard the sound of flesh hitting flesh, followed by several grunts.

"Holy crap, what's she doing?"

"She's…floating!" Robert exclaimed in awe.

"What the hell?" Graham uttered in disbelief. "Grace, if you can hear me, what-the-hell?"

It felt like the air was pushing up beneath me, like hands lifting me toward something that had always been out of reach. My skin was ultra-sensitive to this change and it prickled.

"Make her stop," I heard Uriel shout.

"I can't!" Raphael cried in frustration.

"We must all try together. Michael, Gabriel—help us stop her!"

"We will not," Michael's voice said firmly. "We will let this run its course, as we let you run yours."

Through their argument, I could hear a humming. It vibrated through me, through my veins. Warmth began to chase this humming beneath my skin until it felt like every cell in my body was running to catch up. Golden blips of light flashed in my eyes like internal fireworks, each one growing bigger and brighter and more ferocious.

The humming grew louder as well, and I realized that it and the vibrations it caused were coming from my heart. *It* was racing. But it wasn't because it was about to give in. It was, instead, growing stronger.

"You knew about this, didn't you?" I heard Raphael ask accu-singly. "All of you knew! I'll kill you for this!"

Without even thinking it my body righted itself, my eyes find-ing Raphael as he lunged toward Robert.

"You will not," I snarled, my voice shocking him so greatly that he stopped in mid-air; his hands held out like claws, his face twisted with malice.

"What will you do to stop me? Whine me to death? Throw yourself in front of me?" Raphael gloated.

I laughed. "What is there to stop? You cannot kill anyone, re-member? It is why my mom was created—because you could not do it. It is why you have others do it for you, others whose call it is to obey you because you *have* no calling."

Despite him being unable to do so, I watched Raphael's face pale. "How do you know this? Who told you?"

I held up my left hand and wiggled my fingers. "My mother did."

Raphael's eyes widened and I took advantage of his shocked state. "You're weak; you have no purpose anymore. None of you do. Despite your position as the first four, you have no real power. You've been replaced; over and over again."

From behind me I heard Uriel chuckle. He floated in front of me, blocking my view of Raphael. "No real power? If we have no power than why has humanity feared us for so long?"

My chin rose up defiantly. "Humans don't fear you. Humans pity you. You have electus patronus who serve you only because they feel sorry for you. They call you the undesirables. People like Mrs. Deovo-lente protected you because they knew that you had nothing and you repaid them with betrayal."

"She was human; she was weak!" Uriel spat.

"She gave a damn about you, despite knowing who and what you were. That isn't weakness; that's called being human, and that's something you'll *never* earn the right to be."

From the corner of my eye I saw us being surrounded, the num-bers that had been summoned to fight for Raphael and Uriel swelling to beyond the trees. Robert looked up at me and reached for my hand. All around me, I saw my friends, other angels, their human charges, and the creatures that had come to fight, if not for me, then for themselves and the lives they so desperately wanted to keep. Their faces were a mixture of the familiar and the foreign, but each one looked at me with the same thought.

What do we do now?

"You see," Uriel snorted, "you are outnumbered and your followers have lost faith in you. Your mother's tricks won't save you twice, and they definitely won't save your friends."

I looked nervously at the mob that was closing in on us and saw them with new eyes. They were no different than those who stood with me in the circle, but through their eyes I saw that they all viewed me in the same way. To them, *I* was the monster—the exact same monster, as though the idea had been burned into their eyes.

"You're the one who took over Stacy's mind," I realized out loud. "You set Lem up."

Uriel and Raphael laughed. "He set himself up," Uriel corrected.

"Your mind was so easy to fool; your mother did too good a job at making you believe you were human. All I had to do was leave the pieces there and you would put them together. If Llehmai hadn't been a sentimental fool and his son a complete failure like his mother, you would have been dead months ago and none of this would be happening. Llehmai's death is his fault, and the deaths of everyone here is yours."

"Dead? Llehmai is dead?" I whimpered.

"Yes. He was able to hide from you, but no one can hide from the thrones. Congratulations, Grace; you have done in one night what your mother could not do in over twenty-thousand years: destroy the final wall of man like her creation was supposed to. Now, it's time for you to be destroyed as well."

The strangled cry of desperate souls rang out as the fighting began once more, only this time with far more desperation and need. The dark sky turned red as dozens of angels appeared, their glow surrounding them like a halo of blood.

"Get the dark one first," Uriel commanded to a large group of

604

thrones who were plowing through the mob directly in front of me. "Take his immortality and then take his life. Break him, destroy him. Leave no trace that he even existed."

"Robert!" I cried out with fear, looking at my hand and seeing that he was gone.

And it was my empty hand that finally made the humming in me stop. "This is never going to happen again," I said softly.

"What was that? I'm sorry—I didn't hear you over the apocalypse," Raphael laughed.

My hands grew hot as I looked at my wedding band and my mother's ring. "I said that this is never going to happen again. I won't let you take Robert away from me. I won't let you take anyone away from me ever again."

"And how are you going to do that when you're dead?"

Uriel grabbed one of my legs while Raphael grabbed the other.

"This has gone too far—stop this now," Michael argued.

"If you do not wish to help then do not interfere anymore than you already have," Raphael warned.

"There can be only one outcome here, brother," Gabriel said ominously. "You know this."

"The outcome is *mine* to decide!"

Raphael and Uriel both yanked on my legs. Whether it was to pull me down or to tear in me in two, I don't know, but it didn't matter.

My body wouldn't move.

Around me, the air crackled. It flickered with tiny pops of light that dragged, rather than faded, in the dark. My legs jerked beneath the vise-like grips of the two angels beneath me, while my arms flew out to my sides, my hands stiff, my fingers flexed.

I looked down and then my head flew back as what felt like every scream, every cry for help, every moment I'd ever felt desperate and afraid left me in a column of light. I had no choice but to look at it. It wasn't like shining a flashlight into the sky in the middle of the night.

Nothing passed through this light. Insects flew around it; air seemed to bounce off of it instead of conforming to it.

Time might have slowed down at Raphael and Uriel's request, but for me, it stopped completely when the light shifted from a bright white to an intense, blinding blue. Breathing stopped, and not because you couldn't; it was as if breathing simply didn't exist anymore.

Nothing existed anymore but that light.

It grew, widening, spreading outward and filling every ounce of darkness with a brilliant blue. All sound disappeared except for the hum that had returned, this time making the light glitter and sparkle.

My body jerked again, this time so violently that I knew, even without hearing them snap, that every bone in my body had just shattered. I wanted to cry out, I wanted to scream, but the pain wouldn't let me. Instead, my shoulders pulled back, my arms following as my fingers curled into widespread claws.

The light that poured out of me from my mouth disappeared, blackening the sky and making everything disappear into the darkness once more, the sound of it retreating like the air before a lightning storm.

From behind me, the feeling of sparks and flame licked at my skin. I couldn't move, my chest pushed forward as far as it could go, my back curled inward, stretching even as my chest collapsed. The singeing, arcing feeling of lightning across my skin caused my body to spasm wherever it hadn't been bent and twisted to absolution.

My heart thrummed at a rapid pace, thumping faster and faster as the pain grew in intensity. Each pulse of pain met its twin in my heartbeat; faster, stronger, hotter until there were no pauses, no breaks, no stops, until the two became one entity.

And then time started again, without any warning. Through the thoughts of everyone around me, through their eyes, I saw what was happening to me. My body was bent backwards at such a terrible angle there was no masking the shock that took hold of every living creature that looked on.

My back was glowing an angry red, while blazing white lines branched out from my spine. Those lines pulsed, growing thicker, longer, until they burst through my skin like daggers. They continued to grow, spreading beyond the width of my shoulders and reaching outward. The longer and wider they grew, the higher my body floated, Raphael and Uriel still hanging on, apparently unable or unwilling to let go.

The claws of light that protruded out of my back reached past my feet, hanging like icicles until finally, with my body ten feet off the ground, the points touched the ground. This seemingly innocuous moment was the catalyst that blacked out the vision of anyone who wasn't divine.

Light, pure, opaque light exploded from within me, bursting out of my back and attaching onto the branches that extended out of me, layering light upon brilliant light until wings that were blindingly bright stretched out from above my head to the ground. The sparkling, glittering light didn't hold any real shape, reaching and lashing out at anything that dared to come close.

Like whips, they grabbed onto Raphael and Uriel's hands, curling and oozing around them like golden syrup. Both angels struggled but neither could fight its grip as it began to flow over their bodies, consuming them within its light. But it wasn't done.

Hungry, it continued to spread out, like a ravenous fog. But unlike fog, it discriminated. Its pace quickened and its targets, realizing what was happening, began to run, fly, or disappear into a fog of their own, but the light wasn't going to let them leave.

It mixed with the mist that the angels created, forcing them to solidify before they were drowning along with the others in the greedy light. Stunned individuals who had not been selected or caught by the light watched silently as hundreds of angels, humans, and other creatures were brought up by my wings.

With no warning, the light changed color just as it had done earlier, turning a vibrant blue. Screams—hundreds and hundreds of screaming voices—shattered the night with the horror of what the light was doing. But whatever it was doing, no one could see it, no one could understand it. All anyone knew was that it was agony to be caught in this fog of blue light.

And through their pain, through their fear, I discovered that I was finally able to move. My back straightened, my body feeling incredibly light despite the weight of so many being held up by my wings. I could see and I could hear.

Faces of people that had come and gone passed over my eyes, their thoughts hovering in my mind until I'd accepted them, then floating away to finally find the peace they'd been denied for so long. Mr. Branke, his eyes glittering in the light, smiled at me. A girl with the same smile and the same, glittering eyes stood by his side.

*Thank you.*

Their faces were replaced by Erica's, her beautiful face still full of distaste when looking at me.

*I never hated you.*

That was more than I expected, more than I think I wanted. And it was enough.

Another face appeared; this one only recently familiar to me. It was Patricia, the girl who'd been turned for the sole purpose of destroying me but who'd changed her mind.

*Thank you for not letting me become a real monster.*

The fog of faces disappeared, revealing Robert above me, his arms and his wings held immobile by the two thrones who had tried to attack me earlier. Their faces were frozen in fear as the light surrounded them while avoiding Robert completely.

Robert's thoughts moved like air, and I inhaled them in, desperate for anything he had to say to me to calm me, reassure me.

*I love you, my wife. I love you, my angel. You can do this.*

And with one thought, everything fell; including me. The ground felt like a cushion of air as I landed haphazardly. All light was gone except for a residual glow that emanated from my skin, casting everything around me a soft yellow. The two angels who'd held onto me, whether they wanted to or not, landed just as awkwardly and gracelessly. They tumbled away, righting themselves and glaring at me with angry expressions on their faces.

Raphael hissed at me, but for the first time, there was no pain in my head, no need to flinch or cringe, and I smiled. Uriel, confused, looked at his hand, grabbed at his chest with his uninjured one, and then at me. "What is this?"

His hand was red and blistered…as if it had been burned; physically burned.

"What is wrong with your hand?" Raphael asked before looking at his own bubbled skin. "What is going on?"

Robert came to my side, grabbing my face and kissing me without any restraint. The feeling of him, the scent of him, the very nearness of him was unlike any other time before. This—this moment of unyielding clarity—was my resurrection, and just like my mother, I was reborn with the knowledge of everything. Every question ever asked suddenly had answers.

"Wow," Robert said in awe.

"I know," I replied with a grin before turning my attention back to Raphael and Uriel.

"What's going on is that you won't be hurting anyone else ever again," I promised.

"You think that you being Avi's daughter gives you the ability to decide what any of us do?" he sneered. "You are merely a tool! You were never meant to do anything but ensure that man returns to his rightful place beneath my feet!"

"I am not *Avi's* daughter," I said fiercely, a strange feeling of strength coming over me. My hair began to toss wildly behind me, and I once again found myself floating above the ground, the wings of light returning, crackling with energy.

"I am not Avi's daughter," I repeated. "My name is Grace Anne Shelley Bellegarde. I am Abigail and James Shelley's daughter. I am the sister of Matthew Shelley and the step-daughter of Janice Shelley. I am the best friend of Graham Hasselbeck and Stacy Kim. And I am the wife of Robert Bellegarde.

"And I'm here to make sure that mankind never has to deal with the threat of you ever again. That strange sensation in your chest, that thumping you hear in your ears is called a heartbeat, and those blisters on your hand are what happens when human skin comes into contact with heat."

"A heartbeat? Human skin? What are you talking about?" Uriel barked.

"My mother didn't want to rule over humans like you did, and she didn't want to be used by you to do it, either. She knew that she couldn't stop you—she was a part of it too, after all, thanks to you—so she had to find another way to do it. That's why she had me.

"But she didn't want me to have the same fate as she did: trapped forever to the deaths of human beings. The only way she wanted me to have death in my life was if I chose it. She gave me what no one gave her, and that was choice. She gave me something you could never have as an angel, and she gave me the ability to give it to others.

"So I have."

"What is that supposed to mean? What did you do to us?"

"I've given you the freedom of choice. I've made you human."

He snorted, while Raphael pinched at his arms, wincing at the result. "Human? You expect us to believe that? You? Only the Thrones have that ability."

"Yes, but they don't get to choose when and to who they do it to. But I do, thanks to my mom."

"This is ridiculous. No angel gets to say what abilities or calling another angel receives!"

I laughed. "That's the thing though, isn't it? My mom wasn't an angel when I was conceived. She gave me the calling of her choice because she wasn't bound by the rules anymore; not the way you know them anyway.

610

"See, my mom thought all of this out. It took her a really long time to do it—fifteen-hundred-years, in fact—but she knew what you guys would do and she planned for it. She knew you'd use Sam against me. That night on this field…that light that I thought came from some guardian angel—that was her way of making sure that I could take care of myself.

"It's why I didn't die from my wounds when Sam stabbed me. And it's also why Robert didn't die either. I wouldn't let him; I couldn't. My mother made sure of that when she gave *me* the call that he should have had but couldn't because of how he was born.

"She also knew that you'd do this. She knew that eventually it would come down to me having to choose between my life or the lives of the people I care about. The fact that the Robert and I shared the same second call is not a coincidence.

"I couldn't completely accept being an angel until the human part of me was gone, no matter who told me that that was what I was; I needed to die."

"But you didn't die!" Raphael growled. "You don't die!"

Gabriel stepped forward, his arms wrapped around himself as he looked at me appreciatively. "That's because she's life."

"She's what?" Uriel and Raphael shouted.

"I'm what?" I mimicked.

"You heard what your mother said, about how important you were."

"Yeah; she said I was her life-"

Gabriel cut me off. "No. She said you *were* life. There are two halves to everything in this world. Good and evil; the sun and the moon; life and death. N'Uriel is Death; you are Life; it is how it was meant to be. It is how it should have been. There cannot be one without the other and have balance exist in the world. Your mother knew this but did not realize the imbalance she was creating until after the flood.

"Living amongst the dead is not living at all. And the death of a symptom does not mean the death of the illness; she realized that too late to save the Grigori, the Nephilim, and the humans who'd been killed. But she promised to never let it happen again because even though we forgot what our purpose here was, she never did."

"We're not here to play maids to man! Grow some wings, man! Humans aren't meant to rule—they're weak!" Uriel snarled.

"If angels had been meant to rule this world, we would have been given it. We were only granted the sky," Michael pointed out, his voice calm, though his skin was pale.

"Why do you look like that?" Uriel asked, suddenly concerned.

Michael looked at me and then smiled. "Because I choose to."

Through my human eyes, I'd seen his beauty, but through the eyes I now possessed, I saw something else in him. It lay just beneath his skin like clouds, and as it grew thicker, I knew a storm was forming within him and it wasn't something that would have happened if he were still divine, with no beating heart within his chest.

"I didn't mean...I didn't know," I stumbled.

"Shh—it's not your fault. Your mother knew that this would happen. We asked her to promise us that it would," he said, his smile never fading.

"You asked her to...?"

"Yes. Gabriel and I both knew it was time. We've lived long enough and have done nothing to deserve such a life. It's time we let the first circle die."

My eyes filled with water as the irony hit me: I was life, but I was now responsible for two deaths...even if they hadn't happened yet.

"You aren't responsible for our deaths," Gabriel reassured me. "This is a long time in coming and we've been looking forward to this; truly. And, so have they."

Stacy, Graham, and Lark came to stand beside me and Robert, though they were not alone. I turned around and felt my jaw drop at what I saw.

Before the light, before my wings, the number of human faces in the crowd was limited. But now...now they were all I could see.

"What happened?" I breathed.

"You did. They were all turned against their will; you gave all of these people back their lives. You gave them back their humanity."

The number of people who came forward to thank me was incredible. I didn't know any of them but that didn't matter to them. All that mattered was that they were human again.

*What's going to happen to all of them?* I asked silently to Robert.

*The EPs will take care of them. It's what they do, remember?*

"This is outrageous! You let her destroy us, destroy everything we've done?" Raphael cried.

I don't know why I didn't see it coming; Raphael bent down onto the ground and picked up a large white feather before charging at Gabriel. The unusually long angel's quill pierced Gabriel's heart. I saw it, saw it go through flesh, muscle, more muscle, and finally the organ that, for the first time ever, pumped blood.

I saw through his body, saw the blood seep out through the wound and fill his chest. I reached out for him, my hands instinctively going to his wound.

"No," Gabriel argued as he crumpled to the ground, his hands held as far away from his wound as possible. "Let it run its course."

"Coward," Raphael spat.

Seeing that he was no longer a threat, several individuals came up to hold him, their faces and their thoughts full of rage.

"You're not going anywhere," one of them told him with a sneer.

"Grace..." Gabriel said softly. "Your mother would be so proud of you."

I blinked back tears. "You...you tell her I said I'm sorry for doubting her."

He smiled, his eyes closing. "She already knows..."

Gabriel died smiling, leaving this world with far more love for it than he probably had coming into it. No matter what anyone told me about it, I'd never take credit for that; he came to that decision all on his own.

"Hey, where's the other creeptastic one?" someone asked.

I knew who they were talking about; I looked around for Uriel but he was gone.

"I can find him," Stacy said, sniffing the air.

"No," I said, my eyes moving through the thinning crowd. "Let him go; we can always find him—oh God, no. No!"

I moved without thinking, my body skimming over the ground as my wings of light flew out behind me, seeking, touching whatever it felt needed its help.

Like a stone, I fell to my knees. Mrs. Mayhew was on the ground, her head bent low, her arms wrapped around Dr. Bro whose own arms held her close to him in a loving embrace. The both of them were still, their eyes closed.

"Did I do this?" I sobbed, my hands reaching out to them. "I can fix them. I can bring them back."

"Don't, Grace," Robert said, grabbing my arm as he came up beside me. "They died in peace together; let them remain that way."

"Why? Why can't I bring them back?" I sobbed. "They didn't have to die; they don't have to be dead! What good is being life, or whatever the hell it is that I am if I can't help the people I care about?"

Robert took my hand and squeezed it, his other hand caressing my face as delicately as he could. "Because that's not what they wanted."

"How do you know that? How?"

He chuckled. "It's who I am, remember?"

This didn't help me feel better.

"Grace, I know you want to help fix everything now that you believe you can, but you can't. There are some things you just can't fix."

I reached for him and pulled him into an embrace that mirrored the one locking the couple on the ground together. "I know, but I just…this wasn't supposed to happen."

"That's just it; for them, it was. It was their time and they chose to go together. If only we all were that fortunate; your dad never got that chance."

Stacy fell onto her knees beside us, her face a mixture of emotions. "I don't know if I should be sad or relieved."

"Why?" I asked, confused by the strict contradiction to how I felt.

"Because even though I'm going to miss them, the fact that they died together means that neither of them have to spend the rest of life without the other. You know what just thinking about that feels like. You've seen it in your dad—can you imagine spending forever missing someone like that; especially after how much the both of them have lost already?"

I nodded in understanding. "You're right. You're right... Wait; my dad! My dad still has Janice!"

Robert didn't need to hear me say it or think it; he already knew what I wanted.

"What about Stacy, Lark, and Graham?" I asked as we rose above the ground.

"Don't worry about us; since when did *we* need a babysitter?" Stacy shouted.

"We'll be fine. Go make people better!" Graham added as he trailed behind.

I looked down at Lark's broken frame and swallowed. No matter what I could do, I knew that there was no possible way I could fix her wing. Robert was right: there are some things you just can't fix.

*It's okay. I managed blind, I'll manage with one wing. If nothing else, it adds to my street cred.*

*Street cred? Do angels even have that?*

I saw her head tip up, a smirk forming on her face. *You're an angel for five minutes and you already think you know everything; typical.*

There was no preventing the smile on my face as I waved to the crowd of people who cheered as we left.

"Was that Shawn?" I cried when I spotted a familiar face before they grew too small to make out anyone.

Robert nodded. "He's confused, and there'll be a lot of explaining to do, but he's going to be okay. They're all going to be okay."

I exhaled. "So...Janice?"

"No. First we get your dad then we go and see Janice. Grace-"

"Yes?"

"Your sapphire ring—the star's back."

I looked at my hand and saw that he was right. The white star that had disappeared from the ring that he'd given me for my eighteenth birthday had returned, brighter than ever. "I know why this happened," I said suddenly.

"You do?"

I looked at him and grinned. "Yes. I don't know why, but I do. The star disappeared because I needed it to. My mom said I was her light but I wasn't anymore. Things had gotten so dark for me that I needed as much help as I could get. Now that things are a lot brighter in my life, the star felt it could go back."

"You're talking about it like it's a living thing."

I laughed. "That's because it is."

"If you say so, my love. Now, let's finish putting this family back together."

"And then what?

Robert kissed my forehead and then placed his hand on my abdomen. "Whatever we want."

I sighed. "That sounds like heaven."

# EPILOGUE: GARDEN OF EDEN

"I know that it's hard to believe, but at one point in my life the last thing in this world I wanted to do was wear a dress. But I'm getting used to the idea. I especially like the flowy ones that go all the way to the ground.

"Of course, I still wear my boots. Winter's almost over but the snow keeps falling so I wear them; I don't want people thinking I'm even more of a freak than they already do. After what happened this summer, there's pretty much nothing that'll change their minds about me, but you know what? That's okay. I'm more worried about you and what this will all mean for you.

"I don't want you to go through the same kind of problems that I did in school and in life, period. I mean, it's pretty much guaranteed that you'll be the coolest kid in school, but kids can be awful and the last thing I want is for you to come home one day with a letter from the principal's office saying you got into a fight."

I stopped talking and dipped the paintbrush that I had in my hand back into the can. I pulled the brush out and returned to painting the edges of the wall, making sure that none of the lavender paint touched the pristinely white ceiling.

"Of course, I'm pretty sure that note's going to come with a restraining order of some kind. Stacy's promised you all the Tae Kwon Do lessons you want, and Lark's probably going to teach you how to tear someone's head off, so yeah...I'm worried.

"But I guess that's expected, right? Why am I asking you that?

You're not even here yet!"

I lowered a free hand onto my belly and smiled as I felt the movement beneath it. "Well, you know you don't have to get all cocky about it," I laughed.

The door to the room opened and Robert walked in, a single lily in one hand, a box in the other. "How are my favorite ladies doing?"

"I'm doing fine; our little Maia here is apparently a know-it-all."

He handed me the flower and then lowered his head to my expansive stomach, his lips pressing against the thin fabric that covered it. "She's going to know just enough to get her into trouble and not enough so that her mother can feel like she's helping her out once in a while."

"Oh gee, thanks," I laughed. "What's in the box?"

"A surprise," he said before handing it to me. "Lark and Graham are planning on coming by in an hour so you might want to wrap it up in here and go take a shower."

"But I've got studying to do after this," I groaned.

"You're actually going to study?" he exclaimed, surprised.

"Yes. I don't care if I can read the teacher's mind and see all the answers to tomorrow's quiz; I want to pass on my own merit. Besides, I'm going to take advantage of being snuck in this semester since I'm going to have to miss the next one."

He shook his head, taking mine into his hands and bringing his lips down onto mine in a kiss that made my skin crackle with electricity.

"Whoa," Robert murmured before the kiss deepened, his hands reaching around me and caressing every new curve that had formed on me in the past few months. "I'm going to miss this."

"Miss what? My fat?"

"You're not fat; and I'm going to miss having to hold you sideways because your belly's in the way."

"Oh!" I gasped, hitting his arm with the box.

"Hey! Don't dent that," he laughed.

"Why? What's in it?"

"Open it and find out."

618

I sat down on the floor, Robert joining beside me, and opened the box. Inside laid some tissue paper and beneath that was a photo album. "Did you get this for the baby?" I chirped.

"Open it," he repeated.

I pulled the thick white album out, setting the empty box to the side, and then settled the book into my lap. The cover was a thick, embossed white. It was simple and spoke plainly how well Robert knew me. He smiled at my thoughts and waited patiently as I opened the album.

A small squeak left me when I turned to the first page and found it already filled. A photo of my mom and dad when they got married was there, with a caption beneath that read "Grandma Abby and Grandpa James".

"I know how my mom was able to get pregnant again," I said softly as I took in the smile that lit up the black and white image.

"You do?"

"Uh-huh. It was me. I asked for a baby sister. I wanted one so badly, I snuck into my parents room one night and put my hands on my mom's tummy and asked that she grow me one. It was stupid, and I didn't think anything about it because I was six at the time, but knowing now what I can do…"

"You think that you did the same thing for your mom that my mother did for her?"

"Well…yeah. I think I've proven that I'm pretty capable of getting people pregnant," I said with a short laugh. "Maia's due a bit earlier than she should be if we go on the first time we did it."

"I think my mother explained it to you-"

"Yeah, she said that angels don't get pregnant the way humans do, that they…blend or something."

"It's not blending, it's misting in unison."

"And we didn't do that until…well, it doesn't matter when because Maia's was conceived a lot earlier than that."

"But we did, Grace. Or, at least, I did."

My cheeks flushed at the memory of that night, the first time intimacy had ever been allowed between us. "Oh."

"If we go by that date then it makes sense."

He was right, and I groaned at how obvious it was.

"It's only obvious when you know all of the facts. You can't help not knowing something like this—you were given information about your call, not about how angels get pregnant. Anyway, keep going," Robert said, his shoulder gently bumping mine in encouragement.

Smiling, I turned the page, this one holding a photo of Janice and Dad, with Matthew proudly displaying his new teeth as he waved from Dad's arms. Beneath it read "Grandma Janice, Grandpa James, and Uncle Matthew".

"Did Dad send you this one?" I asked, touching their smiling faces and feeling emotional.

"Yes. I asked him to send one as soon as he got over you being pregnant."

"So you stole this from him then?" I joked.

"Okay…I asked but he didn't respond so I had Janice send it. They took it outside the new house; nice, huh?"

I ran my finger alongside Dad's face. "I still don't know how I feel about him moving back to California. It doesn't feel right, him not being here."

"You know why he left," Robert reminded.

"I know, but I still don't understand why he had to go. Can't EPs do their job like, online or something?"

He laughed. "If only it was that simple. Your father isn't technologically savvy, Grace. He can't hack sites; he can barely remember to check his email. What he's good at is organization. After what happened this past summer, there's a need for that; especially since we lost our registrar."

"But why couldn't he do that here?"

"Because his family is based in California. He needs to be where they are, Grace. He wants to change the legacy of his family—your family; especially now that that family includes us."

I frowned, but accepted his explanation for probably the fifth time this week. I looked at the next page and grinned. Graham was making a pair of glasses with his eyes, his tongue sticking out as his body was held up by Lark, who somehow managed to smile for the photograph.

There was still grief in Graham's eyes, the loss of his father an unintended price that I could not repay. He buried his father next to his grandmother, saying nothing when his mother showed up at the funeral. Ivy tried to reconnect with her son that day, but Graham couldn't let her in. She left the next day for Florida and didn't return.

Graham inherited the house from his father and, after a long talk with Lark and my dad, chose not to sell it after all. Lark, free to choose what she wanted to do now that protecting me was no longer an issue, decided that it was best to continue the ruse she and Robert had started, and finish high school.

"Who took this photo?"

"Stacy."

"And is she-"

"Next page."

Smiling, I turned the page and laughed out loud. "Is she serious?"

Stacy was positioned on one foot, her body tilted so that her other foot was in the air. In her hand was a cup of tea that she sipped with her pinky that stuck out parallel to her leg.

"She thought it was better than a photo of her beating up Graham."

"That's true," I agreed.

I'd asked Stacy a few days after the fight on the field if she wanted to return to being human, to return to the life she had before the cancer returned, and she told me flatly that she did not.

"That life is gone, Grace. I have to move on and this life that I have now, what Dr. Bro allowed me to become is what I want. I'm *doing* something. I'm making a difference. I don't think I could've done that if I were still human."

"You made a difference with me as a human," I said softly.

"Yeah, but that's because you're-"

"Different?" I joked.

"No, you dork. It was because you're special. And no matter where either of us are, you're always going to be one of my best friends."

"Will you stick around?" I asked nervously.

"Why?"

"Because my daughter's going to need an aunt," I said with a sly smile.

"Yeah…like in a dozen years, maybe. You're not thinking about having a kid anytime soon…right?"

"Well, not right away, but maybe in…seven or eight months?"

Very rarely has one ever been able to render Stacy speechless, but I'd done it, and I'd done it at the worst possible time.

"Stacy? Stacy say something."

Her mouth opened, her lips moved, but no sound came out.

"Stacy, you're the first person I've told. I mean, Robert knows but I wanted to tell you first. You can't not say anything after learning my big secret!"

"You're pregnant?"

I nodded and then smiled. "It's a girl—she's already told me."

Stacy's jaw plummeted. "She's *told* you?"

"I know it sounds weird, but it's true."

"When? When did you know?"

"When Lem took me."

"Wow. And you're telling me first; Graham doesn't even know yet?"

"Nope. You get first dibs on the title of auntie."

She never promised that she'd stay, but she hadn't left yet, and that was enough of a promise for me.

On the opposite page of the album, was a photo of Ameila. She was beautiful and serene in her photo, a warm smile crossing her face. She'd been almost as furious as Dad had been when she learned that I was pregnant, but it was mainly because she knew that Robert and I had known before the attack and had chosen not to say anything.

"Why would you risk your child's life like that?" she scolded.

"You knew Grace was going to be fine; why are you so upset?"

"Because my grandchild deserves better than to be treated like an afterthought."

It took a while for her to calm down, but eventually she began to work toward forgiving us, while Robert worked toward forgiving her. We were officially pardoned when we vowed to never call her "Grandma Ameila".

"If you must give me a title, then grandmère is fine. It sounds so much better in French."

I giggled when the caption beneath the photo read "Grandma Ameila" anyway.

I turned to the next page. A photo of Robert and me caught mid-laugh made my cheeks burn. "This was taken at Dad's going away party, after that..."

"After we snuck away and christened our new bedroom," Robert said thickly.

"I'm not sure I'm ever going to get used to this," I laughed.

"To what?"

I put my hand on my belly and sighed. "To us being able to just...live, without worrying about someone trying to kill us, or-"

"Or me trying to kill you."

My nostrils flared in irritation. "Yeah. That."

"I appreciate it, too, Grace. Knowing that I can leave—or that you can leave—to answer the call, and that we will always be able to come home to each other gives me such a sense of contentment and satisfaction. I've never felt that way before; I've always felt right about us, but I was always fearful of its lack of permanence. Now, that's not a worry at all."

My heart swelled at his words, and I pushed myself up to reach his lips, kissing him gently before grabbing the back of his head and bringing down, the kiss intensifying, churning sensations through the lower half of my body. My heart moved like a frantic bird in my chest, and I giggled when I heard his thoughts. "Really? Even when I look like I swallowed Pluto?"

"Grace, if you're implying that you're so big you're planetary—don't. I'm going to be attracted to you no matter what you look like because everything about you is beautiful and sexy to me. Except maybe your strange fascination with that egg-bread thing you like to eat."

"Egg-in-a-hole; and that's the best part of me," I kidded before returning my attention to the album. I turned the page, still smiling at the naughty thought that Robert had allowed me to hear, when my breath caught in my throat.

The page was blank, but the area for a caption was already filled. The page itself didn't match the others in the album—it was thicker and slightly yellowed with age—but it fit perfectly despite that. Written below the empty photo corners in my mother's handwriting was "Grace and Maia: Mother and Daughter".

"I tore this page up," I said in a shaky voice.

"I know. But you forget that I'm an angel; I might not be able to fix people anymore, but I can still fix this."

My vision fogged up with tears. My mother's ring on my finger grew warm, and I could see the moment when she wrote it, feel the emotions that ran through her.

"Your grandmother told her," I said to Robert. "She told my mom everything that would happen and then my mom wrote it on this page. Our entire future was written here on this page and I didn't see it. Or…maybe I didn't want to see it because I didn't believe it was possible."

"And you do now?"

"Yes. I think that anything's possible now."

"Really? Like what?" he asked playfully, his hand tickling my side.

I turned around and put my hand on his chest. I focused, my

eyes looking up at his and never letting them go from my gaze. Beneath my palm, his shirt allowed me to feel the warmth of his skin. The stillness, the quiet that resided there felt odd against my own blatant pulse.

With only a simple thought—a wish really—my pulse was joined by another, the beat weak and tentative at first, but growing more sure, steadier with each passing breath. Only when the beat was strong enough to vibrate through my hand did I finally remove it, waiting for Robert's response.

"Why?" he asked softly.

"Because you will spend the rest of your existence taking the life of others, and I believe that the only thing that kept my mother from allowing the balance to slip through her fingers is the fact that she had a heart beating in her chest. I know that I'm supposed to be your balance, but now…now you have a part of me inside of you, so that if anything happens-"

"Nothing will happen, Grace."

"I know, I know, but there's always a possibility. We don't know what happened to Uriel and he has supporters among your kind."

Robert grabbed my hand and returned it to his chest. "*Our* kind, Grace. They are our kind. And it doesn't matter whether or not he has supporters. The first circle is broken. You are the only remaining legacy to it and no one will try to hurt you because of it. It's quite awesome, really. You're the only reason I'm still alive—the only reason why Heath still exists."

"So what happens if you're wrong?"

"Then we make it right again."

A song began to resonate in my head, the repetition of name and a location that was far from Heath, and I sighed with disappointment. "I've got to go."

"My wife, the working woman," he chuckled. "At least you know that there will be a good outcome from this."

"This is true. I'll probably stop by the hospital and see how Madame Hidani is doing when I'm done. She has physical therapy today."

"Okay. I'll finish up the painting in here."

I grunted and then pushed myself onto my knees, the awkwardness of pregnancy still finding a way to defeat the grace and strength of being an angel. "Thanks."

Robert helped me to stand, and then pushed my hair back so that he could see my face clearly, wiping at a smudge of lavender and then smiling into my eyes. "I love you, Grace."

"I love you, Robert," I said back, my mind suddenly finding an idea that hadn't been broached in a while.

"Oh no," he said, backing away and laughing. "No, no, no. I thought we'd settled this; we are not going to let Bala be our daughter's godmother. No. No, no, no. She's even more protective now than she was before! She'll turn our house into tree, Grace! She'll fill our front yard with man-eating plants! No. Bala cannot be godmother. No. That's final."

I laughed, and braced myself for the argument, glad that this was the worst of our problems.

Life was good.

It wasn't normal, but then again, whose life ever really is?

## ACKNOWLEDGEMENTS

Thank yous have to go out to Alisha, Chyrie, Kerri, Tia, Alan, Allison, Lincoln, Shey, and anyone else who's read and re-read, and re-re-re-read my books and told me what works, what doesn't, and why I shouldn't give up just yet.

To the fans, Robert and Grace made this journey only because of your help and your support.

We owe you our undying gratitude.

24515001R00368

Made in the USA
Lexington, KY
26 July 2013